HOLY DISORDERS

HOLY
DISORDERS

Edmund Crispin

🕑🕑🕑🕑🕑🕑🕑🕑🕑🕑🕑🕑🕑🕑🕑🕑🕑

All the characters and events portrayed in this work are fictitious.

HOLY DISORDERS

A Felony & Mayhem mystery

PRINTING HISTORY
First UK edition: 1945
First U.S. edition: 1946
Felony & Mayhem edition: 2006

ISBN 13: 978-1-933397-28-3
ISBN 10: 1-933397-28-4

Manufactured in the United States of America

To my parents

NOTE

My sincere thanks are due to Mr. Philip Larkin for reading this book in manuscript and making a number of valuable suggestions.

E.C.

Contents

1. Invitation and Warning 1
2. Do Not Travel for Pleasure 17
3. Gibbering Corse 39
4. Teeth of Traps 57
5. Conjectures 73
6. Murder in the Cathedral 91
7. Motive 107
8. Two Canons 127
9. Three Suspects and a Witch 147
10. Night Thoughts 169
11. Whale and Coffin 187
12. Love's Lute 205
13. Another Dead 219
14. In the Last Analysis 245
15. Reassurance and Farewell 253

The icon above says you're holding a copy of a book in the Felony & Mayhem "Vintage" category. These books were originally published prior to about 1965, and feature the kind of twisty, ingenious puzzles beloved by fans of Agatha Christie and John Dickson Carr. If you enjoy this book, you may well like other "Vintage" titles from Felony & Mayhem Press, including:

For more about these books, and other Felony & Mayhem titles, or to place an order, please visit our website at:
www.FelonyAndMayhem.com
or contact us at:
Felony and Mayhem Press
156 Waverly Place
New York, NY 10014

HOLY DISORDERS

CHAPTER ONE

Invitation and Warning

*"Continually at my bed's head
A hearse doth hang, which doth me tell
That I ere morning may be dead…"*
SOUTHWELL

As his taxi burrowed its way through the traffic outside Waterloo Station, like an over-zealous bee barging to the front of a dilatory swarm, Geoffrey Vintner reread the letter and telegram which he had found on his breakfast table that morning.

He felt as unhappy as any man without pretension to the spirit of adventure might feel who has received a threatening letter accompanied by sufficient evidence to suggest that the threats contained in it will probably be carried out. Not for the first time that morning, he regretted that he had ever persuaded himself to set out on his uncomfortable errand, to leave his cottage in Surrey, his cats, his garden (whose disposition he changed almost daily in accordance with some new and generally impracticable

1

fancy), and his estimable and long-suffering housekeeper, Mrs. Body. He was not, he considered (and the thought recurred with gloomy frequency as the series of adventures on which he was about to embark went its way), of a mould which engages very successfully in physical violence. Once one is over forty, one cannot, even in moments of high enthusiasm, throw oneself heartily into anonymous arid mortal battles against unscrupulous men. And when, moreover, one is a finical bachelor, moderately well-off, bred in a secluded country rectory, and with a mind undisturbed by sordid cares and overmastering passions, the thing begins to appear not only impossible but frankly ludicrous. It was no consolation to reflect that men like himself had fought with the courage and tenacity of bears all the way back to the Dunkirk beaches; they at least knew what they were up against.

Threats.

He groped in his coat pocket, pulled out a large, ancient revolver, and looked at it with that mixture of alarm and affection which dog-lovers bestow on a particularly ferocious animal. The driver regarded this proceeding bleakly in the driving-mirror as they entered upon the expanses of Waterloo Bridge. And a new thought entered Geoffrey Vintner's head as, observing this deprecatory glare, he hastily put the gun away again: people had been known to be abducted in taxis, which hovered about their houses until they emerged, and then conveyed them resistlessly away to some place like Limehouse, where they were dealt with by gangs of armed thugs. He gazed dubiously at the short, stocky figure which sat with rock-like immobility in front of him, dexterously skirting the roundabout at the north end of the bridge. Certainly there was only one train which he could have caught from Surrey that morning, in time to get his connection from Paddington, so his enemies, whoever they were, would have known when to meet him; on the other hand, he had had some considerable difficulty in finding a taxi at all, and without exception they had all seemed concerned more with eluding his attention than with trying to attract it. So that was probably all right.

He turned and looked with distaste at the traffic which pursued behind, with the erratic movements of topers following a leader from pub to pub. How people knew when they were being trailed he found himself unable to imagine. Moreover, he was not trained to the habit of observation; the outside world normally impressed itself on him as a vague and unmemorable succession of phantasms—a Red Indian could have walked through London by his side without his noticing anything untoward. He contemplated for a moment asking the driver to make a detour, in order to throw possible pursuers off the scent, but suspected that this would be 'unkindly' received. And in any case, the whole thing was too preposterous; it would do no one any good to follow him publicly through the London crowds on a hot summer's midday.

In this, as it happened, he was wrong.

"Any visit which you make to Tolnbridge you will regret."

Nothing explicit about it, of course, but it had a businesslike air which was far from inspiring confidence. He noticed with that peculiarly galling sense of annoyance which comes from the shattering of some unimportant illusion that the paper and envelope were distinctive and expensive and the typewriter, to judge from its many typographical eccentricities, easily identifiable—provided one knew where to start looking for it. He abandoned himself to aggrievedness. Criminals should at least try to preserve the pretence of anonymity, and not flaunt unsolvable clues before their victims. The postmark, too—thanks to the conscientiousness of some employee of the G.P.O.—read quite legibly as Tolnbridge; which was what one would expect.

The telegram, loosely held in his left hand, fluttered to the floor. He picked it up, shook it fastidiously free of dirt, and

read it through automatically, perhaps hoping to extract from
the spidery, insubstantial capitals of the British telegraph system some shred of significance which had previously escaped
him. That air of callous gaiety, he reflected bitterly, could have
emanated from no one but the sender. It ran:

I AM AT TOLNBRIDGE STAYING AT THE
CLERGY HOUSE PRIESTS PRIESTS PRIESTS
THE PLACE IS BLACK WITH THEM COME
AND PLAY THE CATHEDRAL SERVICES ALL
THE ORGANISTS HAVE BEEN SHOT UP DIS-
MAL BUSINESS THE MUSIC WASN'T AS BAD
AS ALL THAT EITHER YOU'D BETTER
COME AT ONCE BRING ME A BUTTERFLY
NET I NEED ONE WIRE BACK COMING
NOT COMING PREPARE FOR LONG STAY
GERVASE FEN

Accompanying this had been a reply-paid form allowing
for a reply of fifty words. It was with a sense of some satisfaction that Geoffrey had filled it in: COMING VINTNER—a
satisfaction, however, tempered by the suspicion that Fen
would not even notice the sarcasm. Fen was like that.

And now he doubted whether he would have sent that
reply at all had it not been for the telegraph-boy hovering
about outside the door and his own natural reluctance to take
it to the post office later on. Most of our decisions, he reflected,
are forced on us by laziness. And, of course, at that stage he had
not yet opened his letters...There were compensations. The
Tolnbridge choir was a good one, and the organ, a four-manual
Willis, one of the finest in the country. He remembered idly
that it had a horn stop which really sounded like a horn, a lovely
stopped diapason on the choir, a noble tuba, a thirty-two-foot on
the pedals which in its lower register sent a rhythmic pulse of

vibration through the whole building, unnerving the faith-ful...But were these things compensation enough?

In any case—his mental homily prolonged itself as the taxi shot round Trafalgar Square—here he was, involved against his will in some sordid conflict of law and disorder, and in some considerable personal danger. The letter and the telegram in conjunction were proof enough of that. What it was all about was another matter. The telegram, suitably punctuated, sug-gested that some enemy was engaged in a determined attempt to abolish, by attrition, the church-music of Tolnbridge—the reason, presumably, why his own proximate arrival was so much resented. But this seemed unlikely, not to say fantastic. The organists had been "shot up"—what on earth did that mean? It suggested, ominously, machine-guns—but then Fen was notoriously prone to exaggeration, and cathedral towns in the West of England do not normally harbour gangs. He sighed. Useless to speculate—he was in it, with at least nine-tenths of his boats burnt and the rest manifestly unseaworthy. The only thing to do was to sit back and rely on fate and his own wits if anything happened—neither of which aids, he remembered without satisfaction, had done him any very yeoman service in the past. And what was all this about a butterfly-net...?

The butterfly-net. He hadn't got it.

He glanced hastily at his watch, and banged on the glass as the taxi rounded Cambridge Circus preparatory to entering the Charing Cross Road.

"Regent Street," he said. The taxi performed a full circle and headed down Shaftesbury Avenue.

A following cab altered its course likewise.

❋ ❋ ❋

The Regent Street emporium which Geoffrey Vintner eventually selected as being most likely to house a butterfly-net proved to be surprisingly empty, with assistants and customers sweltering in a mid-morning lethargy. It seemed to have been designed with the purpose of evading any overt admission of its function. There were pictures on the walls, and superfluous furnishings, and fat gilt cherubs; while vaguely symbolical figures, standing stiff as Pomeranian grenadiers, supported insouciantly in the small of their backs the ends of the banisters. Before going in, Geoffrey paused to buy a paper, reflecting that any intimations of gang warfare in Tolnbridge would certainly have reached the Press by now. But the Battle of Britain held the headlines, and after crashing into two people while engaged in a search among the smaller items, he postponed further investigation for the time being.

A gigantic placard showing the location of the various departments proved useless from the point of view of butterfly-nets, so he resorted to the enquiry counter. What Fen could want with such a thing as a butterfly-net it was impossible to imagine. Geoffrey had a momentary wild vision of the pair of them pursuing insects across the Devon moors, and looked again, even more doubtfully, at the telegram. But no; it could not by any stretch of the imagination be a mistake; and lepidoptery was as likely to be Fen's present obsession as anything else.

Butterfly-nets, he learned, were to be had from either the children's or the sports department; fortunately both were on the same floor. He examined the lift-girl with a professional air of suspicion as she closed the gates on him, and was rewarded with an exaggeratedly indignant stare ("'aving an eyeful," she confided later to a friend). Thereupon he retired hastily into his paper, and as he was borne upward through the building, discovered and read the following:

ATTACK ON MUSICIAN
The police have as yet no clue to the assailant of Dr.

Dennis Brooks, Organist of Tolnbridge Cathedral,
who was attacked and rendered unconscious while
on his way home the evening before last.

Geoffrey cursed the papers for their lack of detail, Fen
for his exaggeration, and himself for becoming involved in the
business at all. This private ritual of commination concluded,
he scratched his nose ruefully; *something* was going on, anyway. But what had happened to the deputy organist? Presumably he had been banged on the head as well.

The lift came to a shattering stop, and Geoffrey found
himself precipitated into the midst of a vast mêlée of sports
equipment, tenanted only by one plump, pink young assistant,
who stood gazing about him with the resignation and despair
of Priam amid the ruins of Troy.

"Have you ever noticed," he said gloomily as Geoffrey
approached, "the way no sports apparatus is ever a decent,
symmetrical shape? You can't pile it up neatly like boxes or
books—there are always little bits sticking out on all sides.
Roller-skates are the worst." His tone deepened, indicating his
especial abhorrence of these inconvenient objects. "And footballs roll off the shelf as soon as you put them up, and skis you
are bound to fall over, and the moment you lean a cricket-bat
against the wall it slides down again." He looked unhappily at
Geoffrey. "Is there anything you want? Most people," he went
on before Geoffrey could reply, "have given up sports for the
war. I expect they're better off for it in the end. Muscular
development only provides a foothold for fat." He sighed.

"What I really wanted was a butterfly-net," said Geoffrey
absently; his mind still dwelt on the problem of the organists.

"A butterfly-net," repeated the young man sadly; he
seemed to find this information particularly discouraging. "It's
the same with them, you see," he said, pointing to a row of
butterfly-nets propped against a wall. "If you stand them on

their heads, as it were, the net part sticks out and trips you up; and if you have them as they are now, they look top-heavy and disturb the eye." He went over and selected one.

"Isn't it rather long?" said Geoffrey, gazing without enthusiasm at the six feet of bamboo which confronted him.

"They have to be that," said the young man without any perceptible lightening of spirit, "or you'd never get near the butterflies at all. Not that you do very often, in any case," he added. "Most of it's just blind swiping, really. Would you be wanting a collector's box?"

"I don't think so."

"Ah, well. I don't blame you. They're inconvenient things, very heavy to carry about." He scrutinised the net again. "This will be seventeen-and-six. Ridiculous waste of money, really. I'll just take the price off."

The price was attached to the stem of the net with a piece of string that proved impervious to tugging.

"Won't it slip off?" said Geoffrey helpfully; and then, when quite obviously it wouldn't: "Well, it doesn't matter, anyway."

"It's no bother at all. I've got a pair of scissors." The pink young man felt helplessly in his pockets. "I must have left them in the office. I'm always doing that; and when I do remember, they tear holes in my pockets. Just a minute." He had disappeared before Geoffrey could stop him.

The man in the black slouch hat rose from his rather cramped position behind a counter laden with boxing-gloves near the stairhead, and made his way with considerable speed and stealth towards Geoffrey. He carried a blackjack and had the intent expression of one trying to trap a mosquito. The pink young assistant, however, did not stay away as long as he had hoped. Emerging from the office, he took in the situation without apparent surprise, and, acting with commendable presence of mind, put the butterfly-net over the assailant's head and pulled. The blackjack described an arc through the air and knocked over a pile of roller-skates with a horrifying crash. Geoffrey spun round just in time to see his would-be attacker overbalance backwards and collapse into the middle of a vast medley of sports equipment which stood in the middle of the floor. It expressed its unsymmetrical character by general dissolution. A number of footballs were precipitated to the top of the stairs, down which they careered with increasing momentum to the department below. The Enemy freed himself, cursing noisily, from the butterfly-net, got to his feet, and made for the stairs. The pink young man gave him a resounding crack on the back of his head with one end of a ski, and he fell down again. Geoffrey struggled with his revolver, which had become inextricably involved in the lining of his pocket.

Battle was at once engaged. The Enemy, who was showing remarkable powers of recovery, opened a frontal attack on Geoffrey. The pink young man threw a cricket-ball at him, but it missed and hit Geoffrey instead. Geoffrey fell over and upset a heap of ice-skates, over which the assailant in his turn fell. The pink young man tried to put the net over his head again, but missed his arm and overbalanced. The Enemy regained his feet and threw an ice-skate at Geoffrey, which caught him a windy blow in the stomach as he was still endeavouring to get out his revolver. The pink young man, recovering his balance, smote the Enemy with a cricket-stump. The Enemy subsided, and the pink young man banged inexpertly at his head with a hockey-stick until he became silent. Geoffrey at last succeeded in getting out his revolver, to the accompaniment of an ominous tearing of cloth, and waved it wildly about him.

"Be careful with that," said the pink young man.

"What happened?"

"Malicious intent," said the other. He picked up the blackjack, tossed it in the air, and nodded sagely. "I'm afraid that butterfly-net's no good now," he added, with a relapse into his previous melancholy. "Torn to bits. You'd better take another." He went over and got one. "Seventeen-and-six, I think we said." Mechanically Geoffrey produced the money.

A roar of mingled rage and stupefaction from below indicated that the footballs had arrived at their destination. "Fielding!" a voice boomed up at them. "What the devil are you doing up there?"

"I think," said the young man pensively, "that it would be better if we left—at once."

"But your job!" Geoffrey gazed at him helplessly.

"I've probably lost it, anyway, thanks to this. Something of this sort always seems to happen to me. The last place I was at one of the assistants went mad and took off all her clothes. I wonder if I've left anything?" He buffeted his pockets, as one who searches for matches. "I generally do. At least thee pairs of gloves a year—in trains."

"Come on," said Geoffrey urgently. He was feeling unnaturally exhilarated, and obsessed by a primitive desire to escape from the scene of the disturbance. Footsteps clattered up the steps towards them. The lift-girl apocalyptically threw open the doors of the lift, announced, as one ushering in the day of judgement; "Sports, children's, books, ladies'—" shrieked out at the chaos confronting her, and closed the doors again, whence she and her passengers peered out like anxious rabbits awaiting the arrival of greenstuffs. The accidental touch of a button sent the lift shooting earthwards again; from it rapidly diminishing sounds of altercation could be heard.

Geoffrey and the pink young man ran for the stairs.

On their way down, they met a shop-walker and two assistants, pounding grimly upwards.

"There's a lunatic up there trying to break up the stock," said the young man with a sudden blood-curdling intensity which, by contrast with his normal tones, sounded horrifyingly convincing. "Go and see what you can do—I'm off to fetch the police."

The shop-walker snatched Geoffrey's gun, which he was still brandishing, and leaped on upwards. Geoffrey engaged in feeble protests.

"Don't hang about," said the young man, tugging at his sleeve. They continued their precipitate downward rush to the street.

"Well, and what was all that about?" asked the young man, leaning back in his corner of the taxi and stretching out his legs.

Geoffrey deferred replying for a moment. He was engaged in a minute scrutiny of the driver, though obscurely conscious of not knowing what he expected this activity to reveal. No chances must be taken, however; the encounter in the shop indicated that much. He transferred his suspicion to the young man, and prepared to make searching enquiries as to his trustworthiness. It suddenly struck him, however, that this might well appear ungracious, as it certainly would have done.

"I hardly know," he said lamely.

The young man appeared pleased. "Then we must go into the matter from the beginning," he announced. "He nearly got you, you know. Can't have that sort of thing." He proffered his determination to uphold the law a trifle inanely. "Where are you going?"

"Paddington," said Geoffrey, and added hastily: "That is to say—I mean—possibly." The conversation was not going well, and his brief feeling of exhilaration had vanished.

"I know what it is," said the young man. "You don't trust me. And quite right, too. A man in your position oughtn't to trust anyone. Still, I'm all right, you know; saved you getting a lump on your head the size of an Easter egg." He wiped his brow and loosened his collar. "My name's Fielding—Henry Fielding."

Geoffrey embarked without enthusiasm on a second-rate witticism. "Not the author of *Tom Jones*, I suppose?" He regretted it the moment it was out.

"*Tom Jones?* Never heard of it. A book, is it? Don't get much time for reading. And you?"

"I beg your pardon?"

"I mean, I introduced myself, so I thought you—"

"Oh, yes, of course. Geoffrey Vintner. And I must thank you for acting as promptly as you did; heaven knows what would have happened to me if you hadn't interfered."

"So do I."

"What do you mean—Oh, I see. But it occurs to me now, you know, that we really ought to have stayed and seen the police. It's all very well dashing off like a couple of schoolboys, who've been robbing an orchard, but there are certain proprieties to be observed." Geoffrey became suddenly bored with this line of thought. "Anyway, I had to catch a train."

"And our friend," said Fielding, "was presumably trying to stop you. Which brings us back to the question of what it's all about." He wiped his brow again.

Geoffrey, however, was distracted, idly musing on a Passa-caglia and Fugue commissioned from him for the New Year. It had not been going well in any case, and the interruption of his present mission seemed unlikely to prosper it. But not even prospective oblivion will prevent a composer from brooding despondently and maddeningly on his own works. Geoffrey embarked on a mental performance: Ta-ta; ta-ta-ta-*ti*-ta-*ti*...

"I wonder," Fielding added, "if they've anticipated the failure of the first attack, and provided a second line of defence."

This unexpected confusion of military metaphor shook Geoffrey. The spectral caterwaulings were abruptly stilled. "I believe you said that to frighten me," he said.

"Tell me what's going on. If I'm an enemy, I know already—"

"I didn't say—"

"And if I'm not, I may be able to help."

So in the end Geoffrey told him. As precise information it amounted to very little.

"I don't see that that helps much," Fielding objected when he had finished. He examined the telegram and letter. "And who is this Fen person, anyway?"

"Professor of English at Oxford. We were up together. I haven't seen much of him since, though I happened to hear he was going to be in Tolnbridge during the long vac. Why he should send for me—" Geoffrey made a gesture of humorous resignation, and upset the butterfly-net, which was poised precariously in a transverse position across the interior of the cab. With some acrimony they jerked it into place again.

"I can't think," said Geoffrey, after contemplating for a moment finishing his previous sentence and deciding against it, "why Fen insisted on my bringing that thing."

"Rather odd, surely? Is he a collector?"

"One never quite knows with Fen. In anyone else, though—well, yes, I suppose it would seem odd."

"He seems to know something about this Brooks business."

"Well, he's *there*, of course. And then," Geoffrey added as a laborious afterthought, "he's a detective, in a way."

Fielding looked disconcerted; he had evidently been reserving this role for himself, and disliked the thought of competition. A little peevishly he asked:

"Not an official detective, surely?"

"No, no, amateur. But he's been very successful."

"Gervase Fen—I don't seem to have heard of him," said Fielding. Then after a moment's thought: "What a silly name. Is he in with the police?" His tone suggested Fen's complicity in some orgiastic and disgraceful organisation.

"I honestly don't know. It's only what I've heard."

"I wonder if you'd mind my coming with you to Tolnbridge? I'm sick of the store. And with the war on, it seems so remote from anything—"

"Couldn't you join up?"

"No, they won't have me. I volunteered last November, but they graded me *four*. I joined the A.R.P., of course, and I'm thinking of going in for this new L.D.V. racket, but blast it all—"

"You look healthy enough," said Geoffrey.

"So I am. Nothing wrong with me except shaky eye-sight. They don't grade you four for that, do they?"

"No. Perhaps," Geoffrey suggested encouragingly, "you're suffering from some hidden, fatal disease you haven't known about."

Fielding ignored this. "I want to do something active about this war—something romantic." He mopped his brow again, looking the reverse of romantic. "I tried to join the Secret Service, but it was no good. You can't join the Secret Service in this country. Not just like that." And he slapped his hands together to indicate some platonic idea of facility.

Geoffrey considered. In view of what had happened it would almost certainly be very useful to have Fielding with him on his journey, and there was no reason to suspect him of ulterior motive.

"...After all, war hasn't become so mechanised that solitary, individual daring no longer matters," Fielding was saying; he seemed transported to some Valhalla of Secret Service agents. "You'll laugh at me, of course"—Geoffrey smiled a hasty and unconvincing negative—"but in the long run it is the people who dream of being men of action who are the men of action. Admittedly Don Quixote made a fool of himself with the windmills, but when all's said and done, there probably *were* giants about." He sighed gently as the taxi turned into the Marylebone Road.

"I should very much like to have you with me," said

Geoffrey. "But look here—what about your job? One must have money."

"That'll be all right. I have some money of my own." Fielding assembled his features into a perfunctory expression of surprise. "Oh, I ought perhaps to have mentioned it. *Debrett, Who's Who*, and such publications, credit me with an earldom."

Geoffrey summoned up a cheerful laugh, but there was something in Fielding's assurance which forbade him to utter it.

"Only very minor, of course," the other hastened to explain. "And I've never done a thing to deserve it. I inherited it."

"Then what on earth," said Geoffrey, "were you doing in that shop?"

"Store," Fielding corrected him solemnly. "Well, I heard there was a shortage of people to serve in shops, owing to call-up and so on, so I thought that might be one way I could help. Only temporarily, of course," he added warily. "Just as a joke," he ended feebly.

Geoffrey suppressed his merriment with difficulty. Fielding suddenly chuckled.

"I suppose it *is* rather preposterous, when you come to think of it. By the way"—a sudden thought struck him— "are you Geoffrey Vintner, the composer?"

"Only very minor, of course."

They surveyed one another properly for the first time, and found the result pleasing. The taxi clattered into the murk of Paddington. A sudden noise disturbed them.

"Well, I'm damned," said Fielding. "The bloody net's fallen down again."

CHAPTER TWO

Do Not Travel for Pleasure

"A crowd is no company, and faces are but a gallery of pictures, and talk but a tinkling cymbal where there is no love."
BACON

AFTER THE DIM, barn-like vastness of Waterloo, Paddington appeared like an infernal pit. Here there was not the order, the strict division and segregation of mechanical and human which prevailed at the larger station. Inextricably, engines and passengers seethed and milled together, the barriers provided for their separation seeming no more than the inconvenient erections of an obstacle-race. The crowds, turgid, stormy, and densely-packed, appeared more likely to clamber on to the backs of the trains, like children piling on to a donkey at the seaside than merely to board them in the normal way. The locomotives panted and groaned like expiring hedgehogs prematurely overrun by hordes of predatory ants; any attempt at departure, one felt, must infallibly crush and dissipate these insects in their thousands—it would be impossible for them to disentangle themselves from the buffers and connecting-rods in time.

Amongst the crowds, the heat banished comfort, but stimulated the itch to uneasy and purposeless movement. Certain main streams, between the bars, the platform, the ticket-offices, the lavatories, and the main entrances, were perhaps discernible; but they had only the conventional boundaries of currents on a map—they overflowed their banks amongst the merely impassive, who stood at the angles of their confluence in attitudes of melancholy or despair. Observed from ground level, this mass of humanity exhibited, in its efforts to move hither and thither, surprising divergences from the horizontal; people pressed forward to their destinations leaning forward at a dangerous angle, or, peering round the bodies of those in front of them, presented the appearance of criminals half-decapitated. A great many troops, bearing ponderous white cylinders apparently filled with lead, elbowed their way apologetically about, or sat on kit-bags and allowed themselves to be buffeted from all angles. Railway officials controlled the scene with the uneasy authority of schoolmasters trying to extort courteous recognition from their pupils after term has ended.

"Good God," said Geoffrey as he struggled forward, carrying a suitcase with which he made periodic involuntary assaults on the knees of the passers-by, "are we even going to get *on* this train?"

Fielding, still inappropriately dressed in the morning clothes belonging to his recent occupation, merely grunted; the temperature seemed to overcome him. When they had progressed, clawing and pushing, another two yards, he said:

"What time is it supposed to go?"

"Not for three-quarters of an hour yet." The relevant part of the sentence was drowned in a sudden demoniac outburst of hooting and whistling. He repeated it at the top of his voice. "Three-quarters of an hour," he bellowed.

Fielding nodded, and then, surprisingly, vanished with a shouted explanation of which the only word audible was "clothes." A little bemused, Geoffrey laboured to the ticket-office. The tickets occupied him for some twenty minutes, but in any case the train seemed likely to depart late. He waved his bag in optimistic query at a porter, passing on some nameless, leisurely errand, and was ignored.

Then he went, reflecting a little sadly on the miseries which our indulgences cause us, to get a drink.

The refreshment-room was decorated with gilt and marble; their inappropriate splendours cast a singular gloom over the proceedings. By the forethought of those responsible for getting people on to trains the clock had been put ten minutes fast, a device which led to frequent panics of departure among those who were under the impression that it showed the right time. They were immediately reassured by others, whose watches were slow. Upon discovery of the real hour, a second and more substantial panic occurred. Years of the Defence of the Realm Act had conditioned the British public to remain in bars until the latest possible moment.

Geoffrey deposited his bag by a pillar (someone immediately fell over it), and elbowed his way to the bar, which he clutched with the determination of a ship-wrecked sailor who has reached a friendly shore. The sirens lurking behind it, with comparative freedom of movement, were engaged in friendly discourse with regular customers. A barrage of imperative glances and despairing cries for attention failed, for the most part, to move them. Some brandished coins in the hope that this display of affluence and good faith would jerk these figures into motion. Geoffrey found himself next to a dwarfish commercial traveller, who was treating one of the barmaids to a long, rambling fantasy about the disadvantages of early marriage, as freely exemplified by himself and many friends and relations. By pushing him malignantly out of the way, Geoffrey managed eventually to get a drink.

Fielding reappeared as inexplicably as he had gone, dressed in a sports coat and flannels and carrying a suitcase. He explained rather breathlessly that he had been back to his flat, and demanded beer. The ritual of entreaty was again enacted. *"Travelling,"* said Fielding with deep feeling.

"I hope we don't have to get in with any babies," said Geoffrey gloomily. "If they don't shriek out and crawl all over me, they're invariably sick."

❀ ❀ ❀

There were babies—one, at least—but the first-class compartment containing it was the only one with two seats vacant—one of them, on to which Geoffrey at once hurled a mass of impedimenta in token of ownership, an outside corner. He then applied himself to getting Fen's butterfly-net on to the rack, assisted by Fielding, and watched with interest by the other occupants of the compartment. It was just too long. Geoffrey regarded it with hatred: it was growing, in his eyes, into a monstrous symbol of the inconvenience, shame and absurdity of his preposterous errand.

"Try standing it up against the window," said the man sitting in the corner opposite Geoffrey's. His plumpness and pinkness outdid Fielding's. Geoffrey felt, regarding him, like a man who while brandishing an Amati is suddenly confronted with a Strad.

They put this scheme into practice; whenever anyone moved his feet the net fell down again. "What a thing to bring on a train," said the woman with the baby, *sotto voce*.

It was eventually decided to lay the net transversely across the carriage, from one rack to the other. The whole compartment rose—not with any enthusiasm, since it was so hot—to do justice to his idea. A woman seated in one of the other corners, with a face white and pock-marked like a plucked chicken's breast, complainingly shifted her luggage to make room. Then she sat down again and insulated herself unnecessarily against the surrounding humanity with a rug, which made Geoffrey hot even to look at. With a great deal of obscure mutual encouragement and admonition, such as "Up she goes" and "Steady, now," Geoffrey, Fielding, the fat man and a young clergyman who occupied the remaining corner hoisted the net into position. The baby, hitherto quiescent, awoke and embarked upon a running commentary of snorts and shrieks; it grunted like the pig-baby in *Alice*, until they expected it to be metamorphosed before their eyes. The mother jogged it ruthlessly up and down, and glared malignantly at the progenitors of the disturbance. People searching for seats peered into the compartment and attempted to assess the number of people engaged in this hullabaloo. One went so far as to open the door and ask if there was any room, but he was ignored, and soon went away again.

"Disgraceful!" said the woman with the baby. She bumped it up and down even more furiously than before, and cooed at it, adding to its noises with her own.

The net was by now secured at either end, and more or less conveniently placed, except that anyone rising incautiously or coming into the compartment was liable to bang his head on it. Geoffrey profusely thanked his assistants, who sat down again looking hot but pleased. He turned back to transfer the remainder of his belongings from the seat on to the rack. They were now topped by a letter not his own, but plainly addressed to him. The paper and typing looked uncomfortably familiar. He opened it and read:

There's still time to get off the train. We have our setbacks, but we can't go on failing indefinitely.

Ignoring Fielding's curious glance, he put it thoughtfully in his pocket and heaved the remainder of his things out of the

way. In the confusion of a moment before, anyone in the compartment could have dropped that note, and for that matter—
since the window was wide open—anyone could have flicked
it in from outside. He tried to remember the dispositions of
the various persons in the compartment, and failed. He sat
down feeling somewhat alarmed.

"Another?" said Fielding; he raised his right eyebrow in
elaborate query.

Geoffrey nodded dumbly and handed him the note. He
whistled with noisy astonishment as he read it. "But who—?"

Geoffrey shook his head, still refusing to utter a sound.
He hoped to convey by this means his suspicion of one of the
occupants of the compartment. Any open discussion of the
matter might, he obscurely felt, convey information of value to
the enemy. The others were eyeing unenthusiastically this
gnomic interchange.

But Fielding was for the moment oblivious of such innu-
endoes.

"Quick work," he said. "They must have had a second line
of defence ready in case the business in the store failed.
Simply a matter of phoning someone here while we were on
our way. They're certainly taking no chances."

"I wish you'd remember," said Geoffrey a trifle peevishly,
"that *I'm* the object of all this. It's no pleasure to *me* to have
you sitting there gloating over the excellence of their arrangements."

No notice was taken of this. "And that means," Fielding
continued impassively, "that the typewriter they used is somewhere in this neighbourhood—damn it, no it doesn't, though.
The wording of that second note is so vague it could easily
have been got ready beforehand." The failure of his calcula-
tion threw him into a profound despondency; he stared dejectedly at his feet.

Geoffrey meanwhile was carrying out an inventory of the

other persons in the compartment. The man opposite, who had been so helpful over Fen's butterfly-net, had a well-to-do professional air. Geoffrey was inclined to put him down as a doctor, or a prosperous broker. His face was amiable, with that underlying shyness and melancholy which seems always to be beneath the surface in fat men; he had sparse straight hair, pale grey eyes with heavy lids like thick shutters of flesh, and very long lashes, like a girl's. The material of his suit was expensive, and it was competently tailored. He held a thick black book, one of the four volumes, Geoffrey observed with surprise, of Pareto's monumental *The Mind and Society*. Did doctors or brokers read such things on railway journeys? Covertly, he regarded his *vis-à-vis* with renewed interest.

Next door was the woman with the baby. Repeated jogging had now shaken the infant into a state of bemused incomprehension, and it emitted only faint and isolated shrieks. By compensation, it had begun to dribble. Its mother, a small woman vaguely and unanalysably slatternly in appearance, periodically wiped a grubby handkerchief with great force and determination across its face, so that its head almost fell off backwards; while not occupied in this way, she gazed at her companions with great dislike. Probably, Geoffrey reflected, she could be omitted from the list of suspects. The same could not be said for the clergyman sitting in the corner on her right, however. It was true that he looked ready, young, and ineffectual, but these were too much the characteristics of the stage curate not to be at once suspicious. He was glancing occasionally, with anxious enquiry, at the woman with the rug. She, meanwhile, was engaged in that unnerving examination of other persons in the compartment which most people seem to regard as necessary at the beginning of a long railway journey. Eventually, feeling apparently that this had now been brought to the point where embarrassment was likely to become active discomfort, she said to the clergyman, looking sternly at a small wristwatch:

"What time do we get into Tolnbridge?"

This query aroused some interest in other quarters. Both Geoffrey and Fielding started slightly, with well-drilled uniformity, and shot swift glances at the speaker, while in the Pareto-addict opposite Geoffrey some stirrings of attention were also discernible. All things considered, it was not very surprising that someone else in the compartment should be going to Tolnbridge, even though compared with Taunton and Exeter it was an unimportant stop; but Geoffrey at all events was too alarmed and uneasy to make such a simple deduction.

The clergyman seemed at a loss for an answer. He looked helplessly about him and said:

"I'm afraid I'm not sure, Mrs. Garbin. I could perhaps find out—?" He half-rose from his seat. The man opposite Geoffrey leaned forward.

"Five-forty-three," he said with decision. "But I'm afraid we're likely to lose time on the way." He took a gold watch from his waistcoat-pocket. "We're ten minutes late in starting already."

The woman with the rug nodded briskly. "In wartime, we must resign ourselves to that sort of thing," she said, her tone loaded with stoic resignation. "You are getting off there yourself?" she asked after a moment.

The fat man bowed his head. The reluctant and self-conscious democracy of the railway compartment was set into creaking motion. "Have you far to go?" he enquired of Geoffrey.

Geoffrey started. "I am going to Tolnbridge, too," he replied, a trifle stiffly. "The trains are almost always late nowadays," he added, feeling his previous remark to be by itself an insufficient contribution to the general entertainment. "Inevitably," said the clergyman, contributing his mite. "We are fortunate in being able to travel at all." He turned to the woman with the baby. "Have you a long journey, madam? It must be very tiring travelling with a child."

"I'm going further west than the rest of you," said the mother. "Much further west," she added. Her tone expressed a determination to remain in her seat as far west as possible, even if the train should be driven over Land's End and into the sea.

"Such a good boy," said the clergyman, gazing at the child with distaste. It spat ferociously at him.

"Now, Sally, you mustn't do that to the gentleman," said the mother. She glowered at him with unconcealed malevolence. He smiled unhappily. The fat man returned to his book. Fielding sat morose and silent, scanning an evening paper.

It was at this moment, amidst a shrieking of whistles which advertise immediate departure, that the irruption occurred. A man appeared in the corridor outside, carrying a heavy portmanteau, and peered though the window, bobbing up and down like a marionette in order to see what lay within. He then thrust the door aside and stepped aggressively over the threshold. He wore a shiny black suit with a bedraggled carnation in the buttonhole, bright brown shoes, a pearl tie-pin, a dirty grey trilby hat, and a lemon-colored handkerchief in his breast-pocket; his hands were nicotine-stained and his nails filthy; his complexion was sanguine, almost apoplectic, and he wiped his nose on the back of his hand as he trampled in over the clergyman's feet, hauling his case like a reluctant dog after him. It swung forward and struck the woman with the rug a resounding blow on the knee.

"No room!" she said as if at a signal. A confused murmur of admonition and discouragement went up in support of this remark. The man stared aggrievedly about him.

"Wadjer mean, no room?" he said loudly, "Djer think I'm gointa stand aht in the bloody corridor the 'ole journey? Because if yer do, yer bloody well wrong, see?" He warmed to his theme. "Just because yer travelling bloody first-class, yer needn't think yer got a right to occupy the 'ole train, see? People like me aren't goin' ter stand the 'ole way just so you plutocrats can stretch yer legs in comfort, see?" He became indignant. "I paid for a seat same as you 'aye, 'aven't I? 'Ere"— he shot out a finger towards the fat man, who jumped visibly with fright. "You put that there arm up, an' we'll all 'ave a chance ter sit down, see?" The fat man hastily put the arm up, and the intruder, with expressions of noisy satisfaction, inserted himself into the gap thus created between the fat man and the mother and child.

"You mind your language when there are ladies present!" said the mother indignantly. The baby began to bellow again. "There—see what you've done to the child!"

The intruder ignored her. He produced a *Mirror* and *Herald*, and, after slapping the former down on his knee, opened the latter at full spread, so that his elbows waved within an inch of the noses of those on either side. The woman with the rug, after her first sortie, had recognised defeat in the monotonous stream of blasphemy and become silent. Geoffrey, Fielding and the clergyman, afflicted by a bourgeois terror of offending this unruly manifestation of the lower classes, sat impotent and dis-approving. Only the mother, who maintained her intransigence with scornful glances, and the fat man, whose position was more desperate, still showed resistence.

"I suppose," said the fat man, abandoning his Pareto, "that you've got a first-class ticket?"

A deathly silence followed this question. The intruder jerked himself slowly up from his paper, like a pugilist who has been unfairly smitten in the belly and is gathering forces pon-derously together for retaliation. The others looked on aghast. Even the fat man quailed, unnerved by the ominous delay in answering his query.

"What's it got ter do with *you*?" asked the intruder at last, slapping his *Herald* shut. A dramatic hush ensued. "Not the bloody ticket-collector, are yer?" The fat man remained dumb. "Just 'cos I ain't as rich and idle as you, ain't I got a right ter sit in comfort, eh?"

"Comfort!" said the woman with the baby meaningly. The intruder ignored her, continuing to apostrophise the fat man. "Snob, aren't yer? Too 'igh-and-mighty to 'ave the likes o' me in the same compartment with yer, are yer? Let me tell you"— he tapped the fat man abruptly on the waistcoat—"one o' ther things we're fightin' this war for is ter get rid o' the likes o' you an' give the likes er me a chance to spread ourselves a bit."

He spread himself, illustratively, kicking Fielding in the shin in the process. The baby wailed like a banshee. "*Caliban,*" said the mother.

"Nonsense!" the fat man protested feebly. "That's got nothing to do with whether you've got a first-class ticket or not."

The intruder twisted himself bodily round and thrust his face into that of the fat man. "Oh, it ain't, ain't it?" He began to speak very rapidly. "When we get socialism, see, which is what we're fighting for, see, you and your like'll 'ave to show some respect to me, see, instead of treating me like a lot of dirt, see?" Finding this line of thought exhausted, he transferred his attention to the fat man's book, removing it, despite faint protests, from his hands. He then inspected it slowly and with care, as a surgeon might some peculiarly loathsome cancer after removal.

"What's this?" he said. "Vilfreedo Pareeto," he announced to the compartment at large. "*Ther Mind and Society,*" he read. "OO's that—some bloody Wop, is it? 'Ere, you," he addressed Geoffrey. "You ever 'eard of 'im—Vilfreedo Pareeto?"

The fat man looked at Geoffrey appealingly. Treacherously and mendaciously, Geoffrey shook his head. Worlds would not have induced him to admit acquaintance with that sociologist.

The intruder nodded triumphantly, and turned to Fielding. "What abaht you?" he said, waving the volume. "You ever 'eard of this?" As treacherously, but with more truth, Fielding denied it. The fat man turned pale. So solemn were the proceedings, he might have been awaiting sentence from the Inquisition, the only two witnesses for the defence having been suborned against him.

The intruder breathed heavily with satisfaction. Portentously he turned the pages of the book. "Listen ter this," he commanded. "'The principal nu-cle-us in a deriv-a-tive (a non-log-ico-ex-per-i-ment-al the-ory) is a res-i-due, or a number of res-i-dues, and around it other sec-ond-ar-y res-i-dues cluster.' Does that make sense, I arst yer? Does that make sense?" He glared at Geoffrey, who feebly shook his head. "Sec-ond-ar-y res-i-dues," repeated the intruder with scorn. "Lot o' non-sense, if yer arst me. 'Ere"—he turned back to the fat man again, hurling the book on to his knee, "you oughter 'ave something better ter do with yer time than read 'ighbrow books by Wops. And if yer 'aven't, see, you just mind yer own business, see, and don't go poking yer nose into other people's affairs, see?"

He turned back aggressively to the other occupants of the compartment. "Anybody got any objection ter my sitting 'ere, first-class or no?"

So successful had been the process of intimidation that no one uttered a sound.

Presently the train started.

❄ ❄ ❄

All afternoon the train rattled and jolted through the English countryside, towards the red clay of Devon and the slow, immense surge of the Atlantic against the Cornish shore. Geoffrey dozed, gazed automatically out of the window, thought about his fugue or meditated with growing dismay on the events of the day. The possibility—almost, he decided, the certainty—that he had an enemy within a foot or two of him made Fielding's company very welcome. Of the why and wherefore of the whole business he thought but briefly; strictly there was nothing to think about. The occurrences which had followed his arriving down to breakfast that morning, in a perfectly normal and peaceable manner, seemed a nightmare phantasmagoria devoid of reason. Almost, he began to wonder if they had taken place at all. The human mind properly assimilates only those things it has become accustomed to; anything out-of-the-way affects it only in a purely superficial and objective sense. Geoffrey contemplated the attack on himself without a shred of real belief.

Fielding and the woman with the rug slept, shaking and jolting like inanimate beings as the train clattered over points. The young clergyman gazed vacantly into the corridor, and the mother rocked her baby, which had fallen into a fitful slumber, beset in all probability with nightmares. The intruder also had gone to sleep, and was snoring, his chin resting painfully on his tie-pin. The fat man eyed Geoffrey warily, and put down the *Daily Mirror*, which had been forced on him in a spirit of scornful condescension by the intruder, and which he had been reading unhappily ever since the train left Paddington. He grinned conspiratorially.

"Devil of a journey," he said.

Geoffrey grinned back. "I'm afraid you're worse off then I am. But it's bad enough in any case."

The fat man appeared to be considering deeply. When he again spoke, it was with some hesitation. "You, sir, are obviously an educated man—I wonder if you can help me out of a difficulty?"

Geoffrey looked at him in surprise. "If I can."

"An intellectual difficulty merely," said the fat man hastily.

He seemed to think Geoffrey would imagine he was trying to borrow money. "However, I ought to introduce myself first. My name is Peace—Justinian Peace."

"Delighted to know you," said Geoffrey, and murmured his own name.

"Ah, the composer," said Peace amiably. "This is a great pleasure. Well now, Mr. Vintner, my whole problem can be summed up in three words: I have *doubts*."

"Good heavens," said Geoffrey. "Not like Mr. Prendergast?"

"I beg your pardon?"

"In *Decline and Fall*."

"I'm afraid I've never read Gibbon," said the other. The admission appeared to irritate him in some obscure way. "The fact is that by profession I'm a psychoanalyst—quite a successful one, I suppose; successful certainly as far as money goes. The amount of money," he said confidentially, "which some people will pay for information which they could get from three hours' intelligent reading in any public library…However"—he became conscious that he was getting off the point—"there it is. I suppose in London I'm pretty well at the top of my profession. You may think we're all charlatans, of course—a lot of people do"—Geoffrey hurriedly shook his head—"but as far as I'm concerned, at least, I have tried to go about the business methodically and scientifically, and to do the best for my patients. Well, then—" He paused and mopped his brow to emphasise the fact that he was now coming to the crux of the matter; Geoffrey nodded encouragingly.

"As you know, the whole of modern psychology—and psychoanalysis in particular—is based on the idea of the unconscious; the conception that there is a section of the mind in some sense separate from the conscious mind, and which is responsible for our dreams, certain of our impulses, and all the complex manifestations of the irrational in human life." His phraseology, Geoffrey thought, was taking on the aspect of a popular textbook. "From this concept all the conclusions of analytical psychology are derived. Unfortunately, about a month ago, it occurred to me to investigate the origins and rationale of this basic conception. A terrible thing happened, Mr. Vintner." He leaned forward and tapped Geoffrey impressively on the knee. "*I could not find one shred of experimental or rational proof that the unconscious existed at all.*"

He sat back again; it was evident that he regarded this statement as in some sense a personal triumph.

"The more I thought about it, the more convinced I became that in fact it didn't exist. We know, after all, nothing at all about the *conscious* mind, so why postulate, quite arbitrarily, an *unconscious*, to explain anything we can't understand? It's as if," he added with some vague recollection of wartime cooking, "a man were to say he was eating a mixture of butter and margarine when he had never in his life tasted either."

Geoffrey regarded Peace with a jaundiced eye. "Interesting," he muttered. "Very interesting," he repeated beneath his breath, like a physician who has diagnosed some obscure and offensive complaint. "One accepted it, of course, as a thing no longer requiring any investigation, like the movement of the earth round the sun. But I don't quite see…"

"But you must see!" Peace interrupted excitedly. "It strikes at the root of my profession, my occupation, my income, my *life*." His voice rose to a squeak. "I can't go on being a psychoanalyst when I don't believe in the unconscious any longer. It's as impossible as a vegetarian butcher."

Geoffrey sighed; his look conveyed that *he*, at least, could see no way out of the impasse. "Surely," he said, "the matter isn't as serious as all that."

Peace shook his head. "It is, I'm afraid," he said. "And when you come to think of it, isn't psychoanalysis *silly*? Anything can mean anything, you know. It's like that series of sums in which whatever number you start with the answer is always twenty-one."

"Well," said Geoffrey, "couldn't you start a system of psychoanalysis based only on the conscious mind?"

The other brightened; then his face fell again. "I suppose one *might*," he said, "but I don't quite see how it's possible. Still, I'll think about it. Thank you for the suggestion." He became very despondent; Geoffrey hastened to change the subject.

"Have you ever been to Tolnbridge before?"

"Never," Peace replied; he seemed to regard this admission of deficiency as the very acme of his troubles. "It's very beautiful, I believe. Are you proposing to stay long?"

Geoffrey, for no very sound reason, became suddenly suspicious. "I'm not sure," he said.

"My brother-in-law," said Peace didactically, "is Precentor at the cathedral there, and I'm going to see my sister—the first time in several years. I confess I'm not looking forward to it. I don't get on with the clergy"—he lowered his voice, glancing furtively at its representative in the far corner. "I find they regard one as a sort of modern witch-doctor—quite rightly, I suppose," he concluded miserably, remembering his doubts.

Geoffrey's interest was aroused. "As it happens," he said, "I'm going to stay at the clergy-house myself, so we shall probably be seeing something of one another. I shall be playing the services, for a while at all events."

Peace nodded. "Ah, yes," he said, "That organist fellow was knocked out, of course. My sister told me over the phone this morning. Said she wasn't surprised—fellow drinks like a fish, apparently. I suppose it would have been my brother-in-law who asked you to come down?"

"It *should* have been, by rights. Actually it was a friend of mine, Gervase Fen, who's staying at the clergy-house at the moment. Presumably he was authorised." Knowing Fen, Geoffrey was suddenly seized by a horrible doubt. But plainly the Enemy considered him to be authorised, or they wouldn't be wasting their time on him.

"Gervase Fen," said Peace meditatively. "I seem to know the name."

"A detective of sorts."

"I see—investigating the attack on this fellow Brooks, I suppose. And it was he who sent for you to act as deputy? Extraordinary the things the police take on themselves nowadays!"

"Not an official detective—amateur."

"Oh."

"So you're really just holidaying, then?"

"Not entirely. I have to see my brother-in-law about..." Peace suddenly checked himself. "A matter of business. Nothing important." Geoffrey did not fail to notice the alteration in his tone; and he seemed to think he had said too much in any case, for he leaned back and automatically took up the *Daily Mirror* again. Geoffrey felt he had been dismissed. There was one more question he wanted to ask, however.

"Did you by any chance happen to see me pick up a letter from my seat shortly after I came into the compartment?" he said.

Peace looked at him curiously for a moment. "Yes," he said slowly. "As it happens, I did. Nothing alarming, I hope."

"No, nothing alarming. You didn't notice how it got there, I suppose?"

The other paused for some moments before replying. "I'm afraid not," he said at last. "No, I'm afraid I didn't notice at all."

Geoffrey found himself being pursued with a butterfly-net across the Devon moors. The persons of his pursuers were vague, but they moved with great rapidity. He was not surprised to find Peace running beside him. "It is necessary," he said to Peace, "that we should run the unconscious to ground wherever it may be. We can hide there, and besides, I strongly suspect that Gervase Fen will be somewhere in that neighbourhood too." His companion made no reply—he was too much occupied with the baby he was carrying. When they reached the cathedral, the pursuers were a good deal closer, and they ran at full speed to the altar, shouting: "Sanctuary! We demand sanctuary!" They were stopped beneath the rood-screen by a young clergyman. "We can't go on failing indefinitely," he said. "It is impossible for us to go on failing indefinitely." The pursuers were by now very near. Peace dropped the baby. It screamed, and then began to whistle shrilly, like a railway-engine. The noise grew in volume, like the swift approach of a tornado…

The engine of the train passing in the opposite direction swept past the compartment, its whistle at full blast as Geoffrey struggled back to consciousness. Without moving, he opened his eyes and looked about him. Peace slumbered in the opposite corner, the paper dropped from his hands; the intruder still snored; the mother was whispering softly to the baby, which moaned and struggled spasmodically. Fielding sat reading a book—he seemed curiously isolated and strange. Geoffrey felt that if he spoke to him he would turn without recognition in his face, a stranger merely. The clergyman and the woman with the rug were talking together in low tones, their words inaudible above the incessant, monotonous beating of the wheels. Geoffrey sat and stared, first at a disagreeable photograph of Salisbury Cathedral, and then at the "Instructions to Passengers in the Event of an Air Raid," which had been annotated by some passenger with over-much time on his hands:

DRAW ALL BLINDS AS A PRECAUTION AGAINST—nosey bastards. DO NOT LEAVE THE CARRIAGE UNLESS REQUESTED BY A—hot bit.

He blinked sleepily about him, and tried to stop thinking about the heat.

The sirens wailed as the train began braking on the stretch into Taunton. All along the coast, the fierce merciless battle against the invading bombers began. The intruder awoke from his long sleep and gazed blearily out of the window. His hasty movements of departure came as a welcome diversion. He got to his feet, scowled round him, and reached up to the rack above Geoffrey's head, where his heavy portmanteau lay. It was, of course, not entirely surprising, in view of its weight, that he should have let it slip, and if it had fallen directly on to Geoffrey's head as he leaned forward to talk to Fielding, the consequences would have been serious. Fortunately, Fielding saw it coming, and pushed Geoffrey against the back of the seat with all his force. The portmanteau landed with a sickening thud on his knees.

A confused clamour arose. The agent of this disturbance did not, however, wait to make his apologies, but was out of the compartment and on to Taunton platform before the train had come to a stop. Geoffrey sat doubled up with agony, nursing his thighs; but happily the human thigh-bone is a solid object, and Peace showed himself a fairly expert doctor. As to a pursuit, that was out of the question. By the time order was restored, the train was in any case on the move again.

"He might have broken your neck!" said the woman with the baby indignantly.

"So he might," said Geoffrey painfully. Feeling very sick, he turned to Fielding. "Thanks—for the second time today."

Peace had unlocked the case, and was gazing with bewilderment at the medley of old iron it contained. "No wonder it was so heavy," he said. "But what on earth…" Abruptly he decided that this was not the time for investigation. "You'd better do some walking before stiffness sets in," he told Geoffrey. "You'll find it'll hurt, of course, but it's really the best thing."

Geoffrey crawled to his feet, banged his head against the

butterfly-net, and cursed noisily; this, he felt, was the last straw.

"I'll go and get a wash," he said. "One gets so filthy on these journeys." Actually he was afraid he was going to be sick.

"Better let me come with you," said Fielding, but Geoffrey brushed him impatiently aside; he was consumed by a hatred of all mankind. "I'll be all right," he mumbled. He swayed down the corridor like a drunk on the deck of a storm-tossed ship. The lavatory, when he reached it, was occupied, but just as he was passing on to the next a young man came out, grinned apologetically, and stood aside to let him in. Geoffrey was contemplating his features gloomily in the mirror preparatory to turning round and locking the door when he realised that the young man had followed him in and was doing this for him.

The young man smiled. "Now we're shut in together," he said.

❀ ❀ ❀

"Third time lucky," said Fielding cheerfully.

Geoffrey groaned, and again shook himself free of a nightmare. He was back in the compartment, whose occupants were regarding him with some concern; even the baby gaped enquiringly at him, as though demanding an explanation.

"What happened?" Geoffrey asked conventionally.

"I got the wind up when you didn't come back," said Fielding, "and set out to find you. Fortunately, it wasn't very difficult, and we were able to lug you back here. How do you feel?"

"Awful."

"You'll be all right," said Peace. "The blow must have upset you."

"I should damn well think it did," said Geoffrey indignantly. "Where are we?"

"Just coming into Tolnbridge now."

Geoffrey groaned again. "Past Exeter? He must have got off the train there."

"My dear fellow, are you all right? He got off the train at Taunton."

Geoffrey gazed confusedly about him. "No, no—the other. Oh, Lord!" His head was swimming too much to think clearly. He rubbed it ruefully, feeling it all over. "Where's the bruise?" he asked. "There must be a bruise." Peace, who was collecting his things from the rack, looked round in surprise.

"Where he hit me," explained Geoffrey peevishly.

"My dear chap, nobody hit you," said Peace amicably. "You must be dreaming. You fainted, that's all. Fainted."

CHAPTER THREE

Gibbering Corse

> *"And then the furiously gibbering corse*
> *…Shakes, panglessly convulsed, and*
> *sightless stares."*
>
> **PATMORE**

TOLNBRIDGE STANDS ON THE RIVER after which it is named about four miles above the sandy, treacherous estuary which flows into the English Channel. Up to Hanoverian times it was a port of some significance; but the growth in the size of shipping, together with the progressive silting-up of the river mouth, which is now penetrated only by a fairly narrow channel, pretty rapidly took from it that eminence, and it has fallen back into its pristine status as a small and rather inconvenient market-town for the farm products of that area of South Devon. There is still a fishing industry and (before the war at least) some holiday-ing, but the bulk of its prosperity has been transferred to Tolnmouth, a little to the east of the estuary, which as a summer

39

resort is second only to Torquay on the Devon coast. Nor is Tolnbridge of much value from the military or naval point of view; it had received a certain amount of sporadic and spiteful attention from the bombers, but the main part of the attack was concentrated further up the coast, and it suffered little damage.

The cathedral was built during the reign of Edward II, when Tolnbridge was enjoying an unexampled prosperity as the staple port for the wines of Bordeaux and Spain; in style it comes, historically, somewhere about the time of the transition from Early English to Decorated, but few traces of the later method are to be found in it, and it is one of the last, as well as one of the finest, examples of that superb artistry which produced Salisbury Cathedral and many lovely parish churches. Comparatively, it is a small building; but it stands in the centre of the town in a position of such eminence that it appears larger than is really the case. The river rises to a natural plateau, about a quarter of a mile back, on which the older part of the town is built. Behind this again there is a long and steeply-sloping hill, at the very summit of which the cathedral stands—the hill itself devoid of buildings, except for the clergyhouse at the southwestern end. So, from the town, there is a magnificent vista up this long slope, planted with cypress, mountain-ash and larches, to the grey buttresses and slender, tapering spire which over-hang the river. The effect would be overpowering were it not for the two smaller churches in the town below, whose spires, lifted in noble, unsuccessful emulation of their greater companion above, a little restore the balance and relieve the eye. Behind the cathedral, the hill slopes more gently down again to the newer part of the town, with the railway station and the paint factory, whose houses stream down on the northern side to join the old town and peter out to the south in a series of expensive and widely-spaced villas overlooking the estuary.

It is perhaps surprising that Tolnbridge did not share the

fate of Crediton and succumb to the See of Exeter. But Exeter's diocese was large enough already, and Tolnbridge was suffered to remain a cathedral town. About seventy years after the erection of the cathedral, a tallow-maker of the town called Ephraim Pentyre, a miser and a notorious usurer, but a man who gave much money to the Church on the understanding that it should reserve him a front seat at the celestial entertainment, set out by the coast road on a pilgrimage to Canterbury (where he might, had he ever reached it, have encountered Chaucer's pilgrims in person). So niggardly was he, however, that he refused to take servants for his protection, with the consequence that beyond Weymouth he was set upon, murdered, and incontinentally robbed of his offering to the shrine of St. Thomas. This incompetence and stinginess earned him his canonisation, for his bones were returned to Tolnbridge and buried with much ceremony in the cathedral, where their miracles of healing attracted pilgrims from all over the country, Edward III himself visiting the shrine in order to be cured of scurvy (his own legendary abilities in that direction having apparently failed); with what success it is not known. This was the heyday of Tolnbridge's prosperity, none the less welcomed by the inhabitants because they remembered St. Ephraim with dislike, or because worse and blacker crimes than usury had been commonly laid to his account.

After that there was a slow but steady decline. Tolnbridge was too isolated to play any part in the great political and ecclesiastical disturbances which spasmodically racked the country up to the end of the eighteenth century, though upon occasion little symbolic wars were fought out on these issues among the townspeople, only too often with violence and atrocities. The transition from Mariolatry to Protestantism was made without fuss, the more so, as some said, because the old religion was allowed to persist and become vile in secret and abominable rituals. Some emphasis was given to these suggestions by a frenetic outburst of witch trials in the early seventeenth century, and by the equally frenetic outburst of witchcraft and devil-worship which provoked them, and in which several clergy of the diocese were disgracefully involved. It is doubtful, indeed, if there was ever such a concentrated, vehement and (by the standards of the day) well-justified persecution in the history of Europe; there were daily burnings on the cathedral hill, and, that curious feature of most witch trials, free confessions, given without torture, by some hundreds of women that they had had intercourse with the Devil and participated in the Black Mass. After a few years the commotion died down, as these things will, and left nothing behind but the blackened circle cut into the hillside and the iron post to which the women had been tied for burning. There were no further disturbances in Tolnbridge, of any kind; and by 1939 the town seemed to have settled down into a state of permanent inanition.

So at least Geoffrey maintained, in more forcible words, on his failing to get a taxi at the station. What he is actually recorded to have said is "What a damned hole!"

Now this was unjust, and Fielding, looking down past the cathedral at the roofs of the old town and the estuary beyond, felt it to be so. However, it was obviously not the time for argument. Geoffrey was smarting not only with physical pain (this had by now considerably abated), but also with a considerable mental irritation. There are limits beyond which human patience must not be tried; after a certain point, the crossword puzzle or cryptogram or riddle ceases to amuse and begins to infuriate. This point, in the present affair, Geoffrey had long since passed, and his last escape, far from leaving him pleased, maddened him with its pointlessness.

"What I cannot understand," he said for the tenth time, "is why, when they had me exactly where they wanted me, without a chance to resist or cry out, they didn't bang me on the head and shove me overboard."

Fielding regarded gloomily an aged porter who was prod-
ding tentatively at a trunk in the hope, apparently, of provok-
ing it to spontaneous movement. "Perhaps they were interrupted," was all he said.

"You can't be interrupted when you're locked in a lavatory."

"Perhaps they found you were the wrong person and
sheered off."

"The wrong person!"

Fielding sighed. "No, it's not likely. Their organisation
seems very good," he added with a sort of melancholy satisfaction. "Unless you imagined all that."

"Imagined it," said Geoffrey. "Of course I didn't."

"He wasn't just asking you the time?"

"The *time*! You don't follow people into lavatories and
bolt the door simply in order to ask them the *time*."

Fielding sighed again; he breathed out lengthily and noisily. The discussion, he thought, could not profitably be continued. "Is it far?" he asked.

"Yes; *very* far," said Geoffrey, annoyed at being thus
crudely unseated from his hobby-horse; he thought, too, that
he perceived the animal being led away. But something else
had occurred to Fielding, for he turned abruptly and said:

"Those letters."

Geoffrey looked at him in silence for a moment, and then
searched his pockets. The letters were gone.

"Very thorough," said Fielding drily. "When they found
you were coming here despite their warnings, they decided you
shouldn't have any clue to the machine they were typed on."

"So that was it. Damn. But it still doesn't explain why I
wasn't knocked out."

"When you're organising a thing like this, you can't give
your agents a free hand to do whatever emergency dictates.
Besides, this fellow may not even have known what was going
on. I expect he was told simply to get the letters from you, and

when you fainted there was no need to use violence." Fielding whistled gently. "They're fairly thorough."

The heat had grown somewhat less. Peace had made off, presumably towards the Precentor's house, in another direction. The woman with the rug and the young clergyman had long since disappeared. Looking at his watch, Geoffrey found that the train had got in only seven minutes late. He and Fielding started off down the station hill, Fielding carrying both bags, and Geoffrey the inescapable butterfly-net. On their right stood the cathedral, serenely beautiful. The great rose window in the south transept glowed momently at them with a rich, red beauty, and the gulls wheeled and screamed about the slender octagonal spire.

The medley of tobacconists and second-rate pubs huddled round the station soon gave place to a rather dreary street of small villas; and this in turn to the squalid, beautiful houses of the old town. A little beyond the beauty of these two worlds they turned off to the right, and shortly arrived at the wrought-iron gates of the clergy-house, which had been built in the eighteenth century to replace the old clergy-house adjoining the north transept; this being now used for storing lumber, holding choir-practices, and other miscellaneous and untidy purposes. The gates, suspended on either side from pillars of soft, lemon-coloured stone, opened upon a depressing vista of shrubs and lawns, bisected by an overgrown gravel drive which curved round to the front door, skirted the house, and led out beyond the extensive kitchen-gardens on to the cathedral hill itself. Geoffrey entered these regions with circumspection, peering intently at a withered laurel as though he expected it to contain springs, nets and lime for his discomfort.

In this realm of celibacy, the first thing they heard was a girl's voice. "Josephine!" it called; then with more force, and a tinge of irritation: "Come back!"

There was a sound of running footsteps, and a young girl,

plainly the object of these cries, came panting round the side of the house. She could not have been more than fifteen, and she was long, thin, and trembling, with curls of bright gold, tangled and disordered. Her face was red, not only with effort, but also with perceptible anger. She stopped short on seeing the strangers, and after staring at them for a moment, darted off into the shrubbery at one side, whence the diminishing rustle of innumerable graceless plants marked her retreat.

They toiled towards the portico, a little shaken by this welcome, and suspecting, with some dismay, a domestic upheaval. They had not gone more than a few steps before the owner of the voice they had heard appeared also, in unenergetic pursuit. And this at least, Geoffrey thought, was not what one expected to find on cathedral precincts—a girl of about twenty-three, as dark as the other had been blonde, with blue, humorous eyes, a tip-tilted nose, red lips, and a slim, loose-limbed body. Her dress, though rich and sober enough, and her high heels gave, Geoffrey thought, a faint suggestion of the courtesan. Not that he objected to this. Having little experience of women, he classified them, *a priori* as it were, as either amateur prostitutes or domestic helps, and anyone not fitting snugly into one of these categories left him confused, suspicious and uncomprehending (this masculine failing is commoner than perhaps women imagine). Certainly in this case a touch of the *hetaira*, the Lais or Phryne, was present; but there was also a practicality, self-possession and intelligence which softened and diffused the impression.

Fundamentally, Geoffrey was afraid of women. His endeavours to categorise those he had met as either courtesan or domestic had led to dismal misunderstandings, since he had never known anyone remotely resembling either kind. He also laboured, as a result of reading books, under the delusion that every unmarried woman he met was hunting, with all the tricks and subterfuges of her deadly and mysterious sex, for a husband, and congratulated himself inwardly upon hair-raising escapes from several women who in point of fact had never even considered marrying him, and who had merely used him as a convenient temporary paramour and offered him the honourable courtesy of the sex, a good-night kiss at the end of an evening enjoyed at his expense. Beyond the age of thirty, he had gradually shunned acquaintance with these puzzling beings. Consequently, he approached this new example of the species with a trepidation accentuated by her obvious charm.

"Damn the child!" she said, and gave up the pursuit.

"Has she been naughty?" said Fielding simply. He asked the question with the ease and authority of one too essentially courteous to need the formal preliminaries of acquaintance.

The girl met him, with equal ease, on his own ground. "Do you think children should be spanked?" she said. "Girls of that age, that is? I know I was—but Josephine's such a proud, headstrong brat she takes it hard."

"I think you should avoid it if possible," said Fielding with unnecessary seriousness.

The girl laughed—a low, gurgling infectious chuckle. "I see—you think it was me. No, I haven't got to the stage of walloping children yet. Father did it—and I must say I hardly blame him. Would you believe it, Josephine tore up and burnt the whole of the manuscript of the book he was working on?" An almost imperceptible chill came into the atmosphere. There are acts of petulance and ill-temper, and there are acts of deliberate malice. Geoffrey changed the subject with painfully obvious intent.

"We ought to introduce ourselves," he said. "This is the Earl of—the Earl of—What are you the Earl of?"

"It's not of the least importance," said Fielding. He had put down the bags and was despairingly towelling his face and neck with an immense white silk handkerchief. "Don't misunderstand me—if I thought that either of you would resent my being an earl, I should give you the full details immediately. But we might just as well say Henry Fielding, and be done with it."

"Not," the girl said, "the author of—"

Geoffrey interrupted in some haste. "And I'm Geoffrey Vintner," he said. He made the assertion despondently, as though he scarcely expected anyone to credit it.

"How nice," said the girl with business-like conviction. "We often do your Communion Service here. I'm Frances Butler."

"Good. So now we all know each other," said Fielding. He paused and gazed expectantly at Geoffrey.

"Oh, yes," said Geoffrey. "We are looking for Fen— Gervase Fen."

"I thought you were," said the girl, gazing pointedly at the butterfly-net, which he still brandished like a banner in front of him, "because of *that.*"

Geoffrey regarded her gloomily for a moment. "In- sects?" he ventured at last.

She nodded gravely.

"He's out at the moment, and I don't know when he'll be back again. I gather he's going to make some experiment to- night with *moths*, but we told him he couldn't do it here, because poor little Dutton, the Deputy Organist, is terrified of them at the best of times; and as it's got something to do with males flying hundreds of miles to get at a female in a darkened room, we thought that a clergy-house was an unsuitable place for such demonstrations. Besides, in the unlikely event of its succeeding, we couldn't possibly have the place full of moths. So I believe he's going to do it somewhere else."

Geoffrey sighed. "How characteristic!" he said. "He asks me to come down here, and then at the crucial moment disap- pears into the blue. I suppose he didn't mention my arrival?"

"Not a word."

"No." Geoffrey sighed; the burden of Atlas seemed to be upon him. "No, I might have expected that."

"Were you going to stay here?" asked the girl.

"Well, I imagined so. But I can't possibly push myself in if you're unprepared."

"I could manage one of you," said the girl dubiously, "but not both, by any possible means. There just isn't a bed."

"I can find somewhere in the town to stay," said Fielding.

"You'd better go to the 'Whale and Coffin,'" said the girl.

"It sounds terrible."

"It is terrible, but there's nowhere any better. Look, Mr. Vintner, leave your bags in the porch. Someone will take them in later, I dare say. And would you like a wash?"

"What I really want," said Geoffrey, "is a drink. Several drinks."

.   "All right. We'll all go down to the 'Whale and Coffin.' It is after six, isn't it? Then we can talk about things."

"I don't want to drag you away…"

"Away from *what*? Don't be so silly. Come on, both of you. It's only three minutes from here."

Geoffrey had nearly arrived before he realised he was still carrying the butterfly-net. He cursed it inwardly, murmuring under his breath.

"Have a good, rousing swear," said the girl. "You'll feel better."

❋ ❋ ❋

The "Whale and Coffin" turned out to be a large, low, rambling building of indefinite date situated in the middle of the old town. It was provided with innumerable bars, labelled variously: Bar, Saloon, Lounge Bar, Public Bar, Private Bar, and so on; these departments being ineffectually presided over by a small short-sighted, elderly man who hurried con-

stantly from one to another, less with any hope of being useful, one felt, than because it had become a habit and he couldn't
stop it. He peered astigmatically at Geoffrey as he ordered
drinks.

"Stranger?" he said. "Not been here before?"

"No," said Geoffrey shortly. He refused to be kept from
his beer by well-meaning chatter.

"I think you'll like it," said the other without particular
confidence. "It's a good local brew and we get a nice crowd
here." From his accent it was evident that he was not a Devon
man. "Strange name for a pub, isn't it?"

"Very."

"You'd imagine there'd be some story connected with a
name like that, wouldn't you?"

"Yes."

"There isn't, though. Someone just thought it up one day."

Geoffrey looked at him with contempt and moved shakily
back to the others, carrying drinks. They had settled in a remote
alcove. Frances Butler crossed her legs, smoothed out her skirt
with automatic propriety, and said:

"You needn't have worried—Harry never talks to anyone
for more than a minute at a time. I've watched him."

"Do you come here often?" asked Fielding.

"Oh, so-so. I don't haunt the place, if that's what you
mean. But it's the nearest pub to the clergy-house."

"I thought," said Fielding vaguely, "you might have found
a lot of silly prejudice about going to pubs at all—your father
being Precentor, and so on."

"Can't help that," said Frances, and grinned. "I expect
there is some, but they think I'm a tart as it is. Going to pubs
doesn't affect matters much. And Daddy doesn't seem to
mind—that's the chief thing. He brought me up terribly strictly
till I was eighteen, but since then he's just given me a lot of
money and let me do what I like. Poor old Meg—the house-

keeper at the clergy-house—got ill, and one can't get servants for love or money nowadays, so I gave up living with Daddy and went to house-keep there. I don't think the men like it very much, though. Each of them's afraid the others will think he's got designs on me. You've no idea the way they keep clear of my room, and the rumpus they make when they're going to the bathroom."

She laughed, and drank pink gin with a theatrical air of wickedness. It occurred to Geoffrey that she probably got an innocent, childish enjoyment out of pretending to be wicked. He greatly doubted, at all events, if she actually was. But he realised that with his present knowledge of her an adequate assessment of her merits and demerits was out of the question. Certainly she was attractive—very attractive, he suddenly felt. And he sighed, recognising the enormity of his inexperience in love.

"Tired?" she asked.

"No. Just content." It was not, he reflected, entirely a lie, at that. "Do you know," he said, "that I've been attacked three times today?"

She laughed. "Attacked? What on earth do you mean?"

"One man tried to knock me on the head in a shop"— "Store," said Fielding automatically—"another tried to drop a suitcase full of iron on my head, and another locked me in a lavatory on the train. That is to say"—Geoffrey struggled for a more suitable form of words. Put like that, it didn't sound nearly as serious as in fact it had been. "There were anonymous letters, too," he concluded lamely.

"But how awful," said the girl. "No—what a stupid thing to say. I mean"—she gestured helplessly—"Well, *why*?"

"I don't *know*. That's just the point. But I think it's got something to do with the attack on Brooks here."

Frances put down her drink rather suddenly. The movement was a slight one, and in itself unimportant, but it brought a curious unease to the atmosphere. There was a long pause before she said:

"Do you mean that?" Her voice was suddenly very quiet.

"That's all I can think of. If it hadn't been for Fielding, I might now be dead—almost certainly should be, in fact."

When Frances took up her glass again, her hand was a fraction unsteady. But her voice was calm as she asked:

"Was Dr. Brooks a friend of yours?" The question seemed to have a greater urgency, a greater importance, than common sense would allow. Geoffrey shook his head.

"I only knew him slightly—a professional acquaintance." He hesitated. "You said 'was'—"

She laughed again, but there was no humor in it. "No, he's not dead, if that's what you mean. I—" She seemed abruptly to make up her mind about something; with intended deliberateness and ostentation the subject was changed. "And Daddy asked you to come down here and play the services in his place?"

Geoffrey acquiesced, repressing an almost irrepressible curiosity. "Well, no, not exactly. That is to say. I suppose he knew about it. Actually it was Fen who wired me to come." He became uncomfortable. "If I'm not wanted, it doesn't matter. I'm glad of the break, and I shall like to see Fen again…" He stopped, conscious that the words were meaningless.

The girl's tone was lighter now. "Oh, I'm sure you're wanted—I don't know who else would have played, if you hadn't turned up."

"I was wondering—surely there's a deputy? In fact, you mentioned one."

"Little Dutton—yes. But he? sin the middle of a nervous breakdown. The silly boy overworked himself, trying to get God knows what stupid musical degree. The doctor won't let him go near an organ at the moment."

Geoffrey nodded portentously. "That explains it," he said.

In fact, he reflected, it explained very little. Frances had as good as refused to talk about the attack on Brooks—and, confound it, *he* ought to know the facts if anyone ought. He was summoning up courage to reopen the subject when the landlord hurried past, peering intently at a huge pocket-watch supplied with a magnifying-glass which raised the hands and the figures on the dial to grotesque dimensions. When he was almost out of the door he paused and came back to them.

"Didn't recognise you at first, Miss Butler," he said. He clipped his words with the nervousness of the very shortsighted. "How's Dr. Brooks getting on? Any improvement?"

"I haven't heard this evening." Frances spoke shortly. "Harry, you don't know if Professor Fen's in here this evening?"

"What, that tall, mad fellow?" There was something like awe in the landlord's voice. "He might be in one of the other bars. I'll look. But I don't think so."

"If you see him, you might tell him I'm here. And a friend of his, Mr. Vintner."

The landlord's reaction to this last piece of news was unexpected. He took a step back and began breathing very quickly. "Geoffrey Vintner!" he exclaimed.

"Really, Harry. What on earth's the matter with you? You look as if you'd seen a ghost."

The landlord hurriedly pulled himself together. "Sorry," he mumbled. "Didn't quite catch the name. Thought you were referring to a friend of mine, who—who's dead." He stood wavering in front of them for a moment, and then made a little too rapidly for the door.

"Well, I'm damned!" said Frances in frank surprise.

"If it hadn't been for Fielding, I *should* have been dead, too," said Geoffrey aggrievedly. "Who is that man, anyway?"

"Harry James?" said Frances. "Don't know anything about him, really. He's had this pub for about five years—came from up north, I believe. Staunch Presbyterian. Leading light in the local Conservative Club. In fact"—a thought seemed suddenly to strike her—"just the sort of respectable anonymity you'd expect from—" She checked herself, and added humorously: "From what?"

Geoffrey nodded gloomily. "Precisely. From what?"

"I suppose," said Fielding mournfully, "that beer you're drinking is all right?"

Geoffrey jumped visibly. It occurred to him that he was not, perhaps, feeling very well. "Don't be absurd," he said testily. "People don't go putting poison in people's beer. Or if they do," he added with rising indignation, "it's no use worrying about it until it happens, or we shall all go raving mad and have to be put away." He relapsed into sulks. "I shall keep an eye on Mr. James," he mumbled, and then, with sudden irritation: "And where the *hell* is Fen? Really, it's too bad of him not to be here when I arrive." He brooded on his wrongs, cherishing them individually.

"I don't quite understand," said Fielding cautiously, "about these"—he waved a hand, evoking a myriad phantom butterflies—"insects."

"You wouldn't understand," Geoffrey replied, "because you don't know Fen. My better self persuades me that he's a normal, sensible, extremely healthy-minded person, but there are times when I wonder if he isn't a bit cracked. Of course, everyone has these obsessions about some transient hobby or other, but Fen's personality is so"—he hesitated over words—"*large* and overwhelming, that when he gets bitten it seems like a cosmic upheaval. Everything's affected for miles around."

Frances chuckled. "It began," she said, "when he found a simply gigantic grasshopper on the clergy-house lawn. I must say I've never seen anything quite so vast. He put it in a deep cardboard box and brought it in to dinner that night to show us. The bishop was dining." She gurgled, enchanted by the imminent and foreseeable climax. "When he took off the lid, poor Dutton nearly fainted. Then he poked at the wretched thing until we were all ready to scream. 'It's all right,' he said. 'It's biologically impossible for it to get out.' The first leap landed it in the Bishop's soup. I've never seen a man so pale. Finally it ended up in the hearth, where the dog ate it. 'Nature red in tooth and claw,' said the Bishop (we gave him a new plate of soup, but he wasn't happy about it). 'There,' said Fen, 'a perfect specimen, and it's gone. You can stop their noise,' he said, 'by pricking them with a pin.' We said we shouldn't be surprised."

Fielding rocked with silent laughter. Even Geoffrey giggled absurdly. "But I thought," he remarked, "that Fen was busy investigating this business about Brooks. He..."

The girl got up suddenly. In a moment, as it seemed, the laughter was gone. Just so might a child intent on play run out of her own front door into a garden never seen before, and better not seen. Just so might a man turn a casual remark to a friend in a darkened train, and see a dead mask. Frances took two short steps and turned. When she spoke, her voice was not as it had been.

"Sooner or later," she said, "you'll have to know. It may as well be now." She seemed struggling for utterance. "It was kept from the papers, but they would never have printed it in any case. It was—after a choir-practice. Dr. Brooks went back to the cathedral for something. They found him next morning, not unconscious, though there was a bruise on his head." She stopped, and for a moment covered her face with her hand. "Devilry...You'll think I'm mad, but I'm not. Everything isn't well here. Things happen that can't be explained. You—you must—" She was violently agitated.

Fielding half rose. "Look here, Miss Butler—"

But she brushed him aside, and went on speaking more rapidly than before. "I'm all right. Thank God it isn't me. They

took him to the hospital—in secrecy. He's had moments of
sanity, but they haven't been many. He was locked in, and the
key was lying outside—they found it on the grass. An empty
cathedral isn't a good place to be in all night. Ever since they
brought him away he's talked and babbled and raved—about
the slab of a tomb that moved, and a hanging man."

CHAPTER FOUR

Teeth of Traps

"They were in one of many mouths of Hell
Not seen of seers in visions; only tell
As teeth of traps…"

OWEN

*T*HE CLERGY-HOUSE DRAWING-ROOM was a large one, shabby but comfortable, well-lighted, and decorated, not with Pre-Raphaelite Madonnas, but with caricatures by Spy of ecclesiastical dignitaries long dead and awaiting transfiguration, together with one original Rowlandson etching tucked away in a corner. This represented two obese clerics, one throwing bread contemptuously to an equally contemptuous rabble, the other surreptitiously embracing a large and simpering wench, very décolleté; a cathedral which was recognisably Tolnbridge stood in the background. A few scattered books showed tastes not far removed from the worldly: fiction by Huxley, Isherwood, and Katherine Mansfield; plays by Bridie and Congreve; and, in

another but still noble sphere, John Dickson Carr, Nicholas
Blake, Margery Allingham and Gladys Mitchell. The cathedral
clergy are great readers— they have little else to do.

Geoffrey and Frances had left Fielding at the "Whale and
Coffin" to unpack and were sitting together, talking a little
restrainedly. Now they were alone, Geoffrey felt even more
attracted by her, and she quieted his bachelor's misgivings
(which she may have suspected) by an almost timorous
reserve. The evening sunlight lay green and gold on the broad
lawn outside the french windows, glistening on the thickly-
clustered yellow roses and the shaggy chrysanthemum
blooms. A faint scent of verbena drifted in from a plant which
clung to the grey wall outside.

It appeared that since Brooks' arrival at the hospital little
more had been heard of him. The nature and cause of his
insanity were still unknown, except perhaps by the doctors who
attended him, and no friends had been allowed to see him. Of
near relatives he had only a brother, with whom he had been
on the worst possible terms. This brother had been summoned
by telegram, but had not appeared, and indeed it seemed
doubtful whether he would have been the slightest help to anyone if he had. This much Frances knew, and no more.

There was still no sign of Fen.

Geoffrey asked who would be at dinner that night.

"Well, Daddy's coming over," said Frances. "And then
there'll be Canon Garbin and Canon Spitshuker, and little
Dutton, of course—the sub-organist. Oh, and Sir John Dallow's dropping in for coffee—there's to be some sort of meeting afterwards. Have you heard of him? He's the big noise on
witchcraft in this country."

Geoffrey shook his head. "Is Canon Garbin married?"

"Yes. Why?"

"There was a Mrs. Garbin in the compartment we travelled down in. With a young clergyman."

"Oh, that was probably July Savernake. Come to think of it, he did say he'd be back today. I expect he'll be at dinner too."

"What about him?"

"How do you mean?"

"Well, what sort of person is he?"

She hesitated. "Well...he's Vicar at Maverley, about twelve miles from here. Got the living almost as soon as he was ordained." Geoffrey sensed a deliberate reservation behind the recital of facts, and wondered what its cause might be. "He spends half the year buying expensive books and wine, and playing the *curé bon viveur*, and the other half having to economise, and playing the 'poore persoun.' A see-saw sort of existence." Frances laughed apologetically. "That doesn't tell you much, I'm afraid. But you'll be meeting him, anyway."

Fielding came in, and Frances left to supervise the final preparations for dinner. "Hideous little room I've got," said Fielding mournfully as he fell into a chair, "but it will do. How are you feeling?"

"A bit nightmarish."

"It is rather like that. Do you know, I've been wondering if those attacks on you weren't bogus from beginning to end—designed to conceal the reason for something else. Probably the attack on Brooks. All those preposterous warnings! *That* would bring you into the limelight all right—which is just what they wanted. I suppose they didn't care whether you were killed or just injured. Whoever it is, and whatever they're after, it seems they can afford to waste lives like water."

Geoffrey lit a cigarette and sucked at it without pleasure. "It sounds plausible, but there might be some other explanation."

"There's only one way of testing it out," said Fielding emphatically, "and that is by keeping quiet about it. If we once let out that we've rumbled it, they'll abandon the whole business. But if they think it's taking people in, they'll probably try something else—try to kill you again, for example."

Geoffrey sat up in annoyance. "A nice thing," he exclaimed bitterly, "asking me to keep quiet about a beastly theory, so as to encourage somebody to murder me. It's undoubtedly someone *here* by the way. The postmark on that letter was Tolnbridge, and it must have been someone connected with the cathedral to know I'd been sent for..."

He broke off. Footsteps were approaching outside, accompanied by two voices raised in argument, the one shrill and voluble, the other deep and laconic. A touch of acerbity and resentment was audible beneath the tropes of polite discussion.

"...But my dear Spitshuker you apparently fail to realise that by taking the universalist view you are, in effect, denying the reality of man's freedom to choose between good and evil. If we are *all* to go to heaven *anyway*, then that choice has no validity. It's as if one were to say that a guest at a tea-party has freedom to choose between muffins and crumpets when only crumpets are provided."

"I hardly think, Garbin, that you have grasped the essential point in all this, if you will forgive my saying so. You would concede, of course, that the Divinity is a god of Love?"

"Of course, of course. But you haven't answered—"

"Well, then. That being so, His aim must be the perfection of every one of His Creation. You will agree that even in the case of the greatest saint, perfection is impossible of attainment in the three-score years and ten which we have at our disposal. I am inclined, therefore, to believe that there must be an intermediate state, a purgatory—"

The door swung open, and Canon Spitshuker came into the room, closely followed by Canon Garbin. Canon Spitshuker was a little, plump, excitable man, with swan-white hair and a pink face. By contrast, Canon Garbin was tall, dark, morose and normally laconic; he walked soberly, with his large, bony hands plunged deep into his coat pockets, while the other danced and gestured about him like a poodle accompanying a St. Bernard. Their juxtaposition as Canons of the same cathedral was a luckless one, since Canon Spitshuker was by long conviction a Tractarian, while Canon Garbin was a Low Churchman; furious altercations were constantly in progress between them on points of doctrine and ritual, never resolved. Unlike parallel lines, it was inconceivable that their views should ever meet, even at infinity.

The unexpected presence of Geoffrey and Fielding cut short Canon Spitshuker's oration. He spluttered for a moment like a faulty petrol-engine, then recovered himself, dashed forward, and wrung Geoffrey by the hand.

"How do you do?" he said. "I'm Spitshuker, and this"—he pointed at the other, who stood regarding the scene with a faint but unmistakable disgust—"is my colleague, Dr. Garbin."

Garbin slightly bowed, an uncertain and derisive smile appearing momentarily on his face. Geoffrey murmured introductions.

"Henry Fielding?" Canon Spitshuker clucked delightedly. "Not," he added, "The author of *To*—?"

"No," said Fielding rather tersely. Canon Spitshuker seemed a little abashed.

"And you"—he paused for a moment, apparently testing the propriety of the question—"are staying here?"

Geoffrey explained the situation, Canon Spitshuker nodding his head in vigorous and unnecessary affirmation all the time. Canon Garbin crept into the room and deposited his long limbs circumspectly in an armchair.

"You must remember, Spitshuker," he said. "Professor Fen mentioned Mr. Vintner's name at the time of the business about poor Brooks, and Butler asked him to get in touch with him." He paused lengthily; then added, just in time to anticipate Spitshuker's next outburst: "We are very glad to see you. Very glad indeed. We shall greatly appreciate your help."

"Greatly appreciate it," Spitshuker chanted antiphonally.

"I was afraid," said Geoffrey, "knowing Fen, that he'd brought me down unofficially, as it were."

"You heard about Brooks, I suppose?" asked Spitshuker. "Poor fellow, poor fellow. A terrible and mysterious business. Let's hope that nothing of the kind happens to you."

"It *has* happened," Geoffrey was about to retort; but he thought better of it and restrained himself. "You don't know where Fen is?"

"I haven't the least idea. Wasn't he here to welcome you? Very bad, very bad. But I haven't seen much of him since he arrived—don't come into this house very much at any time. The living arrangements are unusual here. No cloisters—the prebends' houses are all scattered about the town. There's a Deanery, of course, and a Bishop's Palace of a sort, but the Bishop isn't there a great deal. Very uncomfortable—don't blame him. This house," said Spitshuker cheerfully, "is used as a sort of general rubbish-heap for minor canons and the sub-organist and any incumbents of the diocese who want to put up for a night or two. Can't think why Fen isn't staying at the Deanery—why you aren't, for that matter. Disgraceful. Still, you'll be comfortable enough here, I dare say. Frances—Miss Butler, that is—is an excellent housekeeper. I'd ask you to stay with me, only my housekeeper is ill at the moment, and to bring in guests, however pleasant, would be a trial." He paused for breath, while Geoffrey uttered sounds expressive simultaneously of deprecation, civility, gratitude, complete understanding, sympathy and sad surprise.

"I think you'll find the choir in very good order," Spitshuker was proceeding irrepressibly, "and the organ, I'm told, is an excellent one." His mind switched subjects with the rapidity of a signalman changing points. "The Precentor has a brother-in-law staying with him, I understand, and is to bring him round this evening. Poor Frances will have yet another to cater for at dinner, I fear." He giggled. "But she can conjure up a banquet out of nothing—a most competent person. The Precentor's brother-in-law is a psychoanalyst, I believe," he pursued without waiting to take breath. "Interesting—extraordinarily interesting. We shall have to see what we can do to challenge his secular interpretation of the workings of the human mind."

Garbin, who had ostentatiously taken up and opened a book during this monologue, now looked up. "Don't be foolish, Spitshuker," he boomed with dreadful emphasis. "Peace has come here on a social visit, not to be dragooned into amateurish debates on serious subjects. My wife, by the way, seems to have travelled down with him this afternoon from London."

"Mrs. Garbin is back, then?" said Spitshuker. "Savernake came down with her, I suppose?"

Garbin nodded gloomily. "That young man," he said, "spends a good deal too much time away from his parish. I'm aware that it's too much to expect any parish priest nowadays to do more than merely conduct the services, but Savernake carries the business of ignoring his parishioners' affairs to an extreme. Butler, I believe, has complained to the Bishop about it."

"You don't mean," piped Spitshuker excitedly, "that Butler is trying to get rid of Savernake? Transfer him to another diocese, that is? I knew he never liked him, but—well—"

"Personally, I am in entire agreement with the Precentor," Garbin stated dogmatically. "Though I think a disciplinary reproof would be sufficient."

"Reverting to the question of Brooks," Geoffrey put in, "has anyone here been able to think of an explanation of what happened to him?"

"One can conceive several possibilities," said Garbin slowly, "but I think it better not to discuss them at present."

"I asked because whatever is going on here seems rather to concern me. There have been today, two attempts on my life."

A dead hush fell unexpectedly on the little group. For what seemed an age no one spoke. Then Canon Spitshuker gasped slightly and said:

"My dear fellow—"

Words failed him. The hush was renewed. Geoffrey said:

"I've heard, you see, what happened to Brooks. And it seems to me that this is no time for false reticence. Of course I know nothing about your affairs here, and in the ordinary way of things wouldn't want to know. But it's quite obvious that my visit here was the cause of those attacks, and we—or the police—will have to start probing sooner or later."

Garbin looked up. He drummed his fingers on the arm of his chair, and seemed to be very carefully weighing his words. "You—or they," he said at last, "will find investigation a particularly difficult business. There is no calling which requires a stricter attention to reputation than the Church. Things do, of course, happen. When they do, they are kept very quiet—very quiet indeed. I don't refer to—serious misbehaviour. Merely small things, which are perhaps more damning in the eyes of the world." He paused, labouring under some obscure emotional strain.

"You know that Brooks is mad—stark, gibbering mad. I hope and devoutly pray that none of us was responsible for that. I think"—he smiled wryly—"that even Spitshuker will agree there is a hell prepared for whoever did that.

"For some human being was responsible, Mr. Vintner. Someone gave Brooks, when he was unconscious, a large dose of some drug—the details I don't know—nearly enough to kill him and quite enough to turn his brain, to make of him an invalid and a maniac for what little remainder of life God may give him. Was it sheer devilry, do you think—or a mistake? Was the intention to kill him, and was he left for dead?

"Brooks knew something, Mr. Vintner. Something which concerned the Cathedral, and which he must not be allowed to say. In his delirium he has often called for the police, has struggled to speak coherently and has never succeeded. The police are always beside his bed. They take down every word he says."

Garbin rose abruptly from his chair, thrust his long, bony hands into his pockets, and crossed to the window. He turned and faced the other three before he spoke again.

"What was it he saw, when he walked alone about the Cathedral? What was it he found there, that no one else has found?"

❉ ❉ ❉

Dinner was over. It had not, from the social point of view, been a successful meal. The events of the last two days weighed too heavily on the minds of those present to allow more than sporadic, half-hearted conversation, always carefully directed away from the obsessing thought. Even the normally jovial Peace, who had come over to dinner from the Precentor's house, where he was staying, seemed affected by the atmosphere, and after opening the proceedings chattily lapsed gradually into a silence from which he emerged only to give occasional startled replies when he was addressed. Frances kept things moving at a rate just clear of open embarrassment and discomfort.

The Precentor had not put in an appearance, so there were eight of them at the table—Frances, Garbin, Spitshuker, the young clergyman Savernake, whom they had seen in the train, Geoffrey, Fielding, Peace and the sub-organist, Dutton, an acutely self-conscious young man with a massive white face spotted with orange freckles, and a shock of pale ginger hair, through which he constantly ran his chubby fingers. There was, it appeared, to be some kind of unofficial meeting of cathedral officers after dinner (without the Dean, who would normally have presided, but who was temporarily away)—obviously to discuss the repercussions of the Brooks affair, though this was not made explicit. The Precentor, Frances' father, whom Geoffrey was curious to meet, would appear for that, and so would the Chancellor, Sir John Dallow. Geoffrey recalled, suddenly, the affair of Josephine and the burning of the Precentor's manuscript, and wondered why the girl was not with them; a casual question, put to Frances, told him that she had gone back to her own home.

Geoffrey found himself next to Savernake, but the acquaintanceship made little progress. After a start of recognition when Geoffrey was introduced to him, the young clergyman became taciturn and nervous. Geoffrey, venturing a straightforward reference to the situation, said:

"The police have made a thorough search of the cathedral, I suppose?"

Savernake nodded. "Thorough—very thorough indeed." He spoke in that exaggerated drawl which so often passes incorrectly for the Oxford accent. "But, of course, it was useless. No one will find—what there is to be found, unless he stays alone there as Brooks did."

"And then?" Geoffrey left the rest of the question unspoken. But Savernake only shrugged, cracked the joints of his long, thin fingers alarmingly, and smiled.

Garbin and Spitshuker engaged in a private controversy on some obscure theological point, which lasted until dinner was over. Peace, Frances (from whom Geoffrey was regrettably distant) and Fielding carried on a three-cornered argument about a recent London play. Dutton was mostly silent, throwing occasional desperate remarks into such conversation as met his ears. Decidedly, not an inspiriting meal.

Coffee was in the drawing-room. There rose to meet them as they came in, Garbin and Spitshuker still engaged in surreptitious altercation, a little old man of phenomenal thinness, with a sharp nose, small beady eyes which never for more than a moment held your own, and a crown of sparse and wispy white hair—Sir John Dallow, Chancellor of the Cathedral. In speech he alternately gabbled and drawled. His mannerisms were at once like and unlike Spitshuker's. There were the same incessant gestures, the same dancing and posturing. But whereas in Spitshuker these were signs of energy, in Dallow, they appeared more as neurotic excitement. Looking at the two men, Geoffrey could think of no better comparison between them than that Dallow was an angle, and Spitshuker a curve; and probably, he thought with amusement, that was due as much to the difference between their figures as to anything else.

Dallow rose with conscious affectation as they came in brushing with the backs of his fingers at an invisible speck of dust on his lapel. He wore no clerical garments of any kind— only a dandified lounge suit and a tie of slightly shocking red. He darted forward to meet Frances as she preceded the others into the room, seized her hand and held it in a lingering parody of the chivalrous man.

"My dear Frances," he gabbled, "you will, I'm sure, forgive my letting myself into the house and settling down in this unconventional way." He had a disconcerting trick of thrusting his face close to the face of the person to whom he was talking. "I realised that I was a little early, and I he-e-sitated"—he drawled out the word, and then went on with a rush—"to *disturb* you...at your meal." His small eyes looked quickly about the gathering "Garbin. Spitshuker. Dutton—and how are you now, my dear fellow? And...?" He glanced at Peace, Geoffrey, and Fielding. Introductions were made. "So pleased," murmured Dallow. "So pleased." He conducted Frances with bird-like movements to a chair, and sat down beside her.

"Butler is not here yet?" he enquired generally. "I hope— indeed I hope—that he will be in time for the meeting. The matter is so urgent—so terribly urgent." With a sharp movement, he began feeling in his pockets, and finally produced a large key. "I have been to the hospital," he said, holding it up, "and the police asked me to return you—this." He laid it delicately on a table beside him.

There was a moment's silence. Then Frances said:

"Is it—?"

Dallow nodded and grimaced. "Exactly. The cathedral key—more properly I should say the key to the door in the north transept. That key which hangs normally"—he emphasised the word—"in the front porch of this clergy-house, for the use of its occupants."

"My dear Dallow," piped Spitshuker in sudden excitement, "are you trying to tell us that that—*that*—is the key which Brooks—" His voice trailed away.

Dallow nodded. "Precisely that." He looked at Frances. "You knew it was missing?"

"I? I hadn't any idea. I never need to use it. Mr. Dutton, what about you?"

The sub-organist shifted. "I never go into the cathedral now. Doctor's orders. Perhaps one of the other two—?"

"But they've been away for three days now. *Nobody* had occasion to notice it was gone. What's more, anyone could have walked in and taken it."

"Precisely what I told the police," said Dallow. "The 'C.H.' engraved on it left no doubt of its provenance. They will probably have to ask questions about it. In the meantime, they're finished with it, and asked me to bring it back. No fingerprints, I gather."

"What I can't understand," said Garbin, "is why Brooks wasn't using his own key to get into the cathedral. He's had one ever since we were authorised to lock the cathedral at seven at nights."

Dallow leaned forward. "My *de-e-ar* Garbin. You miss the point. Brooks *did* use his own key. But whoever was in the

Cathedral with him—used *this* one." He tapped it slowly. "Brooks' key was found on him. This other, as you know, was found lying on the grass outside the north transept."

Fielding looked up. "That's curious."

"Very curious, Mr. Fielding. Why, you would ask, did our intruder not return the key here when he had locked the door behind him?"

"Ah, but our intruder overlooked that. And you must remember that in all probability poor Brooks was left for dead."

"Still less reason for locking it," said Dutton, wedging himself painfully into the conversation. They stared at him with that unanimous surprise which naturally shy people seem always to attract to themselves. You would have imagined that a white mouse was liable to pop out of his mouth at any moment.

"But there was a reason, of course," Spitshuker squeaked excitedly. "That is—supposing our intruder wanted to keep his crime secret for as long as possible. The police try all doors of the cathedral at least three times during the night. If one of them was found open, naturally they would investigate at once. I understand that the longer a body remains undiscovered, the less easy it is to fix with precision the time of death, and so to use the method of investigation by alibi." He seemed to feel that this statement showed too intimate a knowledge of criminology, for he added: "Or so I think I have been told."

"True—perfectly true, my *de-ear* Spitshuker," said Dallow in benign confirmation.

"But that still doesn't account for the fact that the key was thrown away, and not returned," Peace interposed.

"I think I can explain that," Frances replied grimly. "At ten o'clock sharp every night the door of this house is latched. After that time, only the four of us with latch-keys—Notewind and Filts, the two minor canons who live here, Dutton and myself—can get in. Your criminal would hardly risk breaking into the house simply to return a key."

"And that means"—Garbin's deep voice almost startled them—"that those four are thus far freed from suspicion." Frances shrugged indifferently. "If we haven't been talking nonsense—as we probably have—I suppose it does."

"It seems very important," said Geoffrey, "because from what I've heard so far it seems as if the thing may have happened at any time. What time did the choir-practice finish, by the way?"

"It has to be over by a quarter to nine," said Spitshuker, "because the boys must be back at their homes by nine. And if I remember, one of the Decani altos, who was the last to leave, said he got home about ten past. Brooks merely told him that he proposed practising for a while—which I suppose he may have done. But he was nowhere near the organ when they found him." Spitshuker turned to the Chancellor. "How was he, by the way?"

"He is dead."

It was a new voice that had spoken. Simultaneously they turned towards the door. The Precentor, Dr. Butler, stood there looking at them with the coldest eyes Geoffrey had ever seen in a human being. He had the frame and height of a giant, and hair the colour of dirty ice. His face, where the bones showed so prominently, was tanned a dark brown. He was about fifty, prematurely grey.

Frances jumped up. "Daddy…"

The Precentor advanced towards Geoffrey. "Mr. Vintner? It was kind of you to come." He turned back to the others. "Yes, Brooks is dead. About three hours ago he recovered his reason."

"Recovered!"

"Yes. He woke from a long and merciful sleep and asked quite coherently to see the police. Of course, the officer was by his side in a moment, but he seemed so exhausted that he could utter only a few unintelligible words before he went to sleep again. A short while after it was time for him to take some medicine—a solution of caffein, I believe. It was prepared in the dispensary by one of the nurses, and taken out, with other equipment, on a trolley. The foolish girl then left it in the entrance hall of the hospital while she was called away to another patient. The entrance-hall is unwatched, and open to all comers."

He paused, and again the cold eyes glanced round the gathering. His self-possession was almost intolerable.

"She returned," he went on, "and took the medicine in to him. It was criminal negligence, was it not, to leave the glass untended in that way? They roused him, and in front of two nurses and a police officer he drank the caffein solution together with a fatal quantity of atropine. Ten minutes later— rather over two hours ago—he died, in extreme and violent agony." Butler paused again, and again looked round. "And the irony of it is that they thought it was only a return of his delir- ium. For five minutes, before they saw something was seri- ously wrong, they held him down and allowed the poison to do its work."

There was dead silence. No one moved a muscle.

"And now, gentlemen," said the Precentor without emotion of any kind in his voice, "we will proceed with our meeting."

CHAPTER FIVE

Conjectures

"Here's a wild fellow."
SHAKESPEARE

GEOFFREY ORDERED ANOTHER PINT and began to see matters in a more rosy light. He even withdrew himself momentarily from morbid questioning and looked about him. The bar of the "Whale and Coffin" was crowded—crowded with people who knew nothing, he reflected, of what he and the others had heard in the clergy-house drawing-room hardly more than half an hour ago. They chattered with stoic resignation about the state of the war, the quality of the beer, and the minor inconveniences of being alive. They drank, if not with gusto, at least with the appearance of enjoyment—most of them men, though in one corner sat a plump, well-dressed, painted, woman of middle-age sipping in a tolerant, lady-like manner at a glass of oily-looking

stout, while in another a pale, anaemic, characterless shop-girl
drank silently in the company of an equally pale, anaemic,
characterless young man. There was not riotous enjoyment,
but there was at least peace.

The appearance of peace, thought Geoffrey. What is peace?
An ice-cream cornet in the sun? Certainly there was no peace
in Tolnbridge, no serenity. Beneath the placid, quotidian ritual
of the cathedral town lurked unknown forces which were moving ponderously, devastatingly to the surface. Beneath the
familiar mask of any of these people hatred and murder might
lie. The landlord Geoffrey had not seen after his first visit—a
fact which caused him both annoyance and relief: annoyance
because he had returned here determined to confront the man
and demand an explanation of his behaviour earlier on, and
relief because he had not looked forward to the encounter
with any special confidence. The blessings of enforced pro-
crastination! On his left, a soldier was engaged in an inter-
minable narrative about some minor mishap of Army life.

"...So there 'e was in the front o' the lorry, see, and the
'ill full of ruddy 'oles like a sieve, and 'im bumpin' up an' down
like a ruddy marionette, see..."

The voice faded to trite memory. A tall, heavily-built man
came in and elbowed his way to the bar. Evidently he was a
person of some consequence, for conversation wavered on his
arrival, and the thinkers regarded him with curiosity and interest. They appeared to be anticipating from him some oracular
pronouncement. But he only ordered a bitter and a packet of
Players, and the talk became general again.

"...There 'e was, see, the ruddy 'ill pitted with 'oles, an' the
grenades dencin' about in the back like peas in a saucepan..."

Civilised people, thought Geoffrey, react oddly to the
news of violent death. No one had screamed, or drawn in his
breath with an alarming hiss; very little had been said, even,
the party having broken up almost immediately, to allow the

Chapter to get on with their meeting. Frances, refusing an invitation to drink, had gone to her room with a book; Fielding,
whose reactions to the proximity of the sea were conventional,
had announced his intention of going down to the rocks to
potter; Dutton had gone to bed; and Peace had vanished, no
one knew whither. An obscure irritation haunted Geoffrey
that none of these people had felt the need of alcohol as he
had; he felt morally weak. It was true that he had resisted the
temptation for ten minutes when he had made a cursory and
uninspiring examination of the garden, but still, it had mas-
tered him in the end—that and a pressing desire, he added to
himself in hasty and unconvincing extenuation, to see the
landlord of the "Whale and Coffin" again. He, however, was
plainly not here, or else was lurking in some other corner of
his establishment.

The evening was warm, and not conducive to thought;
the drinkers lunged out ineffectually at the flies which sailed
past their noses. There were not, in any case, sufficient data to
make an examination of events. Geoffrey thought first of his
fugue and then, becoming bored with this, as is the way of
artists with their own works, mentally pigeon-holed it, and
thought of Frances instead. The beer slowly toppled him to
the edge of a swamp of maudlin sentiment. Intellect stood
aside and informed him of this fact. He ignored it, abandoning himself to the luxury, and helping it on its way by more
beer. He categorised, by comparison, the charms of his liking,
his true love, his sweeting—"Sweeting," charming word, said
Intellect, vainly endeavouring to divert him into a discussion
of the degeneration of language: pity it's gone out of use. Lips
like—like what? Coral? Cherries? No, no; trite, conventional.
That sort of thing, said Intellect, still trying to stem the tide,
went out with Jacobean literature. *My mistress' eyes*, it quoted,
*are nothing like the sun. Coral is far more red than her lips' red;
If snow be white, why then her breasts are dun; If hairs be*

wires, black wires grow on her head...Emotion replied indignantly with *Shall I compare thee to a summer's day?* but being
uncertain as to how the poem went on, was forced to fall back
on peevish mumblings.

Intellect's victory, however, was only temporary. What,
thought Geoffrey, if I were to ask her to marry me? Bachelorhood, complacent in a hitherto indefeasible citadel, was startled into attention and began to peer anxiously from behind its
fortifications. Discomfort, it whispered persuasively: inconvenience. All your small luxuries, your careful arrangements
for peace of mind, would go by the board if you got married.
Women are contemptuous of such things, or if she should turn
out not to be, why marry her at all? Why have a mirror to
reflect your own fads, to flatter your face? Pointless and silly.
You'd much better remain as you are. Your work, too—a wife
would insist on being taken out just when you were struggling
with a particularly good idea. And what would become of your
Violin Concerto with a baby howling about the house? You're
an artist. Artists shouldn't get married. A little mild flirtation,
perhaps, but nothing more.

Before the undoubted common sense of these remarks, all
that Emotion could do was to mutter gloomily but doggedly: I love
her. And at this a real panic broke out in the citadel. Windows
were banged, the portcullis closed, the drawbridge lowered...

"I wonder if you can give me a light?"

Geoffrey started back to consciousness of his surroundings. The tall man who had just come in was flourishing an
unlighted cigarette questioningly before him.

"Ever since Norway," said the man, "matches have been
getting scarcer and scarcer."

The fact was unquestionable, and seemed to provide little opportunity for comment. Geoffrey produced a lighter and
jabbed viciously at it with his thumb. At the twelfth attempt
the man smiled, a little sadly. "Tricky things," he said.

"I filled it this morning, and I think I overdid it." Geof-frey shook the lighter; quantities of fluid splashed on to the floor. "I'll give it one more try."

The resultant sheet of flame nearly took their faces off. And it was as the tall man was dubiously approaching it with his cigarette that the other thing happened.

There were leading off from the bar three doors which gave access to small private rooms where it was possible for a few people to think in relative privacy. From behind one of these, unnerving sounds were suddenly heard—tremendous crashes, overturning of furniture, curses, grunts, and the noise of rapid movement and heavy breathing; then renewed crashes. The bar listened and gaped in stupefaction. Then the man who had asked Geoffrey for a light strode with an air of authority to the door and flung it open. Geoffrey followed him. The others crowded behind.

At first nothing could be seen but a small room with the furniture somewhat disarranged. From an angle, however, sounds of intense activity could be heard, and someone swear-ing in several languages. Geoffrey and the tall man went in. The crowd behind them stood goggle-eyed with hushed expectancy.

The *bagarre*, when discovered, was not precisely what had been expected. On his knees in a corner was a tall, lanky man. In one hand he held a large glass of whisky, in the other a walking-stick, with which he prodded at some small, mobile object hovering above the floor. This was shortly revealed to be a common house-fly, avoiding the attacks with ease and evi-dent enjoyment. How long this scene might have continued it is impossible to say. But the fly, tiring of the amusement, presently took wing and prepared to depart. Its assailant, plainly maddened by this unexpected manoeuvre, aimed the contents of his glass at it, and missed. The fly flew at top speed towards his nose, made impact, went into reverse, and then with what even to the unimaginative was manifestly a shriek of delight, made off through the window.

The man climbed tranquilly to his feet, dusting his knees in a conventional manner. Dark hair, ineffectually plastered down with water, stuck out in spikes from the back of his head. His cheeks glowed like apples, giving evidence of an almost intolerable health and high spirits. Despite the warmth of the evening, he was muffled in an enormous raincoat, and had on an extraordinary hat.

"Good *God!*" said Geoffrey with deep feeling. Gervase Fen, Professor of English Language and Literature in the University of Oxford, gazed placidly about him. "The trouble about flies," he said without preliminary, "is that they never *learn*. You'd think that if you were as small as that, and landed on an animate object of immense size which heaved and banged and shouted at you, you'd go away and shut yourself up in a cupboard for ever. But not flies. They just circle round and come back again. It's the same with windows. Generations of flies have batted themselves silly against windows without ever discovering that you can't get through them."

The inhabitants of the bar had returned with indifference to their former stations. The tall man who had asked Geoffrey for a light said to Fen:

"I've been looking for you everywhere, sir. No one seemed to know what had become of you."

Fen nodded vaguely. "Inspector Garratt, isn't it? More about Brooks?"

Geoffrey, suppressing his annoyance with difficulty, said: "And I'm Geoffrey Vintner."

"I know that," said Fen.

"Well aren't you going to welcome me?"

"Oh? Oh?" said Fen. "And what can I do for you?"

"You asked me down here to play the services."

"Oh, did I? Did I?" said Fen. "I thought I'd asked old

Raikes, from St. Christopher's. Not that he'd have been any good," he added thoughtfully. "He's been bedridden for years."

Geoffrey sat down, speechless with fury. "To think I come all the way down here, getting myself attacked three times on the way—"

"What's that, sir?" asked the Inspector, turning to him sharply.

"*Attacked.*"

Fen groaned. "More complication. And I came down here for a peaceful holiday. Well, let's get some drinks and have it all out."

They had it all out. First the Inspector, who gave a bare outline of the facts about Brooks' murder, as Geoffrey had heard them, and then Geoffrey, who gave a much less bare— in fact, a somewhat embroidered account of the attacks on himself. He felt this to be justified by the unsatisfactory, and essentially unconvincing, nature of these attacks. Even so, they didn't seem greatly to perturb Fen and the Inspector, which annoyed Geoffrey considerably.

"I shall help," said Fen in a determined manner when Geoffrey finally fell silent.

"Good," said the Inspector. "The Yard warned us we shouldn't be able to stop you." Fen glared. "I think they still remember that business at Caxton's Folly, before the war."

"Ah," put in Fen complacently. "Caxton's Folly. *That* was a case, if you like." A thought suddenly disturbed him. "The Yard?" he added abruptly. "You haven't handed over to them?"

The Inspector sighed. "We haven't made much progress on our own, sir. And the death of Brooks this afternoon has made things worse, not better. Oh, we've questioned everyone within reach, you can be sure of that—though not a second time, of course, since Brooks was killed. That remains to be done." He nodded gloomily, as a general surveying a peculiarly unsuitable terrain before battle. "But what's the use? We don't even know what sort of questions to ask. Brooks hadn't an enemy in the world,—our only pointer is this improbable something he seems to have seen. *So*—the Chief Constable got on to the Yard. I believe they were going to send down one of their best men—fellow called Appleby—"

"Appleby! Appleby!" howled Fen indignantly. "What do they want with Appleby when I'm here?" He calmed down slightly. "I admit," he said, "that he's very good—very good," he ended gloomily. "But I don't see—"

With an effort, Geoffrey leaned forward, hoping thereby to produce an appearance of emphasis. "My dear Gervase: surely in a matter as serious as murder, *anyone* who can help—"

"Don't preach at me," said Fen peevishly.

"Well, we have a free hand for a day or so," continued the Inspector, regardless of interruptions. "If we can't discover something by then, it'll have to be the Yard."

"Of course we can discover something," said Fen magnificently. He paused in some perplexity. "But what? The thing divides itself into three problems, doesn't it? First, the attacks on Geoffrey here; second, the attack on Brooks in the cathedral; and third, the murder of Brooks. We might do worse than to take them separately and see what we can make of each." He considered. "You, Geoffrey, were attacked by three different people—all pretty certainly hired thugs. I wonder what happened to the fellow in the store? Do you think there's any chance of his having got away?" He turned to the Inspector. "You haven't heard anything, I suppose?"

The Inspector shook his head. "No reason why the London people should think it had anything to do with us. But I can ring up and find out." He made a note on a grubby envelope.

"So much for that," said Fen. "Not much use trying to trace the other two men. What happened to the case that was dropped on you, Geoffrey?"

"It was left in the train, I think. Yes, I'm sure it was."

"There might be prints," said the Inspector. "The man who tried to do you in was probably an old lag we've got on record somewhere. Not that I expect it'd do much good if we did pick him up. He wouldn't know much about it. Still, I'll try and get hold of the case. *Routine*, you know. 'The police may not have the dash and brilliance of the amateur investigator, but it is only by their patient and methodical investigation of the smallest details that the criminal, *etcetera, etcetera, etcetera*.'" He fished out his envelope and made another note on it. "The 5:43 in here, wasn't it?"

"Then there were the two threatening letters," Fen went on. "Any idea as to why anyone should want to stop you coming here?"

"I think," said Geoffrey, brazenly plagiarising, "that the whole thing was probably a blind to conceal the real reason for the attack on Brooks—to concentrate our attention on the fact that it was *organists* who were being attacked—"

"Nonsense," Fen interposed rudely. "You don't go to all that elaborate trouble just to cover up." He was prone to slightly out-of-date Americanisms. "Why not the obvious explanation—that they didn't want anyone playing the organ for two or three days?"

"That's silly."

"No, it isn't," said Fen irritably. "Look here. It's pretty obvious that Brooks saw something in that cathedral which incriminated somebody. Suppose it was somehow connected with the organ. Brooks sees it, they know he's seen it, and they try to bump him off." (Here Geoffrey gave a feeble moan of protest.) "Well, and good. They imagine they've succeeded, and that they're safe. Then next morning they get a nasty shock when they find that Brooks is still alive, and quite capable of blowing the words." (Geofffrey moaned again.) "So they make a second attempt, and this time they succeed. But they realise everyone will know by now that there's something of importance hidden in the cathedral (if Brooks had been found dead, no one need have guessed), and they want to get it away. Difficulty the first: the cathedral is well guarded"—Fen glanced at the Inspector, who nodded—"and no unauthorised person can get in except when it's open for services. Difficulty the second: they want to get at the organ-loft, or thereabouts, and that, despite the demise of Brooks, will during services be occupied—by one Geoffrey Vintner, quite publicly summoned for the purpose. Moral: put Mr. Vintner out of action, and keep the organ-loft clear."

"It sounds plausible," said the Inspector. "In fact, it's the only explanation I can think of." ("You didn't think of *it*," muttered Fen. "I did.") "But"—he shrugged helplessly—"what is this mysterious something?"

"Presumably you've had the place searched?"

"It's been searched all right," said the Inspector grimly, "No results, of course—but then, we'd no idea what we were looking for. We did look in the works of the organ"—("*Works*," said Geoffrey faintly)—"but...well, there was nothing that we could see."

"Tombs?" suggested Fen.

"We didn't open them, of course. But then neither, one imagines, did Brooks."

Geoffrey intervened. "You say no *unauthorised* person has been able to get in, except at service times, since Brooks was found. Presumably that wouldn't include the clergy?"

"The gentlemen in Holy Orders? No, sir. But you can be sure that whenever they had occasion to go in, we kept an unobtrusive eye on them."

"Since the cathedral is under suspicion," said Fen, "presumably its sutlers are under suspicion as well."

"Exactly, sir. And that makes it more difficult. It's very awkward, having to try and pry into a canon." The bizarre effect of his phraseology startled the Inspector, and he was silent for a moment. "Well, what now?"

"The second problem," said Fen, "is the attack on Brooks in the cathedral. Any leads?"

"Pretty well nothing. He was knocked out and given an injection of atropine—intravenally, in the left forearm."

Fen interrupted: "I thought atropine was a soporific."

"No, it's an irritant—aphrodisiac—no, not that; what's the word I want?"

"Was it a fatal dose?" Fen asked.

"A fifth of a grain. It should have been fatal, but the action of these thugs still isn't properly understood. A sixteenth of a grain's generally given as the maximum safe dose. They diagnosed it pretty soon—lack of perspiration and saliva, and so on—and treated him with tannic acid, morphine, ether, caffein—everything they had. He would have recovered." The Inspector's voice was for a moment oddly shaken; Geoffrey suddenly realised the heavy responsibility of the man, and saw that it had told on him.

"You didn't find the hypodermic, of course?"

"No."

"It could be quite small?"

"That would depend on the solution. Atropine sulphate's soluble in the proportions one to three in ninety per cent alcohol; one to five hundred in water. But even so, it could have been tiny."

Fen mused, fidgeting slightly and shuffling his feet; he finished his whisky and pressed a plainly inoperative bell to summon more. "An odd method of murder. Gunshot, of course, would be too noisy—but a knife...or strangulation, or—? Messy, all of them. A woman's crime, perhaps. Or a man with a womanish mind." He pressed the bell again; it fell off the wall with a clatter. He regarded it thoughtfully for a moment, and then turned to the Inspector. "Would atropine be difficult to get?"

"I suppose so. Don't really know."

"If you're an inspector," said Fen, "what do you inspect? Tickets?" He laughed uproariously. The others regarded him coldly. When he had finished, the Inspector said: "If you got it at a chemist's, it would have to go on the poison register, of course. As far as the local chemists are concerned, we've been into all that already, and there's nothing in the least suspicious. We can't investigate every poison-book in the country, and besides, I'm pretty sure we're not dealing with a complete lunatic—not in that sense, anyway," he added reflectively. "No, there's nothing to be got from that angle, I'm certain. The knock Brooks got on the head was the usual blunt instrument, one supposes—scientifically placed, to require the minimum of strength: the whole thing suggests medical knowledge. Incidentally, it suggests premeditation as well. People don't go about carrying loaded hypodermics the way they do guns."

Geoffrey proffered an idea at this point, without much confidence. "Perhaps Brooks already knew that something was going on, and *they* knew *he* knew, and decided to silence him once and for all after the choir-practice."

Fen nodded approval. "Very good," he said. "Means? Motive? Opportunity?"

"*Motive*," said the Inspector heavily. "Can we define a little?" As it was evident that both Geoffrey and Fen were ready to define a great deal, and the question had been only rhetorically intended, he hastened to add: "The only clue we have is Brooks' ravings—when he was found by the Verger opening the church in the morning—" He stopped abruptly. "By the way, you'd like to question the Verger, I suppose?"

"No," said Fen.

"Ah," the Inspector replied unhappily. "Well, then. He said a good deal then, and later, when we got him to the hospital, and we got most of it down. A lot of it obviously had nothing to do with the matter in hand—he had some fancies, I can tell you, about that shameless hussy Helen Dukes in the Post Office—"

"Post Office, Post Office," said Fen. "What are we listening to a lot of stuff about the Post Office for?"

"And then naturally there were worries about the cathedral music," the Inspector went on unperturbed, "uppermost in his mind. It seems there'd been a quarrel with the Cantoris Bass over a solo—but that hardly seems to be a motive."

Fen heaved his long, lanky body irritably about in his chair, and fidgeted more than ever. "When are we going to get to the point?" he grumbled.

"Finally, there's a few things he said about the Cathedral itself. They seemed to cost him a lot of pain and fright, but they don't amount to much. You remember that passage in *The Moonstone*, where What's-his-name fills in the blanks of the old doctor's ravings to make a piece of beautifully grammatical English? Never seemed plausible to me: delirium doesn't work like that. The one flaw, I always think, in an otherwise excellent novel, though as *detective* writing I consider it's greatly over-rated, like Poe's stories—"

"Oh, get on," said Fen. "What did Brooks say, anyway?" The Inspector paused; then he took another envelope from his pocket. "Why, sir, this was the burden of it." He read aloud: "*Wires. Man hanging—rope. Slab of tomb moved.*"

There was a brief silence. Geoffrey remembered the circumstances in which he had first heard those words; they affected him hardly less now. "An empty cathedral isn't a good place to be in all night"—even for the unimaginative. He remembered some words read in a story long ago: "In his unenlightened days he had read of meetings in such places which even now would hardly bear thinking of." And even if, as it seemed, the encounter had been material, in such surroundings it might well have shaken a man of strong nerves. This Geoffrey said.

Fen nodded. He appeared unexpectedly gloomy, but those who knew him well would have recognised this as a sign that certain things were becoming clear to him. He said nothing, but collected their glasses, and after a further glance at the offending bell-push, departed to get another round of drinks. Returning, he banged the glasses down on the table, sat down heavily, and said: "Well?"

The Inspector shrugged. "Night thoughts…" he murmured dubiously.

· Fen drew in his breath sharply. "It is always my fate," he said, "to be involved with literary policemen…" He waved his glass in a perfunctory and graceless toast, took a large mouthful of whisky, choked slightly, and went on in tones of bitter complaint: "Why does no one ever take things literally…*wires*. Radio, electricity"—he glared at the defunct apparatus on the floor—"*bell-pushes*. Hanging man—rope: men can hang from rope otherwise than by the neck; they can climb up and down it with definite and possibly criminal purposes in view. Slab of tomb moved: active or passive? Moved of its own accord, or *had been* moved?" He paused. "It seems fairly plain as far as it goes. And what part of the cathedral is inaccessible except by climbing a rope—no staircase?"

The Inspector's eyes shone with sudden comprehension; he half rose. Fen nodded.

"Exactly. The Bishop's Gallery."

Geoffrey gazed uncomprehendingly. "The what?" Fen turned to him. "Of course. You don't know the cathedral well. The organ-loft is high up over the Decani choir-stalls, on the south side of the chancel. From it a narrow gallery runs west, towards the nave, as far as the big column where the south transept begins; it can't be entered from that end. There are only two ways into it: first, from the organ-loft, an entrance which has been bricked up since the eighteenth century; and second, by a spiral staircase which leads down to a small room and then to an outside door, also walled up. In the small room lies the body of John Thurston, Bishop from 1688 to 1705, and the last of the witch-hunters—hence the name of the gallery above it. So apart from hauling down a lot of brick and plaster there's no way in except over the edge of the gallery." He turned to the Inspector. "I suppose the brick and plaster *hadn't* been tampered with?"

The Inspector shook his head; an indefinable sense of uneasiness was growing within him. "That was one of the likeliest places. No, it hadn't been touched—and it's quite impossible to disguise the traces of a thing like that if anyone's looking for it. Not that it wouldn't be fairly easy to burrow through that brick partition from the organ loft: it's thin, and it looks as if it was pretty hastily put up in the first place. But as to this rope business, I admit no one could get up and down from that gallery *except* by a rope—there's that padlocked wall tomb of St. Ephraim underneath, and it doesn't project so there's no foothold anywhere, nor on the columns at either side—they're slippery as glass. But how are you going to get your rope attached in the first place, before you begin climbing up it?"

Fen snorted contemptuously, and gulped his whisky. "This is filthy stuff," he said; and then: "An expert lassoist with a light hemp rope could do it easily. There's a row of crockets or something, along the gallery rail."

"But when you've got down again," the Inspector persisted, "you have to leave the rope hanging there, where someone will notice it."

"No, you don't," said Fen. "Not if your rope's long enough to allow a double length of it to reach the ground. You make a special sort of knot," he said vaguely, "and you climb down one strand, and then when you reach the bottom you pull the other, and it all comes undone." He sat back in a pleased manner.

"Oh," said the Inspector suspiciously, "and what is this knot, may I ask?"

"It's called the Hook, Line and Sinker."

"Why is it called that?"

"Because," said Fen placidly, "the reader has to swallow it."[1]

"But what I want to know *is*," Geoffrey burst out, unable to contain himself any longer: "What are all these people

---

[1] This is outrageous, tantamount to accusing me of invention. The knot does of course exist, is known as the sheet bend, and is much used in climbing.—E.C.

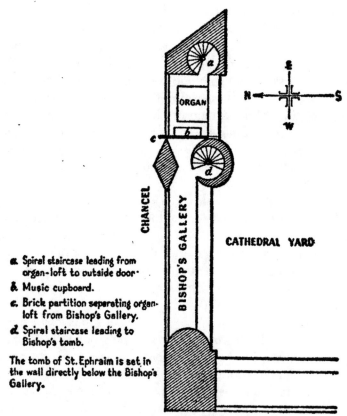

ORGAN

CHANCEL

BISHOP'S GALLERY

CATHEDRAL YARD

SOUTH TRANSEPT

a. Spiral staircase leading from organ-loft to outside door.

b. Music cupboard.

c. Brick partition separating organ-loft from Bishop's Gallery.

d. Spiral staircase leading to Bishop's tomb.

The tomb of St. Ephraim is set in the wall directly below the Bishop's Gallery.

doing shinning up and down ropes? We're no nearer to that than we were before."

"Wires," said Fen gnomically. He got up and began wandering about the room, apparently inspecting its decorations. "We must go over to the cathedral in a minute and visit, somehow or other, the Bishop's Gallery." He looked at the Inspector. "That can be arranged? It's annoying," he added balefully, "because I was going to make a particularly interesting experiment with moths this evening." He interrupted himself and addressed Geoffrey. "That reminds me: did you bring me a butterfly-net?"

Geoffrey nodded, hatred spontaneously arising within him at the memory of that implement. "It's at the clergy-house," he said. "Seventeen and six," he added. Fen ignored this.

"There's one more thing," said the Inspector, "and that's the murder of Brooks. Atropine again—through the mouth this time, of course. Criminal carelessness." His face darkened. "I think it's obvious that none of the hospital people was implicated, and that it was put in the medicine when it was left in the hall."

Fen looked up from his aimless circumambulations. "That's funny. It sounds like the merest chance..."

"Nothing of the kind, sir. The nurse in charge of the dispensary is the scatterbrained kind, and she'd talked about Brooks—talked to every single person who came to enquire after him, I should think. Half Tolnbridge must have known he got that stuff every half-hour, regular as Fate. Just as she was wheeling it into the hall, a bell went—the bell of one of the private rooms she was in charge of—and she went off to answer it. She found the patient sound asleep and no one else in the room. By the time she got back, of course, the damage was done."

Fen groaned. "Oh, my ears and whiskers!" he said. "Adventurous, eh? No one was seen about?"

"Plenty of people were seen about. It was during visiting hours."

"It mightn't have been Brooks' medicine at all. But I suppose they didn't mind about a little thing like that."

(Another sentence came back to Geoffrey's mind: "They can afford to waste lives like water.")

Fen resumed his wanderings, the Inspector his logomachy. "All the people who might possibly be connected with it—all the cathedral people, that is—I shall have to interview again this evening: Miss Butler, Dr. Butler, Dr. Garbin, Dr. Spitshuker, Mr. Dutton, Sir John Dallow, Mr. Savernake, now that he's back..." He reeled off the list with the melancholy relish of a Satanist enumerating the circles of inferno. "But nothing will come of it," he said, suddenly abandoning all pretence and relapsing into a pathetic despair, "nothing at all."

"Come, come," said Geoffrey mechanically.

"I'd be obliged, sir," said the Inspector, pulling himself together slightly and addressing Fen, "if you'd take a look at the cathedral, and the Bishop's Gallery, while I'm seeing all these people. We shall have to get permission from the Precentor to get into the Gallery, but I hope there won't be any difficulty about that. I can give you a note to the men in charge, and they'll help you in every way you need." Fen nodded, and finished his drink. They all rose, the Inspector sighing, and Geoffrey feeling slightly hazy and adventurous with alcohol.

"Well," said the Inspector, "we're not quite as much in the dark as we were, though it's still mostly conjecture. Now we'll see what there really is in this infernal Gallery."

This, however, they were destined never to do.

CHAPTER SIX

Murder in the Cathedral

"To-night it doth inherit
The vasty hall of death."

ARNOLD

*T*HEY WALKED BACK from the "Whale and Coffin" to the clergy-house. Now it was ten to ten and a twilight haze was dusting the roofs of the town, a twilight mist softening the lines of the headland towards Tolnmouth and driving argent channels among the scattered white houses which hung on the low distant bank on the other side of the estuary. The melancholy crying of the gulls was almost silent. The sky, as if in a parting flourish before the on-slaught of darkness, was the palest, most fragile blue. The curious, inexplicable stillness of evening was in the air—a stillness broken only by the cawing of a flock of rooks returning to their nests at the tops of a group of fir trees. Dominating the town stood the cathedral, its spire raised proudly to heaven.

Geoffrey was limping badly; his bruise, he felt convinced,

had grown to considerable dimensions by now, and a second, more formidable stiffness had set in. Moreover, matters were not improved by the speed at which Fen walked; he strode along at a great and unnecessary rate, talking incessantly about insects, cathedrals, crime, and Oxford University, and complaining impartially and slanderously (his normal manifestation of high spirits) about the conduct of the war, his personal comfort, the ingratitude of his contemporaries and the quality of certain proprietary brands of whisky. None the less, Geoffrey was happier than he had been all day. Fen had been found; something of the mystery had been cleared up; and he (Geoffrey) was in all probability the object of incidental and not special malice. He thought suddenly of a way in which the subject by inversion and the subject by diminution could be combined, and sang happily under his breath until even Fen, who was in the middle of some depressing tale about the habits of the common dung-beetle, was driven to comment on it. The Inspector walked for the most part in silence, plainly not listening to Fen, but inserting purposeless monosyllabic comments whenever a suitable opening occurred, like matches thrown upon the body of a stream.

They had not gone far before they met Fielding, on his way back from pottering, the bottoms of his trousers slightly stained with sea-water. He greeted them dejectedly, seeming still to be much afflicted by the heat, and was introduced to Fen and the Inspector.

("Not," said Fen before anyone could stop him, "the author of *Tom Jones?*")

As they walked on, Geoffrey put Fielding *au fait* with the situation, as far as he was able, and Fielding's dejection grew. Such mental inadequacy as he had displayed, his expression implied, boded ill for his hypothetical future as a secret agent. He was however slightly consoled on recognising that he had not known all the necessary facts.

"Things seem a bit clearer," he said to Geoffrey. His brow was puckered with anxiety. "What do you think one ought to do now?" Geoffrey sketchily indicated what plans were afoot, and he nodded.

"Very good," he said, apparently feeling that some comment was required of him. "But who's at the bottom of it all? That's what we've got to find out."

Geoffrey, who was only too ready to out-Watson Watson in this respect, made noises of dissent. "The best thing we can do," he stated dogmatically, "is to keep out of the way and not ask imbecile questions. There are two people in charge of this thing already. And God help the law," he added with feeling, "if people like us are ever landed with enforcing it."

"I think I'd be rather good at it," said Fielding staunchly. A pause. "Geoffrey?"

"Well?"

"Do you think either of these people could help me to get into the Secret Service?"

"Good heavens. Are you still nagging about that? You're unfitted, I tell you, unfitted—"

"I don't see why I'm any more unfitted than anyone else. You don't realise my position."

"I realise it perfectly well. You're a Romantic gone wrong—you're mad... The Secret Service isn't all guns and beautiful spies and codes, you know," continued Geoffrey severely, who knew nothing at all about it. "It's just routine and office work and"—his imagination hastily came to the rescue—"hanging about in pubs listening to soldiers." ("Why?" said Fielding.) "You'll be saying there are spies here next—in Tolnbridge..."

"...And that's another thing," the Inspector was saying complainingly on Geoffrey's left. "There are *spies* here—enemy agents. Bits of information have been leaking out—nothing important, fortunately, but still, symptomatic..."

Happily Fielding did not hear this. Geoffrey paused long

enough to digest the monstrous intelligence and verify the seriousness of the Inspector before hastily diverting the conversation to other channels. Fen paid little attention. Mindful of his hobby, he had begun peering in shrubs and bushes in search of insects.

"How were the rocks?" said Geoffrey.

"Barbed wire," answered Fielding gloomily. "It gets caught in everything. I don't see that *that's* going to hold up an invasion very long, either." He paused in momentary perplexity. "Did you discover anything about the burning of the manuscript by that child?"

"Good Lord," said Geoffrey, startled. "No, I didn't. But I don't suppose that's got anything to do with it."

Fielding shook his head; from the gravity of his expression, it was clear that he regarded the incident as of the last importance. Also, it had been overlooked by the powers that were. He put it away in his mind with the naïve hopefulness of an investor who keeps worthless stock in the hope that it may one day make him immensely wealthy. "You saw the landlord?"

"No. He wasn't there."

Fielding looked at him with mild reproach. "You've been drinking all this time."

"*Certainly* I have been drinking," said Geoffrey with the imagined stateliness which alcohol induces.

"...lays its eggs in a sort of milk-white bubble which refracts the head," Fen was saying. "Then about May the bubble bursts..."

"By the way, sir," said the Inspector abruptly, "we never went into that matter about the tomb—you know, the slab of the tomb that had been moved."

"Oh, my fur and whiskers!" exclaimed Fen. "Nor we did. Did Brooks mean that old reprobate Thurston's tomb, do you suppose? But you said the brickwork hadn't been touched, and there isn't a slab, anyway. Slab. Slab." He flicked his fingers. "Got it! It must be that enormous wall-tomb of St. Ephraim, right under the Bishop's Gallery. That's the only one that hasn't been plastered in—it's got six big padlocks to hold it in position instead. I suppose the keys are somewhere or other." He pondered. "But I wonder why—? M'm. A try-out for a hiding-place, possibly. Perhaps Brooks saw one of the padlocks loose— unpleasantly like *Count Magnus*. We must try and locate those keys, Garratt, and have a look at the tomb."

"All I can say is this," said the Inspector aggressively, as though he were being accused of something, "nothing had been touched that I could see, and certainly none of the tombs that were plastered up." A thought struck him. "Perhaps he was raving after all," he added gloomily.

They rounded a bend in the road, by an evil-looking tobacconist's. Two soldiers sat on the running-board of an Army lorry, smoking and staring with sad absorption at the tarmac. Two shop-girls in short skirts passed by on the other side, giggling and casting *oeillades* after the manner of their kind. The soldiers made sounds jocosely expressive of lustful attention. The girls shrieked with nervous excitement and made off. The Inspector sighed. Fen made futile attempts to put a grasshopper into a match-box. In the distance Frances appeared, a model of beauty, walking towards them. Geoffrey, too, sighed: that lithe perfection of grace could not be for him. Her hair shone a deeper, richer black in the evening light.

"Is the meeting over yet?" Geoffrey asked when she had joined them.

"Ages ago," she said lightly. "They've all gone—most of them, anyway." She did a tiny pirouette in the road.

"You seem happy," Geoffrey ventured.

"I'm excited."

"Why?"

"Oh, I don't know. I shouldn't be, I suppose, with all these awful things happening." She looked at him a little shyly.

"It's nice seeing new people—*you* know. Why did you want to know if the meeting was over?"

"I must see your father about what I've got to play, and when, and where I'm going to see the choir, and try the organ, and—"

She laughed. "Oh, business. Well, you won't catch Daddy at the clergy-house. I can tell you that. He went off up to the cathedral as soon as the meeting was over, half an hour ago at least."

Geoffrey intercepted a swift glance which passed between Fen and the Inspector. "Do you know what he intended doing, miss?" asked the Inspector.

The girl's face clouded. "He said—he said no one could get to know what happened to Brooks unless they did as he did, and stayed in the cathedral alone." She hesitated. "It seems silly."

"It will do no good, miss, if that's what you mean," the Inspector pontificated vaguely. "Nor, I suppose, will it do any harm. The clergy-house key arrived back safely, I take it?"

Frances nodded. "Sir John brought it just after dinner." She turned to Fen. "Are you going to be in tonight?"

"Yes," said Fen gloomily, as though this was the most offensive thing he had ever heard. "I was going to make a most interesting experiment with moths, but apparently that won't be possible now."

"You don't want supper or anything? Are you going back to the clergy-house now? I'm a bit anxious about Daddy—that was why I came to meet you."

"We're going to the clergy-house," said Fen, "to leave the Inspector, who's got some questions to ask about people's movements this afternoon. While he's doing that, Geoffrey and I are going up to the cathedral to have a rather particular look round—and incidentally, to see your father, as you say he's there."

"I shall be glad of that," said Frances a little shamefacedly. "I'm just a tiny bit frightened about his being there alone.

After what's happened…Oh, I suppose I'm making too much of it." She smiled. "Anyway, he's wearing a four-leaf clover for luck, so it ought to be all right."

"He'll be safe enough, miss," said the Inspector automatically. "My men are still on guard there, you know. There's nothing much can happen to him, I fancy." He whistled a few notes, tunelessly and without spirit.

They turned in at the clergy-house gates, traversed the wilderness of unflowering shrubs, and entered by the front door. In the hall they found Canon Spitshuker, small, plump, and excitable as ever, struggling into a raincoat and carolling the Benedicite to himself. "Frances, my dear," he called out as they entered, "you will, I fear, find the house empty, the revellers gone. I alone remain—except, of course"—he fluttered his hands excitedly—"the good Dutton, who has retired to his room with a copy of *The Anatomy of Melancholy* and some tablets of luminal. Hardly the most inspiriting reading for a nervous subject, I should have said, but perhaps it has a quietening effect on some people. And how are the insects, Gervase? The Bishop, I think, will not readily forgive you that last débâcle." He paused, and his face clouded as he glanced at the Inspector. "Strange: I was almost forgetting…poor Brooks…No doubt you will be wanting any assistance we can give you, Inspector, over this new development."

The Inspector nodded. "If you please, sir. It's a matter of routine, you understand, more than anything else. Were you in a hurry to be getting home?"

"No, no. I can stop as long as you wish. No commitments, except for my hot milk and rum before bed." Spitshuker began struggling out of his raincoat again, ineffectually aided by Geoffrey; he emerged from it eventually with the suddenness of a cork from a bottle, and stood gasping slightly.

"I understand, then, sir," the Inspector pursued, "that there's no one except yourself and Mr. Dutton left in the house?"

"Indeed, that is so. Mr. Peace—Butler's brother-in-law—was here talking to me until five minutes ago, but then he went off somewhere: you must have just missed him. We had a most interesting conversation—most interesting. It appears that he is afflicted by doubts, of a crucial nature, about the validity of his calling, but, as I endeavoured to explain to him, when one is dealing with doctrines about the mind which are, in comparison with those of Christianity, so hazy and unscientific—"

Frances came to the rescue. "Do you know if he was going up to the cathedral?"

"My dear young lady, he may have been. He said nothing about his destination. Perhaps he was intent on enjoying this delightful evening."

Fen, who had been pottering about the hall straightening pictures which he fancied were slightly askew, said: "I must meet Mr. Peace." He turned to Frances. "He's staying with your father?" Frances nodded.

"A friendly visit?" Fen went on.

Frances shrugged. "I think he's here on business. It seems odd, though. I've never met him before, and we've never visited him when we've been in Town." Fen made abstracted signs of affirmation: he straightened another picture. "Will you be wanting me?" said Frances to the Inspector. "If not, I must go and deal with things in the kitchen."

"Not for half an hour or so, miss."

"I'll be there or in my bedroom if you want me," she said, and departed.

"Come on, Geoffrey," said Fen, fidgeting about. "Let's get up to the cathedral before it's too dark to see anything." A thought struck him, and he turned to Spitshuker. "Do you happen to know if the Bishop's Gallery has ever been opened or—entered in any way, since it was first blocked up?"

Spitshuker glanced at him sharply, the sudden shrewdness

of his gaze contrasting formidably with the slightly ineffectual mask he presented to the world. "The Bishop's Gallery?—my dear fellow. I think not—no, I think not. At least there is no record of it. It would be possible, I suppose, to climb up from the chancel by means of a rope—one cannot tell if that has been done. But there has been no *public*—as it were—opening of Bishop Thurston's tomb, and if it were ever mooted, much local superstition would be against it. The Bishop was, perhaps, not an ornament of the Church he served, and it is inevitable that there should be…tales. With a gallery thus isolated and containing only the corpse of a man, a trick of the light which made it seem as if someone were peering down…" He stopped.

Fen showed interest—an unusual spectacle. "You fancy you've seen something of the sort yourself?" he asked.

Spitshuker gestured. "As I said—a trick of the light. But we are not forbidden to believe in demons."

"Recently?"

"I think not."

Fen's interest rather noticeably waned. "So the Bishop looks down into the chancel, does he? He's never progressed further, one supposes?"

The Canon laughed, suddenly and harshly. "It is said that there are two—a man and a woman. But I shouldn't bother your head with fairy tales. Dallow will tell you the local beliefs, if you ask him: he is the expert on these things." He paused. "I doubt if your question was framed with a view to ghosthunting."

Fen answered the implicit question. "It's necessary that we should get into that gallery," he said. "For that, we shall need the permission of the Dean and Chapter. Unfortunately we can't afford to wait. Do you think if we climb in over the parapet the Dean and Chapter will wink an eye?"

"My dear fellow, the Church is adept at winking eyes. Among the Jesuits it is known as casuistry. But how do you propose to accomplish this?"

"Geoffrey here will climb up a rope," said Fen firmly.

"Oh no, I won't."

"Somebody will, then. Of course, there's the problem of actually attaching the rope. I suppose there's no one in the town capable of throwing a lasso?"

Spitshuker looked dubious. "Harry James, the landlord of the 'Whale and Coffin,' did some cattle-farming in the Argentine once"—Geoffrey and Fielding flashed simultaneous ocular signals of triumphant finality at one another—"and perhaps you have to be expert with the lasso for that. On the other hand, perhaps not." He seemed dejected by his lack of precise information. "And besides, I fancy it is an aptitude one can quickly pick up—and equally quickly lose."

Mentally, Geoffrey admitted the justice of this; as a piece of evidence against the landlord of the "Whale and Coffin," it was equivocal, particularly since the notion of anyone's having climbed into the gallery at all was still pure theorising. But he was reluctant to abandon any scrap of information about that stocky, sinister, slightly ludicrous little figure who had known his name and who had been so astonished at his presence in Tolnbridge.

"...We'll see," Fen was saying ominously, "what can be managed. It probably won't be possible tonight, in any case, but I want a chance to spy out the land. One other thing; the keys of St. Ephraim's tomb."

Spitshuker stared at him blankly. "The keys...? Oh, ah, yes, to be sure: of the padlocks." He became faintly jocose. "You are not thinking, I hope, of instituting a general disinterment? The keys were in any case lost or destroyed—I forget which—some hundred and fifty years ago. St. Ephraim was originally buried in the chapel dedicated to him—the present tomb is a seventeenth-century erection, to which his remains (not much of them, one fancies) were then transferred. The padlocking is unusual, but not unknown—it's more normal, of course, with sarcophagi. The keys remained with the successive deans…Yes; I believe I have it. The Deanery was burnt down late in the eighteenth century, and probably the keys were lost then. But there again, Dallow would be the man to ask."

"It would be easy enough to take impressions," said the Inspector.

"But my dear Inspector," squeaked Spitshuker, "why, I ask you: why? There is nothing of value behind that immense slab. A lead coffin with some dust and hair—that's all. There *were*, of course, rich offerings to the shrine, but all were seized by Henry VIII, and afterwards the cult died out, except locally."

"We have our own ideas about why, sir," said the Inspector with traditional gruffness, "which, if you'll forgive me, I'll keep to myself for the moment." Rather insubstantial ideas, Geoffrey reflected, but forbore to comment on the fact.

Fen, who for the last minute had been rattling the umbrellas and sticks irritatingly about in the hall-stand, said:

"Let's get off, for heaven's sake. What are we pottering about here for, I should like to know?" Before anyone could say anything more, he had vanished through the front door. Geoffrey and Fielding followed him. Out of the corner of his eye, Geoffrey saw Spitshuker and the Inspector go into the sitting-room.

They rounded the house and passed through the back garden amid a cloud of wordy and incoherent apologies from Fielding for encumbering them with his presence. The gate between the garden and the Cathedral grounds was locked, but Fen had borrowed Dutton's key. He was unusually preoccupied and solemn as they climbed the cathedral hill. The ground was dry and hard beneath their feet, the air preternaturally still; Geoffrey strained his eyes to catch a glimpse of the police who guarded the cathedral doors, but dusk was falling, and once one was actually on the hill, he realised, the trees and shrubs made it extremely difficult to see the cathedral at ground level;

there were only brief occasional vistas, which a step further would annihilate. He thought he glimpsed a figure passing round to the north side of the building, but could not be sure.

They paused by the hollow where the witches had burned. It was overgrown, neglected. Weeds and brambles straggled over it. The iron post stood gaunt against the fading light. They found rings through which the ropes and chains had passed. The air of the place was almost unbearably desolate, but in imagination Geoffrey saw the hillside thronged, above and below, with men and women whose eyes glowed with lust and fright and appalling pleasure at the spectacle to be offered them. And a whisper ran through the crowd, swaying and bending their heads like the fingers of wind plucking at a field of corn, as the cart appeared, and they leaned forward to see better—the justices in their robes, the dean and chapter, the squires, and behind them the many-headed beast, the rabble. A woman they had known—a next-door neighbour, perhaps— a familiar face now become a mask of fear in whose presence they crossed fingers and muttered the *Confiteor*. Who next? And in the breast of that woman, what ecstasy of terror or vain repentance or affirmation? What crying to Apollyon and the God of Flies…? It needed little fancifulness to catch the echo of such scenes, even now. And here, they had accumulated— week after week, month after month, year after year, until even the crowds were sick and satiated with the screaming and the smell of burnt flesh and hair, and only the necessary officers were present at the ending of these wretches, and the people stayed in their houses, wondering if it would not have been better to face the malignant, tangible living rather than the piled sepulchres of the malignant, intangible dead.

"This was the last part of the country," said Fen, "in which the trial and burning of witches went on. Elsewhere it had ceased fifty or sixty years earlier—and then hanging, not burning, had been the normal method of execution. The doings of

Tolnbridge stank so throughout the country that a Royal Commission was sent down to investigate. But when Bishop Thurston
died the business more or less ceased. One of the last celebrated witch-trials in these islands was the Weir business in
Edinburgh; that was in 1670. Tolnbridge continued for forty
years after that, into the eighteenth century, the century of
Johnson, and Pitt, and the French Revolution. Only a step to
our own times. A depressingly fragile barrier—and human
nature doesn't change much."

They moved on up the hill. "It's going to be too dark to do
anything elaborate," said Fen, "and the cathedral isn't blacked
out in the summer." He took a torch from the pocket of his
raincoat and flicked it on experimentally. "It's quite possible, of
course, that we're wildly astray in all our conjectures—though
it seems the good Precentor is with us, up to a point."

"What do you think he's doing?" Geoffrey asked.

"My dear good man, how do I know? Presumably what he
said he was going to do—waiting for the ghost and—Hello!"

They had reached the top of the rise. Over them,
immensely high it now seemed, towered the cathedral, sombre and powerful as a crouched beast in the gathering gloom.
They stood in the angle of the nave and the south transept, in
a stretch of green turf. From where they were, three doors
were visible; none of them was guarded.

Fielding gripped Geoffrey's arm. "Geoffrey!" he whispered. "*Where are the police?*"

❀ ❀ ❀

And it was at that precise moment, in the sitting-room of
the clergy-house, that Canon Spitshuker happened to remark
to the Inspector:

"…And so when I saw you'd taken your men off guard at
the cathedral, I assumed…"

The Inspector was on his feet. "When you *what*?"

"Surely they all left in a motor-car about an hour ago now. Several of us saw them go."

The Inspector gazed at him incomprehendingly for a moment. Then "Holy God!" he whispered, and ran for the telephone.

❊ ❊ ❊

For a moment after Fielding's remark, the three stood stock still, looking. Then the earth seemed to shake under them. In a moment more there came from within the building a dull, enormous crash. After that, silence.

Gervase Fen was the first to stir himself. He ran to the nearest door and tried the handle; it was locked. So also with the other two. They pelted round the cathedral to the other side, and there, to their surprise, almost ran into Peace, who was hurrying anxiously in the opposite direction.

"What was that noise?" he shouted agitatedly. "What was that noise?"

"Don't ask imbecile questions," said Fen shortly, and proceeded to try the doors on the south side. Geoffrey discovered one which was open, and gave a crow of triumph.

"That's no good, you fool," shouted Fen. "It only leads to the organ-loft. You can't get into the cathedral that way. Useless here. Every damn door in the place is locked." They all rushed round again to the north side, vainly trying the west door on their way, and were there rewarded by the sight of the Inspector running like a madman up the hill, waving his arms and uttering unintelligible cries. Subsequently there appeared two constables, summoned by the Inspector over the telephone in blasphemous terms, and toiling up the slope on bicycles.

Fen glanced at his watch. "10:16," he said. "And it's about a minute since we heard that noise. Say 10:15."

"Can we break one of the doors down?" asked Fielding excitedly.

"You can try if you like," said Fen minatorily, "but it won't do the slightest good. We shall have to get a key—or else a rope, and Geoffrey can climb down into the chancel from the organ loft." ("No," said Geoffrey.) "I rather suspect we shall find that the clergy-house key has gone again, but each of the Canons has one."

The Inspector and the constables arrived more or less simultaneously, all greatly out of breath. Fen, with a rapidity and concision which he could very well employ when he chose, explained things to the Inspector, who nodded.

"Some sort of blasted decoy," he said, breathing stertorously. "They're such fools, a little child could take them in. God look down and pity us. Where have they gone, I ask you: where have they gone?"

"Never mind all that," said Fen rudely. "What we've got to do is to get into the cathedral." A constable was dispatched with instructions to get a key; he careered off down the hill at a fine pace.

"I'm going up to the organ-loft," said Fen, "to find out what can be seen from there." They all followed him, toiling up a long spiral staircase. Then, abruptly and without warning, they were there.

The cathedral was sunk in intense gloom. A few last rays of light still struck through the clerestory windows, resting upon capitals stiff with foliage. Enormous shadows moved and flitted with terrifying quickness. Geoffrey could dimly see the big four-manual console of the organ, the structure overhead which bore the tall, painted pipes, and, on his left, a large music cupboard standing against the brick partition which separated the organ-loft from the Bishop's Gallery. He went with Fen and the Inspector to the high wooden fencing which overhung the chancel, and hoisting themselves up, they peered down. Fen's powerful electric torch cut into the darkness;

motes of dust glittered and drifted in the beam; the light created a new world of shadows about them.

And so it was that Geoffrey, looking down, and a little to the left below the Bishop's Gallery, saw the great stone slab which lay poised and rocking, so gently and slowly, on the ground below; glimpsed the huge cavity—the tomb of St. Ephraim—which it had filled; and, as the light shifted, saw the black shoe of a man projecting from beneath that immense stone.

A stifled exclamation came from the Inspector: "There's someone under there. It's..."

He stopped. On the far side of the chancel rattled the wards of a lock, and a door was pushed open. The returning constable, finding no one about, was entering the cathedral. He stopped, startled by the torchlight, looked swiftly up at the organ-lofts and, hand on truncheon, advanced a few steps into the nave.

"Potter!" the Inspector shouted. "Stay by that door! We'll be round in a moment. Don't move from it, and don't let anyone out!" His voice awoke a thousand mocking echoes in the empty building. The constable saluted and returned to the door.

In three minutes they were standing about the stone slab, and the thing which lay under it. Every possible exit from the cathedral was guarded, and no one could get out. The united efforts of all the men had failed to shift the stone more than an inch or two.

"It's uncanny," Fielding whispered to Geoffrey. "No one here, and that damn slab bursting out of the wall as if..." He stopped suddenly, and they both glanced at the ugly black cavity in the wall. In the circumstances no further comment was needed.

The Inspector wiped his brow.

"We shall need a crane to get this thing off," he muttered. "And there's no chance he's still alive: it must have smashed every bone in his body. I suppose there's no doubt—?"

Fen shook his head. "Not very much, I should think...First Brooks, and now Dr. Butler, the Precentor..."

CHAPTER SEVEN

Motive

"Look always on the motive, not the deed."

YEATS

WHEN FIELDING had finally been persuaded to go home: "Resurrection men," said the Inspector agitatedly. "That's what's going on. Two tombs opened in less than an hour." He banged angrily on the table. "I went up that rope into Bishop's Gallery myself—like a Model Home Exhibition, it was. Dust and cobweb of centuries neatly swept into corners. And nothing there. Nor in that smelly tomb place down the staircase. The bird's flown. Whatever it was, gone." He lit a cigarette with as much ferocity as if it had personally offended him.

Fen, his long, lanky body stretched in one of the clergy-house armchairs, drank some whisky and stared blankly in front of him. "Well, that's what we should have expected, isn't it?" he enquired. "It shows at least that we're on the right track." His face hardened. "A strange business, Garratt—very strange. Almost too strange to be real. Accident? No, no. Suicide? Ridiculous. Murder impossible, I should have said—and what a method!" He swallowed more whisky, and gently mused.

It was close on midnight. With tremendous efforts the slab had finally been moved, and the pitiful, mangled remains of the Precentor taken away. Inch by inch, the doors guarded every moment, the cathedral had been searched, and without result; Geoffrey felt he would never forget that grotesque, torch-lit hunting. And now the cathedral was to be watched all night—a further search to be made in the morning. For, unless there was someone still trapped there, what explanation could there be…?

He started when Fen spoke to him. "You told the girl?"

Geoffrey swallowed. "Yes; she was in the kitchen here. She—didn't say anything. I didn't know what to say, either."

"And the mother?"

The Inspector shifted uneasily. "Canon Spitshuker has gone. It seemed the best thing." For a minute they were all silent. "Tomorrow, of course, we shall have to see her our-selves—we shall have to see everyone."

Fen said:

"You talked about resurrection men. Was either of the coffins disturbed?"

"No, no, sir," the Inspector replied. "Not that we could see. A way of speaking merely." He sat down, and said suddenly and frankly: "I haven't the beginnings of an idea about it."

"I have glimmerings," said Fen. He poured himself out some more whisky. "But the whole thing bristles so with prob-lems that one doesn't know where to begin. Take the most obvious point. All the doors were locked, and not a key in any of them, inside or out. No one except Peace about when we got there. No one in the cathedral when we searched (and, incidentally, no chance for anyone to get out anywhere while we waited for a key). All of which seems to dispose of anyone's shoving the slab on top of the poor man. And then, in heaven's name, what murderer is going to get a six-ton slab moved out, climb into a tomb, have the slab put back, and crouch there until his victim happens to come along? It's daft."

"What happened to the padlocks?" asked Geoffrey.

"Don't introduce irrelevancies," said Fen severely. ("We found them piled in a corner," the Inspector explained rapidly.)

"Are you paying attention," grumbled Fen, "or are you not? I don't expect anyone to attend to my lectures at Oxford, though heaven knows I try to make them interesting, and it isn't my fault if I have to talk about rubbish like—" He checked himself abruptly. "What was I saying?"

"Nothing in particular."

Fen glared malignantly about him. "Well, *you* say something, then. No," he added hastily, suddenly recollecting something, "don't for heaven's sake say anything. I want to know what happened to your police guard, Garratt."

The Inspector moaned dismally. "They got a typewritten message, signed by me (not that it isn't easy for anyone to copy my signature if they want to), telling them to get into the car and meet me at once at Luxford, which is a village about fifteen miles away. Off they went, the cretins, and they've only just got back."

"But who gave them the message?"

"Well—that's the odd part of it. It was Josephine Butler— Dr. Butler's other daughter."

Fen whistled noisily. "Well, well!" he said. "This is getting interesting. And who gave it her?"

"We don't know about that yet. But she told the sergeant in charge that she got it from a policeman."

"A policeman!" exclaimed Fen in stupefaction. "You're not wandering in your mind, I suppose, Garratt?" he added with oily kindness. "You didn't send the message yourself?"

"No, of course I didn't," said the Inspector irritably. "And that's what makes it so queer. Why get my men out of the way in order to commit an impossible murder?"

"I should have thought that was an easy one," Geoffrey put in. "It was to give whoever was responsible a chance to get away with whatever it was they'd got in the Bishop's Gallery."

"Lucid," said Fen.

Geoffrey ignored this. "It rather makes one suspect that the two things aren't connected at all. The Precentor may have met his death by accident—in fact, it seems the only possible thing—"

Fen snorted explosively. "Accident!" he said. "Nonsense. Even if he'd unlocked the tomb himself and found the slab was falling out on him, he'd have tried to save himself. And he would have fallen *backwards*, with his head away from the tomb. In fact he was flat on his face, with his head turned slightly inwards towards it." He reflected. "You didn't find the keys to the padlocks, I suppose?"

The Inspector made negative signals. "Not a sign. That rather puts the accident business out of court, too. *Court.* Lunacy court, that's what we shall want. And there's this Brooks business. We haven't even made a start on *that* yet."

"One thing at a time," said Fen tediously. "If at first you don't succeed, try, try, try again." A more useful reflection occurred to him. "While we're on the subject of keys, by the way: who got into the cathedral by means of which keys?"

"Oh, yes, you were right there," said the Inspector grudgingly. They waited until he should explain this gnomic pronouncement, Fen muttering "I'm always right" under his breath. "The clergy-house key was gone again, and what's more, this time it hasn't turned up; so presumably the criminal or criminals used that. As to Dr. Butler, he used his own key. It was found"—he hesitated, as at a distasteful memory—"among his clothes. So that, again, is that."

Fen nodded. "No leads anywhere, it seems. A weird business." He gestured impatiently. "I can't somehow get over the feeling that the whole thing's an accident—that it wasn't intended that way…"

"One other thing occurred to me," said Geoffrey. "And that is that anyone who was in the cathedral might have got out by climbing up a rope into the organ-loft, hiding there when we first came in to look round, and then getting out when we left."

"Not possible, sir," said the Inspector, relieved at the opportunity of making some contribution, however negative, to the proceedings. "For one thing, we should certainly have seen if anyone had been there. For another, there's nothing in that loft or around it to attach a rope to. The organ seat's loose, and can't be fixed, or at any rate hadn't been—I had a look for that—and there's nothing else that would take the strain, or that isn't out of the question for some reason or other. I shall go over the ground again tomorrow, of course, but you can take my word for it there isn't a chance."

"It wouldn't be possible to get in from the Bishop's Gallery?"

"Not unless you flew. You can't see round that partition between them, let alone *climb*—it projects quite a way, you'll find."

"So there's absolutely no way from the organ-loft—or the stairway leading up to it—into the main part of the building?"

"None, sir; you can rest assured of that."

Geoffrey sighed, and abandoned his idea to the limbo of wasted and well-meaning endeavour.

"And in that case…" said Fen and the Inspector simultaneously; they hooked little fingers. "Shakespeare," said the Inspector. "Herrick," said Fen. "And I wish," he added, "that someone would come into this room now who would tell us what this thing is that everyone's so anxious to do murder for."

There was a knock on the door. If the Archangel Gabriel had appeared to announce personally his intention of blowing the last trump in ten minutes' time, Geoffrey could not have been more surprised. What actually happened was that a pale, spectacled young man put his head round the door, and having apparently ascertained that no special perils lurked within, followed it into the room. He was dressed in a slightly greasy overall suit, and carried in one hand a length of wire and in the other an open pen-knife. A cigarette hung unregarded from a corner of his mouth. When he spoke, it was in a vague, abstracted murmur, slightly tinged with a cockney accent.

"Inspector Garratt?" he enquired generally. The Inspector rose.

"Name's Phipps," murmured the young man, scraping at the wire with his pen-knife. "C.I.D., radio. Told me at station I'd find you here. Front door open, nobody about, so just walked in." The telescoping of inessential words gave his conversation a curiously telegrammatic effect. "Mind if I speak you alone a moment?"

The Inspector made brief apologies and followed the young man into the hall. For some minutes Fen and Geoffrey sat in silence, broken only twice, once by Fen saying "Wires," and later by his pointing to the ceiling and remarking: "Privet-Hawk Moth, *Sphinx ligustri*."

In due time the Inspector returned, without the young man; plainly he was much moved. He sat down with caution, stared at the carpet, and said: "That's torn it!" Fen sang a little tune to himself; when he had finished he said cheerfully:

"If it's what it obviously is, no wonder you look glum."

The Inspector looked up. "See here, sir, I oughtn't to tell you this, nor you, Mr. Vintner; but I'm damned if I'll keep it to myself, all the same. You've probably guessed. They've located an enemy transmitting-set here, and they've been trying to narrow it down for the last two days. Pretty unobtrusively they've worked, too—our people never noticed them. There'd been nothing for forty-eight hours, and then suddenly this evening there was a short flash." He nodded grimly. "Just after my men at the cathedral went off on that fool's errand. So it's obvious now what there was in the Bishop's Gallery, isn't it—or, rather, in the tomb down the spiral staircase? And as pretty a hiding-place as you could want, too. But what a nerve—phew!" He mopped his brow.

Fen nodded gently. He was engaged in a remote and pleased contemplation of the moth on the ceiling.

"But there's another thing," the Inspector went on, "which makes it nastier. That set could only have been operated at nights, and that means someone connected with the cathedral must be an enemy agent—someone with access to a key…" His voice trailed off; in a little while he said: "Brooks found out what was going on, and he had to be silenced. And so, I fancy, did Dr. Butler. You understand, sir, that this puts things on a different footing altogether. I shall have to ask the Yard to come down now, as fast as they can travel. I can't deal with this. I should have had a job dealing with the murders, but spying…" He shook his head. "It'll have to be the Yard."

Without shifting his gaze, Fen drank half a glass of whisky. "How annoying," he said mildly.

"Really, Gervase," said Geoffrey in exasperation. "Surely, when matters are as serious as this, purely personal consider-ations…"

"*No!*" Fen howled; he howled with such suddenness that he startled even the moth, which dashed itself frantically against the window-curtains. "I will not be lectured! I know it's very grave, and all that, but I shall only fuddle myself if I try to get solemn about it. I'm not going to abandon the habits of a lifetime just because a lot of rattish transcendentalist Germans happen to be pottering about in my neighbourhood. Kant!" he hooted disgustedly. "There's a passage in the *Kritik der Reinen Vernunft* where—"

"Yes, yes," said the Inspector. "But the fact remains: it'll have to be the Yard."

"Don't keep saying that," replied Fen irritably. "Who will

they send, anyway? I hope it's someone I know. If I get some results before they arrive," he added hopefully, "they might let me be in at the death."

The Inspector got up: "I'm going to write up my notes and go to bed," he said. "It's no use trying to interview anyone tonight. I'll be round here at 9:30 tomorrow morning, and I shall be very grateful for any ideas you may have. The Yard people may be there by then"— ("It'll have to be the Yard," said Fen irritatingly)—"and we shall see," concluded the Inspector without much confidence, "what we shall see." He picked up his hat and moved to the door. "Good night, gentlemen. Not much sleep for me, I fear."

Fen waved a languid hand from the depths of his chair. "Good night, sweet Inspector," he called. "Good night, good night." He finished his whisky; furrows of earnest concentration appeared on his brow. "An odd climax, that wireless business—or anti-climax. Unsatisfactory, like the end of *Measure for Measure*. This is a complex business, Geoffrey. There are oddities…"

Geoffrey yawned. "Lord, but I'm tired. What a day! I can't believe it's only this morning I got your telegram and that letter. God grant I never go through a day like this again." He rubbed his thighs ruefully, and wandered to the door. "Two threatening letters, three attacks; and then on top of that I meet an earl serving in a shop and a landlord like something out of Graham Greene, and I overhear a murder."

Fen smiled sweetly. "I wonder if you're right," he said. "Good night, Geoffrey. *'Let no lamenting cries, nor doleful tears be heard all night within, not yet without, nor let false whispers, breeding hidden fears, break gentle sleep with misconceived doubt; let no deluding dreams, nor dreadful sights make sudden sad affrights…'"*

Geoffrey left him trying to catch the moth in an empty matchbox.

❀ ❀ ❀

Grotesque, thought Geoffrey as he lay in bed next morning, gazing with earnest fixity at the ceiling: a preposterous gallimaufry of hobgoblins and spies. The murders were very well in their way; at least it was demonstrable that they had occurred. But ghosts were inconceivable, enemy agents almost equally so. Daylight, he reflected, restores us to sanity, or at least to that blinkered and oblivious condition which we call sanity. Impossible murders, even, would find it difficult to withstand the penetrating virility of morning light. Plainly, something had been overlooked, or absurdly misinterpreted. The German transmitting set would prove to be the fumblings of a schoolboy of mechanical proclivities. When one came down to facts—well, what? When one came down to facts, Geoffrey was forced to admit, the notorious antisepsis of daylight seemed somehow lacking in effect. Nothing, essentially, had changed since the previous night; the events of yesterday, which, it was evident, the mind was only too willing to write off as perfervid delusions of its own, stood dismayingly impervious to such high-handed attempts at erasure; furthermore, they intruded distressingly upon the mind's naïf and virginal projects for its own placidity during the coming hours—a moral hangover, a blotted and scrawled-upon sheet of the copy-book defying removal. It poisoned all enjoyment. Geoffrey's mood became noticeably more atrabilious. He contemplated with nothing less than malevolence the ravaging incursions of Id upon the tranquil expanses of his personality.

No lust for the hunt, no anguished endeavour to discover the truth possessed him, he observed; and that, presumably, was why he was still in bed. The room had the pervasive melancholy aura of the almost permanently unoccupied; a few personal belongings, scattered about, battled

bravely but ineffectually to make of it a habitation. Plainly the
atmosphere would drive him out of it fairly shortly. But before
that happened, something remained to be debated. Long experience had taught Geoffrey that mental colloquy, however con-
fidently embarked upon, generally ended in irrelevancy, divaga-
tion and chaos; he did not, however, quite realise that it is
impossible for a man to think clearly and rationally about a
woman when lying in bed. The subsequent proceedings of his
mind were therefore confused and for the most part unworthy
of attention. It did, however, emerge from them that although
he might be in love with Frances it seemed in the highest
degree doubtful if she was in love with him; that the thing to do
was to find out about this; and that the time to do it was not the
morning after her father had met with a violent death. Thus
supplied with a course of action and an excuse for putting off
embarking on it almost indefinitely. Geoffrey decided that there
was no point in lying on his back any longer, and got up.

He careened down the corridor to the bathroom, sponge-
bag and towel flowing gently behind him. A faint scuffling
from within, as of rats disturbed at a meal, showed it to be
occupied, conceivably by Fen. Geoffrey cautiously pushed open
the door, and was confronted by the spectacle of Dutton, his
face covered with soap, a cut-throat razor brandished suicidally
in the region of his jugular vein, and making gestures of vague
pudency; Geoffrey retreated. "Breakfast in three-quarters of
an hour's time," a voice pursued him back to his room. "Good
morning," it added as an afterthought.

Dutton having taken himself off, Geoffrey lay in a hot
bath and reflected further on the events of the previous night.
And as he reflected, an idea came into mind. It was an idea so
simple, so plain, so obvious, that he was unable to imagine why
it had not occurred to him before.

And the more he considered it, the more likely it seemed,
though certainly there were smaller problems which it left

unsolved. Not quite a closed box, after all; in fact, not a closed box at all...

He was almost amiable when Fen came in, wearing a violent-purple silk dressing-gown, and looking ruddier, lankier, and more irrepressible than ever.

"I'm going to shave while you're having your bath," he announced threateningly. "Otherwise I shall be late for breakfast." He lathered soap all over his face, flinging it freely about the room, and began making long, tearing passes at his cheeks and throat with a safety-razor: "Did you have a good night? That moth I caught is dead this morning."

"I'm not surprised. Why do you pretend to be interested in insects?"

"Pretend?" Fen examined his face without much enthusiasm in the mirror. "I don't pretend. Essentially I am a scientist, beguiled by chances into the messy, delusive business of literary criticism. You can see that from the clarity and precision of my mind." He beamed at this triumph of autology. "And I don't deny there's a romantic interest as well. Life in the insect world is all melodrama—*The Revenger's Tragedy* without any of the talk."

"And a pretty daft business *that* would be," said Geoffrey. He fished for some invisible object by the side of the bath. "Here's a toy boat." He put it on the water and pushed it to and fro.

"The Elizabethans"—Fen was evasive—"were not strong on plot...The strength of their drama lay in the now lost art of rhetoric. They recognised the superiority of word over action as a means to enjoyable sensations. The Elizabethan groundling was a superior person, in point of culture, to the educated *bourgeois* of today." He paused, and dabbed styptic pencil on a cut. "Whose boat is that, I wonder?"

"Josephine Butler's, I expect: a relic of nonage." Geoffrey was engaged in squeezing water on to it from his sponge, in the hope of capsizing it: "Your groundling had no sense of humour, though. Otherwise he'd never have put up with Beatrice and Benedick." He surveyed the boat thoughtfully, and balanced a piece of soap on the deck; it fell off. "You heard about Josephine's burning her father's manuscript?"

"And being smacked? Yes. It doesn't seem to have much to do with anything. I should like to know what the manuscript was. Garbin would know—or Spitshuker. And it's odd she should have taken that message to the police at the cathedral. Again, it may not mean anything. There are too many peripheral elements in this thing. This centre's a nice convenient blank; the circumference swarms with cryptic sign-boards and notices."

"I think I have an idea."

"It's sure to be a wrong one." Fen blew powder on to his chin from a surgical-looking rubber bulb such as hair-dressers use. He bundled his things indiscriminately into his sponge-bag.

"Don't you want to know what my idea is?"

"No," said Fen in parting, "I don't. And if you stay in that bath much longer you won't get any breakfast, I can tell you that. There's an idea for you to be going on with." He laughed irritatingly, and went out

For Geoffrey, the choosing of a tie had developed into an elaborate ceremonial, involving reference to his suit and shirt, to the weather, and to an imperfect memory of what he had worn during the preceding ten or fourteen days. On this particular morning, having returned with some sense of anti-climax to the tie he had first selected, he gazed for rather longer than usual at his reflection in the dressing-table mirror. The impact of womanhood on one's life, he reflected, is to make one rather more attentive to one's imperfections than is normal. None the less, he did look at least ten years younger than his age; the slightly faun-like mischievousness of his face was, he supposed, not unattractive; light-blue eyes and close-cropped brown hair had, without doubt, their charms...From

these complacent reflections he was interrupted by a subter-
ranean booming which he supposed must mean breakfast. He
bent his attention painfully upon the outside world again, and
hurried downstairs.

Frances, he knew, would not be there; she had returned
to spend the night with her mother, leaving a not inadequate
old person of simple appearance to hold the fort in the meanwhile. Fen was already in the breakfast-room when Geoffrey
arrived, gazing with every appearance of interest at a morning
paper. Dutton shortly appeared, arranging freshly-cut flowers
in a bowl with a curiously feminine competence and delicacy.
They sat down to porridge, Dutton plainly feeling it incum-
bent on him, as the only resident present, to lead the conversation. After several false starts, he achieved the statement
that it was a terrible thing. This as it happened was unfortunate, since conventional expressions were seldom a success
with Fen. He regarded Dutton with interest.

"Is it? Is it?" he said, waving his spoon and scattering milk
about the tablecloth. "I knew very little about Dr. Butler. Not
a communicative man, I should have said, or one easy to get
on with."

Dutton looked cautiously at his plate; plainly he was considering the wisdom and propriety of discussing the dead man.
"Uncommunicative, yes," he admitted eventually. "And liable
for that reason to be—traduced." He offered this linguistic triumph with modest pride. Fen's interest grew. He said:

"He wasn't popular, then?"

Dutton scurried to cover his tracks. "I should hardly put
it as strongly as that. About a man in his position there are
always misunderstandings." A wave of blushes passed up his
face and were engulfed in his ginger hair. It was very awkward.
Fen, possessed of little patience at the best of times, abandoned finesse and said:

"For heaven's sake, don't hedge. What I want"—he pointed

his spoon at the alarmed sub-organist—"is to hear what you know of the relations of all the people round here with the dead man." He became acrimonious. "You'll have to tell the police if they ask, so you may as well tell me. Cast off this skin of discretion," he added, waxing suddenly eloquent; and then, returning abruptly to a more homely plane: "Good heavens, man; don't you *like* gossipping about other people's affairs?"

It seemed that a powerful conflict was raging within Dutton's soul, between discretion and shyness on the one hand, and the desire to be friendly, and the centre of importance, on the other. Quite suddenly, the second party won, and he began to talk, and with hesitation at first, and then, as he found he was enjoying himself, with some zest and vigour. Fen and Geoffrey had little to do except sit and listen.

"Dr. Butler," Dutton said, "made himself out to be, first and foremost, a scholar. As to what he was studying, I'm a bit vague, but I think it was something to do with theology. Garbin's a strong man in that line, too—I believe his book on the Albigensian heresy is *the* work on the subject—and he always maintained that the Precentor's scholarship was half bogus. They had quarrels—one in particular over some important incunabulum which Garbin was editing for the Press and which the Precentor cribbed from for an article in a learned magazine: I think Garbin nearly gave up his prebend because of that. When Dr. Butler died they were both working on a book on the same subject more or less, and the rivalry was terrific." Dutton considered. "I don't know that that would be a motive for murder, though, particularly if Garbin's scholarship was as much superior as he pretended it was."

"We think we know the motive," said Fen, "but I want to get a general picture of all these people. Go on."

"The Precentor quarrelled with poor Brooks over the music, but then precentors and organists are always at loggerheads. I must say, though, that Dr. Butler was quite exceptionally high-handed about the music. But Brooks was a bit of a tactician, and he generally got his own way in the end. Spitshuker and Butler got on well enough on the whole, though Spitshuker's practically an Anglo-Catholic, and Butler was always complaining to the Dean and the Bishop about it, but it never had any effect. He bossed the minor canons about a bit, too. I don't know that there's much else. He seemed to get on all right with his wife and family"—Dutton paused—"at any rate until that Josephine business yesterday. She burned his manuscript, you know—the younger daughter, that is—then ran away round here, and he followed her and gave her the hiding of her life. I must say I think she deserved it."

"How long had he been here?" asked Fen.

"About seven years, I think. He may have had a living before that—I don't know. Anyway, he had pots of money of his own—or, rather, I think it came from his wife. He used to potter about the Continent from library to library—the whole family were in Germany for two years some time in the 'thirties. He was quite poor before he married—scholarship boy, son of a cobbler, or something like that—and I think the money rather went to his head."

An elephant-bell like an inverted sea-anemone, of Birmingham manufacture, summoned in the bacon and eggs; a malodorous alchemistic contrivance for the brewing of coffee was set in reluctant motion. These disturbances over, Dutton returned to his tale.

"Mrs. Butler one can't say much about: she's a little unobtrusive woman without much character of her own. I think he used to bully her rather. Josephine's always been a wild, headstrong girl; she's likely to grow into the sort of woman who'll do anything for a thrill. She used to get some of the poorer kids in the neighbourhood together into gangs and fight round the neighbourhood—sometimes fight nastily and dangerously. But when it came to doling out responsibility she was always the picture of innocence and her father, who doted on her, would never do anything about it.

"Frances"—the young man paused and blushed faintly. "I don't know that I can say anything about her. She—she's a dear." Here, Geoffrey thought, is unassuming adoration; he was unsurprised, but obscurely the fact troubled him.

"Savernake?" asked Fen, piloting the conversation with laborious care over these quicksands. "What about him?"

"July's a pleasant chap—a bit stupid sometimes, that's all. He's—was—by way of being a protégé of Dr. Butler's. He's got the living at Maverley, a few miles out from here. Doesn't seem to spend much time there, though." There was a shade of disapproval in Dutton's voice; evidently he thought severely of such negligence.

"Leaves his sheep encumbered in the mire," put in Fen by way of apposition; then, seeing that the allusion wasn't recognised, became gloomy.

"I've an idea that relations between July and the Precentor were getting strained," Dutton went on. "July wasn't all that Dr. Butler expected him to be. Also"—he hesitated—"July's in love with Frances, and wanted to marry her. For some reason, Dr. Butler wouldn't hear of it—probably suspected he was after the money, or something." A thought struck him. "I suppose they'll be able to get married after all."

Geoffrey contemplated this prospect without pleasure. The possibility of serious rivalry had not hitherto occurred to him. Decidedly, it was disturbing. Dutton was saying:

"Peace I don't know anything about; it seems he's a successful psychoanalyst." He pronounced the word cautiously, as though fearing it might be too much for his auditors. "Spitshuker and Garbin…they're always arguing, but actually they get on very well together. Spitshuker's family's always been rich, and always connected with the Church; he's had an easy, placid life—never got married, he says because of his convictions, but actually I expect it's because no one would have him." He flushed with pleasure at this ingenuous exhibition of worldly wisdom. "Garbin's rather the opposite—a scholarship boy from a poor family with a personal and not a traditional inclination towards the Church. I've told you what he thought about the Precentor. Mrs. Garbin's a shrew—tries to run everything and everybody, including her husband. Curiously enough she hardly succeeds at all: interfering but ineffectual. He's always put up a solid show of passive resistance, and she's come to leave him more or less alone nowadays. She didn't like Dr. Butler, but then"—Dutton frowned in perplexity—"it's difficult to see that she likes anyone very much."

"Soured by a childless marriage?" said Fen.

"Oh, no: there are three children, two boys and a girl. Garbin wanted the boys to go into the Church, but they wouldn't. You know how it is." Dutton waxed philosophic. "Isn't it Anatole France who says that the opinions sons get from their fathers are identically opposite, like the cup moulded by the artist on his mistress' breast?" Suddenly confronted with the enormity of what he had said, Dutton blushed again, and shamefastly restored this treasure of analogy to the private quartets of his mind. "Anyway, the sons are in the Forces—I don't know about the daughter; I've never seen any of them." He hesitated. "Is there anyone else?"

"Sir John Dallow," Geoffrey put in.

"The Chancellor—oh, yes. He's rich, too, but as mean as Shylock." Dutton's discursion was beginning to be enlivened by literary allusions. "He hasn't an awful lot to do, nowadays, of course, though when there was a choir-school he was in charge of that. He's ordained, but he's never 'in residence' nowadays. He's been gradually unfrocking himself, as it were, over a period of years." Dutton waved his hands, to indicate a process of unobtrusive divestiture. "He's an expert on witch-craft, demonolatry—all that stuff. Another of these bachelors, too." From his tone it was evident that he regarded bachelor-hood as *ipso facto* an evil condition. It occurred to Geoffrey that a flame of pure connubial idealism burned probably in the young man's breast.

Fen nodded sagely over his toast and marmalade. "That's the lot, I think, since the Bishop and Dean are away. And now one or two points about yesterday, if you don't mind. Brooks was killed at about six. Where were you then?"

"Out—walking."

"Alone?"

Dutton nodded. "I'm afraid so. I find it difficult to know what to do with myself now that music's forbidden me. I was on the cliffs—towards Tolnmouth."

"And last night—shortly after ten?"

"In my room, reading."

"Did you have the window open?"

Dutton looked perplexed. "Yes. It was a hot evening."

"And did you hear the crash when the slab of that tomb fell?"

"No. Not a sound."

Fen finished his coffee and got up. "Thanks very much," he said. "And now, alas! To work—dishonest, assuming work." Geoffrey and Dutton also rose. Shyness was again engulfing Dutton like a mantle. He hovered about, finally thrusting forward desperately a chromium cigarette-case. They lit their cigarettes. A silence fell.

"Well, I…" said Dutton. He shifted his feet. "I think I have some things to do in my room."

This palpable falsehood was received in stony silence. Dutton became frantic, in a subdued manner. He tottered towards the door, paused and turned uncertainly; and, finally, saying "If you'll excuse me," in a low tone, made a dash for it and got out.

They sighed with relief. "How infectious embarrassment is," said Fen. And Geoffrey:

"He really is rather weird. But the life of a sub-organist is not a happy one. They never have the last word about anything, so they never get any confidence in themselves. Probably next to no money, either—poor as the proverbial church mouse. In fact," said Geoffrey reflectively, "now I come to think of it, Dutton is the proverbial church mouse."

"Natural shyness," said Fen, "is a superb disguise. And shy people have a penchant towards cunning. They must, somehow, act, and since they daren't act in ways that people can see—in the open, as it were...What a lot of hooey I'm talking," he added moodily. "Sounds like the sort of stuff Peace turns out. Come on, we must go." He looked at his watch. "The Inspector ought to be here by now. Thanks to Dutton, we know something about the people we're going to see. Did you notice rather an interesting thing in that account?"

"No. What?"

"About his not hearing the crash."

"Is that important?"

"I'm pretty certain it is."

CHAPTER EIGHT

Two Canons

ITHA: *"Look, look, master; here comes two religious caterpillars."*
BARA: *"I smelt 'em ere they came."*

MARLOWE

"A PLEASANT MORNING."

The Inspector's voice thus greeted them as they passed up the clergy-house drive towards the road. It held a hint of complacency, as if the pleasantness of the morning were somehow of his own contriving. And certainly it was another glorious day, promising much heat and discomfort later on, but for the present as perfect as any man could desire. Tolnbridge sunned itself, opulently and lazily. Its colours took on a new freshness. The estuary glittered—silver tinsel on a vivid blue—and the explosions of the engines of the outgoing fishing boats proceeded peaceably from it. Beyond them, a minute grey warship lay at anchor. The cathedral itself achieved in the sunlight such grace

and lightness that it seemed likely at any moment to be trans-
muted into a fairy place and float gently away into some
Arcady, some genial Poictesme. Decidedly, a pleasant morning.

It soon appeared, however, that the Inspector's comment
was less self-congratulatory than a propitiating gambit in a difficult game. He had rung up the Yard, he said, joining to this
statement a good deal of devious rambling fantasy; they were
sending a man down today; and—here the Inspector's unease
became acute—they considered that unauthorised persons
should be absolutely excluded from any subsequent investigations which might be made.

"The boot," said Fen. "*Anathema sumus.*"

"You see my position, sir," said the Inspector. Plainly he
regretted the outcome as much for himself as for Fen. "As it
is, they're not at all pleased that you know as much as you do.
I suppose"—he stared at Fen unhappily— "I shouldn't have
let either of you in on that radio business." He stared still
harder, becoming acutely unhappy. Fen's spirits, however,
were normally raised rather than lowered by adverse circumstances. "Inspector," he said with evil glee, "I'll beat you to it.
Bet you I get the murderer before you do."

The Inspector nodded pathetic assent. "Very probably,
sir. You can't be much further off from it than I am at the
moment. And, of course"—his eyes twinkled momentarily—"I
can't stop you going round asking people questions if they're
prepared to answer them."

"Have you," said Fen, "got any new information you can
give us before the interdict comes into force? Or is it in force
already?"

The Inspector peered anxiously about him; he appeared
to be seeking for evidences of an ambush. Then, spectacularly
lowering his voice, he said:

"I've had a go at that kid Josephine this morning. Would

you believe it, the little devil still insists that message was given her by a policeman."

"Perhaps it was."

"No: she's obviously lying. But I'm darned if I know how to get the truth out of her. As far as I can see, if she chooses to stick to that story, there's absolutely nothing we can do about it."

"It's odd," said Fen. "I wonder why—?" He shook his head vigorously. "Anything else?"

"Nothing. The *post mortem's* this morning at eleven, and there'll certainly have to be an inquest. God knows what verdict they'll bring in—we can't help them. Is there any other way of violent death except murder, accident and suicide? They all look equally impossible."

"It was murder all right," said Fen with an exuberance unjustified by the nature of the statement. "Oh, by the way. You didn't, I suppose *trace* that radio in any way? There must have been a car to take it away. It occurs to me, too, that they must have been a fair time about it All this whipping transmitting sets in and out of cathedrals must be quite a business. Surely there'd be aerials, or something?"

"Anyway, we didn't trace it," said the Inspector. It was evident that he was sinking to hitherto unplumbed depths of pessimism. "Nor was there anyone in the cathedral when we searched again this morning." He steeled himself reluctantly to action. "I must be off."

"Where are you going first? We don't want our interviews to clash. What a silly waste of energy," said Fen in a pained voice. "Interviewing everyone twice. We're going to Garbin."

"All right," said the Inspector. "Then I'll see Mrs. Butler. It doesn't seem to matter much what order one takes them in."

"I wish," put in Geoffrey, "that you could do something about the landlord of the 'Whale and Coffin.'"

"Do something, sir? Do what? Arrest him because he

happened to know your Christian name? God love us," said the Inspector with feeling, "the things people expect one to do."

"Farewell, Inspector, and God 'ild you," said Fen. "We meet," he added grandiosely, "at Philippi."

"Colney Hatch, more like," said the Inspector.

Parting, however, was not to be yet. They were interrupted by the bustling advent of Canon Spitshuker, greatly out of breath.

"Wanted to catch Mr. Vintner," he gasped. "Music... organist...services." He paused to recover himself, and went on more coherently: "Since the terrible events of last night, the duties of Precentor have temporarily devolved upon me. Mr. Vintner"—he paused and wiped his forehead with a large purple handkerchief —"it will, in view of the circumstances, be *said* Mattins this morning—"

The Inspector interrupted. "Good heavens, sir," he said aghast, "you're not proposing to hold your service this morning as usual?"

"My dear Garratt, of course."

"But really, sir, after what has happened—"

A tinge of impatience came into the Canon's voice. "The Church does not suspend the worship of God on any and every pretext. And if ever there was a time when our prayer and praise were needed, surely it is now."

"Praise!" The Inspector's voice was unexpectedly bitter.

"My dear Inspector, I have simply not the time to argue with your doubtless ridiculous notions about God allowing evil, and so forth. Now, Mr. Vintner—"

"But look, sir." The Inspector was mildly exacerbated. "There's the mess—the confusion..."

"That has all been cleared up."

"*I beg your pardon?*"

"Our cleaners have dealt with it. There is only the slab to put back."

"God have mercy," said the Inspector. "The things people do behind one's back."

Canon Spitshuker looked faintly puzzled. "I fear it was done on my authority. Surely...surely I have done nothing wrong?"

"You may have destroyed valuable evidence, sir."

"It could hardly be *left*, though, could it, Inspector?...Dear me." Spitshuker seemed perturbed. "And I never dreamed...Still, what's done's done."

"No use crying over spilt milk," put in Fen tediously.

"And now, Mr. Vintner: sung Evensong at 3:30, and the choir will be at your disposal at 2:00. Poor Brooks had his practices in the old chapter house—there is a good piano there. Now let me see." He felt in a pocket and produced a bundle of service sheets, among which he scrabbled unsystematically until he found the one he wanted. "For this afternoon we have down Noble in B Minor, and Sampson's *Come, My Way*. All quite familiar to the boys, I think." He thrust the sheaf at Geoffrey. "The music for future services is noted here. I leave it to you to make any alterations that you think fit." He made movements of hasty departure.

"One moment, sir." It was the Inspector. "Did you say you'd made arrangements to have the slab put back?"

Perturbation and alarm again appeared on Spitshuker's rubicund face. "I have, certainly, though if you think it will destroy evidence..." (Was there a hint of sarcasm in his voice? Geoffrey wondered.) "Still, it would hardly be desirable to hold Mattins with the tomb gaping open, would it?" He smiled innocently.

"If it hasn't been done already, sir, I should like to be present. There are certain tests I wish to make." The Inspector's manner was markedly stiff and official.

"By all means. By all means." Spitshuker looked agitated. "I promised to superintend the work myself." He glanced at his watch. "But we must hurry. Mattins is in less than an hour."

In the cathedral they found a group of men gazing at the fallen slab without enthusiasm, under the eye of the Verger. For the first time Geoffrey was able to examine properly the tomb of St. Ephraim. From the space beneath the spire, where the transepts joined the main body of the cathedral, a short flight of steps led up into the chancel; but the stalls of the choir, and of the cathedral officers, were placed some way further to the east, beginning just below the organ-loft. Beneath the Bishop's Gallery, hollowed from the wall, was the cavity of the tomb. The fallen slab normally filled it. In its edges were embedded iron rings, corresponding with others in the edges of the slab, so that when this was in position a large padlock could be passed through each pair to hold it firm. The cavity, though quite shallow, was about ten feet in length and six in height, and the slab was proportionately thick. Amid a good deal of premonitory groaning, it was hoisted upright, and eventually, with titanic efforts, lifted into its cavity. It fitted quite loosely, Geoffrey noticed, the lower edge between two and three feet from the ground, the upper some six feet higher. The Inspector had a chair brought and stood on it, motioning the men away with one hand and holding the slab in position with the other. Then with infinite slowness and caution he withdrew his hand. As yet unanchored by its padlocks, the slab swayed ever so slightly, delicately poised on its narrow base; but it showed no sign of falling of its own accord. The Inspector grunted.

"Wouldn't take much to topple that out," he said. He got down from the chair.

Fen had been unwontedly silent and attentive during these proceedings. Geoffrey stepped back and spoke to him. "Explosive charge inside?" he asked. "Even though the slab doesn't fit exactly, the tomb would be pretty well airtight."

Fen shook his head. "There'd be obvious traces. Any sort of mechanism's out of the question for the same reason."

Geoffrey glanced up to the Bishop's Gallery above.

"Could it be pushed out, by a long pole or something, from there?"

Again Fen shook his head, and pointed. "That projection would stop it. And besides, think of the complications. Very unlikely. And you'd still have to account for how the person concerned got out of the cathedral. The wall between the Bishop's Gallery and the organ is solid brick, remember."

"I think I know," said Geoffrey, "how someone could have got out of the cathedral." Mentally, he fondled his cherished Idea. Fen gazed at him kindly.

"You mean Peace, of course. Just after the crash we find him wandering on the other side of the cathedral. Why shouldn't he just have come out, locking the door after him, and throwing away the key in case anyone should take it into his head to search him? Why indeed? The only snag is that it doesn't fit in with anything else we know about the case."

Geoffrey was peeved at having his thunder stolen; he made obstinate mental reservations, highly unwilling to have his Idea thus facilely disposed of. But he made no comment, since the Inspector was about to make another experiment. The group of men who had hoisted the slab into position, and who had been hanging about since exhibiting that gentle, inane interest in the goings-on of others which is one of the mainstays of the English character, showed as he explained his intentions stupefaction and gloom. He was proposing, in fact, to allow the slab to fall out again.

This, however, was a more difficult operation than at first appeared, chiefly because the slab rested quite flat in its cavity and offered no projection by which it could be pulled. Eventually the Inspector inserted a steel ruler into one side, and standing as far clear as he could, used it as a lever. Slowly the great stone moved, toppled. They watched in frozen silence. The fall at first was slow, rapidly gathering a tremendous momentum. Just before it reached the horizontal,

Geoffrey noted, the lower edge came away from the shelf on
which it rested. And the terrifying, stealthy silence of it! In a
moment it lay flat on the ground, the chair which had been left
beneath it crushed to splinters.

The noise of the impact was shattering, and
yet…somehow, Geoffrey thought, it was different from what
he had heard the previous evening. The deadening effect of
walls and doors might account for the disparity, but it was not
exactly that. Perplexed, he watched the herculean heavings
and groanings begin anew; perplexed, he saw the six padlocks
inserted to hold the slab in position, and the remnants of the
chair cleared away. The Inspector, apparently satisfied, made
off on his own. Fen and Spitshuker, engaged in conversation,
were walking towards the door. After a last look round
Geoffrey joined them.

"…A few questions," Fen was saying as they came out
into the sunlight, "which I hope you won't regard as imperti-
nent." The apology was conventional, and sounded it. "And I
think you ought to know," he added, with an unwonted spasm
of honesty, "that I'm no longer collaborating with the police."

Spitshuker clucked simultaneous dismay and assent. "But
my dear fellow…of course. The police have thrown over your
offer of assistance?" He made clicking noises with his tongue.
"Scandalous, scandalous." This, too, seemed a trifle less than
sincere. "Of course I will answer any questions. If you wish, I
will walk with you towards Garbin's house. I am 'in residence'
at the moment, so I have to say Mattins, but that is not for half
an hour yet." He gathered his short coat about his portly little
figure, and walked down the cathedral hill with them.

"Mainly about times," said Fen. "Six o'clock, and ten to
ten-fifteen yesterday evening."

Spitshuker looked up quizzically. "You are trying to establish alibis," he stated with evident enjoyment. "I have none for
six o'clock. I was alone in my room, working, at that hour. My

housekeeper was in the house, but she cannot possibly vouch for me." He seemed to regard this as a matter for some pride. "Between ten and a quarter-past I was talking to the Inspector in the clergy-house drawing-room. About seven I had set out with Garbin to dine at the clergy-house, and after dinner, when Dallow had given us the terrible news about poor Brooks, we held our little conclave—Dallow, Garbin, Butler and myself."

"Ah, yes." Fen was pensive. "I'm interested in this meeting."

"Unofficial. A purely unofficial affair. Of course the Dean and the Bishop have been communicated with, and are returning at once." The parenthesis confused the Canon, and he paused doubtfully. "The meeting was called when there was, as yet, no question of murder, merely this...accident which had occurred to Brooks, and which necessitated a little rearrangement among ourselves. We had intended, as it were, to clear the ground a little before the Dean returned. I fear that nothing very useful was said. The greater part of the meeting was taken up by a squabble between Dallow and Butler about the legal and financial position of the resident organist, and by some unavailing attempts at armchair detection on the part of Garbin."

"Not a very brotherly affair, in fact?"

"There was, perhaps, a slight undercurrent of unfriendly feeling." Spitshuker hesitated, himself somewhat taken aback, one fancied, by this flagrant understatement.

"Nothing, of course, was decided—about anything." He smiled faintly. "The upshot of it was Butler's announcing that fatal intention of going up to the cathedral and stopping there alone. Had we not been in such a te—had we considered a little, I should say, we should probably not have allowed him to go."

"The meeting ended at what time?"

"About ten to nine, I should say. Yes, that would be it."

"And did anyone else in the house know of Dr. Butler's intention?"

"Everyone, I fancy. He met Frances in the hall, talking to Peace on some trivial matter, as he went out, and informed them. Dutton, I think, was lurking about, too."

"I thought he went early to bed," Geoffrey interposed.

"Dutton, I suspect, does not go to bed without extensive preliminary reconnoitring." Spitshuker nodded his approval of this cryptic comment. "At all events, there he was. I remember noticing him when Butler was arranging to meet Peace up at the cathedral—"

"When *what*?"

Spitshuker was all mild-eyed innocence. "You didn't know? To discuss some business matter, I think it was. Butler suggested that Peace should follow him in about twenty minutes' time and Peace agreed, but I fear we sat so long talking together that it was close on ten o'clock before he—"

"Oh, my dear paws!" Fen exclaimed. "Oh, my fur and whiskers! I knew it. I knew something of the sort—" He checked himself, and asked urgently: "What happened to everybody after the meeting broke up?"

Spitshuker considered. "Dallow and Garbin, as far as I know, went straight home, Butler to the cathedral. I think Frances went to her room with a book. Dutton somehow faded out of the picture. I walked with Butler as far as the gate which leads from the clergy-house garden on to the cathedral hill. I thought he seemed moody, depressed, and a little nervous. I remember that as we stood chatting at the gate he picked a four-leaf clover to put in his buttonhole, which surprised me, because he was always inveighing against such superstitions. But as I say, he appeared nervous. Then I went back and talked to Peace."

"We know about all that," said Fen. "Savernake?"

"I've no idea. He disappeared immediately after dinner, I fancy." Spitshuker looked at his watch. "You must forgive me if I turn back now. I hope I have been of assistance." He smiled and, suddenly, was gone.

Fen seemed little inclined to talk as they walked on; conceivably he was reflecting on what he had heard. Geoffrey, too, reflected, but without much enlightenment, and fell to wondering at the general lack of extreme distress over the Precentor's death. If Spitshuker had been labouring under a burden of emotion, he had not shown it.

"Curious," said Geoffrey, "that all the Butler family should have been in Germany before the war."

"It has its interest," Fen replied. "But for all we know, *everyone* here may have been in Germany. Spitshuker was instructive, don't you think?"

Geoffrey frowned ponderously. "Possibly," he said with judicial caution. "He went off in a hurry. Were you going to ask him anything else?"

"One or two things," said Fen noncommittally. "Whether he was an accomplished church musician, for one."

"Good heavens, why?"

Fen grinned. "That surprises you? It's half a shot in the dark, so I don't wonder. By the way, you might scribble down what people say they were doing at crucial times. It'll be useful for reference. I don't think it's much use trying to pry into alibis on the night Brooks was attacked in the cathedral. If people weren't in bed alone all night, then they ought to have been." He frowned puritanically.

❖ ❖ ❖

Garbin's house and garden were pervasively humid and melancholy. The first characteristic, in view of the unexampled brilliance of the weather, it was difficult to account for; but no other word would describe the listless, damp impression made by the overgrown flowerbeds and drooping foliage which greeted Fen and Geoffrey as they turned in at the gate. In this riot of greenery, through which strug-

gled an occasional misguided and feeble blossom in search of
the light, Niobe must surely have wandered, all tears. Even
the singing of the birds was without spirit, a mere dejected
gurgle.

And the house was no better. Its grey walls seemed to
sweat dampness. Large, Victorian and ugly, its windows stared
upon the world with frank misanthropy. Were it not attached
to his prebend, surely Garbin would not live in it. And yet a
subtle affinity existed between the man and the house, a fun-
damental dull seriousness of outlook, and behind this a complacent if melancholy resignation to things as they were. So at
least it appeared; but Geoffrey reminded himself that, here
and now, no appearance could be trusted.

Mrs. Garbin opened the door to them, dressed in a suit
of drab chocolate-brown. If she was surprised to see in
Geoffrey her travelling-companion of the day before, she gave
no sign of it. Her husband, she said, was working; not, one
gathered from her tone, at anything that was ever likely to be
the slightest use to anyone, even himself. No doubt he would
be delighted to see them; it was one of the penances of a
clergyman's life that he must always be available to anyone
who chose to call; fortunately, he had nothing else to occupy
him.

To this underhanded series of attacks, Fen replied mono-
syllabically. Before they were taken into Garbin's study he did,
however, stop to say:

'You must feel Dr. Butler's death as a great loss."

The woman paused. "Of course," she said. "A very great
loss indeed—to ourselves. It is possible that others may not be
so greatly affected."

"A popular man, I thought."

"A man of strong personality, Professor. And you know what
is commonly meant by personality—an obstinate blindness and
lack of consideration. There were, of course, antagonisms."

"Serious antagonisms?"

"That, of course, it is hardly my business to say." She paused. "The Romish practices of Canon Spitshuker—"

"And the scholarly rivalry of your husband…"

She put a hand on the banisters. The pallor of her face was perhaps a little accentuated. "You had better go in now."

Garbin's study was a large room, unpleasantly panelled in dark pine. Massive mahogany furniture and bookcases added to the gloom. A dark brown carpet was on the floor. There were worn armchairs and a rack of pipes and a pallid bust of Pallas—or more probably of some dead ecclesiastic, since both sex and features were indistinguishable in the crepuscular light—in a niche above the door.

And there, great heavens—Geoffrey felt the sense of unreality which one has immediately on waking from a vivid dream—was a raven. It perambulated the desk with that peculiar gracelessness which walking birds have, ruffled its feathers, and stared malignantly at the intruders.

"You're looking at my pet." Garbin rose from his chair as they came in, his tall, sombre form towering over the desk. "An unusual fancy, some people think. But he came to me quite by chance."

"Indeed?"

Garbin motioned them to chairs. "A foreign sailor with a tragic history sold him to me some two years ago. He is supposed to speak, I think, but I have never heard him do so. He is not"—Garbin paused—"a *companionable* creature, I admit. Sometimes I find his presence actually depressing. I have given him every chance to escape, but he displays only apathy." He stretched out a hand to stroke the bird's feathers. It pecked at him.

Fen, however, plainly was not moved by this recital. "We've come to talk about Butler's death," he said firmly. "There are some odd features about it, and I'm conducting a sort of unofficial investigation of my own." His eye strayed to the bird, and then hastily withdrew. "I don't know if you'd care to cooperate?"

Disconcertingly, Garbin regarded him in silence for a moment. Then he shifted in his chair, to indicate that he was about to speak. "Do you think it wise," he asked in his deep, slow voice, "to pry into these things? Surely the responsible authorities are capable of dealing with it."

"Possibly." Fen's admission was reluctant. "But I should hesitate to rely on them."

"I know you regard this sort of thing as a sport, Mr. Fen. Frankly, I cannot do so. The death of a man seems to me the poorest excuse for a display of personal ability. You will forgive my speaking so frankly."

Fen regarded him thoughtfully. "And you will allow me the same liberty, I'm sure. I shall say that the murder of a man is so serious a business that it concerns everyone who can possibly help in any way, and particularly those who, like myself, have had some experience of these things."

Garbin raised an eyebrow. "Your own vanity is not implicated in any way?"

Fen gestured impatiently. "One's vanity is implicated in everything, as Rochefoucauld pointed out. Action from pure motives simply does not exist."

"There are degrees of purity, none the less."

Fen stood up. "There seems little point in continuing this conversation."

"Please, please!" Garbin waved a hand. "If I was offensive, I apologise. You must remember that I belong to a generation, and a calling, whose standards are strict. Rochefoucauld was not a Christian. Christianity maintains that for a man to act from wholly disinterested motives is possible. Take that away, and the whole fabric of Christian morality falls apart."

"You did not consider it a disinterested action when Butler stole your ideas?"

"The inquisition has begun, I see," said Garbin drily. "No, naturally I did not. But it was forgivable, because Butler was no scholar—he hadn't the temperament. A *poseur* must plagiarise, or he can produce nothing."

"That's a harsh judgment, surely?"

"Perhaps so. God forbid that I should judge anyone. I should have said that—well, that what Butler undertook was beyond his capacities. His sail was too big for his boat."

"Still, you considered his thefts morally reprehensible?"

"Naturally." Garbin smiled slightly. "But surely you're not here to hold an enquiry into my moral standards. I bore him no lasting resentment, if that's what you mean."

The raven rose from the desk, and with a whirring of wings that sounded like a berserk mowing-machine, flew and perched on the bust above the door. Fen and Geoffrey eyed it in fascination. "A literary fowl," Fen murmured; then returned with somewhat of an effort to the matter in hand.

"Mainly," he said, "one wants to know about movements during yesterday."

"Ah, yes." Garbin put the tips of his fingers together. "At six o'clock, the time when poor Brooks was killed, I was alone here. Lenore was out to dinner and bridge."

"*Who?*" The word burst from Geoffrey before he could stop himself.

"Lenore—my wife. So I have no alibi for that time. Between ten and a quarter past."

Fen interrupted. "How about between nine and ten?" The question evidently surprised Garbin as much as it did Geoffrey; he hesitated, slightly but visibly, before replying. "I left the clergy-house shortly before nine, after Butler had announced his intention of going up to the cathedral. I went for a walk along the cliffs."

"You overheard the arrangement Butler made to meet

Peace up at the cathedral?"

"I could hardly avoid it; I fancy everyone did."

"May I ask what was said at the meeting?"

"I hardly think that concerns the death of Butler in any way."

"As you please. But did Butler by any chance say he had definite knowledge about the death of Brooks?"

"Since you ask—no."

Fen nodded. "It might have been necessary," he said, half to himself. "But that depends on the exact time the police guard left...I must find out."

On its perch, the raven ruffled its feathers again. The branch of a tree growing outside the window scraped against the panes. Fen succumbed suddenly to the obsessing temptation.

"Surely," he said—"surely that is someone at your window lattice?"

Garbin glanced over his shoulder. "It's the tree. I am always meaning to have it cut down. It makes the room very dark." Plainly the allusion was lost on him. Geoffrey retired discreetly behind a handkerchief, and went red in the face.

"May I ask how long your walk lasted?" With manifest difficulty Fen had got back to the subject.

"Until about ten-thirty. When I arrived back here I made myself some cocoa, and sat reading by the fire."

"And each separate dying ember," said Geoffrey, "wrought its ghost upon the floor."

Garbin looked at him in mild surprise. "Exactly so. Shortly after eleven Spitshuker came in and gave me the news. We talked for some time."

Fen sighed. "Thank you. You're being kinder than your first words suggested. I wonder if, after all, you aren't anxious to get this thing cleared up?"

A shadow of evasiveness passed over Garbin's face. "Anxious. Most certainly I shall help the law in any way I can. But I cannot disguise from myself the fact that someone—that one of us who are connected with the cathedral must be implicated."

"What makes you think that?"

"It is a question of keys, is it not?"

"Ah, yes. I understand that virtually everyone had a key to the cathedral grounds."

"It seems pointless for people to have a key to the grounds, and not to the cathedral itself."

"Not at all. Suppose I had arranged to meet someone at the cathedral." Garbin paused. "As Butler arranged to meet Peace. I should unlock the gate into the grounds, and lock it again after me, to keep out…intruders. Then I should go up to the cathedral and unlock the door there. Anyone following me up there would thus require a key to the grounds, but not a key to the cathedral itself."

"That seems clear enough. Peace, I suppose, must have had a key to the grounds last night. I wonder whose he borrowed?"

"I'm afraid I can't help you there."

"And possibly Josephine as well."

"Josephine Butler?" Garbin's voice was guarded.

"She took a false message to the police on duty at the cathedral. But what time are the grounds locked?"

"At seven sharp. The sexton sees to it. There are only the north and south gates and that into the clergy-house garden."

"Is it absolutely impossible to get into the grounds otherwise than by the gates?"

Garbin shrugged. "Not impossible, no. Anyone who wished could manage it quite easily. The locking is chiefly a moral preventive."

"Ah, of course. To prevent the incontinent young from necking publicly on the cathedral hill."

Garbin made a gesture of impatience and stood up. This abrupt movement disturbed the raven, which emitted a hoarse, dyspeptic croak and began flying agitatedly about the room. Garbin beat at it ineffectually with his hands. Eventually it settled on the window-sill.

"I must apologise," said Garbin, "for my pet."

"Ghastly, grim and ancient raven from the night's Plutonian shore."

Garbin stared in bewilderment. "A little picturesquely put, perhaps. And now if there's nothing more—"

"One more thing. Are you interested in music?"

Garbin smiled wryly. "I know little or nothing about it; and care less. It always seems to me that it plays far too large a part in our services: there are occasions when the worship of God degenerates into an organised concert." He bowed slightly to Geoffrey. "Please don't think me ungracious. And now, is there anything else?"

"Is there," said Geoffrey, "is there balm in Gilead?"

Fen hastily retired to make a close examination of one of the bookcases. "I see you have here"—he hesitated, and went on in a weak, quavering voice—"many a quaint and curious volume of forgotten lore."

It was at this point that the interview really got out of hand. Geoffrey was hardly able to contain himself, and Fen was scarcely better. The gravity and incomprehension of Garbin made matters worse. What he thought was going on it is impossible to say; perhaps he fancied Fen and Geoffrey to be engaged in some recondite form of retaliation for his earlier outspokenness. At all events he said nothing. Hasty farewells were made. At the door Fen turned to look at the raven again.

"Take thy beak," he said, "from out my heart, thy form from off my door."

"His eyes," said Geoffrey, "have all the seeming of a demon's that is dreaming." Then they went out, in some haste. At the front door, Fen recovered himself sufficiently to ask Garbin one more question.

"Do you know the poetry of Edgar Allan Poe?"

"I'm afraid not. I have no great use for verses."

"Not his poem, *The Raven?*"

"Ah. There's a poem about a raven, is there? Is it good? I know nothing about these things."

"Very good," said Fen with the utmost gravity. "You would find much in it to interest you. Good morning."

CHAPTER NINE

Three Suspects and a Witch

*"I'm not taken
With a cob-swan or a high-mounting bull,
As foolish Leda and Europa were;
But the bright gold, with Danaë."*

JONSON

"**P**OOR BROOKS," SAID FEN as they walked towards Butler's house. "He seems to have rather faded out of the enquiry. But there's much less to get hold of in his case than there is in Butler's."

"Didn't you think it rather odd that Spitshuker should have cleared up the cathedral without consulting the police?"

"Possibly. Or possibly not. It depends on certain medical technicalities which I don't know about."

The sun was hotter now, but a light cooling breeze had sprung up. A cathedral town, Geoffrey thought, is a delightful place—the most perfect practical combination of church and laity in existence. Here one was comfortably lapped about with the tradition and actuality of worship; here, also, one's small vices and peccadilloes drew an added zest from their surroundings. It occurred to him to ask what Fen was doing in Tolnbridge.

"I came here," said Fen sourly, "to see the Dean, who used to be at Oxford with me. He is not here—scandalously inconsiderate. But I suppose he'll be back pretty quickly now. I shall have to go in a few days—term starts early next month, and I've got to lecture on William Dunbar." He sighed. "I feel lost out of Oxford."

"You don't look lost."

"I wonder what sort of a term it's going to be. The undergraduates get more moronic every passing moment. But I believe Robert Warner's new play is to be on locally. In the meantime, I'm getting nothing done about insects. I shall go into this shop and buy a book on them."

This did not take long. "Insects!" said Fen loudly to an assistant, waving his hand impartially at customers and staff. He was found a tattered copy of Fabre's *Social Life in the Insect World*.

In the street they met Fielding wandering vaguely about in pursuit, doubtless, of some private delusive phantom of heroism. He had been reflecting on the case in all its aspects, he told them, but had come to no satisfactory conclusion. They gave him an account of what had turned up since the previous night, but it was evident that he was not enlightened by it. He expressed a vague determination to think things over, and to make what headway he could with the landlord of the "Whale and Coffin." Plainly he resented being excluded from the morning's interviews, but, as Fen said, with more forcefulness than tact, it was bad enough having one useless person hanging about all the time, without adding another. Fielding departed on his indefinite mission, which resolved itself in practice into his playing darts in a public bar.

Butler's house proved to be a substantial, overgrown affair sprouting little valueless wings, outhouses and potting-

sheds over a large and untidy garden. At the gate Fen and Geoffrey met the Inspector, a sad and lonely figure plodding with
pathetic hopefulness from one interview to another. He regarded
them warily, wondering, it was evident, whether they were getting on better than he was. It was like one of those treasure hunts,
Geoffrey thought, in which you have to hide the clues again after
looking at them, and then, when someone else appears on the
scene, put up an elaborate smoke-screen of nescience.

"We're getting on fine," said Fen, with deliberate malice.
"The problem is practically solved. How are things with you?"

"I don't believe a word of it," said the Inspector. "*I* can't
get anything that's any use out of anybody. What is the good of
fussing away about motive and opportunity and so on when
you can't even make out how the thing was done? But I
shouldn't be standing here talking to you about it."

"Has the Yard arrived? How silly that sounds. But it's
grammatical."

"It should be here after lunch some time." The Inspector
was gloomy. "Then, thank God, I can shelve the responsibility
for this thing."

"Inspector, Inspector," said Fen waggishly. "Is that a right
attitude?"

"No, it isn't. But if you were as mixed-up as I am at the
moment you wouldn't stand there carping."

"Carping?" said Fen, offended. "Who's carping?
Carping," he added with more warmth, "your grandmother. I
was trying to find out if anything new had turned up, that's all."

"Well, nothing has, except the details of why Mr. Peace
went to meet Dr. Butler at the cathedral. And those I cannot
give you. That Josephine kid's as obstinate as ever—still says it
was a policeman gave her that message. She's given about
three contradictory accounts of when and where and how he
gave it her, but on the central fact she won't budge. I don't like
the look of her, either—nasty feverish gleam in her eye. Mrs.

Butler's no help—she hardly *exists*. She's about as likely to
know anything about the murder as you are to have climbed
Mount Everest."

"I have climbed Mount Everest."

"That's a lie. Nobody has. You'd say anything for the sake
of an effect, wouldn't you? Savernake's no use, either."

"Is he there too?"

"Staying in the house before he goes back to his parish.
But I don't think he's got anything to do with it. For one thing,
he was in London the night Brooks was attacked. I've checked
on him *and* Peace *and* Mrs. Garbin, and as far as one can possibly tell, they really were there. Incidentally, I've also made
enquiries round the hospital, to see if any of the front line of
suspects turned up there about six yesterday, but it was hopeless. And I've discovered it's quite easy to get into the hospital
by a back way, without anyone in the world seeing you."

"Ah." Fen was thoughtful. "One thing I wanted to ask: do
you know exactly what time the police left the cathedral last
night?"

"As it happens, I do. The joltheads had just enough sense
left to make a note of it. It was five to nine."

"Thank God."

"Why," said the Inspector with dispiriting jocosity, "are
you involving the Deity in this affair?"

"Because if the time had been much earlier all my theories would have gone to Hades."

"You have theories?" The Inspector made it sound like a
disease.

"Many theories, my good, my sweet Inspector. A whole—
what is the collective noun for theories? A gaggle of geese, a
giggle of girls, a noise of boys—of course: a thought of theories."
Fen beamed with enthusiasm. "That's it: a thought. Alliterative
and expressive: shifting, insubstantial, delusive as a thought."
He paused, overcome by this display. "And in return for your
information, I'll give you some advice."

"No one ever took any harm from listening to advice."

"Don't platitudinise. I want you, as soon as the coast is clear, to make a thorough search of Peace's room."

The Inspector gaped in astonishment. *"Peace's* room? And what in heaven's name am I supposed to search for?"

Fen reflected. "The clergy-house key to the cathedral, perhaps. Oh, and a hypodermic, and a phial of atropine solution. I think that will be enough. You ought to find them all there."

"God pity us," said the Inspector, genuinely impressed. "If you're having me on I'll put you in gaol." He turned to go back through the gate.

"Not now. Let us get our bit of nagging over first."

"But there's no time to waste. He may move them."

"We'll keep him occupied and see to it that he doesn't."

"No, I must go back now."

"Really, Inspector, if I'd known you were going to be such a nuisance I should never have told you. You haven't got a search warrant, anyway."

"No," said the Inspector with a wink, "but we'll risk that, I think."

"If you go one step up that path I shall warn everybody in the house that you're proposing to make a burglarious and illegal entry, and we'll all get together and throw you out."

"You devil."

"It's hard," said Fen complainingly. "One gives the police a perfectly sound piece of advice—information almost—and that's the sort of thanks one gets."

The wraith of a smile passed across the Inspector's face. "All right," he said, "all right. Have your own way. I dare say it's all my eye, anyway. It can wait." He turned to go. "But my God, if this is a joke—"

"Don't threaten witnesses," said Fen. "Oh, one more thing—very important. Was there any trace of poison or bullets or knife-thrusts or anything at the autopsy? It is over by now, I suppose?"

"Nothing of the kind."

"Splendid. That suits me admirably."

"What a pity," said the Inspector with heavy irony, "that you've nothing more to find out. You must tell me when you make an arrest."

"Ah." Fen was pensive. "There's the rub. Means, motive, opportunity, all settled. The only trouble is that I haven't at the moment the least idea who did it."

❄ ❄ ❄

They found Peace in the garden, extended fatly in a deck-chair and snoring up into the dappled foliage of the chestnut tree above his head. He had been little in evidence, Geoffrey thought, since the interview in the train; at dinner last night he had been curiously self-effacing, doing and saying nothing that could force itself memorably on the attention. And yet he was, in fact, the only person who could have been in the cathedral when Butler was killed, and it was conceivable that his "business talk" with the Precentor had provided him with an adequate motive. Geoffrey frowned. But a motive wasn't what was wanted—unless, as was quite possible, the phantom radio had nothing to do with the murder in the cathedral. Murder in the Cathedral. Would Butler, like St. Thomas, like St. Ephraim, be canonised now he was dead? Or Murder *ex cathedra*. Peace, of course, would have had time to get to the hospital from the station and kill Brooks; so would Savernake; so would Mrs. Garbin. But the murder of Brooks had depended, it seemed, on a knowledge of the times at which he got his medicine; which none of these people would have had, since he had only been found, and taken to the hospital, the previous morning. Here, then, was a possible means of elimination. It was true that, since plainly more than one person was involved in the affair, a phone call to London earlier in the day could have given the necessary information, but this, surely, was too complicated and unnecessary a method of procedure to be plausible.

Peace still exuded his prosperous and professional air, even in sleep. Slumbering at ease, his face was composed and childlike. He snored, not thunderously, but with a faint and not unpleasant moaning, like the wind in a chimney. His well-cut suit, now creased and crushed, clung about his form unreticently, and his chubby hands lay upon his stomach. Beside him, on the grass, lay *The Mind and Society*, along with a tall glass and two lager bottles, one of them empty. This happy and idyllic scene conveyed no sense of tragedy—either that which had been already enacted or that which was now preparing. It seemed a pity to wake him.

Considerateness, and sensitivity to conventional atmospheres were not, however, Fen's strongest points. He advanced boisterously, making a formidable amount of noise. Peace jerked into alarmed wakefulness; then noticing the source of the commotion, heaved painfully to his feet and stood ineffectually brushing himself and blinking blearily and without enthusiasm about him.

"Awake, Æolian lyre, awake," said Fen, "and give to rapture all thy trembling strings."

"Rapture?" Peace peered at him anxiously. "Liar?" He paused dubiously. "That seems a little hard."

Fen settled himself on the grass. "And so," he said, "is the ground. Are there no more chairs? Phyllida and Corydon may have enjoyed this sort of thing, but not I." He rummaged in a dandelion root. "Ants," he said.

"The Arcadian myths"—the dominie in Peace became very evident—"are plainly sexual in origin. Always they concern pursuit. Pan is the incarnation of male desire, Syrinx the elusive, fleeting object of his lust. Almost one might say that the myth involves the whole contradiction and antithesis of the male and female characteristics. Or possibly"—he became thoughtful—

"not."

Fen grunted. "Do you ever get tired of rummaging about finding psychological parallelisms?"

"Yes. Very tired. But if one regards it as an amusing and preposterous game it can help to pass away a dull evening. The Faust legend, now: there's endless material in that—the stored dream-fantasies of a whole ethic division of humanity. And the principles of the game are so simple that, as they used to say about labour-saving machines, a child can operate it. Water is always the unconscious—I haven't the least idea why. If you dream about tumbling into the sea and swimming about underneath it means your unconscious has triumphed, or"— he paused—"that you're dyspeptic. Anything round or hollow is the womb, the feminine principle." He picked up the empty lager bottle and tapped the bottom of it. "This, for example— a mandala-symbol. Anything else is a masculine principle, in all probability. Also, there are primal old men with beards."

"It appears to me," said Fen gravely, "that we are in the presence of a radical breakdown of faith."

"Faith." Peace nodded. "That's it precisely. Not intellectual doubt, but a breakdown of faith. The witch-doctor loses confidence in his paint and headdress and amulets." He was silent.

Geoffrey sought for a means of turning the conversation to more relevant matters. "Did you," he enquired cautiously, "get any light from your conversation with Spitshuker last night?"

Peace glanced at him sharply; the ruse was transparent. "He offered to substitute his own faith for my own. He said it was at once much more rational and much less so and would consequently be twice as satisfactory."

"What do you think?"

"I suppose he's right. I confess I feel *drawn* to the Church in a way I've never experienced before. The transition shouldn't be difficult. It isn't *what* one believes that mat-

ters, it's the emotional need one's beliefs satisfy. Plainly I'm
one of those people who need a faith—what kind doesn't
much matter. Patriotism might do equally well."

Intellectually, Geoffrey thought, the man was stronger than
he at first appeared to be; but that constituted only the surface
of his mind. Where was the emotional centre? A woman? That
was possible. A scientific passion?—but what he said conveyed
little of that impression. Money? Creativity in some line? A
man's life may be wholly bound up with a passion for basket-
work. Or after all, was there no such centre? Was the shell really as hollow as it sounded? In himself, Peace was a perplexing
problem. Somehow he lacked inwardness, lacked a self—the
result, perhaps of constantly attending to the inwardness, the
personalities, of others.

Fen, who was playing around with one of the lager bottles, said mildly:

"The *minds* of people, as such, are always less interesting,
because more uniform, than the façade they present to the
world. Dr. Butler, for example." He paused deliberately, to allow
the change of topic to settle. "How little one knew about him."

Peace resigned himself. "He was a curious man. I knew
little about him, for I saw him seldom. He disapproved, arbitrarily and without consideration, of my profession, which was
one of the things that induced me to continue in it. For the
rest, if you'll believe me (though it doesn't depend on that), he
was entirely selfish. His calling required of him a certain show
of charitableness, but it never went beyond the bare minimum
of *bienséance*. And that was why I came down here."

"Oh?" Fen's voice deliberately lacked interest.

Peace leaned forward; he spoke slowly and emphatically.
"My father died a rich man. There were only two of us children. As I was already on the road to prosperity and Irene, my
sister, had nothing, he left his money to her—on the understanding that should my fortunes ever fail, half was to come to

me for the benefit of my children. The capital, you realise, could not be touched." He paused and fingered his tie.

"That understanding Butler effectually wrecked when he married Irene. He persuaded her, in fact, that the whole of the inheritance should be left to their own children, and poor Irene, who never had a great deal of spirit of her own, was forced to agree. The man was a bully, and I fancy he had an easy job of it." There was real feeling in Peace's voice now, Geoffrey noticed.

"Naturally, I want as good prospects for my children as I can possibly get, and just recently things haven't been going so well with me. People have had to draw in their horns a bit, and the war's induced them to stop fussing so much about themselves—which is a damned good thing. But just recently, too, Butler had been trying to get Irene to transfer the money to him, for better safety, as he said." Peace's lip curled contemptuously. "I knew once that happened there'd be no more hope for me and my family. Writing was no good, so I came down to talk things over with him. That's why I went to see him up at the cathedral last night. We'd had a few words about it earlier, when I first arrived, and he'd been pretty cool, I can assure you. Said he'd give me his final word later. *His* decision!" The man was agitated; he got up and paced restlessly up and down. "Well, he never did. But you see the injustice of it—the vile impertinence and lack of all moral decency. It isn't as if I'd wanted a lot; it isn't as if this understanding about the money were a fabrication of mine—I've got letters to prove it. And yet he—*he*, who had lived in comfort on that money for nearly twenty years—was going to 'give me his decision' as if I were a beggar, a poor relation soliciting at his door!"

Here was the man with a vengeance, thought Geoffrey: sincerity was plain in every word he spoke, a sincere sense of outraged justice, a sincere affection for his family; and it was hardly necessary to add, a sincere and plausible motive for murder. Fen asked:

"Was the reason for your visit here generally known?"

"He'd broadcast his own account of it pretty widely, you can be sure—the sponging relative."

"Ah." Fen was thoughtful. "And the money is very important to you?"

Peace grinned suddenly. "Very. I'm not quite so successful at my job as I made myself out to be to you, Mr. Vintner. I've done well enough, I suppose. But really I've always been a square peg. Most men fit their jobs, but I don't. I don't know what I should have been—an actor, I sometimes think."

Fen stirred himself. "How dreadful."

"And do you know, if I *had* found my proper place in the scheme of things, I don't think I should have bothered about this business at all, however poor I was."

Fen made vague signs of concurrence. "Dissatisfaction always breeds demands, even if they're not for the particular satisfaction that's lacking." He appeared rather pleased at this utterance.

"You see why I'm telling you all this." Peace sat down, something of his normal diffident good-nature restored. "I have, as far as I know, the best motive yet discovered for killing Butler, and obviously it's no use trying to cover it up. Also, I was the only person who could have been in that cathedral when he was killed. So I quite see that things don't look too good for me." He hesitated. "Personally, Mr. Fen, I know of you only as a literary critic. But I've been told that you've had a good deal of experience of these affairs, and that's why I put the facts before you. Not—heaven forbid!—in any frenzied attempt to prove my innocence, but in the hope that they may help to prove someone else guilty."

The man was no fool; very clearly he recognised his position. But, on the other hand, frankness and willingness to help might be an excellent pose; he might, in fact, be drawing attention to one motive in order to divert suspicion from another.

Fen cleared his throat, noisily and at great length. "You've told all this to the police?"

"Naturally."

"Of course, of course. The truth in all circumstances. I suppose you know they'll arrest you?"

Peace sat up. "Good God! Surely it's not as bad as that?"

"They're certain to get round to it sooner or later," said Fen with malignant delight. "Tell me about your movements."

"Movements? Ah, yes, I see. At the relevant hours. The train arrived more or less on time, and I came straight here. Characteristically, there was no one in when I arrived, but Irene and Butler turned up in about ten minutes—say at a quarter past six. No alibi for the Brooks murder, you see. Butler and I were both supposed to be going to the clergy-house for dinner, but he cried off at the last moment. Couldn't stand the sight of me, I suppose. After dinner, when the meeting was going on, I sat in the summerhouse, but I got bored with that and went back shortly before nine. It was then that Butler arranged to meet me privately up at the cathedral, at about twenty past. I got talking to Spitshuker, and although I saw how the time was going, I thought it wouldn't do him any harm to wait. And besides, Frances was getting anxious about him. She said she was going out to look for you at the 'Whale and Coffin' and would I wait and let her walk up to the cathedral with me to make sure he was all right. The poor kid seemed really scared. Anyway, she was the devil of a time, so I set off alone just before ten—rather more than five minutes before you arrived—and I was just pottering about trying to find a door that was open when I heard that crash. The rest you know."

"Convenient," Fen murmured. "Extraordinarily convenient. The trouble is that one can't check the extra minute or two here and there which counts. Ultimately it doesn't matter, though."

Peace grimaced. "It matters to me."

"And what is the situation now about this money?"

"I suppose I shall get it now that Butler's dead. Which makes matters look worse. Do you think if I abandoned all claim—"

"Give up a lot of cash!" Fen howled indignantly. "Certainly not. Don't be so daft. No one ever leaves *me* any money," he complained darkly, "despite my frenzied efforts with rich old women. It's an extraordinary thing that the people who really deserve money—" He suddenly lost interest in what he was saying, and climbed to his feet. "Never mind that. I must see Savernake and the girl. Are they about?"

"Somewhere." Peace seemed indifferent. "But you haven't advised me what to do."

"Do!" exclaimed Fen. "If it were done when 'tis done, then 'twere well it were done quickly."

"What is that supposed to mean?"

"It isn't supposed to mean anything. It's a quotation from our great English dramatist, Shakespeare. I sometimes wonder if Hemings and Condell went off the rails a bit there. It's a vile absurd jingle."

Frances and Savernake were in another part of the broad, rambling garden, talking quickly and earnestly. Geoffrey wondered if Dutton had been right, and if after all they would get married now. Love imposes a sense of proprietorship; and though Geoffrey had no possible claim on the girl, he felt an active resentment at Savernake's easy air when he was with her. One should not, in any case, treat so much beauty with an easy air. Beauty, as Dr. Johnson remarked, is of itself very estimable, and should be considered as such. Geoffrey found himself disliking Savernake, and not entirely for reasons of jealousy—disliking his affectation, his evasiveness, his nervous jumpiness. As they approached, he stood twisting his long, thin fingers together, his sparse, corn-coloured hair meticulously brushed back and his grey eyes moving with great rapidity from person to person; just on the edge of downright shiftiness.

He opened the conversation unfortunately by a reference to Fen's butterfly-net. Geoffrey riposted with a feeble sarcasm, Fen being temporarily engaged in trying to catch hold of a dragon-fly. The atmosphere perceptibly worsened. It was not that there was any particular gloom about it. Frances quite candidly admitted that though she had been reasonably attached to her father, she was affected by his death more as something shocking than as something melancholy. But there was a tinge of what could only be called irritability in the air, a neurotic rather than an emotional reaction. Everyone was on edge.

"Poor Mummy," said Frances. "Daddy used to bully her rather, I'm afraid, but I think she's more affected now than anyone else. Isn't that always the way?"

She wore a light dress of plain black, with white collar and cuffs, which modelled her figure to perfection. Even Fen, who, being comfortably married, had some time ago, more from a sense of wasted effort than from any moral scruples, given up looking at girls' figures, was manifestly impressed. "O my America! my new-found-land!" he murmured; and despite an outraged glare from Geoffrey, who happened to know his Donne, continued to gaze in frank admiration. This inspection was, however, peremptorily interrupted by Savernake, who said insultingly, in the irritating drawl which unfortunately he did not always remember to assume:

"Is there anything in particular we can do for you?"

Now this was a mistake. Fen turned upon him a look of quite distressing vehemence. "Yes, you sheepshead," he said, forgetting the proper respect due to the cloth, "you can go and dance a rigadoon at the bottom of the garden. A nice thing, to be treated in that cool way when one comes along, bursting with sympathy"—Fen contrived to look suitably inflated—"to lend a helping hand. Apologise!" he howled in conclusion.

"My dear sir, I can only imagine you're mad."

"You fopling!" said Fen with great contempt. He was enjoying the scene. When not occupied with speaking, he beamed with enthusiasm and delight. "You numbskull!"

"Now look here—"

"None of that," said Fen sternly. "Either you answer my questions, or you don't."

"I don't."

"Oh." Fen seemed a little taken aback. "Well, in that case—"

"Oh, come on, you two," said Frances impatiently. "Don't squabble. Of course we'll answer any questions you like, Mr. Fen. Won't we, July?" She looked straight at the young man for a moment; then he nodded.

"I'm sorry."

"And so," said Fen without much conviction, "am I."

"Let's walk, shall we?" said Frances. "I can't bear standing about." They wandered across a lawn embryonically laid out for putting, towards the orchard.

The subsequent conversation, however, elicited little of value. On the monotonous problem of alibis, it proved that Savernake had one which, barring collusion, was virtually unassailable for six o'clock, having walked with Mrs. Garbin to the house where she was dining and playing bridge and stopped there some time with her. He had then gone straight to dinner at the clergy-house, only stopping to leave his bag at the Precentor's. After dinner he had walked—whither and with what purpose it was not clear. He had, however, met some local worthy and talked to him between 9:45 and 10:20, arriving home just in time to hear the news of Butler's death.

As for Frances, she had been down shopping in the town until just after six, when she had returned to the clergy-house to find the tail-end of the Josephine disturbance going on and to meet Geoffrey and Fielding as they came in from the train. She had gone to have a drink with them, as they knew,

returned, got the dinner, gone to her room with a book afterwards, come down to deal with some problem or other of
housekeeping in the kitchen and found the meeting breaking
up, gone straight to the kitchen and done what she had to do,
become a little anxious about her father, set out to find Fen,
Geoffrey, Fielding and the Inspector and walked back with
them; afterwards staying in the kitchen until Geoffrey had
come to tell her of her father's death.

"Let's get the movements of this family straight," said Fen.
"What exactly was your mother doing between five and seven?"

"She was out having tea with a friend, and got back about
a quarter past six, meeting Daddy almost at the gate; they
found Mr. Peace had arrived. By that time Daddy had found
out about Josephine and his manuscript, followed her round
the clergy-house, spanked her, and returned home."

"Does that mean," Geoffrey asked, "that your father was
in the clergy-house when we arrived?"

"Yes. He must have left just after we set out for the
'Whale and Coffin.'"

"Ah," said Fen obscurely. "Is Josephine about? I must see
her if it's humanly possible."

"She's somewhere in the house, I think."

"Good." Fen seized an apple from off one of the orchard
trees, crunched it, and said indistinctly: "So far so good. And
your account checks up with Peace's."

Geoffrey saw Frances exchange a swift glance with Savernake: so did Fen.

"Don't hedge," he said threateningly through a mouthful
of apple. "I saw you."

Frances said: "Don't you think, Mr. Fen, that Peace
ought to have had the decency to clear out when this happened?—and particularly since he and Daddy got on so badly
together."

"I see." Fen's tone was guarded. "A business matter, wasn't

it?"

"Business!" Frances' eyes blazed suddenly with indignation. "He was trying to sponge on Daddy."

"My dear girl," said Savernake with a sneer, "be more
realistic. You must expect that sort of thing. Money attracts
men of that type like wasps round a jam-pot."

Fen took another bite from his apple. "I think," he stated
mildly, "that there's probably more than one side to the matter...But don't let's talk about that now." Manifestly he was
impatient to get away from the subject. "What really matters
is that except for Dallow we've now got where everybody was,
or say they were, at six o'clock last evening; to wit—

"Spitshuker was alone in his room, working—unchecked
and apparently uncheckable;

"Garbin was alone in *his* room—ditto;

"Dutton was out for a walk—ditto;

"Peace was hanging about here—ditto;

"You, Savernake, and Mrs. Garbin were together;

"Dr. Butler was smacking Josephine at the clergy-house;

"You, Frances, were returning from shopping;

"Your mother was at a friend's for tea;

"Geoffrey and Fielding were walking to the clergy-house
from the station;

"And I—what was I doing?" Fen frowned with concentration. "Yes, I have it: I was just going into a pub. I knew there
was something familiar about six o'clock. If *everybody* had had
the sense to go into pubs as soon as they opened their doors,
this thing wouldn't have happened. Interesting lack of alibis,
isn't there?" He finished his apple and threw the core at a bird.
"Well, no more talking. I must see Mistress Josephine. She's in
the house, is she?"

"Yes. July, be a dear and show Mr. Fen into the house and
find Josephine for him." Savernake consented with an ill grace,
and the two went off together. Geoffrey and Frances walked

into the vegetable garden. Geoffrey felt that his moment had come.

Bachelorhood was engaged in a tour of his defences, but without much confidence in their efficacy; it resembled more the last, sentimental walk round a long-familiar dwelling, now for ever to be abandoned. Staring with exaggerated interest at a row of radishes, Geoffrey meditated subtleties; and it was his inability to think of any rather than a sense of fitness which led him to ask at last, quite simply:

"Are you engaged to be married?"

She shook her head; the question seemed quite natural.

"Then would you marry me?"

She stopped and gasped. "But Mr. Vintner— Geoffrey...We've hardly met."

"I know," he said unhappily. "But I can't help it. You see, I'm in love with you."

The admission sounded so dismal that she burst out laughing. Geoffrey stared harder than ever at the radishes. Brutish roots! What did they know of the agonies of a middle-aged bachelor proposing marriage? He said, "I'm sorry," less because he felt it than because he could think of nothing else.

She stopped laughing quickly. "That wasn't very civil of me; I didn't mean to hurt you." Her eyes were soft. "But— well, do you think this is quite the time—?"

"No. I'm a tactless creature. I shouldn't have said anything."

"It's so sudden: that's the funny thing about it. I—well, it just took me aback."

"Will you think about it?"

"Yes," she said with real seriousness, "yes, I'll think about it. And"—hesitating a little—"I think you're sweet."

"No, I'm not sweet, really. You ought to know the sort of bargain you'd be getting." Bachelorhood was contriving rather a cunning oblique counter-attack. "I'm fussy and old-maidish and selfish, and fixed in my habits and disagreeable at breakfast and—"

"Don't!" She laughed a little breathlessly. "After all, I'm not such a prize-ticket as all that." She hesitated. "We must talk things over—soon."

"What about Savernake?"

"Oh, you know how it is: one drifts into an understanding without really wanting it. But don't worry. All that is— would be—my side of the business." She paused. "Look, I must go in and see Mummy now, but let's walk—and bathe— tomorrow before breakfast. All right?"

"Lovely."

"I shall be sleeping at the clergy-house again, and I'll wake and bang on your door. We'll go really early, so that there won't be a lot of people about. Then"—she smiled—"well, we shall see."

They looked at one another in silence for a moment. Deepest, darkest, raven hair, blue eyes, red lips, and the body of a goddess. But banal! Our loves are separate and incommunicable; not all the poets who ever wrote begin to express what we feel. And yet it's only something pleasant and quite simple. And it doesn't cloud the vision, or how could one observe the radish-tops, caught in a momentary breeze, nodding their pygmy approval? Ecstasy is simplicity itself. Oh my America, my new-found-land!

Then she was gone, the glory departed. Even the radishes settled again to their vegetable loves, dull roots merely. Edible roots, however; Geoffrey pulled one out of the ground, wiped it clean, and ate it.

❀ ❀ ❀

Fen and Josephine sat opposite one another in the big, gloomy library, he serious and not very talkative, she sullen and even less so. Her tousled hair fell over her eyes, unnaturally bright and with the pupils dilated. Beneath the black frock, her body was thin, and she trembled now and again, very slightly, crouching back in the armchair as though she were glad of its pressure against her back.

"Why did you burn the manuscript?" he said quietly. The child stirred. "I don't see why I should tell you."

"Nor do I really. But I could help you a lot if you did." She considered; this seemed reasonable if it was true, but then it mightn't be true. "How could you help me?"

"I could get you the things you like."

"I don't know...whether it's one of the things I'm allowed to tell. I felt sick suddenly, and giddy, after I'd—after...My head went all sort of funny and I didn't know what I was doing. Then he beat me. I'd rather have died than let him lay a finger on me." She wiped her nose with the back of her hand.

"And who gave you the message?"

"A policeman." The reply was automatic.

"That isn't true."

"A policeman." She smiled suddenly and foolishly. "It was a policeman."

"Who gave it to you?"

"I'm not allowed to tell, or I won't be given what I want."

"And that is?"

"I'm not allowed to tell."

Fen smiled, and with infinite gentleness and patience tried again. "Why did you mind so much having your father beat you?"

"It wasn't fair...I felt sick, I didn't know what I was doing." She suddenly buried her head in her hands.

"Poor kid," said Fen. He leaned over and touched her on the shoulder, but she flared up at him.

"Don't touch me!"

"All right." Fen sat back again. "You ought to have had a doctor if you didn't feel well."

"I was told I wasn't to allow Mother to get a doctor. I had to pretend I wasn't ill."

"Who told you?"

"It was—" Her eyes suddenly shone with childish cunning; for a moment the extended pupils seemed enormous. "You're trying to catch me out I'm not allowed to tell."

"Very well." Fen seemed indifferent. "But you still haven't said why you so hated your father beating you."

"It was a"—she struggled over the word—"a desecration. Only one man is allowed to do that sort of thing." The spasm of shivering caught her again.

"Who is that one man?"

"The Black Gentleman."

Fen sat up. Understanding was beginning to come to him. "Apollyon," he said.

"You know."

"Yes, I know," he answered. "*Maledico Trinitatem sanctissimam nobilissimamque, Patrem, Filium et Spiritum Sanctum. Amen. Trinitatem, Solher, Messias, Emmanuel, Sabahot, Adonay, Athanatos, Jesum, Pentaqua, Agragon…*"

"*Ischiros, Eleyson, Otheos,*" she said, her voice rising shrill above his own, "*Tetragrammaton, Ely Saday. Aquila, Magnum Hominen, Visionem, Florem, Originem, Salvatorem maledico…Pater noster, qui es in coelis, maledicatur nomen tuum, destruatur regnum tuum…*"

So the monotonous stream of foolish blasphemy went on, until at last there was a pause, and Fen said:

"You see, I'm one of you. You can trust me." He pulled a cigarette-case from his pocket. She looked at it greedily and he glimpsed her expression. "You'd like one?"

"Yes, give me one—quickly." She snatched a cigarette and put it in her mouth. He lit it for her, and watched in silence while she smoked, inhaling deeply. But after a minute she threw it away with a cry of disgust, almost of desperation.

"It's not the right kind!"

Fen stood up. "No," he said, and his voice was hard. "It's not the right kind. The Black Gentleman gives you the right kind, doesn't he?" she nodded. "I came only to test your faith. *In nomine diaboli et servorum suorum.*"

"My faith is strong." The child's voice was confident, but hysteria lay beneath. "My father died in the bad faith."

At the door Fen turned. "I am one of you. Tell me who is your director."

For a moment all hung upon a thread of gossamer. Josephine hesitated, shivered again. Then she looked up at him and smiled.

"I'm not allowed to tell."

Fen met Geoffrey at the gate, and his eyes were cold with rage.

"You've seen Josephine?" Geoffrey asked.

Fen nodded. "She has been systematically drugged," he said deliberately. "Probably with marihuana—a form of haschisch; at any rate with something in cigarette form. She must be taken to a hospital for treatment at once—I'm going to phone the Inspector about it now." He paused. *"And it's got nothing to do with the murders at all*—except that the same person is responsible: mere, gratuitous devilry, corruption for the sake of corruption. And it's not only her body, it's her mind. There's something else."

"What?"

"She's a witch."

Geoffrey stared. "A witch!"

"In Tolnbridge, it seems, the old tradition dies hard. Yes, by ordinary definition Josephine is a witch. She burnt the book of Christian theology her father was writing. She wished to keep herself pure from his hands, for what beastliness we shall, I hope, never know. She told me he died in the bad faith. She has seen the Devil and taken the Black Mass."

CHAPTER TEN

Night Thoughts

"Hatred and vengeance, my external
portion,
Scarce can endure delay of execution."
COWPER

*F*OR GEOFFREY, the afternoon was spent first taking a choir practice, and then in playing Evensong. The choir was as well-trained, and the organ as excellent as he had expected, and no special difficulties arose. The moments of respite afforded by lessons and collects he occupied in considering the account Fen had given him of his interview with Josephine. Even at second-hand, it seemed an appalling business. And Fen had said it was actuated by pure malice and had nothing to do with the murders—though how he could know this Geoffrey was unable to imagine. There remained Dallow to be seen—the affected, slightly epicene little Chancellor who was an expert on witch-craft. What was it Frances had said?—"takes rather more than a scholarly interest in the subject." There should, at all events, be something of interest and importance here.

Dinner was over before they set out for his house. Fen had spent the afternoon meandering about the countryside in search of insects, and was in high spirits. He walked at his usual exhausting pace, talking incessantly all the while. Josephine had been taken away from Tolnbridge for expert treatment, he said, out of harm's way.

"She'll recover all right," he added. "Though she won't enjoy herself for the first few weeks. But I shall be interested to discover which of all these people has the sort of mentality which regards the systematic drugging of a child of fifteen as an entertainment."

Sir John Dallow lived in one of the new, large, expen-sive villas overlooking the estuary. And no sooner had the servant opened the door than the extreme and depressing fastidious-ness of the man became apparent. There was something more, too: the study into which they were shown exhibited tastes so depressingly morbid as to be almost incomprehensible outside a madhouse. A repellent little vampire-sketch by Fuseli hung on one wall; beyond it, an elaborate drawing by Beardsley of the fifth circle of the Dantean inferno; and dominating the whole room, over the fireplace, a meticulous, distorted paint-ing of a torture-scene by an early German master. A bad reproduction of Dürer's *Melancholia*, which completed the decorations, did, however, contrive to lend his miniature chamber of horrors a respectable, even a conventional air. The bookshelves were loaded, and as Sir John had not yet put in an appearance, Fen and Geoffrey inspected them fairly thor-oughly, and with a growing sense of depression. Certainly there was an almost unparalleled collection of works on witch-craft: the *Daemonolatreia* of Nicholas Rémy in the original edition of 1595; a modern private printing of the *Malleus Maleficarum*; Cotton Mather's *Wonders of the Invisible*

World; the *Sadducismus Triumphatus*; and inevitably, all the standard text-books on the subject. But there were also other books which suggested a propensity to enjoy as well as to study the night-side of Nature: Toulet's scabrous study of sadism, *Monsieur du Paur*, de Sade's *Justine*, and many other recondite volumes of perverted semi-pornography. Fen regarded them thoughtfully.

"At least he doesn't keep them in cupboards," he said. "And I somehow fancy that people who enjoy that sort of thing in books never do much harm in real life. The fact that they go to books at all suggests something very like impotence. Still, one never knows."

In another minute Dallow minced into the room, his wispy white hair straggling chaotically all over his head. "My *de-ear* Professor! And Mr. Vintner! But this is charming! And I *cannot* apologise too much for my disgraceful negligence in not being here to greet you. I have been toying—toying—with the most depressing cheese *soufflé* you ever saw. Nothing more important than that. My foolish woman didn't tell me you were here. But you must make yourselves at home."

The furniture was modern and luxurious. Geoffrey sank with some relief into an armchair. Dallow gabbled on:

"But you've no idea the life I lead here—so lonely. Visitors are really a treat to me. Mr. Vintner, how did you find the choir?"

"Admirable, thank you," said Geoffrey. "No difficulties at all."

"Good. Good." Primly, Dallow folded his hands. "The boys are not what they were in the days when there was a choir-school, of course."

Probably not, thought Geoffrey, with a headmaster whose reading was de Sade; but perhaps Dallow had been different then.

Fen roused himself from a sort of stupor to say: "We're making an unofficial enquiry into Butler's death. Would you care to co-operate?"

"But of course—*delighted.*" None the less, Dallow's tone was more guarded now. "How can I help?"

"It's about your movements."

"My *movements.*" Dallow giggled foolishly, crossed and uncrossed his legs, and unnecessarily straightened his tie. "The good Inspector has already examined me on the subject, so you see, I have my story ready. I have an alibi, my dear Professor, for six o'clock. I was *here,* and talking to my servant, at precisely that hour. But at ten-fifteen—no. I left that foolish meeting and went straight to discuss some business with a local contractor. Unhappily, he was out, and I had my long tramp for nothing. I arrived back here at, I suppose, half past the hour."

"What hour?"

"But *ten—of course.*" Dallow twisted his lips into a thin phantom of a smile. "I dined about seven, alone here. At five-fifteen I went down to the hospital to visit Brooks, but they wouldn't let me see him. That must have been about the time he recovered his reason. It was then, by the way, that the excellent Inspector gave me the clergy-house key to the cathedral to bring back."

"Ah, yes, there's a point there. To whom did you return it?"

"Strictly, I suppose, to dear Frances. And *she* put it back in the vestibule, where normally it hangs. I saw her do it."

"That seems clear enough. Have you any ideas about Butler's murder?"

"None," said Dallow definitely. "Except that it was a blessing we had not dared to hope for."

"Blessing?" Fen stared. "You disliked him, then?"

"If we are to be candid, my *de-ear* Professor, I disliked him intensely. The man was a fool—neither scholar, nor artist, nor priest. More accurately, he was nothing, devoid of all talent and interest. And besides, he threw contempt on my studies. Human vanity being what it is, the last is the obvious

motive for my detestation of our lamented friend." Dallow was
slightly and absurdly flushed with annoyance.

"And Brooks?"

"Ah, Brooks I liked. He was a musician to his fingertips.
He made those boys sing as I have never heard boys sing
before. *He*, my *de-ear* Professor, was an Artist." Dallow got up
and paced lightly about the room. "*O ces voix d'enfants*," he
exclaimed, "*chantant dans la couple!*"

But Fen waved this Mallarméan ecstasy a trifle brusquely
aside. "Why should anyone murder Brooks?" he enquired.

The Chancellor paused to finger one of three huge
orchids in a Chinese vase. "I dare say," he murmured, "that
Butler was responsible."

"No."

"As you say." Dallow resumed his pacing with an elaborate shrug. "Brooks had no enemies that one knew of, Butler,
on the other hand, had a great many, myself included. But as
to who killed them, I haven't an idea."

He was at least frank, thought Geoffrey. But oh, the permu-
tations of frankness and deceit—the double, triple, quadruple
bluffs that were possible! Moreover, Dallow was quite intelligent
enough to put on an act. The *poseur* so successfully hides his real
self that he makes falsehood difficult to detect; where there is no
apparent truth, there can be no obvious lie.

Fen, however, who had little of the traditional persistence
of the investigator, was becoming bored. He shuffled his feet
impatiently about and shifted the conversational ground. "Is
St. Ephraim a revenant?" he asked.

Dallow stared, for the moment uncomprehending. "St.
Ephraim?"

"I gather there have been rumours locally about the curious method of Butler's murder—the tomb."

Dallow's face lit up with understanding. He suddenly
clapped his hands with childish glee. "I see! No, St. Ephraim

has never, as far as is known, disturbed the peace of the living. The most active spirit in the neighbourhood is, of course, Bishop John—that excellent ghost."

Outside, a soft warm rain had begun to fall. Beads of water gathered on the window-pane, joined, parted, joined again. Fen stared abstractedly out at the garden.

Geoffrey looked perplexed. "I wish I knew something more about it."

"Spitshuker," said Fen, "told us you could give us some information about the Bishop. The bare fact that he caused a number of unfortunate young women to be burned, we know. But his spirit, it appears, rests uneasily in his odd tomb, and seems likely to be more uneasy still after having it desecrated."

Dallow was plainly delighted at the turn the conversation had taken. "So the people believe," he said. "I have heard rumours of it already—and very possibly it is true. The story of why he chose to be buried in Bishop's Gallery is curious. It seems he could not bear the idea of being, in death, completely enclosed—a sort of posthumous claustrophobia." Dallow giggled. "The Gallery provided, as it were, an outlet into the world—and not one person, but many, have seen him hovering behind its parapet. He—and a woman."

The rainclouds were obscuring the light, and the room was darker now. Geoffrey shifted uncomfortably. This was a waste of time, and yet…And yet not for all the world would he have missed hearing more about Bishop John Thurston. He scented mystery. And he was not mistaken.

"The tale," said Dallow, "is an interesting one. The Bishop was only twenty-five when he came here in 1688. As was so often the case in those days, such positions were obtained by influence, and the suitability or experience of the candidate hardly canvassed at all. Certainly that must have been so in his case. He was a curious problem of a man—an inconsequent mingling of rakehell and Puritan. His father had been one of Cromwell's men, and had made a late marriage with a woman of good position in a Cavalier family. And there was something of both parents in the boy: the father's severity and dull moralism; and the mother's light-headed looseness of character. He went to Eton and then to King's College, Cambridge, and entered the priesthood at the age of twenty-three. He remained, as was normal in those days, unmarried, but when his parents died and left him considerable means, he was able to buy his sexual pleasures out of a glutted market, and there seems little reason to suppose that he restrained himself in any way. Such, in brief, was his history when he arrived here. I ought perhaps to have said that he was no fool—that he was, in fact, a man of considerable education and ability."

Dallow was absorbed; his affectation and self-conscious-ness were gone. It occurred to Geoffrey that he was probably a born romancer; except that this was not fiction...

"Curiously enough," Dallow went on, "it was not from Thurston that the persecution of the witches began in the first place, but from the townspeople themselves, who saw, or fancied they saw, the black art being carried on in every hole and corner. And there seems little doubt that several covens were operating in the district. Why, one wonders? Why at one particular time and in one particular place? Why in Salem? Why in Bamberg? Why in Tolnbridge? And yet it was so. And recusant priests of the diocese were involved, as it is said they must be, in the celebration of the Black Mass. That brought the ecclesiastical authorities, chief among them Thurston, to the centre of the persecution. Suspicions and accusations multiplied, because the best defence against suspicion of oneself was to accuse another. There's no evidence that the Bishop, in the first instance, particularly encouraged or enjoyed the proceedings. But soon there came a change." Dallow paused. Fen was lighting a third cigarette from the end of the second; he seemed more than usually thoughtful.

. "You must know," Dallow continued, "that it was the custom to torture witches in order to extort confessions from
them—though it often happened that they confessed without
torture. And it was necessary, at least, that the confession should
be reaffirmed without torture. But there was slow, methodical
flogging and the hot witch's chair, and thumb-screwing and
leg-crushing and hoisting by weights. And it came to be
observed that Bishop John Thurston was more frequently—
though always unobtrusively—present at these scenes than his
office warranted. He was present, too, at the executions, and
it was said that it was he who had instituted the custom of
burning as opposed to hanging the malefactors. Certainly
some extraordinary legal quiddity must have been involved—
though I have never succeeded yet in properly discovering
what the legal position was—because elsewhere in England
witches were invariably hanged and not burned. And one has
no means of telling whether or not the imputation was correct.
At all events, Bishop John was beginning to read Glanvil, and
the *Malleus*. And one sees how this ready-made, well-sancti-
fied moral issue would appeal to his underlying Puritanism—
and how the methods used in dealing with it would appeal to
his sensuality. For many of the women were young, and some
beautiful. So it was in 1704, the year before he died."

Dallow went to the cupboard, and took from it one of
several thick, leather-bound books. Reverently he opened it,
and turned over the pages.

"Here," he said, "is the Bishop's personal diary, for the
last months of his life."

Even Fen showed signs of intelligence at this.

"It is," Dallow continued, "one of the most complete
first-hand records of a haunting in existence, and there seems
no doubt of is authenticity. The Bishop left orders that the
diary was to be destroyed at his death—unread. But such is

human curiosity, and so extraordinary was his account of the last months, that it passed into the keeping of the then Chancellor, and so came to me. Mr. Vintner"—Dallow crossed to Geoffrey's chair—"perhaps you would care to look at it—to read it to us, even. I never tire of hearing the story. And the diary itself gives the whole thing, without any need for commentary. You are not in a hurry, Mr. Fen?"

Fen shook his head, and Dallow gave the book to Geoffrey. It was heavy, and the writing was neat, large, and fastidious. Leaning over Geoffrey's shoulder, Dallow turned the pages, and at last pointing to an entry:

"You might perhaps begin here…"

So Geoffrey read, as the rain hissed softly on to the garden, and the yellow, veiled light of the sun came and went, cloud-driven, across the stiff, thick pages.

"27 Febr. A^0 1705. We are advis'd in one of those Sermons of Dr Donne of St. Paul's that have so justly been rever'd as sound Doctrine, that the pleasures of the Senses are right to be employ'd insofar as they interpose no veil between the soul and its Maker; that is to say, moderately employ'd. Yet Donne himself was a notorious Rakehell in that earlier part of his life that preceded his reception in the bosom of the Church of Christ, a man of great profligacy and extravagancies, an associate of London whores and conycatchers. If therefore in Youth a man may overtop the limits of moderation and yet be due to Repentance and Charity later defy the pains of Hell, why should I being yet in ye flower of mine age and full of natural energies be hinder'd through exercise of my Holy Office from the relaxations that are everywhere enjoy'd by common men? It is written that even the Sons of God lusted after the daughters of men. True it is that their Desire was Impiety by the disparity in Kind between the Angelic Substance and the bodies of those Jewish Women; but let there be no such disparity, and where is the sin? If we believe, our crimes are expiated as soon as committed.

"Often upon my pillow I think of my youth in London, of the Playhouses and those comedies of Mr Wycherley, and the darkness and the smell of the women's hair and the gleam of their naked throats; and take out sometimes the *Ars Amatoris*, to read that Passage that concerns the wooing of a woman in the Playhouse (thus inaccurately paraphrased by Mr Dryden.) These things for me are past by, but I desire them still. Here I am among Bumkins, having neither Wit nor Grace of body or mind. Their women are like sacks.

"See that this be regularly lock'd away, after perusal.

"*4 Mar.* Have seen her come twice this week into Mattins, most modestly veil'd; but was able to perceive the extraordinary Texture and richness of her Hair.

"*6 Mar.* I have found that she is nam'd Elizabeth Pulteney, being niece of a woman burn'd last year by my order as a Witch. Her bodily perfection and Grace of carriage argue a higher origin than in that low station to which as I am assur'd she belongs. She is devout, yet there have been accusations against her. Four Women were burn'd this week. The crowds grow less continuously.

"*21 Mar.* Return'd from the flogging of a woman to extort confession. It was not long. She was stripp'd and beaten with triple knotted thongs of leather. The screams were unusually piercing. I took no pleasure in it, as I should do, were I properly concern'd with the chastening of Satan through this punishment. My thoughts were continually elsewhere.

"*26 Mar.* Spoke to her this morning for the first time. Her Skin is remarkably soft and fine. She is meek and reverent. I have offer'd her regular spiritual Guidance. She will come to me often now. To chasten that Submissiveness into active pain! But these are idle Fancies."

(Here Geoffrey omitted a number of entries dealing with the work of the diocese. The next reference to Elizabeth

Pulteney was dated April 23rd.)

"Tonight her fourth visit. I stress'd to her the need of Absolute submission to those set in Authority over her, and set her the
test of unclothing straightaway before me. She demurr'd greatly
and it was long before I persuaded her (by various Means) to do
it. Her modesty excited me beyond all caution. Learn'd she is but
seventeen years of age, but remarkably well-inform'd, and the
tresses of her Hair coiling long and golden about her…Milton, in
his great religious Poem, tells of the naked beauty of Eve and of
her hair. So also Donne in that Elegie.

"She realis'd my purposes early, and seem'd afraid. I
twisted the Hair about her throat and pretended to be about
to kill her. She is a foolish child, with her talk about being the
Bride of Christ. As I said to her, is not the Church Itself that?
But the threat of Persecution as a Witch silenc'd her.

"Feel unusually depress'd. The house is over-silent, and it
is not good to be alone. Must get to my bed and drive these
thoughts and scruples away with recollections of the Pleasure
I have had. But first to lock this away downstairs. The house
has echoes, and I have always hated the dark. I dare not leave
it here. The Servants have long since retir'd.

"13 Aug. All goes well, and I have not had sufficient
Leisure to write in here previously. Since I must to myself be
honest, I have fear'd to face the doubts which have lain about
me. I have reason'd with my self and see no cause for fear in my
actions. If I have chasten'd her body, there is Authority and
Precedent enough, as in the history of the early Church. She
grows very silent and unresponsible, and my interest dies. I shall
not see her again. Why do I feel so continuously the enormity
of my acts, when Reason itself does not condemn them?

"15 Aug. The worst has happen'd, and she is with child by
me. But the threat of burning will keep her silent.

"16 Aug. Met her this day secretly, in the coppice beyond Slatter's Close. She is recalcitrant, and will own the par-

ent of her child. It seems that even the Threat of torture as a Witch does not deter her. But there is no other course. Her Ravings against me will be held the evidence of demoniac Possession. She is resign'd, as it seems, to penitence and Expiation. Oh, the Follies of these religious women! I would spit upon their hateful Piety.

"23 Aug. The Danger is pass'd. Her accusations against me were as I had anticipated an added condemnation of her self. It was Madness ever to fear that she would be believ'd. Today the thumbscrews to extort Confession. When that fail'd, hoisting by weights. The Confession greatly Circumstantial, led me to suppose her in fact a Witch. And what more likely than that the Devil through her employ'd his arts to surprize my steadfastness? I am convinc'd that this is the Truth.

"Throughout her eyes fix'd upon me, though she no longer spoke against me. I do not like the Memory of that.

"29 Aug. Deus misericorde me. Today she burn'd. I thought it might last for ever. Her hair was first shav'd, and burn'd separate. There was some Cavill and Murmuring in the crowd, that the Sergeants were forc'd to employ their Authority in the maintenance of a due silence and respect. Adjur'd to confess publickly, she kept obstinate silence, only as she came by me saying 'Keep fast your doors against those that will wish to visit you.' Then was hurried to the Stake, bound, and the Faggots kindl'd. She seem'd little more than a Child.

"I know not what she mean'd by this, but the house is cold, and I were better in bed. Without doubt I acted rightly, and she was a Witch.

"4 Sept. We are cruel punish'd for our Follies, and I, most miserable sinner, with hardest stripes. As I lay in bed last night, the curtains of the bed drawn upon three sides, and the fourth open to admit the light of the candles set upon my table, that fourth curtain (no Person being in the room) was drawn sudden in upon me, when I was left in the darkness.

And some Creature of the Night, moving without, seem'd trying to crawl beneath the curtains, and plucking at the bedclothes, so that I scream'd out loud, and one of the Servants
came running, but nothing was there. Had him stay with me
the remnant of the night, in great fear and perturbation of
mind, with every light burning. Shall see that all doors be fast
lock'd but I fear 'twill make no difference. I dare confide in
nobody. But, Christ the Lord will protect me against the consequence of my Evil.

"5 *Sept*. Today went about the house, setting the Pen-
tagram upon the sills and thresholds, after repeating the rite of
Exorcism. With these cares, I shall live long and happy. She
shall not filch from me the time to expiate my sins. Though the
Autumn is cold and windy, the house grows uncomfortably
warm. Being just come in from Mattins, ask'd one of the servants if he had notic'd this, but he said no. Seeing he seem'd
surpriz'd at my appearance, ask'd him the reason. 'Why sure,'
said he, 'I thought your Grace was in the Studdy, for not ten
minutes hence I heard someone walking to and fro there.'
When I went up no one was there.

"10 *Sept*. I have seen It for the first time, and pray I may
never again. God have mercy on my Soul, and rescue me from
the horror. Hell is not Anguish, but Fear, such as this. Tonight
late in going to my Chamber, pass'd by the Studdy door, and
there saw one of the serving-maids (as I thought) bending to
make up the fire. I went in to reprove her for not being retir'd
to her own quarters, when the Thing straighten'd suddenly
and put its arms about me. I fell to the floor in a Faint, but one
of the men happening to be by, came to my assistance, but saw
no thing. I cannot write more. Christ, have mercy on me.

"13 *Sept*. There is Whispering in the town that all is not
well here, and Whispering against my own Person. Seven of
the servants have left. Burning coals found scatter'd about the
library, though there was no fire there. The warmth grows

insufferable.

"*19 Sept.* A servant today found all the hangings of my closet ablaze. The conflagration was hard to extinguish.

"*2 Dec.* Praise be to God for all His mercies! Two months gone and no Incident, and the heat likewise evaporated. That Devil's minion Elizabeth Pulteney sent at last to her right Account. Virtue can command even the Powers of Hell. My mind is at last at rest, and I can apply my self with renew'd vigour to the affairs of the Diocese. God has allow'd this as a Testing of my Faith, and I am emerg'd triumphant. The evil Phantasms are gone.

"*3 Dec.* I shall not see Christmas. This morning enter'd one of the Sextons to tell me that a woman would see me by the North Transept of the cathedral. Poor fellow, he knew not what manner of thing it was bade him fetch me forth. As I stood looking about me for the Woman, I saw it crouching in the shadow of a buttress. The skin is like parchment, peeling from the Skull, that shows through in white patches. There are no Eyes. The Hair is still beautiful, beautiful. But I must not see it again..."

The writing trailed away. Geoffrey turned on; the rest of the book was blank. There was a long silence. Geoffrey looked enquiringly at Dallow.

"The night of the twenty-fourth," said the Chancellor softly, "was cold and windy, and on Christmas morning there was snow. They found Bishop John Thurston lying in his bed. There were burns on his face, and he had died of suffocation. There was no sign of a struggle, but his mouth was full of hair."

Geoffrey closed the book and put it on the table beside him. He made no comment.

"An ugly, frightening tale," said Fen, who had let his cigarette go out and was now relighting it. "The history of Tolnbridge Cathedral is evidently more lurid than I'd imagined." He turned to Dallow. "Is there devil-worship in Tolnbridge now? I've reason to believe there may be."

To Geoffrey's surprise Dallow nodded. "A singularly childish cult of demonolatry exists—in no sense, you understand, a continuation of the tradition, but merely a trumped-up, unspontaneous affair. It appears to give certain people a mild *frisson* of excitement."

"I think," said Fen, who was beginning to fidget and shuffle his feet, "that it may have some remote connection with the murder of Butler. You don't run it yourself, I suppose? From the contemptuous way in which you referred to it, I should imagine not."

"You imagine rightly, my *de*-ear Professor. I have been once or twice to the Black Mass, but much of it was always so incompetent and—if I may use the word— uncanonical, that I have recently discontinued my attendance."

"You never thought of reporting it to the police? It is illegal, you know."

"But so *harmless*! If you could only *see* the poor dears—" Dallow stopped, glanced at his watch, and suddenly beamed. "Half-past eight. And yesterday was Thursday. Now, does Friday come after or before Thursday? *After*, isn't it?"

"Why?" Really, thought Geoffrey, this amiable posturing was a little much.

"Because I think it is on Fridays that they devil-worship. Every Friday—just like a *churchwardens' meeting*, my dear sirs. If we were to go to their place of resort we might find them at it. Would you like that?" Dallow might have been organising a Sunday School treat.

"It seems a good idea," said Fen. "Let's visit them. But first tell me more. Who runs the racket?"

"My *de*-ear Professor, I haven't—I really haven't—the least notion."

"You don't *know*?" Geoffrey exclaimed.

"It may be the Bishop *himself*." Dallow giggled irritatingly, and balanced himself on the tips of his toes, looking for a moment like a drawing by Edward Lear. "Both celebrants and participants are masked, you understand. Identification of your neighbour is made virtually impossible. And that reminds me that we too shall have to be masked." He went to a cupboard, and took three weird contraptions from it. "Animal masks, you see. Rather beautifully designed. They are of Hindu origin. They will do." The masks were of a pig, a cow, and a goat.

Fen put on the cow's mask. His pale blue eyes stared disconcertingly from the eyeholes. Geoffrey took the pig, and Dallow the goat. They surveyed one another without enthusiasm.

"You both look pretty silly," said Fen. He mooed experimentally, and then, seeming pleased with the sound, did it again. He continued to moo all the way to their destination. There were times when Fen could be very irritating indeed.

❊ ❊ ❊

The Black Mass proved to be in progress in an old wooden Scout hut, situated in a deserted spot a little way off the road from Tolnbridge to Tolnmouth. It still bore traces of its former occupancy, in the shape of cardboard beavers, otters, and other amorphous-looking fauna pinned to various parts of the hall, and which stared down at the goat, pig and cow which came and settled themselves at the back. They looked very absurd, but no one took any notice of them.

There were quite a number of people present, all masked, and mostly women. Two masked and black-robed figures pottered ineffectually about by an improvised altar. There was no talking. Presently the business of the evening commenced, and very dull it was. It consisted, as far as Geoffrey could judge, of the ordinary Latin Mass, with the *Confiteor* and *Gloria* omitted. Geoffrey, Dallow and Fen made no attempt to communicate, and no one seemed to expect them

to. There were no diabolic ecstasies—but then, Geoffrey
reflected, there were seldom any noticeable ecstasies at the
Divine Mass. There was no human sacrifice, or obscene ritual.
Geoffrey had seldom spent a less interesting half-hour. Fen
became very fidgety indeed, and could scarcely be restrained
from stalking out. Geoffrey wondered how it would end; perhaps they would play God Save the King, or the Doxology,
upside down.

Eventually, however, things seemed somehow or other to
come to a stop. The Celebrant and Acolyte departed to a room at
the back of the hut, and the participants, after a little whispering
and sniggering together, melted away into the growing dusk.

"I thought they always had an orgy after the Mass," complained Fen, removing his mask.

"An orgy." A trace of humour appeared in Dallow's voice.
He waved a hand at the surroundings. "Hardly the right
milieu, do you think? One would require to be very determined indeed to have a satisfactory orgy here."

The hall, except for themselves, was now completely
empty. Geoffrey went to the altar, and examined the Cup and
the Host. The latter, he found, was a large section of turnip
painted black, apparently with creosote.

"That is traditional," Dallow explained. "I expect they got
it out of a book," he added contemptuously.

The Cup proved to be a revolting concoction with a basis,
it seemed, of quinine.

"Keep them healthy, anyway," said Fen cheerfully. "I'm
going to interview the priests of these rites," he added, making for the door into the back room.

"Then I shall leave you," said Dallow pleasantly, "to your
investigations. I think you may have difficulty. The rule of
secrecy is very strictly observed, and—for obvious reasons—
particularly by the Celebrant. However, I wish you luck. You
may catch me up—I am a slow walker. In case not, a very good

evening to you, with a murderer behind every door." He giggled, and with a limp wave of the hand left the hut.

Fen turned the handle of the door, and pushed it open. It was ill-fitting and scraped on the floor. They found themselves in a room structurally identical with the one they had just left, only much smaller. It was unfurnished, except for a single cheap table and chair.

The Acolyte had gone, but the Celebrant was unrobing, his back turned towards them. When he heard them come in, he replaced his mask unhurriedly: then faced them.

"Well, gentlemen?" The voice was clearly disguised. But Geoffrey found it impossible to identify the original.

"We hoped to be able to make your acquaintance," said Fen.

"I'm afraid that that's impossible. Absolute anonymity is the rule. You yourselves should be masked."

"That's rather absurd."

The Celebrant made a gesture which might have been humorous resignation. What he actually did was to take an automatic from beneath his robes and fire it at Fen.

CHAPTER ELEVEN

Whale and Coffin

*"Why, what a disgraceful catalogue of
cutthroats is here!"*

OTWAY

BY SOME MIRACLE, the shot went wide. Looking back on
it afterwards, Geoffrey thought that the Celebrant's arm became
entangled in his robes; and there was no doubt that he was
extremely nervous. Fen, who had fought in the Great War, fell
flat on his face, with well-drilled precision. Geoffrey, who had
not, remained immobile, gaping in frank stupefaction. And the
Celebrant was seized with panic. There was no logical reason
why he should not have killed both of them there and then. But
he hesitated, and as he hesitated, there came a sound of running
footsteps outside; someone had heard the shot. Grotesque in his
robes and mask the Celebrant rushed to an outer door, flung it
open, and vanished. Almost at the same instant someone pounded

across the hall, and came in through the door by which they themselves had entered. It was Dallow, dishevelled and alarmed. More automatically than courageously, Geoffrey followed the Celebrant out. As he went, he was aware of Fen climbing to his feet and grumbling quietly to himself.

The Celebrant had a good start. Like some fantastic crow, with his black robes flapping in the wind, he was running across the wet fields into the gathering dusk. Grimly Geoffrey set off in pursuit, though with no very clear plan of action in mind. The chase proved abortive, for before very long the Celebrant stopped, turned, and fired his automatic at Geoffrey. As an offensive measure this was perfectly useless, since the shot must have fallen at least a hundred yards short. But as a deterrent it was good enough. Geoffrey slowed down, stopped, and stood watching as the figure plunged on and was eventually lost to view in a small clump of trees. Then he returned to the hut. It was not heroic, but it was sensible.

"I don't know what good you expected chasing him to do," said Fen peevishly when he reappeared. "I am covered," he added with more concentrated malevolence, "in bruises."

He inspected himself tenderly.

"I lost him," said Geoffrey rather obviously.

Dallow, who apparently was now acquainted with the situation, moaned faintly in deprecation. "I confess, my de-ear Professor," he said, "that I lingered, fearing trouble of some kind. But this I did not anticipate."

Fen pressed himself experimentally, and let out a sudden howl.

"Perhaps you might tell us," he said when the noise had subsided, "why you were so anxious."

The Chancellor had his answer ready—almost too ready, it seemed to Geoffrey. "In the first place," he pronounced, with the air of one embarking on a lecture, "there were ritual considerations. In the second, the compelling need of anonymity in this business. I suspected your intrusion would not be welcome, though I never thought…" He stopped, not even pretending to simulate incoherence.

Fen grunted. He inspected the place where the bullet had buried itself in a wooden joist, and then the room. It contained absolutely nothing beyond the table, the chair, a quantity of dust, and themselves.

"Useless," he exclaimed disgustedly. "Let's go."

"You will perhaps allow me, my *de*-ear Professor, to accompany you as far as my house?"

Fen gave a grudging and uncivil permission. They set off, walking moodily and in silence. It was the measure of Fen's absorption that he passed by three dragon-flies, a golden beetle, and a nest of flying ants without even deigning to notice them. Geoffrey thought, rather unintelligently and quite fruitlessly, about the case. What Dallow was thinking it was impossible to tell, but he appeared to be reciting sections of *The City of Dreadful Night* to himself at brief intervals. It was only when they were nearing his house again that Fen exclaimed:

"Oh, my dear paws!"

Dallow was not aware of Fen's recourse to the White Rabbit in moments of high excitement. He looked round with mild surprise.

"What a fool I've been," said Fen.

"I know this stage," put in Geoffrey. "You tell us you know who the murderer is, we ask you, and you won't inform us, though there's no reason in heaven or earth why you shouldn't."

"Of course there's a reason why I shouldn't."

"What is it?"

"Because," said Fen solemnly, "you did it yourself."

"Oh, don't be so daft."

"All right, I know you didn't. But seriously, there is a good reason why I shouldn't. An all-important reason. You'll know it finally."

"Are you certain you know what you're talking about?"

"Logically certain. I can't think why I didn't see it before. Unfortunately, there isn't a shred of material proof—nothing that would hang the person concerned. For that reason I've got to go warily. (It's the Butler murder I'm talking about, by the way.) But the identity of one person concerned is as certain as anything on this earth. Or rather…"

"Well?"

"There's one snag." Fen was very thoughtful. "Just one. And it depends on something I must ask Peace. At least—" He hesitated. "Yes, it must depend on that."

"You mean Peace isn't guilty?"

"Certainly not."

"But he's the only person who could have been in that cathedral…"

Fen groaned. "I know, I know. But just the same, he's *not guilty.*"

"He had the best motive."

"Don't be so foolish. We know perfectly well what the motive was. And it wasn't money. I should have thought you would have known how Butler was murdered, if anyone did."

Geoffrey was blank. "Me?"

"Certainly."

"But didn't you say that the police would find incriminating evidence in Peace's room?"

Fen sighed and shook his head, like one dealing with a particularly backward child. "Oh, Geoffrey, Geoffrey…Perhaps this will give it to you. Peace left to go up to the cathedral before we got back to the chapter-house last evening, didn't he?"

"That was what Spitshuker said."

"Well?"

"Well what?"

Fen shook his head again. "Never mind. You ought to know, and so ought everyone else. I expect we shall find Peace at the police station. They'll have found the stuff in his room by now, and either arrested him or detained him for questioning."

"I don't see how you knew anything would be in his room."

"No," said Fen rudely. "You wouldn't."

At this point the argument ceased, as they had arrived at Dallow's house. The Chancellor bade them an affected good night, and went in. They continued down the hill into the town.

"It occurs to me," said Geoffrey, "that this Black Mass business might, if suitably handled, and with the help of drugs, be a very good way of getting military information out of the wives of people in the know—they were mostly women there."

"Yes, that's true. In spite of the horrid boredom of the whole business, I really believe the majority of those people must have thought they were doing something wicked and exciting and important."

They walked on in silence. Thanks to the rain-clouds, it was considerably darker now than it had been on the last evening, when they had gone up to the cathedral and found Butler dead. Looking at his watch, Geoffrey was surprised to see that it was only half-past nine.

"Still time for a drink," said Fen laconically when informed of this fact.

"Why didn't you want to tell me who the murderer was?" asked Geoffrey. "Was it because Dallow was with us? Is he in on this business?"

Fen frowned in perplexity. "He may be. That's just what one doesn't know. There must be more than one person concerned—perhaps three even, though I doubt if there are likely to be more. All I know is that one person was quite definitely concerned in the murder of Butler, and *may* be the brains of the whole business."

"You say *concerned* in the murder…"

"Well, there must have been more than one of them in the cathedral when Butler went up there, in order to get that radio away." Fen paused. "Geoffrey, are you very famous as a composer?"

"No. Church musicians would probably know about me. Very few other people. Why the change of subject?"

"I was thinking about the landlord of the 'Whale and Coffin' knowing your Christian name. He might just be a knowledge-able music-lover, overwhelmed at being confronted by you in the flesh." (Geoffrey glared.) "But it doesn't seem very likely." (Geoffrey snorted crossly.)

"We must tackle him on the subject. They're occasionally inefficient, these people. But I've no doubt the same idea will have occurred to them, and they'll be ready for us. Anyway, we must see Peace first."

❀ ❀ ❀

They found the Inspector standing on the steps of the police station, smoking a cigarette and gazing blankly and purposelessly up the street. He brightened somewhat when he saw them.

"Ah, here you are, sir," he said to Fen. "You were right about that stuff in Peace's room. We found it easily enough, under the traditional loose floor-board: the clergy-house key to the cathedral, a phial of atropine solution and the hypodermic."

"Any finger-prints?"

"Not a thing. They'd been wiped clean."

"Yes, I rather expected that. What have you done about it?"

"Arrested him. Or rather the Yard people have. He's here now, but we haven't got a thing out of him more than he told us before."

"Oh," said Fen. "So the Yard's come, has it? Appleby?"

"No, unfortunately." The Inspector looked uneasily over his shoulder, and lowered his voice. "A couple of great churls, they are. Most uncooperative. They think they've got the whole business cut-and-dried, now they've arrested Peace. Won't do anything but sit in the station playing rummy and smoking foul pipes."

"It seems to me," Geoffrey interposed, "that they'll have to make up their minds which motive to go for. If they think it was the radio…"

"The point is, sir, that they regard the money motive as simply a cover for the real one."

"Is all that money business a fake, then?"

"No, it isn't: and that's what worries me. We've checked on it, and things are exactly as Peace said, even to the fact that Butler was trying to get his wife to transfer the dibs to himself. Now it's all very well to say that's a cover for the spy business. But it seems to me the crisis over the money came up pretty conveniently just at the time when the murder was necessary. Somehow, it doesn't really seem plausible. Not that they haven't got a pretty good case without that."

"For instance?" queried Fen.

"Well, the stuff that was found in his room."

"Could have been a plant. The fact that there were no fingerprints suggests it, in fact."

"That might have been only an additional precaution. But I agree, mechanically speaking it *could* have been a plant. I've checked times, access to Peace's room, and so on, and you can take it from me that *anyone* remotely connected with the case could have put the things there. But there's other things, the chief being that only Peace could have been in that cathedral when Butler was murdered. They had it in for me, I can tell you, for not searching him for the key immediately afterwards." The Inspector stared aggrievedly. "Not that he couldn't have hidden it somewhere, and recovered it afterwards."

"The point is," said Geoffrey, "that one can't see why he kept it at all. He could quite easily have put it back in the clergy-house or left it where he'd hidden it. He didn't need it again."

"Exactly, sir. That's another point in his favour. But there's more to it yet. According to his own account, Peace got to Dr. Butler's house at five past six, and was there till a quarter past, when Dr. Butler and Mrs. Butler returned. Now, the poison was put in Brooks' medicine at six o'clock, and we've no proof at all that Peace didn't go straight down there from the station and *then* back to Dr. Butler's house, since there weren't even any servants in to receive him. Mr. Vintner, you didn't happen to notice which way he went when he left the station?"

"I didn't, I'm afraid."

"Well, there it is. It's possible, though it doesn't seem to me likely."

Fen, who had been shuffling his feet and showing other signs of impatience, now demanded:

"But what about the first attack on Brooks—in the cathedral? I thought it was quite certain Peace was in town that night. And why should be have the *hypodermic* in his room?"

"Yes," said the Inspector, scratching his nose thoughtfully. "If your theory about a plant is right, that was a serious mistake. Even those ruffians from London"—he pointed a thumb at the interior of the police station—"admit that he couldn't have been responsible for that. But then, we know there's more than one person concerned, don't we? And the evidence against Peace on the other two accounts is pretty black."

"Except," said Fen, "for the business about the key and the mixed motives. But I suppose there are ways of getting round that."

"The trouble is, sir, that I don't know where else to look, even though I'm inclined to agree with you that Peace isn't guilty. They're mainly concerned with the spy business, mind you, and of course that's quite right. But they think they can get at it through Peace, and they're hardly bothering about anything else."

"Can I see Peace? There are a couple of rather important questions I want to ask him. If I get the answer I want to the first of them, I think I shall be on to something at last."

"I don't see why you shouldn't, sir. I shall have to ask those churls' permission, though. And they'll probably want to be present."

Fen nodded, and all three passed inside. As they went, Fen asked if Josephine had been got away safely.

"Nasty business that, sir," said the Inspector. "What decent person'd want to do a thing like that to a little kid? It was clever of you to tumble to it. Yes, we got the doctor to look at her, and she's been sent to a private nursing-home up north for expert treatment. Mrs. Butler wanted to go with her, but we headed her off. She was in a rare taking when she heard about it, I can tell you. I don't think she had anything to do with it, though."

"No. Still, it was wiser not to let her go. Did you get anything more out of the girl?"

"No, the doctor wouldn't let us ask any questions."

The churls were, as the Inspector had predicted, playing rummy and smoking foul pipes. He went over and engaged in a muttered colloquy with them, while Fen stood with a poker-faced expression which made him look like something loose from a mental home, but which was evidently intended to be noncommittal. After a while they all set off to Peace's cell, which was small and comfortable-looking. Peace was sitting on the bed, smoking a cigarette and reading *The Mind and Society*. He seemed pleased to see them.

"Ah," he said, "you've come to visit the condemned man. Have you been hearing about the case against me?

"It all sounds rather unpleasant. And as I keep telling these people, I'm damned if I know how those things got into my room." His tone was light, but Geoffrey sensed great strain and anxiety behind it.

"You'll be out of here in no time," said Fen. "That is," he

added minatorily, "if you give the right answer to a question I'm going to ask you."

"Well?"

Fen hesitated. Even Geoffrey, who had no idea of what Fen was getting at, felt somehow the importance of the moment. Even the churls took their pipes from their mouths.

"What time," Fen asked, "did you leave the clergy-house to go up to the cathedral and meet Butler?"

"It was"—Peace paused—"just before ten."

Fen turned to the Inspector. "According to Spitshuker, five minutes before we got to the clergy-house." The Inspector nodded; Fen turned back to Peace.

"Now this is the point." He leaned forward and spoke with emphasis. "When you left the clergy-house, did you go straight up to the cathedral?"

Peace stared. "Yes—I…"

"Damn!" Fen began pacing about the room. "No, it can't be. I can't be wrong. Think again. Think, man, think. Didn't you delay at all? Everything depends on this."

Again Peace hesitated. "No, I—wait a minute, though. I did."

"Well?" There was a fury of impatience in Fen's voice.

"I went straight out on to the cathedral hill. Then I stopped for five minutes to look at the burning-post. I was thinking about the psychological impulses which go to make witches and witch-burners…"

"Only five minutes?' Fen broke in. "Are you sure?"

"I'm sorry," said Peace helplessly. "It couldn't have been more than that. If as much."

"That would mean you got up to the cathedral at five past ten—at the latest. It was 10.15 when we arrived and heard the crash. What were you doing in the other ten minutes?"

The two Yard men looked at one another. "It seems to me, sir," said one of them, "that you're just doing our work for us. In that time we have reason to believe that he went into the cathedral, knocked Dr. Butler out, dropped the slab on him, and slipped out, locking the door behind him. Then he met you as you rushed round."

"He did nothing of the sort," said Fen offensively. "And don't interrupt."

"Actually," said Peace, "I wandered round the cathedral trying all the doors. I couldn't make out why Butler didn't hear me."

"*All* the doors? On both sides?"

"Yes, of course. Several times."

Fen took out a handkerchief and mopped his brow; Geoffrey had seldom seen him show so much emotion. "Thank God!" he said. "It is possible, then. Or rather"—he became suddenly anxious again—"it's possible provided we can find out what that innkeeper was doing all evening."

"Harry James?" enquired the Inspector.

"Yes. There's a third conceivable snag, and that is that none of these people we're thinking of had anything to do with it at all. But no, that's impossible. It must have been someone connected somehow with the cathedral, for reasons we've discussed. One more point," he added to Peace. "What key did you use to unlock the gate between the clergy-house garden and the cathedral hill?"

"I borrowed Spitshuker's."

"Good. Well," said Fen, recovering something of his normal boisterous manner, "we shall have you out of here in no time. Try not to get into any mischief," he adjured Peace with tedious facetiousness. Then he nodded farewell, glared at the Yard, and marched out, accompanied by Geoffrey and the Inspector.

They paused on the steps, and the Inspector remarked:

"I didn't quite see what you were getting at, sir."

"No," said Fen rudely; "you're too stupid. And let me tell you another thing: I have to report an attempted murder."

The Inspector stared. "What? Attempted murder of who?"

"Of me."

"Good heavens." The Inspector stared even more. "But how?…why?…"

Fen explained about the Black Mass, and what had followed.

"Black Mass!" the Inspector exclaimed. "Holy God, what shall we be having next? Here, you'd better come in and make a formal statement about all this."

"I haven't time," said Fen shortly. "They'll be closed in half an hour. Besides, I've got to write things down on pieces of paper, to clear up my ideas a bit. If it's devil-worship you're worried about, then you can take it from me that's not likely to crop up again after this evening's *fracas*."

"But what about you?"

"I'm all right," said Fen irritably.

"They'll try it again."

"No, they won't. That was just a panic impulse, because the fellow thought we'd find out who he was. Very silly. Come on, Geoffrey, we must go."

"Just as you like," said the Inspector with theatrical resignation. "It's your own funeral. But you might tell me what this idea of yours is. It won't be much good to us if you're bumped off without telling anyone."

"You go and think up an idea of your own," Fen replied. And without more ado he strode off towards the "Whale and Coffin."

"Seriously, though," said Geoffrey when they were out of earshot of the Inspector, "why don't you tell him?"

"Because, my dear Geoffrey, he'd insist on at least detaining the person concerned, and that's the last thing I want. They're not quite such fools that they won't have provided against the contingency of arrest. Whatever work they have to do will be done in any case. By far the best thing is to leave them free, imagining we don't suspect them, and then see if

we can't somehow ferret out what their methods are. But it's
going to be difficult. Damned difficult."

❖ ❖ ❖

The public bar of the "Whale and Coffin" was crowded,
and they went round to the lounge, where it was still possible to
sit; not, however, before collecting Fielding, whom they found
playing darts. A spasm of remorse seized Geoffrey as he realized that he had not once thought of Fielding during the past
few hours; after all, the man had twice saved his life. He
seemed as dejected and purposeless as ever. Geoffrey resolved
to make amends for his past neglect.

They discovered the innkeeper, Harry James, and Fen
questioned him. He seemed quite ready to reply, and suspiciously prompt in his details. Last evening, he said, he had been
in the bars uninterruptedly from opening time (six o'clock) to
closing time (10:30). From 9:30 to 10:30, he said, he had been
talking to three regulars, whose names he was prepared to give.
(Geoffrey noticed with surprise that Fen heaved a sigh of relief
at this intelligence.) Fen asked if he had himself opened the
doors at six o'clock. He said he had, and that several customers
who had been waiting outside would bear him out. It was all
very natural, and not unexpected, but Geoffrey found himself
disliking more and more the little man, as he stood there with
his small eyes blinking through the thick lenses of his glasses,
and fingering incessantly his watch-chain. There was something
almost physically repulsive about him.

"I was wondering," Geoffrey put in, "how it was you came
to know my Christian name last night."

"Why, Mr. Vintner"—James smiled, and his glasses
flashed, as he turned, in the electric light—"I know of you as
a composer of Church music. I'm afraid you must be too modest about your reputation."

"You said at the time that you were thinking of someone who was dead."

"I didn't wish to embarrass you," James replied smoothly. "I deplore the habit of pestering well-known men."

"You're interested in Church music, then?"

"Very much so. I've made it a life-long study." Geoffrey simulated interest with, he secretly thought, a good deal of success. "It's unusual to find a layman who knows anything about it. We must have a talk some time. What is your favourite setting of the evening service?"

James smiled again. "I'm a Presbyterian myself, so I'm not well acquainted with the settings of the Anglican service. But of those I've heard, I have a sentimental liking for Noble in B minor."

"Personally I prefer Stanford in E flat." Geoffrey waited breathless for the answer. But James only raised his eyebrows and said:

"In E flat? I've never heard of it. The B flat is delightful, of course, and the less-known G."

Geoffrey cursed inwardly; the man had the better of him. Aloud he remarked:

"You should come to Mattins at the cathedral tomorrow. We're doing Byrd's eight-part setting of *In Exitu Israel*."

"Ah." James beamed, and Geoffrey's spirits rose. "I'm afraid the only one I know is the Wesley." Geoffrey's heart sank; his ruse had failed again.

"May I before I go," James was saying, "thank you for your own delightful Communion Service. The Creed is particularly fine, with that recurrent rising crotchet figure in the accompaniment...Well, gentlemen, if I can't help you further. Jenny!" He called to a passing waitress. "These gentlemen are my guests for the evening. A glass of the special whisky for Professor Fen here. A very fine liqueur whisky," he added confidentially to Fen. "You'll like it, I'm sure. Good night to you all." He beamed at them, and was gone.

"Whisky!" said Fen with great satisfaction. None the less, he tasted it circumspectly when it came.

"Flummoxed," said Geoffrey in disgust. "Amazing what a day's intensive study of the text-books will do."

"Personally," Fen remarked, "I like Dyson in D. It's a battle of religion and romance, of Eros and..." He checked himself abruptly. "Never mind that. I've got what I wanted to know. Let's get down to work now."

He produced from a pocket a number of grubby, crumpled sheets of blank paper, and from another an assortment of blunt, stubby pencils. Then he and Geoffrey settled down to work out individual timetables for each of the persons likely to be concerned in the case, Fielding proffering valueless conjectures and advice the while. Eventually, after some acrimonious argument and mutual accusations of defective memory, the following list was produced:

Garbin. At 6 p.m. was alone in his house (unconfirmed); about 7:30 arrived at clergy-house; stayed to meeting after dinner.

Left the clergy-house shortly before 9 and went for walk along cliffs (unconfirmed). Arrived home at 10:30.

Spitshuker. At 6 working in his room at home (unconfirmed). At 7 set out with Garbin for the clergy-house, arriving towards 7:30.

Vouched for from then to the end of the meeting (*circa 8:50*). Walked to the clergy-house gate with Butler.

From then till just before 10 talking to Peace.

Met on the point of leaving, at 10, by Geoffrey, Fielding, Fen, Frances, the Inspector.

From 10:05-10:15 talking to the Inspector.

Dutton. At 6 out walking (unconfirmed).

At 7:30 returned to dinner.

After dinner retired to his room, but was seen about when Butler was arranging to meet Peace at the cathedral.

Remained there for the rest of the evening (unconfirmed).

Dallow. At 6 talking to his servant at his house. Had an early dinner, and went down to the hospital to see Brooks. Then returned to clergy-house, arriving about 8. Stayed to meeting, left about 9, and went to see a local contractor on business; found him out, and returned home about 10:30 (unconfirmed).

Savernake. At 6 was walking with Mrs. Garbin from the station to the house where she was dining, and stayed there for some time. Returned direct to dinner at the clergy-house, only stopping to leave his bag at Butler's house.

After dinner went for a walk (unconfirmed). Talking to one of the aldermen between 9:45 and 10:20. Returned home just in time to hear the news of Butler's death.

Peace. At 6 had arrived from the station at Butler's house and found no one there (unconfirmed), but met Butler and Mrs. Butler when they returned at 6:15. Dinner at the clergy-house at 7:30. After dinner sat in the summer-house (unconfirmed) but went back shortly before 9. Arranged with Butler to meet at the cathedral at 9:20. Stayed talking to Spitshuker till just before 10, then set off for the cathedral. Found outside the cathedral at 10:16.

Butler. At about 6 was smacking Josephine at the clergy-house.

Returned home at 6:15, arrived at clergy-house about 8.

Left meeting to go up to the cathedral about 9. Was found dead at about 10:20-10:25.

James. From 6 to 10:30 in the "Whale and Coffin."

Frances. At 6, shopping down in the town (unconfirmed). Returned to clergy-house, meeting tail-end of Josephine disturbance and Geoffrey and Fielding at about 6:10. Got dinner, went to her room with a book afterwards, reappeared as the meeting broke up (8:50). Did some work in the kitchen (unconfirmed), set out for a stroll, met Fen, Geoffrey, Fielding, the Inspector at about 9:50 and returned with them to the clergy-house, subsequently going to the kitchen (unconfirmed).

Josephine. At 6 was being spanked by her father in the clergy-house. Subsequent movements uncertain, but took a false message to the police at the cathedral at 8:55.

Mrs. Garbin. At 6 was walking with Savernake to a friend's for dinner and bridge. Remained there till 11.

Mrs. Butler. Returned at 6:15 from tea with a friend, accompanied by Dr. Butler. Remained at home for the rest of the evening, with Dr. Butler till shortly before 8, after that alone (hence unconfirmed) until Spitshuker brought her the news of her husband's death.

At the bottom of the last sheet Fen had scribbled:

(1) The police left the Cathedral at 8:55;
(2) The implications of the tomb-slab—unpremeditated;
(3) The plant in Peace's room—mistake about the hypodermic;
(4) The cathedral grounds are locked in the even-

ings, but anyone who really wanted to could easily get in without a key (Josephine did).

On the point about Geoffrey's Christian name, and the lasso, James may be involved; one other may be involved.

From the evidence of the timetables and the points listed above, *one person was quite definitely involved in Butler's murder, may have been the murderer, and is almost certainly the brains of the spy-ring.*

Fen looked at Geoffrey and Fielding. "Do you get it?" he asked.

"No," said Geoffrey.

"Nincompoop," said Fen.

CHAPTER TWELVE

Love's Lute

"0 Love's lute heard about the lands of death!"

SWINBURNE

*T*HE NEXT DAY BROKE in a haze of fierce, shimmering heat. Geoffrey's night had been uneasy, beset with dreams which were just on the edge of real nightmares. He had woken, restlessly slept, woken again. And when towards morning he did sink into a deeper sleep, he was disturbed almost at once (as it seemed) by a light tapping on his bedroom door. He opened his eyes a little way, perceived without enthusiasm that it was quite light, and uttered that choking, miserable sound which those newly conscious employ to indicate their ready comprehension of what is going on around them. From behind the door, Frances' voice said:

"I've finished with the bathroom. For the Lord's sake don't

be too long, or we shan't have time to really do anything before breakfast."

Geoffrey looked at his watch, saw that it was only shortly after six, shook his head at the lack of veracity of womankind, and succeeded eventually in getting out of bed.

When he arrived downstairs she was waiting for him, dressed in an open-necked check shirt and a pair of dark blue slacks. He wondered afresh at the dark beauty of her hair, the unblemished milk-white skin, just relieved from pallor by, here and there, a touch of red, the breath-taking perfection of her body. This morning she looked, somehow, almost a child; and the sparkle in her eyes, and her impatience to be away, added to the impression. He wondered just what she felt about her father's death. And as if reading his thoughts, she said:

"You think it's rather shocking that I should be going out to enjoy myself when my father's been killed."

"I don't think so a bit."

She smiled, a little sadly. "I suppose it is shocking, really. But...Well, damn it all, one can't *force* oneself to feel sorry when one doesn't."

"Weren't you fond of him?"

"Yes, I was. That's the funny part. But only in an aloof sort of way. I mean..." She laughed suddenly. "How absurd that must sound! I don't know how to express it, really. Of course it was a horrible shock when...when you came and told me, but somehow it didn't last long. None of us ever knew much about him, really. He was always shut up with his work."

They went out of the house and through the garden, taking the road which led up to the cliffs between Tolnbridge and Tolnmouth.

"I hope nobody sees us," said Frances. "I really *oughtn't* to be gadding about."

"No one in his senses will be up at this hour."

She turned to look at him, and grinned. "You really are an old maid."

"Yes, aren't I? I think that's why women don't like me. They like a man to be a man—large, hairy, masterful. A sort of D. H. Lawrence gardener or pit-boy."

"What utter nonsense. All women like different things about men. Don't make specious generalisations like that. Men who generalise about women simply show that they don't know anything about them."

"1 don't know anything about them."

"I know. That's partly what makes you so nice to be with. A man who's really shy about a woman is a lovely change."

"Is Savernake shy?"

She looked at him quickly. "You would drag him into it."

"It's because I'm jealous."

"Are you really? How nice. Well, he isn't shy, if you want to know. He's bumptious."

"Are you still engaged to him?"

"Yes." She answered shortly, almost hurriedly.

"Frances…I meant what I said yesterday…"

She put a hand quickly on his arm. "Please, Geoffrey, I don't want to talk about that. Not now, anyway. Later, perhaps."

He felt an irrational tinge of resentment; she seemed to sense this.

"We'll discuss things later."

And, after all, he thought, I've only known the girl less than forty-eight hours. I've no right to try and burst into her personal life like this. Perhaps no right to do it ever. Perhaps I don't even want to do it. To marry her would mean giving up a lot of things I don't want to give up. But then I don't know whether she'd want to marry me.

Almost, he wished he had not come. She was beautiful, she was desirable, but if he committed himself…He wanted more time to think. Then he cursed himself for an idiot and a coward, and, his sense of humour suddenly reasserting itself, he laughed out loud.

"What are you laughing at?"

"My own absurdity."

"I suppose you are rather absurd. Let's not talk for a while."

They walked on in silence. The sun, still low in the heavens, burned hotter, its edges ragged with fire. They turned from the hot, dusty road and climbed a path which led over a steep ramp into a wood hanging in the hillside. In the wood it was cool, a green, liquid coolness. Dying bracken, and brambles were twisted together between the trees. There were one or two wild roses, and some sour-looking small blackberries. The path, which led up the hillside, was narrow, and sloped at the edges, like a trough. The centre was full of stones, and yellow mud still wet from the water which flowed down it, so that once or twice they stumbled as they went on upwards.

Coming out of the wood was like emerging from a cavern. They found themselves on a wide expanse, dotted with rough stones and encircled with gorse. Overhead the gulls glided, their wings stiff, in long, immensely rapid flights. Their harsh shouting was the only sound except for the distant murmur of the sea. The young ones were ugly, speckled with brown. One came so low that they could see its throat throbbing with the sound.

In another moment they stood above the estuary-mouth, looking out to sea. Below them stretched the brown cliffs, with a strip of sand at the bottom strewn with the wreckage of a disused quarry: a rotting wooden landing stage; two lopsided trucks; rusted rails, broken and uneven, leading to nothing. The grass was short, hard, coarse, and brown with drought. A faint wind, brushing the surface of the sea into rows of tiny corrugated wavelets, played about their faces. Frances stretched out her arms in sheer animal pleasure.

"Lovely!"

They went on along the cliff path, towards the sea itself. Tiny fishing-boats, blue and brown and red, with little triangular sails at the stem, chugged along below them, convoyed by gulls. After a time Frances beckoned to Geoffrey, and they both went to the very edge of the cliff. Beneath was a wide stretch of clean, almost white sand, a cove where the water ran out clear as glass as far as the eye could reach.

"That's nice," said Geoffrey rather prosaically.

"Come on."

"Good heavens! I can't climb down there. It'd be mad. We'd break our necks."

"There's a way down," she said, "if you know how. I do. It's quite easy."

"It doesn't look easy to me."

"No one else knows about it. Or next to no one. You can always rely on getting it to yourself."

"I should like my coffin to be of lead, if there's anything recognisable to put in it."

Tant bien que mal, by a series of hair-raising athletic feats, they achieved the climb.

"Lord," said Geoffrey, panting, when they reached the strand, "I hope we can get back again."

"It's much easier to climb up than down." Frances performed a couple of tiny dancing steps on the sand. "Isn't it wonderful? We're quite alone. Let's have a bathe."

"But I haven't got any things."

"It doesn't matter. Nor have I."

He stared at her. "Do you think we've really known one another long enough?…"

She laughed infectiously. "Oh, Geoffrey, don't be a prude. Wouldn't you *like* a swim?"

"Yes, but…"

It was too late. She had already begun to take off her clothes. Apprehensively, Geoffrey followed suit. When they had finished, they looked at one another for a moment in silence; then simultaneously burst out laughing.

"Don't *stare* so!" she said with mock indignation. "It's

rude." They raced each other into the water; it seemed to Geoffrey very cold.

Frances swam quickly out, with a swift, competent crawl. Puffing slightly, Geoffrey followed her.

"It's a pleasant sensation," he said, "but I feel very immoral." In the clear water, fathoming beneath their feet, they could see one or two small fish going about their esoteric affairs.

When they had come out, and were drying themselves on some rocks, Geoffrey put his arm round her shoulders, but she pushed him away.

"Not till I've got some clothes on." Geoffrey suddenly and unexpectedly blushed.

Then, as soon as they were dressed again:

"Frances."

"Well?"

"You know I'm in love with you?"

"Yes: I think I'm in love with you, too." He was almost troubled at the sincerity in her voice.

"I should like to marry you."

For a long time she was silent. Then she said: "Geoffrey, I'm sorry, but...I can't."

"Why?" He took her almost fiercely by the arm.

"Don't. You're hurting me."

"It's Daddy. I've been thinking, and after what's happened I can't leave Mummy. You do understand, darling?"

"Yes, but you've got your own life to live. And besides, all that can be got over. Your mother can live with us—and Josephine as well." He made the offer with a certain gloom.

"That's sweet of you, but I mustn't promise anything—just now." She laughed. "Promise—as though I was conferring some kind of privilege. It does sound vain."

"You're not refusing because of Savernake?"

"No. No." The denial was quick and eager. "I shan't marry him in any case."

"You did say you were fond of me."

"I am. Oh, my darling, I am. I love you so very much. But don't you see...I'm confused. It's all so quick. We can wait, can't we?"

"I don't want to wait."

"We must. All that's happened...Oh, darling, what *did* happen to him? Was it an accident? It must have been an accident. Surely not even Peace..."

"They've arrested him."

"I know." It was like a shadow between them. "Has Professor Fen discovered anything?"

He put his arms round her. "Don't bother about all that. Other people will look after it." He tried to put his lips to hers, but she pulled her head away. He stood back. She looked at him with eyes in which there was a hint of tears.

"Let's go home."

But when they were again at the top of the cliff, she turned and pulled him to her and for a moment kissed him warmly. Then they walked back, in silence.

Thus began the third day.

❀ ❀ ❀

Geoffrey afterwards looked upon it as the day when, quite suddenly and as if at a signal, the talk ended and the final struggle began. Hitherto they had dealt with characters single, isolated from one another, mere waxworks lined up for questioning. When they had turned their backs one of those figures had moved, and there had been killing. But now some sixth sense told him that the end was near, that the pretence could no longer be kept up. He felt that they stood at a cavern-mouth, waiting for some creature to spring at them from the darkness, and yet not knowing what kind of thing it would be. And there was no more time for conjecture now; they were committed, at last, to fight.

When he had played Mattins, he set out with Fen and Fielding to a little pub on the outskirts of the town, where Fen was proposing to put some plan of action before them, since they were less likely to be interrupted or overheard there than at the "Whale and Coffin." Fen carried a large map of the district, which he persisted in opening as they walked along and refolding the wrong way, so that it became crumpled and torn.

"I don't think," he said, "that these people can possibly be operating from the centre of the town exclusively. It would be too dangerous. I've been trying to find out if there are any likely hideouts nearby—a pretty impossible business."

"Did you discover anything about the wireless messages they sent out?" Fielding asked.

"I'm going to ring up the cipher department, but I don't expect they've decoded the stuff yet. That sort of thing takes time. But the trouble is," he added waspishly, "that it's all so vague. Ten to one nothing will turn up at all."

At this point there was an interruption. They were going down a narrow path, flanked by high yew hedges, which skirted the churchyard. And from the other side of one of these hedges they suddenly heard a voice.

"*You may seek it with thimbles,*" said the voice informatively, "*and seek it with care, you may hunt it with forks and hope…*"

Fen stopped dead. "I know who that is," he said gloomily.

"*You may threaten its life with a railway share,*" pursued the voice, "*you may charm it with smiles and soap…*"

"Charlemagne!" Fen bawled suddenly. The voice stopped, and there was a scraping sound on the other side of the hedge.

"That, I fancy," said Fen grimly, "is the Regius Professor of Mathematics."

A gruff, hairy, little old man put his head over the hedge.

"What are you doing here, Charlemagne?" asked Fen minatorily.

"I am holidaying," said the head, "and it was impolite of you to interrupt a total stranger in that ungentlemanly way."

This made Fen so indignant that he uttered a little shriek. "Don't you know me?" he said irritably. "Don't you know me, you stupid old man?"

"Yes, I know you," said the head. "You are the New College buttery boy." It then disappeared.

Fuming, Fen rushed on to the next gap in the hedge. The Regius Professor of Mathematics arrived there simultaneously.

"*But oh, beamish nephew,*" he chanted, wagging his finger at Fen, "*beware of the day if your Snark be a Boojum! For then*"—he lowered his voice to a bloodcurdling whisper—"*you will softly and suddenly vanish away, and never be met with again! It is this, it is...*"

"Stop all that," Fen commanded peremptorily. "It's nothing but affectation. You know perfectly well who I am. I'm Gervase Fen."

"You might be," said the R.P.M. "I remember a much younger man."

"Oh, it's no use talking to you," said Fen. "Come on, you two."

"Where are you going?" said the R.P.M. He said it with such suddenness and severity that they all started.

"That's no business of yours," said Fen. "But if you must know, we're going to have a drink."

"I shall come too."

"Oh, no, you won't. We don't want you."

"I shall recite you *The Hunting of the Snark.*"

"We'd rather do without that, thank you."

"I shall accompany you," said the Professor with such firmness that even Fen was daunted.

"Are you quite sure you want to?" he asked feebly.

"I am sure of nothing," said the Professor, "except the differential calculus. And I'm not as good on that as I used to be."

Fen moaned and shrugged his shoulders, and they all set off. "He's all right, really," Fen said to Geoffrey in a penetrating whisper. "Only he's dishonest. He steals things. But I don't think it'll hurt to have him with us. And I don't see," he added with more venom, "how we'd get rid of him even if we wanted to."

Beside them, the Professor placidly continued reciting Lewis Carroll. The public bar of the "Three Shrews" was empty when they arrived there, apart from the landlord, who stood polishing glasses in the detached, otherworldly manner of his kind. They ordered beer, for which Fen prodded the Regius Professor of Mathematics into paying. Then they all sat down at a table, listened patiently to the conclusion of Fit the Seventh, and began to talk.

"It seems to me," said Fen, "that our general strategy has got to be (a) to try and find out where these people's headquarters is and (b) when we've done that, to discover precisely what their plans are."

"As simple as that?" said Geoffrey.

Fen glared at him. "Well, if you can suggest anything else," he grumbled, "you suggest it. It may not be as difficult as it sounds. What we must *not* do is to start arresting them right and left without knowing what arrangements they've made for just that contingency."

"No."

"Very well, then." Fen opened the map. "I've been making enquiries about deserted buildings in the neighbourhood." He pointed at a section of the map, and Geoffrey, glancing idly at it, caught the words "Slater's Wood." "And I've come to the conclusion that apart from the Scout-hut, there's only one…"

It was at this moment that Fielding interrupted him. And before many hours had passed, Geoffrey was bitterly to regret that interruption.

"I don't see how you know," said Fielding, "that it's anywhere *out* of the town at all."

"I know," said Fen severely, "or I *think* I know, because I've been making discreet enquiries about the general activities of the person chiefly concerned in all this. And I've discovered that that person has had a habit of taking frequent jaunts in the surrounding country, and always in the same direction. They may have been pleasure trips, of course. But I rather doubt it."

Here the landlord, who had momentarily vanished on some obscure mission, returned with an envelope in his hand.

"Excuse me," he said, "but is any of you gentlemen named"—he stared at the envelope—"Gervase Fen?"

"Me," said Fen ungrammatically.

"I just found this note for you on the mat. Heard it slipped in through the letter-box."

With this pronouncement he returned to polishing glasses. Fen tore the letter open; it was typewritten.

Clever of you to find out who I am. But you won't have me arrested, will you? There's not sufficient evidence. And I have enough deputies to look after things if you do. Let us have a talk some time: I shall be about this afternoon as usual. (And my apologies for that foolish shooting at the Mass: of course it wasn't my doing.) My best regards.

"But this is *fantastic!*" Fielding exclaimed. "Criminals just *don't* write letters like that."

"I rather agree," said Fen thoughtfully. "There's something half-phoney about it. But the impulse to swank is quite genuine, I think. I wonder..." he mused. "Oh, Lord, I wish I knew what to do. The trouble is, that letter's quite right. There really isn't enough material evidence—cigarette-ash, footprints and so on—to convict the person concerned; just times, and an odd method of murder."

"They don't seem to be worrying very much about anything you can do," said Geoffrey.

Fen looked at him queerly for a moment. "No, they don't, do they?" he said slowly. "And after all, what can I do? Threaten them with a revolver? They'd give me no information, and I should get arrested myself."

"We might whisk them away and torture them," put in Fielding hopefully.

"I can't help feeling that if we tried that we should end up with bullets in our backs."

"Dear, dear," said the Regius Professor.

"Oh, shut up, you," said Fen. "But what I *am* going to try and do is ring up the War Office and try and find out if they know anything yet about the radio messages. McIver's the man. Now, what on earth's his number? Whitehall something."

"Look it up in the Directory."

"It isn't there. And enquiries won't give it you, either."

"It's a national secret. But it's got a five and a six and an eight and a seven in it. 5-8-6-7; 7-6-8-5; 7-8-6-5...Nothing sounds right."

"We'd better work out all the possible combinations," said Fielding, "and try the lot."

"That's going to take a time."

"I'll work out the combinations," said the Regius Professor of Mathematics eagerly. He grabbed hold of a pencil and a piece of paper.

"Couldn't you try someone else?"

"He's the only man I know. No one else would listen to me."

"Well, come on, then."

The Regius Professor laboured for five minutes. Then he gave them the complete list of possible combinations. Geoffrey looked at it and said: "*You've forgotten 5687.*"

"Impossible," said the Professor. "I worked it out by the factorial four."

"Well, you've still forgotten 5687."

The Professor gazed at the list intently. "That's funny," he admitted.

"Oh, come on," said Fen impatiently. "I'll do it. You see, you put each number first, in turn…"

"Try the ones you've *got*," said Geoffrey. "Look at them. Does any of them strike a chord?"

Fen looked at the list for a long time, and finally said: "None."

"Let's go, then."

"There's a telephone in the passage outside. I saw it when we came in."

Fen finished his beer with a disgusted expression, and they all trooped out. The pub still seemed completely deserted. They put Fen in the telephone box and he got in touch successively with the offices of a Warden in Lunacy, a large undertaker's, a theatre, the Prime Minister, and Mr. James Agate at the Café Royal (something must have gone wrong with the mechanism at this point). They all turned out their pockets for coins, and rushed to and fro procuring change from the bar. Eventually, and rather to everyone's surprise, he got the number he wanted.

"Hello, is that you, McIver? This is Fen…I don't care if you're busy; you just pay attention for a minute…No, I am not drunk. Listen."

He explained the circumstances. There was a prolonged crackling from the other end.

"Information about military and naval dispositions," said Fen. "Yes, I was afraid of that. Well, it'll be all your fault if we lose this war. You'll wake up tomorrow with Himmler in the chamber pot…" He turned to the others. "Go away, all of you. I'm going to gossip." Obediently they trooped back to the bar.

There they ordered more beer, and consumed it. The day was already drowsy. Geoffrey lay back in a pleasant stupor. Flies buzzed on the window. Somewhere in the distance a car started up and drove off. The landlord polished glasses with wearisome persistence and no appreciable result. Geoffrey looked at the note which Fen had just received. The amiability of the wording was hateful. He remembered that whoever wrote it had helped to drug a child of fifteen, to drive a man mad and then poison him, to crush another man to a blood-flecked jelly...Despite the warmth of the day, a shiver of sheer repulsion seized him. He handed the letter to the Regius Professor of Mathematics, who was sitting drinking his beer and staring blankly in front of him.

"I haven't the least idea what all this is about," said the Professor, "but I agree there's something wrong about this letter. The tone is so indifferent. Almost as though it were intended to lull someone into a sense of false security..."

Geoffrey and Fielding sat up. The same thought flashed across both their minds.

"Fen's taking a devil of a time over that call."

Almost in one bound they were at the door, sick apprehension in their hearts. The passage was empty, and the door of the telephone-box stood open. There was no one there. But the receiver hung, swaying gently, at the end of its wire, and a faint smell of chloroform sweetened the air.

The Professor, who had followed them out, paused by the empty booth.

"He has softly and suddenly vanished away," he said gravely. "The Snark *was* a Boojum, you see."

CHAPTER THIRTEEN

Another Dead

"An intellectual hatred is the worst."
YEATS

*T*HE FIRST THING TO BE DONE was obviously to rush out into the road and discover if anything was to be seen. But even as he went, Geoffrey remembered the car he had heard drive away, and knew it was useless. There were wheelmarks in the gravel court, but they lost themselves in a fringe of macadam adjoining the road, and it was impossible to tell which way the car had gone. For the rest, not a soul was about. As a kidnapping it was not only daring but flawless.

Then there was the Inspector to telephone. The language with which he received the news fitted in well with Geoffrey's mood. He promised to use what resources he could in tracing the car, and suggested that Geoffrey and Fielding should come down to the station at once to discuss a plan of action. They set off, leaving the Regius Professor of Mathematics drinking gravely and peaceably on his own, and never saw or heard of him again.

But while they walked, Geoffrey realised the utter hopelessness of what they had to do. For Fen had not told them the name of the criminal, and they could not find him in that way. He felt none of the excitement of the chase—only a nausea, a dull despair, and a sense of bitter self-reproach. What a perfect trap that note was, and what a blind imbecile he had been not to see through it!

The Inspector listened with a glum expression to what they had to tell him, and seemed devoid of constructive ideas. The churls from the Yard, it appeared, had returned to London early that morning with a view to making certain investigations into Peace's past career. Fielding asked rather irritably what Peace could have been supposed to have had to do with it, since he was locked up in his cell when Fen disappeared, but even Geoffrey saw the logical flaw in this: they were dealing, after all, with a gang. The only slender clue they had to go on, as the Inspector pointed out, was the possible complicity of Harry James, the landlord of the "Whale and Coffin."

· Certainly a search-warrant could be produced, to enable them to look at his premises; but equally certainly, that move would have been anticipated. The Inspector had had one or two fresh pieces of news since they saw him last, but all of a negative kind: the case which had been dropped on Geoffrey in the train could not be traced; nor could the man who had dropped it; and nor could the assailant in the shop, who had made his escape through one of the other departments in the general confusion. But these, at the moment, were matters of very secondary importance. The Inspector had thought that he might be justified in pulling James in for questioning. Now that Fen had been kidnapped, however, he was less certain of the wisdom of this. If he was not dead already (Geoffrey turned sick inside), such action might simply precipitate his murder.

In the end, Fielding persuaded them that as a resident of the "Whale and Coffin" it would be easier for him than for them to do a little unobtrusive snooping. Neither Geoffrey nor the Inspector seemed very willing to leave this to him alone. The "Whale and Coffin" was, after all, their only chance. It was finally decided that while he was investigating Geoffrey should be stationed in the bar, as a second line of defence; and that, as a third, a constable should remain unobtrusively outside, ready to summon more help if necessary.

And so it was that a quarter of an hour later, with a quick-beating heart, Geoffrey stood once again in the crowded little public bar of the "Whale and Coffin," waiting. Fielding's plan of action had simply been for a general search, as far as that was possible: and it had been agreed that if he did not return within twenty minutes, the place should be turned inside out. Geoffrey sipped whisky, and saw the minute-hand of his watch crawl through aeons of eternity from four to five, from five to six...All about him, the serious business of drinking continued tranquil and unregarding. It was impossible to suppose that their enemies had not anticipated this move, that they were not conscious of what was going on. Geoffrey became more nervous every second, and was profoundly grateful that he was surrounded by a crowd. The landlord was nowhere to be seen. He wondered what Fielding was doing.

In point of fact, Fielding had already found what he was looking for. He found it at once, and the chance nearly cost him his life. He had set off from his own bedroom down the narrow, panelled corridor, bending his head to avoid the low beams, and feeling slightly less enthusiastic about secret service work than usual. As it happened, he was gifted with a fairly high degree of physical courage, but it had occurred to him, as to Geoffrey, that they were hardly likely to take whoever they were looking for unawares, and the reflection not unnaturally depressed him. Experimentally he tried the first door along the corridor on the right. It was not probable that criminal evidence would be lying about in such a public spot, but one had to be methodical. The door yielded, and he found himself in a low white-panelled sitting-room, well-lighted and pleasantly furnished in chintz. It was empty, but from a closed door on the other side came the sound of voices. He tiptoed towards it, and put his ear to the keyhole. Fragments of conversation reached him.

"...tell you there's never been a conger caught on this coast longer than twenty feet."

"...you get them bigger in Cornwall."

"The trouble is, the local men haven't got the pilchard to bait the lines. And there's so little good eating on a conger..."

This sounded unpromising, and he was about to creep away again when he thought better of it. If the people in there were guests of the hotel he could easily apologise. If not...Gently he turned the handle, opening the door a fraction of an inch. From within, a surprised voice called out:

"Hello! Who's there?"

So there was nothing for it but to go in. He opened the door wide and stepped across the threshold. There were two men there talking. One was Harry James, and the other...

Savernake.

They sat at either side of a table, with beer in front of them. The room was a rather smaller replica of what he had just left. Apart from a few books which, his eye passing rapidly over them, Fielding recognized as being textbooks on Church music, it gave no sign of permanent habitation. Savernake said cheerily:

"Fielding! How pleasant to see you. I'm sorry we haven't been able to see more of one another since you arrived."

James said:

"Well, sir! Anything I can do for you? You're quite comfortable, I hope?"

Savernake said:

"Join us for a drink. I very rarely do this, myself—one has one's reputation to look after—but I like to have a talk with Harry about fishing now and again."

He got up and put himself between Fielding and the only door, that by which he had entered. Fielding saw that the one large window was heavily barred, looking out on to a deserted courtyard at the back of the inn. He realised he had to fight. The two men were looking at him queerly. He felt suddenly helpless, and tried to speak, but the words stuck in the back of his throat.

Then he pulled over a table, and kicked a chair at the innkeeper. James stumbled momentarily, then righted himself. Neither he nor Savernake made any other movement. Fielding fell back slowly into a corner, scraping his left shoulder against the wall.

"Why, Fielding," he heard Savernake say, "whatever's the matter?"

Sick fright closed about his heart. For an age it seemed to stop beating. Then he filled his lungs to shout.

The room turned suddenly to blood. He was vaguely conscious of an explosion, a sudden tearing jolt which spun him hard against the wall and drove him fathoms down to a smashing concussion with the floor. Lying there, he struggled frantically both to keep consciousness and to suppress (biting his tongue) the terrible panic of the mind at the first realization that a part of the body has been destroyed. Obscurely he knew that he must keep consciousness, in case they said anything that would help him to find Fen; he must make them think he was dead…The lights of a million roundabouts whirled and pirouetted before his eyes; the pain was just beginning. Echoing strangely through mile-long tunnels and labyrinths, their voices came to his ears.

"What did you want to shoot for, you fool?" James was snarling. "That's the second time playing about with that gun has nearly finished us. Do you want the whole neighbourhood in here?"

"No one will have heard it. Please remember that I am in charge here. I shall do what I think best."

"Sweet Fanny Adams. What are you going to do now, Mr. Clever? You know Vintner's downstairs and a copper outside the door?"

"We must get out, of course. Destroy the stuff and get out. If we can reach Scotland…"

"*If* we can reach Scotland! That's pretty."

"Go and dope Vintner's drink. We can put him in a back-room and leave word that he was taken ill. That will give us a little more time."

"You bloody, over-educated bungler…"

"I should not have the slightest compunction about using this gun again—on you. In fact, it would make my own departure a good deal easier."

"Listen. Someone's coming…"

"No, they're not. No one heard that shot. Get out, will you, and fix Vintner's drink."

"And Fen? What are you going to do about him?"

"He'll be dead by now."

"I don't think. Not with the trickle of gas you let out of that tap, and the room not properly sealed. Your blasted little bit of sadism's going to fix us properly. We ought to go out to the old asylum and finish him off."

"*There's no time, you f—— swine. Go out and fix that drink.*"

James went, and Fielding, unable to hold on any longer and incapable of warning Geoffrey, fell into a dead faint. In five minutes the landlord was back—five minutes during which Savernake paced about, wiped the perspiration from his long, thin face, smoothed back his corn-coloured hair, and twisted his fingers nervously together. His narrow upper lip was quivering slightly, with fright, and a muscle twitched continually in the corner of his right eye.

"Took it like a lamb," said James briefly. "I've left word what's to be done with him when he passes out." He turned and inspected Fielding. "He's not dead. If you can't kill a man at that range, you'll better leave that gun alone."

Savernake produced the gun again.

"No, you don't," said James. "We were lucky first time— nobody downstairs heard—but we mayn't be again. There are quieter ways of finishing him than that. Here, give me a hand."

Together they dragged Fielding over to the gas-fire. It was of the movable kind, attached to the tap in the wall by a length of flexible tubing. James removed the tubing from the fire, and inserted the end into Fielding's half-open mouth. Then he took a roll of surgical tape from his pocket, and plastered up Fielding's nostrils and the corners of his mouth. He turned the gas-tap full on, and they stood back for a moment, listening to the gentle hiss, and watching the blood from his wound spreading slowly on the uneven floor.

"That'll fix him," said James. "Now let's scoot. If we once get to Bristol, G. will have a plane to take us to Scotland, and we can snap our fingers at the lot of them."

"I'd better look through his pockets."

"For Jesus' sake, hurry. If you aren't down in five minutes, I'll take the car without you."

"I'll be down."

James went out, slamming the door behind him. Savernake bent over the recumbent body.

❀ ❀ ❀

But Geoffrey was not doped. With a perceptivity unusual in him, he had observed that the last whisky he ordered was not drawn from the bottle suspended above the bar, but brought in from outside by the woman in charge, on the excuse of its being a better brand. He saw, too, that there was someone watching him through the chink of a door marked 'Private" beside the bar. With an ostentatious gesture he turned his back and pretended to drink, actually pouring the doped whisky down his collar inside his shirt. It felt extremely uncomfortable, but his buttoned coat hid the broad stain, and fortunately none of the other customers had noticed, or shown surprise at, this unusual manoeuvre. Wiping his mouth, he turned back to the bar, put his empty glass on it, and with some facetious remark ordered another. The woman went off to get it, and Geoffrey leaned idly on the bar until, out of the corner of his eye, he saw the door by the bar softly close, and knew that for a moment he was safe. He knew, too, that Fielding had been caught, and what he must do.

He strolled carelessly to the door leading on to the street, and standing there for a moment, whistled a bar or two of "Widdicombe Fair." In response to the pre-arranged signal, the constable moved gently away; but once out of sight of the windows, he ran. It was only five minutes' walk from the "Whale and Coffin" to the police station. Geoffrey calculated that in little more than ten the place could be surrounded.

He turned back to the bar, and pushed his way through to the lavatories. From them, he remembered, there was a second exit into the hotel proper. But once there, where to start looking? The place was an absolute warren of rooms and passages, in which the unknowledgeable might easily get lost. He considered, as well as he could. He knew at least where Fielding's room was, and it was by no means unlikely that he had started his search from there, working outwards. Also, it was plain that he had not had time to search far. The upshot of it was that in another minute Geoffrey was entering that outer room which Fielding had entered a few minutes before.

As he stood on the threshold, the door leading into the inner room opened, and Savernake came out, shutting and locking it carefully behind him. Savernake! But Geoffrey did not pause to consider. He would not have paused to consider if it had been the Archbishop of Canterbury. He performed a sort of flying leap across the room, and landed on top of Savernake before the clergyman had even become aware of his presence.

Like most struggles, it was a hazy, chancy, unscientific business. But Geoffrey had the advantage of surprise, and Savernake was unable to get his gun out of his pocket. Moreover, Savernake was smaller, weaker and less wiry than Geoffrey. The end of it was that he fell, smashed his head against the skirting-board, and lay there, dazed and moaning.

Geoffrey was not waiting to make sure of him, however; the smell of gas from the inner room was becoming too insistent for that. He burst in, turned off the gas, tore the tape from Fielding's mouth and nostrils, and applied what methods of first aid he could think of. Fielding was still breathing. Somewhere below Geoffrey heard a car start up and drive off. Then in a little time other cars drove up, and the police were on the stairs. Geoffrey pulled Fielding from the inner room to the other. He found Savernake had gone, and wondered momentarily if it had been he who had been in that car. But no; there would not have been time for him to get downstairs and out.

The Inspector had brought with him a doctor, who set about applying restoratives to Fielding, and dressing his wound. Geoffrey explained what little he knew.

"Savernake!" the Inspector exclaimed. "So that was it. Though I still don't see..." He checked himself. "Never mind that. We'll get him."

"I think James must have left in a car."

"We'll get him, too. I'll telephone the county police and the military authorities, and we'll arrange for a cordon." He disappeared abruptly from the room.

"He's coming round," said the doctor. He pillowed

Fielding's head in his arm. "Someone ring the hospital and tell them to send an ambulance."

Fielding opened his eyes and was violently sick. He groaned and struggled to speak.

"Keep quiet," said the doctor. "You'll be all right. I don't think the wound's serious," he added to Geoffrey. "It must just have missed the right lung."

"…James…Savernake…" Fielding said. His speech came slowly, broken by long, retching gasps, and his face and finger-nails were blue with cyanosis. "Fen gassed…in…in…" His voice became incoherent. Geoffrey leaned forward.

"Yes?" he said. "Yes?" His whole body was itching with impatience.

Fielding tried again, but only succeeded in retching air. Then he fell back, with his eyes closed.

"For God's sake," said Geoffrey to the doctor. "For God's sake try and bring him round somehow. He knows where Fen is…Fen's life depends on it…You must bring him round."

"My dear sir," said the doctor with a touch of irritation, "you're demanding the impossible. That is…Well, I could try, but it would be infernally dangerous. It would probably kill him."

"He'd want you to do it."

"Perhaps," said the doctor drily; "but that hasn't got any-thing to do with it."

"I should say it had everything to do with it."

The doctor looked at Geoffrey steadily for a moment. Then he said:

"All right. I shall get struck off the register, and probably had up for manslaughter into the bargain. My wife and chil-dren will starve. But I'll try. Give me that bag."

❀ ❀ ❀

Fen had awoken from a dream in which he was being pursued by a gigantic praying mantis down the steep slope of a railway cutting, to find himself constricted in a large white contraption which he only slowly recognised as a strait-jacket. After trying to sort out the implications of this unusual situation for a moment, he devoted himself to being quietly sick. Then he looked up to see Savernake and James, who were standing silently watching him.

"Hello," he said with as much cheerfulness as he could muster. "You look pretty silly."

Savernake sneered. "Not as silly as you do, I assure you. There's a certain appropriateness about your surroundings, don't you think? This is the old lunatic asylum, you know."

"Indeed," said Fen briefly. He made experiments with his limbs, and found that his legs also were tied.

"Don't bother to try and get free," said Savernake. "It will be a waste of energy."

"Why did you kidnap me?" -

"To be able to kill you quietly and conveniently."

"Thanks so much...Excuse me, gentlemen, but I'm going to be ill again...your blasted chloroform..."

"Do."

When he had finished, Fen said: "And what now?"

"We shall be obliged to dispose of you."

"Do talk English," said Fen with a touch of acerbity. "And try to stop imagining you're in a book."

"My dear Professor, I am the last person you are ever going to speak to. You might pretend to be civil."

Suddenly Fen laughed. "How old are you, Savernake?"

"Why?"

"I just wanted to know."

"I'm twenty-six." Fen laughed again, and Savernake snarled: "What the devil's so funny?"

"It's only that I know your type of undergraduate so well. It's always existed in Oxford—over-clever, incapable of concentration or real thought, affected, arty, with no soul, no morals, and a profound sense of inferiority."

Savernake stepped forward and kicked Fen in the face. After a minute:

"That hurt," said Fen mildly, "and you've knocked out one of my teeth." He spat it on to the floor. "Why do you conspire against your country?"

"That has no relevance at present, and I am not prepared to discuss it. I find a certain charm, however, in the fact that Nazism muzzles the fools, the public-bar wiseacres, the democratic morons."

"It kills a lot of people."

"That does not matter."

"No, I suppose it wouldn't to you. When you're being killed it will, though. You'll find it most unpleasant, and at that moment you'd give your soul to spend the rest of your life listening to public-bar wiseacres."

"Like all democrats, you are a sentimentalist."

"I think killing people is a bad thing, that's all," said Fen, still mildly. He sighed. "Well, what are you going to do with me?"

"Turn on the gas."

"The gas?" Fen was surprised. "But I thought this place was deserted. It'll be off at the main."

"It's being taken over by the military authorities the day after tomorrow," said James. It was the first time he had spoken. "The gas has been very conveniently put on again."

"Where is this, anyway?" Fen asked.

"Five miles out of Tolnbridge," Savernake replied, "a mile from road or cottage in every direction. If your nerve fails and you scream, as you very probably will, no one will hear you. But we shall gag you before we leave, just in case."

Fen thought for a moment. Then: "I think," he remarked, "that I'd rather have a quicker death than gassing."

"Very well," Savernake's voice was totally indifferent. "Shoot him, James."

James took a revolver from a shoulder-holster, opened the magazine, and shut it again.

"Do hurry up, man," said Savernake in the same lifeless tone. "We can't stop here all night. And for God's sake put your glasses on. You might not do it properly first time, and we don't want a filthy mess."

James nodded, without speaking. He drew a case from his pocket, opened it, took out the glasses, polished them carefully and put them on. Then he cocked the pistol, pointed it at Fen's head, and tightened his finger on the trigger.

Fen abruptly changed his mind. "I think I'd rather be gassed," he said very rapidly, and added, as James with a shrug lowered the gun: "*Plutôt soufrir que mourir, c'est la devise des hommes.*"

"Oh, we'll try and arrange for you to suffer," said Savernake. He went over to the gas-jet in the wall, and experimentally turned it on. There was a sharp hiss.

"Admirable," he said. "But that would make it rather too quick." He turned the tap down to the lowest possible point. "Now, let's see. The windows are closed, but the room won't be properly sealed, so there'll be some escape. I should say that with the gas at that strength it will take about an hour and a half."

"That seems bloody foolhardy to me," muttered James. "Suppose someone finds him before the time's up?"

"No one will. How can they? And we must leave him a little time to meditate, mustn't we?" To Fen: "I'm afraid we must gag you now. We'll make it as comfortable as possible." Then, when it was finished:

"Goodbye. I won't say that I'm sorry to have to do this, because it delights me. Come on, James."

Fen, being incapable of other utterance, nodded his head in dismissal. They went out, locking the door behind them. Fen found the silence a relief. He bent his head towards the jet, which was on the other side of the room, but the issue of gas was so weak that it gave no sound. Then he did a little struggling, without other effect than to accentuate his cramp and send spasms of sharp pain through his limbs. The strait-jacket made him extremely hot, and he soon desisted. The room offered no promise of assistance, being large and totally devoid of furniture—the warden's office, he judged. Germans, he reflected vaguely, seemed to have a neurotic obsession about mad-houses—there was *The Cabinet of Dr. Caligari*, for example and *The Testament of Dr. Mabuse*. But these were Nazi agents, and the Nazis had driven out Wiene and Lang…He pulled himself together. These vague meanderings would not do. He was conscious of an insistent regret at the prospect of dying.

❀ ❀ ❀

Fielding's eyes were still closed. The doctor put his things back in his bag and looked up at Geoffrey. "Sorry," he said. "No go. I can't bring him round."

"Oh, God…He isn't worse, is he?"

"No. He'll pull through all right. Is that the ambulance? About time we got him out of here. I'll let you know the moment he utters a word."

Geoffrey stood helpless, irresolute. "If they only catch James or Savernake…No, it's hopeless. Fen'll be dead by then."

"They're swine, aren't they?" said the doctor simply. It was more comforting than an elaborate assumption of concern.

Fielding was taken out on a stretcher. He seemed hardly to be breathing. The doctor followed. Geoffrey cursed viciously and racked his brains. Where had they put Fen? What way was there to find out? He sought desperately for a clue, but none came. Gassed…a tap in a wall…gas, gas…gasometers…gas company…

He emitted a sudden yell. "Idiot!" he shouted to the

empty room. "Idiot!" It gave a surprised and slightly mocking echo. Geoffrey rushed like a lunatic down the stairs.

He met the Inspector coming away from the telephone. "So far, so good," said that worthy, blandly unaware of Geoffrey's pressing desire to communicate with him. "The cordon's out, and I don't think that car'll get through it. Savernake must be on foot, or on a bike. I'm going after him…"

"Never mind all that," Geoffrey interrupted him excitedly. "Get back to that telephone!"

The Inspector stared.

"The Gas Company!" Geoffrey bawled. "The Gas Company…"

Five minutes later, beneath some four thousand lunches in the last stages of preparation, the gas flickered and went out. The supply for the whole district had been cut off at source.

Three times already Fen had been violently sick, and twice he had only just prevented himself from going under. There must be a good deal of gas in the room by now, he thought, and his mind was by no means clear.

What the time was, and how long had passed since James and Savernake had left, he had no means of telling. His face hurt badly, but the gas had a little anaesthetised the pain. He found he could no longer focus the room properly. He sighed inwardly, and devoted himself to meditating on the First and Last Things.

A quarter of an hour later, he found to his surprise that he was still meditating on the First and Last Things. The shock was sufficient to clear his brain a little, and to allow him to observe that the sun was appreciably higher than it had been when he had last looked. Moreover, the room was coming back into focus, and his face was hurting more. A mood of mild curiosity seized him. Perhaps there was something peculiar about his lungs which made him immune from gas. The thought amused him so much that he made himself sick again trying to laugh at it, and to be sick with a gag in your mouth is not a pleasant experience. He calmed down a bit.

But two hours later still, when Geoffrey, the doctor, and two constables broke into the room, he was feeling lively, irritable and obscurely aggrieved. The first thing he said, when they had taken the gag out of his mouth and he had painfully forced his jaws into working order again was:

"I'm immune from gas."

"Don't be silly," said Geoffrey. "It was turned off hours ago at the mains. And oh, you old devil, how glad I am to see you again."

While they helped Fen down to the car, Geoffrey explained what had happened. "Eventually," he concluded, "I remembered that when we were in the 'Three Shrews,' you pointed to some place on the map which you said might be the gang's centre of operations. Then Fielding interrupted you, and we never heard what it was. But I noticed a name near where you were pointing. I couldn't remember what it had been—you know that sort of complete mental blank—but I knew it had something to do with the ghost story and Thurston's diary. I rushed round to Dallow's house, and looked at the diary again. There it was—'met her today secretly, in the coppice beyond Slater's Close.' Of course—Slater's Wood. The police knew there was only one empty building near there—this one. So here we are."

"Ah." Fen was unusually laconic. "Well, it was a pure guess on my part, but a lucky one. Thank heavens for all of you." After a while he said grandiloquently: "I have saved the country." He went on saying this for some weeks afterwards, but as no one took any notice of it, he finally gave it up.

They drove back to Tolnbridge, to the police station.

But when they got there, the cupboard was bare. Which is to say that the Inspector and most of his men were out on the search for James and Savernake. From an excitable

Sergeant left in charge, his head evidently full of heroic deeds and high responsibility, they learned that Fielding was going on as satisfactorily as could be expected; that it was almost certain James was still in the area, since the cordon had been quickly and tightly organized; and that no sign had been discovered of Savernake, who, it was supposed, had gone to earth in some part of the town. They decided to wait in the hope of getting some news. It was now nearly teatime, and a constable brewed them a thick, oily concoction of tea. They went away and saw Peace—still in his cell, still reading *The Mind and Society*—and told him everything that had happened. He seemed bewildered.

"Well, I never liked Savernake," he said. "But I wouldn't have thought he had the mentality to organise a thing like this." He embarked on an account of psychologically ideal types, to which nobody paid much attention.

Meanwhile, the Inspector pursued his ways, alone and full of a righteous indignation. He had organised the men at his disposal so as to cover the places at which Savernake was most likely to be found, and had chosen, for himself, to return to Dr. Butler's house. Savernake, he reminded himself, had frequently stayed there and might at least have looked in to collect money or belongings. In this he was proved to be right. Frances met him in the drive, pale-faced and frightened.

"Thank God you've come!" she exclaimed. The words tumbled over one another. "It's July—Savernake. He's been here with a gun. What's been happening? Is Geoffrey all right? Did July kill my father? He disconnected the phone and we couldn't reach anyone, and we didn't dare come out of the house, in case he was still about. He took all the money we had."

"How long ago was this?"

"About ten minutes."

"Do you know which way he went?"

"No. We didn't see. Mummy's in a terrible state."

"Listen," said the Inspector. "Will you do something for me?" His normal easy-going manner had vanished, and a brisk, formidable coldness had taken its place.

"What?"

"Go down to the station and tell them what's happened. They'll know exactly what to do."

"I...I daren't. I'm frightened." She hesitated. "And I'm afraid to leave Mummy alone."

"Take her with you. You've nothing to worry about. Savernake's too busy trying to get away to bother about you." He looked at her steadily. "Will you do it?"

"I...All right."

"Good girl."

The Inspector ran back to his bicycle and mounted. From the gate he shouted:

"Was he on foot?"

There were three ways Savernake might have gone. One was back into the town—a wholly foolhardy undertaking, unworthwhile even for the sake of bluff; a second was down to the waterfront, which he must have anticipated would be guarded; and the third was along the estuary and round the cliffs to Tolnmouth. Here it might just be possible for a man on foot to elude the watchers, and the Inspector decided it was his best chance. He would, of course, make an admirable target, on his bicycle, for a stray shot from a copse or thicket by the roadside; but that had to be risked. The Inspector, normally a peaceable, easy-going man, kind to his wife and family, fond of books, genial in his enforcement of the law and very generally liked in Tolnbridge, had now become a formidable machine, practically insensible to ordinary fear. He recognized, wryly, that he would probably be a good deal less bold running with the hare instead of hunting with the hounds. But he remembered also the many unamiable characteristics of his quarry, and deliberately stifled that pity for the defeated which springs up infallibly in the English mind. He liked England, without thinking very much about it, and he objected, with more intensity than he would have admitted, to people who tried to interfere with her. Moreover, he liked to think of England as standing solidly against her enemies, not buffeted by treachery from within; that offended his sense of symmetry. *"Je hais,"* he might have said if he had known enough French, *"le movement qui déplace les lignes."*

He was glad to have his gun with him. The only time he ever gave himself wholly up to resentment and dislike was when he engaged in target practice. At such times he vaguely felt himself to be engaged in destroying some undefined power of evil; the target became his personal enemy, and he fired at it as though it represented some amalgam of the forces of oppression—Capitalism, Fascism, Bolshevism (he seldom particularised further)—incarnate in shadowy, insubstantial, infinitely menacing figures. It was the only form of day-dreaming he allowed himself, but it made him peculiarly dangerous when he had his gun and something legitimate to shoot at.

In the meantime, it was exceedingly hot.

In a quarter of an hour he had arrived at the top of the cliffs, near the deserted quarry which Geoffrey and Frances had seen on their walk that morning. It was possible that he had missed Savernake on the way. But he knew that half a mile on there were guards, and he decided to climb up among the gorse-bushes on a small knoll and discover if anything could be seen. And it was just as he was laying down his bicycle—no longer practicable on the rough track—that he saw Savernake.

He was working his way quickly, silently, and apprehensively through the bushes only about fifteen yards away, and by a lucky chance had not observed the Inspector's approach. It was possible to see the sunlight gleaming on the sweat which poured from his brow, and the limp, tousled condition of his corn-coloured hair. The Inspector sighed his satisfaction as he crouched out of sight: it was too simple. He waited until Savernake, glancing nervously about, had arrived in the open and turned his back to go further, and then drew his revolver and stepped out after him.

"Stop and hold up your hands!"

Savernake stopped, stiffened, but did not turn. Then he began in a sudden fury of desperation to run, doubling back away from the direction he had been going, and the guards. The Inspector went after him, but he was the heavier man, and Savernake was impelled by panic fear. The Inspector stopped and aimed his gun.

Twenty yards now separated them, and the shot was a difficult one, with Savernake in swift, dodging flight. He staggered for a moment at the impact of the first bullet, but still went on—more slowly now, tripping on stones and gorse-roots, and clutching at the spines for support, The Inspector fired again; missed. A third time, and Savernake fell. But he went on crawling away, still alive, as a chicken will run about a farmyard with head severed. Perhaps he was remembering what Fen had told him about his own death, only three hours before; no one ever knew. For the Inspector also was remembering things—the killing of two men, the dreary blasphemy of the Black Mass. He fired a fourth time, and the shot smashed Savernake's backbone as he crawled. He stopped, seemed to be trying to get to his feet, and then fell hard on his face and lay still. So he was dead.

❀ ❀ ❀

Fen and Geoffrey walked back from the police station to the clergy-house. They had grown tired of waiting, and when Frances had arrived to announce that the Inspector was on Savernake's track, had made up their mind to return, It was with a full heart that Geoffrey saw Frances again; he realised now that he had never really expected to. But a hand-press and a smile were somehow all he had been able to manage.

Of James nothing had so far been heard. The guards were positive that his car had not been able to get through, and thought it extremely unlikely that he had succeeded on foot. But Geoffrey was only too willing to leave the job of finding him to the police, and so, it seemed, was Fen. Although now doped and patched by the doctor, he had grown noticeably more bilious, irritable and depressed. He refused to indulge in any explanations, merely saying:

"I'm going to my room to lie down until dinner. I'm ill," he added severely. "You think things out on your own." He tramped upstairs, while Geoffrey settled down in the drawing-room to think.

Harry James got up from the armchair in Fen's bedroom as Fen flung open the door and strode in. His eyes, small and black as a pig's, glistened behind the thick lenses of his glasses, and the hand which held his revolver trembled slightly. His clothes were dusty and dishevelled.

"Come in, Professor," he said softly. "I was waiting for you. Close the door quietly and don't try to shout."

Fen did as he was told. He felt very tired.

"You were mad to come here," he said. "And you certainly won't get away."

The innkeeper's hand was trembling more. "I know that. But I decided I wanted to settle things with you first. If you hadn't been so bloody interfering, we should have been all right...No, keep your hands up."

"It's uncomfortable," Fen complained.

"Never mind. It will only be for a minute."

Fen thanked heaven, with perhaps more fervour than was normal, that he was standing behind a chair, with his feet and legs out of sight of James. He blessed the inefficiency of the housekeeper, who had left a small pebble lying there, where he had dropped it yesterday when emptying out what he had imagined was a praying mantis, but which proved to be a deformed grasshopper. The only other problem was of not betraying in the upper part of his body the movement of his leg—that and getting the pebble in the right direction without moving his eyes from the man with the gun. Of course, the chance was so frail as to be almost ludicrous, but there was no other, and he had at least the advantage that James was in a highly nervous state. His glance strayed to the full-length cupboard set in the door; it had been convenient because of its lack of a keyhole. He hoped the damned things hadn't all killed one another by now. It was a pity he was not near enough to James to risk a leap at the crucial moment, but that couldn't be helped.

Aloud he said:

"What I can't fathom is why the hell a man like you gets mixed up in a business like this at all."

"Don't try to gain time. It won't help you." James' finger tightened on the trigger.

"For heaven's sake give me a minute or so."

"So you want to know why I joined the Nazis, do you?" It suddenly occurred to Fen that for James, too, every minute of life was now precious; the thought encouraged him.

"Then I'll tell you, Mr. clever-bloody-professor. I joined 'em because they pay well, see? A fat bloody lot I care what government there is. That doesn't affect men like me. But I can tell you one thing: if I'd had the running of this business things would have turned out very differently..."

Now, thought Fen, now: no use putting it off. His eyes fixed unwaveringly on James, he kicked the pebble. His heart almost stopped until he heard the slight tap and clatter as it hit the cupboard door. Inwardly he vowed libations to the gods; outwardly he gave a slight start, and ostentatiously paid no attention. From now on it depended on acting.

James had heard. He stepped quickly back to bring Fen and the cupboard door simultaneously within his range of vision. Then he jerked his head towards it.

"What's through there?"

"Nothing," said Fen rapidly. "It's only a cupboard. Why?" (Oh, the strain of not over-acting one's acting!)

"I think you know very well why. There's someone behind there." (So the trick *had* worked.)

"Nothing except my suits, I assure you." Fen kept glancing rapidly and with heavily concealed expectancy at the door. James' nerves were getting worse, and he also was unable to keep his eyes off it. The problem now was to keep his mind off the realities of the situation. From his point of view, it hardly mattered if the whole Devon constabulary were behind that door; he had chosen to make his own escape impossible, and he would still be able to carry out his purpose of killing Fen. At the same time, he evidently had no wish to die at once, which would almost certainly happen if there were someone behind the door, and besides, the motive of curiosity is a very powerful one. Fen was relying on these two factors. And it was therefore with intense dismay that he heard James say:

"But is doesn't matter, does it? It doesn't make any difference to our little quarrel."

It seemed to have failed. But still the curiosity and the fear must remain, waiting to be aroused again. And plainly James did not suspect the origin of the noise, for the pebble was a small one, and moreover had bounced out of sight. Fen noted with slight satisfaction that if James moved to the door he would be in range of a quick jump; but the difficulty was to get him there.

"I wonder if you'd mind," said Fen, "if I got something out of that cupboard...in a pocket of my suit..."

"Don't try that on me...and don't move." The trigger-finger was tense again.

"Perhaps you'd get it: a photograph…"

"And perhaps I wouldn't." James' eyes were uneasy again. The sweat was beginning to trickle down his cheeks, and his glasses were misting over—an added advantage, Fen thought, as he dare not attempt to wipe them. Suddenly he burst out:

"You leave that bloody cupboard alone! How do I know it's not a door with one of your fine friends behind it?" Anger, and fear, had triumphed, and Fen felt a moment's real hope. But it rapidly faded. The innkeeper recovered his self-possession. His nerves had come very near breaking-point, but they had not broken. He was breathing quickly and heavily now, as a man breathes whose heart is beating too quickly.

"I've had about enough of this," he snarled. "I'm going to finish you now, before you can get up to any more of your tricks." Again his finger grew tight.

Fen was desperate. He must get the man's attention back to that door, or perish. A start in that direction? It would have to be very carefully judged. Too little, and it would be ineffectual; too much, and James' already overstrained nerve might break, and the fatal shot be fired. But that must be risked.

For a fraction of a second Fen resigned himself to eternity. No explosion came. But now James could stand it no longer. The sweat was literally dripping on to his collar, and his hand shook almost uncontrollably.

"How do I know it isn't all a bloody trick!" he shouted suddenly. "How do I know that! There's no one there! I'll prove it! And by Christ, I'll make a mess of you when I have!"

He strode towards the cupboard door. Fen closed his eyes in gratitude. He had done all he could. It rested with them now. New anxieties seized him. Perhaps they had fought and killed one another. Perhaps the darkness had made them torpid. Perhaps…He calculated distances, and braced his muscles for a jump.

A faint drowsy murmur, the murmur of a hayfield in summer, filled the air. James backed towards the cupboard, stood pressed against the wall, felt for the latch, lifted it, and, after a moment's hesitation, half opened the door.

It was enough. Out of it, like the battalions of hell, poured a seemingly unending swarm of bees, wasps, and hornets, assembled there by Fen for the purposes of experiment, and maddened by their dark and prolonged imprisonment. Since James was the nearest animate object, they attacked his face with the utmost ferocity. It would have needed a superman to keep his head in such an extraordinary situation, and James' nerve was already gone. His attention was diverted just long enough for Fen to take a running kick at the gun in his right hand. It went off, smashing three fingers of his left. The insect horde turned its attention to Fen. When Geoffrey, startled by the shot, came racing upstairs, he found James babbling and moaning on the floor and Fen beating fiercely but unavailingly at his vengeful collection.

Since Fen was rather badly stung (though not as badly as he made out), they put him to bed, swearing terribly and crying for whisky.

CHAPTER FOURTEEN

In the Last Analysis

"Here she comes; and her passion ends the play."

SHAKESPEARE

*F*ROM AMONGST A MASS OF BANDAGES which the doctor was now unwinding, a bleak, pale blue eye glared at the assembled company. "I'm not well enough," said a familiar voice from beneath the bandages. "I am not well enough to be unwound yet."

"Nonsense," said the doctor in the brisk, heartless manner of his kind. "You're perfectly well. The swelling's practically gone—you must have a skin like leather. And you can't go about for weeks looking like a mummy."

"You're most unkind," said Fen, feeling his restored features tenderly. "I have been gassed, bludgeoned and attacked by the third plague of Egypt. But does anyone sympathise? No. They stand about jeering." He sat up in bed and scowled.

It was the following evening, and they were all gathered in Fen's bedroom, which only the prolonged exercise of Flit had succeeded in clearing of insects. Geoffrey thought that the occasion had the solemnity of the unveiling of a monument. Frances, Garbin, Spitshuker, Dallow, Dutton all stood or sat about the room. Various formalities had prevented Peace's being released yet, but he would be out shortly. And the Inspector, who as Fen told them, was superintending the final break-up of the cordon, had promised to look in a little later.

Of course they wanted an explanation, and, after a good deal of grumbling, Fen consented to give it.

"The motive for the murders of Brooks and Butler," he said, "was obvious from the start—as was the whole of this business," he added with some vehemence, "to anyone with even a speck of brain."

"Control yourself," said Geoffrey.

After a mild fit of the sulks, Fen went on:

"That motive was, of course, the wireless hidden in the Bishop's Gallery in the cathedral—an admirable hiding-place, blamelessly public and yet easily available for use at night to anyone with access to a cathedral key. Brooks found out about it—how, and how much, we don't know, but enough to make it necessary to put him out of the way. The first attempt, after the choir-practice, failed; the injection of atropine wasn't fatal. So he was murdered in the hospital before he recovered sanity enough to tell what he knew. But in the meantime the cathedral had been put under guard, and it was imperatively necessary to get the transmitting set away to some spot less under the eye of the law. The only time to do it was during the hours of service. The organist was dead, and the deputy organist temporarily out of action; it would be possible to burrow discreetly through to the Bishop's Gallery from the organ-loft, concealing the hole behind the big music cupboard which stands against the partition. Apparently they hadn't contemplated the possibility of another deputy coming at once; so when your arrival was announced, Geoffrey, it gave them a bit of a shock. They tried to put you off with threatening letters and they tried to put you out of action. No good. Another way had to be devised."

"Then it was Savernake," asked Geoffrey, "who put that letter on my seat in the train?"

"Almost certainly."

"He must have written it and had it ready in case of emergency. But I suppose it was the merest chance that I happened to get into his compartment."

"I think so. If you hadn't, he would have got it to you just the same. As to his writing it…" Fen's blue eyes glanced easily round the gathering.

"Well?" Geoffrey felt a sudden, unaccountable tension in the air.

"Apparently it hasn't occurred to any of you," said Fen, "that if Savernake had the brains to run a spy-ring, he hadn't the personality; and if James had the personality, he hadn't the brains. What's more, Savernake could not have systematically drugged Josephine, since he was out at Maverley most of the time; and for James it would have been nearly impossible."

They were silent.

"And there's another thing," said Fen, "which doesn't seem to have suggested itself to any of you. *Both James and Savernake had alibis for the murder of Brooks.*" Geoffrey felt a sudden sickening premonition. Nobody made any movement, or said a word.

Fen nodded slowly. "No, you're quite right. We haven't got them all yet." He paused and leaned back against the pillows.

"The murder of Brooks provided no handle. Someone— one of a number of people without alibis—knew of the arrangements at the hospital, slipped into a room and rang the bell for the nurse who was bringing his medicine punctually at six o'clock. Then, evading the nurse as she came up, went down and put atropine in it. There were no fingerprints on the bell; there was no clue of any kind, any more than there was in the first attack on Brooks, in the cathedral. But the death of your father, Frances, was different."

Again Fen glanced at them. Again nobody moved or spoke.

"There were two features in that which no sane man could stomach for a moment. One was the method—the tomb-slab; and the other was the fact that Butler quite unexpectedly announced his intention of going up to the cathedral, and must have arrived there only five minutes after the police guard left.[1] Do you see the point?"

"No," said Geoffrey. "For God's sake get on and tell us." His voice sounded strained and harsh.

"We heard the slab fall at 10:15—nearly an hour and a quarter afterwards. The purpose of getting the police away was to remove the wireless. Do you suppose they'd wait an hour and a quarter to do that? Of course not. They'd get on with it at once, which would mean they must have arrived just before, or simultaneously with, or just after Butler. So what was he doing during that hour and a quarter? Looking on and giving helpful advice?"

Dallow cleared his throat, a little nervously. "Surely, my *de*-ear Professor, it is possible that he was himself involved?"

"I considered that. But other evidence, which I'll come to in a moment, went against it. No, the plain fact is that he must have been killed almost as soon as he arrived in the cathedral."

"Then the slab was a decoy!" Geoffrey exclaimed. "No, wait, you can't *counterfeit* a noise like that. And, anyway, how was it got to move? There was no one in the cathedral, and no one except Peace could have got out. How was it toppled on top of Butler?"

"I will interrupt the classic perfection of my narrative,"

[1]See pp. 150 and 201.

said Fen severely, "to digress on that point. It's more or less guesswork, and it has no relevance to the identity of the...person with whom we're concerned. But you should have realised, Geoffrey. What was the one part of the cathedral we paid no attention to, thinking it could have nothing to do with the affair?"

"The organ loft," Garbin put in. His deep voice momentarily startled them.

"Precisely. And you remember there's a thirty-two-foot stop on the pedals which literally shakes the cathedral..."[2]

"Good God!" Geoffrey exclaimed.

"You remember how delicately that stone was poised once the padlocks were out. Two notes played together at the bottom of the pedal-board would topple it out in a moment. You remember, too, that you noticed a difference between the crash we heard and the Inspector's experiment. The first crash was preceded by a marked vibration, the second by absolute silence.[3] That alone made me pretty certain I was on the right track. And you must recall how little attention we paid to the organ loft. It would have been perfectly possible in the general confusion for anyone to get out *that particular* door.

"But that didn't really matter." Fen waved the point indifferently aside. "What did matter was why this elaborate business had ever been contrived. Butler was dead a long time ago, you understand. Probably he was thrown over the edge of the gallery immediately over the tomb, and the idea was improvised on account of his position. To move him about would leave dangerous traces. Some pretty quick thinking was done. But why?

"It was not to falsify the *manner* of death, since the autopsy found no trace of weapons or poison. So it must have been to falsify the *time* of death. The slab had three advantages: *(a)* it produced the same physical results—crushed and

[2]See p. 4–5.
[3]See pp. 104 and 133–134.

broken bones—as the fall from the gallery; *(b)* it made medical assessment of the time of death impossible; and *(c)* it made the devil of a noise. The plan must have been improvised at lightning speed—that was why I emphasised all along that it was never intended. But still—why?

"It might have been to create an alibi; it might have been to incriminate someone else; or both. Before long it became plain that it was the second possibility that mattered. To supply a personal motive for the murder might still divert attention from the spying (they knew nothing about the C.I.D. radio van). So I hunted about for likely personal motives, and, of course, the most glaring was Peace's money.

"Now I began to understand things—with a vengeance. I remembered that a number of people knew that Peace was going to the cathedral to meet Butler at 9:20. *But in fact he didn't go then; he went at 10.* Now imagine the mental processes of the criminals. Butler is dead. They have removed the wireless and locked the cathedral, throwing the key away somewhere, to be found later and used as evidence against Peace. But no Peace appears. *Rigor* is setting in, and if he does not come up to the cathedral soon it will be impossible to connect him with the crime, on medical evidence alone. Someone returns to the clergy-house and finds he has an infallible alibi, talking to Spitshuker here. What they decided to do, you know. They decided to drop out the slab and create a false impression of the time of death."

Fen paused, and lit a cigarette. Geoffrey saw that Frances, crying a little, had crept out of the room. He felt a pang of pity, but worlds would not have moved him from the spot.

"So far I got," Fen was saying; "And then for a long time— like a fool—no further. Even when Dutton told me that he hadn't heard the crash of the slab from the clergy-house— right on the edge of the cathedral grounds—I didn't properly realise its importance. Even when I learned that those grounds

were locked at night, so there would be no casual wanderers,
I didn't see what it meant. And then, suddenly, I realised.

"Someone *had* to hear the slab fall."

Fen glanced quizzically around. "Someone had to be got
up to the cathedral at about the right time—when Peace was
up there. Some reliable person—you, Geoffrey, or myself, or
Fielding, or even the Inspector. Perhaps all four of us…The
crash wouldn't be heard outside the grounds, and there would
be no lovers to listen, since the grounds were locked…

"Do you remember who we saw, when we came back
from the 'Whale and Coffin'? Spitshuker, of course, but he had
an alibi for almost the whole evening. And Fielding—but if he
was involved, why did he prevent you, Geoffrey from being
put out of action at a time when it was essential you should be?
There was only one other person to decoy us to the cathedral.
That person expressed great anxiety about Butler, and asked
us to see that he was safe. That person learned that we were
going up to the cathedral on business of our own—very satisfactory information…"

"Stop!" Geoffrey almost shouted the word.

Fen turned to him. "I'm sorry, Geoffrey," he said quietly.
"Yes, I'm very sorry. Of course it was Frances."

❀ ❀ ❀

What Geoffrey thought in that moment he never afterwards remembered. It was too turbulent and too vilely painful.
But he left the room at once and went downstairs and out of
the house. There he saw Frances again.

She was walking rapidly towards a car which stood in the
drive, a small attaché case clutched tightly in her hand.. She
swung round as she heard him, and a small automatic was in
her other hand.

"Don't interfere with me," she said briefly. "Our sentimental relationship is now at an end. A one-sided affair, I'm afraid, but I enjoyed my little piece of acting. If you make the slightest attempt to move, to stop me, or to shout, I shall shoot you without hesitation. One more fool dead will be no loss to me or to anyone else."

She got into the car. He stood silent, watching her drive off. There was no movement from inside the house.

Of course the cordon had not been removed. She drove into the barrier on the Exeter road at seventy miles an hour. They said afterwards that there was no point in even attempting to shoot. A piece of jagged metal tore open the carotid artery in the left side of her neck, and before they could get her out of the wreckage she had bled to death.

CHAPTER FIFTEEN

Reassurance and Farewell

"Should she to death be led
It furthers justice, but helps not
the dead."

DRAYTON

A DAY MORE, and both Fen and Geoffrey were packing to leave Tolnbridge: Geoffrey with an elaborate, old-maidish care, Fen chaotically. Dutton had been pronounced by the doctor fit to take on the services again until a new permanent organist should be appointed, so Geoffrey was no longer needed; and Fen had to attend an educational conference in London before returning to Oxford.

Geoffrey's mind was numb. The three days he had been in Tolnbridge had produced so many shocks that he was incapable of assimilating them. And the death of Frances...For a long time it would be in his dreams. But he knew that sooner or later it must go. It would take months, perhaps, but in the end he would forget. He knew now, too, that he could never have loved her, being what she was. Perhaps it had never been more than an infatuation: love, he remembered, was supposed to triumph over all the defects of its object. But not that; not that. He trembled involuntarily. But it would be all right in the long run. Bachelorhood, with returning confidence, surveyed with new pleasure the green and smiling expanses of his demesne.

He found the manuscript jottings for his Passacaglia and Fugue, and his spirits lightened somewhat. There was always work, and his cats, and his garden, and Mrs. Body...He snapped the case shut; and after a brief glance round the room to make sure that nothing had been left, went in to see Fen.

He found the Inspector, Dallow and Peace with him, Peace newly released, and bearing as ever *The Mind and Society*. Fen's ruddy face, still swollen slightly and blue from Savernake's kick, glowed with effort, and spikes of hair stuck up obstinately from the crown of his head. He was smoking a cigarette, throwing things wildly into a suitcase, striding about the room and drinking whisky.

Geoffrey marvelled at his powers of recovery.

"So James confessed," the Inspector was saying, "as soon as he heard Miss Butler was dead. And confirmed pretty well everything you said. It was he who made the first attack on Brooks in the cathedral, and injected the atropine after knocking him out; but it was Miss Butler who put the poison in his medicine at the hospital. And Butler *was* toppled over that gallery—by Savernake, with Miss Butler looking on. They tried to knock him out and kill him more quietly, but he put up a fight, and it was a near thing that Savernake didn't go with him. They were expecting him, of course—as soon as she heard he was going up there, she pretended to go to her room, but actually slipped up ahead of him to warn Savernake. James had taught him to use the lasso, you see, and it was he who was deputed to get the wireless out. Well, Butler was killed, and

Savernake took the wireless off, while Miss Butler waited in hiding for you, Mr. Peace, having conceived the idea of pinning the murder on you. But you didn't come. She slipped back to the clergy-house and found you talking to Spitshuker, so the second plan—the tomb-slab—had to be improvised."

"I suppose," said Peace to Fen, "that you thought of the plant in my room as the obvious sequel of the attempt to incriminate me."

"It seemed likely," said Fen mildly. "To leave the hypodermic was a mistake, though." He shook his pyjama-trousers free of a wasp. "But you see why I was so interested in two things: whether James had an alibi for the time of the faking (he had) and whether Peace had gone straight up to the cathedral when he left Spitshuker. Savernake, of course, I didn't know about at that time, but there was a certain amount of reason for suspecting James. Anyway, it was obvious that he couldn't have been concerned in the murder of Butler or the faking. Then I remembered that Peace left the clergy-house to go up to the cathedral *before* we returned there with Frances. To my mind that meant either that it *wasn't* Frances who played about with the organ and made the tomb-slab fall out, or else that you, Peace, somehow delayed on your way up to the cathedral, and enabled her to get there ahead of you. (I was a bit worried about whether it was *her* key you borrowed to get into the grounds, but fortunately it wasn't.) Of course, she must have got a frightful shock when she got back to the clergy-house with us and found you'd already gone; because you promised to wait and walk up with her when she got back. That was simply a means of keeping you *in situ* until she'd collected her witnesses. Savernake, of course, imagined when he left with the wireless that you were going to be there at 9:20 according to your arrangement with Butler, and so never returned. He just disposed of the wireless and provided himself with an alibi for the rest of the time. So she had to do everything herself. That was what made me think she must be the leader—no subordinate would have taken that amount of responsibility."

"It was an extraordinary chancy affair," said the Inspector reproachfully, as though Fen were somehow responsible for this.

"Certainly it was," said Fen a trifle irritably. "It was a rapidly improvised emergency scheme. Ten thousand things might have gone wrong. We might never have gone up to the cathedral at all. As it happened, it went more or less right. But, of course, it was the merest idiocy to attempt to incriminate the good Peace at all. I think something like personal malevolence may have been involved, to judge from what she said about you the other day in Butler's garden. Because there was no earthly reason why she shouldn't have left Butler lying where he was. As an accidental fall, it would have appeared improbable, because the parapet of the Bishop's Gallery is high, and because of what had already happened to Brooks. But it would have left the murderer in complete obscurity. It was the fatal desire to round things off by incriminating you, Peace, which did for the scheme—a plan much too hastily conceived not to have loop-holes all over it.

"Actually, the loop-holes made it all the more confusing. And I admit that (but for one point) my own processes of deduction were chancy, too. When you're dealing with a gang of unspecified dimensions they have to be. That's one reason why I hope this affair won't go into the Chronicles of Crispin.[1] Still," Fen went on indignantly, like one accused of some disgraceful negligence, "they weren't as chancy as all that. Once one had grasped the reason for the use of the tomb-slab, and the fact that someone had to be about to hear it fall, it became pretty clear. Spitshuker couldn't have been involved. Nor could Fielding, because he rescued you, Geoffrey, from being

[1] Vain hope.—E.C.

knocked out when it was most desirable that you should be. And that left Frances. She had no real alibi for the crucial times. She tried to make certain that you, Peace, didn't leave until she got back with us—another point. And the last confirmation was when I found out from McIver that there weren't more than three agents working here in all. I saw Savernake and James with my own eyes when they kidnapped me, suspecting I already knew too much. Both of them had alibis for the time of the faking, so that, again, left Frances."

"Some supplementary questions," put in Geoffrey. "Was the wireless found?"

"It had been taken to bits, sir," said the Inspector, "and hidden in various parts of the 'Whale and Coffin.' One of the women in the bar there, by the way, knew something was going on and cooperated with James, but didn't know what. We pulled her in. The stuff they used, materials for making keys to the tomb, atropine, radio parts and so on—must have been smuggled over here from Germany before the war." He gestured, as though in apology for making so elementary a point.

"That's another thing," said Geoffrey. "Why make keys to that tomb?"

"I got that from James," the Inspector replied. "In case of an invasion, it was to be filled with explosive and the whole cathedral blown sky-high, as a signal. Nasty, isn't it? You see, they had to get the stuff in there beforehand, since it had to be ready at a moment's notice, any hour of the day or night. But they hadn't started on that when the attack on Brooks was made, and afterwards, with the police guard and so on, it was impracticable." He smiled grimly. "The whole business is a very pleasant commentary on the celebrated German efficiency. A flop."

"You might remember," said Peace, "that I was nearly indicted for murder."

Fen took a cardboard box and emptied the dead bodies

of a number of insects out of the window. "I've finished with
these nasty things," he said. The butterfly-net, forgotten and
unused, stood in a corner. He glared at it for a moment, then
broke it across his knee; subsequently he deposited *Social Life
in the Insect World* in the waterjug. "Like Prospero," he
announced, "I have broken my staff and drowned my book."
He looked round complacently, but no one was paying much
attention.

"One thing more," said Geoffrey, "and that's about
Josephine and the Black Mass."

` "James disapproved of all that," the Inspector explained.
"The devil-worship business was a private toy of Miss Butler and
Savernake. Of course, sir"—turning to Fen—"it was Savernake
shot at you—in a panic, more or less."

Fen nodded. "I thought so. A recusant priest is supposed
traditionally to celebrate the Mass."

"As to drugging that kid," the Inspector went on, "and ini-
tiating her into their filthy goings on, I confess I can't understand it. Of course, she was useful as a tool—as in taking that
message to my men at the cathedral—but it seems to me most
of it was just sheer devilry."

"The manuscript had nothing to do with it, then?" Peace
asked.

"No," said Fen, "I think that was probably just a fit of
blind rage at being deprived of the stuff too long. It was given
her in cigarette form, you know. Marihuana generally is."

Peace sighed. His plump, red face was creased with
worry, and his grey eyes were sad. "It's going to be a business
looking after Irene," he said. "She wasn't very fond of Butler,
but Frances she loved. I'm taking her—and Josephine, when
she's better—under my own wing, you know. Of course the
money comes to me—not that I want it now."

"You might be able to explain these people's psychology
to us," Fen suggested.

"Not any longer," said Peace firmly. "I'm giving all that up and going into the Church."

They stared. "The Church!" they all exclaimed.

Peace seemed mildly hurt at their incredulity. "It seems the best way out of my doubts," he explained. "And I confess I've always thought the life attractive."

So there was no more to be said about that. But Fen was still worrying the question of psychology.

"James one can understand," he said. "He had a purely mercenary motive. Savernake, too—he was the superficially clever type to whom Fascism makes an immediate appeal. But Frances...she was in Germany, of course, but that doesn't mean anything. I suppose we shall never know now."

For the first time, Dallow spoke. "Isn't it possible, my de-ear Professor, that there may have been something in the blood?"

"What do you mean?"

"She was of Tolnbridge blood on her father's side—a very old family in these parts. And there were real witches here— they were not all Elizabeth Pulteneys. I always think"—he glanced apologetically at Peace—"that psychology is wrong in imagining that when it has analysed evil it has somehow disposed of it."

"Then she was—"

"Witches ally themselves with the forces of the Devil wherever, and however, they appear. It isn't just a matter of participating in the rites of Walpurgis Night, nor of killing the neighbour who has slandered you. There is political evil as well."

"She made her sister a witch," said Geoffrey.

"It has always been done. The mother initiates her daughter; neighbours, sisters, each other..."

There was a long silence.

"One thing struck me," said Fen at last, turning to Geoffrey. "Do you remember when she met us, just after seeing her own father killed?"

"Yes."

"Did anything particular strike you about her?"

"I thought she seemed happy."

"Yes. I think she was."

There was again silence. From the lawn below, where Garbin and Spitshuker were pacing together, fragments of argument floated up.

"It seems to me that when you insist on regarding the Old Testament simply as a historical record of the search of the Jewish people for God you are falling into the Marcionite heresy. Marcion…"

"You've made no attempt to answer my point about the literal interpretation of Genesis…"

"My dear Garbin…"

Towering beyond the garden stood the cathedral, restored again to quiet and worship, abandoned to the ghosts of Bishop John Thurston and Elizabeth Pulteney—*requiescant in pace!* The sky was clouding over, and a fresh wind presaged a gale later. But it was a clean, strong, cool wind.

Fen, who had finished packing, put on his raincoat and his extraordinary hat. "Come on, Geoffrey," he said. "We've got to catch this train, and we must look in on Fielding on the way. How is he, by the way?" he enquired of the Inspector.

"Better," said the Inspector. "That C.I.D. chap Phipps has been talking to him, and I think promised to try and get him some routine office job connected with the counter-espionage. He's not well enough to bounce about with joy yet, but he would if he could."

"Some people," said Fen, "simply never learn from experience." He moved towards the door.

"I still think," said Geoffrey, following him, "that as detection this business simply won't do."

Fen turned in the doorway. "It wouldn't but for one thing."

"Well?"

"You remember Spitshuker told us about Butler picking a four-leaf clover at the gate from the clergy-house garden into the cathedral grounds? After Butler had decided to go up to the cathedral, Frances, according to her own account, went straight up to her room. Even if she had looked out she couldn't have seen at that distance what her father was doing. And we know that he wasn't in the habit of wearing four-leaf clovers in his buttonhole. So when she met us and told us he was wearing one, do you see, that rather gummed up the works. If she knew he was wearing it, she must have been at the cathedral. And if she was at the cathedral she must—mustn't she?—have seen him die."

The Hangman's Song

The Hangman's Song

JAMES OSWALD

HarperCollins*Publishers*Ltd

HarperCollins Publishers Ltd
2 Bloor Street East, 20th Floor
Toronto, Ontario, Canada
M4W 1A8

www.harpercollins.ca

Library and Archives Canada Cataloguing in Publication
information is available upon request

ISBN 978-1-44344-111-7

Printed and bound in the United States of America
RRD 9 8 7 6 5 4 3 2 1

This one's for Zos, Dregs, Fergus, Felix
and of course
'Doctor' Eleanor Austin

1

'The important thing is to get the drop right. Nothing else matters, really.'

He stands on tippy-toes, balanced on the precarious chair, hands behind his back like a good boy. His fingers are trembling slightly, as if in anticipation, but he's not struggling. I knew he wouldn't. Not now. He wants this, after all.

'Of course, to work that out I need to know your height, your weight, your build.'

I tug at the rope. Good, stout hemp; none of that nylon rubbish for a job like this. Getting it over the beam was a struggle, but now it's secure, ready. His eyelids flutter as I slip the noose over his head, gently snug it around his neck past his ear, let the excess loop over his bare shoulder.

'Height? No, height is easy, as long as you're not wearing platform shoes. Clothes can be deceptive though, make a thin man seem fat. And then there's build.'

He doesn't respond, but then why would he? He's not here any more. I can see the movement of his eyes under closed lids, the flick, flick, flick as he watches something far off in his mind. I reach out, run the backs of my fingers down his cheek, his arm, the muscles of his taut stomach. He is young, so young. Barely a man yet and the world has already dragged him down. Young skin is so soft and pure, not corrupted by the cankers and blemishes of age. A pity the same cannot be said of young minds. They are so fragile, so hopeless.

'Muscle is so much denser than fat. A well-muscled physique will weigh more than a lazy body. It is essential to take that into account.'

The spirit shivers in me, drinking deep from the well of despair that fills this room. There is nothing here worth saving, only the joy of release from a life not worth living.

'A handshake is usually enough. You can tell so much from a person's hand, their grip. I knew as soon as I met you how long a piece of rope we would need.'

I let my hand drop lightly down, stroking him with my nails. He rises to the occasion, ever so slightly, a soft moan escaping from his lips as I reach in, cup his barely dropped testicles, tickle them with my fingertips. The touch is both exhilarating and revolting, as if some tawdry sex act could ever be as intimate as what we have, this man child and me.

He shivers, whether from cold or excitement I will never know. I withdraw my hand, take a step back. One second, two, the pressure builds as the spirit rises within me. I see the rope, the knot, the chair, the table. Clothes neatly folded and placed on the bed a few feet away.

There is a moment when I push the chair away. Anything is possible. He floats in the air like a hoverfly, trapped in that instant. And then he is falling, falling, falling, the loops of rope untwining in lazy, slow-motion rolls until nothing is left.

And then.

Snap.

2

'You sure about this, Tony?'

Detective Chief Inspector Jo Dexter sat in the passenger seat of the Transit van, staring out through a grubby windscreen at the industrial wasteland around Leith Docks. Street lights glowed in orange strings; roads to nowhere. The first tinge of dawn painted the undersides of the clouds, marching north and east across the Forth to Fife. The high-rises that had sprung up along the northern shoreline were dark silhouettes pocked by the occasional light of a shift-worker coming home. This early in the morning there wasn't much activity, least of all from the dark bulk of the freighter they were watching. It had docked two days ago, a routine trip from Rotterdam bringing in aggregates for the new road bridge. As if they didn't have enough rock and sand in Scotland already. A team had been watching around the clock ever since, acting on information thought to be reliable. Beyond the unloading of a large quantity of gravel, nothing interesting had happened at all.

'According to Forth Ports, she sails on the tide. In about two hours' time.' Detective Inspector Anthony McLean checked his watch, even though the clock on the dashboard told him it was almost five in the morning. 'If nothing happens before then, we've been played for fools. I dare say it won't be the first time.'

'Easy for you to say. You're not the one having to justify the overtime.'

McLean looked across at his companion. He'd known Jo Dexter of old. She'd joined up at the same time as him, but had hit the promotion ladder early. McLean was happy for her, though he preferred his own niche; a career of chasing prostitutes and pornographers had hardened Jo Dexter's once pretty features so that she looked far older than her thirty-nine years. Vice did that to a person, he'd been told. And now he was finding out first hand thanks to bloody Dagwood.

'Well, you're the one reckoned the tip-off was good.' The temperature dropped by several degrees. Even in the darkness, McLean could see that this was the wrong thing to say, no matter how true it was. The letter had appeared in his in-tray on the first day of his secondment to Jo Dexter's team in the Sexual Crimes Unit. It didn't have a stamp on it, and no one knew how it had got there. Nevertheless, the information in it showed that whoever had written it knew a great deal about the sleazy underbelly of Edinburgh's sex industry, and the final nugget had concerned a highly organized people-smuggling operation and this very ship.

'It's just that normally these things happen in container ports. How the hell do you smuggle people off a boat like that without being seen?'

'Your guess is as good as mine.' McLean switched his focus away from his temporary boss, across the empty yard to where a large box van had appeared at the security gate. After a short pause, the guard let it through. It continued its slow journey around the seemingly random

4

piles of rocks, sand and other unidentified materials that were the port's stock-in-trade, headed in the general direction of the ship.

McLean picked up his radio set, called the guardhouse. 'Who was that?'

'Catering firm. Provisions for the ship's galley. Guess they've got to eat, aye?' The guard sounded bored. Hardly surprising given his shift.

'They check out OK?' McLean asked.

'On the roster, aye.'

'OK then. Keep your eyes peeled for anything unusual.' He put the radio back on the dashboard as the box van arrived at the ship's side. In the semi-darkness, with nothing to compare it to other than the distant buildings, the ship had seemed small. Now with the van alongside, McLean could see just how big it was, high in the water without its ballast of rock.

'You think they might try something here?' Jo Dexter stretched as best she could in the confined space. She'd have been better off in the back, were it not for the half-dozen officers already in there, snoring gently.

McLean picked up the binoculars he'd appropriated from stores earlier that day, focused on the box van as the driver got out. A single lamp lit the steps leading up from the dockside to the deck, casting more shadow than anything else.

'Even if we weren't here watching, nothing gets out of this bit of the port without the excise boys checking it. There's no way they'd be able to smuggle anyone out unless they'd paid somebody off.'

'Stranger things have happened, Tony. What can you see?'

The driver opened up the back of the van and clambered into the darkness. After a moment he jumped back out again, grabbed a box and carried it up the steps. At least that's what McLean assumed he'd done. The way the van was parked, it obscured the foot of the steps, and the top was in shadow. Only a small part in the middle was visible, and by the time he'd adjusted the focus, the driver was gone.

'A man unloading groceries, by the look of it. Yup. There he goes again.' Movement at the back of the van, and the driver once more grabbed a box, heading for the steps. McLean flicked the binoculars up a fraction, and caught a fleeting glimpse of someone before the darkness swallowed them. It wasn't much, but there was something wrong. He couldn't put his finger on it; the way the driver moved, perhaps?

A moment later and the figure passed across his view again, heading up the steps with a baker's tray in its hands. But that couldn't be right, could it? How had he missed the driver coming back down the steps? Unless there were two people in the van. That would make more sense anyway.

Another figure cut across the narrow pool of light, this time carrying a large cardboard box, struggling under its weight and bulk. McLean squinted through the binoculars, wishing the magnification was better. This figure seemed different from the first and second. There couldn't be three people working the van, could there? And how much in the way of provisions did a cargo ship need to make the crossing from Leith to Rotterdam?

Dropping the binoculars back onto the seat, McLean

started the engine, slammed the Transit into gear and shot forwards. Beside him, Jo Dexter grabbed for the handle above the door, too stunned to say anything.

'Not smuggling them in. Taking them out. Wake up you lot. It's time to go to work.' McLean shouted to the team in the back. A couple of muffled grunts and a high-pitched yelp were all the answer he got as he accelerated as hard as he could, covering the distance to the ship in less than a minute. The back of the box van was open, and as he swept round behind it, the Transit's headlights threw aside the shadows, revealing what was inside.

'Go! Go! Go!' The team burst out of the back of the Transit, fanning out and securing the van. A commotion up on deck was followed by a shout of 'Armed police. Drop your weapons.' McLean and Dexter watched from the Transit as a large cardboard box fell from above, twisting once, twice, before smashing against the concrete of the dock in an explosion of oranges.

It was over in seconds. The sergeant in charge of the armed-response team came over to the Transit and signalled the all clear. McLean didn't need to hear it; he could see with his own eyes. Out of the back of the box van they began to clamber into the light. Pale, almost cadaverous some of them, scantily clad despite the cold and all bearing that same terrified expression. A dozen or more young women, no more than girls, really, though their faces showed they'd seen more than any girl their age should ever see.

'Well, that's not quite what I was expecting.'

McLean leaned back against the cool concrete wall

7

outside the back of the station, watching as the last of the young women was escorted into the station. Dawn had already painted the overcast sky in oranges and purples, promising rain for later on. A quick glance at his watch showed that it was almost shift-change time. Not that he worked shifts any more.

'Not what I was expecting, either.' Jo Dexter pulled deeply on the cigarette, held the smoke for just long enough for it to do its worst, then let it spill upwards as she let her head clunk lightly against the wall. 'Remind me about that tip-off again?'

The letter. McLean reached into his jacket pocket and pulled out the photocopy the forensics team had given him. He knew that they'd not managed to lift anything from the original, but he still wasn't allowed to have it back. It didn't matter, the words were still the same. Date, time, place, ship name, it was all there. He even had a suspicion he knew who had sent it, but it wasn't a suspicion he cared to share. He tapped the edge of the folded-up paper against his hand.

'It all checked out. You know that as well as I do, otherwise we'd never have got this lot authorized.' He nodded at the Transit van as the last of the armed-response team jangled back into the station, Kevlar body armour unstrapped and dangling.

'You're right. I thought it was legit. But this? Trafficking prostitutes away from the city? Taking them to Rotterdam and then God only knows where.' Dexter shook her head, sucked once more on the cigarette as if the answer might be in there somewhere. The smoke billowing out into the lightening air gave up no answers.

'I . . .' McLean began, but was interrupted by his phone buzzing in his pocket. It had been on silent all through the stake-out and arrests. A quick scan of the screen showed an instantly recognized number. Dexter must have read something from the expression on his face, said nothing as he took the call. It wasn't a long one, not even time enough for her to finish her cigarette.

'Bad news?' she asked through a haze of smoke.

'Not sure. I have to go.' He saw the scowl forming on Dexter's face. 'Won't be long. It's just . . . I have to go.' And he scurried off before she could stop him.

3

McLean didn't even wait for Doctor Wheeler to greet him, just started off down the corridor and expected her to keep up. He'd known her what . . . almost six months? Quiet, competent and impossibly young for someone with such a detailed knowledge of the human brain, she had given him hope that Emma would recover eventually, promised to let him know as soon as anything happened.

And now something had.

The guilt had been there ever since her abduction, when poor, mad Sergeant Needham had smashed her over the head, and all because he'd let Emma get close to him. He'd visited her every day, even if it was sometimes only for five minutes. He'd watched her, as he'd watched his grandmother before, wasting away bit by bit, her mind somewhere else, her body kept alive by machines. Day after day, the hope being ground away like a mountain succumbing to the onslaught of weather. Slow, but inexorable. He'd been steeling himself, rebuilding the walls that she'd been the first in a decade to breach. Hardening himself for the time when he'd have to bury another.

But something had happened.

'You said on the phone there'd been a change?'

'Indeed there has, Inspector. But you mustn't get your hopes up. She's still unconscious.'

The route to the ward was imprinted on McLean's

memory, but he still had to run the gamut of patients out and about, trailing drips on wheeled stands or revealing more flesh than it was comfortable to see through skimpy backless gowns. Even though it felt like he'd spent half of his life in them, he still couldn't get used to hospitals; their smell of disinfectant, bodily fluids and despair. The institutional beige walls didn't help, and neither did the bizarre collection of artworks hung along the corridors. No doubt chosen by some psychotherapist with a view to creating the optimum healing environment. Either that or a six-year-old child.

'Unconscious is not the same as in a coma though. She's going to come round soon.' Was that a desperate hope in his voice, or just weary resignation?

'I believe so. Yes. And yes, you're right, unconscious isn't the same as coma. The brainwave patterns are different for a start. There's more happening. She's shifting to something more akin to sleep.'

They had reached the door to the ward, but before McLean could push on through, the doctor reached out and stopped him.

'Inspector . . . Tony. You need to face up to the fact that there could be permanent damage. There almost certainly will be permanent damage.'

'I know. But this happened because of me. I'm not going to abandon her now.' McLean was about to open the door when it pulled away from him of its own accord. A startled nurse stood on the other side.

'Oh, Doctor. I was just coming to look for you. The patient's started talking. I think she might be about to wake up.'

Just like McLean's grandmother had been for the eighteen months it had taken her body to die, Emma was surrounded by the machinery that kept her alive. She had been propped upright, her shrunken form pale even against the white pillows of the hospital bed, her unruly mop of black, spiky hair tamed by some well-meaning nurse, far longer than she would ever have worn it. As he approached, McLean could see the change in her in an instant. Her eyes fluttered under eyelids, twitches in her face almost reminding him of her mischievous smile, then creasing into a frown. And all the while she muttered, quiet whimpers of terror. He was about to take her hand as he had done every day since she'd been brought here, but before he could, Doctor Wheeler once more stopped him.

'Best to wait just now. A touch could bring her out too quickly. Let her come at her own pace.'

'What's happening to her? She looks scared.'

'Difficult to be sure, but she's probably reliving the last few moments before she was knocked out.' Doctor Wheeler consulted the clipboard at the end of the bed, then pulled a pager out of her pocket. McLean hadn't even heard it ping. 'Gotta go. I'll check back as soon as I can.'

It was a special kind of hell, sitting there, watching the emotions skim across Emma's face, wondering what it was that Needy had done to her. Just the bash to the skull, or had there been something more? McLean found it hard to recall the events clearly himself. Too much smoke inhalation and blows to his own head. Too much dealing with the past he thought he'd finished with but which didn't want to let him go.

'Oh my god. No.'

The voice was barely more than a whisper, but it was hers. McLean looked around to see if any of the nurses in the ward had noticed. They were busy with the other patients and their machines. He reached out, about to take Emma's hand where it lay on the covers, fingers flexing minutely. Before he could, she drew her hand away.

'No, no, no, no. No!' Louder now, and Emma started to shake. Her heart rate monitor pinged a warning, but still the nurses were oblivious. McLean went to stand, meaning to get some help, but a tiny hand whipped out and grabbed him by the wrist, surprisingly tight. He snapped his head around as Emma sat bolt upright, eyes wide open.

'It took their souls. Trapped them all. They were lost. I was lost.'

And then the grip was gone. Her eyes flipped up into her head and she dropped back into the pillows. McLean could only watch as the nurses gathered around, alerted by the motion. He couldn't move, could only stare at Emma's face as they bustled around her, checking monitors, adjusting drips, whispering urgent messages to each other. Did this happen whenever a patient woke from coma? Was there some procedure they followed?

Slowly, the commotion died down. Everything that could be checked had been checked. The patient was asleep, heart rate steady. It was going to be OK. Everything was going to be fine. Still he sat and watched, oblivious to the passing of time. Minutes, hours, he didn't really care. This was his fault, after all. He wasn't going to shirk that responsibility. Not now. Not ever.

She woke more slowly the second time; colour coming back to her cheeks as her breathing changed from deep and regular to shallow and swift. Her eyes opened slowly, a hand reaching up to her head as if feeling for the damage that had been inflicted. Then she noticed the tube taped to her arm, the needle.

'It's OK,' McLean said, hoping to fend off the panic with a familiar face and voice. 'You're in hospital. You've been unconscious.'

Emma slowly rolled over, her head too heavy for the wasted muscles in her neck to control. She squinted against the light, even though it was muted in the ward, and it took her a while to focus on him. Even longer for her to speak. He'd hoped for a smile, but was rewarded only with a frown. Her voice, when it finally came, was cracked and dry. The words as terrible as they were inevitable.

'Who are you?'

4

'We've got sixteen girls who between them seem to speak about eight words of English, a Dutch captain screaming blue murder, Leith Ports chewing my ear off about a freighter that was meant to leave at dawn, and you go running off just because of a phone call. Jesus Christ, Tony. No bloody wonder Dagwood wanted shot of you. Five hours you've been gone. What took so bloody long?'

Jo Dexter stood in the middle of the main room housing the Sexual Crimes Unit, arms folded across her front. She looked as if she'd been waiting for McLean to come home, like an errant child. Any moment now she was going to start tapping her foot.

'It's Emma. She's woken up. I had to be there. Sorry.'

'Shit. There you go again. I can't even give you a proper bollocking, can I?' The DCI slumped back against an unused desk, dropped her hands to her sides. The room was almost empty, just a couple of PCs on the back shift manning the hotline phones and pretending they weren't playing Words with Friends on the vice squad special computers; the ones that weren't blocked from the worst of the internet. 'How is she?'

'It's . . . complicated.' McLean pictured the scene in his mind. That face he had watched for almost two months now, suddenly come back to life only to be covered with confusion and fear. 'She doesn't remember anything. Well, apart from her name.'

'You need time?' McLean could see that Dexter really didn't want him to say yes. Like everyone else, they were permanently short-staffed. That was why he was here, after all.

'No. She's going to be in the hospital a while yet. Think I'd rather throw myself into the job right now. Otherwise I'm just going to fret.'

'Fine. Well, you and DS Buchanan can make a start on processing these girls then. We can't keep them in the cells much longer. Immigration'll be here soon, and I'd like to find out who put them on that ship before they get here.'

'Why were they taking you onto that boat? Where were you going?'

McLean sat at the table in interview room one, the nice one where they put people who were 'helping the police with their enquiries' rather than the more skanky holes where the low-lifes were questioned. Opposite him, the young woman stared at her hands, folded in her lap. Her long blonde hair had a natural curl to it that was almost hidden by the layers of grease and grime. Her face was thinner than a supermodel's, sharp cheek bones poking out through skin the colour of curdled milk. Her eyes were sunken pits, the traces of bruising yellowing them like some weird attempt at alternative make-up. He was fairly sure she understood everything he was saying, but like all her companions from the van, she was playing the silent act.

'Were you trying to get home, was that it?'

She looked up at him then, fixed him with a stare from her grey-blue eyes that left no doubt as to just how much of an idiot she thought him. Still she didn't speak, scratching at the inside of her left elbow with the long fingernails of her right hand. The track marks were easy to see, but old.

'Look, I know you speak English. I know you've been working as a prostitute somewhere in the city. I know that probably wasn't your idea. You thought you were coming here to get a job cleaning, or maybe working in an office. But the men who brought you here had other ideas, didn't they.'

Alongside him, Detective Sergeant Buchanan shifted in his seat impatiently. McLean tried to suppress a grimace, but something must have shown on his face. The girl looked straight at him, flicked her eyes across to the other detective and back again, then raised both eyebrows. It was the briefest of interactions, but it was the most he'd got out of any of them so far. Eight down, seven still to go.

'You couldn't get us some coffee could you, Sergeant?' McLean voiced it as a question but even the dumbest of officers should have realized that it was a command. Buchanan opened his mouth as if to say something, then closed it again with an echoing pop. He dragged his chair backwards as he stood, the noise setting McLean's teeth on edge. Ambled slowly to the door and paused before opening it.

'Black, no sugar for me.' McLean tried not to flick his head in a gesture of dismissal, but he might have failed a little.

17

Buchanan left the door open. Whether on purpose or because he lacked the basic motor skills to close it, McLean didn't want to guess. He got up, closed it, and sat back down again. The young woman said nothing, but her eyes followed him all the time. Only when he was back in his seat did she finally speak.

'You're not like the others. I've not seen you before.'

Her voice surprised him. He had assumed she was from Eastern Europe, but she spoke with a Midlands accent.

'I'm on secondment. Filling in while they decide who gets to be promoted.'

'You must have fucked up pretty badly to get sent here. What did you do?'

What did I do? My job. Only it was bloody Dagwood who got made up to acting superintendent when we broke open that cannabis operation, and he didn't want anyone around pissing on his chips. McLean kept silent, studied the young woman's face for a moment, trying to see past the Slavic features that had made him jump to such an erroneous conclusion earlier on.

'The other girls. They from England too?'

'Nah. Most of em's Poles, Romanians, think I might've heard some Russian spoke too. Don't really know them that well. We only got picked up a couple days ago.'

'Picked up?'

'There an echo in here?' The young woman pushed back her greasy hair, scratched at the side of her nose, sniffed. For an awful moment McLean thought she was going to spit on the floor, but she swallowed instead. He wasn't sure which was worse.

'There were sixteen of you in that van, being loaded onto a ship bound for Rotterdam. Normally we have to deal with people coming the other way. I'm curious as to why you were being trafficked out of the country.'

'You not even going to ask my name?'

'Would you tell it me if I did?'

'It's Magda. And yeah, I know that's Polish. My grampa came over in the war and never went back.'

'So what's the score then, Magda? Why were you being sent overseas?'

'Cos I speak Polish, probably. Cos of the way I look. Mebbe they thought I was like all the others. Mebbe I tried to tell them and got a smack in the face for my trouble. Mebbe they didn't care who I was. Long as they get the numbers.'

'Numbers for what, though? Where were they taking you?'

Magda gave him an odd, quizzical look, as if she couldn't quite believe what she was hearing.

'You know I'm a whore, don't you? You know what that is, y'know, apart from the whole sex for cash thing?'

McLean didn't answer. He wasn't quite sure he could.

'Means I'm a piece of meat, dunnit. Owned and traded. I get passed from one pimp to the next and I don't get any say in that. Who'm I gonna complain to anyway, the filth? Ha, that's a laugh. You lot either don't give a fuck or just want a free one. I got no rights, no protection. Just a habit needs feeding and only one way to feed it. So when Malky says I'm going with Ivan now, I don't argue. Cos what's the fucking point, eh?'

'You don't know where they were taking you.'

'Top marks for the inspector.' Magda clapped her hands together in mock applause. For a moment something like the ghost of a smile spread across her face, and then the door clicked open. DS Buchanan appeared, arse first, carrying two mugs of coffee. By the time he'd turned around and placed the mugs on the table, Magda's face was blank, eyes down, staring at the hands folded in her lap, fingers worrying at the scars of track marks on her inner arms. It was almost as if the whole conversation had been no more than a dream.

'Thanks. Not having one yourself?' McLean picked up the mug with black coffee in it, nudging the other one carefully across the table to Magda. Buchanan opened his mouth, looked at the two mugs, then shut it again. He pulled out his chair and sat down heavily.

'You don't know where they were taking you.' McLean tried to pick up the threads of the conversation, even though he knew he was in for a struggle. 'But you know who took you. Who's Malky, Magda? Who's Ivan?'

Buchanan looked sideways at McLean as he spoke the young woman's name, a quizzical eyebrow raised. McLean wondered if he could find some other way to send the sergeant away. He was clearly not helping.

'Malky'd be Malky Jennings. Typical lowlife scumbag runs a dozen hookers out of Restalrig.'

Maybe helping a bit. 'Go on,' McLean said.

'He's small beer. We usually let him get away with a caution if he pushes too far. Known quantity, if you get my meaning. We lock him up and who knows what'll float up to take his place. He has his uses.' Meaning he was someone's informant. Or supplier.

'And Ivan?' McLean directed his question at Buchanan, but looked at Magda. He couldn't catch her eye though; she was finding her lap increasingly fascinating, those marks on her inner arm more itchy by the minute.

'Ivan, I haven't a fucking clue.'

'Magda, who's Ivan?' McLean let the question hang in the silence that followed, just watching the young woman across the table. She kept her gaze down for long seconds, the only sound the scrit, scrit, scrit of her fingernails on the flesh of her inner arm. She'd be breaking through soon, adding to the scars already there. Perhaps finally realizing what she was doing, she stopped, raised her head and fixed him with a stare through her lank blonde ringlets. There was something more than anger and defiance in that stare. There was fear. And then the quickest of flicks across to the detective sergeant and back. Then she dropped her head and said no more.

'Tell me about Malky Jennings.'

McLean leaned against the wall by the whiteboard in the SCU main office, looking out over a cluster of empty desks. The blinds were drawn on the windows at the far side of the room, slants of sunlight painting stripes onto the grubby carpet tiles. This wasn't a place people generally liked to spend much time in; you never knew what new degradation or atrocity was going to appear next.

'Not much to tell, really. Scumbag just about sums it up.' DS Buchanan lounged in the one good chair in the office, feet up on his desk. Observing the small team at the SCU in the few days since he'd arrived, McLean recognized the Alpha Dog, or, perhaps more accurately, the frustrated Beta Dog, lording it over the junior ranks but never quite having the nerve to challenge for the top spot. He was an old-school copper, which in the case of Grumpy Bob was a good thing; less so with Buchanan. Where DS Laird affected an air of laziness but got the work done, Buchanan was the kind of policeman who always seemed busy, but was actually doing bugger all.

'We got a file on him?'

'Should have.' Buchanan made a show of taking his feet off the desk, pulled his keyboard towards him and started tapping away. McLean pushed himself off the wall and came around to see what appeared on the screen.

'Malcolm Jeffrey Jennings.' Buchanan poked a greasy finger at the glass. 'Thirty-six years old. Lives in one of the tower blocks down Lochend way. He's got form for drugs, but strictly small time. Mostly he runs prostitutes in that area. Nasty little shit. Violent, but he's bright enough not to hit them in the face. Prefers a baseball bat to the ribs, way I hear it.'

McLean peered at the image on the screen. A thin, ratty-faced man peered back. Narrow, long nose, broken sometime long ago. Hair in lank, greasy straggles down to his shoulders. Eyes set just that little bit too close together, giving his face a permanent angry frown. Deep bags under them suggesting some form of habit, barely under control.

'And we tolerate this why?'

Buchanan sighed, clicked the cursor on a series of thumbnail images taken by a surveillance team. The first showed Malky Jennings walking along a street with a woman beside him. McLean hadn't noticed in the mug shot, but Jennings liked to dress flamboyantly. Not necessarily with any sense of style, but the purple velvet smoking jacket and ruff-necked shirt were certainly noticeable.

'Malky's a known quantity. We keep an eye on him, haul him in if he gets too far out of line. But there's no point locking him up. He's not the problem.'

McLean scanned the top of the list of convictions and cautions. 'He looks like a big problem to me.'

Buchanan snorted. 'You're new here, so you wouldn't understand.'

'No, I don't. Explain it to me.'

'OK then.' Buchanan put on his best school teacher voice. 'Malky Jennings is a scumbag, but one whose behaviour we can predict, possibly even control to a certain extent. Lock him up and someone else moves in on the territory. Someone we don't know anything about, maybe. Someone trying to make a name for themselves, establish their place. That means violence and disruption, and that makes the Chief Constable unhappy. So we leave Malky Jennings well alone.'

'Lesser of two evils.' McLean understood the concept, but that didn't mean he had to like it.

'Now you're getting it.'

'There's just one thing you seem to be missing though. This Russian fellow, Ivan or whatever. He's a new player, right?'

Buchanan nodded. 'Looks like it.'

'And he's taken a whole load of Malky's prostitutes, put them on a boat headed for the Continent and God knows where after that.'

23

Again with the nod. McLean could almost see the thoughts linking themselves together in Buchanan's head.

'So at the very least we need to talk to Jennings and see what's going on, wouldn't you think? Bring him in and let's make him sweat a bit. If we're giving him our tacit approval, then he can bloody well give us something back in return.'

5

'Is that a genuine weejy board? Christ, I thought those things went out in the seventies.'

She's not the prettiest girl he's ever met, but there's something about her he finds impossibly attractive. Maybe it's her hair, cut like his mum would have had it back when she was that age. Or perhaps it's her easy smile. Not a 'come and get me, boys' flash of the teeth, but a selfless sharing of genuine joy. She's always happy, and that's so rare. It's almost infectious, though it would take more than a winning smile to lighten his mood these days.

Of course, it helps that she's weird. Everyone loves weird.

The evening started well. Just a few of them out for a drink after work, winding down at the end of another shitty week. Some lucky bastard's leaving do, otherwise he'd not have bothered. He's not a big drinker – can't afford it – but there's a certain sad fun to be had watching the girls slowly lose control. He's not interested in exploiting their drunkenness for anything so tawdry as sex; that's not his style at all. What would be the point, anyway? He's still got to work with them, day in, day out. Most of them think he's gay, and he's never really bothered to correct them on that. It's not true, of course, but women seem to be far more comfortable around a gay man.

And then they'd met this strange, mad, intoxicating

woman. He wasn't really sure whose friend she was, or whether she'd simply attached herself to their party. She reminded him of someone, but he couldn't put his finger on the name. Every time he thought he'd got it, she'd caught him looking at her and flashed him a knowing smile. And every time he looked into her eyes it was as if his brain switched off and had to reboot.

Someone had suggested going to a club, but no one was keen. There were pubs that stayed open pretty much all night, but they'd had enough of pubs. Like him, she was on soft drinks anyway. He'd noticed that and she'd noticed that he'd noticed. They'd shared a smile then. And she'd suggested they all come back to her place.

Put like that it sounded corny. A come-on, but not a come-on. Not unless she was hoping to have an orgy with all five of them. That was his nervousness showing through, to think about sex at a time like that. Of course, sex was the furthest thing from her mind, this strange, intoxicating woman. She wanted something different from them. A séance.

'Automatic writing has been a favourite of mediums for thousands of years.' She lays the board out on the table, places the planchette in the centre. He can't help noticing that this isn't an ancient artefact. The wood is shiny with varnish, not age, and the letters are clearly machine-stencilled. The company logo 'Hasbro' in tiny letters in one corner is a bit of a giveaway.

'It's not the board, silly. It's what's going on in your head.' She smiles again, slaps him gently on the arm. That's something else he's noticed about her. She likes to touch. A light brushing of the fingers here, a firm hand on the arm there. It's almost as if she doesn't know she's doing it. He doesn't think the others have noticed, anyway. But then they're all half cut, tucking into the bottle of wine she found in the cupboard under the sink in her kitchen.

'OK then. What are we meant to do?'

'First we all need to sit in a circle and hold hands. Here.' She holds out her left hand to him, fixes him with a stare that can't be denied. Before he knows it, he's in her grip, with Mandy from Accounts on his other side. The others all join together too, without any of the joking and complaints he would have expected. An expectant hush falls on the gathering.

'Spirits from the other side, hear our call. We have questions and seek your wisdom.'

Is it his imagination, or is the room just that little bit colder? And were the corners of the room always so dark and shadowy? Did they always move like that?

'Come to us, spirits. Answer our call. Is there anybody out there?'

The planchette, shaped like a tiny wooden heart with a hole hacked through the middle of it, moves slowly across the board. Scrape, scrape, scrape of wood against wood as it inches towards the circle marked 'Yes'. He stares at it for long moments before realizing that none of them are touching it. He looks sideways at her, unable to break the bond that links them all together in their circle. For the first time since he was a wee boy waking in the darkness of the middle of the night, he feels genuine fear. She is hunched over, her eyes squeezed tight shut, her lips moving as if she is speaking some silent language. It's impossible

27

to shake the feeling that there is something in the room with them. Some*one.*

Too late, he realizes that there is. Looming out of the shadows on the far side of the circle. Only there is no circle now, no weird, happy, smiley girl. No Ouija board. Just him and a face with eyes of fire. A devil's grin splits in two, all teeth and sharp, pointed tongue, lips as red as fresh-spilled blood. It speaks a voice from far away and long ago. A voice that opens up the darkest depths of his soul, lays bare his hopelessness and despair.

'You are mine.'

6

Against all the odds, there was a parking space just a few yards away from the front door to Emma's tenement. McLean had picked her up from the hospital earlier; with her mother in a care home in Aberdeen, there was no one else to do it, and he couldn't face the thought of her taking a taxi. Given the way she'd looked out the window all the way across town, it was probably just as well. He was reminded of a small child on her first visit to the big city. Eyes wide at each new wonder, mouth hanging ever-so-slightly open.

'Is this it?' she asked as he parked the car and killed the engine. No spark of recognition at all.

'Yup. This is it. You've been renting it since you came down from Aberdeen about eighteen months ago, remember?'

She looked along the street, eyes gliding over her own front door as if it meant no more to her than any other. 'Nope.'

'Well, let's go inside. See if you recognize your stuff.'

Emma had been skinny to start with, but two months on a drip had left her skeletally thin, and weak with it. The hospital had tried their best since she'd woken; regular physiotherapy sessions and the stodgiest food McLean had seen since his school days, but still she moved like someone twice her age. He had to suppress the urge to put his arm out and help her. That, he had already learnt, just pissed her off. Some things were still the same about her, he was pleased to see.

'This one.' He pointed at the door she was about to walk past. 'Here.'

He dug the keys out of his jacket pocket and handed them over. The little plastic gnome hung from the key ring, its hair a bright pink shock of colour. She looked at it with the same intense fascination she'd shown on the journey over, but showed no interest in the keys.

'This is mine?'

McLean nodded.

'I have no recollection of it at all. Did I buy it? Did someone give it to me? Did you give it to me?' With this last question Emma stared at his face, examining his features in a way that McLean found deeply disturbing. It was a look he knew well. One he had used in many an interrogation over the years. She even left the silence hanging, waiting for him to fill it and condemn himself with the answer.

'Not guilty, your honour.' He held up his hands in denial. 'Are you going in or not?'

Emma frowned in confusion for a moment, then seemed to notice the bunch of keys hanging from the fascinating key ring. 'Oh. Right.' Pause. 'Umm. Which one is it?'

It had been like this for almost three weeks now. Doctor Wheeler felt that Emma was improving all the time, but McLean couldn't see it. Yes, there were occasional flashes of the old Em, but mostly there was this uncomfortable, awkward person who didn't seem to know much about anything at all. She had latched on to him with such an intensity that at first he'd thought it was something of their relationship coming back. But as the days had passed and he'd done all he could to help her recuperate, so he'd begun to suspect that she clung to him because his was the first face she'd seen on waking. Even now there were times when he caught her staring at him with something closer to fear than anything else. She didn't treat him like an equal, didn't act like an adult. It was almost as if the blow to her head had regressed her to a child.

'Here, let me.' He reached for the keys. She shrunk away from him, just a little, then realized what she was doing and checked herself. Almost reluctantly she handed over the key ring, fingers clinging to the little gnome as he pulled it away. He selected the right key, slid it in the lock and opened the door.

Inside was dark. What little light that could make it through the grimy window halfway up the stairs was swallowed up by a large, dead pot plant on the windowsill. McLean had been here a couple of times a week since Emma had been taken to hospital, checking her mail and making sure the flat was OK. In all that time he'd never seen the plant watered and only now it occurred to him that this might be because it was hers. She paused on the stairs as they passed it, feeling a leafy frond between bony fingers. For a moment he thought it might be sparking a memory, but she just shook her head and moved on.

She didn't recognize her front door, and when he pushed it open to let her into the apartment, she hesitated on the threshold, peering in as if expecting monsters. McLean stepped inside and reluctantly Emma followed. If this was meant to start the process of bringing back her

31

memories, as the good doctor had suggested, then it didn't seem to be working.

'I'll make some tea.' He left her standing in the hallway. 'Why don't you have a look around. I've done my best to keep the place clean and tidy.'

'You said I rented this place.' Emma had followed him into the tiny kitchen and now stood close as he filled the kettle. 'Who's been paying the rent whilst I was . . . you know?'

'Don't worry. It was all taken care of.'

'I must owe you a lot of money.'

The assumption that he'd paid for it all was correct, but it surprised him she'd made it nonetheless. Technically she was on sick pay and there were damages due for being injured in the line of duty. Either the Scenes Examination Branch or the police should have been picking up the tab, but in the end he'd just taken it on himself. It was much easier than waiting for the internal bureaucracy to run its course, and it wasn't as if he couldn't afford it.

'It's not a problem. You've got to get better first.' The kettle popped off, steam billowing out into the frigid air. The whole apartment was cold, now he thought about it. Tucked down in a narrow street, away from the sun. Perhaps he should have had the heating on.

'I knew there was something I should have got. Milk.' McLean opened the fridge in the hope that magic pixies might have put some there, but they were on holiday this week. 'You mind your tea black?'

'Not much of a tea drinker, really.' Emma stepped back into the hall, pulled open the bathroom door and peered in. 'So this is where I live, then?'

'Yup.'

'What about you?' She closed the door, turned to face him with a stare that was almost the old Emma. Almost, but not quite. 'You live here too?'

McLean felt a reddening about his ears and wasn't quite sure why. 'No. I live over the other side of town.'

'But you and me. We were . . .'

'Yes. Not for long, but . . . Yes.'

'That's so weird.' She opened the bedroom door, paused a moment and then darted in, grabbed the stuffed animal toy off the bed, hugged it to herself. 'Potamus! I remember him. Mum bought him for me when I was eight. Christ, that feels like it was just a couple of years ago.'

She kept the stuffed hippo with her as they moved into the living room. The largest room in the apartment, it was filled with mementos, books, photographs. As far as McLean was aware, even the furniture had moved down from Aberdeen with her, so if anything was going to jog her memory, this should. Emma stood in the middle of the room, looking slowly around. Then she noticed the low bookshelf by the window, its top lined with photos in frames. She picked one up, showing herself and a bunch of young women McLean didn't recognize, peered at it, shook her head and set it back down again. The same routine went for all the others until finally she got to the one of her mother.

Grey-haired and frail, the old lady slumped in a high-backed armchair that looked too big for her. She wasn't smiling, wasn't even looking at the camera properly. Something in her eyes had died long before the photograph was taken. McLean only recognized her because he'd travelled

33

up to Aberdeen to introduce himself, try somehow to explain to Mrs Baird what had happened to her daughter and assure her that he'd do everything in his power to speed her recovery. What he had found had been a husk, a 65-year-old body with no mind. Emma had told him her mother was in a care home; what she'd failed to mention was the severity of her dementia.

'This looks like my gran, only different.' Emma placed the photograph back down on the bookshelf, one finger caressing the glass as she slowly turned away. 'It's my mum, isn't it?'

'She's had Alzheimer's for seven years. She's getting the best care possible.'

'Why don't I remember any of this? The last thing I remember about Mum is talking to her about going to college. I was seventeen. I don't even know how old I am now.'

'Do you really want me to tell you?'

Emma walked across to the mantelpiece and stared at her reflection in the mirror hanging over it. 'No. It'll just depress me. Why can't I remember?'

'It'll come back. Give it time. Doctor Wheeler said . . .'

'I know what Doctor Wheeler said. But she doesn't have to live with it, does she?' Emma swept one arm around in an arc encompassing the room. 'She doesn't have to live in a place filled with stuff I don't remember buying. Or worse, photographs of people twenty years older than I remember them.'

'You want to go somewhere else? I've got a spare room. You're more than welcome.' The words tumbled out before he'd really considered them. It sounded almost like he was asking her to move in with him. The thought filled him with conflicting feelings; hope and despair. And guilt. There was always guilt.

Emma took one more slow look at the living room, eyes finally settling on him with a desperate stare. 'Please.'

It took almost an hour to get across town, fighting the traffic chaos caused by the construction work for the trams. By the time the car crunched over the gravel and came to a halt at the back door, the afternoon was almost gone. McLean was grateful that Jo Dexter had given him the time off, but sooner or later someone was going to phone him and drag him back to the station.

'Just the one spare room?' Emma asked as they walked towards the house. She seemed more relaxed here somehow. Perhaps it was easier being somewhere she wasn't expected to recognize anything. McLean was searching for a suitable reply as he opened the door, but something large and furry trotted out, twining itself around Emma's legs, tail high and purring like a badly tuned engine. He felt a moment's irrational jealousy. Mrs McCutcheon's cat had never shown him that kind of affection.

Emma bent down, stroked the cat. It nudged her hand, rubbing the side of its head on her arm, tail quivering with pleasure at meeting an old friend. She picked it up and it started to nuzzle at her face. And then McLean saw tears in the corners of her eyes.

'There was a fire. Everyone was killed. Only the cat survived.' She turned to face him. 'The cat and you.'

'There you go. Extra towels in the airing cupboard. I'm not sure how comfortable the bed is, but the sheets are clean.'

McLean stood just inside the guest bedroom, pointed at the door across the way that led to the en-suite bathroom. Emma sat on the end of a king-size bed looking as pale as the white sheets as she stared around the room. It was one of five spare bedrooms in the house, not counting McLean's own room and his grandmother's. Or the old box-rooms up in the roof where in times past the servants would have slept. Not for the first time he wondered why he kept the place. It was way too big for him.

'It's very nice. Thank you.' Emma fiddled with the strap on her bag. Awkward. Beside her, Mrs McCutcheon's cat had leapt onto the bed and was pawing at the bedding, purring as it nuzzled her free hand.

'I'm just across the landing. Shout if you need anything. I'll leave the light on.' McLean cringed at his words, treating her like a child. But in some ways that's what she was. Scared, alone, unsure of anything. He couldn't begin to imagine what was going through her mind. Only that she didn't seem to remember much that had happened since she had turned sixteen.

'Tony?'

He turned in the doorway as he was about to leave. Emma pushed the cat aside, stood up.

'We had something, didn't we?'

An image in his head, unbidden. Lying on a cold bed, staring up at the ceiling. Rolling over to see spiky black hair poking up out of the top of the hogged duvet. A hand reaching out, touching his side. Warmth as the duvet and the body it contains envelope him.

'Yes. We did.'

Another image. Older. A body lies in the dark, cold

36

water, naked and splayed out. Long dark hair tugged by the current into a fan like seaweed. A loss as deep and wide and cruel as the gaping cut across her neck.

'You're a kind man.' Emma was suddenly very close, her hand touching his, those dark eyes staring straight at him. He saw her face properly for the first time in months. Those eyes sunken in their sockets like a junkie three days into Cold Turkey. Her cheekbones pushed up through grey skin as if trying to escape something terrible inside. And her hair, once spiky with a life of its own, now hung lank around her scalp, streaks of white mixed in with the black. But she was still Emma. There was a spark in her he recognized. Damaged, flickering, but there.

She reached up, lightly touched the side of his face, stood on tiptoes as she leaned forward to kiss him. And then she stopped, just inches away. A shudder ran through her, she dropped her head into her hands, started to shake. McLean went to touch her, but something stopped his hand before he made contact.

'You'll be OK.' He tried to make the words as soft and reassuring as possible, but she still flinched at them, as if he'd slapped her. Mrs McCutcheon's cat jumped down off the bed, scowled at McLean in a way that only cats can, and started to weave itself in and out of Emma's legs until she bent down, stroked it, picked it up. The two of them stared at him until he felt uncomfortable. It didn't take long.

'If you need anything, just ask.' He stepped backwards out of the room, leaving Emma to close the door behind him. Time, that was what Doctor Wheeler had said was needed. Time and stability. Well, he'd try to give her both, but in the morning he was going to have to start looking for help.

Something woke him in the dead of night. One moment McLean was asleep, the next he was fully awake, staring up at the darkness and the shapes of his fading dream. He strained his ears, searching for the sound that had woken him. A cat yowling outside perhaps, or a car horn in the distance. He glanced over at the bedside table. 3.14 a.m., according to the red glow of the alarm clock. At the same time as he registered the meaning of the numbers, he heard the lightest of creaks, a floorboard outside his bedroom. And then the door latch clicked.

There was no light from the landing, just the feeling of air displaced. Soft footfalls on the threadbare carpet and then a body pulled back his duvet, clambered into bed beside him. Emma smelled at once familiar and deeply different. There was an antiseptic quality to her, as if after spending months in hospital her skin had absorbed the aroma completely. The arm that reached across his chest was stick-thin and bony. She pulled herself tight to his side, nestled her head against his shoulder, shivered slightly in her heavy cotton pyjamas. After a couple of moments, she started to mutter under her breath. He couldn't make out the words, but she sounded scared.

McLean lay perfectly still, unsure quite what to do. There was nothing sexual in Emma's behaviour, not like her earlier awkward advance. This was more like a child climbing into bed with a parent because something in the darkness has terrified it. He tilted his head gently, tried to listen to her voice. It sounded different, almost foreign. In the dull glow of the alarm clock he could see that her eyes were tight shut. After a while, the words drifted away to silence, her breathing slowed and she relaxed into proper sleep. How long was it since he'd bade her good night? How long had she lain alone and frightened in a strange room? And how the hell was he going to get any sleep himself with her lying there? And yet he didn't dare move, couldn't bring himself to disturb her.

A flicker in the darkness, shadow upon silent shadow. His eyes darted to the dresser, sitting in front of the window. A different kind of black filtered in from outside, tinged with a distant orange glow of the night-time city. In its diffraction he saw an outline, the unmistakable shape of Mrs McCutcheon's cat. There was no way he could see in the gloom, but he knew it was watching him.

Watching them both.

7

It had to come sooner or later, that much McLean knew. He wasn't a betting man, but it was going to be either Ritchie or MacBride. Grumpy Bob could cope with pretty much anything Dagwood threw at him, and the newly promoted Acting Superintendent Duguid still had some small respect for Bob Laird. Either that or fear; Grumpy Bob knew where a surprising number of bodies were buried.

Bad enough Dagwood being in charge of CID, but until the Powers That Be decided how Scotland's new Single Police Service was going to work, he was running the whole station – uniform, plain clothes and civilian staff. If he'd been insufferable before, it was as nothing compared to him now. Dagwood had always been of the 'management by bullying' school, and with no one to keep him in check, morale was taking a battering.

In a way, Dagwood had done him a favour sending him over to the SCU, although McLean knew damned well that had never been his intention. It meant that he didn't have to deal directly with the man on a daily basis, although there was still a mountain of paperwork to get through. For some reason he couldn't quite fathom, he seemed to be in charge of the overtime rosters for half a dozen investigative teams, even though he wasn't actually running any of their investigations himself. Dagwood had made it quite clear early on in his tenure that he didn't trust McLean to run a sweepstake, let alone something as complex as a murder enquiry. Hence he had been placed under the watchful eye of DCI Dexter. Which was why he was currently sorting through sixteen sets of interviews, none of which yielded any useful information. DS Buchanan was supposed to be following up the lead on Malky the pimp, but so far he seemed to have gone to ground. The phone was a welcome distraction.

'McLean.'

'Umm. Sir. Sorry to call you. Didn't really know who else I could ask.'

So Detective Constable MacBride had been the first to break.

'What's the problem?' McLean set aside his report and leaned back in his chair.

'I'm looking into a suicide. Apartment down in Trinity. Bloke hung himself.'

'Hanged.'

'What?'

'Hanged, Constable. A picture is hung, a man is hanged. Who's the senior officer in charge?'

'Erm, that'd be me, sir.'

Bloody brilliant. True enough MacBride was a competent detective, but he was just a constable, and not long in plain clothes either. If there was a dead body, there should have been a detective inspector involved at the very least.

'Where's Ritchie?'

'Dag–... Err... Acting Superintendent Duguid's got her organizing the door-to-doors on the missing schoolgirl search.'

Which should have been uniform's gig.

'OK. What's the problem with this suicide then?' McLean rubbed his face and stifled a sigh. Looked at the reports in front of him, the mound of papers teetering over the edge of his in-tray. 'No, forget that, Stuart. Give me the address and I'll come have a look for myself.'

The posh bit might have been home to Edinburgh's judges and lawyers, but time was you wouldn't have dared walk through the back end of Trinity in uniform on your own. Even a pair of beat officers might find themselves in a sticky situation if the locals were in the mood for a fight. Parts of it were still bad, but the money pouring into Leith had begun to filter out sideways now, spreading middle-class civility like spilled extra-virgin olive oil as it went. Nowadays the violence stayed behind closed doors, more often emotional rather than physical though there was plenty of that too.

The address was for a small development just off the Ferry Road. McLean couldn't really tell what the building had been before it had been gutted and turned into flats, only that it had never been intended for habitation. Who-ever had done the work had been looking to maximize profits though; the individual apartments were tiny.

An ambulance blocked the entrance to the parking bays behind the building, so McLean left his car on a double yellow line behind a familiar mud-and-British-Racing-Green Jaguar with a 'Doctor on Call' sticker shoved in the windscreen. A pair of bored-looking paramedics were loafing around at the bottom of a set of stone stairs lead-ing up to the first floor of the old building. They nodded

42

at McLean as he passed, either recognizing him or not caring if anyone approached what might be a crime scene. At the top of the stairs, a uniform PC guarded the door with almost as much professionalism. She struggled to attention as she saw him.

'Inspector. Sir. I'm sorry. No one told me. I thought . . .'

'Don't worry. I'm not really here.' He stopped, looked around. Saw no battered white Transit van. 'And neither's SEB by the look of things.'

'They're on their way, sir. '

'What's the situation, then? Who found the body?'

'I'm not sure, sir. You should probably see DC Mac-Bride. He's inside with the pathologist.'

'Body's still here, I take it.' McLean nodded at the paramedics, didn't wait for an answer.

The door opened onto a narrow hall. Little more than a corridor with delusions of grandeur. There appeared to be four apartments shoe-horned into this tiny space, but only one had a gaggle of people clustered around its open doorway. McLean recognized Tracy Sharp, assistant to the city pathologist, Angus Cadwallader. No doubt the man himself was inside.

'Is it safe to go in?' McLean stopped at the door, peered through. Doctor Sharp might have been wearing a white coverall, but the assembled constables were in uniform. No latex gloves, no over-boots.

'Don't think you could contaminate the scene any more than it's already been, Tony. Come on in.' Angus Cadwallader stood in the middle of a small, open-plan apartment. There wasn't much in the way of furniture, just a futon, a couple of bookshelves and a desk shoved into one corner.

The chair that should have gone with the desk lay on its side in the middle of the floor alongside a small table. Above it, the old roof was opened up, exposing sarking board, purlins, joists and beams. A stout rope had been slung over one of these, its other end wrapped in a professional-looking noose around the neck of a naked and very dead young man.

Death had not been kind to him. His eyes bulged, and a swollen blue tongue poked out between his lips, shiny crinkles of saliva running off it down his chin and onto his chest as if slugs had been crawling over him. The shock of the hanging had loosened his bowels and made a nasty mess of the threadbare rug that covered the polished floorboards.

'So, a suicide then.' McLean wrinkled his nose as he got closer.

'Certainly looks that way,' Cadwallader said. 'No sign of a struggle, no obvious marks to suggest he was forced. His hands aren't tied.'

McLean peered closer, and sure enough the young man's hands hung loosely by his side.

'Was there a note?'

'On his computer.' This from DC MacBride, who was hunched over the desk. He was wearing latex gloves, McLean noticed.

The computer was a small laptop, tethered to the desk by an external keyboard and mouse. The desk itself was as far removed from McLean's own as to hardly warrant the same name. It was tiny, like everything else in the apartment, and it was as tidy as a cleaners' convention. There were no papers strewn across it, no piles

44

of reports in the in-tray awaiting attention. No in-tray for that matter. Just a clear expanse of fake wood. He pulled a pair of latex gloves from his pocket, squeezed his hands into them and slid open the top, narrow drawer.

'I had a look already,' MacBride said. 'There's not much to see.'

It was true. The drawer held pens, neatly lined up and sorted into colours. A pair of small scissors, a stapler, a ruler. Nothing out of the ordinary. The drawer below yielded a lined A4 writing pad and some envelopes. The bottom drawer held a hole punch and a couple of power adaptors for mobile phones, the cords neatly tied as if they'd never been used.

'What about this message then?' A screensaver image looped and twirled mesmerically about the screen until MacBride nudged the mouse. The image steadied to a word processor, a few words typed out, the cursor blinking as it waited for more.

Ive had enugh. There's no reasen too go on. The world hates me well it can do without me now. To whoever finds me, Im sorry. Good bye.

'That it?'

'That's all there was when I got here.'

'We know who he is?' McLean looked back at the naked man.

'Neighbour says he's Grigori Mikhailevic. Doesn't know him well.'

'That who found the body?'

45

'Aye. Door was open as she walked past. Says she didn't come in, and I'm inclined to believe her.'

'Where's she now?'

'Back in her flat. PC Gregg's with her.'

Sandy Gregg. Poor woman. Well, at least she wouldn't have to do any talking. McLean looked around the apartment. It wasn't just the desk that was tidy; everything had a place and everything was in its place. What little furniture there was sat square, aligned with the walls. Even the table upon which the chair had been balanced was centred neatly. Perhaps that was a necessary adaptation to living somewhere so small, but he'd seen places smaller still where chaos had been allowed to reign. No, this was the apartment of a tidy man. Meticulously tidy. Anally retentive, as the Freudians would have it. And there he was, hanging from a stout hemp rope slung over his own beam.

'We're done here, if you want to cut him down.' Cadwallader straightened up from his crouch with an audible popping of bones.

'Your crime scene, Constable. I'm not here, remember.' McLean nodded at MacBride.

'Oh. Right. Yes. Carry on, Doctor Cadwallader.'

'Any more thoughts, Angus?' McLean asked.

'Well, if it wasn't suicide it was a very good fake. If I had to put money on it now, I'd say he killed himself. I'll run blood tests in case he's been given something to make him compliant, check one or two other things at the PM. But I'm not seeing any evidence of foul play here.'

'But you think there's something fishy.' McLean turned to DC MacBride.

'It's hard to put my finger on it, sir, but there's something not right. I'd like to look into it some more, but you know what Duguid's like. He'll want this written up and forgotten by the end of the day.'

'We wouldn't want you going out and finding new crimes to investigate. Just think what that would do to the statistics. Let alone the budget.'

'I don't know, sir. It's just . . .'

'I think you're right, there's something hooky here. This is a man who arranges his pens by colour and lines things up so they're nice and square. There's no mess in here at all, no clutter. That sort of person doesn't hang himself, it's too prone to things going wrong. That sort of mind isn't normally suicidal at all. More likely to be homicidal, especially if the neighbours don't put their recycling in the right bin.'

'So you think I should keep looking?'

McLean watched as the two paramedics manhandled the body onto the stretcher they had wheeled in, careful to avoid the mess on the rug.

'Yes. And I'd start with that laptop. The note's a joke. It's impersonal, could've been written by anyone. And it's riddled with typos and spelling mistakes. I'll bet you a purple beer token there's not a single error in any of the other documents on there.'

The door to Chief Superintendent McIntyre's office was closed; that was the first thing that McLean noticed. For three years it had stood ajar, no barrier between the chief and those who worked under her. Janice's desk now stood unattended and cleared of anything that might be deemed personal. Jayne McIntyre's open-door policy had been one of the few positive things about the station, but now she had moved to better things, or at least he hoped so. Anything to do with the setting up of the new Police Service of Scotland was a double-edged sword. McLean couldn't begrudge her the chance to progress up the greasy pole, but there was part of him that wished she was still here, or at least that the person who'd been promoted to fill her shoes was less red-faced, balding and generally useless.

Taking a moment to compose himself, he knocked quietly on the door, waited for the gruff 'enter' and then did as he was bid.

Acting Superintendent Charles Duguid had taken no time to impose his own lack of style on McIntyre's office. The casual area, with its bookshelves, coffee machine and curiously uncomfortable armchairs, was gone, replaced by a wall of whiteboards and a long conference table. The pictures on the wall were gone too, presumably to Tulliallan. Neutral ground for the new HQ so that no one region could dominate. As if that wasn't going to happen any-way. Duguid hadn't bothered to replace them yet, no doubt finding comfort in the discoloured patches they had left on the walls. The desk itself was the same one McIntyre had used, but where under her tenure it had usually been heaped with papers, reports and other signs of busy-ness, now it was almost clear. And behind it, scowling at McLean as he finished his telephone conver-sation, the man of the hour.

'What is it, McLean?' Duguid made no effort to hide the impatience in his voice.

'You wanted to see me, sir. The duty sergeant –'

'That was hours ago. Where the hell have you been?'

McLean suppressed the urge to look at his watch. He was fairly sure Sergeant Dundas wouldn't have sat on the message for more than a few minutes, and he'd been in his office for the past two hours trying to make some sense of the overtime figures foisted on him by one of Duguid's own investigations.

'Well, you're here now, I suppose.' Duguid leaned back in his enormous leather chair. That was new, and expen-sive by the look of things. A pity he hadn't bothered to provide one on the other side of the desk. McLean stood with his hands behind his back, trying not to let his temper rise. That was, after all, exactly what Duguid wanted.

'I've been reviewing your cases since your promotion.' Duguid nodded towards a closed brown folder that was pretty much the only thing on his desk. There was noth-ing on the outside to indicate that it was what he said it was, and judging by its thinness, it was more likely a review

49

of Duguid's own caseload, but McLean said nothing. He knew better than to provoke the beast this early in the conversation.

'Not much of a clear-up rate, is there. Not many arrests and convictions. When was the last time you gave evidence in court?'

'A couple of years ago. The Broughton Post Office raid.'

'You were still a sergeant then.' It wasn't a question. McLean resisted the temptation to add 'Detective.'

'So, since making inspector you've put how many criminals away?'

That depends on how you count, doesn't it? The drug bust that gave you your bloody promotion was effectively down to my lead, so you could say something of the order of two dozen awaiting trial just at the moment. And there's the small matter of the forensic photographer who was posting crime scene photos on the web. I caught him, but you took the credit for that one, even after you'd tried to pin it on someone else. McLean bit back the obvious retort.

'There's Christopher Roberts. He's in remand right now. The PF's finalizing the case.'

'Ah yes. Roberts. The unlikely child snatcher. He claims he was coerced, I understand. Put in an impossible position by a very powerful and influential man. A man who should have been arrested for murder, abduction and many other things. What happened to him, McLean?'

'As I understand it, sir, his bodyguard killed him. Poetic justice, I'd say.'

'Of course you would. And no doubt you'd say it was

poetic justice that the bodyguard died a week later in hospital. You were the last one to visit him before that, I'm told. And the doctors aren't really sure what killed him.'

Don't rise to it. Don't give him the satisfaction.

'If you're unhappy with my performance, sir –'

'Of course I'm bloody unhappy with your performance, McLean. Why do you think I asked you here?'

Because you're a prize arse who likes to bully people and I'm the only one who dares to stand up to you? 'I assumed it was to allocate me a new case, sir. I understand there's a gang of pickpockets have been working the festival. Organized, probably East European and tied into something larger. I know it's sergeant work, but then I don't really expect anything more complicated from you, sir.'

Duguid's already florid face reddened. 'With that attitude, McLean, it's hardly any surprise. You've no respect for authority, and every time you start investigating someone they end up dead.'

'With respect, sir –'

'Don't give me any of that shit. Gavin Spenser, dead. Alison Kydd, dead. Needy –' Duguid broke off. So that was it. Three months on and still the enmity. Forget the fact that Sergeant John Needham had abducted, raped and murdered three women, tried to kill a fourth. He was an old-school copper and they stood up for one another.

'Would it have been better if he'd gone to trial, sir? After what he did?'

'He'd have been found insane.'

'And that would have been OK, I suppose.'

'Dammit, McLean. You're just trouble wherever you

go. I don't know why McIntyre put up with you, but I'm sure as hell not going to.' Duguid picked up the folder, flipped it open. 'What were you doing over at that suicide case in Trinity?'

It took McLean a moment to process the change of direction. 'What?'

'The suicide. Chap hung himself. Why were you poking your nose in there when you're meant to be helping Jo Dexter out in Vice?'

'I wasn't "poking my nose" in anywhere, sir. DC Mac-Bride was appointed SIO. He's only a constable.'

'What of it? The way I hear, it was suicide, plain and simple. Even left a note. Doesn't take a detective inspector to fill out an incident report, does it?'

McLean suppressed the urge to sigh. It was like dealing with a particularly obstinate toddler. 'A person died in unnatural circumstances, sir. At the very least, the Fiscal will want a basic investigation. DC MacBride thought there was something unusual about the case. He called it in so he could get a second opinion. No doubt a sergeant would have done, but there weren't any available. I was going that way anyway, so I thought I'd drop in and see what he was on about. Turns out he was right.'

Duguid's eyes narrowed, a sure sign that he was trying to think. 'What do you mean, he was right?'

'There's a lot about the hanging that doesn't add up, sir. Enough to make me suspicious.'

'And we're going to pay for this hunch-following how, exactly?'

'I wouldn't call it a hunch, sir.'

'No, you wouldn't. But that's what it is. And we don't

have the budget to go digging where there's nothing to find. The PF doesn't want to waste money on lengthy enquiries either. If it looks like a duck and sounds like a duck, then it's a duck, McLean. Now get MacBride to write up the report and file it.'

McLean held his breath, just for a few seconds. Duguid stared at him from the other side of the desk, his face a mottle of crimson and white. There wasn't really much point arguing with the man when he was like this, and besides, he had somewhere else he needed to be.

'If you say so, sir.'

'I do. Now get out of here. Some of us have work to do.'

A hubbub of quiet noise filled the echoing hall of the sale room, the collected murmurs and whispers of over a hundred punters settled into ranks of chairs lined up to face a stage at the far end. A simple lectern stood to one side, a stand to the other presumably for books to be placed upon. Fortunately there was little mention of the man whose books were on sale, and no photographs. Perhaps it was the notoriety of the collection, or maybe antiquarian book sales were always like this. It was the first time he'd ever been to one, so McLean couldn't be sure. He wasn't even sure why he'd come at all.

The sale catalogue had plopped through his letterbox a month or so earlier. At first he'd thought it was some kind of cruel joke. Then he'd noticed that it had been addressed to his grandmother, not him. Yet another mailing list woefully out of date. Donald Anderson's shop on the Canongate had already been sold and was apparently going to become a trendy wine bar. Now it was the turn of his substantial collection of rare and ancient books. The money raised, so the introduction to the catalogue stated, was to go to the Sick Kids Hospital and the Zero Tolerance campaign. Such had been Anderson's last wishes, conveyed to his solicitors just the day before he died.

McLean hadn't read any more than that, consigning the catalogue to the bin in the corner of the kitchen where all the junk mail went to die. But something about it had stuck with him, and two days later he'd fished it out again. Every so often he'd find himself idly leafing through it as he drank tea at the old kitchen table, wondering what possible use he might have for an obscure sixteenth-century hagiography or a bound fragment of an illuminated manuscript from an unverified source but thought to be of the St Kilda school. He had noticed a first edition of Gray's *Anatomy* that looked like the sort of thing Angus Cadwallader would have loved, but why he'd noted the date and time of the sale in his diary and made sure the afternoon was free, he had no idea. Even less so why he'd actually come along.

'Inspector. What a pleasant surprise.'

McLean looked around to see a large woman approaching. At least he thought she was a woman, though she had the largest hands he'd ever seen. She wore the sort of outfit you might expect to be taking tea in Jenner's on a weekday afternoon, an overemphasis on tweed and heavy makeup. She was either wearing a wig or had spent the entire morning at a very skilled hairdresser's, one who most likely trained in the 1950s. Still slightly bemused to be at the sale, it took him too long to make the complex series of connections to a name.

'Madame Rose.' He nodded, shuffling sideways in his seat as she dropped herself indecorously beside him, too close for comfort. Not she at all. He. McLean remembered now, the so-called medium and fortune-teller with the shop at the bottom of Leith Walk. She'd helped . . . dammit, he'd helped out with the ritual killing cold case a year or so back. Had a vast collection of occult rubbish, including many ancient books, tucked away at the back of the shop. Madame Rose was also a friend of Jayne McIntyre, which had to count for something he supposed. He wondered how they'd met.

'Just Rose is fine.' Madame Rose settled into the seat, which creaked in protest at his considerable bulk. 'I must say I didn't expect to see you here. What with your connection to Anderson and all.'

'I never really expected to come here myself.' McLean tapped the rolled-up catalogue against his leg, considering the possibility of getting up and leaving. A few minutes earlier he might have got away with it. Now, having been recognized, it would only draw attention.

'And yet here you are. Had your eye on anything in particular?' The medium nodded at McLean's rolled-up catalogue. 'There's some rather wonderful first editions of Wendell's *Treatise on Babylonian Magic*. I do hope they don't go for too much. Rumour has it they once belonged to Aleister Crowley.'

A red-faced gentleman in a too-tight suit appeared at the lectern before McLean could say anything in reply, or make good his escape.

55

'Good afternoon, ladies and gentlemen, and welcome to this sale of rare and antiquarian books, the collection of the late Donald Anderson.'

The auctioneer lost no time in getting stuck into the collection, rattling off quick descriptions of each book as it was placed on a stand beside his lectern by a pair of assistants. Bidding was brisk, with some pieces fetching quite ridiculously large sums of money. So much for a double-dip recession.

Sitting beside him, McLean could feel Madame Rose twitch with each new sale, as if he were a football fan at a cup final. The medium hadn't bid for anything, seemed just to be there to watch. Every so often he would make little notes in the catalogue. Names of who was buying what.

'Lot thirty-two. Gray's *Anatomy*. First edition, published London in 1858 by J. W. Parker. Not in brilliant condition, but originally the property of a Mr A. Conan Doyle according to the inscription in the front. That has not been verified, although it is entirely possible. Who'll start me at five hundred pounds? Five hundred? No? Four hundred then? Three hundred and fifty? I don't need to remind you that there are no reserves in this sale, but all proceeds are going to a good cause. Three hundred then. Surely someone? Thank you, sir.'

McLean look around to see who had made the first bid, then realized that it was him.

'Three hundred I've got. Who'll give me three-fifty. Yes? Four?'

And so it went on. Someone across the hall was in for a fight, but McLean had decided he wanted this book. So

he kept upping his bid. When the hammer finally came down he discovered he'd paid almost fifteen hundred pounds, plus auctioneer's commission, for a book that probably had nothing to do with Sir Arthur Conan Doyle whatsoever.

For some reason he didn't care.

'You come very highly recommended, Miss Nairn. Do you have much experience working with younger patients?'

She had arrived not long after he'd come home, deflated after the curious excitement of the sale room. Her feet crunching up the gravel drive had given him a few moments' notice before the doorbell rang. At first he'd thought she was lost; she certainly didn't look like the kind of person who lived in this part of town.

He'd forgotten about the appointment, of course, but the letter from Doctor Wheeler was legitimate, so he'd let her in, ushering her into the library for an impromptu inter-view. It was either there or the kitchen, and that seemed just a little too informal. From the CV sent by the hospital, he'd been expecting someone perhaps a little older than the young woman sitting opposite him, perhaps a little less, what was the word, Gothic? No, that wasn't right. She had more of an Earth Mother thing going, but with black leather DMs that laced almost up to her knees and pierc-ings in places that surely weren't meant to be pierced. Still, there was no denying her credentials. Or his desperation.

'I started off in trauma rehabilitation, Detective In-spector. Most of my patients were in their teens or twenties. Motorbike accidents, a few soldiers injured in Iraq or Afghanistan.'

57

So she'd done her homework too. That was a good sign, wasn't it? McLean knew better than to judge someone purely by their outward appearance. Emma herself was hardly conventional.

'Did Doctor Wheeler tell you about Miss Baird's condition?'

'A little, but she's bound by patient–doctor confidentiality. I understand Emma has some memory loss, she was in the ICU for several months. Other than that, not much. Is she here?'

'Upstairs.' McLean glanced at the ceiling. In truth Emma had hardly come out of her bedroom in the days since she'd arrived, apart from her regular early-morning visits to his own room, his own bed. He'd lugged a television up there for her, but judging by the gaps in the bookshelves, she was filling her time mostly with reading. She ate the food he put in front of her, but he didn't think she helped herself to anything whilst he was away at work. He was pretty sure she'd not left the house, except for the two appointments with Doctor Wheeler back at the hospital. It had been at the last one where he'd broached the subject of a full-time carer. Miss Nairn was, he hoped, the answer.

'If you don't mind me asking, what's your relationship with Emma?'

Cut right to the chase, why don't you?

'She's my girlfriend. Was. Is? I'm not sure. She was abducted, possibly drugged, certainly had a very severe blow to the head. About four months ago. She was in a coma for almost two months. When she finally woke up she couldn't remember anything about the last fifteen years.'

Miss Nairn uncrossed her legs, leaned forward in her high-backed armchair. She wore a thin tie-died skirt over black leggings, white T-shirt and a suede leather jacket. Her blonde hair had been cut tight to her scalp, the furrows on her brow as she frowned reaching up into the short fuzz.

'That sounds unusual, for physical trauma. Has Emma seen a psychiatrist?'

'Not yet, but it's early days.'

'Early days, yes.' Miss Nairn tapped at her cheek with a finger, making a hollow pop, pop sound. 'So what is it you want me to do, Detective Inspector?'

'Whatever you can, really. I can give her a roof, a bed, feed her, but Emma needs company and I can't give up work to look after her while she recovers.' Even as he spoke the words, McLean saw the lie in them. He didn't need to work at all. If Miss Nairn saw the lie too, she didn't let on.

'And you think a carer specializing in physical-trauma victims is what she needs?'

'You were Doctor Wheeler's suggestion. If you don't think you're right for it, I'm sure she can give me other names.'

'No, no. I think I can help.' Miss Nairn levered herself out of the chair and McLean realized how he'd been played. If nothing else, she was smart. That had to be worth something.

'You're OK with doing this full time? Staying here?' McLean asked.

'It's usually the best way. And it looks like you've got the space.' Miss Nairn smiled, half twirled around, her

59

outstretched arms taking in the over-large room. Her skirt flared out like a flamenco dancer's, a brief moment of exuberance before it settled back down against her legs. 'Shall we go and meet Emma then?'

9

'You got a minute, sir?'

McLean looked up from the report he'd been trying to force into his brain for an hour. The elfin, freckled face of Detective Sergeant Kirsty Ritchie peered around the door-jamb, not trusting itself to commit fully to a relationship with his office.

'A minute, an hour. Anything's got to be better than this.' McLean dropped the sheaf of paper onto his desk, where it nestled in amongst many others of its kind. He thought that Dagwood had sent him off to work in the SCU, but that hadn't stopped the acting superintendent from passing on every half-baked criminal psychology paper that came his way as well. Read, digest, condense into little words for the hard of thinking.

'I've been working with Stu– . . . DC MacBride on the suicide case. You know.' Ritchie leaned against the door, still not actually entering the office.

'I visited the scene, yes.' And got a bollocking for it. 'What did you make of it?'

'The scene? I think he's right. There's something odd about it.'

'But you can't be more specific, right?'

'Yeah. And that's what's bugging me.'

'You want to go deeper? Do a profile on the victim?' McLean dug around in the recesses of his memory for anything specific about the case. Came up with less than he'd have liked. 'Did we have a name for him?'

'Grigori Mikhailevic, according to his neighbour. Lithuanian. Of Russian descent if that name's anything to go by. Apparently he was over here studying accountancy. I guess that's enough to turn anyone to suicide.'

'Family?'

'Working on it. I've put in a call to the embassy, but you know how long it can take to get a response these days, especially if they think it's a suicide.'

'You haven't told them you think it's suspicious?'

'Well, that's the problem, isn't it. I can't.'

Ahh. So that's what it's about. 'Let me guess.' McLean raised a finger in the direction of the ceiling and the floor above. Not that the office in question was immediately over his own; that would have been far too demeaning for Dagwood.

'As far as he's concerned it's a simple case of suicide. He's already chewed MacBride's ear off once for even calling out SEB without asking first. Wants it written up and filed away ASAP.'

And they made this man acting superintendent. Put him in charge of an entire station. McLean slumped back in his seat, resisted the urge to bury his head in his hands.

'I know. He chewed me off a strip just for going along to have a look.'

'He does know that any dead body has to be investigated for foul play?' It was a question, but not one that should have needed answering. McLean just shrugged.

DS Ritchie looked over her shoulder into the empty

corridor beyond, as if expecting the object of their scorn to appear at any moment.

'I've not been here long, sir. But if you want my opinion, I think he's struggling to cope. He shouldn't even have been made up to super, let alone put in charge.'

'You won't find me disagreeing with you, Kirsty, but there's not a lot I can do. I'm just a humble detective inspector. It was hard enough dealing with him when he was just a DCI himself.'

'What about McIntyre? Is there nothing she can do?' There was a desperation in Ritchie's question, like a small child about to scream 'but it's not fair!'

'Last time I spoke to Jayne she was running to stay still. The phrase "poisoned chalice" comes to mind. This whole Police Scotland is a bugger's muddle and no mistake.'

'Aye, I thought as much.' Ritchie's face dropped, as if the last hope had died and unremitting hardship was the best she could expect from now on.

'What's he got you doing, then?' McLean asked.

'Anything. Everything. Mostly running around after DI Spence. That and responding to every petty burglary call that comes in like I was a beat constable. Not much actual detecting, though.' Ritchie nodded at McLean's desk. 'Paperwork. Lots of it. Beginning to wish I'd stayed up in Aberdeen.'

McLean looked at the piles on his desk, up at the clock on the wall. He'd been reading for at least three hours. Wasting time. 'Is MacBride about?'

'Down in the canteen last I saw him.'

'OK. Go and get him. I'll meet you out the back in ten minutes.'

63

'Where're we going?' The spark of intrigue in Ritchie's face was worth the trouble McLean knew he was inevitably going to get himself into.

'The City Mortuary. Let's see if Angus has had a chance to look at this dead Lithuanian student.'

McLean paused at the door to the CID room where all the detective sergeants lived, wondering whether going in was a good idea or not. Sooner or later word would get upstairs, and then there'd be consequences. On the other hand, if his instinct was right, and young MacBride's hunch was good, there was every chance a murder was about to go uninvestigated just so the crime statistics would look good. A sophisticated and well-planned murder at that, which meant either that there was more to Grigori Mikhailevic than was immediately apparent, or someone had acquired a taste for killing. Neither option was particularly appealing.

Or, of course, it was a suicide and he was going to look a right tit.

A series of desks cluttered up most of the space, reminding him more of a school room than an office. Perhaps it was the way they all faced the whiteboard wall. Or maybe it was the mixture of the hard-working and the semi-comatose sat at those desks that reminded him of hot summer afternoons and Latin declension. Detective Sergeant Carter was in earnest conversation with some uniform PCs and barely looked up as he walked in. A couple of other sergeants glanced around from their desks, phones clamped to their ears, eyes slightly wide with the fear of being caught looking at naughty pictures hidden inside a textbook. Both of them hung up without a word when they saw who it was had interrupted their afternoon; no bollocking from Dagwood today, no need to pretend they were busy.

McLean spotted his quarry over in the corner, feet up on his desk, face bathed in warm sunshine from the large window. Grumpy Bob had the look about him of a man who has fallen asleep reading a report. His balding head was tilted back, mouth slightly open, eyes tightly shut, but as McLean approached, before he could even say anything, the detective sergeant had swung his legs off the desk, scooped up his report and begun leafing through the upside-down pages. Then he saw who it was.

'Oh, it's you, sir. I thought . . .'

'Dagwood that bad, is he?'

'Don't get me started. He pops in here about once every bloody five minutes. No wonder he never gets anything done.'

'Well, you never know. HQ might even choose someone before Christmas. Then again, they might decide to make his position permanent.'

'Oh Christ. Don't.' Grumpy Bob groaned at the thought. Behind him, McLean heard several others.

'You got a moment, Bob?' he asked.

'If it gets me out of here, aye.'

'Well, it might. You know that suicide DC MacBride's been investigating?'

'Aye.'

'Well I want you to have a look at it too. Go over his report. Stick your nose in at the scene if SOC are finished with it.'

65

'Give it the benefit of my many years of experience, you mean.'

'That's the one. Just keep it low profile.'

Grumpy Bob raised his eyes heavenward and frowned. 'I take it this is not a sanctioned use of investigative resource.'

'Not exactly, no.'

'Nae bother, sir. I'll get right on it. Got to be better than wading through all this pish.' Grumpy Bob thwapped the sheaf of paper down on his desk. 'New procedures for community policing, my arse.'

'Aye, well. You can get off it and go have a nosey. On the quiet'd be best, but if Dagwood finds out and kicks up a fuss, tell him I sent you.'

'Oh, don't you worry about that, sir. I will.'

Hidden away down the Cowgate in the bowels of the Old Town, the City Mortuary was an easy place to overlook. That might have been the idea behind putting it there, of course. No one likes to be confronted by their mortality. A fresh breeze blew in off the Firth of Forth, whistling as it picked up speed down the narrow, canyon-like confines of the street. Throwing rubbish around their feet like playful paper dogs as they approached the entrance.

McLean held open the door, then followed Ritchie and MacBride into the air-conditioned lobby. The little party barely got a nod from the security guard; he'd seen them often enough before. They scribbled their names on the visitor pad anyway, before heading into the cool interior.

Angus Cadwallader was two-finger typing at an ancient computer in the office off the examination room when

McLean rapped his knuckles on the open door. The pathologist looked around, peering over half-moon spectacles, eyes taking a while to regain their focus before a broad smile spread across his face.

'Tony. It's been ages. I was beginning to think I'd done something.' He cast an eye over McLean's shoulder to the two officers standing behind him. 'The team's all back together, I see.'

'Not quite. Grumpy Bob's off down to Trinity. I thought the rest of us deserved a break from the office. Wondered if you'd had a chance to look at our Hanged Man yet.'

'And you decided to walk rather than phone? Things must be bad.' Cadwallader grabbed a pair of latex gloves from a box by the door, then led them through to the cold store. A bank of stainless steel refrigerator doors, about two foot square and each with a heavy handle, were set into one wall. Behind each, a body awaited, ready to give up its secrets.

'This one, I think. A pity Tracy's not here. She knows where everyone is.' Cadwallader opened a door, slid out a long shelf with a corpse on it, draped in a white sheet. Rolled back, this revealed the face of the young man McLean had last seen dangling from a stout hemp rope. His face was still distorted, his neck mottled with bruises.

'Grab that trolley will you, Constable.' Cadwallader pointed across the room. Startled, DC MacBride complied, and together they transferred the cadaver on its tray to the examination table through in the next room.

'You've done him already,' McLean said as the pathologist rolled the sheet down further. A brutal Y-shaped incision across the dead student's chest and down to his crotch had been sewn up with delicate care, no doubt the work of the missing Doctor Sharp.

'Yesterday. I'm still waiting on the results of the tox screening to come back. I was making a start on the report when you arrived.'

'The edited version?' McLean nodded at the young man on the slab, wondering why Cadwallader had wheeled him out.

'In a word, odd.'

'Odd?'

'Yes. Odd. I couldn't put my finger on it at first. But see here.' The pathologist lifted one of the dead student's hands up, splayed out the fingers. They were puffy and red where blood had pooled in them as they hung at his sides after death, but otherwise they looked well enough kept. The nails were trimmed neatly but would have needed doing again in a week or so. Had their owner not died.

'What am I looking at?' McLean asked. Behind him he could sense DS Ritchie leaning in for a closer look. No doubt DC MacBride was backing off. No fan of the dead, he.

'It's what's not there.' Cadwallader put down the hand and picked up the other. Here the fingernails were pared right back, the pads of the fingers thick.

'A guitarist.' McLean turned to MacBride, surprised to find him watching closely. 'Was there a guitar in the flat, Constable?'

'I think so, sir. I can check.'

'You're missing the point, Tony. Either that or being deliberately obtuse.' Cadwallader put the hand back down, rolled the white sheet back over the body. 'I've checked those hands thoroughly and there's no sign of any damage to the fingers. No splinters or wood fragments at all. It's just about possible he might have got that rope up over that beam without damaging his hands, but it's unlikely.'

'It's not much to go on though, is it?'

'On its own, no. But you saw his nails. They were quite clean, but it's amazing what gets left behind even after a good scrub. I could tell you a fair bit of his history over the twenty-four hours leading up to his death going by what was under those nails. Probably longer if I had the time and resources. But there was one thing very notable by its absence. No hemp fibres.'

For a moment McLean wondered what cannabis residue had to do with anything, but then the penny dropped.

'The rope.'

'Exactly, Tony. The rope. Your man there may have hanged himself, but if he did, then someone else put the rope up over the beam and around his neck.'

News had obviously run ahead of him. McLean could tell by the way the few other plain clothes officers he met on his way up to the third floor looked at him like he was a marked man. It was a stare he was all too familiar with; that mixture of anger that he'd poked the hornets' nest and relief that the little buggers were going to be focusing their attention on someone else for a change.

Duguid's office door was open, and McLean almost walked straight in as he would have done back when Jayne McIntyre was in charge. A self-preserving sixth sense stopped him. That and a quiet 'ahem' from the desk to one side of the door. He looked around to see a pale-faced constable manning the barricades.

'He's, um, expecting you, sir.'

McLean raised an eyebrow. 'Anyone else had a strip torn off yet?'

'I couldn't say, sir. DS Laird was in earlier though.'

Poor old Grumpy Bob. Well, he'd been dealing with the likes of Dagwood for long enough to develop the necessary thick skin. McLean took a deep breath, then advanced upon the open doorway. Across the room he could see the object of his scorn hunched over his desk, peering myopically at the screen of a tiny laptop computer. He rapped lightly on the door frame. Acting Superintendent

Charles Duguid stopped what he was doing, looked up and scowled.

'About bloody time. Come in and shut the door.'

McLean did as he was told, approaching the desk like a man who wasn't in fear of his life. Better to close on your enemy fast.

'The Leith suicide. Did I not make it clear I wanted it wrapped up quickly?'

McLean nodded, said nothing.

'And yet you asked DS Laird to go and check it over again today.'

McLean shifted slightly, stopped himself from fidgeting. Again said nothing.

'And now I hear you've taken DC MacBride and DS Ritchie down to the mortuary for . . . what exactly?' Duguid's scowl deepened. 'For Christ's sake. You're meant to be working with Jo Dexter in the SCU. Is Edinburgh so chaste you've got time to go nosing into every suicide?'

'It –'

'There's plenty of work for all of us without you sniffing out more, McLean. Don't go complicating things. It's a simple case. Young man couldn't face it any more, hanged himself. End of.'

'It wasn't a suicide sir.'

Duguid's stare hardened, his face starting the journey from red to purple.

'What the fuck are you talking about? There was no evidence of foul play. I've read the report. Have you?'

'Sir, I've just been talking to the pathologist. There's no trace of fibres from the rope under his nails. He didn't

71

touch it. That means at the very least he had an accomplice. Someone helped him.'

Duguid let out a noise halfway between a sigh and a roar. 'It's never easy with you, McLean. You can't leave well enough alone, can you.'

McLean held his tongue. No point deliberately poking the bear, especially now he was in charge.

'I don't know what arrangement you had with Jayne McIntyre, but from now on it will be proper channels. You understand? No new investigations without approval. We don't have the manpower to go playing every hunch. You know our budget's being cut like everyone else's.'

'I understand, sir. Which is why I came to see you as soon as I knew there was something amiss.'

'Dammit, McLean. Are you listening?' Duguid thumped the desk in time with his words. 'Proper channels. You report to DCI Brooks. He decides whether or not to take it up with me. You deal with the sergeants, they deal with the constables. Chain of command. Christ, what did they teach you in Tulliallan?'

How to think for myself. Obviously a lesson you missed.

'I'll speak to DCI Brooks right away, sir.'

'No, McLean, you won't.' Duguid slumped back into his expensive leather chair. 'You're here now. I'm not so bloody stupid as to send you off around the houses. Brooks will only come bleating back to me like the rest of them.'

'It won't take much manpower, sir. DC MacBride's done a good job so far. He and Bob Laird can do the leg-work. I'll keep an eye on progress, make sure they're not spending too much time on it. We just need to find out a little bit more about the victim. Speak to his friends, fellow students, tutors.'

'Contrary to what gets said in the canteen, I do know how to run an investigation, McLean.'

Yes. And it mostly involves having someone else do all the work and then taking all the credit. 'Sorry, sir. I just meant it shouldn't take more than a few days.'

'Make sure it doesn't.' Duguid nodded a dismissal and turned back to his laptop. McLean breathed out a silent sigh of relief and turned to leave.

'Oh, and McLean?'

'Sir?'

'Don't think this gets you off Sex Crimes. You want the work, fine, but you're reporting to DCI Dexter as well as John Brooks. Don't come running to me if they expect you to work twenty-four hours a day.'

11

He's happy to get out of the club. Pounding noise they call music, strobe lights threatening to induce epilepsy, drinks costing half a day's wages for a single round. He's never seen the attraction of the places. You can't even talk to anyone; it's all by eye contact, a smile, a nod. Is it any surprise a bloke can get confused? Take the wrong message from a throw of the head?

Not that it's a problem this time. There's a crowd of them leaving all at once, bubbling out into the cool night street like school kids at the bell. Only they're school kids with a nice dull alcohol fug and ears that don't hear too well, enveloped in a warm fuzziness that's almost unsettling. There'll be whining in the morning. Tinnitus by the time he's forty, if he's that lucky.

He doesn't really know where they're going. Christ, he doesn't even know half of the people in the group. But there's Kizzy and Len and a couple of girls he recognizes from the college. The others all seem friendly enough. Either that or they're on something. Someone mentions a place nearby. Was it another club or someone's house? He hopes it wasn't another club. He couldn't really face that.

Maybe it's the cold air, but he can't really focus on anything. Or is it that he can only focus on one thing at a time? He doesn't feel drunk. Not like he's felt drunk before. Not like those wild undergrad days when he'd stagger back from the pub in the wee small hours, stiff-legged, trying to use the lines between the paving slabs to keep himself straight. Usually failing. And besides, he hardly had anything. Couldn't really afford it. But there's the group, and then there's a house. A bottle getting passed around. Wine? Laughter, smiling faces. Blink and he's somewhere else. Blink and there's a hand on his forehead, eyes gazing deep into his own. Blink and they're still there, burrowing into his soul. Blink.

Home. His home? Yes, he thinks so. Or is this a dream? It feels a bit like a dream. Is there someone here with him? He can't see anyone, but he can hear a voice in his head calming him, reassuring like his mum that time he had the flu. Maybe that's it; he's got the flu. That would explain why he's naked. Getting ready for bed. Sleep would be good; sleep cures everything. There's no worrying about the lack of cash when you're asleep. No fretting about the bills mounting up, the drudgery of a life that's fallen so far short of all the promises he was made. No wondering when the axe is going to fall. Wouldn't it be wonderful to sleep for ever. To fall into that warm, sweet, dark embrace and never leave.

The ground far, far away. His feet on a precarious chair. Hairy like a Hobbit. There was a girl once, long ago, said she loved him for his feet. But she left him all the same. What would she think of those feet now? Those hairy legs?

The voice calls to him. Is it her? It tells him to step off the chair. Just jump off and everything will be fine. There's something around his neck, a light pressure resting on his shoulder, brushing the skin of his naked back. But that's

75

OK. He doesn't need to worry about that. He doesn't need to worry about anything any more. Just a quick bend of the knees and jump down to the ground. Falling, falling, slow like they decided they didn't need gravity after all.

12

'Jesus wept. What is that smell?'

McLean stood at the entrance to a narrow alleyway running down the back of an anonymous row of prefab concrete garages. It was a place where things went to die: bits of old car, rusted beyond recognition; rotting mattresses, springs escaping like metal insects; an exercise bike bent as if it had been in a collision with a truck; the inevitable purloined shopping trolley. Mostly it was decaying black bin bags, ripped open by seagulls and urban foxes. Chip pokes, foil containers scraped clean of their biryani and saag aloo, pizza boxes stained with grease. Here and there a used condom, as if this foetid hole were the perfect spot for a bit of romance. And in amongst it all, thrown out with the rest of the trash, the decomposing body of a man.

At least, he assumed it was a man. It wasn't easy to tell from what was left. No doubt finding them tastier than rancid pizza, the foxes had taken his fingers down to stubs, and something had eaten away at his face. It had to be a man's body, though. No self-respecting woman would dress up like that.

'Putrefaction, Tony. Enzymatic breakdown of the body's cells. Bacterial decay. And I dare say the garbage doesn't help.' Squatting close to the dead body, the city pathologist, Angus Cadwallader, lifted a flaccid arm and inspected what was left of a hand. McLean stayed put at the end of the alley, to avoid contaminating the crime scene, of course. Although if truth be told he was more worried about ruining his shoes. He doubted forensics would get anything useful from here.

'What's the prognosis then? You think you can save him?'

Cadwallader levered himself back up to his feet and picked a careful route back from the body. His white over-alls were stained a riot of greens and browns around his legs, black wellingtons slimed with things best not thought about. 'I can't be hugely accurate until I get him back to the mortuary, but given the weather we've been having lately and the state of the insect life living inside his mouth, I reckon he's been there at least a fortnight.'

McLean took a step back and turned slowly on his heels. The garages were surrounded on all sides by squat, six-storey tower blocks. Ugly concrete and pebble-dash, each apartment with a wide balcony affording views across the Forth. Or the back of the next block if you were unlucky. At least half of the balconies had washing draped on airers or dangling from railings. Many hundreds of people lived here, looked out these windows, saw what was going on. For two weeks, no one had come forward to report the rotting corpse chucked out with the bin bags.

'He was covered up, aye?' McLean asked the uniform sergeant who'd first greeted him when he'd arrived on site.

'Reckon so, sir. That many foxes round here these days, they must've dug down and pulled him up.'

'How'd we find out about him then?'

'Anonymous tip-off. Probably someone round here got

sick of the stench.' The sergeant nodded in the direction of the nearest flat as another squad car drew up. A couple of uniforms were trying to placate a small mob of garage-owners, no doubt anxious to know when they could get back in and dispose of all the stolen goods and pirated DVDs that were hidden inside. It might be an idea to use the body as an excuse to search all the lock-ups in the close, but they'd need a lot more manpower if they were going to do that. A riot squad too.

The short figure of DCI Jo Dexter climbed out of the squad car and ducked under the cordon tape. McLean watched her size up the whole site as she approached. Her eyes darted from tower block to parked car to garage and finally to the group of people standing at the opening to the narrow alley.

'One for us, Tony?'

'Not sure. I thought you might want to take a look. It's not pretty, mind you.'

Dexter gave him the sort of look his grandmother had reserved for the times he said something really obvious. He held the stare for a couple of seconds before conceding defeat.

'Over here then.' He pointed at the alleyway and the two of them stepped carefully into the shade, as close as they dared.

'He's certainly dead,' Dexter said. The body lay on its back, sprawled almost as if it had fallen into the soft embrace of the bin bags. Or more likely been thrown.

'SEB haven't been yet. Not sure I want to be the one to tell them they've got to go through all this shit.'

'Waste of time anyway. He wasn't killed here.' Dexter

79

inched closer, testing each footfall as if she were creeping over thin ice. 'Why'd you think it was something
for us?'

'The jacket he's wearing. Look familiar to you?'

Dexter took one more step forward. Swore. It could
have been because she'd trodden in something that meant
her shoes would have to be incinerated, or it could have
been that she, too, had been looking through mug shots
that morning.

'Malky Jennings?' McLean asked as they both retreated
from the alleyway.

'Malky fucking Jennings,' Dexter echoed. 'Either that
or someone's nicked his clothes.'

'Subject is male, Caucasian. One metre seventy-three
tall. Extensive damage to the extremities, most likely from
wild animals. Decomposition consistent with having
been dead for at least two weeks, given current weather
conditions.'

McLean stood some distance off from the examination table as Angus Cadwallader dictated his observations
into the microphone slung from the ceiling. Doctor
Peachey was on hand as witness to the proceedings, with
Doctor Sharp assisting as she ever did. He felt like a gate-
crasher at a very exclusive party.

'Can you narrow that down at all?'

'Ah, Tony. You always ask, even though you know what
the answer will be.' Cadwallader pulled open the deceased's
mouth, shone a light into the depths within. 'I've sent off
a collection of the more interesting insects we found
inside him at the scene. There's an entomologist at the

university who's a marvel with bugs. She'll be able to tell you to the hour when the eggs were laid. Probably who the father was too. But it takes time.'

'What about cause of death, then?'

'You want me to speculate, or would you rather I carry out this post-mortem first and then tell you?'

McLean bounced on his feet, didn't answer. Cadwallader was right, of course. He always was. The only reason for being down here in the mortuary was to get away from the station for a few hours. There was nothing to be gained from watching the gruesome spectacle of Malcolm Jeffrey Jennings being cut open, his most intimate secrets revealed. If it really was Malky Jennings of course, lying there on the slab. Identification was going to take a while, even if the corpse had been wearing those distinctive clothes. They'd need to run DNA, and that could take days. Even dental records might be a challenge. From what little he knew of Jennings, visits to the dentist were fairly low on his list of priorities, and someone had mashed his face in anyway. Perhaps he needed to attack the problem from a different direction.

'Let me know if anything unusual comes up, will you?'

Cadwallader looked up from the corpse, frowned. 'You not staying to the end?'

'No. I've got a better idea.'

'Oh yes? What?'

McLean grinned as he reached for the door handle. It wasn't often he found something to be cheerful about these days. 'I'm off down the East End to see if I can find me a prostitute.'

*

81

Mid-afternoon was the wrong time of day, of course. No one would be plying her trade on the streets at this hour unless she was really desperate and stupid. On the other hand, you had to be pretty desperate to be in this line of business. Stupidity? Well, there were different kinds.

The address Magda had given when she was processed turned out to be a fourth-floor flat in one of the seventies concrete blocks that backed onto the square and lock-ups where Malky Jennings had been found. If it was Malky Jennings. Scaffolding clung to the frontage like a parasite, but there was no sign of workmen. Just a bucket on a rope, looped over a winch at the top and tied away out of easy reach.

The entrances to the flats on the fourth floor were spaced along a long concrete walkway, open to the brisk wind off the Firth of Forth. Fine in the summer, when a breeze kept away the stench of the courtyard below. In the winter, with a cold north-easterly throwing wet snow against anything more than a few feet high, it must have been miserable. Pity the poor buggers who lived on the next two floors up. As he approached the one he was looking for, McLean saw why the scaffolding was there. The rough harling on the parapet running along the outside of the walkway had succumbed to years of Edinburgh's coastal weather, cracked away to reveal loose bricks behind it. The missing workmen had knocked out a fair few of these, no doubt clearing back the rot before repairing the wall. He peered over the edge at the car park far below, felt his muscles tighten involuntarily. It was a long way down.

McLean was about to knock when he realized he'd

come alone, what that meant. He should have found a uniform PC, or better yet DS Ritchie, to accompany him. She was good at this sort of thing, and it always helped to have a female police officer with you. It added balance. But he had to admit he'd been avoiding the station recently, falling back into bad habits. Anything to avoid Duguid, Brooks or more often the pleading of his fellow officers for him to do something about it, please, for pity's sake. Replace 'it' with whatever asinine thing one of his superiors had done that particular day.

Movement further along the walkway caught his eye. The door to the neighbouring flat stood open and a young girl sat outside on the concrete. She was playing with a pair of naked, armless dolls, and as she looked up, McLean could see that her face was grimy, her hair matted in places. She gave him an adult's scowl and returned to her play. One to mention to social services? Or would they just scowl at him themselves and tell him to mind his own business? Probably.

The door opened almost before he'd knocked on it. A middle-aged woman stared at him, not who he'd been expecting. She was shorter than Magda, not much more than five foot tall. She wasn't dressed particularly like a prostitute either, although he didn't really know what a prostitute dressed like when she wasn't working. Jeans, a hoodie maybe. Comfortable slip-ons. This woman looked more like someone who worked in an office. Slacks and a blouse, sensible jacket, heavy handbag slung over one shoulder. She gave McLean a look almost as unfriendly as the little girl.

'What you want?'

83

'Is Magda Evans in?'

The woman turned, shouted into the depths of the flat. 'Magda! I thought you said you'd packed that in.'

A distant voice, coming closer. 'What? What you talking about?'

Magda appeared, barefoot, stained jogging bottoms and a sweatshirt two sizes too big for her. Her quizzical expression turned blank when she saw McLean standing in the doorway. 'Oh. It's you.'

'You know him? One of your Johns?' The short woman managed to fit a long list of derogatory comments into that one word.

'Polis.'

If anything, the short woman's expression grew even frostier. She crossed her arms over her chest. 'Can't youse lot leave her alone, aye? She's no doin' that any more. Not for you. Not for anyone.'

An inkling of what was going on began to form in the back of McLean's brain. He recalled how Magda had reacted to DS Buchanan, how much more willing she was to talk to him without the other officer present. And the short woman, well, his best guess was social services or some shelter. Maybe he should have phoned ahead. Here he was dealing with things as if this were a murder investigation, but there was more to it than that.

'Detective Inspector McLean.' He held up his warrant card so that the short woman could see it. Let her know that he wasn't afraid of her being able to identify him. Could work two ways, he supposed. 'I wanted to have a word with Magda about Malky Jennings. That's all.'

If his words had reassured the short woman, she gave

no sign of it. Magda's face changed at the name, a look of anxiety creeping over her Slavic features. She stood perfectly still, as if frozen by indecision.

'Look, I don't know who you are.' McLean addressed the short woman. 'But I assume you're some kind of helper. I need to talk to Magda, either here or at the station. If it's here, now, then you're welcome to sit in and observe. But I'm dealing with a murder investigation here, and I've not got a lot of patience right now.'

'Murder? Malky's dead?' Magda spoke quietly, but McLean could hear the hope in her voice.

'Someone's dead. It might be him. I'm trying to find that out.'

'Well you'd better come in then,' the short woman said.

Her name was Clarice Saunders, pronounced the way Anthony Hopkins does it. She worked for a charity rehabilitating former sex workers, or at least that was what she told McLean once they were settled in Magda's sitting room. It could have been a wonderful place to live, with a floor-to-ceiling window giving views across the city towards Arthur's Seat and the castle that anywhere else would have been worth hundreds of thousands of pounds. Here, in the Schemes, surrounded by the junkies, the unemployed and the just trying to make the best of their lives with what little they had, a nice view counted for nothing. The single-glazing, rattling in the wind, didn't help. Neither did the mould blackening the corners, reaching up from the floor and down from the ceiling; the flaking paint on the window frames; the peeling strips of faded flock wallpaper. Magda's furniture had seen better days, too. Probably in the mid-seventies from the look of it. But the mugs in which she brought them tea were clean, and the packet of biscuits was within its sell-by date, just.

'Tell me about Malky Jennings,' McLean said once Magda had taken a seat. She perched on the edge, knees close together, legs tucked to one side like a debutante. Her nails had been painted in alternating shades of red and gold but the varnish was beginning to crack and flake away.

'What's to say? He's a toerag who likes to beat up women. You reckon he's dead? I say not soon enough.'

'He was your pimp, right?'

Clarice let out a sharp little bark of a humourless laugh, like a terrier poked.

Magda took a long drink of her tea before replying. 'He owned me. Like I told you back at the station. Right up until he sold me to that Russian.'

'How does that work?'

Another long pause. 'He told me when to work, who to go with, how much to charge. He took all the money and let me sometimes have a little back for food. If he didn't think I was working hard enough, he hit me. If he thought I was trying to hold back some money, he hit me. If he felt like it, he hit me. Never the face, you understand. Always here, here.' She touched her sides lightly. 'You can still give blow jobs even if your ribs are broken.'

'Why did you stay with him? Why –'

'– didn't she go to the police?' Clarice finished a different question to the one he'd been going to ask, but not all that different. 'You're new to the Sex Crimes Unit, aren't you, Detective Inspector. You don't really know how it works.'

86

'I'm beginning to get an idea.'

'You arrest someone like Malky Jennings, another wee shite pops up to take his place. Only first he's got to make his name, ain't he? So he puts his fists about a bit. Maybe picks on one girl and puts her in the hospital. Keeps everyone else in line.' Clarice perched on the edge of the tatty sofa, knees together, elbows planted firmly on them, hands cupped around her mug of tea as she leaned forward earnestly. 'Your lot know this, so they don't arrest people like Malky Jennings. Turn a blind eye. Maybe in exchange for a few favours. Information. Wouldn't surprise me if there was cash involved too. Off the books.'

McLean cast his mind back to the series of interviews, the sullen young women, tight-lipped and nervous. How none of them had said anything much at all, except Magda and then only when DS Buchanan was out of the room. Was it really like that in the SCU? He couldn't believe Jo Dexter standing for that kind of nonsense. At least not the Jo Dexter he'd known back in training college. No doubt it was something he'd have to look into, and no doubt it would make him unpopular, but that wasn't really why he was here.

'Tell me more about Malky, Magda. What was he like, physically?'

' He was average height I guess. Skinny. Big nose. Bad teeth. He used to wear these flash clothes, like he thought he was something out've the movies, you know? Only he wasn't nothing special. Just another violent shit of a man.'

'Could you identify him?' Christ, how to put this delicately. 'If you couldn't see his face?'

87

Magda's brow creased, then her mouth split in a meagre grin. 'Did he fuck me, you mean? Do I know what his scrawny little body looks like? Yes, inspector, he did fuck me. But he wasn't really one for cuddling and intimacy, you know? More a throw you against the wall and bang you up the arse kind of a guy. That or a quick face-fuck with a knife at your throat.'

Sounds charming. McLean fidgeted with the folder he'd brought with him, the case notes so far and photographs of the body. It was beginning to look like this was a dead end, at least for now. No point trying to find out why someone might have killed Malky Jennings if they didn't know for certain he was dead.

'That him?' Magda pointed at the folder. 'Can I see?'

'It's not a pretty sight. If we could ID him from his mug shots I'd not be here right now.'

'I'm not squeamish, Inspector. Show us.' Magda reached out for the folder. Reluctantly, McLean opened it up, selected a full-body shot from the mortuary. Naked and laid out on the slab, the corpse was pale and mottled, skin yellowing around the bloody stumps that had once been hands, sightless eyes staring out from lids chewed away by something that didn't care what it ate. He handed it over, noticing that Clarice strained forward to try and get a look herself, then recoiled in shock.

Magda's reaction was slower, more measured. Her eyes darted over the A4 print, sipping at the details one at a time before going back for more. Her frown came back, and she peered closer still, her nose almost touching the page before she finally went to hand it back.

'It's him. About as certain as I can be from a photo.'

'How can you tell?'

'He has a scar, down here.' Magda pointed to her crotch. 'I gave it to him. Reckon I should be able to recognize it again if I see it.'

13

'Well, that's a pretty positive ID on Malky Jennings. I think we can safely say it's him.'

McLean dropped his coat over the back of the chair currently sat in front of the desk they'd given him in the SCU office. It wasn't the same, comfortable chair that had been there when he'd left that morning; that was groaning under the weight of DS Buchanan at the other end of the room. He'd nick it back when the sergeant left, early as usual, and so the game would continue until he managed to get out of the place altogether.

'Who confirmed it?' DCI Dexter asked from her perch on the edge of one of the several empty desks. The SCU control room was large, dark and empty. As far as he could tell, there were only about five officers working full time in the place, and they tended to avoid it if they could. Behind the chief inspector's head, a whiteboard had acquired some photographs of Malky Jennings in his final resting place, and laid out on the mortuary slab. A few half-hearted early-investigation questions had been marked in. Across the room, the board for the white slave trafficking investigation was fuller, but held much less promise.

'One of the girls we picked up off the boat.'

'You trust the word of a pro?' Jo Dexter raised an eyebrow in mock incredulity.

'She's no love of Jennings. And she was able to identify a unique body marking. On account of she was the one gave it to him in the first place.'

DS Buchanan snorted. 'What'd you offer her in return?'

McLean turned on the sergeant. 'What do you mean?'

'These girls aren't our friends.' Buchanan paused just long enough to be rude before adding, 'Sir.'

'No? That's not what I'm hearing. Some of them seem to be very friendly indeed. To some officers.'

Buchanan's face hardened, his joy at McLean's apparent naivety turning quickly into anger. Suspicions confirmed then.

'You reckon she's reliable, this witness of yours?' DCI Dexter pushed herself off the desk, neatly blocking the space between McLean and the sergeant.

'I think so, yes. She's trying to get out. Being sold into white slavery may have changed her priorities a little. She was with a Clarice Saunders when I met her. You've come across her, I take it.'

This time DS Buchanan's laugh was more of a guffaw. 'The midget? Aye, we've all heard of her. Interfering wee busy-body.'

McLean peered around Jo Dexter to where Buchanan was still sitting at his desk, but the sergeant had his head turned away, fascinated by whatever he was reading.

'You got a moment, Tony?' Dexter asked, nodding towards the door. He followed her out, across the corridor and into her own office. She closed the door firmly behind them, then dropped wearily into her seat, indicated for McLean to take the other one.

'I don't think Pete likes you.'

'Well, if half the things I've heard about him are true, I don't much like him either.'

'Oh they're true. I've no doubt about that. Old hand like him's bound to be a bit bent.'

'And you're OK with that?'

'OK's a strong word. I think it's the least bad alternative.'

McLean rubbed at his face, not sure what to say.

'Look, I know why you've been sent here, Tony. Can't say as I didn't see it coming.'

'Far as I'm concerned this is my punishment for calling Dagwood an idiot to his face. On balance I think I'd rather be here than having to deal with him. Sadly I have to do both, it would seem.'

Jo Dexter slumped back in her seat. 'You really did call him an idiot then.'

'Well he is. And it was my lead that cleared up the cannabis-farming operation, for all the good it did us. But he got the promotion.'

'You sound like a little boy, you know.'

'Oh I'm not bitter about that. Not really. I don't want promotion. I just wish they'd give the job to someone who actually knows what they're doing.'

'Dagwood's cannier than you give him credit for. He sent you here, after all. What is it he always says about you, Tony? You over-complicate things? Something like that.'

'And he over-simplifies. I don't . . . Oh.' Stupid, really. He should have seen it straight away.

'He wants to shake things up here. He's known Pete Buchanan for decades, knows all about how the SCU works, the compromises we make to get results. And he doesn't like it. So he chucks you in here like a grenade. And who benefits when it all explodes?'

'But surely there must be a better way of doing things than . . .' McLean tailed off, trying not to think too hard about exactly what was being done already.

'If we had unlimited resources, yes. If people weren't prepared to pay for sex, maybe all the hookers would find better jobs elsewhere. Maybe there wouldn't be drugs in the Schemes if there was work for everyone. But there isn't. Policing by containment, that's the best we can hope for here. We tread a fine line, and the last thing we need is someone coming in and trampling over all that.'

'I can't turn a blind eye if an officer is taking bribes, Jo. Whatever form they come in.'

Dexter stared at him, her hard face pinched.

'I know. And I shouldn't either. Christ, I'd like to clean this operation up, but there's never a right time. We implode and who knows what's going to happen on the streets?'

'Worse than letting the likes of Malky Jennings operate because we're scared what might come along if he's put behind bars? Worse than rounding up prostitutes and shipping them out to the Middle East to be slaves?'

'Aye, well. About that.' Jo Dexter straightened in her chair, the confessional over. 'This pro of yours, you've got some kind of rapport with her?'

'Jesus Christ. She's not a "pro". She's a young woman with a name, a history. She made some shitty decisions in the past, now she's trying to change.'

'OK. OK. Sorry.' Dexter put her hands up in mock defeat. 'I get your point. Really, I do. But whatever she is, you've got something going there. She won't talk to anyone else, but she might talk to you.'

'You think she knows more than she told us already?'

'She didn't tell us anything, Tony. Neither did any of the others. But they know exactly who took them and why. We need to find this Russian, whoever he is. That should be our top priority.'

'What about Malky Jennings?'

'What about him? He's dead, Tony. You think it's any coincidence he was killed just a few days after his girls have been lifted off the streets?'

'Find the Russian, find who killed Malky. You think it'll be that easy?'

Jo Dexter gave him a weary smile. More like a hopeful grimace, really. 'I never said it'd be easy, Tony. Just do what you can, eh?'

'There is no Russian. You know that, right?'

McLean put down the phone, fresh from speaking to some loon at Serious and Organized in the vain hope that they might both have something helpful about the prostitute-smuggling operation, and be prepared to share it. So far it didn't look good on either count, though there was always the chance his initial enquiry would kick something off and he'd be passed a melodramatic brown envelope in a dark car park sometime. He looked up from his temporary desk in the SCU main office, over to where DS Buchanan was pretending to work.

'What d'you mean?'

'There's no Russian. We'd have heard of him already if

there was. That whore of yours made him up. She's given you something that'll keep you running around for days. Meantime she gets a bit of freedom, chance to find a new pimp.'

'You know her? Magda?'

A moment's hesitation. Not much, but enough for McLean to see the lie coming. Buchanan shook his head. 'Her? No. But I've seen the type plenty.'

'Her type?' McLean didn't try to keep the disdain out of his voice. Couldn't see the point.

'Aye. She's a serial escaper. Stuck in the life, tries to get out. Probably succeeds for a while thanks to someone like your new friend Clarice.' Buchanan made a meal of the name. 'Only thing is, she doesn't know how to operate without a man like Malky telling her what to do. Sooner or later, usually sooner, she'll come crawling back to her old haunts. There'll be a new Malky in charge then, of course. Who knows, we might even have broken him in.'

McLean shook his head. 'You think this is all just a game, don't you.'

'Well it is, isn't it? And one we can't win.'

'So why d'you stay at it? Why not get a transfer out?'

Buchanan shrugged. 'Tried it. Didn't like it. Ended up crawling back here.'

'Hey, Tony. You any idea what time it is?'

He'd been heading out of the station, walking to his old car. Tapped the name in his phone book without thinking, forgetting that his oldest friend had moved to California three months ago, along with his new wife, to take up a

95

very lucrative professorship at a very prestigious university. It wasn't until he heard Phil's voice that he realized what he'd done.

'Come off it, Phil. You're what, ten hours behind?' McLean glanced briefly at his watch. 'Even you should be up by now.'

'You're forgetting the delights of scientific research. I've been up all night checking Assays. Only got to my bed about an hour ago.'

He knew it was a lie, at least the Assays bit. Still, what was the point of having friends if you couldn't lie to them?

'Sorry. Been pulling a few all-nighters here too.'

'Let me guess. You wanted someone to have a pint with and hit speed dial. I knew I shouldn't have let Rachel put our new number into your phone.'

McLean considered pretending there'd been a different reason for his call, found he really couldn't be bothered. 'Something like that, aye. It's been a shitty few days. Shitty few weeks if I'm being honest.'

'You should book yourself some holidays. Come over here and visit. We've got a spare room. You can even see the beach, if you stand on a chair and crick your neck.'

It was very tempting. Hell, he could just hand in his notice and walk away. Except that he knew he'd never do that. 'I'd love to, Phil, but it's complicated. What with Emma and everything.'

'No change, I take it.' Even thousands of miles away, Phil's concern was as genuine as it was a knife to the guts. Had he really forgotten to tell his best friend?

'Christ, did I not say? She woke up, about a month ago.'

'A month! Jesus, Tony, have you any idea what Rae's going to do to me when I tell her? How is she?'

'It's . . . complicated.' McLean settled into the car seat, phone clamped tight to his ear and started telling the tale. He'd hoped he might get a pint and a blether, but right now he'd settle for one of the two. Worry about how he'd not spoken to his best friend in over a month some other time.

Mrs McCutcheon's cat stared up at him from the middle of the kitchen table when McLean let himself in through the back door. It was late, he was tired and the last thing he wanted was to have an argument with a cat.

'You really shouldn't be on there, you know,' he said, shucking his coat off one arm whilst he dropped the pile of case files that he'd foolishly agreed to look over onto the nearest chair. The cat held his gaze for just long enough to let him know it was considering what he'd said, then jumped elegantly from the table and trotted out through the door to the front hall.

The light was on, and the sound of music leaked from the closed door to the library. His brand new Linn stereo system was in there, along with a couple of dozen vinyl LPs he'd picked up in the months since his flat had burned down. Christ alone knew how long it would take to rebuild his collection, amassed over a lifetime and something he'd always meant to catalogue. Perhaps it didn't really matter; it wasn't as if he ever had time to sit and listen to music any more.

The other thing that was in the library, of course, was his whisky. And that was something he felt he deserved, especially after a day like today. What he didn't really want was to have to spend time with people. Old habits died hard, and he'd lived alone for so long. It was a struggle adjusting to having two young women under his roof. Still, needs must when there was a dram at stake, and if he was going to make it through the case files, perhaps more than one.

Emma was sitting on the floor, cross-legged and with her back to him when he opened the door. Jenny Nairn slouched on the sofa, reading a book. She looked up almost guiltily as he entered, that flicker across her eyes something he'd seen countless times in interview rooms. Emma must have noticed it too, as she looked around, straining her neck rather than getting up. A big smile spread across her face when she saw him.

'Tony! We were just talking about you. How was your day?'

An endless round of meetings, paperwork and management issues that meant he'd done no actual investigative work at all. Hence the case files that had followed him home. 'Same as usual.'

'You never were a good liar.' Emma levered herself up off the floor, hopped over and gave him a hug, a chaste kiss on the cheek.

'You ladies get up to anything interesting while I was gone?'

'Jen's been making me do crossword puzzles and stuff. It's meant to work my brain, apparently.'

'She's making good progress.' Jenny put her book down, took her stockinged feet off the cushion and placed them carefully on the floor. Her movements were supple, careful. She reminded McLean of a cat. Nothing done without careful consideration. 'Tell Tony about the camera,' she said.

'Oh god, yes. I almost forgot.' Emma hurried over to the antique writing desk at the far end of the room, came back with a clunky old digital SLR camera he dimly remembered his grandmother buying, around about the same time she'd discovered the delights of the internet.

'Where'd you find that?'

'I was going through the desk, looking for a pen.' Emma's face dropped. 'I hope you don't mind.'

'Not really, no.'

'But the thing is, I know how to use it. See.' Emma popped off the lens cap, twisted a few knobs, put the camera to her face and took a picture. The flash starred his eyes, so McLean had to blink to see the image on the small screen on the back. He looked like he was sucking on a lemon, but then he'd never liked having his photo taken.

'Very nice,' he lied.

'Not that, silly.' Emma's thumbs tapped at the tiny buttons on the back of the camera, flicking from menu to menu with the dexterity of a teenager on an Xbox. Things happened that McLean couldn't begin to understand, but the image changed, turned black and white, cropped, swivelled.

'I know it inside out. It's like I've had one for years, used it every day. But I don't remember ever owning a digital camera at all.'

McLean thought back to the first time he'd met the SOC officer, at a crime scene in Merchiston, snapping away like a paparazzo at a celebrity wedding. She was a dab hand with photo-imaging software, too; a skill that had almost seen her locked up, accused of posting crime scene photographs on dodgy websites.

'You're a trained crime scene photographer.' McLean knew as he said the words that they were the wrong thing. It was so difficult to know how to deal with Emma these days. Her mood swung back and forth like a small child at a birthday party.

'Yes, but I don't remember.' Emma waved the camera about like a club. 'It's like there's this other person inside me who knows all sorts of stuff, but she never talks to me. Just steps in and takes over when it pleases her.'

'Perhaps you need to let her. Encourage her.'

'Actually, that's not a bad idea,' Jenny said. 'You should take loads of photographs. We can make a project of it. Get you outside a bit.'

Emma looked nervously at the window, even though the curtains were drawn. 'Outside?'

'You'll be fine, Em.' Jenny stood up and took the camera. 'We'll start in the garden. You can take pictures of the birds. We won't go any further until you're happy, OK?'

Emma nodded, even though she didn't look happy. As soon as outside had been mentioned the life had fled from her. The sky still seemed to terrify her.

'I think it's probably bedtime anyway.' Jenny handed the camera to McLean, took Emma's hand like she was a child. Unlike a child, she didn't throw a tantrum, just muttered a quiet 'Night' and allowed herself to be led out of the room.

*

Much later, a hefty dram consumed and most of the case files at least skimmed over, McLean glanced at the clock on the mantelpiece. One in the morning was not such an unfamiliar time to him, but it was still late. He knocked back the last of the whisky, stacked the files neatly on the desk and headed for bed.

The hall was dark, no lights on in the rest of the house, so that when he switched off the library light he was plunged into darkness. Shapes re-formed slowly as his eyes adjusted, the ever-present orange glow of the night-time city filtering in through the skylight high above. The dark didn't bother him, not in this house where he'd grown up. He knew all its secrets, the feel of the air in different rooms, the way the floorboards creaked as he walked over them. In the almost-black, with just the faint, distant roar of the city as a background noise, this was his place. He didn't need lights to know it.

The door to Emma's room was closed, which was a relief. It had been a few days now since she'd climbed into his bed for security, like a child frightened of the dark, but her mood swing earlier, and the mention of going outside, had worried him. It wouldn't surprise him at all if he woke to find her alongside him again.

He trod quietly across the landing, the reflected glow of the clouds shining through the big glass skylight over the stairwell, casting evil shadows of deeper black, twisting sinister shapes out of the banisters. His own room was at the far side, opposite Emma's, and as he reached for the door handle, he noticed something out of place. Froze.

When she'd taken on the job of Emma's full-time carer,

Jenny Nairn had insisted on taking one of the attic rooms, rather than any of the main spare rooms that McLean had offered. He wasn't sure why; maybe the opulence bothered her. Or maybe she felt that as a hired help she should of course live in the servants' quarters. Perhaps she felt a need to be above everyone else and looking down. Whatever her reasons, now she was sitting on the narrow back stairs leading up to her room.

'Thought you were never coming up. You work too hard, Inspector.' She pushed herself upright, stepped from the shadows towards him. For a moment he wondered whether this was some kind of awkward advance, but she stopped just outside his personal space.

'You could have come and talked to me downstairs. If there was something you wanted to ask.'

'Nah. You were busy. Looked like you wanted some time to yourself too.'

Nothing could have been further from the truth, really. What he wanted was the company of the Emma Baird he'd met all those months ago. Someone he could go down the pub with, forget about the slow torture that was work in a station run by Acting Superintendent Charles Duguid and his band of cronies. But he couldn't have that, of course.

'Not really,' was all he managed to say. 'This about Emma, I take it?'

'Yes. No. Sort of.' Jenny studied her fingernails for a moment. 'It's kind of, well . . . I don't really know you, but you seem open-minded, right?'

McLean said nothing, wishing she'd get to the point.

'It's just, I've got this idea of something that might

help. Help Em, that is. Only most people, if I mentioned it to them they'd scoff.'

'Doctor Wheeler thinks highly of you. That counts for a lot in my book. If you think there's something that can help Emma, please don't hold back.'

'You sure? OK. Well I was going to suggest you try hypnotic regression therapy.'

Of all the crazy ideas that had skimmed his mind, this wasn't the most loony. At least not quite. 'Hypnosis. As in Derren whatsisname? Brown?'

Jenny's shoulders slumped. 'There you go. It's so hard to shake the old magic trick aspect of it. Hypnosis is a well-researched therapeutic tool. And Doctor Austin is the most skilled hypnotherapist I've ever encountered. She helped me, way back when my folks died. I really think she could work wonders with Emma.'

McLean stifled a yawn born only from lack of sleep. He didn't know much about Jenny's background beyond the basic checks he'd done before hiring her, but the news of her parents' death struck a chord. No stranger to him, that experience. She worked well with Emma and, despite her rather unorthodox appearance, didn't seem the type to suggest something lightly.

'You say Doctor Austin. This is a qualified practitioner?'

'Eleanor's a psychiatrist, yes. She has a private practice in the New Town and teaches at the university.'

'OK. It's not something I'd normally consider, but I'll run it past Doctor Wheeler at Emma's check-up tomor-row. If she's happy, then we'll go see your Doctor Austin.'

'Thank you, Inspector. You won't regret it.' Jenny's face

broke into a wide grin, her teeth flashing white in the semi-darkness. She darted forward, grabbed his hand and squeezed it for a moment in a peculiarly old-fashioned gesture. Then without another word she turned and scampered up the black, narrow staircase to her attic room.

14

'Well, this is all a bit of a fucking mess, isn't it.'

McLean stared out through the grimy windscreen at the long line of traffic not in any way moving down Queen Street. Digging up the roads to put in tram tracks had been one of Edinburgh Council's more inspired ideas. Buggering up the procurement contracts in true civil service fashion so that the job was going to take twice as long was just the icing on the cake. There were times when the city just ground to a halt, and this seemed to be one of them. He suspected the traffic wasn't what was bothering his old friend though. Sat beside him in the passenger seat, Grumpy Bob was for once living up to his name.

'Dagwood making life miserable again?'

'He's a walking disaster area, breaking up teams for no bloody reason. You know what he's got Ritchie doing now?'

McLean did, but he knew better than to get in the way of one of Grumpy Bob's rants.

'She's down in the basement doing Needy's old job. Filing. I mean, for fuck's sake. She's a detective. What's that all about?'

'It's only short term. A week at the most.' McLean indicated, turned down towards the Colonies, got a hoot of the horn from another frustrated driver. Serve him right. Idiot had been half asleep and missed his chance.

'You know as well as I do why she's been sent there and it's got bugger all to do with them needing a sergeant at short notice. There's half a dozen would've come back out of retirement to do the work part time.'

'You think he's really that vindictive?' McLean was going to use the word petty, but thought the better of it. He was searching the corners of the buildings, looking for the street sign whilst at the same time trying to avoid driving into the back of another car.

'What do you think? First thing he did when he took over. Jayne McIntyre's seat wasn't even cold and he'd split up our team. Sent you off to the SCU? Young MacBride running around after Spence like he's a sergeant with years under his belt.'

'He's not making you work for a living is he, Bob?' McLean found the street he was looking for, slowed down as he saw the blue and white tape across the road.

'Ach, you know what I mean, sir. He's just changing things 'cause he can. Fucking us around 'cause we pissed him off. Great man management that is.'

'You're not telling me anything I didn't already know, Bob. Not a whole lot I can do about it though.' McLean killed the engine, climbed out of the car. They were in a tiny street, both sides blocked in by neat terraces of houses. Once upon a time these three-storey buildings would have been single residences, the basement levels the realm of servants. Now they were all split up into as many flats as the landlords thought they could get away with. Tiny little bedsits shoe-horned into rooms that had been small by the standards of the New Town to start with. All the activity seemed to be focused around an upper flat, reached by a flight of stone steps from the pavement. McLean showed his warrant card to a uniform PC who looked about twelve. 'Who's SIO?' he asked.

'Umm. You, sir?' The PC looked confused.

OK. Start again. 'Who's in charge of the crime scene?'

'I'm not exactly sure, sir. Detective Constable Mac-Bride's inside. He seems to be giving orders.'

And so it begins. The breakdown in the chain of command.

'This is a dead body we're dealing with here, Constable?' Grumpy Bob asked the question before McLean had the chance.

'Aye, sir. Hanged hisself.'

'And they sent a detective constable to take charge? No sign of DI Spence or DS Carter? Anyone else?'

'No, sir. Just Stu– ... DC MacBride. Duty doctor's been too.'

Bloody marvellous. McLean looked around the street, the rows of wheelie bins, the gates in the metal railings where steps led down to basement flats, the tightly parked cars with their permits proudly displayed, the gathering faces at windows.

'Right, well, I guess it's up to me then. I want this cordon moved further down the street. Take in the houses either side of the crime scene. I want to know who owns all these cars. I want a list of all the neighbours, this side and across the road. And I need someone to go and tell everyone who's rubbernecking to get back inside. We'll start interviewing as soon as I've seen the body. OK?'

The constable stared slack-jawed, rooted to the spot by the impossible list of tasks.

'Well, get on with it, lad. Don't stand there like you're wanting your arse kicked.' Grumpy Bob stepped in with his size nines. With what might have been a frightened yelp, the young officer jumped to attention, then scurried off in search of help.

'Right then. Let's go see what we've been saddled with, shall we?' McLean said, and headed up the stairs.

There wasn't a lot of room in the tiny flat, and most of it was taken up by the body dangling from a rope tied up in the skylight. Judging by the smell and what little McLean could see as he approached, the deceased had been there quite a while.

'Another suicide?' he asked by way of a greeting. Detective Constable MacBride turned a little too quickly and almost tripped over his own feet, wobbling precariously as he tried not to touch the body. The look of worry on his face eased as he realized who had spoken.

'Oh, thank Christ for that. You back from Vice then, sir?'

'No, Constable, and it's the Sex Crimes Unit, as well you know.' McLean gave the constable a reassuring grin, even though he didn't much feel like it. 'And I'm not here. Just cadged a lift from Bob, OK? He'll be SIO on this one.'

MacBride nodded, he was quick on the uptake that way. Might make sergeant soon, inspector in a couple of years if he was unlucky. He turned back to the body, flattening himself to the wall to make room for McLean and Grumpy Bob to see.

'Looks like a suicide, sir. Jammed a broom handle in the skylight, threw the rope over it, stood on a chair at the top of the stairs. There's even a note through in the room there.'

'But you don't like the look of it.' McLean took a step closer to get a better view of the body. It was male, that much was obvious enough. Judging by the smell, the bloating and the discoloured skin, it had been hanging for weeks rather than days. Flies buzzed around the corpse, a few battering themselves against the glass skylight, most happy to be locked in with such a prize.

'The pathologist been yet?' Grumpy Bob asked.

MacBride shook his head. 'Just Doctor Buckley.'

'Well, we can't do anything here until Angus has done his bit.' McLean scanned the narrow hallway, seeing just two doors leading off it other than the one they'd come in through. 'Where's this note then?'

'This way, sir.'

MacBride inched past the hanged man, careful not to disturb the body. McLean followed, trying not to breathe as much to avoid the stench as anything. Grumpy Bob stayed back. 'I'll just wait, in case Cadwallader turns up, aye?'

As if he wouldn't be able to find the body by himself. 'Fine, Bob,' McLean said. 'Fewer of us in here the better. You know what SEB are like if we contaminate their nice clean crime scenes.'

The door on the right-hand side of the hall opened onto a bedsit room scarcely big enough to stun a kitten. A single bed, unmade, was rammed into one corner, a cheap Formica-topped table within easy reach of it forming a desk of sorts. The only chair in the place was lying on its side in the hallway, not far from the dangling feet of the hanged man. A narrow window peered out through years of grime onto the back of the terrace and the slow-moving

Water of Leith. Underneath it, a kitchen sink, electric water heater and two-hob cooker all filled a space only marginally bigger than a tea tray. The dirty plates in the sink had begun to grow some interesting new life forms, but looking around the tiny room, McLean suspected that was only because the deceased had not been discovered for a week or two. Generally, the place was shabby, cluttered, but not dirty.

'The note's here, sir.' MacBride stood beside the table-cum-desk, studiously not touching anything. A pile of textbooks were wedged up against the wall, the little coloured tags on their spines telling of overdue library tickets. Alongside them, a stack of cheap spiral-bound notebooks and an elderly mobile phone, a broken tin pencil case with a random collection of cheap pens in it. All had been moved to the sides to make space for the single sheet of paper, green biro spelling out the last confused thoughts of a man about to hang himself.

There is no hope, only blackness.
I can see no point in going on.
To whoever finds me, I am sorry.
Farewell, cruel world.

'It's a bit melodramatic, isn't it?' McLean leaned close, inspecting the page for any marks without actually touching it. The notebook it had been torn from lay on the top of the pile, the leaky plastic pen alongside. Everything was very neat, almost perfectly lined up square. He turned and scanned the room again; shabby, not chaotic, but neither was it somewhere an obsessive lived.

A noise from outside dragged his attention back to the door through to the hall, the unmistakable sound of the city pathologist, Angus Cadwallader, arriving on the scene.

'Oh good Christ, Bob. Not another one?' Two footsteps on the wooden steps and then, 'Oh shit. Tracy!'

McLean rushed to the door, fairly sure what sight was going to greet him. Sure enough, frozen in tableau, Angus Cadwallader and his assistant Tracy Sharp stood in the hallway, with Grumpy Bob silhouetted behind them by the daylight outside. Closer still, the body hung from its stout hemp rope. As he watched in horrified fascination, its head slowly shifted sideways and up, as if the hanged man were trying to look his dissector in the eye. And then with a horrible sucking, tearing sound, like pulling a foot from wet mud, it sheared off completely, rotted flesh of neck no longer able to hold the weight of the body beneath it, vertebrae snapped by the drop that had killed him. The body didn't so much fall as slough to the floor, exploding in a mess of foetid liquid, a water bomb balloon filled with diarrhoea that splattered over walls, doors, pathologist and assistant alike. McLean sprang back, gagging at the smell as the rope, released of its tension, flipped the severed head in a neat arc through the open doorway. It landed with a horrible thud, rolled over once and came to a halt at his feet, dead eyes staring sightlessly upwards. He stared back, aware of nothing but the noise behind him as Detective Constable MacBride threw up on the threadbare carpet.

The stench of rotting flesh was still in his nostrils three hours later as McLean sat in a chair in Doctor Wheeler's office, Emma beside him. No one had mentioned it, but he was sure they could smell him. Just too polite to say anything.

It had taken almost two of those hours just to get out of the tiny little bedsit room. Once the body had exploded all over the hall, he and DC MacBride had been effectively trapped; no way out except to wade through a morass of decaying flesh and noxious fluids. Angus Cadwallader had done his best to inspect the remains in situ as quickly as possible, but removing them had proven tricky. In the end one of the neighbours had produced a ladder and they'd climbed out of the window. McLean had sent the constable back to the station for a shower and a change of clothes, with the advice that he might want to think about burning those he had been wearing. There hadn't been time for him to do the same, even with Grumpy Bob ably handling the crime scene. McLean had barely made it to the hospital on time, meeting an anxious Emma and scowling Jenny Nairn in the lobby with minutes to spare.

'These are remarkable. Very good indeed.' Doctor Wheeler shuffled slowly through a pile of photographs printed off earlier in the day. Not only could Emma handle a camera like a professional, she had taken to the photo-editing software like a teenager with a new video game. The results were costing him a fortune in printer ink and glossy paper, but it was worth it to see the spark in her eyes as she worked.

'You've been going outside, I see,' Doctor Wheeler added. 'Is this a park somewhere?'

'The garden,' McLean said. The doctor made no reply,

merely raised an eyebrow and peered more closely at the photograph.

'There's a squirrel lives in that tree.' Emma leaned forward, tapping the photo. 'Mrs McCutcheon's cat tries to catch it, but it's too quick for her.'

'Mrs McCutcheon?'

'Her?'

McLean and Doctor Wheeler spoke at the same time. Her question was understandable, his less so. He'd never given the cat a name, true. And he would always think of it as Mrs McCutcheon's cat. But he couldn't recall ever telling Emma that. Nor had he any idea what gender it was.

'You've been visiting a neighbour?' Doctor Wheeler asked.

'Ah. No. Mrs McCutcheon lived in the ground floor flat in my Newington tenement. She . . .'

'She died in a fire.' Emma's finger slid from the photo, her hands slowly coming together in her lap. Her voice was different, an echo of her old self. 'It was so sad. Only one of her cats survived. Tony took it in. Like he took me in.' She looked sideways at him and a shiver ran through McLean's whole frame. Was that how she thought of him? As the man who took her in and gave her a roof over her head? It was true, in a way. But it was also deeply depressing. They'd had so much more, and now she thought of him as . . . what? A cross between a knight in shining armour and a parent?

'Well, these are very good anyway.' Doctor Wheeler shuffled the photographs into a pile, banging the edges against the desk with a little more noise than was necessary.

'You're making progress. And it shows us that the memories are still in there somewhere. We just need to find the right stimulus to shake them free.'

'Did you have something in mind?' McLean asked. Alongside him, Emma had retrieved her stack of photos and was leafing through them as if no one else was there.

'Ah, the detective's leading question.' Doctor Wheeler smiled. 'As a matter of fact I did. Something a bit unusual, I'll grant you, but a colleague of mine over in Glasgow's used it a couple of times with good results.'

'What are you suggesting?' McLean had a horrible feeling he knew already.

'It's called cranial-electro stimulation therapy,' Dr Wheeler began.

'Shock therapy.' It wasn't a question.

'Not exactly, no.' Doctor Wheeler's voice changed, taking on the tone McLean suspected she used on her students. 'Not like *One Flew Over the Cuckoo's Nest*. That's electro-convulsive therapy. ECT. That would be counter-productive in that it's designed to eliminate behaviours and tends to destroy memories. What we're trying to do is stimulate Emma's brain into rebuilding the lost connections.'

'But you still want to pass an electric current through her head.' McLean slumped back in his chair, let out a long noisy breath. He'd thought maybe some new drug, something behavioural.

'You're sceptical.'

'Does it show?'

'Just a bit.'

He thought about the odd conversation the night

before. 'Probably no worse than what Ms Nairn suggested last night.'

Doctor Wheeler gave him an odd little look, half a smile, half a frown. 'Let me guess. Hypnotherapy.'

'You think it's hogwash?'

'No. quite the contrary. It's a useful part of the recovery process, especially where memory loss is concerned. It would probably be good for Emma, certainly shouldn't do her any harm.'

'I sense a but in there.'

'So easy to read?' Doctor Wheeler shrugged. 'It's not so much the what as the who. I take it Jenny's talking about Doctor Austin.'

'That was the name.'

'Well, Eleanor's good at what she does. I'll give her that much. Silly of me, really. We had a bit of a falling out many years ago, which is probably why I wouldn't have suggested her myself. But she helped Jenny, many others too.' Doctor Wheeler shook her head as if trying to dislodge something stuck there. 'No. You'd be as well taking Emma to see her.'

15

'Why were you even there, for fuck's sake?'

Chicf Superintendent McIntyre's office, early morning. McLean tried to focus on Duguid, not stare past him at the pattern of rain on the window. Too easy to be swept away by the endless motion, tune out the droning noise of that voice. It was a skill he'd perfected through innumerable endless morning briefings as a sergeant, but now was not the time for it, no matter how much he wanted to just ignore his superior.

'You were meant to be assisting Jo Dexter with a murder enquiry, not swanning about poking your nose into messy suicides.' Duguid grasped the sheaf of paper that was Grumpy Bob's initial report on the hanged man as if the act of terminal desperation had been meant only for his personal inconvenience. McLean held his tongue, kept his eyes on the acting superintendent, just the occasional sideways glance about the room. No matter what the man did to the place, it would always be Jayne McIntyre's office as far as he was concerned. A place where problems were shared, dissected, solved.

'Are you even listening to me, McLean.'

'Yes, sir. I'm sorry about the suicide scene. I wasn't meant to be there, but I was getting a lift across to HQ when the call came in. It was on the way, we thought it would be a five-minute detour.'

Duguid sneered. 'That old Morse-mobile of yours not working then?'

It took a while for McLean to realize what the acting superintendent meant. He'd not been using his grandmother's old Alfa much; it wasn't really suited to modern cities with their gridlocked traffic. Somewhere on his list of things to do was buy a new car; he couldn't carry on living across town without one. It was just that pretty much everything else on the list was higher priority.

'Why do I fucking well bother, McLean?' Duguid dropped the mangled report back onto the desk, ran a bony, long-fingered hand over his face and through his hair, like a face-hugging alien. 'You're determined to stick your nose into every little investigation going.'

'With respect, sir. I don't think this is a "little" investigation at all. If you've read the report you'll know that DS Laird thinks it's suspicious. Might not be a suicide at all.'

'Oh Christ. Here we go again. Haven't I heard this before? You said there was something hooky about the last suicide but we couldn't find anything. God only knows how many man hours we wasted interviewing the poor bastard's friends and they all said he was depressed as fuck.'

McLean gritted his teeth. Why couldn't the man see? It was plain as the knobbly lump on the end of his red nose.

'I know what they said, sir. I've read DC MacBride's interview transcripts. Mikhailevic wasn't happy, true, but there's a long way between that and stringing a rope up, looping it round your neck and jumping off a chair you've balanced on the edge of a table. And no one's been able to explain how he did all that without getting any rope fibres under his nails.'

117

Duguid stared up at him with his piggy little eyes, an expression on his face of utter bemusement. 'I just don't get you, McLean. Suicide note – check. Suicidal tendencies – check. None of the neighbours saw or heard anyone else. What more do you need to convince you that he killed himself? A fucking home video?'

'I'd be the first to admit it's tenuous, sir. But I thought we were supposed to investigate crimes. If Grigori Mikhailevic didn't commit suicide. If someone –'

'If someone what, McLean? If someone somehow managed to string him up without him struggling? If someone persuaded him to write a suicide note, climb up on a chair, jump off to his death? Have you heard of Occam's Razor? Educated man like yourself, I'd have thought you would.'

'To be honest, sir, I'd accepted Mikhailevic's death as suicide. Not happy about it, but I get that we don't have limitless resources. I don't consider the time we put into investigating it a waste, either. We'll put that down to different priorities, shall we?'

Duguid opened his mouth to speak, the red anger rising in his face. McLean cut him off before he could start.

'But yesterday's hanging opened up a whole new angle. There were too many similarities for it to be coincidence. They both used the same phrase in their notes: "To whoever finds me, I am sorry."'

'That's hardly enough to launch a murder enquiry,' Duguid scoffed.

'No, sir. It's not. But it's not a normal thing to find in a suicide note. Generally speaking the last thing these people are doing is thinking about the impact of their actions on others. I think we need to consider the possibility that these two suicides are connected. I'd like DS Laird and DC MacBride to reopen the Mikhailevic case, combine the two investigations. Just in case there's some sort of suicide pact going on. You know, like happened down in Wales a few years back?'

Duguid fell silent. Were it not for the drumming of rain on the window, McLean felt sure he could have heard the cogs turning slowly in the acting superintendent's brain. He stood still, hands clasped behind his back, almost at attention. Said nothing while he waited. No point rushing a decision out of Dagwood; you'd only end up regretting it.

'Not Grumpy Bob, no,' Duguid said eventually. 'He's part of Spence's team on the Braid Hill investigation. Technically MacBride is too. You want to look into this suicide so desperately, do it yourself.'

Ah yes, the notorious Braid Hill flasher. Not seen since the students went down for the summer holidays. Just the sort of high-profile, manpower-hungry investigation that needed a detective inspector, a detective sergeant and a detective constable to pursue. Nothing to do with the fact that a certain acting superintendent lived just across the road from the last reported sighting.

'What about DS Ritchie?'

'What about her? She's busy.'

'You've got her running the evidence store, sir. She's an experienced detective sergeant. She transferred down here from Aberdeen to help with investigations, not piss around in the stores. It's bad enough you being shifted to admin without losing anyone else from CID. We're short enough as it is.'

Duguid looked up suddenly at McLean's words, sharp enough to catch the veiled compliment, searching for the joke but not finding it.

'What about the evidence store? We need someone with half a brain to run it.'

'Bring Tam Ferrers out of retirement, or Pete Dundas. He made enough noise about having to quit before his time anyway.'

Duguid's stare narrowed as he considered the idea, as if his hatred for McLean was warring with the realization that it was a sensible suggestion. McLean decided it was time to play his trump card.

'If you bring an ex-copper back in on contract, it's a direct cost, sir. You can run it through the admin budget rather than payroll.' Not as if he'd wasted a morning discussing it with Heather in HR.

'Very well.' Duguid gave his head the lightest of nods. 'You can break the news to her yourself. And set up something with Human Resources to get a replacement in.'

Of course, because it's every detective inspector's job to sort out the station's admin staff needs. McLean nodded back in acknowledgement, turned to leave.

'And McLean.'

'Sir?' He didn't turn around.

'I want this done by the sergeants and constables. Use PC Gregg or someone else from uniform. There's plenty wanting a shot at being a detective. None of your hands-on, sticking your nose in everywhere stuff. You're an inspector now. You manage the investigations. Direct. Leave the grunt-work to those on a lower pay scale.'

'Sir.' Another nod. McLean ground his hands into fists

and willed himself calm. He left the office without another word, closed the door firmly behind him. He'd got what he wanted; it was just a shame it had come at such a high cost.

'I don't know what you did to get me out of there, sir, but I owe you big time.'

Detective Sergeant Kirsty Ritchie sat in one of the uncomfortable chairs in the CID room, leaning back against the wall. She'd only been in the evidence store a week, but already she had taken on the pale and unhealthy pallor of those who dwelled underground.

'Me? I didn't do anything.' McLean feigned ignorance as he set to cleaning the scribbled notes of a long-abandoned investigation from the whiteboards that filled one wall of the room. He thought he'd been clever, stopping by the major incident room and nicking a whiteboard eraser and a handful of pens, but time had welded the ink in place. Now he was doing his best with a damp cloth he'd found in amongst the detritus around the coffee machine in the far corner of the room. He suspected it was meant for drying up mugs. If so, no one had explained to the detectives who used the place that they were supposed to wash them first.

'That's not what I heard. And there's no way Dagwood could've come up with the idea of bringing back Sergeant Dundas from his retirement.'

'And yet there it is. His own idea, fully formed and costed in his head.' McLean polished a coffee smear from the now usable whiteboard and took a step back. Where to start? He took a red marker pen out of his pocket and

121

wrote 'Grigori Mikhailevic' in capital letters at the top. Pulling out another pen, blue this time, he reached across to write the next name a couple of feet away. Paused.

'The second hanging. What was his name again? Paul Sanders? Pete?'

Ritchie dropped her seat back down, pulled the folder off the desk beside her. 'Patrick Sands. Twenty-five years old. Works in a call centre off Leith Walk. Studying part time for his banking exams.' She gave a little snort of disbelief. 'I didn't even know there was such a thing.'

'Every day's a good day when you learn something new.' McLean wrote the name down and stepped back again. So far the only thing linking these two was the fact that they were both written on this board here in the CID room. Now all they had to do was fill in the big blank space between them.

'Where do we start?' Ritchie asked, standing beside him now. She had the Mikhailevic file in one hand, tapped the corner of it lightly against her chin. McLean caught that slight whiff of perfume off her and realized he'd not smelled it for a while now. Duguid had done a fine job of ripping his team apart.

'There's a list of Mikhailevic's friends and co-workers in there.' He pointed at the folder. 'Don't worry, it's not long. Contact them all and see if any of them know Sands.'

'I'll get on it. What have we got on Sands so far?'

McLean picked up the other folder, slimmer even than the one Ritchie was holding. 'Bugger all. Name, place of work. Not much else. MacBride did what he could, but he's got a lot else to deal with.'

'He going to be helping us with this one?'

McLean let out a long sigh. 'It would make sense. He was the first detective at both scenes. But like I said, Mike Spence has got him running around after every call that comes in. And Dagwood said no. See if you can get PC Gregg to help, or one of the other more resourceful uniforms.'

Ritchie gave him a sceptical look. 'What about Grumpy Bob?'

'Did I hear someone calling my name?'

McLean and Ritchie both turned at the same time, narrowly avoiding a nasty collision. Grumpy Bob stood in the doorway, a newspaper tucked under one arm, coffee mug in the opposite hand. Little tendrils of steam wafted off the top, bringing a warm, rich aroma to the room. Not from the canteen then.

'Morning, Bob. You still working that burglary case?'

'Got the little toerag down in the cells as we speak, sir. Can you believe he tried to flog some of his ill-gotten gains across the road.' Grumpy Bob nodded towards the window in an approximation of the direction of the pub used almost exclusively by police officers just off their shift.

'Surely nobody's that stupid,' Ritchie said.

'You've not been in Edinburgh long, lass. We take pride in the idiocy of our petty criminals.' Grumpy Bob dropped his newspaper onto his desk, pulled out the chair and sat down. He took a long slurp of coffee, staring at the white-board all the while.

'Mikhailevic. That's the chappy hanged himself, aye?'

McLean nodded.

'And Wee Paddy Sands would be the one we had to scrape up off of his own floor yesterday.'

McLean resisted the urge to ask who Bob thought 'we' was in this statement, since as far as he was aware, the detective sergeant had kept well away from the clean-up operation. 'That's the one.'

'What makes you think there's a connection?'

'Come on, Bob. Two hangings in quick succession? Similar profile to the two victims? The same phrase used in both suicide notes?'

'The same rope, too.' Grumpy Bob grinned and for a moment, McLean was a wet-behind-the-ears detective constable again.

'You noticed that.'

'I noticed that, aye. And it's not just any old rope either. Good solid hemp, three-quarter inch thick. You got photos in those folders?' Grumpy Bob pushed himself out of his seat like a much younger man, reaching for the reports. He shuffled through the first one, coming out with a couple of glossy sheets, stuck them to the whiteboard under Mikhailevic. By the time he'd finished, Ritchie had done the same for Sands. McLean stood back, watching them at work.

'You'll only get that at a ship's chandler's.' Grumpy Bob tapped at one of the photographs showing a close-up of the rope still tight around the victim's neck. The second picture was just the rope laid out, the knot still tight. 'There's only a couple in the city, probably worth paying them a visit.'

'While you're at it, see if you can find an expert on knots,' McLean said. The two sergeants stopped what they were doing.

'Knots?' Grumpy Bob asked.

'Knots. Yes. I don't know much about them. Sure I couldn't tie one of those hangman's nooses, but they look very similar to me. Everything else is circumstantial so far, but if we can show that these two knots were tied by the same person . . .' McLean let the sentence go unfinished, stared at the two photographs, that all too familiar chill forming in his gut as the implications of what he was seeing started to build.

16

McLean found Jo Dexter at her desk, poring over some photographs that would almost certainly get anyone else arrested, should they be found in their possession. It looked like she was comparing images to see if the same child appeared in more than one. The scowl on her face when she looked up as he knocked at the door showed just how little she enjoyed the task.

'Thought you were coming in earlier,' she said by way of greeting.

'I was, but I had to go and see his majesty first. Seems I'm now working Vice and Homicide. It's a good thing I don't need to sleep.'

Dexter tried to smile at the joke, but it didn't really sit well with the job she'd been doing. Everyone referred to the Sexual Crimes Unit as Vice, except the poor bastards working there. Nothing glamorous about dealing with paedophiles and rapists day in and day out. Never mind the prostitution and all its associated ills.

'Still buggered sideways till Tuesday?'

'Something like that. I don't know whose brilliant idea it was to put Dagwood in charge, but they'd better make a decision soon about a permanent station head.'

'What if they decide to give it to him?'

McLean looked at the DCI's face, searching for any

hint that she was joking. Finding none. 'They wouldn't. They couldn't. Could they?'

'They thought he was good enough to fill in.'

'Yes, but that was just temporary. I mean, Jayne had to move out sharpish when . . .'

Now the smile, a wicked cracking around the eyes. It was a tired one though, as if the possibility of Superintendent Charles Duguid, not acting, was too terrible even for the darkest of comedies.

'What's he got you working on then?' Dexter shuffled the photographs back into a pile, pushed them into a brown folder where she wouldn't have to look at the one on top. At least not for now. McLean told her about the two suicides by hanging, DC MacBride's initial suspicions and the anomalies that had come to light after just a brief investigation.

'I can see why he's not happy throwing a lot of manpower at it,' Dexter said after a while. 'I mean, it sounds suspicious to me, but in the end it's a couple of lonely blokes with no prospects both deciding to top themselves the same way. You'll probably find there's been a documentary about a hangman on the telly recently. Something like that. Just bad luck it struck a chord with both of them.'

McLean rubbed at his eyes. 'Thanks for the support.'

'Hey. I'm just saying. You may be right.' Dexter held her hands up in surrender. 'Anyways, I'm guessing that's not what you came to chat about.'

'No, I was wondering where we were with Malky Jennings. I missed the morning briefing.'

'Wouldn't've made any difference if you'd been there. Nothing's changed. We've as much chance of catching whoever did him as I have of making Detective Super. Acting or no.'

'Interviews all done?'

'Aye. Every single apartment in that square. Even the ones that look out the other way. Half the folk living there are on the dole. They'd've been in all day watching telly. Or stoned out of their heads. Nobody saw a bloody thing.'

'And he was killed somewhere else, dumped in the night?'

'That's what the SOCOs and your pathologist friend think. Beaten to death with a stick or a bat and then thrown into the garbage pile at the back of the lock-ups. No real surprise he was there; half his pros live in those apartments.'

McLean thought of Magda Evans in her mouldy fourth-floor flat, standing at that floor-to-ceiling window and looking down as someone beat her pimp into a pulp. Or had she already been on her way to the boat then? He'd got more information out of her than anyone else so far. Perhaps he should go and talk to her again. Might be worth speaking to that charity wifey as well, if he could remember her name. Sanders or something.

'You've got that look on your face again, Tony. What're you thinking?'

'Just what you said. Half his pros live there. Might be worth having another chat with them.'

'I'll get Pete onto it. He knows everyone down there.'

'That might not be the best idea.' McLean pulled up a chair and sat down. He knew this was going to be difficult; no reason for it to be uncomfortable too.

'What is it with you and him? You don't like his methods? He gets results.'

'He scares people into giving him what he wants. From what I've heard that's not always information. I'd not be happy working with someone who took that sort of thing if it was offered, let alone demanding it with menace.'

'Like I said, he gets results.' Dexter sat back in her chair, shoulders slumped. 'I don't like it any more than you do, but it gets to you, this job.' She swept a weary hand in the direction of her desk, the envelope filled with pictures of young children having their innocence stripped away along with their clothes. 'Some of us just get bitter, drink too much. Others get it out of their system in different ways. Pete Buchanan has been here longer than anyone.'

McLean shook his head. 'It's no excuse. And it's no help here. You saw how those girls we took off the boat clammed up when he was interviewing them. They're not going to help us if he's about.'

'And you think they will if it's just you?'

'No. But they might if I get Clarice Saunders in.' Judging by Dexter's expression he'd got the right name.

'Jesus, Tony. Dagwood said you'd be a breath of fresh air in the place. He didn't say anything about a tornado. You want to bring that woman in here?'

'I want to find out who killed Malky Jennings. I've a suspicion it's the same people who pulled all those women off the streets and put them on a boat to the Continent. Next stop the Middle East and Christ alone knows what.'

'And all Clarice Saunders will want to do is tear a strip off any officer she can buttonhole for more than two minutes.'

'If Buchanan's the best we can do then maybe she's got a point. Look, we can do this at my own station, use some of the CID sergeants. New faces.' McLean stopped speaking, aware that Duguid would have a fit if he found out. Dexter stared at him, silent for what felt like an hour. He said nothing, just met her stare and waited.

'Fine,' she said eventually. 'Bring Little Miss in. Interview your girls without any of us to help.'

'Thank you.' McLean stood, opened the door. Dexter waited until he was just about to leave before speaking again.

'Just don't blame me when it all blows up in your face.'

The CID room was empty when McLean popped his head round the door several hours later. The whiteboard had begun to fill up, evidence of some work going on at least. He had to hope that Ritchie and Grumpy Bob were off interviewing friends and associates of the late Patrick Sands, or maybe following up something from the pathology report.

Thinking of it, McLean realized he'd not seen anything about Sands since his partly liquefied remains had been scooped up and taken away for closer examination. That was one post-mortem he was pleased not to have had to witness. But it was frustrating nonetheless. Being split between two teams meant he couldn't concentrate fully on either. Nor could he give Emma the attention she really deserved.

Without realizing it, McLean had entered the room and crossed to the whiteboard. Grumpy Bob's and Ritchie's desks faced each other close by, and he started to scan the papers lying on them for anything that might look like a pathologist's report. He almost jumped when the door opened across the room, starting like a guilty schoolboy. But it was only DC MacBride who entered.

'Afternoon, Stuart. You seen the path report for Sands?'

'Erm. Couldn't rightly say, sir.' MacBride looked very uncomfortable, as if he were a child recently scolded.

'Someone been picking on you, Constable?'

MacBride's cheeks went pink, his forehead shining like a beacon. He was going to have to work on that if he wanted to make a good interviewer.

'It's Dagwood, isn't it. Let me guess. He told you not to work on any of my cases, and if I bullied you into it to let him know. Am I right?'

'Actually it was me, but the sentiment's the same.' Mac-Bride spun around as the door he'd just entered pushed open. He was so close that it almost caught him on the chin, not that the man behind it would have cared.

'Come on, MacBride. Out the way.' Detective Chief Inspector John Brooks blundered into the room, closely followed by his sidekick, Detective Inspector Michael Spence. Or Little and Large as they were universally known in CID. Behind them, a gaggle of DCs clustered nervously, no doubt awed by the presence of such powerful men.

'I thought you were working Vice these days, McLean.' Brooks dropped his heavy frame into the nearest available chair, glanced up at the whiteboard. 'Oh yes. Your pet theory about the suicides. Charles did mention something now I think about it.'

Charles. McLean stifled a laugh. As if Brooks hadn't

spent his entire time in CID calling Duguid every name under the sun. Now they were best buddies and on first-name terms. Or maybe he was just trying to impress the new recruits.

'You know me, sir. I don't like unanswered questions.'

'Problem is you see questions where there aren't any, McLean. Don't you. And you just keep on asking them regardless of the cost.'

'I prefer to think of it as being thorough. Sir.'

'Well go and be thorough somewhere else then. I need this room for a briefing.' Brooks nodded at the assembled constables, all of whom were staring at him like first-years in front of a prefect. Except MacBride, McLean noticed. He at least had the decency to look embarrassed.

'Unless of course you'd like to sit in and give us the benefit of your thoroughness.' This from Little Detective Inspector Michael Spence. Until he'd said it, McLean might have considered staying to listen, if only to annoy Brooks. On his own, Mike Spence was OK, but something of the toad crept into him when he was with his boss. Together they could be as catty as schoolgirls and he really wasn't in the mood for being on the receiving end of that.

'It's OK. I wouldn't want to get in the way.' McLean turned his back on the detectives, caught MacBride's eye as he left. 'You see DS Ritchie, let her know I'm looking for her, aye?'

MacBride nodded, but said nothing. McLean left him, sitting with the others and yet painfully apart. Well, the lad was going to have to learn about politics if he wanted to go anywhere.

17

He doesn't really know why he's come here. Well, that's not true; there's the pain, that's the main reason. But this isn't a place for pain, not exactly. The hospital's for pain. They give you drugs that don't really take it away, just make you not care about it so much. Except that he does, care that is. He can feel it, even through the stupefying, thought-muddying fog of medication. The grinding of bone upon bone, the stretch of scar, ripping deep inside muscle, the impossible weariness of constantly feeling his whole body falling apart.

'Jonathan. Welcome. I've heard so much about you. Please, take a seat.'

He folds himself into the chair as gently as possible. Even so his skin screams at the touch of soft cushion and old leather. Somewhere deep inside he knows that it can't really hurt, not sitting in a chair, but that part of his brain is no longer wired to the rest of him.

'You were in an accident, they tell me. Badly hurt.'

He tries to focus on the person speaking to him, but the words take him straight back to that day. He remembers it all, cannot help living it over and over again. The screeching noise like an animal mortally wounded, brakes locked, rubber on tarmac. It only took seconds but he pictures it in years. The slow inevitability of it all is almost as bad as the pain. Tiny details present themselves: the

expression on the driver's face, more annoyance than surprise; the pattern of cracks in the windscreen that will
shatter and rend his skin to mincemeat; the broken wiper
arm that will knife him like a jealous lover, vent his spleen.

'You've been in a lot of pain, yes? Even though your
body has healed, it still troubles you.'

He isn't healed. Not nearly. He can hear the shotgun
cracks as his bones pop, feel the wind rush out of him as
the van hits. He is flying through the air, helpless as the
street bin rushes up to meet him. Better if he'd not been
wearing his helmet. Then it would have been over quickly.

'I can help you. I can make the pain go away.'

A touch, light on his hand. It sends shivers of purest
agony pulsing through his arm. He looks up, sees no face,
no body attached to that point of contact. Just two eyes,
blazing like the headlights that took away his life. Something surges through him, a force that would be impossible
to resist, even if he wanted to resist it. But he doesn't.
This is why he came here, after all. To be rid of the pain.
To be rid of it all.

'You are mine!' The voice is triumphant, gloating
almost as if it has won some great victory. He no longer
cares. Longs only for it to end.

'Yes. I am yours.'

18

He'd been expecting something different. McLean wasn't really sure what; maybe a bit more mysticism, some occult paraphernalia, even a picture of Paul McKenna or something. Instead the offices of Doctor Eleanor Austin were light and airy. More Feng Shui than Doris Stokes. They had sat in a room that could have been the reception area for a dentist or an accountant, plied with coffee and pleasantries by a young assistant who had introduced himself as Dave. The wait had been short, and now they were in the therapy room with Doctor Austin herself. She was older than he'd thought she'd be. Much older than Doctor Wheeler, certainly. And yet she held herself with the poise of a younger woman. She sat in a high-backed leather armchair on one side of a low table. Emma had a similar seat to herself and he was relegated to a sofa arranged along one wall so that he could see and be seen by both of them.

'So tell me, Emma. What's your most vivid memory from before the . . . trauma?'

'I'm not really sure. It's all such a blur.'

'That's the recent past. We'll get to that. Tell me something that you remember from a long time ago. Home, perhaps. A birthday, or maybe Christmas?' Doctor Austin's voice was soft, calm, reassuring, with the slightest hint of a sing-song lilt to it, an accent McLean couldn't place.

'I never liked Christmas. Mum was always sick, and Dad . . . I don't want to talk about Dad.'

Emma was still pale, even this long after coming out of her coma. The high-backed chair she sat in almost swallowed her, making her look even more like the child he sometimes thought she had become. As far as he was aware, no actual hypnotism had taken place yet; this was just a getting to know you session.

'What about university then? I understand you went to Aberdeen, read biology.'

'I don't remember. I mean, yes. I understand on some level I must have. I know a lot about it. Just don't know how I know, if you know what I mean.' Emma's voice had begun to take on that edge McLean had become all too aware of. The tone that said she was verging on panic as she tried to sort the memories in her head. He'd tried gently questioning her himself, teasing out details and helping her build a trail in her mind back to where they'd originally come from. It usually ended badly. He couldn't begin to imagine what it was like, to know something but not know how you knew. To understand that a large chunk of your life was missing. He'd be treading on the edge of terror himself, if it had happened to him.

'OK. Let's leave that for now.' Doctor Austin was obviously sensitive to the mood too. Then again, you'd have to be in her line of work, surely. It was all about the empathy, after all. 'We'll try something different.'

'Are you going to hypnotize me?' Emma asked.

'Not straight away, no. I just want you to relax. Close your eyes. Listen to my voice.' Doctor Austin began to recite a slow, quiet litany, her voice even softer than it had been before. It took him a while to make out the actual words, longer still to realize that he, too, had closed his eyes. With an effort, McLean opened them. The room turned darker, and colder too. An involuntary shiver ran through his body. Emma had almost disappeared into the back of her chair, her head drooped, eyes closed, arms folded loosely on her lap. Opposite her, Doctor Austin was in complete contrast, ramrod stiff, upright, chin jutting out. Her eyes too were closed, but McLean could see flickering movement behind the lids as if she were reading some script off the inside of them. She crackled with an energy that was both reassuring and alarming. He shook his head, not realizing until he did that it was fuzzy, as if he'd been drinking on an empty stomach. With the motion, the room brightened, the scene shifted almost imperceptibly, Doctor Austin's words drifted away to nothing.

'Did you fall asleep, Tony?'

McLean shifted his gaze at the question. Emma was no longer sitting in her chair, but had somehow stood and crossed the room to where he was sitting without him realizing. He looked up at her with a mixture of confusion and surprise. She loomed over him, the ceiling light making a halo of her spiky hair, and she was smiling at him with a grin that went right up to her eyes. It was the first time he'd seen her smile like that since she'd woken in the hospital, and it filled him with hope that chased away the strangeness of the past few minutes.

'I did? I guess I was more tired than I thought.'

'Can we go home now?' Emma turned a little, towards where Doctor Austin was still seated, and the effect of the lights disappeared. Without the halo, the smile, she was once more the frightened little girl in a woman's body. Her whole posture was different, hunched into herself as if she had no self-confidence.

McLean hauled himself out of the sofa, knees protesting as if he'd been sitting there for hours. A quick glance at his watch, but no, only twenty minutes had passed since they'd been ushered into the room by Dave.

'Are we finished?' he asked Doctor Austin.

'For now, yes.' The doctor stood, touched a hand lightly to Emma's elbow and steered her towards the door. 'I'll need to see you again in a few days. Then we'll try a little hypnosis.'

McLean followed the two of them out of the room, through the reception area where Dave was forcing coffee and biscuits on another customer. He felt removed from the scene, as if his hearing were dulled by listening to loud music, but as he stepped out of the building into the
street and the clear, bright sunlight, the noise of the city returned, enveloping him like the embrace of an old friend.

The downside of taking the morning off to see Emma through her session with the hypnotherapist was that he had a mountain of paperwork waiting for him when he finally arrived at the station. McLean had taken the unusual step of closing his office door in the hope that nothing would disturb him. Now an unpleasant electronic imitation of an old-fashioned bell broke his concentration as he fought to understand a set of overtime forms that appeared to have no bearing on any of his active

138

cases. He dropped the sheaf of papers and reached gratefully for the phone, noting the flashing light for the front desk.

'McLean.'

'Ah. Glad I caught you, sir. There's a fellow down here asking for you by name.' Sergeant Murray was working the desk this afternoon, it would seem.

'You couldn't be a bit more specific could you, Pete?'

A short pause as if the desk sergeant were trying to find the right words. 'It's, errr . . . personal, sir.'

Oh bloody hell. 'OK. I'm on my way.'

McLean hung up, took a quick look around his office in an attempt to fix it in his mind. It wouldn't be the first time he'd been called away on a false errand only to find on his return that things had been moved. He could lock the door, of course, but somehow that felt like ceding victory to his tormentors before the game had even begun. And there was always the possibility this was a perfectly genuine matter requiring his personal attention. A slim possibility.

The station was quiet as he strode the corridors, which either meant everyone was out fighting crime or they were all avoiding him. He pushed through the security door into the reception area, seeing a well-dressed elderly gentleman with a large leather Gladstone bag. No one else had seen fit to bother the police at that precise moment, and a quick glance over his shoulder showed that Sergeant Murray was nowhere to be seen. Ah well, might as well play along.

'You wanted to see me, Mr . . . ?' McLean approached the elderly gentleman, who looked up, startled by the voice. He was thin, long-fingered bony hands folded

139

neatly across his lap, head somehow too large for his body. His suit fitted perfectly, but whereas on a younger man this would flatter, on him it only emphasized how much he needed a really good meal. McLean had seen enough cadavers to know better than to use the adjective cadaverous lightly, but this time he felt it was perhaps justified.

'Detective Inspector McLean?' The well-dressed man stood up as if his muscles had been replaced with rubber bands. Standing, he was taller than McLean had been expecting. He held out a hand to be shaken. 'Jeremy Scranton. From Garibaldi and Sons.'

'The tailors?' McLean took the hand, surprised to find it was warm and not mortuary cold.

'The same. I've come for your measuring, as arranged. Would you like to do it here, or is there somewhere a little less, ahem, public? I've brought some material samples for you to consider as well.'

It didn't take a genius to work out what was going on. McLean looked back over his shoulder to the reception desk, hidden behind its screen of bullet-proof glass. Sergeant Murray was nowhere to be seen, which rather confirmed that he'd been in on the joke. Like most pranks, it was hilarious to the people who'd thought it up, and no doubt they'd be sniggering at how well they'd fooled him, but this poor old man had done nothing. He'd come here, taken up his precious time, expecting to be paid, and now he was going to have to go back to his shop empty-handed. Worse, if McLean ever wanted to buy something from Garibaldi and Sons, who were by all acknowledgement the finest tailors in the city, if not the whole of Scotland, then he was going to have to do some serious apologizing.

Or he could just go with it, and get a nice suit into the bargain.

'Thank you so much for coming, Mr Scranton. Please, follow me.'

A parcel sat on the kitchen table waiting for him when McLean let himself in late. He fully expected to get a couple of fine suits out of the prank, but being measured up had taken a lot longer than he'd anticipated. And the paperwork he'd been avoiding all day had still needed doing after Mr Scranton had left.

The house was quiet, even Mrs McCutcheon's cat barely stirred from its place beside the Aga, just lifted its head and fixed him with a beady stare for a moment before going back to sleep. He strained his ears for sounds that anyone was still up, but at this hour he doubted it. The clock in the kitchen suggested it was more tomorrow than today. So much for work–life balance.

One good thing to be said about having two women living in his house was that there was always food in the cupboards. Jenny was a vegetarian, something that had not come as much of a surprise to him, and Emma had taken her cue. Consequently most of what was in the fridge could be labelled under the broad term 'salad' and everything in the cupboards looked distressingly healthy. There was beer though, and wine. Through in the library there would be whisky too. He set about making himself a cheese sandwich, debating long and hard before adding a couple of lettuce leaves and a smear of mayonnaise. Poured himself a glass of Riesling from the bottle he'd started yesterday and took his spoils to the table.

The parcel was a little larger than A4, and as thick as a box file. His name and address were on a label printed out and stuck across the front, but there were no franking mark or stamps. Taking a bite of sandwich, he pulled the parcel towards him, turned it over. The name of an old city auction house had been printed on the back, and at the sight of it he remembered. The auction of Donald Anderson's books, the curious impulsion to buy this copy of Gray's *Anatomy*, purportedly from the collection of Sir Arthur Conan Doyle.

'A nice lady dropped it round earlier.'

McLean twisted round in his seat, sending a slice of pain up his neck in the process. In the shadows by the door through to the hall stood Jenny Nairn. He'd not heard her come in; a quick glance showed bare feet poking out from the legs of her sweatpants, hoody with the hood down on top, arms folded as she leaned against the wall. Her nose ring glinted in the light, her eyes dark shadows that were hard to see. How long had she been standing there watching him?

'I say lady.' She pushed herself away from the wall, padded into the light. 'But he was plainly a man dressed as a lady. You have strange friends.'

'Madame Rose. She . . . He runs a, well, I'm not sure what you would call it. A psychic centre, I guess. Palm reading, Tarot cards, that sort of stuff. Out of an old flat down Leith Walk. He's also something of an expert on medieval books and manuscripts, especially the more esoteric stuff. Not sure I'd describe him as a friend. He brought this round himself?' McLean hefted the parcel.

'Just winding you up. Everyone knows Rose.' Jenny

grinned as she drew out a chair and slumped into it. 'He dropped in back of six. Think he was a bit disappointed you weren't home.'

'That makes two of us.' McLean took another bite of his sandwich, carefully peeled open the parcel and slid out the book inside. There was a bill of sale from the auction house and a handwritten note.

'May I?' Jenny nodded at the book.

'Sure.' McLean handed it over.

'You went to see Eleanor today,' Jenny said.

'Doctor Austin? Yes.'

'I'm so glad you did. She helped me out when my folks died. Don't think I'd be here if it wasn't for her. She'll sort Emma out, don't you worry.'

'Your folks?' The words were out before McLean remembered. 'Oh yes. You said. I'm sorry.'

'No worries.' Jenny tapped a slender finger on the cover of the book as she spoke. 'It was a few years back now. Christ, near enough ten. You deal with it. Move on, y'know?'

'As it happens, I do. Sort of. I was four when my parents died. My gran raised me. Here in this house. Seemed somehow appropriate given I was born here.'

'Here? In this house? For real?' Jenny's face cracked into a wide grin as she echoed his words. 'How'd that happen? Your mum not trust doctors?'

'Far from it. Gran was a doctor. Ended up a pathologist, but she was working as a GP when I was born. She wouldn't hear of my mother slumming it in some hospital.'

'So which room, then? Where did the great Detective Inspector Tony McLean take his first breath?'

The question surprised him, not so much for its personal nature as for the wild-eyed enthusiasm that had come over her. He'd not thought about the facts of his birth in years; well, it wasn't something you dwelt upon, really. He remembered his gran bringing it up at dinner parties or whenever he invited a girl home. Her little way of embarrassing him to show she cared.

'Oddly enough, it was in the attic. Mum was up there doing all the sorts of things pregnant women are told not to do when they're close to term. I arrived earlier and quicker than expected. Gran just rolled her sleeves up and delivered me on the attic floor. That's how she tells it, anyway. Told it, I should say.'

Jenny's smile faded slightly. 'You miss her. Your gran.'

'She was more of a mum than my mother ever had the chance to be. But like you said, we deal with it, move on.' He shook his head slightly, trying to dislodge the feeling that he was lying to himself. No doubt sensing the awkwardness, perhaps feeling it herself, Jenny opened up the book near the back and started leafing forwards. McLean watched her for a moment before realizing he was still holding the note Madame Rose had written to him.

My Dear Inspector, it began. *I trust this finds you well. I hope to speak to you in person, but if you are not around then this note should suffice for now. My investigations have, alas, yielded little to corroborate the signature in the front of this book. It is of the correct type and age for a medical student of that time, and if Donald had it in his collection then it is likely he thought it genuine.*

McLean stopped as he read the name. Donald. So informal, as if he and Madame Rose had been friends. But then there was really no reason why they should not have been. Anderson was older, of course, but he'd been another expert in the same small field. They'd have known each other well. McLean shook his head, dispelling the train of thought, and returned to the note.

The grapevine informs me that your paramour is returned to consciousness. I would be the last to indulge in idle gossip, but I trust that Miss Baird fares well and is making a speedy recovery. You and I both know the malign influence to which she was exposed, however, and you have unique experience of the evil that can come of it. It is my most fervent hope that her encounter was brief and has led to no permanent harm, but should you suspect otherwise, please know that you need only ask and I will do all in my power to help.

Ever yours
Madame Rose

'Arthur Conan Doyle. Who'd've thought it?' Jenny Nairn snapped the book shut as McLean stared at the note and its curious contents. He placed it on the table, then laid the bill of sale on top of it, though he couldn't really be sure who he was hiding it from.

'We don't know it's real,' he said eventually, taking the book back and opening it up. The dedication and signature were there on the top of the first page. Just the sort of place a young and impecunious student would mark his valuable possession.

'We don't?' Jenny arched an eyebrow. 'It looks like his signature, doesn't it?'

'That's easily faked. Apparently the ink too. There's a big market for Conan Doyle memorabilia, particularly in the States. Something like this could fetch a lot of money if it were verified.'

'But that's not why you bought it, is it.' It wasn't a

question, which was just as well. McLean looked at his half-eaten sandwich, the red lettuce leaves poking out through the cheese and mayonnaise like a bloody gash in dead, white flesh. His appetite vanished, and even the glass of wine had lost its appeal. He felt suddenly very tired.

'You should go to bed. It's late.' Sitting beside him at the kitchen table, Jenny sounded just like his grandmother. An impressive feat given her age. He couldn't argue with her logic though, started to clear up his plate and glass.

'I'll sort that out, don't worry.' Jenny took them from him, bustled over to the sink.

'I didn't hire you as a maid, you know.'

She ignored him, carried on acting like one. 'She's in your bed again. Emma.'

McLean sighed. It was difficult to sleep with her there. He'd been alone so long before she'd forced her way into his life, and he couldn't help remembering her warmth, her vitality, her intoxicating scent. Having her so close, so intimate and yet unattainable was a special kind of torment.

'There's not many would put up with that. Not without taking advantage.' Jenny came back to the table, picked up the book and the two sheets of paper all together, slipped them back in their packaging and handed them to him. 'You're a good man, Tony McLean. Don't spoil that.'

And then she walked past him, bare feet silent on the floor as she disappeared into the darkness of the hall.

19

Way too early in the morning, McLean stifled a yawn as he waited for the foul-tasting coffee from the office vending machine to have some effect. The interview room was cold, which helped a bit. If the heating didn't kick in soon though, he was likely to slip into a hypothermic coma. The clunks and gurgles from the tiny radiator suggested it was trying, at least.

The door clicked open and the cheery face of Grumpy Bob peered through. 'You ready, sir?'

'Aye, Bob. Send them in.'

The door pushed wider to let in two women. Magda Evans wore jeans torn at the knee and a padded bum freezer jacket, gold with little sparkly flecks in the material. She'd tied her hair in a messy wedge on top of her head and stood upright, as if a great weight had been taken off her shoulders. She towered over the diminutive form of Clarice Saunders, swaddled in a long black woollen overcoat.

'Thanks for coming in, both of you.' McLean stood and motioned for them to take the seats on the other side of the table. Unexpectedly, Magda took the extended hand, shook it vigorously. Her touch was warm, a welcome bit of stolen heat in the chill room. McLean studied her face in the instant of that contact. She had less makeup on than the last time they'd met, and she looked healthier for it. Or maybe it was just the knowledge that her pimp was dead and she might actually escape the life she'd lived.

'This is about Malky Jennings?' Magda seemed reluctant to release his hand, so McLean tugged it gently away. Clarice had already sat down and was staring at the two of them like a disapproving parent.

'Among other things, yes. Please, sit.' He pointed at the chair and waited until Magda complied before taking his own.

'Any chance you could rustle us up some tea?' Grumpy Bob stood in the doorway. He nodded at the request, pulling the door closed behind him as he left.

'No second officer as witness?' Clarice asked.

'This isn't a formal interview, Ms Saunders. You're here because you agreed to come in. I can record things if you want.' McLean pointed at the tape machine on its shelf just in case she didn't know how it was done.

'And if we hadn't agreed to come in? Would you have arrested Magda again?'

'Again? I wasn't aware we'd arrested her before.'

'You held her here for twenty-four hours. After she'd been abducted and shoved in the hold of an old boat bound for God knows where.'

'That was the other thing I wanted to talk to Magda about, actually.' McLean shifted his gaze from the stern, tiny woman to her companion, knowing full well that it would take more than that to shut her out.

'I already told you all I know about that, Inspector.'

'I don't doubt that you believe that, Miss Evans, but I'd like to go over the events one more time, just in case we missed something. First though, Malky Jennings.'

'Malky Jennings. What of him?'

'Let's not beat about the bush. You hated him for what he did to you, aye?'

'You're not suggesting Magda here –' Clarice butted in. McLean cut her off before she could get into full flow.

'No, Miss Saunders, I'm not. Otherwise this interview would be under caution and there'd be another officer present. I know Miss Evans here had as much motive to kill Jennings as anyone. Any of his prostitutes had plenty of motive, but I don't think any of them killed him, OK?'

'He was a total bastard.' Magda's voice was quiet, matter of fact. 'But then all men are. Most men, maybe.'

McLean let that slide. 'He had control over you though, didn't he. Fixed you up with drugs, stopped you from going elsewhere. I've heard he was a violent man. Very possessive.'

'It sounds like you knew him better than most, Detective Inspector,' Clarice said. McLean ignored her again.

'You tried to leave him a couple of times though.' The sheet on Magda Evans was surprisingly short for someone who'd worked the streets in Edinburgh for as long as she had, but there was a pattern to the cautions she'd been given. Two separate occasions when she'd been found far off her normal patch. One short stint in a notorious Marchmont massage parlour that had been just a little too blatant even for the city council's laissez-faire policy, another incident in Sighthill. Both far from Restalrig and the little empire of Malky Jennings.

'He always found me though. Didn't matter how far I ran.'

'How did he know where to look?'

Clarice snorted a dismissive little laugh. 'You don't know much about how these people operate, do you, Inspector.'

'Like I said, he had control over you. And he had connections.' McLean slumped back in his chair so that his focus was no longer solely on the ex-hooker. 'He was low-level, true, but he dealt drugs and pimped a dozen, maybe fourteen prostitutes in and around Restalrig. And we let him, I'm sorry to say.'

'Can I get that in writing?' Clarice was actually smiling. It made her look slightly mad.

'Sadly I don't speak for the entire police service, Miss Saunders. I do disagree with the way things have been run here, but I also have to follow orders. Malky Jennings was largely left to his own devices because he was a known quantity.'

'This isn't anything I didn't already know.' Clarice Saunders' smile had gone, now she had her serious face on. 'I've been trying to help these women for ten years now, and every time I've reported the likes of Malky Jennings to you lot, there's been minimal response. Pulled in for questioning, maybe a fine for possession. Never anything about the women he regularly beat black and blue.'

'And you'll know why we did it, too, Miss Saunders.' McLean addressed his next question directly to Magda. 'Would you have testified against him in court if he broke your ribs?'

Her lack of response was answer enough.

'No, you wouldn't. I don't blame you, if I'm being honest. You put him away, he's out again in six months, a year. Like you said, he always managed to find you. Don't suppose it'd be just your ribs he broke the next time. And while he's away, who takes over? How do they go about asserting their authority?'

'So what? You just give up? You let the likes of him run the place? I thought you swore an oath to protect and serve?'

McLean hadn't the heart to correct Clarice Saunders on that point. It was a fair summary of what he'd thought the job was about, after all.

'Let's just say I don't like it, OK? But it's true. Malky might have beaten his girls around, but he stopped anyone worse from coming along and putting them in the mortuary. Now he's gone and I really need to know who's trying to take over his patch.'

A long silence filled the room. Earlier on in the interview, McLean hadn't been able to avoid Magda's stare, but as the conversation had turned to Malky, so her gaze had dropped. Now even her head was bowed and her shoulders slumped.

'Magda's put that world behind her, inspector.' Clarice Saunders reached over and placed a hand on her companion's arm. 'She doesn't know. Doesn't want to know.'

'You think that was wise, sir? Going all confessional on them like that?'

Grumpy Bob leaned against the wall in the corridor outside the interview room. He had a mug of tea clasped in his hand and a rolled-up newspaper shoved under his arm. A uniform PC had taken Magda Evans and Clarice Saunders out through the back, where McLean had organized a taxi to take them home.

'My Gran always told me it was best to tell the truth, no matter how painful.'

'Aye, but she didn't work for the polis, did she.'

'Not directly, no. Not sure what she'd have made of all this, either.'

All this. A nice, easy way of summing up a godawful mess. Despite her initial enthusiasm for the interview, and the different location, Magda Evans had managed to give them zero new information. McLean wasn't fooled by Clarice Saunders' stories either. Maybe the charity worker believed her new best friend was making a break from her old life. Maybe it was even true. But it didn't take a genius to see that Magda knew damned well who had muscled in on Malky Jennings' patch, and she had a very good idea who'd taken her and the other girls onto that boat. Chances were she knew why they'd picked her, too, and the story about her being half Polish didn't wash.

'So what's next?' Grumpy Bob asked. McLean eyed him up, the tea, the paper.

'Looks like you're set for a session in an empty incident room, if you can find one.'

'That depends on whether you can make me a better offer or not.'

'How're you getting on with the Braid Hill investigation? Keeping you busy?'

Grumpy Bob's answer was to pull out his newspaper and flip it open with his one free hand. The headline was easy enough to read. 'Flasher Caught!'

'Students back already?'

'Post-grad. They never really go away. Stupid bugger tried to climb over a garden wall in his flasher mac. Didn't realize it was topped with smashed glass until it was too late. He's in the hospital now. Not going anywhere in a hurry. Not on his own two feet, anyway. Probably won't be fathering many children either.'

McLean winced, but only briefly. 'So you're at a bit of a loose end right now.'

Grumpy Bob lifted his mug to his mouth, took a noisy slurp of tea. 'Mebbe. Why?'

'Ritchie's off on some bloody Police Scotland thing, but she left me a list of ship's chandlers who stock hemp rope. Thought I might go and see if any of them recall seeing either of our hanged men.'

The Captain's Rest sounded more like the name of a seaside pub than a place you'd buy bits and pieces for your yacht. There was no mistaking what it was once you approached the place, though. Stacked on the pavement outside the door, rolls of blue nylon rope, buoys, wicker lobster pots for the tourist trade and heavy ironmongery dared the casual thief to have a go. The windows displayed more expensive and easily pocketed equipment, shielded from the sun by a thin film of rumpled yellow cellophane on the inside of the glass. If you wanted to buy a dead wasp, this was clearly the place to come, too.

Inside was everything McLean expected. Head-high shelving formed narrow aisles, funnelling the shopper towards a wooden counter at the back. Deep-sea fishing gear hung from hooks on the ceiling, along with shackles, ratchets, pulleys and other impressively engineered gear he had no name for. Over to one side a rack of heavy-duty wet-weather clothing gave testament to the reality of sailing in the Firth of Forth and North Sea. No high fashion here, just survival in an environment where exposure could kill you in minutes.

Behind him, Grumpy Bob closed the door with a jingling rattle from a collection of karabiners hung on the frame, then set off into the shop to look at a stack of charts and navigation aids. McLean squeezed himself down the nearest aisle, stepping over a cardboard box that had escaped from the shelves, and approached the counter. At first he thought there was no one in, but a shuffling noise from under the wooden counter-top turned out to be a very small man with a great profusion of bushy, white hair, most of it on the lower part of his face and neck. The captain, no doubt.

'Good morning, sir. What can I do for you today?'

'I was wondering, do you sell hemp rope?'

'Ah, the old-fashioned kind. Much the best for the older boats. What is it you sail, sir? You look like a clinker-built man to me.'

McLean fished around in his inside jacket pocket, brought out his warrant card and a couple of photographs.

'Actually I'm not a sailor at all. I'm investigating a couple of suspicious deaths.'

The shopkeeper retrieved a pair of ancient wire spectacles from a chain around his neck, placed them on the end of his nose and peered at the warrant card. He stared at the image, then up at McLean, then back at the image. For a moment McLean thought he was going to carry on like that for ever.

'McLean, McLean. Any relation to Johnny McLean?

Has a twin-master in South Queensferry. Did the round-the-world a couple of years back.'

'Not that I'm aware of, no.' McLean retrieved his warrant card.

'Are you sure? You look like him.'

'Quite sure. About the hemp rope?'

'Oh yes, of course. We stock some quarter inch, half inch, three-quarter and inch. Anything bigger we'd need to order up from the manufacturer. It's foreign, of course. Comes from India. Seems like we don't make anything over here these days.'

'Quite.' McLean laid out the photographs on the counter. Grigori Mikhailevic and Patrick Sands. 'Both of these men bought three-quarter-inch hemp rope recently. You recognize either of them?'

'It's not a crime, selling rope you know.' The shopkeeper took up the photograph of Mikhailevic and gave it as close a scrutiny as he had McLean's warrant card. His spectacles were scratched almost opaque and smeared with greasy fingerprints. How he saw anything through them was a mystery, but something must have got through the mess.

'This one I recognize.' He put Mikhailevic down and picked up Sands. 'Came in and bought twenty metres of three-quarter inch, oh, a month back? Bit more probably.'

'And the other?'

'Never seen him in my life.'

'Twenty metres. That's what, sixty feet?'

'More like sixty-five.'

'Good length that.' Grumpy Bob sauntered up to the counter. 'What would you do on a boat with twenty metres of rope?'

155

'Depends on the boat, really,' the shopkeeper said. 'You'd not use it for sheets, right enough. But you might use it to tie up a smaller craft. Course, most people buying rope don't want it for boats, do they. Not everyone comes in here's a sailor. You gentlemen, for instance.'

'You say you recognize this man, Grigori Mikhailevic?' McLean held up the photograph to attract the shop-keeper's attention before he launched into another random segue.

'Aye, didn't know that was his name. Don't think he sounded foreign, mind. I'd remember something like that.'

'You remember how he paid? You have any record?'

'Probably cash. Why?'

'I was hoping you might have been able to pinpoint the sale,' McLean said. 'If we know when he bought the rope, we can trace his movements immediately before and after. I'm trying to build up a picture of his movements.'

'He hanged himself, didn't he. The shopkeeper grimaced. 'Not much else you can do with that much good three-quarter-inch hemp on dry land.'

He bent down below the counter again and came out with a large hard-bound ledger. Dropped the spectacles off his nose, licked an index finger and began leafing through the pages.

'My boy wants me to put all this on his damned computer, but I find this much easier to work with.' It didn't take long for him to find what he was looking for. He spun the book around so McLean and Grumpy Bob could see.

'There you go. Two months ago. Cash sale. That's your chappy, God rest his soul.'

*

Of the two other chandler's shops on the list, only one stocked hemp rope and hadn't sold any for months. Nylon, it would seem, was the thing these days. Only old bufties insisted on the traditional stuff. They'd visited a couple of big hardware stores as well, just in case, but it seemed to be very much a niche product. The afternoon was winding out towards evening as McLean and Grumpy Bob crawled through the traffic on the way back to the station. A whole day of successfully avoiding Duguid and in the meantime doing some actual detective work. It felt good; a change from the dull drudgery of constant staff management, report writing and time wasting.

'Where're we going with this, sir?' Grumpy Bob sat in the passenger seat of the pool car McLean had managed to secure by luck more than good judgement. Not for the first time it occurred to him that life would be much easier if he just bought a proper car for himself and used that, like every other detective he knew.

'Not exactly sure, Bob. But we know now when and where Mikhailevic bought his rope.'

'Aye, but two months ago? He didn't kill himself till what, three weeks ago? Why'd he hang on to it for so long?' Grumpy Bob grimaced at the unintentional pun, but let it slide anyway.

'I don't know. Maybe he meant to kill himself two months ago, then had second thoughts.'

'I guess so.' Grumpy Bob stared into the middle distance, a clear indication that he was thinking things through. 'That kind've makes it more likely this is just a simple suicide though, doesn't it?'

'How so?'

'Well, I'm no expert, but I'd imagine if you'd decided to do that, to hang yourself, you'd need to get some rope from somewhere. That shop's not far from his flat, so chances are he'd have known about it. He goes in there, buys it with cash, takes it home. Has second thoughts maybe, leaves it under the bed for a while. Comes home after a particularly shit day and does the deed. No need for any complications, really.'

'You're forgetting one little thing though, Bob.' McLean feathered the brakes, coming to a halt at the end of a long line of stationary cars. The pool car was a pig to drive, its clutch heavy, gearbox notched as if it had been driven by monkeys all its short life. Probably not far from the truth. 'He bought twenty metres of rope. Sixty-five feet, near as doesn't really matter.'

'And he only used thirteen to hang himself.' Grumpy Bob got it.

'Exactly. So where's the rest? Wasn't in his flat, so did he give it to Sands? And who buys rope for someone else to hang themselves with? How does that even work?'

'You think there's some kind of suicide pact going on here?'

'We don't even know if they knew each other. There's nothing obvious to link them. Well, apart from the hanging of course.' Dip clutch, release handbrake, ease forward a few more feet. Maybe one of those new-fangled semi-automatic gearboxes he'd read about. It would certainly make driving in the city easier. 'Give forensics a call, see if they can match the two pieces. Problem is, even if they do match, that still only makes twenty-six feet. Where's the other forty?'

'Christ, you really think there's more of them out there?'

McLean eased the clutch out again as the lights turned green, mistimed it, stalled. Behind him the horns started before he could even get the engine going again. He really needed to get himself a car. Anything was better than this heap of shit.

'I really don't know, Bob, but we need to find that rope.'

20

A note on McLean's desk belied the quiet that had settled over the station by the time he and Grumpy Bob got back in. 'See me tomorrow, first thing. D.' First thing was underlined twice, never a good sign where the acting superintendent was concerned. McLean screwed it up and threw it in the bin, took a quick look at the piles of reports and overtime sheets that had been placed where some poor bastard of a secretary had obviously hoped he would see them when he sat down. No chance of that, not now. He closed the door on the trouble that would only get bigger, and went off in search of something more enjoyable to contemplate.

The quiet extended to the CID room, only two desks occupied by detectives. DC MacBride was on the telephone, furiously scribbling down notes and occasionally nodding his head in agreement with whatever was being said on the other end. DS Ritchie looked up from her computer screen as he entered.

'Hive of activity here,' McLean said.

'DCI Brooks has taken the team off to the pub to celebrate.' Ritchie snapped shut the notebook she'd been transcribing onto the computer and slumped back in her chair.

'The Braid Hill Flasher, I heard. Hardly cause for a piss-up though.'

'Not that. They caught the gang that's been hitting post offices over in the West End. Three of them holed up in a flat in Comely Bank. They had the whole street blocked off, sent in an armed-response team. It'll be all over the evening news.'

McLean thought about the note on his desk upstairs. 'This come in before or after Dagwood knocked off for the day?'

'After, why?'

'I've got a bollocking diaried for tomorrow, first thing. Maybe he'll have a change of mind.'

'That'll be DS Laird, sir.' McLean looked around. Detective Constable MacBride had finished his telephone call.

'What's Grumpy Bob done this time?'

'Gone off with you when he was supposed to be working with DI Spence. Least that's what I heard in the canteen.'

McLean pinched the bridge of his nose and let out a heavy sigh. He'd never really been sure why people did that at times of stress or exasperation, but oddly enough it helped.

'You get that list of friends and co-workers for the two suicides?'

DS Ritchie swivelled in her chair and looked at Mac-Bride, by way of passing on the question. McLean rolled his eyes at her.

'What? Dagwood said you weren't to use him for your investigation. He said nothing to me. I'm just delegating my workload to the available detective constables. Aren't I, Stuart?'

And this is what happens when you promote a detective chief inspector beyond his level of competence. 'OK, then. Has anyone got a list of friends and co-workers for the two suicides?'

'Here, sir.' MacBride held up a sheet of paper. It was split into two columns, one for Mikhailevic, one for Sands. None of the names were repeated in both columns, but that was hardly surprising as there were only half a dozen in total.

'So few?'

'That's all I've been able to come up with so far. Neither of them were exactly sociable.'

'You've spoken to their workplaces? Their bosses?'

'Mikhailevic was a student, but he had a job in a bar on Leith Walk. Sands was working in a call centre, some online bank outfit. He was a temp, paid through an agency, but he'd been there almost a year. Apparently he was studying for his banking exams. According to his manager it'd be a miracle if he ever passed them. Diligent but unimaginative was the exact phrase he used.'

'Sounds perfect banker material to me.' McLean looked at the list again, checked the time. 'Mikhailevic worked in a pub, you say?'

'The Bond Bar, down the bottom end of Leith Walk.'

'Well then, since DCI Brooks obviously didn't see fit to include you in his celebrations, I think I'll have to buy you both a drink.'

The Bond Bar was one of those places old men went to nurse grudges, a pint of heavy and a wee nip of an afternoon. The smoking ban had cleared the air inside, but nothing could get rid of the miasma of stale beer, body odour and mould that hung about the place. Early evening and a dozen or so punters were staring at a screen showing some indeterminate football match. It wouldn't be a long wait to be served.

'What you having?' McLean asked Ritchie while at the same time trying to catch the barman's eye. DC MacBride, perhaps with an eye on his future in the police service, had politely turned down the opportunity to go for a drink, claiming he had a mountain of paperwork to process. McLean couldn't blame him, really. If Dagwood was generous with anything it was with his animosity to anyone who helped those he didn't like.

'I'm guessing a white wine spritzer's not going to cut it here.' Ritchie stared across the bar at the rows of optics behind. Cheap spirits and a couple of prize bottles of malt whisky arranged on a deep shelf with smeary shot glasses and postcards from the Costa Del Sol. There might have been a bottle of wine in the chiller cabinet under the till, but there was no telling how long it had been open.

'Best stick with the beer.' McLean pointed at a fake pump handle as the barman finally sauntered up, scarcely taking his eyes from the football. 'Two pints of Eighty Bob please.'

They took their dubious prize to a table as far away from the screen as possible, McLean making sure his back was turned to the flickering lights. He hefted his glass, said 'cheers' and took a long drink, watching Ritchie do the same. The Eighty Bob wasn't bad. Which was to say it was cold, wet and not particularly sour. He wasn't sure it had any discernible flavour either.

163

'How was the task force? You know all there is to know about Police Scotland?'

'About as much as anyone, I guess. Which is to say bugger all, really.' Ritchie took another long swig. 'Christ, I didn't realize how much I needed that. Thanks.'

'You're welcome. Though I'd rather have gone somewhere a bit more upmarket.'

'Yeah, it's not exactly the most welcoming of places. I presume we're here to talk to the barman.' Ritchie nodded at the dour man, absent-mindedly polishing a glass with a stained bar mat whilst he watched the television. 'Why the wait?'

'Three reasons. One, he'd be less likely to help us if we just came in and started asking questions. Two, half time is in about five minutes. All these people will want another drink, and then there'll be about ten minutes of men called Brian discussing the game so far. We're far more likely to hold his attention then.'

'Didn't know you were a footie fan, sir.' Ritchie raised a thin eyebrow. They'd never really grown back properly since the fire she'd dragged him out of.

'I'm not. Can't stand watching sport, to be honest. But it helps to know how the other half live, eh?'

'What about three then?'

'Three?' McLean lifted his pint, took a long deep draught before continuing. 'Three was I really needed a drink.'

The referee called half-time five minutes later. McLean watched as the collected punters headed either to the toilets or to the bar before returning to their tables in readiness for the second half. After her initial thirst, Ritchie had slowed down, but he'd more or less finished his own pint. Ah well, it was all in the line of duty. He threw back the last of it and went in search of another.

The barman was a little more friendly this time, in the same way a room at minus eighteen is a little warmer than a room at minus twenty.

'Two more, aye?'

McLean nodded, waited for the drinks to be poured, handed over a ten-pound note.

'Grigori Mikhailevic. Used to work here on the late shift,' he said as the barman handed over his change.

'What of him?' Back down to minus twenty.

'I was wondering if you knew him at all.'

'Why?'

McLean produced his warrant card. 'You know he hanged himself?'

'Aye, I heard that. Didn't much surprise me, like.'

'What, miserable was he?'

'No' exactly miserable, but he didn't say much, ken? Kept to himself.'

'Was he a good worker?'

'Good enough, I suppose. Turned up, did the job. Didn't complain. Just never went out of his way, ken? No' a great one for the chatter.'

'What about friends? He ever meet people here?'

The barman made a noise that sounded exactly like 'Ppphhhttt'. Shook his head. 'Not that I remember.'

'You ever see this man before?' McLean slid the photograph of Patrick Sands across the bar. The barman peered at it, but didn't pick it up.

'Nope,' he said after just long enough a pause for McLean to trust he was telling the truth. In the mirror behind the bar he could see the television screen, footballers running back onto the pitch.

'Well, thanks anyway.' He picked up the two pints, turned to go back to the table where Ritchie was staring at her smartphone with an expression of horror on her face. No doubt some impossible demand from their gallant leader. Christ he wished Jayne McIntyre would come back.

'There was one time, now I think of it.'

McLean did a one-eighty, managing somehow not to spill any of the semi-precious liquid. 'Aye?'

'That's right. I remember now, ken. Not long before he . . . Well. He was here wi' a lassie.'

'A young woman?'

'No' so young, ye ken. Thought mebbe she was his mother at first, but the way they was carrying on. And him being foreign and all, well, she didn't look like she was Russian.'

'You remember when this was?'

'I dunno. Couple of days before his last shift?'

'You remember what she looked like?'

The barman's eyes flickered away towards the television screen, back again. 'Quite tall, aye? Bit of grey in her hair. She had a long coat on. Black, I think. They sat over there where you're sitting just now.'

He pointed, and McLean turned to look. Ritchie was still glowering at her phone. When he turned back, the barman had picked up his glass and cloth, eyes glued to the television where the match was back in play. Well, it was more information than he'd hoped for, even if he didn't know what it meant. He nodded a quick 'thanks' to the barman, receiving the most minimal of grunts by way of reply, then set off across the empty bar towards Ritchie. She looked like she needed a distraction.

'Get anything?' She asked as McLean plunked her pint down beside the now-empty glass.

'Depends what you would consider anything.' He told her about the conversation with the barman, the mysterious older woman.

'Lecturer, tutor? Could be almost anyone. I don't suppose they have CCTV in here.'

'Doubt it, and even if they did they'd be unlikely to have kept recordings from that far back.'

'But you think she's important, don't you.'

'We're working on the assumption these two suicides are linked, aye?'

Ritchie nodded, said nothing.

'And we know that Mikhailevic hadn't handled the rope he used, so someone must have helped him.'

'Could've been Sands. If the two of them knew each other. You know. One helps his mate hang himself, then goes home and tops himself.'

McLean could see by Ritchie's expression that she didn't really believe it. Too far-fetched.

'It doesn't really stack up. Sands would stay close if he was going to do that. Not traipse halfway across town before hanging himself. He must've died before Mikhailevic, too. The way he was.'

'So we're looking for a third party.' Ritchie took a sip of

her beer, placed the glass back carefully on the dog-eared beer mat, exactly central.

'It's an avenue of enquiry, and this woman Mikhailevic was seen with is a loose end. Anyway, we can go and talk to the college tomorrow. Maybe we'll get lucky and find a tall, greying lady in a long dark coat there.'

Ritchie grimaced. 'Erm, not me, I'm afraid. Got an email from Dagwood. He wants me at Tulliallan for eight. More bloody Task Force Action Groups or whatever pish they come up with next.'

McLean put his glass down before he broke it. The pettiness of the man never ceased to amaze him. 'Don't suppose you feel like calling in sick?'

'And have him come round my flat to check?'

'Fair point. I'm sorry, Ritchie, this is my fault.'

'It's not your fault he's a dick. Sir,' she added.

'Aye, but it's my fault he's picking on you and MacBride. Christ, I wish Jayne McIntyre was back.'

'I'll drink to that,' Ritchie said, and raised her glass.

They didn't stay much longer at the Bond Bar; it wasn't really the place for a session, and Ritchie had to be up early for her trip to Tulliallan the next day. McLean watched her head off towards the New Town and her tiny flat before shoving his hands in his pockets and walking in the opposite direction. He'd probably flag down a taxi before long, but it was always good to walk, especially when you had things to think about.

It wasn't long before he realized he'd picked up a tail; the man wasn't exactly trying to hide it. McLean slowed, hand clasping his mobile phone as he allowed his pursuer to catch up. He had a sneaking suspicion he knew what this was all about.

'So you're the idiot went round to see Razors MacDougal about his daughter, eh?'

'What of it?' McLean looked at the man walking alongside him. Say what you liked about the Scottish Crime and Drug Enforcement Agency, they enjoyed their cloak and dagger. No doubt this loon with his long dark overcoat in the autumn, wearing shades even in the half-light of the gloaming, had been watching and waiting for a chance to approach unseen. Too easy to just phone. Or stick something in the internal mail system.

'Takes some balls, I'd've thought. Going into the house of a man like that and accusing him of sexual assault on his only child.'

'Is that what you wanted to talk to me about? MacDougal? Only I've not seen him since we closed the case.'

'Nah. MacDougal's low priority right now. We're keeping an eye on him, mind. And you too, McLean. He likes you, for some reason I can't begin to fathom. That might be useful to us sometime.'

'So this is about Ivan the Russian then.'

'If he even exists.' The SCDEA officer swung his arms like a soldier marching. Quite likely he was ex-Services. 'It's an odd one, I'll give you that much. People smuggling's nothing new, but normally they're coming over here. Not often we see a bunch being freighted back the way. And it's not as if they were prime meat, either.'

McLean stiffened at the words. Bad enough getting that attitude from an old dinosaur like Buchanan, but a young Turk from the drug squad ought to know better.

On the other hand, he had a point. None of the young women they'd pulled off the boat had been remotely healthy. The word 'used' sprung to mind.

'You say "if he exists". You really have no idea about him?'

'Not a Scooby, mate. But we'll be looking into it. The boss don't like it when stuff happens he hasn't sanctioned. Know what I mean?'

McLean didn't, but decided not to say so. 'You'll let me know what you find out?'

'If I can. Depends what we turn up.' The SCDEA officer tapped the side of his nose with single finger, a gesture McLean felt singularly inapt for the occasion. 'Be seeing you, Inspector. But don't expect to see me.' And with that he turned down a side street to nowhere. McLean paused for the briefest of moments, shook his head at the idiocy of it all, then carried on his long walk home.

21

Edinburgh was full of them, tiny little institutes and further education colleges trading on the name of the bigger universities. Grigori Mikhailevic had, according to DC MacBride's notes, been studying accountancy at a place called Fulcholme College, based in Newhaven. Its centre of operations was a large detached house, the front garden flattened and laid to tarmac. Wide stone steps led up to the front door, with an impressive sign beside it claiming accreditation from a body McLean had never heard of.

Inside was much like any of a thousand large houses dotted across the city, once the homes of prosperous merchants, bankers or clergy. The only real difference between this place and his Gran's house was that he didn't have a reception desk set up in the hallway. He was disappointed to see the receptionist was a young man, not the greying, tall lady he'd hoped for. It was never that easy.

'Can I help you, sir?'

McLean showed his warrant card. Before he could say anything, the receptionist had picked up a phone and hit a button for an internal call.

'Professor? There's a policeman here. Detective Inspector McLean.' He palmed the microphone end of the hand-piece, looked up. 'It's about Grigori?'

McLean nodded, pocketing his card as he looked around. Four closed doors, each with a modern plastic plaque screwed to the dark wood. Room 1, Room 2, Room 3, Room 4. They didn't go in for creativity much at Fulcholme, it would seem. Stairs climbed up the back wall, past a mezzanine window, chest-height dark-oak panelling sucking the light out of everything, even on this bright summer morning. The most notable thing about the whole place, however, was the complete lack of students. He'd have expected at least one or two to be loitering around the hall waiting for a tutorial to start; there were sofas arranged around an empty fireplace that looked to be just for that purpose.

'Professor Bain will be with you in a minute, Inspector.' The receptionist hung up his phone at almost the exact moment one of the doors clicked and swung open. A round-faced man appeared from Room 1, saw McLean and approached with hand extended. His hair was white, and grew only from the sides of his head and his ears.

'Terrible business, terrible.' Professor Bain gave McLean's hand a vigorous shake. 'Come to my office, please. Trevor, can you organize some coffee? You do like coffee don't you, Inspector?'

McLean found himself being bustled into Room 1, which turned out to be a large study. At one end, surrounded by floor-to-ceiling bookshelves, a desk had been positioned to give commanding views out of the window onto the back yard. At the other end, near the door to the hall, a couple of sofas and four armchairs clustered around a low table. A flipchart board stood to one side, scribblings from the last tutorial group still evident on the final page.

'Please excuse the mess. Here, have a seat.' Professor Bain indicated the armchairs before dropping himself onto a sofa. 'I must say, I'm surprised to see a detective inspector out here. It's about poor Grigori, you say.'

'You call him Grigori. First name. He was popular here, I take it.' McLean sat on the edge of the armchair, unwilling to trust himself to its depths. He wanted to maintain eye level with the professor, not be talked down to like an undergrad.

'I try to be on first-name terms with all my students, but, yes, Grigori was special. A model student in many ways. And a nice person, too. Always ready to help his classmates. If they needed it, that is.'

'I'd very much like to talk to them, if I could.'

'Shouldn't be a problem. They're all in lectures right now. But why the interest? I mean, I'm glad you're investigating, of course. But poor Grigori took his own life, didn't he?'

'Yes, at least we think so. But there are remarkable similarities between his death and that of another young man at much the same time. Tell me, does the name Patrick Sands mean anything to you?' McLean slid the photograph out of his pocket and handed it over. Professor Bain studied it a while before handing it back.

'He doesn't look familiar. But then I see so many faces come through here every year. Sands, you say? I'll ask Trevor to check the register, see if we have anyone of that name on file.'

'Thanks.' McLean took back the photo. 'Tell me, Professor Bain, were you surprised when Mikhailevic killed himself?'

There was the tiniest of pauses before the answer. 'Yes, I think I was. But do we ever really know people?'

173

'He was doing OK in his studies?'

'Top of his class. A very diligent student.'

McLean remembered the tiny bedsit flat, the neatness of the place, the pens lined up in their drawer. 'What about fees? Did he have money problems?'

'His fees were all paid up for the year. Grigori wasn't rich, but he worked hard. I think he had a job in a bar? I'm sure money was tight, but not enough to drive him to suicide.'

'What about family? He was from Russia, I understand. Did he miss them?'

'Lithuania, actually. But of Russian descent. He never mentioned his family though. If he missed them, he didn't say. I don't think that would be reason for killing yourself anyway. No.'

'And yet when I asked you if you were surprised by what he did, you hesitated.'

'Did I?' Professor Bain looked down at his feet, then back at McLean. 'I suppose I did. It's difficult to put it in words. Grigori was . . . Well, distant isn't right. But there were times when he would just disappear into his head. He'd be sitting there, like you are, contributing to the tutorial group one moment, and then the next you'd ask him a question and he'd not hear you. It was almost like a kind of epilepsy. A little seizure if you like. But instead of going into convulsions, he'd just stop.'

'Did he realize this was happening?'

'Well, there's the thing, Inspector. I'm not sure he did. Or if he did he didn't want to admit to it. That's the only time I've seen him depressed though, when I asked him if he was all right.'

*

174

Students really were getting very young these days. McLean had thought MacBride was fresh-faced, but Grigori Mikhailevic's tutorial group made the detective constable look ancient by comparison. The group was not large; just five other students appeared to be studying for whatever accountancy qualification Fulcholme College could offer. McLean felt he should maybe find out, but as he interviewed the group he was increasingly convinced this was a dead end in the investigation.

There were three women and two men, all foreign though none from Mikhailevic's country. All of them spoke English so fluently it shamed his pathetic schoolboy French. None of them knew Mikhailevic well, it seemed.

'Did you never go out for a drink after tutorials? Go clubbing at the weekends?' McLean pitched the question to the whole group, he could see no point in interviewing them separately. One of the women, Claudia from Spain was how she'd introduced herself, seemed to have appointed herself as spokesperson.

'No, no. Grigori was always working. Working here on his studies, working in that horrible little bar. We asked him, did we not, Eva?' This, directed to one of the other young women, received a nod of assent from the whole group. 'But he didn't have much money. And I think he was a bit shy, you know.'

'Did he ever meet anyone here? A woman perhaps. Or maybe he mentioned something?'

A vigorous shake of the head from Claudia, followed by something that was almost a laugh. 'No. Not Grigori. He would never do something like that. He would die of shame.'

'What about his family back home. Did he ever mention them?'

'We never really talked much about that sort of thing.'

'But he helped you? With your studies, when you were struggling?'

Claudia rolled her eyes as if such a suggestion were madness, but Eva spoke before the older woman could say anything.

'He helped me, from time to time.'

'Go on.' McLean tried to make his voice sound encouraging.

'I couldn't, how do you say it, get to grips with value added tax.'

You and me both, McLean suppressed the urge to say. He let the silence linger until Eva felt the need to fill it.

'Grigori spent some time explaining it to me. He was very bright, and very kind.'

'Did you talk about other things?'

'Not so much, but I think there may have been something going on. Just before he . . . You know.' No one seemed able to say the words 'hanged himself'.

'Why do you say that?'

'Well, I don't know. It's just that he was different. Not more cheerful, particularly. Grigori was never very cheerful. But he acted like he had purpose. Does that make sense?'

Like a man who has decided he's going to take his own life. A man who finds a certain sense of peace in the short time between making the decision and carrying out the act. Or maybe a man who has met someone who has a profound effect on him?

'And he was different in his routine, too.' The third young woman spoke finally and McLean revised his opinion of her nationality. Edinburgh born and bred, if he was any judge. 'He left here earlier, got in later. It was only a few days, but he was such a creature of habit. I thought maybe he'd met someone. Y'know, like, a girlfriend. Only, well, Grigori? It didn't seem likely. He was so shy.'

The phone rang, vibrating in his pocket as he stepped out of the building and into the mid-morning sun. Overhead, seagulls wheeled and screamed, which made it hard to hear what was being said at the other end of the line.

'McLean.'

'Ah, Tony. How delightful. I was expecting the answering machine.' The clipped tones of Angus Cadwallader.

'It's your lucky day, Angus. My phone is both working and switched on.'

'So it would seem. Might be your lucky day too.'

'Oh aye?'

'Your two hanging victims. Mikhailevic and Sands. I've got some interesting lab test results just in.'

'Interesting how?'

'Interesting as in something rather unusual was going on in their brains when they died. Both of them have abnormally high levels of dopamine in their systems.'

'You think they were drugged?' McLean stopped. 'Someone maybe slipped them L-Dopa?'

'Would that it were that simple.' Cadwallader paused and over the screeching of gulls McLean could hear the sounds of the examination room in full swing. Perhaps the pathologist really had been hoping for the answering machine. 'Look, any chance you could pop round the mortuary later on this afternoon? I've a shed load of PMs to do, but I think you'll want to see these results.'

'I'll do that, Angus. But you know I won't be able to concentrate now, what with you tantalizing me like this.'

'Well, sorry about that. Must dash. See you later.' And the phone went dead.

McLean paused beside his old Alfa. Stared at nothing in particular as he tried to remember his old university days and neuropsychology lectures. Dopamine levels. Weren't they tied into suggestibility? He'd need to phone Doctor Wheeler. She'd know.

'Nice car, mister.'

The voice jarred him out of his thinking, a young boy on a BMX bike hurtling down the pavement in contravention of lord only knew how many health and safety laws. McLean smiled to himself, opened the door and climbed in. It was a nice car, he had to admit. Just bloody useless for his line of work.

Midday traffic was relatively light on the outskirts of the city, but the sun high in the sky cast a merciless heat over everything. McLean watched the temperature gauge rise past the central point and on towards the red, despite managing to keep some airflow over the radiator as he drove along. So the old Alfa might have been designed for Italian summers, but somewhere in the intervening forty years since it had been built, the cooling system had lost most of its ability to actually cool.

The heat was seeping into the cabin too, warm air flowing through the ventilation ducts despite the lever being pushed as far over to cold as it would go. He had the windows wound down on both sides, not an easy feat when you don't have electric motors to do the work for you. Even so it was sweltering, worse when he had to stop for traffic lights.

Thoughts of ice-cold air conditioning were cut short by the buzzing of his mobile phone where it lay on the passenger seat. It had fallen face down when he'd thrown it there, so he couldn't see who was calling. Probably Cadwallader with more complications. No hands free, but there was a gap in a line of cars parked along the side of the road. He pulled over, grabbed the phone before it went to voicemail.

'McLean.'

No voice at the other end, just a noise McLean couldn't immediately identify. Then a clattering as if the phone had been dropped. Distant voices, male, harsh, the words unintelligible, their intention all too obvious from the tone. Then a woman's voice shouted in pain. More noise of things being broken. A scream.

McLean stared at the screen. It was a mobile number, not one stored in his address book or anything he recognized. Scrabbling in the glove box he found a notebook and pen, jotted it down. He pushed the button for speakerphone and listened in horror as someone was systematically beaten at the other end. Should he listen in for clues, or hang up and try to find out where this was happening?

A second's indecision was punctuated with another scream. It was a woman being beaten, of that much he was certain. How many women had his mobile number

179

and weren't in his address book? Immediately he thought of Emma. Had someone broken into the house and disturbed her? But both hers and Jenny Nairn's numbers were in his phone's memory.

The sound of something hard hitting a sack of wet potatoes. Who else, dammit? Not Ritchie; and all the DCs would be using Airwave sets. It had to be a civilian. Someone who might find themselves in danger. Someone he'd given his number to. His card.

Shit. McLean killed the call as the screams faded to low moans. Flicked through his address book until he found another number. It rang once, twice. Come on.

'This is the Sexual Crime Unit –' McLean killed the call as it went to answerphone. Where the hell was everyone? He thumbed through his contacts list until he found another number, hit dial, listened as it rang. Hoped to God it wouldn't be another message.

'Aye?' DS Buchanan's voice was gruff, almost as if he were out of breath from running.

'Thank Christ for that. McLean here. Have you got a mobile number for Magda Evans on file?'

'Magda who?'

Oh for fuck's sake. 'Magda Evans. Come on, man, you remember. The prostitute we took off that boat. The one who ID'd Malky Jennings.'

'Oh right. Her. Why, you fancy one, do you?'

McLean ground his teeth. 'Sergeant Buchanan. Do you or do you not have a note of her mobile number? Be careful how you answer that question if you want to continue being a sergeant.'

Silence for long seconds. In his imagination McLean

could still hear the wet slapping sound of a body being repeatedly hit with a blunt object.

'Aye. I've got it here in my notebook.' Buchanan reeled off a number. It was the same as the one that had called him. 'What's this about then, sir?'

'She's just phoned me. Sounds like she's being beaten to a pulp. Where are you right now?'

A pause, then Buchanan answered. 'Sighthill. Got a call out on a kiddie fiddler hanging around the school playground. Don't think there's anything to it. Just someone spreading rumours.'

'Well get over here sharpish. Tag a squad car if you have to. And call control. I want backup at Magda Evans's flat by the time I get there.'

McLean didn't wait for an answer. He dropped the phone onto the passenger seat again and pulled out into the traffic. U-turn to the sound of mixed horns, he had a moment to wish he had a pool car; one with the hidden blue lights in the front grille. On the other hand, the Alfa was light, nimble and fast. He floored the throttle, best speed to Restalrig.

It didn't come as a huge surprise to find that there was no squad car waiting for him when he arrived at the block of flats. McLean parked as close as he dared, locked his car and sprinted to the stairs. Halfway up he realized he was heading without backup into a situation best described as perilous. Where the hell was that squad car?

He stopped on the walkway below Magda's floor, peered down at the cars parked below. His Alfa stuck out like a sore thumb, but as yet had drawn no attention. Then again, the residents of this block hadn't noticed a dead body a hundred yards away until he'd started to smell so bad even the urban foxes wouldn't touch him any more, so why should they notice this? Not much he could do about it anyway.

Peering up at the underside of the walkway above, he strained his ears for any noise of a fight. It was impossible to make out anything over the howl of the wind all around, and he couldn't see the front doors of the flats from where he was, the scaffolding obscuring the view even more than the damaged parapet wall. He was going to have to go in.

The walkway on the fourth floor was empty this time; no small girl playing with a doll with no arms. He checked the doors as he approached, but they were all closed, lace curtains or blinds drawn against the prying eyes of casual thieves. A silence and stillness settled on the scene as he approached Magda's front door. There was a dusty imprint of a boot where it had been kicked in, the security chain hanging uselessly from the jamb. He stopped by the window that looked onto the small hallway inside, peered in around the edge. It was hard to make out anything. Nothing moved.

McLean checked his watch. Twenty minutes since he'd called in. Where was that bloody squad car? The wind swirled dust around his feet in little eddies, and was that a groan from inside? In his mind he heard the sounds from the phone call, the thwack of something hard being smashed against something soft and wet. A baseball bat like they'd used to beat Malky Jennings to death? He couldn't wait any longer for backup, he had to go in.

The door pushed open silently. The thin rug had rucked up as if something had been dragged towards the open door at the far end. The living room if he remembered correctly. McLean stepped carefully over the splinters, keeping as silent as possible as he crossed the hallway and sneaked a look.

It hadn't been the most tidy of flats to start with, but now it was like a war zone. The sofa had been turned over, its cushions ripped open and foam padding spread all around; the coffee table was smashed, a broken chair leg poking out through the shards of the glass top; the television lay face up, the screen scratched and torn. Something had been smashed hard enough against the glass wall that it had cracked and crazed, star-patterns radiating out from a bloody smear.

There was no sign of Magda.

No sign of anyone. McLean picked his way carefully through the mess, into the kitchen beyond. Whoever had been to the flat had kept their work to the living room, in here was tidy by comparison. At least until he looked down. Blood smeared across the cheap lino, towards a door at the other end. He followed it, careful not to step in anything. Pulled on a pair of latex gloves before opening the door. Beyond was a short corridor, lit only by narrow lantern lights above a couple more doors. Bedrooms, presumably. The flooring here was cheap carpet, but the blood smear continued to the end, a similar mark along the wall just below shoulder height, where someone might place a hand to steady themselves. It stopped at the far end of the corridor. A neat hand print marked the painted wood with blood like some plague warning.

It was the bathroom, of course. Where else would she go in the state she was in? McLean pushed the door open, eyes following the blood smear across the floor to the shower. Magda had crawled in, huddled against the wall with the shower curtain pulled down off its rail across her. At least he assumed it was Magda. It was difficult to tell by looking at her face.

Her eyes were puffed closed, black and red. Her nose wasn't so much broken as exploded. Blood and mucus and cartilage smeared together in a glutinous mess. Her cheeks were gashed deep, the same knife cruelly carved a cross-hatch pattern in her forehead, but it was her mouth that was the worst, slit at either end in the Joker's rictus smile. He couldn't tell whether she was alive or dead. A part of him wished it was the latter; these were not injuries that were going to heal well. That had no doubt been the point.

'Magda?' He knelt down close as he dared, not wanting to spook her. 'Magda? It's Detective Inspector McLean. You phoned me.'

Her right hand clasped the shower curtain tight, her left arm was plainly broken. Still clothed, it was impossible to tell the extent of her other injuries, though he was in no doubt they were severe. McLean was about to lean in and check for a pulse when she stirred, breathed out a bubble of blood and spit through her ruined lips. Moaned in soft pain. He stepped back, nothing he could do for her here.

'Help's on its way.' He remembered the squad car that should have been there fifteen minutes earlier, checked his phone to see if there were any new messages. Nothing. Where the hell were they? He was reluctant to leave her, but he was bugger all use standing there staring at her. He had to do something.

A towelling dressing gown hung on the back of the bathroom door. He carefully tucked it around Magda's shivering body, then retraced his steps to the front door, dialling the station as he went.

'I need an ambulance here right away. And where's the backup that was meant to be here half an hour ago?' McLean peered out and down to where his Alfa was beginning to draw a crowd of ne'er-do-wells. He was about to yell at them when they scattered anyway. Then a squad car appeared from around the side of the neighbouring block, lights flashing lazily on its roof.

22

The City Mortuary was a haven of tranquillity after a long and hectic day. McLean stepped from the oven-like heat of the Cowgate into the air-conditioned chill and let out a sigh of relief. There might be complications here, but at least no one would be chewing his ear off about staffing costs, or complaining about his methods.

The examination room was empty, the stainless steel tables clean and shiny, the tools that looked like they should have been in a carpenter's workshop all tidied away. McLean found Angus Cadwallader in the open-plan office adjacent, still wearing his green scrubs and two-finger typing at an elderly computer. His assistant, Tracy, looked up as he rapped on the frame of the open door.

'Ah, the prodigal son returns.' Cadwallader wheeled around on his chair, the grin on his face turning to a worried frown. 'Good God, Tony. You look like you haven't slept in weeks.'

Until his friend said it, McLean hadn't really considered himself tired. Now it had been mentioned, he wondered how he'd not noticed. He rubbed at his eyes and stifled a yawn.

'It's been a very long day, and I've not been getting much sleep lately either.'

'Oh aye? Emma keeping you up late, is she?'

'Not in the way you're thinking, Angus.' McLean

explained about the late-night visitations, stressing their entirely Platonic nature. For once the pathologist refrained from making any obvious joke.

'I'm sure she'll get better. It just takes time.'

'I don't know, Angus. It seems like there's a bit of her missing. If that makes any sense?'

Cadwallader didn't answer that, which was perhaps for the best.

'What about these test results? Abnormally high dopamine levels, you said.'

'Yes, of course. I was forgetting.' Cadwallader twirled his chair back around to the computer screen and tapped away at the keys for a few uncertain seconds before looking up at his assistant. 'Tracy? How do I get the path lab screen up again?'

Tracy caught McLean's eye and shook her head in despair before hauling herself out of her seat and around to her boss's computer. A couple of clicks was all it took. 'There you go,' she said.

'It was so much easier when it was all paper based.' Cadwallader fetched a pair of half-moon spectacles from where they hung on a slim cord around his neck, placed them on his nose and leaned close in to the screen. 'Ah. Here we are.'

McLean stared at the columns of figures and chemical symbols. 'What am I looking at?'

'Here.' Cadwallader stabbed at the screen, leaving a smear of what McLean hoped was grease on the glass. 'This is the first one, Sands. Dopamine levels off the scale. Serotonin's quite high as well. Same here with the second one, Mik– . . . whatsisname.'

187

'So Sands was the first victim,' McLean said. 'Thought that was probably the case.'

'What gave it away?' Cadwallader twirled his chair around again, this time leafing through a stack of papers flowing out of his in-tray.

'Oh, you know how it is. Hang around with pathologists long enough and you pick up a few tips here and there. The putrefaction got me thinking, though.'

'Yes, he was a bit ripe. Unlike your Russian fellow.'

'Lithuanian.'

'Eh?'

'He was Lithuanian, not Russian. Of Russian descent, I think is how it was explained to me.'

'Yes, well. Russian, Lithuanian. It's not important. What is important is that he died second, like you suspected. The other fellow'd been hanging for at least a couple of weeks beforehand. Makes you wonder about the neighbourhood though, if no one noticed the smell until he'd been decomposing for a fortnight. Possibly even a month.'

Brilliant. More complications.

'But that's not important.' Cadwallader tapped the screen again. 'This is important. This profile in one suicide would be interesting but not enough to be suspicious. You get outliers in any population and anyone who puts a noose around his neck's got some pretty hooky brain chemistry going on. But two? Well, that starts to look like an outside influence to me.'

'They were drugged?'

'If only it were that simple, Tony. Well, it is that simple. L-Dopa, like you mentioned on the phone this morning.

188

Very good at raising dopamine levels. But there's one small problem.'

'Only one?' McLean raised a quizzical eyebrow.

'Quite. But back to the matter in hand. L-Dopa leaves traces, not least of which is a paper trail. None of them are here.'

'So what else could account for these results?' McLean squinted at the screen again. It still didn't make any sense to him. 'You said serotonin was high too? What does that mean? My neurobiology's a bit rusty.'

'It means they were both very relaxed. That's the serotonin. And very suggestible, judging by the dopamine.'

'So what you're saying is that someone could have just told these two to go hang themselves and they were so laid back they'd have done it?'

'Pretty much, yes.'

'So how did they get like that? What were they given?'

'As far as I can tell, nothing. Their own brains produced those levels. Both of them.'

An anxious-looking Jenny Nairn met him in the kitchen as he let himself in an hour later. McLean had driven home straight from the mortuary, not wanting the hassle of going back to the office. He'd have to write up everything Cadwallader had told him, though he had a nasty suspicion it wouldn't be enough to sway Duguid from his cost-cutting.

'Something up?' The agitation on Jenny's face instantly brought up dreadful scenarios. And where was Emma anyway? Normally the two young women were joined at the hip.

'It's Wednesday. Remember?'

Wednesday. Of course. Jenny's night off. He'd left that morning before either of them were up, and if he was being honest with himself, had hardly considered what day of the week it might be. It wasn't as if he was counting up to the weekend or anything.

'Sorry. Completely forgot.' He glanced up at the clock on the wall. Ten past seven already. 'You want me to give you a lift into town?'

'In that old bucket of yours?' Jenny shook her head. 'No, it's OK. I've got a cab booked. Should be here any minute. I was just getting a bit worried about having to send him away.'

'You should've phoned. I can get a bit carried away with the work sometimes. Not used to having people at home.'

'I had noticed.'

'How is she today? You two get up to any mischief while I was away?'

'She's been photographing things again. That camera's something of a lifeline for her right now. We spent most of the day up in the attic going through old trunks of clothes and stuff.' Jenny paused, no doubt considering what she'd just said. 'You don't mind, do you?'

'God no. It needs clearing out. Some of that stuff belonged to my great-grandparents. There's probably boxes there that haven't been touched since before the war.' Or at least in the twenty-five or more years it had been since he'd grown out of playing up there in amongst the dust and spiders' webs.

Lights played across the window, accompanied by the crunch of wheels on gravel. 'Your taxi,' McLean said, as if there were any doubt. 'Look, I'll be late going in tomorrow morning, so don't worry about rushing back.'

'Thanks. I'll bear that in mind.' Jenny grabbed her bag and headed for the door.

'Going anywhere interesting?'

'Maybe. We'll see. Friend of mine runs a séance group. You know, Ouija boards and astral projection. She's as mad as a coot, but a lot of fun. Especially when there's been a bottle or two of wine consumed.'

'Well, be careful.' McLean wasn't sure whether he should be taking her seriously or not. That was the problem with Jenny Nairn. Her sense of humour was so dry it could be used to cure leather.

'Oh I will. Have no doubt about that, Inspector.'

'Please, Tony's fine,' he said. But she was already gone.

He found Emma in the library, hunched over the computer. She'd obviously been there for hours, daylight slowly leaching out of the room as dusk set in. The glow from the screen painted her face pale, emphasizing how sunken her eyes still were, how angular her cheekbones. He stood silent in the doorway for long moments, just looking at her as the tumble of the day ebbed away from his mind. Absorbed in whatever task she was doing, she was almost the Emma of old; that streak of rebellious obsessiveness was obviously a trait that had established itself early on in her life. It was, he realized, both what had allowed her to break through the barriers he'd put up after Kirsty's death, and what had attracted him to her enough to let her get close.

Something must have broken her concentration. She

191

looked up and saw him standing there in the doorway. A grin spread slowly across her face, but it wasn't the welcoming smile of a friend, or a lover, so much as the delight of a child.

'You're back.' She didn't stand up, or run across the room to give him a hug. Whatever was on the screen held her fascination too much for that.

'I'm back,' McLean confirmed. 'And Jenny's just left. What're you doing there?'

'Don't like Jenny any more' was all he got by way of response to the question. Emma's gaze flicked back to the screen, then to him again, as if she were fighting to maintain her attention.

'You don't like her? I thought she was your best friend.' McLean flicked on the lights, though whether it was that or the suggestion that made Emma pout like a teenager he couldn't tell. He walked across the room to the drinks cabinet, artfully hidden behind a fake bookcase, poured himself a glass of whisky then went to see what she was finding so fascinating. She wrinkled her nose at the smell as he put the glass down on the desk, but shuffled over a bit anyway so he could see what was on the screen.

'More photos?' A series of thumbnail images arranged across the page, dark and difficult to make out at this resolution. 'I thought you were up in the attic playing costumes.'

That got him a nudge in the ribs, not too hard but sore nonetheless. It was an oddity of Emma's condition that whilst she often behaved like an eight-year-old girl, if you treated her like one it rarely went well.

'Not playing. Looking for stuff. And taking photographs. And talking to the ghosts.'

The statement was so matter of fact, McLean didn't at first register it. He was still staring at the tiny thumbnails when it finally sank in.

'Ghosts?'

'Mmm hmm.' Emma clicked the mouse and a full-size picture came into view. 'Ghosts, see?'

It was the attic, that much he recognized. There were several rooms up in the roof space of this big old house. One was a servant's bedroom, now occupied by Jenny Nairn. In olden times it would have been shared by more than one serving girl. Alongside it at the top of the narrow stairs was a tiny washroom; a luxury indeed for a time when most servants would have been expected to use the facilities in the coach house. That was now the garage, but had also housed the male servants before the First World War. Back when a house this size would have employed at least five full-time staff. The final room was what McLean had always referred to as the attic; one large, long room with a couple of skylights and a narrow slit window at the gable end. It was where unwanted stuff went to die, and Emma had captured that well in her photograph. There were the stacks of boxes and trunks bearing the initials of long-forgotten ancestors; the heavy old oak wardrobe he had no idea how anyone had managed to get up there. He'd spent many a wet winter afternoon searching for the door in the back that would take him to Narnia. Across from the wardrobe, an old leather Chesterfield sofa and a couple of armchairs had been the *Tirpitz* and Lancaster bombers to his young imagination. They didn't appear to have moved an inch since the last great battle, but neither were they empty as he expected.

Three wispy white figures sat on them, staring at the camera. You couldn't exactly call them people, but neither were they something to do with the lens, some light flare or reflection.

'What on earth?'

'I told you, silly. They're ghosts. Look.' Emma clicked through a half dozen more photographs, each showing a different angle on much the same scene. In some of the pictures there were only one or two figures. But they were always there, like someone had run across the view on a long-exposure shot.

'How did you do this?' McLean asked after a while. 'Is it some kind of software manipulation?'

That got him another jab to the ribs. 'They're ghosts. Spirits.' Emma paused for a minute, stopped looking at the screen and turned to him. 'And you can see them.'

'Well, yes. I mean, I can see something. Ghosts if you say so.'

'No, I mean you can actually see them. Like here and here and here.' Emma jabbed at the screen, setting it to a perilous wobble.

'Umm. Isn't that the whole point? You showed me the pictures.'

'But Jenny couldn't see them. Or she wouldn't see them. Sometimes I think she's just humouring me. Just being nice 'cause she's paid to. She swore blind there was nothing in these photos but the furniture and boxes.'

McLean bent down to get a better look, staring long

and hard at the image with its curious misty lines. He couldn't have said exactly what it was he was seeing, something from an age when photography was new and people believed in faeries, perhaps. But there was something on the photographs. Of that he was sure. Of course, it could have been an elaborate joke; wouldn't have been the first one Emma had played on him. Her posture and the palpable feeling of excitement radiating off her made it unlikely though. This close, he could feel her warmth, smell the scent of shampoo in her hair. He pulled away before he lost himself in it.

'So what are these ghosts doing up in the attic?' The question was only half joking, though he didn't realize that until he'd asked it.

'Nothing. They're just memories.' Emma clicked on the little x in the top corner of the screen and the ghostly images disappeared.

23

Patrick Sands hadn't been the most popular of employees. That at least was the impression McLean got from talking to his team boss at Chartered Eagle Bank. It was a typical downtown call centre, just off the London Road. Driving past you might mistake it for a DIY warehouse or a cash and carry store. Only the lack of windows at ground level and the omission of any car parking spaces gave the game away. McLean and Ritchie had arrived early for their appointment, but their contact, Ashley Coombes, hadn't mentioned anything about it. She'd welcomed them in and been nothing but helpful. He only wished all interviews were as easy.

'So the last time he came to work was two months ago. Didn't anyone say anything? Try to find out where he was?' McLean sat in a surprisingly comfortable low-backed leather armchair in a small office off the main hall of the call centre. An expensive-looking machine had given him a very nice cup of coffee and the woman sitting opposite him, separated by a low table, had apologized profusely for the lack of biscuits, having spent five minutes searching through every cupboard in the room just in case.

'Patrick came to us through a temping agency. We contacted them about him, of course, but they just sent a replacement.'

'How long had he been working here?' Detective Sergeant Ritchie asked the question, which was just as well since McLean was enjoying his coffee too much.

'He started here on January 3rd. Here. I've made a copy of his file for you.' Coombes picked up the slim brown folder she'd brought in with her and handed it to Ritchie.

'What was he like, as a person?' McLean reluctantly placed his empty cup on the table, wondered idly if it would be rude to ask for another.

'Quiet, I guess. Competent. He got on with the job. We've taken on a few of the temps as permanent employees. Offered it to him, but he wasn't interested.'

'And yet he was studying for his banking exams.'

'Was he? I didn't know that.' Coombes looked genuinely surprised.

'Would you say he was depressed at all?' McLean picked up his coffee cup, rolled it around in his hand then realized what he was doing and put it down again.

'Not especially, no. Here, let me.' Coombes took the cup over to the machine, punched some buttons to produce more coffee. 'Like I said, he was quiet. He didn't socialize much with the rest of the team. After hours, you know. Sometimes they all go off to the pub together, but Paddy would always just go home.'

'Paddy?'

'That's what everyone called him, yes.' Coombes paused, a slight frown rippling across her forehead as a thought scuttled through her mind. 'Now I think about it, he wasn't really all that happy about it.'

'Probably not enough to make him commit suicide though.'

197

'No, I guess not.' The frown disappeared, replaced by a smile. 'How's the coffee?'

'Lovely.' McLean raised his cup. 'I don't suppose we could have a quick chat with his co-workers?'

'Umm. Here? Now?' The frown came back.

'It won't take a minute. I can speak to them at their desks if it's easier.' McLean swallowed the last drop, put the cup down on the table. 'I just want to see if anyone noticed anything strange in the last few days he was here.'

The open-plan office echoed with a hundred different voices, a study in desperate busy-ness. Most of the workers were seated in front of large flat-screen monitors, heads down and concentrating on selling mortgages, personal loans, insurance or whatever it was the bank did. At one end of the hall a large screen displayed the number of calls currently being answered, and the number stacking up to be dealt with. The air was filled with a sense of desperation so thick you could almost taste it. Or maybe that was just the odour of sweat and unwashed bodies.

Coombes led them to a far corner, where ten or so people worked in a space blocked off by low partitions. The rest of the room was similarly split up, reminding McLean of nothing so much as a livestock market, beasts waiting nervously for their turn in the ring, or the short walk to the killing house.

Everyone was busy when they arrived; no one looked up to see the new arrivals. Coombes stood in the middle, peering over shoulders at screens as if the rapidly changing pages meant something to her. There was a moment's indecision as she tried to decide which of two calls were going to end soonest, and then she dived in, tapping a young man on the shoulder. He clicked a single key on his keyboard before swivelling around in his chair to face them all.

'John, can you spare a moment?' As if the poor bastard had any choice. He nodded, eyes flicking from Coombes to McLean to Ritchie and back to Coombes again.

'These two police officers want to ask everyone about Paddy Sands. It won't take a moment.' The last was not a question so much as a statement, and seemed to be directed at the two detectives rather than the hapless John.

'You worked with Sands?' McLean asked.

John nodded.

'Where did he sit?'

John pointed. 'Over there. It's Steve's station now.'

'You talk much?' Even as he asked, McLean realized it wasn't the most intelligent of questions. No doubt if you spent enough time in this place you'd get used to it, but he was having a hard time filtering out one voice from the constant babble.

'Break time, maybe. Sometimes on the afternoon shift it's a bit quieter.' John glanced quickly over his shoulder at the big screen.

'You ever go out after work. The pub or something?'

'With Paddy? Nah. He wasn't really into that.'

'What about the last few days he was here? Was he different in any way?'

'Couldn't really say. We all have off days, y'know?'

'Who sat next to him? Same people as now?' He nodded his head in the direction of the workstation now occupied by Steve.

199

'Nah, was Jen. She left about a week before Paddy. And Charlie there sat on the other side.'

McLean was about to go and speak to Charlie when the young woman sitting next to John tapped her keyboard, slipped off her headset and swivelled around to face him.

'There was that one night Paddy came out with the rest of us. Must be, what, couple months ago?'

John looked momentarily confused, then the light came on behind his eyes. 'Aye, that was right, Maeve's leaving do. I think he was a bit soft on Maeve.'

'Him and every other person in here with balls.' The young woman shook her head. 'Except for Ben, of course.'

This was obviously an in-joke at Ben's expense, whoever Ben was. Both of them laughed anyway.

'You all go somewhere together then? For this leaving do. Sands as well?'

'Oh God, I don't remember much,' the young woman said. 'Had the day off after, so I drank more than was probably wise. I think a bunch of them went off after the pub but I was well gone. Last I saw Paddy he was talking to Jen.' She shook her head. 'No, that can't be right. Jen'd left by then, hadn't she?'

'Yeah, but she came back for Maeve.'

'And this was just before Sands left?' McLean asked.

John scratched at his cheek for a moment before saying 'Yeah. Couple days maybe. It all blurs into one after a while, mind.'

'I can imagine. And thanks, you've been a great help.'

McLean left the two of them to their calls, turned to where the young man called Charlie had been pointed out to him. All the people working here seemed to be young. Or maybe he was just getting old. Charlie was staring intently at his screen, fingers battering away at his rackety keyboard as he spoke into the microphone dangling just in front of his lips. Busy. And probably wouldn't have any great insights into the state of Patrick Sands' mind.

'Are we done here?' Coombes took his hesitation as a cue to move the distraction away from her workforce. McLean couldn't bring himself to be annoyed. Time was money in these places, after all, and she had given him two cups of very good coffee.

'I think so.' He let her lead them towards the exit.

'There was one thing,' he added as they reached the door. 'There was a young woman worked alongside Sands for a while. Left a bit before he did.'

'Jen. Yes. What of her?'

'I was wondering if you could tell us how to find her.'

Coombes looked a little askance, as if McLean had asked her what her preferred sexual position was. 'I can't hand over confidential personnel information like that, Inspector. Not even to the police. I'm sorry.'

'I understand, of course. Perhaps you could point me in the right direction though. Was she another temp? What's her full name?'

'Oh. Right. Yes. She was a temp. Worked for the same agency as Paddy. They might be able to contact her for you, I suppose. And it's Nairn, her surname. Jennifer Nairn.'

24

'So this is where you work. It's nice.'

Jenny Nairn didn't try to hide the irony in her voice as she lounged back in her uncomfortable plastic chair. The interview room was probably the best available, but it was still a small room in a police station. And whilst this might be an informal session, it was still 'helping the police with their enquiries'. The easy-going young woman McLean had shared his house with for the past month had disappeared almost as soon as he'd suggested she might like to make the trip down. Now she was almost as unhelpful as Emma in one of her more childish moods.

'Miss Nairn. I understand that you worked at Chartered Eagle Bank, in their call centre in London Road, for the first four months of this year.' DS Ritchie asked the question. She had a long list that she and McLean had put together for the interview. Now he sat silently beside her, all too aware of the awkward situation he was in. Technically Jenny wasn't a suspect, but the fact that he was her current employer would no doubt give Duguid something to complain about when he read the report. If he read the report, though of course this would be the one, the only one, that he did.

'What of it?'

'Did you or did you not work at Chartered Eagle bank?'

'Yes, yes. I did. Shithole that it was, I worked there.'
Jenny tipped her head back, tilting the chair onto two
legs, pushing as far as it would go without losing her
balance.

'Why? I thought you were a registered care nurse.'

'Yeah, well. There's not always jobs for registered care
nurses, are there. I'd been looking after an old bloke in the
New Town up to Christmas, but he died. Money was a bit
tight so I took the call centre job to tide me over.' Thump
as the chair came back down. 'Look, is this important?
Only I can't see how.'

Ritchie almost recoiled, stopped herself at the last
moment. 'Sorry. You're right. Not important. This isn't
really about you, so much as Patrick Sands.'

'Yes, Tony mentioned that.' Jenny looked straight at
McLean. The way a shark might look at a passing fish. A
smile that was all teeth.

'You worked in the same team as him. Alongside him in
fact. You must have talked.'

Jenny gave a little humourless laugh. 'You been to that
place, right?'

'We have, yes.'

'Well, you'll know there's not much time for idle chit-
chat. Even when the calls were light, Ms Coombes didn't
like us talking too much.' Something about the way Jenny
pronounced Ms as Mzzz suggested she hadn't much cared
for the woman. It was perhaps not all that surprising.

'Is that why you left?'

'No. I left because I was fed up. That and a friend
of mine at the hospital told me about a carer's job that
might be coming up. You know, coma patient woken with

memory loss? Needing full-time care while she recovers? Ring any bells?'

'Tell me about Patrick Sands then.' Ritchie quickly changed the subject.

'Not much to say, really. Paddy was nice enough. Shy. He didn't hang out with everyone after work much, but then neither did I.'

'Did he struggle with his shyness?'

'How do you mean?'

'Did it depress him?'

Jenny made a sour face. 'What am I, his therapist?'

'I don't know. Were you? You have a degree in psychology. Maybe he asked you for help. Maybe he made a pass at you. I don't know. I'm trying to find out what sort of a person he was, not criticize you.'

Round one to Miss Nairn. McLean noticed the twitch of a smirk around the corners of her mouth. He'd played this game with plenty of interviewees down the years. Ritchie presumably less so. Either that or she'd let Jenny get the upper hand on purpose. It wasn't a bad strategy to take with a hostile witness.

'OK. One thing. He never made a pass at me. He was too busy ogling Maeve's chest for that.'

'Did he ever make a pass at her, then?'

'Wouldn't have known how to. Poor wee thing. He wasn't good at talking to people, specially not women. He used to blush every time he asked to borrow my stapler. It was sweet, in a way. But creepy, too.'

'So it's possible he was badly affected when Maeve left. You'd already been gone what, a month by then?'

'Something like that. Said they were all going out for

drinks and did I want to come. I was surprised as the next one when Paddy was there too.'

'Did the evening go well?'

'What do you mean? Did I get off with anyone?'

'Did Sands?'

'Ha! As if. No, of course not.' Jenny paused, then added, 'least not while I was there. He might've done later. Or he might've passed out from all the Dutch courage he was drinking. Here, maybe he was going to propose to Maeve or something. I don't know, declare his undying love to her. She'd've laughed like a drain at him if he had, drunk or no'. That might be what tipped him over the edge.'

Ritchie paused a moment before speaking again, as if she found the thought objectionable. 'This Maeve. You have a contact number for her?'

'Somewhere, aye. Won't do you much good though. She went home to Canada the day after the party. Far as I know she's still there.'

'Far as you know? You don't keep in touch then?'

'Not like we were best buddies or anything. I worked with her in that shithole call centre a couple of months. She's hardly been gone that long. Don't think I even spoke to her that much the last time I saw her. Like I say, Paddy was drinking, so he might've tried something on with her. I left early, no idea what happened later.'

'Why?' Ritchie asked. 'Why'd you leave early?'

'Job interview.' Jenny pointed a finger straight at McLean's chest. 'Had to have a clear head so's I could make a good impression on the boss.'

*

A heavy silence filled the car as McLean drove across town, headed for home. Beside him in the passenger seat, Jenny Nairn stared ahead. He'd glanced at her a couple of times, under the guise of checking his mirrors, but her expression was unreadable. He hoped for Emma's sake that she wasn't going to hand in her notice as soon as they arrived.

The interview hadn't been a complete failure, but neither had it yielded much in the way of useful information about Patrick Sands. Maybe he'd be able to get some more out of her, away from the station and its unmistakable reek of police authority.

'Look, I'm really sorry about all that back there.' McLean nodded his head backwards, as if the station were still directly behind them. Jenny said nothing, continued her stare into the middle distance. McLean knew that she was leaving a silence for him to fill; he wasn't exactly a novice at this game himself.

'I'd have talked to you at home, informally, if I could have done. Soon as your name came up though, I had to do it all by the book.'

'Why?' Jenny hadn't moved, hadn't turned to face him, but the question was a good sign.

'I'm your employer right now. That's a relationship, a connection between me and Patrick Sands beyond the fact that I'm investigating his death. My boss is . . . Well, he insists on everything being done by the book, and lately he's been double-checking everything I do. Making sure it's all above board.'

'You cock up somewhere?'

'That depends on your definition of cock up. If you mean did I solve his case for him and not make a fuss when he took all the credit, then yes, I cocked up.'

That brought a ghost of a smile. It didn't last long though.

'I don't like police stations. Don't trust you lot.'

'I know. I read your file.' Arrested during the G8 protests. No charges pressed. A couple of minor altercations at other rallies, lots of cautions but always managing to stay out of court and jail. Clever, but angry.

'And you still hired me?'

'Well, I should probably have read it before taking you on. That would've been an inappropriate use of my privileged access though. I've bent a few rules in my time, but that's not somewhere I'd be all that happy going.'

'Why'd you read it now, then?'

'Because your name came up in connection to my investigations.'

Jenny didn't respond at first, just carried on staring out the window as they neared their destination. Finally the wheels scrunched on the gravel drive and McLean pulled the car to a halt outside the house. Only then did she turn to him and speak.

'So are you going to fire me?'

'I don't think Emma would let me, even if I wanted to.'

'You don't mind about all the . . . stuff?'

'Far as I can see you've not committed any actual offence. You might find it hard to believe, what with this house and everything, but I'm not a huge fan of the one per cent either. You do a good job, Jenny. Emma likes you, and that's all I care about. I really am sorry that I had to drag you down to the station. If I could've done it any other way, I would have.'

McLean pushed open the car door and climbed out. That was the other thing about old sports cars; they were low to the ground, and he wasn't getting any younger. His back creaked in protest as he straightened up. Perhaps he should get a Saab. He'd read somewhere they had the best seats of all modern cars. But they'd gone bust, hadn't they?

Shaking his head at the random thought, he trudged across the gravel towards the back door. Only then did he realize that something had been bothering him. A step back and a quick look. The front door was wide open.

A horrible cold sensation settled in the pit of his stomach. The front door was never opened these days. Everyone came around the back, through the little utility room and straight into the kitchen. Standing on the other side of the car, Jenny had noticed too.

'Em wouldn't have gone out into the garden on her own.' It wasn't a question.

Both of them hurried to the front door. Jenny was about to dash in, but McLean stopped her, held up a finger to his lips. He went in first, listening for any sounds that shouldn't have been there, hearing none. No noise from the television either. Across the hall, the library door hung open like the front door, as if Emma had just got up and walked out in a daze. McLean looked inside, but she wasn't there. When he turned back, Jenny was at the doorway that opened onto the narrow corridor past the scullery and butler's pantry to the kitchen. She shook her head.

Together they checked the other ground floor rooms, then the upstairs and finally the attic. The garden was empty, as was the coach house, except for Emma's light blue and rust Peugeot 106 which had been put into storage there months before. There was no getting away from the fact. She was gone.

25

'About five two. Black hair with a life of its own. Skinny as a rake. Kinda scruffy, aye?'

McLean sat at the kitchen table, watching as Jenny Nairn spoke on the phone. He'd already called everyone he could think of; now she was putting the word out among a different stratum of Edinburgh society. He stared down at his mug of tea. It had gone cold, a surface scum congealed on the milky top. Up to the clock on the wall; half past four. Two hours since they'd found Emma gone; four since she'd been left happily watching telly, maybe five.

'I should have got someone in to look after her,' he said as she hung up. 'Shit. I should've just talked to you here, not taken you down the station.'

'Em was fine when I left. She said she was OK being on her own in the house for a few hours. You know that, I know that. If anyone should be kicking themselves, it's me, right? I'm the one being paid to be her carer.'

McLean didn't answer that, didn't want to suggest it was true when he'd been the one who'd dragged her away from her job. All so he could cover his own arse.

'Look, she can't have gone far. She's on foot, doesn't much like being out in open spaces. Chances are she's at one of your neighbours drinking tea and chatting about flowers.'

Jenny didn't look like she believed what she was saying.

McLean almost laughed. 'That's my line, you know. Reassuring the worried parent, other half, whatever.'

'Maybe I should have been a copper then.'

'You'd make a good one. Family liaison, that kind of thing.'

'Not finding missing scatterbrains though.' She twirled her phone around on the kitchen table for a moment, then snatched it up. 'Sod this, I'm going to look around the garden again. There's a gate through to the dell. Over in the far corner, right?'

'It's padlocked tight, rusted up. Hasn't been opened since I was a boy.' McLean knew that he'd checked it, but felt the pull all the same. It was always possible, just, that Emma had found a way to open it and wandered off into the woodland, down to the river maybe. Except that he had checked it, not half an hour ago. It was unlikely to have changed in the interim. He let Jenny go anyway. Better to do something, even if it was a waste of time, than to sit around and wait.

'I'll have a look up in the attic again. She's had a fascination with the place for weeks now. Probably crawled into an old trunk and fallen asleep.'

They set off in their different directions, Jenny out the back door, McLean up the main stairs and then the echoing, wooden servants' staircase to the attic. The door creaked theatrically as he pushed it open onto the void under the rafters. Afternoon light speared in through the window at the end, shadows moving as the wind outside played with the branches of nearby trees. Dust hung in the warm air, gravity and thermodynamics in perfect balance. He remembered the pictures Emma had shown him, just a few nights earlier. Those ghostly figures sitting on the empty sofa, standing around the wardrobe. In his mind's eye they reminded him of Victorian spiritualist photographs, simple double-exposure fakes from a time when photography was new and anything was possible. Conan Doyle had been a true believer, hadn't he? Taken in by the hoaxers in his later years. Sad to see the mind that had invented Sherlock Holmes believing in faeries like a little child.

For a moment McLean stood still, wondered where the thought had come from. Then he noticed something lying on the floor beside the old sofa. A book. The book he'd paid a king's ransom for at auction. The book that had once belonged to Donald Anderson, and possibly before that to Sir Arthur Conan Doyle. His feet echoed on the floorboards as he walked over and picked it up. The note from Madame Rose had been folded in half and used as a bookmark. An indentation in the sofa cushion showed where someone had sat whilst reading, but when he put his hand to it, there was no warmth. Emma had been here, yes. Not recently though.

With the book tucked under his arm, he worked his way around the space methodically, checking trunks, the old wardrobe, and even the half-height cupboard doors that opened up onto the roof eave space. There was ancient wiring in there, and no loft insulation worth talking about, but no missing women.

He stopped by the window in the gable wall, stared out through the dust and cobwebs at the tiny form of Jenny Nairn stalking back across the garden. Hers had been a futile search as well, it would seem. In the light from the window, he opened up the book again, flicked idly through the pages as if he might find Emma in there. Looking up, he realized he was standing in the exact spot she must have taken the first of her photographs from. There weren't any ghosts to be seen.

'Where are you, Emma?' It wasn't a question he expected to have answered, but as he spoke, the bookmark slipped from the pages and fell to the floor. He stooped, picked it up and unfolded it, seeing the neatly inked handwriting of Madame Rose's letter again. And as he read the first line, he heard a voice call faintly from below.

'Halloo! Is there anyone home?'

Shoving the note back in the book, McLean rushed out of the attic, taking the stairs two at a time. From the first floor landing he couldn't see into the hall, but halfway down the stairs it hit him. He knew that voice, had heard it in his head as he read the letter. And sure enough, there she was. There he was. Whatever. Standing in the little porch that separated the main hallway from the outside. Madame Rose in all her Jenner's Tea Room finery. And beside him, her, dwarfed by the transvestite's bulk, the tiny, frail form of Emma.

'Oh my god! Where have you been?' McLean rushed down the stairs and was halfway across the hall before he stopped. Emma was a state, her hair even less kempt than ever, her face muddy. The clothes she had been wearing that morning hung from her as if she'd been on a diet for months, and her feet, good Christ, her feet. He stared at the blood-stained mess poking from the bottom of her sweatpants. 'You went out without shoes?'

'Calm yourself, Inspector.' Madame Rose put a gentle arm around Emma's shoulder and steered her into the house. At the same moment, Jenny Nairn appeared from the kitchen clutching a familiar-looking pair of trainers. Her eyes widened at the sight, the shoes tumbling from her hands as she ran across the hall and gathered Emma into a large embrace.

'Where did you go? I thought you were lost.' She pulled back, briefly looking Emma up and down and then added: 'Why'd you not put on some shoes? Why'd you not –'

'I think a cup of tea is in order, don't you?' Madame Rose looked around the hallway, eyes finally alighting on the door through which Jenny had just come. 'Kitchen this way, is it?'

McLean leaned against the Aga, unsure what to say as he waited for the kettle to boil. Madame Rose had taken a seat at the large wooden table and was leafing with great interest through the copy of Gray's *Anatomy*. Emma sat beside her, him, dammit. Clingy like a child while Jenny fetched a basin and filled it with warm water. Soon the air was filled with that school-familiar smell of antiseptic.

'Here, Em. Let's have a look at your feet.' Jenny knelt down and lifted one of Emma's legs, gently resting it on another chair so that her foot was taking no weight. Then she set about the task of cleaning away the blood and grit, tutting all the while as she worked.

'Where did you find her?' McLean pulled the boiling kettle off the hotplate and poured water into the teapot. He placed the pot on the table and took a seat opposite the large medium.

'Well there's the strangest thing.' Madame Rose care-

214

fully closed the book and put it down in front of her before continuing. 'I was doing a card reading for a client. Lovely chap, comes in once a week. Every time his tarot's the same, but he insists it will change.'

'And Emma?' McLean interrupted before Madame Rose could get into full flow.

'I was coming to that, Inspector. Anyway, I was reading the cards and all of a sudden, out of nowhere, I found myself thinking about Donald Anderson's shop.'

'Anderson?' A lump of ice began to form in McLean's guts.

'We'll get there much quicker if you don't keep interrupting me. Tea?' Madame Rose nodded at the teapot. Instinct kicked in, and McLean began the ritual of pouring. Milk. Two sugars. He should probably have offered biscuits.

'Thank you.' Madame Rose accepted a mug. 'As I was saying, I found myself thinking about Donald's shop. Not just an idle "I wonder what's happened to the old place" kind of thing, you understand. This was a portent. Something had thrust the idea into my head. Well, I couldn't ignore such a thing, so I finished with Mr Mortimer and then closed up for the afternoon. Took a taxi to the Canongate. You know, people still step off the pavement as they pass that place, without noticing they're doing it. But she was there.'

McLean's gaze slid from the medium to the skinny woman sitting beside her. 'Emma? At Anderson's shop?'

'Apparently she'd been there almost an hour. Just standing by the door, staring at it.'

'How do you know that?'

'Am I being interrogated, Inspector?' Madame Rose placed a theatrical hand over her fake bosom. 'How exciting.'

'I'm sorry. I should be thanking you for finding her. For bringing her here.'

'You were worried sick, Inspector. You and Miss Nairn both. I can see that plain as my hands.' Madame Rose put down her mug and waved them about, just in case McLean didn't know what a man's hands looked like. 'I know the old fellow runs the coffee shop just across the road from Anderson's place. He told me he'd seen Emma standing there. He'd been about to call the police.'

'But what was she doing there?' McLean turned to Emma, realized as he did so that she hadn't said a word since she had been brought back. 'What were you doing there, Emma?'

Slowly, as if half asleep, Emma raised her head, stared at him with deep, black eyes. It was like being gazed upon by the abyss.

'I lost something. Looked everywhere for it. I thought maybe it was there.'

'You lost something? What did you lose, Emma?'

A frown creased her forehead and those eyes shifted focus, took in his face rather than his soul. 'I don't know.'

Madame Rose placed a hand on Emma's shoulder. 'Don't you worry dear. Your Auntie Rose will help you find it.' Then: 'Jenny, why don't you take Emma upstairs. I'm sure she could do with a long hot soak after her ordeal, don't you think?'

Jenny Nairn looked across to McLean for confirmation. He nodded, wondering how it was that Madame

Rose knew her. Something to do with Ouija boards and séances, no doubt. He watched silently as Emma allowed herself to be led from the room, more childlike now than she had been since first waking. Only when she was gone, and the door was closed behind her, did he speak.

'Why do I get the impression you know more about this than you're telling me?'

'Because you're a detective inspector?' Madame Rose took a long, unladylike slurp of tea. 'Or maybe because you know what this is about but just don't want to accept it.'

'What are you talking about? Emma? She had a nasty blow to the head.'

'Her brain has recovered. That's not what's wrong with her.'

'If it's not her brain, then what?'

'Think, Inspector. Use that mind your grandmother was so proud of.'

That set him back a step. First Emma, then Jenny Nairn. Now his grandmother. Was there anyone in his life this strange transvestite medium didn't know? McLean suppressed the urge to ask. Kept his mind focused on the task at hand.

'Why was she at Anderson's shop?'

'Ah. Now we're getting somewhere. Why do you think?'

'She had nothing to do with that place. Apart from being part of the SOC team that went over it after we found it had been used again.'

'And you think that might be it? That maybe it was one of her last memories before she had her blow to the head?'

Damn, this was worse than a session with Grumpy Bob. 'It's a possibility.'

'Possible, yes. But it's not why she went there.' Madame Rose put down her mug and picked up the medical textbook. 'Why did Anderson kill those women? Why did Needham?'

'Anderson was a sick bastard who got off on pain. Needy went mad when his dad died leaving him with a million quid in death duties to pay.'

'OK. Let's try that again. Why did they both claim they killed those women?' Madame Rose dropped the book back on the table. McLean knew damned well what he, she, whatever, was doing. That didn't mean he had to like it.

'The *Book*. The bloody *Book of Souls*. It doesn't exist. Never did. It was just Anderson trying to get off with an insanity plea. It didn't convince the jury and it didn't convince me.'

'Even after what you saw in the fire?'

'How do you know what I saw in the fire? How do you even know about the fire at all?'

'I make it my business to know what's going on at the fringes, Inspector. You might not be ready to accept it, but you are part of that world. I know what you saw in the fire. I know what happened when the book burned. The souls trapped inside it were released. There isn't a medium in Europe can call themselves that who didn't feel it when those souls were freed.'

McLean used the excuse of taking a sip of tea to study Madame Rose more closely. The man was a fraud, of that he was sure. For a start, he was a man dressed as a woman. That was a deception up front. She, he, whatever, peddled fortunes to the gullible, no doubt held séances too. That was probably how Jenny Nairn fitted into the picture, and no doubt how Madame Rose knew so much about him.

At least, that was what the rational, trained detective in him said. That was the simplest of explanations, the truth revealed after everything else had been pared away. On the other hand, there was a seductive quality to the argument. It fitted so well with the things he had seen and done. And there was no denying that Madame Rose believed in it completely. Even heavily made up as he was, you could see it in his face. And the way he held himself, the way one hand absent-mindedly stroked the cover of the copy of Gray's *Anatomy*.

And, of course, he had found Emma. Brought her home.

'Needy did have a book,' McLean said after a long pause. 'But it wasn't anything special. Just a prop. An old ledger or something he'd got from the evidence stores. It burned in the fire, but to be honest I don't remember much about what happened back then. I was concussed for one thing, and there wasn't much air.'

'Well, let me spell it out for you then.' Madame Rose gathered her hands together, leaned forwards with her elbows on the table, eyes boring into McLean's. 'The *Book of Souls* existed. Donald Anderson stole it from the monastery where he was librarian for many years. He tried to read it and failed. It consumed his soul and you know what happened next. When you caught him, the book went into hiding. It ended up in your evidence stores, where Sergeant John Needham found it. He tried to read it, and you know what happened to him.'

'You're saying Needy did what he did to those women – to Emma – because he had no soul?'

'The book did those things. It just used the man as its vessel.'

'And the women? Emma? Kirsty?'

'The book traps the souls of the victims as they die. You cannot destroy a soul, Inspector, but you can capture it and feed off it.' Now Madame Rose was staring straight at him, her eyes wide and intense. 'Or at least so I am told.'

'But Emma didn't die.'

'No, Inspector. She didn't. But I fear your Sergeant Needham made her read the book. I fear it took a part of her, and that missing part is what she was looking for today, why she can't remember anything from her adult life and why she's becoming more childlike day by day. She has lost a piece of her soul. There is really no hope of recovery until she gets it back.'

The sound of Madame Rose's taxi disappearing down the drive on its way back to Leith had long since echoed away into the background hum of the city. McLean sat at the kitchen table, a mug of cold tea in his hands, staring at nothing as he played the conversation back in his head. Half-remembered snippets flickered through his mind, suppressed memories of the fire that had claimed Sergeant John Needham, the strange underground chapel beneath the house, the factory bursting into flames spontaneously.

No, it hadn't been spontaneous. He'd taken a candle in there with him, dropped it when Needy hit him with that bit of two by four. Old, dry timber. A factory that hadn't

220

been used in years, methane gas seeping up from ancient coal mines. No wonder it had gone up like a bonfire on Guy Fawkes night.

But there had been a book, hadn't there? Needy wouldn't give it up even when the flames took him, caught that ridiculous cloak he'd been wearing, went through his hair like a knacker-man singeing a pig. McLean put down his tea, scrunched his hands into his eyes as hard as he could stand in an attempt to erase that image. A man on fire, screaming as much in frustration and rage as in pain. Or was that his imagination, his brain filling in the gaps where memory had been erased by the heat, the smoke, not enough oxygen?

Pulling his hands away from his eyes left ghost images dancing in the dim kitchen light in front of him. Spirits rising up from the ashes of a book, burned by a mystical flame. The souls of countless victims, trapped down the years. Victims and murderers both; the innocent and those who had sought to test themselves against evil and found themselves wanting. Needy had been there, a man broken by the weight of expectations laid upon him. Anderson too, small and frightened, a little boy abandoned by his parents and never understanding why. And then the women they had abducted, tortured, raped, killed. All because a book told them to? Well, was that so hard to believe, after all that had been done in the name of the Bible, the Koran?

They were naked. Does he remember that? Or is it the memory of the post-mortem slab, the endless photographs of dead bodies he has seen. No, they were there. Surrounding him, keeping the flames away until rescue came. Kirsty.

A noise and flurry of movement. At the same moment he registered that he'd heard the cat flap clatter in the back door, Mrs McCutcheon's cat was on the table in front of him. The normally unflappable beast looked wild, its fur straggled and unkempt, mud spatters all along one side.

'Jesus, you gave me a shock.' McLean rocked back in his chair, feeling his heart bashing away in his chest like a cheap horror movie. The cat just looked at him, sat down and started to clean itself.

'Where've you been anyway?' He didn't expect an answer and wasn't disappointed. It occurred to him that Mrs McCutcheon's cat had not been there when he and Jenny had returned from the station. Normally it would present itself at some point soon after he came home; ever since Emma had come from the hospital it had been her shadow. And then he knew exactly where it had been. Halfway across town and back. Following Emma all the way to the Canongate and Donald Anderson's shop. Only when Madame Rose had brought Emma home in a taxi, she hadn't noticed the familiar. Poor bloody thing must have run the whole way back.

'Let's get you something to eat then.' McLean pushed himself up from his chair, ignoring the creaks and groans from his knees as he did so. The cat stopped its cleaning, watched him with glass-black eyes as he went to the cupboard where the cat food lived. It stayed where it was, sitting in the middle of the kitchen table, until he'd bent down and brought out the box. Then with a disdainful flick of the tail it jumped down to the floor and trotted off into the hall.

26

He must have been a drummer, once. He has one of those little round stools with the padded top that rises on a screw thread. The drum kit has long gone, no doubt to pay off debts, or the rent, or just to eat; he looks like he hasn't been doing enough of that. But he kept the stool. I like that. A reminder perhaps of a better time, when life was full of possibilities.

Now the possibilities are all gone, and there is just the stool. Unwound to its fullest extent, he teeters on the edge, wobbling slightly, toes flexing as he tries to maintain his balance. He really is a skinny thing. Not an inch of fat on him. There's muscle in his legs but it's wasting away now, and his arms, his torso, are weedy. Naked, I can see the scars all around his middle and yes, there across his buttocks. Dark purple stains in the skin, slashed with shiny, white tissue. He looks like some mad headmaster has flayed him to within an inch of his life. Some malevolent first mate gone at him with the cat-o'-nine-tails, but kept the strokes low. Even if I couldn't taste the despair in his soul, I could see it written all across his ruined body. Once he was alive, fit, strong. Now he is reduced to a hobbling, pain-wracked mess of a boy. No future at all. The spirit sings in me to end him.

'You are in your safe place now. Nothing can harm you here.' My voice fills the room like smoke, spreading into every corner, pushing its way deep into the boy's mind. It is always like this when the spirit is with me. The power sends shivers deep into my core. I take the rope from my bag. Not much left now; I will have to send the next one out for some more. Heavy, rough hemp, my hands work it as if I had done this all my life, the knot appearing without any thought, perfect, deadly. I pull a chair over from the nearby table, climb up and throw the other end of the rope over the ceiling beam. I have no idea what I am doing, and yet I know exactly how long the rope must be, how far the drop. I have done since I first saw this boy, first shook him by the hand and sized him up, first knew that his struggle would soon be over. The spirit guides me in this, as it has always guided me. Since we first came together in our perfect union.

'We are close, you and I. Much closer than lovers could ever be.' I whisper the words into his ear as I lower the noose over his neck. His eyes are closed, little fluttering movements under the lids. He breathes lightly, slowly, his hands hanging loose beside him like branches swaying in the gentlest of breezes. This close, I can smell his musk, an intoxicating mixture of sweat and hormones, soap and shampoo. His mouth is shut, but his lips are pursed, dark red, full like a girl's. I have to suppress the urge to kiss them, though I feel no attraction to him. The spirit would not want me to sully myself, not when it can offer me so much more.

'Not long now and we shall be joined so perfectly you cannot begin to imagine it.' I step lightly from the chair, put it back where it came from. A quick look around the room, the shelves of bric-a-brac, the boxes strewn here and there, the thin glass panes set into the top of the old garage doors. So much bigger than the hovels the last two lived in, and this is a house, not some dingy bedsit squashed into the back of a tiny terrace. Once he had a future, this poor, poor boy. Once he might have been something. All that was taken from him in a squeal of brakes, a moment of lost attention, a terrible accident. The van that broke his bones might not have killed him straight away, but it killed him nonetheless.

I feel the spirit rising up in me now. Its power is overwhelming and pure. I give myself to it without pause or regret. The world expands in my sight and I can see every tiny detail laid out before me. The note pinned to the corkboard over the workbench. The door, slightly ajar, leading through to the kitchen where this beautiful, damaged boy took off his clothes and folded them neatly over a chair. The pores on his skin, glistening as the effort of keeping his balance brings a sheen of sweat to his cheeks and forehead. The slow, relaxed beat of his heart and the steady rhythm of his breathing.

'Come to me, now.' And my voice is a command so strong even I take a step. The boy responds without hesitation, without fear. Forward, forward.

And down.

'I want you to close your eyes, Emma. Take a breath. Hold it. Now let it out slowly.'

The office of Doctor Eleanor Austin, early morning. McLean sat on the low, comfortable sofa, cradling a cup of coffee. As ways to start the day went, it wasn't too bad. Just a pity he'd been awake since half past four, when Emma had crawled into his bed, sobbing and shivering in her sleep.

'That's good. Concentrate on my voice. Take a breath. Hold it.' A pause, and McLean found himself struggling to breathe out. 'And let it out slowly. Good.'

Emma's nocturnal visits had become regular as clockwork in the days since her disappearance. She'd started talking in her sleep, too. Low whispers that he could never quite understand. There was no mistaking the distress in her voice. Or the fact that it often didn't actually sound like her voice at all.

'Now, concentrate on your breathing. In. Hold. Out. Good. I want you to keep that rhythm.'

McLean struggled to keep his eyes open, took a long sip of coffee and looked around the room. There wasn't all that much to it. His sofa, the two high-backed armchairs one facing the other, a bureau under the window at the far side of the room. There were no pictures on the walls, just a pair of antique mirrors, candle holders set into the frame dripped with wax. A similar pair hung in the living room in his grandmother's house. He couldn't remember them ever having held candles, but presumably they must have done once. Back in the days before electric light. Before he was born. Before even his grandmother was born.

'Now I want you to think back to your earliest memory. Keep breathing. In. Hold. Out.'

His hand in someone else's. His mother's, perhaps. An adult's, certainly. He has to reach up almost above his head. He is standing alongside a car, staring into fog that swirls about the trees. Everything is white, and yet at the same time dark. The car's headlights spear through the fog, making it seem like the road is a tunnel leading to who knows where?

'And breathe – Inspector, really!' The tinny warbling of his mobile phone cut through McLean's dream. He scrabbled around, trying to get the damned thing out of his pocket, succeeding only in pouring lukewarm coffee all over his trousers.

'I'm sorry. I could have sworn I'd turned the thing off.' Finally McLean pulled the phone out, just as it rung off. Caller ID told him it had been DC MacBride. He stood up, the room swaying gently as he shook away the last vestiges of sleep. 'I'd better phone this in. Sorry.'

'I think we've probably got as far as we're going to today anyway.' Doctor Austin turned her attention back to Emma, who was trying hard to suppress a smirk but not really succeeding. 'Now I need you to practise that breathing exercise every day. Jenny will help you. It's important to learn to relax.'

McLean left them to it, heading out the door and into the small reception area as he tapped the recall button on the screen. Dave looked up at him with a slightly startled expression, but said nothing. The phone rang twice before it was answered.

'What's up, Constable? I said I'd not be in until later.'

'I know that, sir. And sorry to phone, but I thought you'd want to know as soon as. We've got another hanging.'

'You have got to be fucking joking.'

McLean stood in the small yard outside a nondescript fifties detached house in Colinton, looking in through the opened doors to a garage that like most of its ilk was not actually used for the housing of cars. This one had been pressed into the inevitable storage role, with a distinct theme of bicycle about the place. There were also a work-bench, table, some chairs. And a naked man hanging by a rope, his toes just a few inches off the ground.

'Why do they always take their clothes off?' Detective Constable MacBride slammed the door of the pool car and came to join him, unwilling to go any further into the crime scene. Probably best to leave it to the SOC officers who were even now swarming over the place like well-trained, white boiler-suited ants.

'That, Constable, is a very good question. Would you like to hazard an answer?'

MacBride said nothing, which was probably a good thing. McLean looked around the street, a long line of identikit dormer bungalows each with its pitched-roof garage alongside. Homes for Edinburgh's swelling middle

228

class at a time when the motor car was every man's dream and global warming hadn't been invented yet.

'Maybe there's a sexual element to it?'

'What?'

'The nakedness, sir. Maybe it's a . . . I don't know, a fetish or something.'

'What, like auto-erotic asphyxiation? Aren't we missing a couple of items here? A broom handle and an orange?'

It was difficult to tell whether the young detective constable was blushing or not, his face was always pink. The way MacBride turned away from the dangling man, full-frontal but not exactly stimulated, suggested he was. McLean looked back too, distracted by a car as it drove slowly along the street, almost stopping as the driver tried to get a look at what was going on.

'Why's this street not been cordoned off? Jesus, who's the officer in charge?'

'Umm . . . I just got here, sir. With you?'

'Well go and find out, won't you? And while you're at it get someone to tape off this road, at least fifty yards each way. See if the SOC boys have got a screen they can put up to stop the gawkers seeing your man there in all his glory.'

MacBride scurried off on his errands. McLean shoved his hands in his pockets and approached the nearest SOC officer. She looked at him with a scowl, her eyes dropping to his feet in a deliberate, slow motion. He stopped, backed away from the scene.

'I just need to know who's in charge, OK? I won't come inside and spoil anything.'

'Speak to him. And don't come in here without a suit. Better yet don't come in at all till we're done, aye?' The

SOC officer pointed towards the front door to the house. The porch was open, little more than a slim shelter to keep the rain off as you entered. A thin haze of blue-grey smoke hung around it, the telltale sign of someone sneaking a crafty smoke. Sure enough, as he rounded the corner, McLean was confronted with the sight of two uniform constables and one plain clothes detective sergeant keeping well out of the way.

'Everything under control is it, Sergeant?'

'I . . . Sir . . . No one told me . . .' Detective Sergeant Carter hurriedly dropped his half-smoked cigarette and scrunched it under his foot. The two constables with him hid theirs behind their backs, shuffling in the tight porch to put the DS between them and McLean.

'You two. Go see DC MacBride. We need to secure this crime scene. I want someone at each end of the street, too. Only let people in who live here, and take their names. Get started on a list so we can go house to house and speak to people.'

'Sir, is that really necessary? Silly bugger topped himself. It's not as if –'

'A man's dead, sergeant. I don't consider that silly in any way.' McLean had a head's height on Carter, and the advantage that the DS was backed into the porch.

'I was waiting for the pathologist, sir. I didn't think there was any rush. Suicides don't normally get high priority.'

'Were you aware that two other people have hanged themselves in this city in the past fortnight?'

'Ah. Way I hear it we get about two hangings a week, sir. No' that unusual a way fer folk to top themselves.'

'Like that?' McLean nodded in the direction of the

dead man, hidden round the corner of the building, and now, finally, by a hastily erected screen. Carter didn't answer, instead shifted his weight from foot to foot like a schoolboy needing to be excused.

'And no doubt you were aware that I was investigating whether they were in fact suicides at all. I seem to recall DCI Brooks making some derogatory comments about it during his briefing yesterday morning.'

'Sir, I'm sorry. I . . .'

'Forget it. Just bring me up to speed, OK?' McLean itched to tear him off a strip, preferably in front of as many junior officers as he could find, but that had happened more than enough to him in the past, and he knew just how counterproductive it was. Carter paused a while, as if considering whether to apologize or just get on with his job. He wasn't a bad detective, McLean knew, just a touch on the lazy side. And he'd been cosying up to Spence, Brooks and the rest of the cabal whose mission these days seemed to be to make life as difficult as possible. As if the job wasn't hard enough already.

'Suicide . . . That's to say the victim's name is John Fenton. Local boy as far as I can tell. Lived here all his life.'

'How was he found?'

'Neighbour.' Carter nodded towards the house on the other side of the garage. 'Said he dropped round for his bike. Fenton was the local repair man. Mad keen cyclist. Worked as a cycle courier until about six months ago when he had an argument with a Transit van and came second.'

McLean looked back at the body, still dangling from its rope. Was that stout hemp? The same as the other two?

231

'He didn't try to get him down, this neighbour. Most people would do that, wouldn't they?'

'He's one of ours, sir. Constable Stephen. Works with traffic and knows his way round a crime scene. He could tell Fenton was dead, thought it best not to disturb anything.'

'That's something at least. He at home now?'

'Had to go for his shift. We can get in touch with him easily enough.' Carter pulled a hefty Airwave set from his jacket pocket.

'Jesus. You actually carry one of those things around?'

'We all have to now, sir. And they're not so bad, really. Not the new ones, anyway. Save a fortune on the mobile, too.'

'Well, set up an interview for the end of his shift. His clock, not ours. I'll square it with his sergeant if there's any kickback. Now grab us a couple of monkey suits and let's go look at poor old John Fenton.'

'PC Stephen, sir. I was told you wanted to see me.'

McLean looked up at the noise, seeing an officer standing at the open door to his office, one hand held up high where he had knocked quietly on the door jamb. Police Constable Kenneth Stephen was not what he had been expecting. Truth be told, he'd not really been expecting anything at all, but if he had been, this surely wasn't it. He was young, for one thing; mid-twenties at the most. And he was dressed in police-issue cycling gear, a helmet stowed under one arm. Traffic, that's what DS Carter had said. Well, traffic cops rode bikes, especially in the city centre. He knew that but had somehow failed to consider exactly what it meant. Sweat, mostly, it would seem. Had the man just cycled here at full speed?

'Yes. Thank you. Ummm. Have a seat, if you can find one.' McLean nodded in the direction of where a seat might be, were it not covered in a mound of boxes and paperwork.

'I'm OK standing, sir. I take it this is about John.'

'Fenton, aye. You knew him, I understand.'

Stephen shook his head. 'Thought I knew him. Never thought he'd be the type to . . . well . . . you know.'

'So he wasn't depressed then?'

Stephen paused before answering, a frown wrinkling his damp brow. 'Actually, now you mention it, he had every reason to be depressed, just didn't seem to show it.'

'How d'you mean?'

'Well, sir. See, John's a bicycle nut. That's why I was away round his place this morning, to fetch my road bike. He'd been fixing the brakes and making me a new wheel.'

'Yes, I saw the bikes in his garage.'

'He was an off-road racer. Semi-pro. Endurance stuff mostly. Don't think I've ever met anyone as fit. Used to work for a cycle courier firm in the city. Wheel Deliver, I think they're called. Told me it was his ideal job. He kept race fit, and they gave him time off to compete. Spon-sored him for a while too, I think.'

'Sounds like a man with every reason to be happy.' McLean leaned back in his seat until his back hit the wall. He still had to crane his neck rather more than was com-fortable to look the standing PC in the eye.

'Well, he was. I mean it was sad when his mum died, but

233

that was a few years back. Told me he'd never known his dad, but he and his mum were close. I guess that's why he kept the house. Could've sold it for a fortune if my rent's anything to go by.'

'So if he was happy enough in his job and he'd got over his mum's death, why was he depressed? Sorry, that's not what you said. Why did he have every reason to be depressed?'

'He was in an accident, sir. About six months ago I think. No, more like eight. Got hit by a Transit van that pulled out of a side street without looking. We got the bastard, lost his licence for two years. You ask me, they should've locked him up and thrown away the key.'

'Fenton was badly injured, I take it.'

'Broke his pelvis in three places. Right femur too. Doctor reckoned he was about a millimetre away from severing the artery. Would've killed him in seconds. He'd've bled out.'

McLean made a mental note to tell Cadwallader, then realized that the pathologist would look up Fenton's medical file long before he started examining the dead body.

'How long did he take to recover?'

'He wasn't really back to full mobility yet, to be honest, sir. He was in hospital for three months, then a wheelchair and crutches for a couple more. But I saw him out on his bike recently. Going slow, but steady. Thought he was doing OK. And he was always cheerful when you talked to him.'

McLean scratched a little question mark in his notebook underneath the line where he'd written 'John Fenton'. He hadn't actually taken any notes. He hastily added 'Wheel Deliver. Cycle Couriers'.

'Thank you, Constable. You've been very helpful.' He snapped the notebook shut and stood up. 'We'll need a proper written statement, too. Let's see if we can find DC MacBride and get that done before your shift's over.'

Stephen nodded, then stepped aside to let McLean out of the office. He fell into step alongside as they walked up the corridor towards the CID room.

'Can I ask a question, sir?' Stephen asked after a few seconds.

'Of course.'

'John hanged himself. I could see that clear enough when I found him this morning.'

'That's not a question, Constable.'

'No. I mean, well, it is. Sort of. Only I called it in, soon as I found him. SEB were on the scene pretty sharpish, and that DS Carter arrived with a couple of constables to check everything over. But they didn't seem all that interested.'

'Still not an actual question.'

'No. Sorry. What I'm trying to say is, if this is just another suicide, then why's a DI looking into it? I mean, I'd expect a report to go across your desk. You might even read it before signing off the investigation costs. But asking questions? Getting involved?'

They had reached the door to the CID room, and McLean pushed it open, ushering PC Stephen inside. MacBride looked up from his desk in the far corner, saw them and picked up his notebook in readiness.

'You go speak to Detective Constable MacBride there.' McLean pointed him out. 'And if you ever fancy a change to plain clothes, give us a shout. I'm always on the lookout for officers not afraid to ask questions.'

He was on his way back to his office and the ever-renewing stack of paperwork when his phone vibrated in his pocket. He managed to get it out before it switched to voicemail.

'McLean.'

'Ah, Detective Inspector. Good. Jemima Cairns. From the forensic labs. We met briefly at the hanging crime scene in Colinton. John Fenton.'

McLean tried to remember who he'd spoken to that morning. Failed.

'What can I do for you, Miss Cairns?'

'You asked for someone to look at the rope used in the earlier two hangings. I've been comparing them with the one we found this morning.'

'Are they all from the same length?' He paused mid-stride, all too aware how much hinged on the answer.

'It's . . . complicated. I really think you should see for yourself.'

'So this is what you wanted me to see then? Would it not have been easier just to send me some photos?'

McLean stood in the middle of the Scene Evaluation Branch main lab, trying not to touch anything in case it brought yet another scowl from the short, round woman beside him. She had introduced herself as Jemima Cairns, but he had a feeling she was always going to be Miss Cairns to him. Either that or Ma'am. She didn't have the look of a Jemima.

'Photographs can only show so much, Inspector. Much easier if you can actually handle the objects. Here.' Miss Cairns handed him a pair of latex gloves, which he dutifully pulled on. She was already wearing a pair, and bent down over the bench to pick up the first of the three objects that had brought him all the way across town at her summons.

It was a noose, expertly tied. Good hemp rope. Three-quarter-inch stock, but then that much he already knew. The knot was still intact, a neat cut through the loop showing how it had been removed from its last user. This one had come from either Mikhailevic or Fenton, as it wasn't stained with the juices of decomposition.

'It's a noose,' he said, aware that he was stating the obvious but needing something to say.

'It's not just a noose, Inspector. This is a hangman's knot. Thirteen loops, see. Makes sure it doesn't slip, and it's unlucky.' Miss Cairns carefully twisted the rope around until the intricate loops could be seen in the best light. 'It's been tied by an expert. Someone who's done it many, many times before.'

'I can barely tie my shoelaces, so I'll take your word for it. These are all from the same piece of rope?' McLean pointed at the other two knots on the bench. Miss Cairns carefully put down the one she was holding and picked up the next, again angled it so that the knot itself was easy to see.

'As far as we can tell, yes. Which is to say the chances of them not being the same piece of rope are vanishingly small. A lawyer might try reasonable doubt if a trial hinged on it, but I'd be happy to square up to him if he did.'

I bet you would. McLean stopped himself from taking a step back. Miss Cairns might have been short, but she made up for it with girth and an indefinable presence that set his self-preservation alarms ringing.

'That's not the interesting part though. See?' She held up the second rope for a closer inspection. Judging by the reek coming off it, this had been the one that had seen Patrick Sands through into the next world.

'Like I said, not an expert in knots.' McLean backed off this time. Miss Cairns gave him a look that was a mixture of disappointment and pity, then shook her head and put the noose back down again. She didn't bother picking up the third, but as far as he could tell it was exactly the same as the other two.

'Well, as it happens, I am. Member of the International Guild of Knot Tyers and a registered forensic expert in knots and ropes. Dad was a trawlerman, worked out of Crail. He taught me a thing or two about tying rope. They're a bit like signatures, you know. Knots. Sure, the knot might be the same, but everyone ties it differently. A twist here, a bit tighter there. I could always tell when I was mending the nets who'd tied them before. And I can say with absolute certainty that these three knots weren't tied by three different people.'

'You're sure of that?' McLean saw the scowl, raised his hands in defence. 'I mean, of course you're sure of that. But is there any, I don't know, objective way of measuring this? I don't mean to be sceptical, but I've never heard of the science of knots before.'

'I'm sure of it, and, yes, I have done an objective analysis. And that's where it gets complicated.' Miss Cairns turned her attention to a computer nearby, clicking away until three photographs of the three nooses were lined up.

'This works better if you've got the 3D goggles on, but you'll get the picture.' She clicked again and the first noose shifted on top of the second. It wasn't a perfect fit, but it was damned close. Another click and the third noose shifted onto the other two. If it weren't for the discolouration on one of the ropes, courtesy of the late Paddy Sands' decomposition fluids, McLean might have thought he was looking at the same rope photographed three different times.

'I've never seen anything quite like it before, Inspector. In all three dimensions these knots are virtually identical. That's after they've been tied and then used to standard-drop hang three very different people.'

'That's pretty impressive,' McLean said, not really knowing what Miss Cairns was getting at. The SOC officer glared at him as if he were an imbecile, which given the circumstances was perhaps fair enough.

'No, it's not. Not impressive at all. What it is is impossible.'

28

'So we've got three deaths by hanging. All very similar MO. Two I could put down to coincidence, but three's just too much. And besides, I don't believe in coincidences anyway. This could be some kind of suicide pact, but if it is, it's a very odd one. Looks like all three nooses have all been tied by one person, probably using one length of rope. To my mind that makes this at the very least manslaughter.'

The CID room, early, for an impromptu briefing and catch-up. McLean looked upon his gathered team with a mixture of relief and despair. True, they were all people he'd worked with in the past and all people he trusted to bring something to the investigation. But they were also very few in number. Grumpy Bob lurked at the back, his feet up on his desk, cradling a mug of coffee that quite plainly hadn't come from the vending machine in the canteen. DC MacBride perched on the edge of the neighbouring desk, pink and scrubbed and eager. DS Ritchie had somehow managed to avoid being sent up to Tulliallan for more Police Scotland workshops and was gracing them with her presence, along with a delicate whiff of some perfume McLean couldn't immediately identify. Unless that was coming from PC Sandy Gregg, on secondment and fair quivering with the excitement of being in plain clothes for a change. DS Carter had put in an appearance a few minutes before the start of the briefing, and for a moment McLean thought he might have defected. As soon as he'd realized what was going on, he'd grabbed a folder from his desk and darted out of the room. No doubt to report back to Spence and Brooks that the upstart McLean was conducting investigations and what were they going to do about it?

'They knew each other?' This from Sandy Gregg. No one else would try to state the obvious so, well, obviously.

'That's our working hypothesis. We've not managed to find any solid links between them yet, other than the rope and the knots.' McLean turned back to the whiteboard where he had taped up photographs of Patrick Sands, Grigori Mikhailevic and John Fenton.

'The deaths are approximately three weeks apart. All left suicide notes. You should have copies of them in the packs MacBride handed out earlier. I think you'll be as struck by the similarities between them as I was.'

Cue a rustling of sheets as everyone leafed through their paperwork. Except Grumpy Bob, who just took a slow drink of his coffee.

'All three of them were naked when they hanged themselves, and all three used the standard-drop method to do it.'

'Standard drop?' This from Ritchie, sitting at the front like teacher's pet.

'Standard drop is between four and six feet, though these were all at the lower end of that. As opposed to long drop, where the optimum drop is calculated for each individual to be hanged. The idea's to snap the neck cleanly and swiftly so the hanged man is dead before he starts swinging. Problem is, it's not very reliable. How far you need to drop depends on your weight, height, body type. There's a whole load of calculations. You just string someone up and let them fall three or four feet, chances are it's not enough to break their neck and they suffocate to death. Or if it's too much, their head pops off, which is messy.'

The whole group turned as one to DC MacBride, the font of this unusual wisdom. His pink face turned even redder under the combined scrutiny.

'Is that usual?' Sandy Gregg asked. 'The standard thingy?'

'Actually, no. Hanging's one of the most common methods of suicide; about half of the annual total. But it's usually just a form of self-strangulation. It's not easy to engineer a drop, and even if you do, most people underestimate, choke themselves to death. All three of these men put a chair on something, or over a drop, so they knew what they were doing.' MacBride shrugged at the collection of dropped jaws staring at him. 'What? I looked it up. OK?'

'Just as well someone did. Thank you, Constable.' McLean turned his attention back to the whiteboard and its three photographs. 'These three not only opted for a very complicated way of killing themselves, they also all succeeded. PM results show three clean breaks. Only Sands possibly overdid it a bit, which is why . . . well, you've seen the photos. They died instantly and painlessly, not slowly strangling to death, which I'm told is a nasty, protracted and agonising way to go. They also all used nooses that were tied by one person. Could have been one of them, could have been someone else entirely.'

'So they all used the same rope. One of them tied the nooses. And Grigori Mikhailevic bought the rope from The Captain's Rest in Newhaven?' Acting DC Gregg ran her finger down the page of the report as she asked the question.

'That's how it looks,' McLean said.

'But Patrick Sands died a fortnight before Mikhailevic. Isn't that right?'

McLean stared at the constable in consternation. He'd forgotten that the sequence of deaths wasn't the same as the discovery of the bodies.

'That's a bloody good point,' Grumpy Bob said. 'What's the timeline for these suicides? How's it all fit in with when the rope was bought?'

All eyes turned to DC MacBride again. He shrugged, then dug out his notebook, flicked through the pages.

'According to the pathology report, Patrick Sands died sometime in the first week of July. Grigori Mikhailevic hanged himself on the twenty-second and Jonathan Fenton was found yesterday, seen alive the day before, so died sometime on the night of the thirteenth.'

'Oh bugger.' Grumpy Bob had his own notebook out, but McLean didn't need to see what was written in it to know what was upsetting him. If the shopkeeper was right both in his identification of Mikhailevic and his book-keeping, then the rope hadn't been purchased until the second week of July, when Paddy Sands was already hanging from the skylight in his tiny Colonies flat. He might have used the same type of rope, but it hadn't been cut from the same length.

'What? Did I say something wrong?' PC Gregg looked

backwards and forwards between the two senior detectives, a horrified look on her face.

'Far from it, Constable. You stopped us making complete tits of ourselves.' McLean slumped into a nearby chair. It wasn't like him to miss something as obvious as that, but then he wasn't normally working for two different teams.

'OK then, people. Where does this leave us?'

DC MacBride looked like he was about to answer, but then the door to the CID room swung open and Detective Sergeant Carter poked his head through.

'You come to join us?' McLean asked. 'Only we could use some intelligent input.'

Carter made a quizzical face, which wasn't far off his normal one. 'No. I mean . . . Sorry, sir. It's Dag– . . . Acting Superintendent Duguid, sir. He wants to see you in his office.'

'I'm kind of in the middle of something here.'

'He knows, sir. Think that's why he wants to see you.' Carter had the decency to look embarrassed.

'OK. I'll go and see what he wants.' McLean hauled himself out of the chair, paused at the door to address what he hoped would still be his team in an hour. 'Let's start from scratch here. Set up a timeline, go over the interviews with friends. These three people are linked. Find out how.'

'You know your problem, McLean? You make everything more complicated than it needs to be.'

Jayne McIntyre's office. Well, technically Acting Superintendent Charles Duguid's office, but he was damned if

244

he was going to give in and start calling it that. McLean stood in front of the wide desk like a persistent trouble-maker called up in front of the beak. On the other side, Duguid flicked through the latest in a long line of tedious and time-consuming daily reports with the air of a man who really couldn't be arsed reading the thing.

'The way I see it, you've got it in your head these deaths are suspicious, and now you're going looking for the evidence to back up your theory. Feel free to correct me, but that's not how I was taught to conduct an investigation.'

Deep breath. Try to keep a lid on the anger. That's what he's trying to do, after all. Goad. 'With respect, sir. Three very similar deaths by hanging in the space of just over a month is suspicious enough to warrant a second look, wouldn't you say?'

'We went over this already. People commit suicide every day, McLean.' Duguid stopped a moment as what he'd said sunk in. 'I'm not saying that's good or inevitable or whatever. It's just that we can't go treating every single one as if it's a potential murder.'

'Seven hundred and seventy-two in 2011, sir. In Scot-land as a whole that is. So yes, about two people a day take their own lives. And about half of that total hanged them-selves in one way or another. I know the stats.'

'Like I told you before. Someone hangs themselves in this country every bloody day. And yet you think these ones are so important you've got two sergeants working them, three if you count Carter on this latest case. God only knows how many constables running around after you. And that's just CID. I dread to think what the uniform count is. All just for a couple of suicides. Have you any idea how much this is costing?'

More than you, in all probability. 'It's three deaths actually, sir. And I don't think they're suicides. At least not just suicides.'

'I don't care what you think. You were only meant to be using DS Ritchie for this investigation. Not half the bloody station.' Duguid threw the report down on his desk. It missed the edge and tumbled to the floor.

'Ritchie's on the local liaison group for the new Police Scotland, sir.' Which you know perfectly well, since you were the one who ordered her to do it. 'She's not here most of the time. And DS Carter's back working with Spence and Brooks, which is frankly the best place for him. I've got Grumpy Bob co-ordinating the investigation with MacBride and Gregg helping him out. I'd hardly call that half the station.'

'Gregg?' Duguid's confusion spoke eloquently of his skill at personnel management. Christ, this man was supposed to be in charge. Of the whole station.

'PC Gregg, sir. She's on probation with CID. You know. You suggested her for my team earlier.'

'Oh, that Gregg.' Duguid shook his head as he spoke, suggesting he didn't really have a clue who McLean was talking about. He looked around for the report, made a show of bending down to pick it up and place it on the desk between the two of them. 'It's still too much manpower. This PC Gregg could collate the forensic, pathology and background reports on her own. Deliver the whole lot to the Procurator Fiscal's office and the job's done.'

Gods, it's like dealing with a four-year-old. 'I could ask

her to do that, sir. Or DC MacBride, since he was the officer initially investigating the first one. But he thought there was something odd even then, and everything that's happened since has only confirmed that for me. These three hangings are all linked.'

'And yet for all the manpower you've thrown at the investigation so far, you can't find anything except circumstance and supposition. Dammit, McLean, you had a hunch and it didn't pay off. Happens to all of us. Let it go and move one.'

'Is that an order, sir?'

'If it has to be. Wrap it up, and get back to the SCU. I've had Jo Dexter bending my ear all day about your beaten-up whore and her dead pimp, not to mention the Port Authority calling me about a freighter that's still impounded and clogging up their docks. Get on top of things, man. Or move aside for someone who can cope.'

Time was he'd been able to take a meeting with Duguid in his stride. Brush it off in the full and frank knowledge that the man was a complete arse and anything he said was deserving of as much attention as a tabloid headline. But recently McLean had been finding it hard to shrug off the man's incompetence, and his latest meeting had been a particularly bruising one. Bad enough Duguid was fixated more on keeping costs down than on finding out what had happened, but that last jibe had cut deep.

He couldn't face going back to his office and the inevitable stack of paperwork to deal with. Neither was he in any great hurry to get back to Jo Dexter and her team, although he'd have to check in on Magda sooner or later.

No, what he needed was to sit down with Grumpy Bob and thrash out this case that Dagwood wanted closed.

But first he needed coffee, and possibly a bacon buttie if there were any left.

The canteen was in mid-shift quiet mode, just a few uniforms catching a breather and a couple of admin staff huddled in the corner with a stack of papers. McLean grabbed his booty and was almost out the door when a low voice stopped him short.

'The streets must be safe if the great Detective Inspector McLean feels there's time to get himself a coffee.'

He could have ignored it, could have pretended he'd not heard, walked out the door, but it had been a shit day, really. He turned to face his accuser, unsurprised to see DI Spence was not alone. On his own, little Mike Spence would never have had the temerity, but the presence and bulk of his fat superior emboldened him. Or perhaps made him more rash.

'I'm guessing all the really bad criminals are tucked away in jail if the two of you can spare the time to sit and hold hands.' Not his most brilliant riposte, but hey, he was busy. Mike Spence's face crumpled at the words, but alongside him, DCI Brooks flushed an angry red. His hands were on the table, cupped around a gently steaming mug. A plate that had once held a large portion of lasagne and chips sat on the table between the two men, but it wasn't hard to work out which one had eaten it.

'Heard you'd been hauled up in front of Dagwood again. What you do this time, lose your girlfriend in the park?'

Had he not been carrying a Styrofoam cup and a bacon

roll, McLean would have clenched his fists, might well have swung for the DCI. As it was he slopped hot coffee on his hand, the splash of pain diverting his attention just long enough to stop him from doing anything rash.

'Actually, sir' – he emphasized the title by clenching his teeth as he said it – 'the acting superintendent is very concerned about budgets and wanted to know where all the manpower was being directed. I showed him my team roster, think he was just about satisfied there was no wastage. No doubt he'll be wanting to see yours soon.'

Brooks scowled, which just made the rolls of flesh on his face wobble. 'Why are you still here, McLean?'

The question took him by surprise. McLean looked around the canteen, then hefted his booty. 'A man's got to eat. You of all people should know that. Sir.'

The scowl deepened, folds of skin rippling across Brooks' damp, ruddy forehead. 'Don't get cocky with me. You know damn well what I meant.'

'I do? Come on then. Say it out loud. Everyone's been dropping enough hints to start a war. About time someone said it to my face.'

'You don't need to do this job, man. Way I heard it you inherited big time when your grandmother died. So why are you still here? Why don't you fuck off to the country or something? Let us get on with our jobs.'

McLean let out a long slow breath he hadn't realized he'd been holding. Finally, someone getting to the bloody point. A shame it had to be a senior officer he'd get into trouble for being insubordinate to. He put his coffee cup and bacon buttie down on the table, pulled a handkerchief out of his pocket and dabbed at the damp spot on

249

his hand. Taking his time and keeping his eyes on Little and Large while he did so. Normally he'd have just shoved the hanky back in his pocket when he was done, but this time he folded it neatly before tucking it away. Finally he picked up his cup and roll again. Maybe thirty seconds of silence had elapsed, but it felt like a week.

'You're a detective, sir. Why don't you see if you can work it out, eh?'

29

'Your man Fenton. Now there's an interesting case.'

Angus Cadwallader sat at his untidy desk in the little office off the main examination theatre of the City Mortuary. For so late in the day, his green scrubs were very clean, which probably meant he'd had to change. McLean leaned against a long workbench by the door, happy to be out of the station and the idiot politics of the place for a change.

'Interesting for you, or for me?'

Cadwallader smiled. 'Oh both, I hope. But mostly me. It's not often I get to see reconstructive surgery so soon after it's been done. The work on rebuilding his pelvis is masterful. Just a shame they couldn't do much about his femur. Poor bugger would always have walked with a limp, and I doubt he'd have ever been completely free of pain.'

'So what's interesting for me then?'

'You mean apart from the warm glow of knowing you've rescued what was otherwise a particularly rubbish day for me?' Cadwallader grabbed a pair of latex gloves from the desk beside him, stood up. 'Come.'

McLean followed his old friend out into the examination theatre and over to the banks of chill stores. It was a route he'd trodden far too many times before. Cadwallader opened a door that wouldn't have looked out of place on a commercial catering refrigerator, slid out a drawer holding a corpse covered in a heavy rubberized sheet. Pulled aside, it revealed John Fenton as naked as he'd been the day before, dangling from his rope.

'Don't need to get him up onto the table, really.' Cadwallader pulled on the gloves, then picked up one of Fenton's hands. 'The other two suicides you're looking into had no traces of hemp fibre under their nails, you'll recall. Well, this one's just the same.'

'He never touched the rope?'

'I'm not saying that. Not never touched it. But certainly not any time soon before he died. It's possible he strung up the rope, then went away and had a thorough scrub, but he'd still have had to touch the bloody thing to get it over his head and tighten it up.'

McLean looked down at the young man's face, pale in death. His hair was short, recently cut, and he was clean shaven. Were those the actions of a man in the pit of despair? He didn't know. Time was he'd been close himself, but he'd still managed to keep clean and tidy, so maybe there wasn't anything suspicious about that.

'The lack of fibres is interesting enough,' Cadwallader continued. 'It suggests a similarity between the three that goes beyond chance. And it's a puzzle of course. But there's something else I thought you might like to see. Here.'

The pathologist covered up the mortal remains of John Fenton and pushed him back into his chill rest, then led McLean back to the examination theatre. Where the old x-ray examination light boards had once been, now a sleek set of flat panel screens hung from the wall. Cadwallader flicked these on and fiddled around with the controls a bit until he had three images side by side.

'It's much easier when Tracy's here. She's brilliant with all this modern stuff.'

'I was going to ask where she was, actually. You've not done away with her and buried her under the patio have you?'

'No. She's off on some orientation workshop to do with all this new single body bollocks. Police Scotland, what a waste of time and money.'

'I keep on losing DS Ritchie to the same thing. Bloody nuisance if you ask me. I'm still not sure what problem it's meant to be solving.'

They fell silent for a while, staring at the images on the screen. McLean had seen enough x-rays in his time to recognize neck vertebrae and the signs of a clean break.

'These are the three hangings, I take it,' he said eventually.

'Indeed, yes. Sands, Mikhailevic and here the new boy, Fenton.' Cadwallader prodded the screen with a finger, causing it to change to a menu of options. A little cursing and poking brought the original images back.

'They all died quickly then.'

'Oh yes. Instant for all of them. And that's the problem, really.'

'It is?'

Cadwallader fixed McLean with one of his best teacher stares. 'How much do you know about the science of hanging, Tony?'

He thought back to the morning's briefing. Something about short drops and long drops that had made his neck hurt in sympathy. 'Not as much as Detective Constable MacBride.'

'Ah yes. Stuart. A quick learner. Well, I'll give you a brief summary.' Cadwallader pointed at the first fracture, careful not to touch the screen this time. 'The idea of hanging, at least in semi-civilized countries, is to swiftly dispatch the condemned. A broken neck is ideal, but it's not as easy to achieve as you might think.'

McLean remembered now. 'You need to get the drop right, that's what I was told. Too short and you choke to death, too long and your head comes off.'

'Something like that, yes. But there's more to it than just velocity. You need to jerk the head in a particular way to get a clean break. That's why the knot of the noose is usually placed here, under the left ear.' Cadwallader laid his hand on McLean's left shoulder to demonstrate.

'Sometimes it's put under the chin in an attempt to get the head to snap backwards. Putting it to the back is almost guaranteed to cause death by asphyxiation, and none of these victims showed signs of that. Most suicides will put the knot directly behind their head, straight up.' Cadwallader made the universal 'being hanged' motion, sticking his tongue out and scrunching his eyes up as he did so. 'That doesn't work. Just strangles you.'

'I'm still not sure why you're getting so excited about it though. This was supposed to happen, right?' McLean pointed at the three snapped necks. 'So what's the problem?'

'Two things, Tony. Since you're determined to be slow on the uptake today.' Cadwallader shook his head in disappointment. 'First, whilst this is the desired outcome, it's extremely difficult to achieve. I was impressed at the first one, surprised at the second. A third is unprecedented.

Law of averages says at least one of these three would have botched it.'

'I thought Sands did. That's why his head came off.'

'Only after he'd been rotting for the best part of a month. Would likely have happened to the other two if they'd been left long enough.'

'So what's the other thing, then?'

'Here. Here. Here.' Cadwallader pointed out the three fractures. 'The hangman's fracture. Subluxation of the C2 and C3 vertebrae if you want me to get technical. These injuries are almost identical in all three cases. All caused by the noose being placed under the left ear, as per the hangman's manual.'

'There is such a thing?' It would certainly make life easier if they could find evidence the three men had read it.

'I was being facetious, Tony. No doubt there's endless stuff on the internet about hanging. That's how young MacBride found out, I'd guess. But the point is most suicides don't know this stuff.'

'So you're saying these three didn't kill themselves.'

'I can't be as definite as that, Tony, no. None of them struggled at all before they dropped, which would suggest they at least partly wanted to kill themselves. But I can tell you they all had help. Either they all got their information from the same place, or one of them found it and then shared it with the others. It's possible they even helped each other, which would explain the lack of fibres.'

'Are you suggesting there's someone else out there?'

'That's your department, Tony. All I'm saying is that none of these three died alone.'

*

It wasn't until he'd climbed into his car and started the engine that McLean noticed the brown paper envelope wedged under the windscreen wiper. Climbing wearily out, he snatched it up before sinking back into the seat. A4 size, not very thick. There was nothing written on the front of it, and just the manufacturer's logo and part number stencilled on the back. It had been sealed, and for a moment he considered taking it straight to forensics for examination. Only for a moment though. He knew exactly what it was, and from whom.

He still put a pair of latex gloves on before switching off the engine and using his car keys to open the envelope from the wrong end. Inside was a very slim report, printed on anonymous office laser paper. The title on the front page read 'Magda Evans/Ivan ? (Russian)'. Beneath it, the cheap printer had done a poor job of reproducing a pair of mug shot photos of Magda.

McLean skim-read the text, then went back and read it again properly. It was mostly snippets of information taken from other reports; mentions of Magda in connection with ongoing or completed investigations. There were a few redacted black lines, but it didn't take a genius to work out that she'd just been a pawn in the games of bigger players for most of her working life, and that had started painfully early. At the back was a copy of the hospital report detailing her injuries, which at least meant the SCDEA were up to date with their information gathering. He flipped over the last page, noting that the surgeon expected his patient to need at least eighteen months of reconstructive surgery and rehabilitation. Flipped back again when he realized there was nothing more. Bloody typical of them to leave the job half done, much like it was bloody typical of them to hand over the information to him in such a stupid, faux-spy manner. Anyone could have seen the envelope there and helped themselves to it. Unless someone was watching him even now, waiting to see what he did so that they could report back to their ringmaster. And Duguid thought he was wasting time and money.

'Bloody idiots.' McLean slid the report back into its envelope and dropped it onto the passenger seat. Peeled off his latex gloves before starting the car. Of course, it could always be that Buchanan was right and there was no Russian called Ivan. Which begged the question: who had beaten Magda to within an inch of her life?

30

McLean wasn't sure what he'd been expecting. Perhaps something a bit more Bedlam. After all, cranial electric therapy brought to mind Victorian asylums, high-ceilinged rooms tiled in white porcelain and with the windows set too far up the wall to see anything but the sky. Or for anyone to see in from the outside and realize what was going on. There should have been a dreadful contraption of a bed, with heavy leather restraints for head, arms and legs, and alongside it something that looked like the control system for a city-scale power station. There should, in short, have been more wires.

Instead, the room into which Doctor Wheeler had brought him and Emma was pleasantly bright, with a long window showing views out onto city rooftops and the far-distant castle. There was a reclining chair, and it had restraints, but they were slim and padded with what looked like sheepskin but was presumably more hypoallergenic than that. The machinery that would do the actual shocking was disappointingly small. It looked a bit like a transistor radio designed by someone with a knob fetish.

'You sure you want to go through with this?'

Emma was standing very close, hand clasping onto his as if it were her only lifeline. Her eyes were wide as she took in the room, perhaps seeing it very differently to him. She was the one who was going to have a million volts zapped through her head, after all.

'I don't have much choice, do I.' She squeezed his hand and then let it go.

'OK, Emma. If you'd like to take a seat.' Doctor Wheeler pointed at the chair. 'Tony, you can sit over there if you want. This won't take long.'

McLean reluctantly retreated to the far side of the room, where a couple of uncomfortable armchairs had been pushed against the wall. As he sat down, Doctor Wheeler pulled some thin wires from the small machine on its trolley beside Emma's chair.

'Right then. We just attach these here.' She reached around, clipping something to Emma's earlobe. 'And here. That's not uncomfortable, is it?'

Emma shook her head very slightly, but McLean could see her hands clenched tight to the arms of the chair, knuckles white as if she were on a rollercoaster. He couldn't begin to imagine what was going through her head just now, and that was before the voltage was applied.

'Now, this isn't electro-convulsive therapy, so we don't need restraints or muscle relaxants. The machine takes a little time to power up, but don't worry. You won't feel anything.' Doctor Wheeler flicked a couple of switches on the box, which began to emit a high-pitched whine, like a terrier left on the wrong side of a door. From the corner of his eye, McLean thought he saw movement at the door, but when he turned to look there was nothing. When he dragged his eyes back to Emma and the machine, Doctor Wheeler had placed a hand on Emma's for reassurance.

259

'Don't worry. I've done this hundreds of times. It's perfectly –'

Emma froze. She had been staring at McLean, but her eyes rolled up in their sockets so completely all he could see was whites. Then she started to shake, so fast it was almost a vibration running through her whole body. Her mouth opened and a sound came out like nothing he had ever heard before. It went straight through his head without passing his ears. A million voices clamouring to be heard, a thousand thousand different tongues.

In an instant, Doctor Wheeler had flicked off the power. Emma continued to wail for a second that seemed like an hour, then relaxed like a puppet that has lost its master, flopping forward in the chair. The silence left an echo ringing in McLean's ears, doubt already creeping over the memory of what he thought he'd just seen.

'Is she all right?' He pulled himself out of the seat, feeling an ache as if he'd been sitting for days. Doctor Wheeler was at Emma's side, checking her pulse, shining a tiny pen torch into a forced-open eye.

'I think so. She seems to have fainted. Never seen that happen before.'

McLean crossed the room, knelt down and took Emma's hand. She stirred gently at his touch, but didn't wake. After a moment he turned his attention to the control box, pulled at one of the thin cables. A thin wisp of smoke rose up from it in a single tendril.

'What . . . What just happened?' McLean pulled himself up, his whole body aching as if he'd been the one being shocked, and at a much higher voltage.

'I really don't know.' Doctor Wheeler stared at the cable

he'd pulled out. One end was still attached to the electrodes taped to Emma's head, the other was a lump of molten plastic and wire.

Mid-morning after a late start. Emma hadn't woken from the failed electro-cranial stimulation therapy for an hour, and had gone straight to bed after he'd finally brought her home from the hospital the previous evening. McLean had hoped for a good night's sleep himself, but she'd climbed into his bed at half four again and he'd not slept a wink after that. He felt dog-tired, and a dog that had been kept awake for weeks by howling cats at that.

For once, the CID room was a hive of industry as he entered; all the desks occupied by sergeants and constables quietly going about their tasks uninterrupted by the demands of senior officers for a change. It couldn't last, not least because he was about to ruin the moment, but it was nice to see.

DS Ritchie noticed him first as he stood in the open doorway. She tapped a couple of keys on her computer as if to make a point before standing, grabbed her notebook and wound her way through the desks towards him.

'You after something, sir?' There was a hint of desperation in the question. As if anything was better than being sent off to Tulliallan again. McLean could only sympathize.

'Updates, mostly. Grumpy Bob about?'

'He sloped off with his paper about fifteen minutes ago. Find an empty meeting room and that's probably where he'll be.'

'What about MacBride?'

At the question, a round face poked up from behind a nearby screen, freshly scrubbed and pink. 'Here, sir.'

'You got a moment?'

By way of an answer, MacBride leapt to his feet, notebook at the ready.

'OK then. Round up Gregg and let's see if we can find Grumpy Bob's meeting room. We need to go over these hangings again.' McLean turned back to the door, only to find a rather frightened-looking young PC standing in the doorway, struggling with an enormous wicker hamper.

'Package for Detective Inspector McLean. I was told I'd find him in here?' The PC almost tripped forward, and McLean had to grab the hamper to stop her from dropping it.

'Steady, Constable. Here, let me take that off you.'

'Thank you, sir. Thought I was going to drop it. Weighs a ton.'

McLean could only nod in agreement as he took the full weight of the hamper. It was about the size of a trunk and if he was any judge was full of expensive delicacies. He staggered over to the nearest clear table and set it down as carefully as he could.

'Any idea who this is from, Constable?' he asked.

'Van had Valvona and Crolla written on the side, sir. Oh, and I've to give you this as well.' The constable pulled an envelope out of her jacket pocket and handed it over. McLean thanked her and she scurried off with obvious relief. Confused as to who might be sending him gifts, he slid open the envelope and pulled out the note. The last time it had been a bottle of very expensive single malt whisky from one of Glasgow's more notorious thugs.

This looked even more expensive, and he wasn't aware of having helped out anyone recently.

'You've got an admirer, sir.' DS Ritchie was trying not to peer over his shoulder at the note as he unfolded it. Not a note at all, but an invoice for almost two grand still outstanding, addressed to him care off the station.

'What the . . . ?' McLean handed the invoice to Ritchie. He looked at the hamper, noticed for the first time that it had already been opened. No doubt some key item had been removed by whichever smartarse had ordered the thing in his name in the first place.

'I don't get it. You ordered this, sir?'

'Does it look like Christmas to you, Ritchie?' He immediately regretted snapping at her. 'Sorry. No, I didn't order this. Someone pretending to be me ordered this, and I'll bet you a fiver it's the same person who opened it and removed the most valuable item.'

He unlatched the clasps holding the hamper closed and lifted the lid. As might be expected, it was full of extremely expensive delicacies. There was even a helpful printed sheet detailing everything. Sure enough, the bottle of VSOP Brandy was missing. Hard not to notice given the large gap right there in the middle, between the Colston Bassett Stilton and the Royal Beluga Caviar.

'What kind of outfit sends out something like this without payment up front?' It was DC MacBride who asked the obvious question. His eyes were wide as he looked at the invoice. Not surprising given it was probably more than he earned in a month.

'Well, if you can't trust a policeman, who can you trust?' McLean appreciated the cunning of the prank as he said it, if not the outcome. And the final touch, making sure the CID room was full when his extravagant purchase was delivered. That was a touch of genius. By the end of the shift, every officer in Lothian and Borders would know of it.

After such a good start, the day could hardly fail to get better. McLean hid the hamper in his office, covering it with paperwork where no one would think to look. He cadged a ride over to HQ and the offices of the SCU, mindful of Duguid's words the day before and all too aware of how little time he was spending there. Not that he was spending much in CID either. Split between both meant not really being able to do anything properly.

DS Buchanan was sitting at his desk in the SCU main office, peering myopically at his computer screen when McLean arrived. The sergeant looked up with something close to a sneer on his face as he saw who it was.

'You back then?'

McLean fought down the urge to call him out on his insolence. It was, after all, exactly the sort of thing Duguid would do. Better just to let it slide.

'Where are we with the Malky Jennings murder?'

'Report's over there.' Buchanan nodded in the direction of the desk McLean had been allocated when he'd first arrived. It was almost as deeply covered in paperwork as his desk back at CID, much of it of no relevance to him whatsoever. The Malky Jennings file was at least on the top, and easily identified. It was also very slim. Transcripts of the door-to-door interviews filled the bulk of the file, and they were almost all identical. 'Din't see nothing, aye.'

Or words to that effect. Scanning through, McLean could see that they had got precisely nowhere since Magda Evans had positively identified the body. He could sort of understand why. Nobody much cared if a drug dealer and pimp was beaten to death and left for the foxes to eat. There'd be more effort going into finding out who was taking over his patch, working out how best to contain them. If forensics couldn't come up with anything, then a conviction was about as likely as Duguid taking early retirement.

'We ever find a murder weapon?' McLean flicked through the front pages of the report, barely taking in the words.

'Nah.' Buchanan shook his head once, went back to his screen. Sod you then.

'How'd you get on with your kiddie fiddler?'

'You what?' Buchanan looked up again, a puzzled frown on his face.

'Playground stalker over in Sighthill? You know.'

For a moment it looked like he genuinely didn't. Then realization dawned across the detective sergeant's face. 'Oh, aye. The kiddie fiddler in Sighthill. Aye. One of the Sex Offenders Register boys. He's not meant to go anywhere near the primary school. Local plod got a call saying they'd seen him hanging around during playtime. Wanted me to go have a word. He's harmless, really, but. You know.' He shook his head again, went back to whatever it was he was doing. Conversation over.

McLean flicked through the report again, looked down at the desk to see a thicker one for the prostitute-trafficking case. There was a stack of the all-too familiar overtime sheets attached to it, and a pile of requisition orders to sign off. Home from home. He shuffled around to the business side of the desk, dropped into the seat and realized it wasn't the comfortable one he'd nicked back from DS Buchanan's desk the day before. Sod it, the sooner he got started, the sooner he could go home, and starting an argument with a stroppy sergeant was just going to waste precious time. With a sigh, he reached for the first in an impossibly large pile of forms.

31

He was driving home when the call came through. No hands-free in his little Alfa, so normally McLean would ignore his phone on a short trip, pick up the message when he got wherever he was going. Maybe it was the slow-moving traffic, maybe just chance, but something made him pull the phone out of his jacket pocket this time, glance at the screen. Jenny Nairn.

To a chorus of irate horns, he indicated and swerved over to the kerb, hit the hazard lights whilst accepting the call and clamping the phone to his ear. There was only one reason why the young carer would phone him at work.

'Thank fuck for that. Where've you been for the last three hours?'

'Umm. Jenny?' McLean frowned, even though there was no one there to see him.

'Too bloody right, Jenny. I've been trying your phone for ages. Check your messages why don't you.'

McLean looked at his phone, but in call mode he couldn't see if there were messages waiting or not. He didn't remember there being any, and, anyway, the thing had been in his pocket all day. He'd have heard if it rang.

'I'm sorry, OK? I'm here now. What's the problem?'

'It's Emma. She walked out again. Ran, more like.' Jenny sounded winded, breathing heavily as if she were running.

'I thought you were with her.' McLean stared in the rear-view mirror as the traffic snarled up behind him even worse than it had been before.

'I am with her. Now. Can barely keep up.' More heavy breathing and the sound of cars in the background.

'Did you not try to stop her?' He knew it was a stupid question even as he asked it.

'Yes, and if she's broken my nose you're paying for the plastic surgery. She's a lot stronger than she looks, you know.'

Now he listened carefully, there was something of a more nasal quality about Jenny's voice.

'Look, where are you. I'll come and get you. OK?'

'Just past IKEA at Loanhead, walking towards Bilston.' Jenny wheezed and coughed. 'More like jogging. Jesus, she's going like a train.'

McLean flicked his indicator, saw the narrowest of gaps in his mirror and pulled out into the traffic, only then remembering that the hazard lights were on. He floored the throttle and shot forward to another chorus of horns. With the phone still clamped to his ear, he couldn't change gear, so he red-lined the engine, spinning the back wheels around as he did a U-turn. 'I'm on my way. Just don't lose her.'

He hung up before Jenny could come up with a witty rejoinder, chucked the phone onto the passenger seat and grabbed second gear. Loanhead. Bilston. He knew exactly where Emma was going.

Needham House was no longer the fine mansion it had once been. Truth be told, it had been falling down from

268

neglect for over a generation. Too expensive for the two career policemen who had been its last owners to keep up, but too much family history for either of them to sell. Old man Needham had flogged the paintings and family silver to pay death duties when his father died, which had left only a rattling, empty shell for his son to take over. That hadn't stopped the man from the revenue from valuing the place high enough to demand a seven-figure sum in inheritance tax, which had probably been the final straw that broke poor Needy's mind.

Poor Needy. The words hung in McLean's mind as he approached, driving carefully now he was off smooth tarmac and onto rutted, pot-holed driveway. Sergeant John Needham had murdered three women in his madness, abducted Emma and very nearly killed McLean himself. And yet for all that McLean couldn't bring himself to blame him. Not now, and not seeing what had become of the once grand house.

It was a ruin now, the roof gone, the insides burned away. Behind it the bulk of the McMerry Ironworks, the source of the Needham family's wealth in an earlier century, was being bulldozed away. Plans submitted for a development for four hundred starter homes, if McLean remembered rightly. So far the legal wheels were still turning over exactly who owned the remains of the house and its grounds.

McLean had made good time from the city centre, mostly by flouting all the traffic regulations and speed limits that he could. The gods were obviously on his side, as there were no patrol cars on the route. He'd still had a few heart-stopping moments, and no doubt the switchboard would be buzzing with calls about the nutter in the old sports car burning up Liberton Brae. He'd just have to square it with Traffic later.

Jenny appeared from around a half-demolished wall as he arrived, hugging herself against the chill wind dropping down off the Pentland Hills. She'd come out without a coat, which was fair enough given that she'd probably not counted on walking the best part of five miles. As soon as she saw the car, she trotted over and had clambered in before McLean had switched off the engine.

'Took your time.' She stared at the minimalist dashboard before working out how to switch the heat on. Cranked it up full.

'I was in the middle of the city. Got here as quick as I could.'

'I meant three hours ago, when Em first got it in her mind to take off on a little jaunt. Why didn't you answer?'

'Give me my phone and I'll tell you.'

'Eh?' Jenny looked at him as if he were mad.

'My phone. You're sitting on it.'

'Oh.' She shuffled her bottom, reached underneath and pulled out the phone. McLean was relieved to see the screen unbroken. He clicked the menu for missed calls, held it up for Jenny to see. Nothing.

'Where's Emma now?'

'Round the back, in the rubble.' Jenny scowled at the phone as if that would make it change its mind. 'I told her not to go up there, but she's . . . well, you'll see.'

The front of the house, with its ornate fascia and grand hallway, had largely survived the explosion and fire. The back of the building hadn't fared nearly so well. Someone from the council had put up metal barriers and a notice that read 'Danger of Death. Unsafe Building.' As if that was going to stop the local youth from coming here to play. As he walked around to the back, McLean saw the empty lager cans and cider bottles, dog-ends and used condoms, the graffiti that marked it as turf for one gang or another. At least there didn't seem to be any syringes or needles. Not yet.

He found Emma crouched down on the top of a pile of rubble, pulling at the rocks with bloody hands. She was wearing trainers this time, but still only dressed in a T-shirt and sweatpants. Unlike Jenny, she didn't seem to have noticed the cold. Mrs McCutcheon's cat sat just behind her, cleaning a paw as if this was the most natural place for it to be. McLean climbed slowly and carefully up the pile until he was standing beside them both.

'Down under all the rocks. Can't reach it. Sure it's here.' Emma muttered under her breath as she pulled first at one rock, then another. She was reaching out for a point too far away, would surely overbalance and tumble over the edge, when McLean touched her on the shoulder.

The contact sent a shock up his arm like static from a cheap rug, set up a ringing in his ears that sounded almost like a clamour of high-pitched voices far in the distance. Then with a pop, it was gone. Emma stiffened at the contact, fell back onto her heels, leaning hard against him. She looked around like a person who has just woken up somewhere very different to the place they went to sleep. Then she saw her hands, bloodied and torn, fingernails ragged where she'd been digging at the rubble. She held them in front of her face for long moments, turning them this way and that as if they were someone else's. Finally she held them up for him to see, like a child suddenly realizing they aren't alone in the world. Mouthed a single word.

'Tony?'

And then she collapsed.

'I've really never seen anything like it. Frankly I'm baffled.'

Doctor Wheeler stood beside the hospital bed as a nurse tended to one of Emma's hands. The other had already been cleaned and bandaged and lay across her chest. She hadn't woken since collapsing at Needham House and was now hooked up to a drip and an EEG monitor.

'Is she in a coma? Is this some kind of relapse?' McLean really didn't want to ask the question, didn't want to face the possibilities an answer would bring.

'Not in a strict medical sense, no.' Doctor Wheeler bent down to peer at the monitor, adjusting a dial that seemed to have no effect on the jagged lines plotting themselves across the tiny screen. 'It's almost like she's asleep and dreaming. But the patterns are too chaotic for that. How long's she been out?'

'About an hour, I'd say. Maybe a little less.' The journey to the hospital had been slower than the drive out, McLean unwilling to chance his luck with the traffic gods any further. Emma had been comatose on the rear seat all the way, covered by his jacket but shivering anyway. Mrs McCutcheon's cat had, perhaps predictably, jumped into the car as soon as McLean had put Emma inside. It hadn't done anything useful like lie on her lap to keep her warm though. Jenny had said nothing beyond a grunt to keep the heat turned up and a moan that her feet hurt. She was off parking the car now; at least that was what McLean hoped she was doing. She'd been gone a long time. Hopefully the cat wouldn't try to find Emma here in the depths of the hospital.

Doctor Wheeler put a hand to Emma's forehead, forced open one of her eyes and shone a tiny pen torch into it, took a pulse. All things she'd done twice already in the last half hour. McLean knew displacement activity when he saw it.

'You're worried this is a side-effect of the electro-therapy treatment.'

She turned to face him. 'Am I that obvious?'

'Detective Inspector, remember.' McLean watched as the nurse tidied up her tray of bandages and bustled out of the room before continuing. 'To be honest, I'm worried too. She seems to be regressing ever further back. When she woke up it was like she was, I don't know, twenty-one or something. Lately she's been acting like an eight-year-old.'

'Like I said, it's got me baffled and believe me, I've read up everything I can find, put the word out to everyone I can think of. The CAT scans don't show any sign of further damage, far from it. Her brain's as good as it ever was, so there's no reason she should be getting worse. If anything, memories should be starting to come back by now.'

McLean walked around to the other side of the bed and slumped into a chair. He should really have been getting back to the SCU and the ongoing investigations there, but he was dog-tired. Maybe he could get away with sitting here for an hour or so. He could always drop in on Magda on the way out. That counted as work, surely?

'How's she been getting on with Doctor Austin?' Doctor Wheeler asked the question almost too casually.

'Early days. Emma seems to like going there. Me, I just fall asleep as soon as the session starts.'

'Yes, Eleanor can have that effect on people.' Doctor Wheeler looked at her watch, the universal sign that she needed to be somewhere else. 'I'll leave you here with her then. The monitor will let the nurses know if she's waking up.'

'I can't stay long. Just a little while.'

'You look like you need a good sleep, Inspector. I could arrange a camp bed if you'd like.'

'Don't tempt me.' McLean scratched at his chin, feeling the need for a shave.

'Well, just get a nurse to page me if you need anything, OK?' Doctor Wheeler gave him a smile that was warm but as tired as he felt, and then she was gone.

32

A bored PC sat on an uncomfortable-looking plastic chair outside the room where Magda Evans was recovering. He saw McLean approaching and scrambled to attention, dropping what looked suspiciously like a copy of a Mills and Boon romance.

'Sorry, sir. No one told me you were coming.'

'Don't worry, Reg. You know if she's awake?'

'Couldn't say, sir. Nurse was in about a half-hour ago, so she might be.'

'Well, I won't be long anyway.' McLean knocked gently on the door, listened for a reply. He could hear the soft noises of a television playing, so he let himself in.

Magda was lying on her back much like Emma on the other side of the hospital. Only where Emma was now sleeping peacefully, and encumbered only by the bandages on her hands, Magda was surrounded by stands and apparatus supporting her legs and one arm. Her toes, poking out of the ends of the heavy casts, were blue, though whether that was from bruising or lack of circulation, McLean couldn't be sure. The cast that encased her hand ended in a curious arrangement of metal spikes that held her fingers in place. Her attackers had broken them methodically, at least that's what the surgeon had told him. It was doubtful she'd ever regain more than very rudimentary use of them, and they'd had to amputate the crushed remains of her thumb.

But it was her face that was the worst. McLean remembered the young woman he'd first encountered when they'd raided the boat. Was it really just a month ago? She'd been rake thin then, and hardly what you'd call a looker. But she'd had a certain elegance to her features. Now the bandages hid most of the damage, but she would need a lot of reconstructive surgery if she was ever going to have a nose again. The razor cuts to her cheeks would always be scars, twisting her mouth into a Joker's rictus grin.

She was barely awake, drowsy with morphine and watching the television that had been thoughtfully hung on the wall. Whatever was on was not so engrossing that she was unable to drag her attention away from it as he entered. She squinted at him through eyes still puffed almost closed, reflexively tried a smile and then winced in pain.

'Just thought I'd pop in and see how you were doing.' Now he was here, McLean realized it wasn't the most brilliant idea he'd ever had. Magda couldn't talk. She struggled with her one good arm to reach something on the table beside the bed. Good being a relative term, as her hand was stitched and taped up, two fingers spliced together. Her hand connected with a small spiral bound notebook, and she grimaced as she knocked it to the floor, letting out a little squeak of pain. McLean bent down and picked it up, flipped it open to find only blank pages. Hardly surprising given her injuries. The woman couldn't feed herself, let alone hold a pen.

'What are you doing in here? You mustn't disturb her.'

McLean was startled by the arrival of a nurse, cowed by the withering look she gave him. She bustled around Magda's bed, checked the monitors and finally squeezed the morphine drip to send the patient back into sedation.

'I was just seeing how she was.' Even as he said it, he realized it was a lie. He'd wanted to talk to Magda, ask her questions. As she slipped away, he realized that had been a forlorn hope. She wasn't going to be in any position to talk for days, possibly weeks.

'You really shouldn't have gone to see her alone, Tony.'

Jo Dexter leaned back in her chair, stifled a yawn. She looked like she'd been up for days, her face lined and ashen, her hair even less kempt than normal. McLean shuffled uncomfortably, trying to ignore the leering presence of Detective Sergeant Buchanan. He'd been offered a seat but seemed determined to stand.

'I was just checking she was OK. Reg was outside the whole time.'

'Yes, but he should have been inside, shouldn't he. I should tan his hide for letting you in anyway.'

'For what it's worth, she didn't say anything. Couldn't say anything to be honest. Whoever attacked her did a real job of work. They're keeping her heavily sedated.'

'I know. I've read the medical report.' Dexter flicked a sheaf of papers that was perched atop the mess of reports and general detritus strewn across her desk. McLean thought his office was a study in chaos, but maybe he was just an apprentice.

'Probably had it coming to her, right enough.'

277

McLean and Dexter both stared at the detective sergeant, who looked slightly surprised himself at the words that had come out of his mouth.

'I'll pretend I didn't hear that, Pete,' Dexter said.

'Well, I won't.' McLean was on his feet in an instant. 'What do you mean by that, Sergeant?'

Buchanan stared at him with that all too familiar mixture of disdain and loathing. 'Nuthin. Just saying. She's a whore. Getting beat up comes with the territory.'

'No. It's more than that. You've seen the photos. That's not a pimp knocking one of his girls around. That's someone making a statement. You know anything about that, Sergeant?'

'What the hell d'you mean by that?' Buchanan pushed himself away from the wall, his face flushed red, eyes threatening. McLean stood his ground, squared up for the fight. He'd had enough of Buchanan's attitude to last him a lifetime. Quite looked forward to taking the man down a peg or two.

'Enough. Both of you.' Of course, Jo Dexter was never going to allow it to come to blows. Then there'd be paperwork and she obviously had quite enough of that already.

'Let's get back to the point, shall we? Tony, sit down. And you too, Pete. Stop lowering over us like some great ogre.'

McLean caught himself waiting until Buchanan had sat before doing so himself. How swiftly the pettiness came. But lately even the smallest of things had been getting his back up. There wasn't really any reason to react to the detective sergeant the way he had done. Maybe he was as tired as Jo Dexter looked.

'Right then. I've had another demand from the Port Authority to release the freighter. What d'you reckon, we let it go?'

'Forensics came up with nothing,' McLean said. 'Captain's story checks out. He really didn't know anything about it. Don't think there's anything to be gained from holding on to it any longer.'

'OK, I'll let them know.' Dexter leaned forward and placed a tick against a paragraph scrawled on a piece of paper at the top of her piling system. 'So where does that leave us with the investigation, then?'

McLean looked over at Buchanan, who shrugged and said nothing.

'None of the girls will say anything. They wouldn't before, and once they hear what happened to Magda they'll be even less helpful. Most of them just want to get away. We've been working with Clarice Saunders and her charity on that.'

'What about the van driver?' Dexter ticked another paragraph.

'Just a delivery boy. Paid a chunk of cash, no questions asked. He'll do a bit of time, but I've seen his type before. He won't say who paid him. Even if he knows.'

'Pete? You got anything to add?'

'What he said.' Buchanan nodded in McLean's direction. 'It's a waste of bloody time. We put away the driver and the second mate on the ship. Case dies there. Meanwhile the gangs keep moving these whores around under our noses.'

'Thanks for that upbeat appraisal, detective sergeant.' Dexter ticked another paragraph, then drew a line through it. 'So what about Malky Jennings then? We any closer to finding out who put him out of our misery?'

'Dead end.' Buchanan seemed to have warmed to his theme now. 'No one saw anything. Forensics can't find anything useful. There's plenty folk wanted him dead, but we can't arrest them for that. If we had the murder weapon, we might get somewhere, but we don't even know where he was killed. Let alone what with.'

McLean was about to say something, but the way Dexter scored out the next paragraph on her list stopped him. No one was going to spend too much time and effort trying to find the killer of a scumbag, it would seem.

'Which just leaves us Magda Evans.' Dexter lifted the medical report off her desk, then dropped it back down again. 'What's the low-down there?'

McLean looked at Buchanan, who was slouching in his seat as if he hadn't a care in the world. He caught the gaze, sneered.

'What? Not my case, is it.'

'You've done nothing about it?' McLean asked.

'Why should I? You're SIO, right?' Buchanan's sneer turned into a cheeky grin.

'I told you to take over when I went with her to the hospital. What the hell have you been doing since then?'

'My job, of course. Not yours.'

'Your job is to do what I bloody well tell you to do, Sergeant, and I told you to take over the Magda Evans crime scene. Are you telling me you've done nothing about it at all?'

Buchanan shrugged, as if that were enough of an answer. 'I set a couple of constables on door-to-door.

SOC came and dusted for prints, took some photos. Wasn't a lot more we could do.'

'So where's your report? What's the situation with the crime scene now?'

'DC Watson was typing up the report. Far as I know the crime scene's secure. Council were sending someone round to fix the door and board up the window. Local toerags'll break in soon as they know the place is empty otherwise.'

McLean realized he had clenched his hands into fists, willed himself to relax. How many days had passed since Magda Evans had been attacked? He'd been so busy he'd lost count. And he was partly to blame, too. If he'd been on top of things he'd have checked what Buchanan was up to more regularly.

'So I think it's fair to say we're nowhere with the investigation, then.' Jo Dexter summed things up with a shrug.

'I'll get on it right away.' McLean stood, ready to leave. Beside him, Buchanan still slouched in his seat.

'You do that, Tony.' Dexter gave him a weary smile, which disappeared as she turned on the detective sergeant. 'And as for you, Pete, consider this a formal warning. If you can't run an investigation without constant supervision, then you're not fit to be a sergeant. There's plenty of young constables looking for promotion.'

Something finally seemed to get through to Buchanan. He struggled to his feet, straightened his jacket and nodded at Dexter, adding a gruff 'Aye, ma'am.' Then he turned and left without another word.

*

'What the hell's your problem, Buchanan? You looking to be reported to Professional Standards or something?'

Out in the corridor. McLean had barely shut the door to Jo Dexter's office and Buchanan was heading off in the direction of the canteen. He'd picked up a slight limp somewhere along the line, McLean noticed. Maybe that was why he'd not wanted to sit down. Didn't explain the general surliness though.

'You want to know what my problem is, sir?' Buchanan emphasized the title in a manner McLean couldn't help recognizing. It was exactly how he addressed Duguid, DCI Brooks and pretty much any other senior officer who was pissing him off. The detective sergeant came back up the corridor towards him, trying hard to hide the limp, but grimacing every so often when something twinged in his leg. Serve the bugger right, really.

'You're my problem. That's what. Swan in here with your high and mighty ideals. Stick your nose in an investigation then bugger off back to your own station for days, leaving me to do all the legwork.' Buchanan shifted his weight as he said this, leaning on his left side. So it was his right leg giving him gyp. McLean wondered what he'd done to hurt it. Fallen down the stairs drunk, most likely. He kept silent on the matter though. Buchanan was in a mood to talk, and a wise man took the opportunity to listen.

'And then you go visit a witness without anyone to corroborate what you've said. A witness in secure custody, for Christ's sake. What if we need her testimony in court and some smart-arse lawyer finds out you've been coaching her?' Buchanan shook his head. 'Duguid's bloody well right. You're the liability. Should be you in front of Professional Standards, not me.'

Buchanan turned away again, stalked off towards the stairs. McLean let him go, stung by his words. It wasn't a fair appraisal, of course, and the detective sergeant was ten times worse. But there was a nugget of truth in what he'd said, and the truth always hurt.

33

The rumbling echo of an expensive V8 engine burbled in through the open window of his office, but McLean barely paid it any attention. A couple of the detective chief inspectors drove cars way above their pay grade, and it was almost a job requirement if you were a superintendent to have a Range Rover, even if your area was entirely urban. Something about this rumble suggested exotic and pricey; no doubt there'd be a gaggle of young constables ogling whatever it was when it parked up in the visitor space in the yard behind the station. Shaking his head, he focused back on the report that was failing to come to any meaningful point.

Something of the noise was still in his head five minutes later, when the phone rang. He knew as soon as he saw the light that indicated it was the front desk, the arrival had to be connected. Either someone high up in the organization wanted to give him a bollocking in person or another in a seemingly endless line of tiresome pranks was afoot.

'McLean.'

'Ah, I thought you'd be in, sir. There's a gentleman in reception to see you.' Reg on duty this time. Usually not one to muck people about, so maybe he wasn't in on it this time.

'Did he say what it was about? Only I'm up to my ears here, Reg.'

'Something about a car, sir. Was yours being fixed?'

'I'll be right down.' McLean hung up, secretly glad to be shot of the report, even though he knew it would still be waiting for him when he got back.

The reception area was busy this afternoon, but it was easy enough to spot the man waiting for him. He might have been wearing a designer suit, but he had car salesman written all over him. Something about the shiny face, slicked-back hair and bad skin.

'Inspector McLean?' He took a couple of steps forward, holding out a hand.

'It's Detective Inspector, actually. What can I do for you?'

A flicker of uncertainty in the man's eyes, quickly recovered. 'A man like you, must be always busy, I'm sure. That's why it's no problem at all to bring her out for you to see.'

'Her? I'm sorry. Who are you?'

'Johnny Fairbairn? Northern Motors? You booked a test drive?' That flicker was back, growing into a full puzzled frown. Johnny Fairbairn glanced around the reception area as if searching for another Inspector McLean.

'I did?' McLean held in the sigh he so desperately wanted to release. Of course he had, although if the call had been recorded, the voice he used to make it would sound very different to the one he normally used. 'Oh well, you're here now. Might as well show me.'

Escorting Johnny Fairbairn through the station to the parking yard at the back, McLean couldn't help but wonder what it was that his colleagues had set him up with this time. Something flash, for sure. And expensive. He'd

285

accepted the other pranks with as good grace as he could muster, but somehow he didn't think this time he'd be getting out his wallet.

'Sergeant at the desk tells me you drive a classic Alfa. Always been a great fan of the marque myself. Had a Sud when I was at college. Great little car for chucking round the corners, and that lovely growl off the boxer engine. But the rust? Bloody thing had more holes than a tea bag.' It wasn't hard to have a conversation with the salesman; all you had to do was listen. McLean had tried the occasional nod and 'yes', but they really weren't necessary. It didn't take long to get through the station, but by the time they emerged into the sunshine he knew considerably more about the man than he really needed to, whilst also knowing almost nothing at all.

'And there she is. Conti V8. A good bit cheaper than the twelve, but a nicer car if you ask me.'

McLean stared. Much like the dozen or so constables who had gathered around, some with their camera phones out. The car was red, very red. He'd not really been keeping up with things as much as in his misspent youth, but even he could recognize the Bentley logo on the back. Conti, Johnny Fairbairn had said, so this must be the new Continental GT. It had to be well over a hundred grand's worth of car, easy. And for something with just two doors, it was huge.

'Shall we take her out? See what she can do away from all these . . . ahem . . . Policemen?' Johnny Fairbairn pulled something that didn't look much like a key out of his jacket pocket and handed it over. Solid, weighty and with the Bentley logo in shiny enamel, it had a button set into it exactly where your thumb fell whilst cradling it in your palm. McLean pressed it and was rewarded with a flash of the indicator lights and a solid thunk as the car unlocked itself. At least two of the constables jumped, turned around with guilty faces. They all knew who he was, of course, even if he could probably only name about four of them. Soon they'd be telling their fellow officers all about the brand new car DI McLean had bought.

Not that he was going to buy it, of course. Although sinking into the comfortable and supportive leather seat and seeing the obvious craftsmanship that had gone into making the thing, he was tempted. The thunk of the door closing was echoed by the salesman as he climbed in on the other side. McLean hadn't really been aware of the noise outside but, sealed in, he was aware of the silence. It was a release of a pressure he hadn't realized was there. He would have been happy to have just sat back and breathed in the smell of leather and walnut veneer for a while; forget that he was a detective with a heavy caseload and a bunch of colleagues he wouldn't piss on if they were on fire.

'It gets me like that every time.' Johnny Fairbairn managed to ruin the moment by speaking. 'It's like a little oasis away from life's worries and stress.'

McLean looked at the salesman. How much of a line had he been spun to believe that a DI could afford a car like this? OK, so technically he could afford a car like this, and he was a DI, but that wasn't the point. 'Mr Fairbairn . . .'

'Please, call me Johnny.'

'Mr Fairbairn. I feel I need to get something straight

here before I even start the engine. I have no intention of buying this car.'

'Ah, you say that, sir, but just wait until you start her up.'

Well, he'd tried. McLean studied the fob, finding out how to extract the key from it. The engine fired up with a satisfyingly deep rumble, accompanied by a complicated sequence of lights flashing across the dashboard. There were controls and levers everywhere, unlike the nice and simple gear stick and indicator stalk in his Alfa. He'd driven plenty of cars in his time, though. This couldn't be all that difficult. It was an automatic, after all.

The Bentley garage was out on the Niddrie road, heading towards Musselburgh. He'd noted the address on the discreet dealer badge in the rear window. McLean thought it best to take the car straight back, rather than waste too much of Johnny Fairbairn's time. Or his, for that matter. It was true, this was a most pleasant distraction from a particularly boring report, but this wasn't really something he should be doing during working hours. Wasn't really something he should be doing at all, if he was being honest.

'You might want to head for the bypass. Open her up a bit.'

McLean ignored the suggestion. 'Like I said, Mr Fairbairn. I'm not going to buy this car.'

'If you're worried about the finances, we have some very good offers on.'

'I could write you a cheque for the full amount right now. The money's not the problem, and the car is superb.' McLean snatched a sideways glance at his passenger, seeing the ever-cheerful face form into a confused frown.

'I don't understand, Inspector. Why did you ask me to bring her out for you to see if you weren't interested in buying her?'

'I have to apologize to you, Mr Fairbairn. And frankly that makes me quite angry. I never called you, never asked about a test drive. My colleagues at the station have recently taken to playing pranks on me, and like all pranksters they see only the amusement of making a fool of me, not the inconvenience they cause to everyone else involved.' McLean suddenly noticed the little flappy paddles behind the steering wheel. He flipped one, and the car magically changed down a gear, the engine note deepening to a fruity bellow as they shot forward. Fortunately the road was clear.

'I'm sorry,' he continued. 'You were never the brunt of this joke, but you're the one who's lost a couple of hours work. I'm happy to pay for your time, and for the chance to have a go in this car. It's great. Better than anything I've driven before. I do need a car, can't keep using the old Alfa. But this isn't exactly inconspicuous. Not the sort of thing I could park up at the side of the road and watch a suspect from.' McLean blipped the throttle again, feeling a bit like a schoolboy. 'Dare say if he did a runner I'd be able to catch him though.'

Johnny Fairbairn smiled. 'That you would. Nought to sixty in four point eight. Ah well. We don't sell them every day anyway. No harm done, and I maybe should've done a few more checks before hurrying out. But like you say, she's great. Any excuse to get out, really.' He patted the dashboard with a light hand, fell silent for a while. McLean piloted the car down the narrow lanes that were a feature of this part of Edinburgh, where the city gave reluctant way to the countryside. They were almost at the garage before the salesman spoke again.

'So you need something a bit less conspicuous, considerably less expensive, I'm guessing. And you're an Alfa fan.' He had a schoolboy grin on his face, back in full salesman mode. 'You know I might just have something you'd be interested in. And as it happens, it's also a GT.'

Six grand lighter of pocket, but with a nearly new car being given a service before delivery, McLean was hurrying back to his office when a voice he really didn't want to hear bellowed out down the corridor.

'Where the fuck have you been? I've been trying to find you all bloody afternoon.'

Constables scattered like extras in a war movie as Acting Superintendent Duguid advanced. His face was its usual florid red, blotchy around his forehead where no doubt he'd been kneading it with his thumbs to try and force out a coherent thought. McLean pulled out his phone, checked the time. He'd not been out of the station more than two hours.

'I had to go out, sir. You could have called.'

'Aye, road testing some flash sports car. That's what I heard. Exactly how does that fit in with the working day?'

'I wasn't road testing anything, sir.'

'No? And what about arranging for a tailor to come and measure you up for a suit? That didn't happen either, I suppose. And you know you're not supposed to have personal items delivered here. We don't let the constables do it, so what the hell makes you think it's OK for inspectors?'

Duguid's head looked like it might explode any minute, which would at least have made life a bit easier for everyone. McLean glanced past him at the surprisingly large number of officers, uniform and plain clothes, who just happened to be passing that very spot at that very moment. Well, if they wanted a show, who was he to deny them?

'About that delivery, sir. I wasn't going to mention it, but since you brought up the subject, here in this rather public place, were you aware that there's a thief here in the station?'

You could almost see the cogs whirling in Duguid's brain. 'What are you talking about?'

'That delivery, sir. The one that shouldn't have come here?' McLean pitched his voice just a little too loud not to be overheard. 'You're right. I know the rules as well as the next man. Which is why I never made the order in the first place.'

'Don't be ridiculous, McLean. It was a delivery for you. Bloody great luxury hamper. Sergeant Murray signed for it at reception. It was logged in.'

'I'm aware of that, sir. What I don't know is why it then took three hours for someone to bring it to me. I don't know why it was given to a constable, who found me in the CID room. I don't know who pretended to be me and ordered the bloody thing in the first place. And most of all, I don't know who opened it and took out a very expensive bottle of brandy, thus ensuring that I couldn't return the whole package. Strange that, the way everything's logged and noted and checked through the system, and yet nobody knows who opened up a parcel that wasn't addressed to them and took something out of it.'

A puzzled frown wrote itself across Duguid's brow. 'I don't –'

'It was a prank, sir. An expensive one at that. Someone phoned in that order, persuaded a very reputable city business to deliver two grand's worth of goods here on invoice rather than demanding payment up front, then made sure I wouldn't be able to return the goods once I received them. I paid up because I didn't want to tarnish the reputation of the police.'

'Don't you dare suggest –'

'I'm also getting a pair of new suits, thanks to whoever it was phoned up Garibaldi and Sons pretending to be me. And yes, I've been out for the last two hours placating a car salesman who thought he might make a one hundred and twenty-five thousand pound sale. That one I wasn't prepared to take on the chin. Sir.'

Duguid was sweating now, his anger mixed with confusion and not a little worry. He glanced around at the collected officers as if unsure whether to shout at them or not. McLean had thought he was complicit in the pranks, but now he wasn't so sure. It was a shame; a blustering Duguid who nevertheless knew he was really in the wrong was easy enough to deal with, but a Duguid realizing that serious misconduct had happened without his knowledge was another matter entirely.

'So you're telling me you're not responsible for any of these . . . things?'

'No, sir.'

'Then why the fuck didn't you come to me?'

Really? 'I didn't think it was important, sir. Figured if I

acted like it wasn't happening, then whoever was doing it would get bored and stop soon enough.'

Wrong thing to say. Duguid advanced on him, visibly shaking as he tried to control his rage. He stabbed McLean repeatedly in the chest with a finger as he spoke. 'That's precisely why you'll never be more than an inspector, McLean. Christ, it's amazing you even made it this far. You don't cover up this sort of thing and hope it goes away. These miscreants are wasting police time. We arrest people for that.'

'Sir, I hardly think —'

'My point precisely. Think, McLean. That's what you're paid to do. Even if you don't actually need the money. I want a list of all of these so-called little incidents on my desk by the end of the day. OK? And if you've any suspicion who might be behind them, then don't be shy about saying so. We're professionals, not fucking schoolboys. I expect my senior officers to behave as such.' And with that, Duguid turned and marched off in the direction of his office.

McLean let out a sigh of relief, then realized that the corridor was still half full of constables and sergeants. He caught the eye of one in particular. DS Carter, favoured lackey of DCI Brooks and DI Spence, Little and Large. He had a haunted, guilty look on his face, and quite probably a bottle of expensive brandy in his locker.

'It ends. Now.' McLean waited for the sergeant to respond, took the tiniest of nods as all the confirmation he needed.

34

No one paid him much attention as he climbed the stairs to the fourth-storey walkway, although McLean noticed one or two sideways glances. It was an open secret that prostitutes worked out of some of these flats; no doubt they thought he was just another John, here for a bit of executive relief.

The window to Magda's flat was broken, a torn flutter of blue and white police tape the only thing stopping the locals from climbing in and helping themselves to anything they wanted. Tape also covered the door, and this at least didn't look like it had been disturbed. McLean tried the handle, unsurprised but nonetheless angry to find that the door pushed open to his touch. Buchanan said the council had been round to seal the flat up, so either he was lying or someone had cocked up big time.

Inside, it was obvious that Scene Evaluation Branch had been and gone. Every surface that might have held a fingerprint had been dusted, faint grey powder everywhere, at least in the hallway. Through into the living room and it was less clear that anything had been touched. The place still looked like a small explosion had ripped through it. The window wall opposite was still cracked, that horrible smear of blood now turned black as it dried. A stench hung in the air, part rot, part something more human. McLean pulled a pair of latex gloves out of his jacket pocket and snapped them on. More concerned with inadvertently touching something unpleasant than with contaminating a crime scene. If SEB had decided there was nothing more to be found here, then moving things around was hardly going to be a problem.

He'd been the first on the scene, and as he stood in the middle of the living room he tried to picture it as he'd seen it then. The sofa and armchairs had been turned the right way up, pushed against one wall with the broken television piled on top of them. The coffee table's glass top had been cleared away completely; fragments taken back to the lab to test for fibres and fingerprints no doubt.

The floor had been swept too, some poor bugger would have had to go through that lot with a magnifying glass. Cleared of debris, it was possible to see the blood stains though. McLean crouched down, imagining the scene played out. The door had been kicked hard enough to break the security chain, but the latch wasn't broken. That meant Magda must have answered a knock at the door. He glanced back from the living room. Yes, there was a security spy hole, and the window, of course. So she would have known who was outside. Someone she knew well enough to open the door and talk, but not trust to let in? Or someone she didn't know at all, but had no reason to feel threatened by? Impossible to tell, but either way they'd kicked the door down anyway. Hauled her across the hall to the living room. Picked her up and thrown her across the table, shattering it. Dragged her up and smashed her against the window, her head cracking the glass and leaving that bloody smear. Thrown her back down onto the floor, catching the television as she went. Two parallel smears of blood showed where she'd tried to break her fall. And then, what?

And at what point had she phoned him? When whoever it was had come to the door? That would suggest it was someone she was wary of. Someone she both knew and knew not to trust.

He turned slowly on the spot. Something was bothering him, but he couldn't put his finger on it. He should really have done this before the forensic team started moving things. Sure, they'd have photographs, but that wasn't the same.

His eyes came to a rest on the sofa and chairs. They had been upside down when he'd first arrived, stuffing ripped out of the cushions. Peering close now, he could see no blood on them, so the damage at least had been inflicted directly on the furniture, but why?

McLean pulled out one of the cushions, surprised that it hadn't been bagged and taken away for further analysis. The cuts to the cheap leatherette had been done by something sharp. A Stanley knife, most likely. The same one that had been used on Magda's face? Or had someone come in afterwards and done this with a different knife? At the time he'd not given too much thought to the damage. It was just the result of a frenzied attack. But now he could see the pattern to the cuts. Not random slashes, but a cross, opening up the cushion to get at something hidden inside. He looked carefully at the cuts, the wad of foam left inside. Then at the other cushions, one by one. They'd all been done the same way. Impossible to tell which had been done first, but to the naked eye there was no sign of blood on any of them.

McLean put the final cushion carefully down and looked over the scene again. This time the scenario painted itself differently. The assailants had still broken in when Magda hadn't been expecting anyone, but this hadn't been a simple case of beating her up as a warning to the other prostitutes in the area to keep in line. No, they'd been looking for something, even knew where it was hidden. But his best guess was that they'd not found it, hence Magda's injuries.

He stepped carefully over to the window, realizing for the first time just how high up the central point of the fracture in the glass was. Higher than his eye line by a good couple of inches. Magda wasn't small, but she was shorter than him, which meant whoever had smashed her against the glass had lifted her off her feet. Strong, then, throwing her around like a rag doll.

Through in the kitchen, McLean found the source of at least one of the odours. Someone had taken the bin out from under the sink and placed it on the counter. Several warm days and no open window, it was buzzing with flies. Trying not to breathe in, he went through to the corridor beyond and the bathroom where he'd found Magda. He'd assumed she had half staggered, half crawled here after her attackers had gone, but if they were looking for something and she wouldn't tell them where it was, then the bathroom became a torture chamber, an interrogation room.

The shower curtain was gone, wrapped around her as she lay on the trolley the paramedics had used to get her out of the flat. Dry black blood caked the walls, but in the sink hole it had retained enough moisture to clog the air

297

with a foetid smell. More flies buzzed lazily around, fat on the stench. It was all McLean could manage to stay in the small bathroom for thirty seconds. He backed out into the corridor, taking shallow breaths of the slightly less foul air, debating whether to go back in for another look. Again, there was that niggling thought in the back of his mind, that he had missed something.

McLean picked his way back through the flat and out onto the walkway, climbed carefully through the unbroken police tape and pulled the door closed. He'd have to get on to the council to come out and fix the lock and window. And then it hit him. The first thing he'd noticed when he'd arrived after Magda's call. The door had been kicked in, the security chain splintered off and a dirty great boot print in the wood. But now there was nothing showing on the paintwork at all.

He stared at the door for long minutes, searching his memory, trying to convince himself he hadn't just imagined the boot print. He leaned in close, inspecting the surface for any telltale signs that it had been cleaned. He thought there might have been something, but it was impossible to see in the half-shade from the walkway overhead. Then a slight noise to one side distracted him.

The little girl's face was still dirty, and her doll still had no clothes and no arms. She stared at him with wary eyes and said nothing. He was useless when it came to children, but McLean guessed she must have been five or so. Maybe older if she didn't get enough to eat; something all too common in this part of town. No doubt there'd be a huge telly in the flat, and the girl's mum would have the latest model of mobile phone though. Probably spent a tenner a day on cigarettes, too.

'Do you know the lady who lives here?' He crouched down until he was almost at her level, but didn't come any closer. In response, she clutched the doll to her grubby chest and leaned away. She reminded him of nothing so much as a cat, wary of something strange but unwilling to cede any territory too easily.

'I'm a policeman.' McLean put his hand in his pocket, brought out his warrant card. It had his photograph on it, which was probably the only thing that would make any sense to the little girl. She still didn't respond.

'She was attacked a few days ago. Some people came here, broke in. Did you see them?' He shouldn't have been doing this, Jo Dexter would tan his hide, and DS Buchanan would sneer at him about protocol. You couldn't question a child without a parent or guardian present. On the other hand, no one else was going to help him.

The little girl shook her head, but something about the way she clamped her mouth shut made McLean think that maybe she was just unwilling to say. He wondered whether it would be possible to get someone from Child Support in to question her. Perhaps in the right environment she might open up.

'Senga. Stop playing with that fucking doll and get your arse in here.' An expression of pure terror swept over the little girl's face and she looked away from McLean towards the door. He was halfway to standing when a woman appeared in the opening.

'Who the fuck are you? You a fucking nonce?'

The woman took her eyes off McLean for a moment

and barked: 'Get inside and clean up the kitchen.' The little girl darted past, narrowly avoiding a skelp to the back of the head in what was obviously a practised move.

'I'm a police officer.' McLean held up his warrant card, still in his hand. 'That your daughter?'

'What the fuck is it to youse?'

She took a step out onto the walkway, and McLean could see the woman properly. His first impression was of fat, in stark contrast to the tiny, skinny girl. Probably her who ate all the pies. She was dressed in sweatpants that had probably once been black but were now faded to grey, stained and pock-marked with burn holes. Her T-shirt was no doubt the largest you could buy from Primark, but still too small by an order of magnitude. It clung to her in all the wrong ways, emphasizing the rolls of fat around her middle, her sagging lumpy breasts. Fat hung in pendulous loops from her arms, wobbling as she lifted a cigarette to her mouth. She barely looked at his card, sized him up and down in a brief glance as if wondering whether he was worth eating or not.

'Fuck you looking at anyway?'

'You know your neighbour was badly beaten a few days ago?'

'Fucking whore. Deserved it, din't she. Men coming and going all hours of the day. Screaming all fucking night. You know they made these fucking buildings out of paper, aye?'

'Did you see anything? Anyone coming you might recognize again?'

'Do I look like I give a fuck?'

'A woman was beaten near to death. Her face has been

cut open, her arms and legs broken. Her assailant smashed her so hard against the window it nearly shattered. This happened here, in the middle of the afternoon. You happy with that sort of thing going on around your daughter?'

The fat woman gave him an angry stare. 'She coming back?'

'I've no idea. For a while, maybe. Once they let her out of hospital. Won't be for at least a month, the way she is at the moment.'

'Then I get a month's fucking peace. Might as well enjoy it.' The fat woman flicked her dog-end over the parapet, turned her back on him and waddled inside, slamming the door behind her. McLean heard her voice shouting obscenities at the little girl from inside. He took out his notebook, scribbled down the address. He'd put a call in to social services in the morning.

35

The Scene Evaluation Branch labs were busy when McLean stuck his head round the door later that afternoon. He'd thought of phoning, but coming here in person meant he'd most likely get a response to his questions quickly; they were always keen to get rid of visitors. And it meant he could stay away from the station for a while too. There was an office-shaped stack of paperwork waiting for him, and no doubt an irate acting superintendent.

'Is Miss Cairns in today?' he asked the first passing lab tech who was foolish enough to let him catch his eye. The young fellow looked alarmed, but indicated another door before scuttling off about whatever task he had been assigned.

The door led through to an office, which was a relief. McLean had visions of wandering into some clean room and being shouted at for destroying a day's work. Miss Cairns had her back to him as he entered, working at a large flat-screen monitor that displayed an image he wouldn't be able to un-see in a long while. She turned as he knocked on the doorframe, scowled when she realized who it was.

'You know this is a restricted area, right?' As friendly greetings go, it was almost as welcoming as the fat woman back at the tower block in Restalrig

'I was told you were here. No one said I couldn't come in. Sorry.'

Miss Cairns tapped a keyboard and the image disappeared, replaced by a wallpaper picture of sunny skies and clouds over a hilltop. 'Well, you're here now. What can I do for you, Inspector?'

'The Magda Evans case.' This drew a blank. 'You know. Tower block over in Restalrig, woman beaten near to death. You were the crime scene manager for that one, weren't you?'

Miss Cairns frowned some more. 'I guess. We've not really done more than a preliminary sweep so far.'

It was McLean's turn to frown. 'A preliminary sweep? I thought you were finished.'

Miss Cairns actually laughed. 'You'd be lucky. You any idea how backlogged we are? Case like that we only do the stuff that has to be done, then seal the place off. No point treating it as a murder scene if your wifey gets better and tells us who did it.' A fresh frown wrinkled her forehead. 'She's no dead, is she?'

'I . . . No. She's in intensive care, but she should pull through.' McLean struggled to make sense of what he was being told. 'You sealed off the crime scene then?'

'Well, not me personally, no. Bloke from Housing was coming round to board up the window and the SIO should have the key for the front door.'

'I'm the SIO.'

'Well, there you are then.'

'But I don't have the key. I've just been at the scene and it's far from secure. Door unlocked, broken window. Chances are every Ned in the scheme's been in there for a nosey.'

'You are joking, aren't you?' Miss Cairns was wearing the frown again.

'I wish I was.' Christ, he was going to get a bollocking for this. 'Don't suppose you remember who was actually there when you left? I had to go the hospital with the victim.'

'Pete Buchanan was swanning around the car park. Don't think I saw him up on the fourth floor though. There were a couple of new constables I had to tell not to come inside. One of them would have been waiting for the chippy to come and board up the window.'

'Oh bloody hell.' McLean withered under a disapproving glare from the SOC officer. 'Sorry. It's just I get told off for not delegating stuff, then when I take my eye off the ball it all goes ti– . . . wrong.'

'Welcome to senior management. You should see what this lot get up to when my back's turned.'

McLean looked for any sign of a smile on Miss Cairns' face, but found none. The silence hung heavy for a while as he tried to find anything that might even partially salvage the situation.

'You've got crime scene photos?' he asked finally.

'One or two, aye. You want to see them?' Miss Cairns turned back to her keyboard and mouse, clicked away until a page of photo thumbnails appeared on the large monitor. It reminded McLean of Emma, how she'd manipulated the images so quickly he couldn't begin to keep up. This was where he'd first met her, not much more than a year ago, wasn't it? And it was her skill with the image software that had made him suspect her of posting crime scene photos to dodgy internet forums. That as much as anything was what had brought them together, and look how much good that had done her. He really would be better off alone.

'Here you are.' Miss Cairns' voice snapped him back into the present, and McLean's eyes focused on the screen. It was like a hundred other sets of crime scene photographs he'd stared at, a dozen or more pictures all showing the same thing, then a dozen showing something else, or the same thing but from a different angle. Digital cameras were great, but a modern day crime scene photographer could take hundreds if not thousands and some poor bugger then had to go through the lot of them.

'Have you got any of the front door?'

'Should have.' Click, click, click. 'Here you go.'

And there it was, the front door. A dirty great boot print just by the handle.

'Do you know if anyone took any samples from this?' McLean pointed at the photo.

'I'd've thought so. That's outside. More difficult to secure for later examination. I can check for you, but it'll take a while.'

'Thanks. You're a star.' McLean would have kissed her, but that might have given her ideas.

'I'm doing it for Emma, OK? Not you.'

'Well, I'll be sure and tell her. And thanks anyway.' McLean left her to her work, headed back to the door, then stopped.

'Actually, could I ask one more favour?'

'You can ask.' Miss Cairns didn't turn to face him, just spoke to her monitor.

'Can you send a copy of all the photos to Grumpy . . . Sorry, DS Laird. Not the SCU. The analysis on that boot print, too. When you've time.'

Miss Cairns turned this time, raised a quizzical eyebrow

and then smiled. It suited her better than the scowl or the frown. 'Aye, I'll send it all to Grumpy Bob.'

'Thanks. I owe you.' McLean ducked out of the room and headed back towards his car, pulled out his phone to call Grumpy Bob. It was just possible that this was all a giant cock-up, but it felt like something a lot more deliberate to him. It would be hard enough to prove, though And as SIO, he was going to have a hell of a job convincing anyone he wasn't just trying to cover his arse.

'My office, Tony. Now.'

McLean had barely walked in through the SCU door and Jo Dexter was shouting at him. He knew what it was about, took a quick look around to see if his chief suspect was in. A small gaggle of constables sat in the far corner, heads down and nattering about something. No sign of DS Buchanan though.

'Now, Tony.'

It wasn't wise to make Jo Dexter ask for something twice. He followed her along the corridor and into her office. The mess on her desk hadn't improved much since their morning meeting.

'I've just had a call from SEB about the Magda Evans crime scene. Seems someone forgot to make sure it was secure before everyone left.'

'I . . .' McLean started, but Dexter waved him silent.

'I know it wasn't you, Tony. How the fuck could you have? You were at the hospital, not running the crime scene. Who was SIO?'

'That's the whole point, Jo. I was. I am. I should have made sure everyone was doing their jobs properly.'

'That's bollocks, Tony, and you know it. You delegate, that's how it works. You must have left someone in charge when you went to the hospital.'

'Aye, I did. DS Buchanan. Remember? I told you.'

Dexter must have read his expression. Certainly McLean didn't make any effort to hide it. 'What, you think he did this on purpose? Why the fuck would he do that?'

McLean told her about his visit to Magda's flat, the slashed cushions, the missing boot print. He didn't tell her he'd asked for what little forensic evidence there was to be sent to Grumpy Bob for safe keeping.

'I rang Buchanan when I got Magda's call. Said he was over in Sighthill, but he confirmed it was her number. I asked him to put a request in to control, get a squad car over ASAP, but it didn't turn up until I'd been there twenty minutes myself.'

'That's hardly damning. You know what patrols can be like.'

'Pretty much what I thought. But Buchanan told me on the phone the Sighthill call-out was a false alarm. When I asked him about it this morning, he spun me a completely different story.'

'You don't think he was there at all.' Jo Dexter slumped back into her seat.

'No, I don't. I think he was at Magda's flat beating the shit out of her.' McLean recalled the conversation, how Buchanan had sounded out of breath. Like he'd been walking uphill. Or smashing up someone's flat. 'He got out of there sharpish, called control when he was far enough away.'

Dexter said nothing for a while, the thoughts flickering

across her face in a series of frowns. 'I still think it's a hell of an assumption. I mean, why? What possible reason could he have?'

'I don't know, but whoever beat Magda up was looking for something. Drugs, money, who knows? They turned the place upside down, cut open all the cushions. It wasn't just random.'

'Still. I mean, Pete's methods aren't always strictly legit, but that's a hell of a leap to make. We're talking attempted murder here, not GBH. It's a miracle she survived at all.'

A horrible thought crept into McLean's mind. 'Where's Buchanan now?'

'I've no idea.' Dexter pushed herself out of her chair, swept past McLean on her way to the door. He had to rush to catch up as she went back to the main SCU room and its cluster of constables.

'You lot, any idea where Pete is?'

They looked at each other, then around. One or two of them even got up. Eventually a spokesman was elected by silent consensus. 'Not sure, ma'am. He went out about an hour ago. Said something about the hospital?'

'Shit.' Dexter stopped a moment. 'Find him. Call him. Track his Airwave. I want him in my office right away.'

With a scraping of chairs, the constables hurried about their new task. McLean already had his phone out. 'Who's guarding Magda right now?'

Dexter looked at him with horror. 'You can't think . . .'

'I'm not taking any chances.' He spooled through the contacts list on his phone, looking for the hospital switchboard. Magda was in intensive care, and you couldn't have mobile phones or Airwave sets anywhere near. 'Bollocks. It'll be quicker if I go there myself.'

He sped down the corridors, skirting around startled nurses and slow-moving patients. In the back of his head he could hear his headmistress shouting at him to stop running, but she was long dead and he never much cared about those rules anyway. At least enough of the staff here knew who he was and had the sense not to try and stop him.

Through the final set of double doors, McLean saw the reassuring sight of PC Jones sitting on his uncomfortable plastic chair by the door to Magda's room. The constable looked up at the noise, folding his paper and setting it down on the floor when he saw who it was, then standing when he realized that McLean was running.

'You all right, sir?'

'Magda. She OK?' McLean sucked in air in big gulps, wondering when it was he had become so unfit.

'Fine, I think.' PC Jones shrugged. 'Pete Buchanan was in a half hour or so ago. No one else been since.'

McLean said nothing, just pushed past the constable and through the door. He already knew it was too late.

Magda stirred as he entered, but didn't wake. Someone had put a vase of flowers on the bedside table. Otherwise the scene was pretty much the same as the last time he'd been in. It might even have been the same television programme playing.

'She's OK.' McLean shifted uncomfortably, not sure what to do with his hands. Constable Jones poked his head through the doorway.

'Is there a problem, sir? Only I was told no one on their own.' PC Jones hovered in the doorway.

'You said Sergeant Buchanan was here. He see her alone?'

'No, sir. I know the rules. I was in here with him at all times.'

'Was she awake then?'

'I think so, maybe. Difficult to tell with the amount of morphine they keep pumping into her. He didn't say anything, mind. Just stood there, where you are. Looked at her for a couple minutes and then went.'

'He bring the flowers?' McLean pointed at the vase and its gaudy contents.

'That was Ms Saunders, sir. She came not long after you were here. One of the SCU detective constables was with her. Patterson, I think. They come and go so quickly I find it hard to keep track of their names.'

'I know what you mean, Reg.' McLean took one last look at Magda as a nurse came in. She gave them both a disapproving scowl, then went to check the monitors. A couple of clicks to a button just out of the patient's reach and Magda relaxed back into her pillows. Intravenous morphine could cure a multitude of ills.

'What are you doing in here disturbing the patient?' The nurse rounded on McLean as soon as she had finished. For once, he didn't know her name, but he could tell she wasn't one to be messed with.

'Sorry. Emergency. We thought someone was trying to kill her.' McLean backed out of the room as the nurse held up a finger to her mouth.

'Quiet. She may be drugged, but she can still hear you.'

*

Outside, with the door firmly closed, McLean let out a long breath and collapsed against the wall. Had he been wrong about Buchanan?

'You all right, sir?' PC Jones asked. McLean turned to face the old constable. Solid Copper, one of the old school. But then so was DS Buchanan.

'Fine, Reg. Thanks.' He pushed himself off the wall. 'I think I may have made a huge cock-up though.'

As if to underline the point, his mobile phone started to ring. He pulled it out of his pocket, looking for the off switch. The 'no mobile phones' posters taped at ten-foot intervals all along the corridor left little to the imagination. And for those who couldn't take a hint, the scowl he received from the nurse, who had stopped mid-stride halfway to the swing doors, should have hammered the point home. The screen told him it was DCI Dexter calling, though.

'Just don't let anyone in there unsupervised until I get back to you, OK, Reg?' McLean pointed back at the door to Magda's room as he hit 'answer' and hefted the phone to his ear, jogging away from the ICU as fast as he could.

'. . . fucking right I'll shout. Accuse me of deliberately sabotaging an investigation . . .' McLean pulled the phone from his ear, checked the number and name on the screen. Definitely Jo Dexter. Not her voice he was hearing. He put the phone back to his ear again.

'Jo? You there?'

'Ah, Tony. Sorry about that.' The sound muffled, but McLean thought he heard Dexter shout: 'Just get out. If you can't act like a police officer, then don't expect me to treat you like one.' Then the voice came back clear. 'Where are you now?' In the background he heard a door slam.

'The hospital. Magda's OK. Buchanan was here seeing her though.'

'I know. That was him just now. Seems he's got wind of your accusations and isn't all that happy about them.'

'Well, tough shit. If he wasn't such a prize arse then people might give him the benefit of the doubt. I seem to recall you thought he was our man too.'

'Yes, well. That was before he had a decent excuse for pretty much everything you accused him of. He may be a prize arse, Tony, but he's a well-connected prize arse. You need to tread carefully.'

'With respect, Jo, fuck that. If I suspect an officer of misconduct I'll bloody well investigate it. And if I find anything suspicious I'll have Professional Standards on it like a ton of bricks.'

'Even after what they did to you last year?'

That gave him pause, but only for a while. 'They did what they had to given the circumstances.'

'Oh don't sound so fucking pompous. They fucked you over, Tony. Rab Callard and his cronies. If it hadn't been for that forensics girlfriend of yours you'd be in Saughton right now.'

'I was innocent. I have to believe that would have come out eventually.'

'Aye, in eight to ten years. Look, I know you don't get on with Pete, but a lot of the senior detectives like him. He's one of them, came up through the ranks with them, except he got stuck at sergeant. And he gets results. The high heidyins see that and turn a blind eye to everything else.'

McLean had been pacing all the while and was now in

the public waiting area at reception. The walking had calmed him down a little, but his nerves were still fizzing.

'I still think it's him, Jo. Or there's something in it for him. It's too bloody convenient to put it down to incompetence.'

'Yeah, well. You'd better be damned sure about that before you start making accusations again. And don't be at all surprised if Duguid tries to rip you a new one when he hears about this.'

Duguid. Of course. Brilliant.

'I've coped with worse.'

'Of course you have, but you can cope with it tomorrow. It's been a long day. Go home, get some rest and we'll pick up the pieces in the morning.'

Mrs McCutcheon's cat paused, halfway through the routine of cleaning its arse, and gave him an old-fashioned stare that would have done his grandmother proud. McLean sighed as he closed the back door and dropped the bundle of papers he'd brought home with him onto a chair. He could have put them on the kitchen table, except for that look from the cat, sitting there right in the middle, next to the uncovered sugar bowl and the salt and pepper pots.

'I ought to tell you to bugger off, but what would be the point?' He pulled off his jacket and draped it over the chair back. The constant heat from the Aga made the kitchen by far the most welcoming and warm place in the house. At this time of year it could even get a bit stifling. He knew people who let their ranges go out over the summer months, but that felt wrong. There was something dead about a kitchen with a cold Aga in it.

Bored of him, or perhaps of cleaning its back end, Mrs McCutcheon's cat stood up, stretched and then leapt off the table, walking swiftly towards the door that led to the rest of the house. As it passed through, McLean noticed the sound of music. He glanced at the clock, wondering if Emma was still up. He'd left her asleep in his bed, curled up in her fleecy pyjamas with the cow print on, far too early in the morning and only scant hours after she'd woken him by crawling in. He headed through to see, hoping for a glimpse of her cheerful smile to lift his mood after a weary day. The papers could wait another hour, surely.

Wafts of smoky scent hung in the hallway air, the half-open door to the library spilling out the muted tones of Liz Fraser as she wailed her way through 'Pearly-Dewdrops' Drops'. He'd not replaced very many of his old records yet, turned to so much vinyl slag by the fire that had destroyed his Newington tenement flat, but McLean had managed to find a set of early Cocteau Twins albums in a charity shop on Clerk Street one rare after-noon off. They crackled a bit, but the music still held its magic, even thirty years on. Thirty years. Christ, but that made him feel old.

Jenny Nairn was sitting cross-legged on the sofa. She'd pulled the table close and spread open some reference books, bending low to see the text in the soft light from a standard lamp and scribbling notes on a cheap, lined A4 pad. The source of the scent was smoking away mer-rily in a little holder, filling the room with an aroma that the detective inspector in him immediately thought was there to mask something else. McLean could see no evidence of illicit substances though. Nor of Emma. The first was a relief. The second, he was surprised to find, something of a disappointment. It put him strangely in mind of being a teenager, hanging around the Victoria Street boutiques in the hope that a girl he fancied might show up. More often than not she didn't, and even if she did he'd not have had the courage to go and talk to her. Not when he was on his own. But on those days when she was there, he'd felt, well, happy. And when she wasn't, then the world was a little more grey.

McLean rubbed at his forehead self-consciously, trying to scrub away the adolescent memory. Maybe it was the music, taking him back all those years. He couldn't even remember the girl's name, for heaven's sake. But she had flame-red hair and freckles all over her nose. He remembered that.

'Oh, you're back.' Jenny unfolded herself from the sofa, flipping the books closed and coming to her feet in one fluid, catlike movement. McLean envied her, for a moment. His bones ached even at the thought of sitting cross-legged, let alone being able to stand again afterwards.

'Oh my god. Sorry.' Jenny noticed the joss stick smoking away merrily, lunged forward and pinched out the end. 'I should have asked if it was OK.'

'No, it's fine.' McLean waved in the general direction of the table and the dresser beyond, where his fabulously expensive turntable was clunk-hissing its way around the end of the record. 'Emma gone to bed?'

Jenny gave him an odd look, almost as if she couldn't believe he was asking. Fair enough, it was a pretty stupid question. But maybe it was more that she hadn't been expecting him to care. He'd been so busy these past few weeks he'd barely been in the house, let alone had time to sit and chat.

''Bout an hour ago. Yeah. Why?'

'Just wondered what she'd been up to. Sometimes I worry she might think I'm avoiding her on purpose.' He went over to the drinks cabinet, poured himself a small measure of whisky and topped it up with some water. Turned back to Jenny. 'You want one?'

'Bit late for me, thanks. I probably ought to be heading up myself.' She yawned, paused long enough for McLean to savour a taste of his dram. 'She doesn't, though. Think you're avoiding her. Not exactly.'

'Not exactly how?'

'Well, she knows you're busy with work, but she misses you. What she's going through, it's not easy. Her memory's not so much gone as shattered. Bits come and go, disjointed, things shoved together that shouldn't be, big holes where she can do stuff but doesn't know how she knows how. If that makes sense. I see it all the time I'm working with her. The conflict inside.'

McLean said nothing, just nodded. Took another sip of his whisky even though the flavour had gone out of it.

'But you're something she can latch on to. She remembers . . . Well, not you exactly. Not the life you had together before. But part of her deep down trusts you, and it's more than just because you've taken her in, put a roof over her head and not taken advantage of her.'

Jenny bent down and gathered up her books, took the joss stick and shoved it and its little ceramic pot-stand into the pocket of her hoodie.

'I miss her too, you know.' McLean surprised himself by saying the words he was thinking. Jenny just looked at him, head slightly cocked to one side like a dog trying to work out what the idiot human was doing.

'Well, she's here,' she said finally, then left him alone with his dram.

36

McLean sat at his desk, staring sightlessly at the stack of reports, overtime sheets, memos and other junk that had somehow grown in his absence. He was fairly certain he'd squared everything away just a couple of days past, so this new load was yet one more play in the tiresome game. Like Duguid's constant demands, the secondment to the SCU and the dispersal of his team to the four corners of Lothian and Borders, it was all part of a concerted attempt to get him down. And it was all just spiteful jealousy.

He could take it in reasonable spirit from the junior ranks. There wasn't a day went by when some cocky sergeant or constable didn't ask him if they could borrow a hundred quid. Everyone knew he was loaded, didn't really need to work, and that pissed off the senior ranks for reasons he couldn't quite fathom. OK, so they might think him a jammy sod, but it wasn't as if he'd always been wealthy enough not to have to worry about working. He'd struggled up through the ranks like the rest of them, proven his worth time after time, and yet now they treated him like some kind of dilettante. Or worse, the station pariah.

There were those who blamed him for Needy's death too, mad though that was. If anything they should have been thanking him for saving their old friend from the shame of a trial, or worse being sectioned and sent to a secure mental hospital. But that wasn't the logic of coppers. No, McLean had been there when Needy had died, so it was somehow McLean's fault. Brilliant. And this lot were meant to solve crimes.

With a sigh, he reached out and pulled the first item on the pile towards him, praying as he did so for some form of distraction. It arrived in the form of a round-faced young detective constable knocking on the frame of the open door.

'Morning, Stuart. What can I do for you?'

'I was putting together the final report for the Mikhailevic and Sands suicides, sir. Wondered if you'd had a chance to look over the case notes I left you.'

McLean stared at the pile on his desk. It was news to him that either investigation had been concluded. 'In here somewhere, are they?'

MacBride took two steps into the room, reached towards the precarious stack of papers and whipped out a slim folder with commendable dexterity. The pile rocked slightly, but didn't fall. 'No one else uses the right folders. It drives Elsie in filing mad.'

McLean took the report, noticed the official stamp and file number on the cover. He opened it up and looked at the neatly typed notes inside. Closed it and handed it back. 'You couldn't give me the executive summary, could you?'

'Both men died from snapped vertebrae as a result of hanging. There's no direct evidence to suggest anything other than that they did it to themselves. They appear to have used rope from the same manufacturer, possibly bought from the same store, but forensics can't say that with a hundred per cent certainty. Likewise, the knots appear to be identical, but there's a million and one sites

319

on the internet that tell you how to tie the things. The blood profiles of both men are similar, unusually elevated levels of dopamine and serotonin, but Doctor Cadwallader couldn't find any evidence this was due to outside agency. It could just be that you need to be in that state of mind to want to kill yourself.'

'No luck finding any links between them, then.'

'We've looked, but they don't seem to have any friends in common. Don't think we've been as thorough as we could've been there though. Could've done with a bit more manpower.'

But there was no way Duguid, or Brooks, would sanction that. Not for a couple of unimportant young men with no immediate family clamouring for answers and no press interest bringing pressure to bear. 'What about the suicide notes? You look into those?'

'I ran a textual analysis, sir. They were different enough that it seems unlikely they were written by the same person. Mikhailevic's was odd. Full of spelling mistakes and grammatical errors where his other writing was meticulously correct. Again, that could just be a result of his state of mind.'

'No one thinking straight would put a rope around their neck and jump. Right enough. So the conclusion is suicide in both cases, similarities notwithstanding.'

'That's what the report says, sir.' MacBride tapped the offending article against his arm. 'Also I checked the TV schedules. There's been a documentary about Albert Pierrepoint on BBC4 recently. It got repeated half a dozen times. Last showing was six weeks ago, just before

Patrick Sands hanged himself. Add it all up and suicide's the obvious conclusion.'

'I sense a but in there, Constable.'

'Well, it's bollocks isn't it. A blind man could see the two are hooky, and connected. This latest one too.'

'So why the final report then?' McLean nodded at the folder clasped in the young detective constable's sweaty hands. 'I don't remember asking for one.'

'Lar–... DCI Brooks wants it all squared away, sir. "If there's no obvious sign of foul play, then we can't keep digging until we find some" were his exact words.'

That sounded about right for Brooks, especially if Dagwood was breathing down his neck. 'What about John Fenton?'

'That one's still open, sir. But only because we're waiting on the forensic report. Chances are it's going to be the same as the other two.'

'You want to do some more digging? See if you can come up with anything to link the three together?'

MacBride wore his worried expression openly, like all his other expressions. Guile wasn't a part of his nature. Not a brilliant trait in a detective.

'It's all right. You can make calls from here if needs be, and if anyone asks, I told you to do a bit more background on Fenton, OK? I can sit on those case notes for weeks if you want.' McLean swept an arm across the air above his desk, taking in the expanse of paperwork awaiting his attention. 'It's not as if I've nothing else to do, and there's another desk just like this one waiting for me over at the SCU.'

A knock at the door stopped MacBride from answering.

DS Ritchie stood in the doorway, a thick padded envelope in one hand.

'SOC sent this lot to Grumpy Bob, sir. He's out with DCI Brooks. Asked me if I could pass them on to you.'

'Thanks.' McLean took the package. 'You back with us then?'

'For now. God only knows when they'll want me back up at Tulliallan though. Still, it beats being stuck down in the cellars. At least I get to see the sun.'

Opened, the package revealed a thick sheaf of photographs, printed on a better-quality colour printer than the one up the corridor. Proper glossy paper, too. There was a note with it, but McLean didn't need to read it to recognize Magda's smashed-up flat.

'Anyone fancy a trip down to Restalrig?'

MacBride looked crestfallen. 'Sorry, sir. I've got to report to DCI Brooks in half an hour. Wrap-up briefing on the post office robberies.'

'I'll come along, sir.' DS Ritchie smiled. 'It's been a while since I did any actual detective work.'

McLean shuffled the photographs back together and slid them into their envelope. He wanted to compare them with the scene now, if it hadn't been even further contaminated. 'Excellent. You can sort us out a car then.'

McLean piloted his old Alfa down Leith Walk, heading for Lochend and Restalrig. He wasn't too happy using it in heavy traffic in the heat of late summer, but DS Ritchie had sworn blind there were no pool cars to be had anywhere in the entire Lothian and Borders area. McLean could well believe it, though there was always the possibility she just wanted another drive in the classic car.

'What's the score here?' she asked as they crawled through the permanent traffic nightmare caused by the tram works.

'Ex-prostitute. One we picked up off that boat a month or so back, you remember? Someone gave her a punishment beating. Left her almost dead.' McLean brought Ritchie up to speed. By the time they reached the tower block, she knew as much about it as he did.

The car park in front of the block was surprisingly full. McLean parked directly beneath the front of the building, too close to the concrete walkways and the scaffolding for comfort.

'I can see why you wanted a pool car,' Ritchie said as she looked up and around. A couple of smashed breeze blocks just a few paces away had obviously been heaved over the parapet several storeys up. Probably for shits and giggles, but there may have been more malicious intent.

'Yeah, well I should be getting something a bit less conspicuous in a day or two.' McLean made a mental note to give Johnny Fairbairn a call. 'Let's just get this over with as quickly as possible, aye? Sooner we're gone, the less likely someone'll notice.'

They took the stairs to the fourth floor, not trusting the elevator to work and sure that it would smell worse than the stairwell. Glancing along the concrete walkway at each floor as they passed, McLean saw only one person; an old lady who scowled at him from her doorway, flicked her cigarette butt over the parapet and went back into her flat. He winced at the thought of the dog-end bouncing over his shiny red paintwork, but it was too late to do anything about it.

The window beside Magda's front door had been boarded up, so the message had finally got through to Housing. Stable door and horses bolting sprang to mind. The door itself appeared to have had a new lock fitted, as well. Beyond it, the little girl was in her favourite spot, with her armless, naked doll. She looked at him wide-eyed, but said nothing. Another mental note he needed to do something about.

'I don't suppose you've got the key, sir?' Ritchie reached for the door handle. It clicked as it turned and the door swung open. 'Ah, we don't need one, it would seem.'

She was about to step inside, but McLean stopped her. Something about this didn't feel right. No, everything about this didn't feel right. He raised a finger to his lips for quiet, then motioned for Ritchie to step back. When they were both clear of the doorway, he nudged it wide with his foot and peered inside.

It was empty, and just as messy as when last he had been here. The council services department had only boarded up the window and repaired the lock, thankfully. He took a step into the hallway, which was when he heard a voice coming from the living room.

Backing silently out onto the walkway, McLean closed the door and pulled Ritchie back towards the stairs before speaking. 'Get onto control. I want backup here as soon as possible.'

Ritchie made the call while McLean kept an eye on the door in case whoever was in there decided to come out. The little girl watched him with large, round eyes; he was obviously providing far better entertainment than her doll. Really he should have sent her back inside, but the thought of another confrontation with her mother filled him with dread. And there was no way it could be done quietly, either.

'What do you suppose they're doing in there?' Ritchie asked in a low whisper.

'Destroying evidence? Looking for something? Could just be local kids being nosey, for all I know.' McLean took a couple of steps towards the door. Stopped. Came back to where Ritchie was standing by the stairwell.

'You got your pepper spray?'

Ritchie opened up her shoulder bag and guddled around inside. Brought out the small canister and held it up.

'Right then. Stay here and wait for backup. If anyone comes out and tries to get away, let them have it.'

He didn't wait for her to argue, instead went straight back to the front door. No point in being subtle, and perhaps he'd be able to catch whoever was inside off guard. Surprise was always an advantage. McLean reached forward for the handle.

The door swung open before he could touch it, revealing the startled figure of Detective Sergeant Buchanan.

'What the fuck are you doing here?' McLean thought the words, but it was Buchanan who spoke them.

'What the –? How dare you speak to a senior officer like that?'

'I'm sorry, sir.' Buchanan emphasized the title with little effort to hide his sarcasm. So that was what it sounded like. 'You took me by surprise. I was just checking over

325

the crime scene. Bit of a cock-up with housing not turning up to board up the window. But they've done it now.'

Far too rehearsed to be the truth. McLean looked back to where Ritchie was standing. She had her phone in one hand, the other holding the slim can of pepper spray. She had seen them both, started to approach, but McLean waved for her to stay where she was.

'OK then.' He turned to Buchanan, fumbled in his pocket for his own phone. 'Let's go in and see what you found.' As they stepped through the doorway, McLean saw the little girl clasp her doll to her chest with one hand, and with the other point straight at Buchanan. He pointed at the detective sergeant's back and mouthed 'him?' at her. She nodded, her face very serious, then got up, crossed the walkway and went into her own flat.

Buchanan wasn't hanging around, which gave McLean enough time to find the record button on his phone. He slipped it into the breast pocket on his jacket as he walked into the living room.

'About that little cock-up' he said. 'Why'd you not wait for them to turn up? Housing, that is.'

Buchanan scowled at the question. 'It was your bloody crime scene. Besides, it's usually forensics who arrange that sort of thing.'

'You mean you didn't even call Housing? You didn't even check to see if someone else had done?'

'Like I said. Not my crime scene.'

'Actually it was. Right from the moment I stepped into the ambulance. But I don't really give a fuck whose crime scene it was. Even if Charles bloody Duguid was supervising in person, it would still have been your responsibility

326

to make sure the scene was secure. You and every other bloody officer on site, plain clothes or uniform. You don't leave the scene without making sure it's being processed properly and someone is in charge.'

Buchanan snorted a humourless laugh. 'Don't quote procedure at me like you're some kind of perfect copper. Everyone knows you take short cuts, McLean. Get people killed, too.'

McLean stared at the sergeant, let the insubordination slide this time. Buchanan was angry and on the defensive; hardly surprising if the little girl outside was telling the truth. Pushing him now might reveal even more nasty little secrets.

'You know she phoned me, when her attacker arrived?' McLean looked around the living room as he talked. It was still a mess, but a different mess to the one he'd seen previously. The chairs that had been stacked on top of the sofa were now lying on the floor, their cushions scattered about. Someone had been poking around for sure, none too carefully either. It didn't take a genius to guess who.

'I found her phone under that chair when I got here.' He pointed at the metal and velour monstrosity that was the only piece of furniture not broken or upside down. 'She must've dropped it when her attacker came in. Heard the whole thing as I was driving over here.'

'Oh aye? Why've you not arrested the bastard then?' Buchanan stood with his back to the window. McLean couldn't help but notice that the blood stain at the point where the glass had cracked, where Magda's head had been smashed against it, was almost exactly the same height above the ground as Buchanan's shoulders. Maybe a bit higher. A head higher.

327

'All I could hear was screaming, and the noise of things being broken. Sounded like an army.'

'Must've been a gang of them, the damage they did.' Buchanan kicked lightly at the edge of the upturned sofa. 'To this place and the prozzy.'

'You were over in Sighthill when it happened, weren't you.'

Buchanan twitched at the question, thrown by the change of subject.

'That's right, aye. What of it?'

'Nothing, really. Just that you told me at the time it was a crank call. Then you said it was a kiddie fiddler hanging around the school playground.' McLean crossed the room as he spoke, picking his way through the debris over towards the destroyed sofa. Someone had definitely been through the pile of cushions.

'Nah. You're imagining things. It was just a hoax call in the end. Had to check it out mind. You know what it's like with the register.'

McLean picked up one of the cushions and made a play of inspecting the slashes across it. Put a hand inside and felt around as if looking for something. 'Yes, of course. Can't take a chance where children are concerned. You have children, Pete?'

'What?' Buchanan's gaze had been fixed firmly on the cushion. Now it swung back to McLean's face. 'No. Never married.'

'The two are no longer mutually exclusive. I bet ninety per cent of the kids living in these blocks have parents who never married. But still, I'd've thought a detective of your long standing and experience would have known that it's the school holidays right now. Kids won't be back in the playground for a couple of weeks yet.'

'Ha. That the best you can come up with? School's out? Come on, McLean. A playground's a playground whether it's got kids in it or no. You're on the register, you're not allowed anywhere near. We get a call saying someone's been seen in the wrong place, we investigate. Plain and simple.'

'Why'd you go alone, then? Why not take a constable with you?'

'That, coming from the great Detective Inspector McLean, just makes my day.'

It was a fair point, even if it didn't answer the question. McLean dropped the cushion back onto the pile and took a good look at Buchanan's shoes. Heavy-duty, thick soles. Built more for the beat than plain clothes, but a lot of coppers wore them. He opened up the envelope Ritchie had given him, pulled out the sheaf of crime scene photographs and leafed through them until he found the one he was looking for. The living room, as seen by SOC when they first arrived, looked much as McLean recalled it himself. He paced around the room until he found the spot where the photographer had stood, lifted up the picture for comparison. It was still a bomb site, but whereas before the furniture had been scattered around more or less at random, now it was arranged in piles, as if someone had been systematically going through the place. Looking for something.

'You use an Airwave set, sergeant?' McLean didn't look directly at Buchanan, instead shuffling through the photographs until he found another interesting one.

'I did. Had it nicked out of a squad car a couple of days back. Thieving bastards. What of it?'

'Aye, I heard that. Unfortunate, but they'll give you another, I guess. Just wondered if there'd be a record of our conversation. You know, when I called you and asked about Magda's number? Why do you suppose they did this?' He turned on the spot to encompass the whole room. Buchanan seemed reluctant to respond to the question. He hadn't moved from the spot near the cracked window since they'd entered the room, as if he was defending it. Now his gaze was firmly on the stack of photographs.

'Nothing? No? Well, here's my theory. I think he was looking for something. Money, probably, or some money equivalent. Could be drugs, but that doesn't seem like Magda's style. She wouldn't tell him where it was, so he threw her around here a bit. She still wouldn't tell him where it was, even after he'd cut her up in the shower.' McLean noticed that Buchanan's eyes shifted to the door that led through to the corridor and bathroom. 'He kept on looking though. Can't have been anything too large. Otherwise why bother cutting these cushions open?' McLean picked one up again, then dropped it back onto the remains of the sofa. 'Something tipped him off though. Either that or he found what he was looking for. He was long gone by the time I got here.'

'It's all very interesting conjecture, sir. But why do we care, exactly? I mean, she's just another whore got herself beaten up as a warning to the others. I tried to explain it to you when you first came into the SCU. We tolerated Malky Jennings because he was a known quantity. We could control him, more or less. Soon as he's gone, someone else decides to make this their turf. Best way to do that's to make an example of one of them. You saw what they did to this one. She'll never work again. The rest of 'em will be handing over their takings like good little girls now.'

McLean shuffled the photographs again until he found the one he wanted. The front door with its boot print. The next picture in the pile showed a detail of the locks. The deadbolt was unlocked, as you'd expect with Magda at home. The snub lock was in place, but there was no sign of it having been forced. Only the security chain was damaged, hanging from the door, its anchor in the frame ripped out. A picture began to form.

'I reckon Magda knew her attacker. She opened the door to him but was wary enough to keep the chain on.' He turned his back on Buchanan, felt a chill run down his exposed neck as he walked slowly to the hallway.

'Didn't do her much good though.' He peered through the spyhole as he spoke, seeing the distorted image of Ritchie on the walkway outside, before turning back again. Buchanan was very close behind him. Too close for comfort, really.

'I don't think you were in Sighthill at all, Sergeant. I think you were here. You do realize that it's the control centre that logs the location of the Airwave sets, not the sets themselves? Conversations too.' McLean opened the door wide, took a step out onto the walkway, then held up the photograph for comparison. The one was suspiciously clean given the grime all around; the other showed a neat boot print. 'What do you reckon, Ritchie? This Buchanan's size?'

Buchanan let out a low snarl and launched himself at

McLean, hands reaching for his throat. McLean lurched backwards, tripping over his own feet in his rush to get away. He was dimly aware of movement further along the walkway as Ritchie started towards them, and then Buchanan screamed as he lost his balance, swept past in a lunge towards the parapet. McLean could see what was going to happen with a horrible certainty. He pushed himself up, grabbing at the detective sergeant's jacket, fingers gripping the fabric of one arm as Buchanan hit the crumbling blockwork, which broke away and disappeared. A split second later the sound of breaking glass and crushed metal underscored Buchanan's scream as he toppled over. McLean thought he had him by the wrist, but Buchanan's hand slipped past his own until he was holding only the sleeve. The weight almost pulled his arm out its socket, and he slammed up against the remaining brickwork with a force that winded him. He could see the mortar failing, harling cracked and bowing as his weight combined with Buchanan's threatened to pull them both over.

'Hold still, dammit.' McLean grunted the words as Buchanan flailed about. They were close to the scaffolding, but just too far to reach the rope that hung from a pulley up above. Each swing bowed the weak wall of bricks a little more, and McLean could feel himself being dragged across the concrete towards the drop. His fingers ached and his arm felt like it was going to pop off at any moment. Then Ritchie was there, kneeling by his side. She grabbed McLean by the waist so he could lean further over the parapet, try to get a hold with his other hand. Buchanan looked down, then raised his head up, staring straight into McLean's eyes.

'Don't you fucking dare let go.'

'Well, stop swinging around like a fucking monkey then, you idiot.' McLean spoke through gritted teeth, barely able to breathe with the effort. Ignoring him, Buchanan made another swing for the rope, his out-stretched fingers just reaching. At the same moment, there was a terrible ripping sound. McLean fell backwards onto the walkway, the sleeve of Buchanan's jacket still in his hand as the weight suddenly disappeared from his arm. Struggling to extract himself from Ritchie's embrace, he could see the rope snaking up to the pulley high overhead. It swung wildly, then started to run through the wheel as a heavy weight pulled it down. It stopped suddenly as a knot jammed in the pulley, then hung straight and taut.

McLean scrabbled to the edge, trying to make sense of what he was seeing. Buchanan had reached the rope, but somehow in his fall it had tangled around his head. He hung there, four storeys up, neck quite clearly snapped, body swaying gently from side to side.

'Oh fuck.' Ritchie crawled to the edge beside him on all fours. Peered down with wide eyes. She shuffled away from the drop and slumped against the doorframe of Magda's flat. McLean leaned back against solid parapet, drinking the air in deep gulps and staring at the sleeve in his hands. He shook his head once, then looked down at the walkway. Lying in the middle, exactly where a man attacking another man might place his foot and slip, lay the crushed remains of a doll, naked and with no arms.

37

It was probably delayed shock. That at least was what he kept on telling himself as he walked slowly around the car park, staring at things but not really seeing them. The place was full of uniforms, scurrying around securing the scene, attaching tape to anything that didn't move, interviewing anything that did. The irony of it all wasn't lost on him: when Malky Jennings had been found dead around the back of the tower block, there'd been a cursory investigation but nothing serious. When Magda had been beaten within an inch of her life, the investigation had been a cock-up from the start. Now that a detective sergeant was dead though, the whole of Lothian and Borders were crawling over the scene.

McLean stopped pacing, vaguely aware that someone had spoken, possibly to him. His feet had brought him back to his Alfa, its windscreen smashed, roof and bonnet dented by falling brickwork. High up above, a team of firemen were working to get DS Buchanan's body down.

'You OK, Inspector?'

The voice finally broke through his musings. McLean looked around to see the SOC officer, Jemima Cairns, standing beside him. He couldn't immediately work out how she had got there.

'Miss Cairns,' he said.

'Well, at least that much is working.' The SOC officer

peered at him in an all too familiar manner. 'You really shouldn't be here. You're in shock.'

'I'm fine. Really.'

'No, actually. You're not. And you're messing up my crime scene. Why don't you go see Wally over at the van. He'll give you a cup of tea.'

Miss Cairns put a hand on his shoulder and steered him away from the cars. There was enough truth in her words for McLean to allow himself to be led. And, besides, it was never wise to turn down a cup of tea. Who knew when the next one would come along?

DS Ritchie was already at the van, cradling a mug between her hands. She always looked pale, her north-eastern complexion never that well attuned to the sun. But now her eyes matched the whiteness of her skin, the freckles across her cheeks dark spots across a bloodless canvas.

'This is so fucked up,' she said as McLean sat down next to her. The SOC officer called Wally handed him a mug of hot tea and he drank, noticed the sweetness and didn't care.

'Ever the master of understatement.'

'I keep seeing it in my head, but it makes no sense. How did it . . . ? How did he . . . ?'

McLean saw an image in his mind. DS Buchanan staring up at him with more anger in his eyes than fear.

'You saw what happened, right?'

'I saw something happen. Not quite sure what. You came out of the doorway, said something I couldn't hear. Next thing there was a shout and Buchanan came charging out through the door. He didn't even scream. Just went over and –'

335

'He was trying to get to the rope, stupid bugger. If he'd stayed still I could have got a better grip on his arm instead of . . .' McLean shuddered, suppressed the urge to look up and see if the body was still there. For some reason he couldn't immediately process, it wasn't a simple case of putting up a ladder and bringing Pete Buchanan down.

'But he was shouting – no, screaming – at you when he came out. Looked like he was going to throttle you.'

'Actually I think he wanted to push me over the edge.'

'Christ. Why?'

'I'm hoping Magda Evans might be able to shed some light on that, just as soon as she can talk.' McLean took a sip of his tea. It really was disgustingly sweet. 'I'm fairly sure it was Buchanan who beat her up. I'm just not sure why.'

'Oh God. Here we go.'

McLean looked at Ritchie. She had been staring into her mug, but something had attracted her attention. He followed her gaze past the SOC van towards the road. A shiny silver Range Rover had pulled up and was even now disgorging Detective Chief Inspector John Brooks. A second figure climbed out behind him. McLean expected little DI Spence, but instead the balding ginger and grey head of Acting Superintendent Duguid emerged. Just what he needed.

'You reckon Wally'll let us hide in the SOC van?' But it was too late. Duguid had scanned the scene and spotted them.

'What the fuck's going on, McLean? A man's dead and you're sitting around drinking tea?' Ever the master of observation. DS Ritchie struggled to stand as Duguid marched up to them. McLean put a hand on her arm to stop her.

'It was an accident, sir. DS Buchanan came out of one of the fourth floor flats at speed, tripped on something lying in the walkway and went through the parapet. Bloody thing should have been repaired by now. That's why the scaffold's there. And the rope.' He looked up now, as did Duguid. The view was partially obscured by a high access platform that had backed into the car park, blocking everything else in. You could still see the body hanging there though.

'Dammit, man, what were you even doing here?'

'Would you believe conducting my investigation?'

'Don't get smart with me, McLean.'

'Sorry, sir, but I just saw a man die and I couldn't do anything to save him. You'll understand if I'm not at my best right now.'

Duguid looked around for something to sit on before leaning against the bonnet of the nearest car. He ran a hand through the remnants of his hair. 'OK. From the beginning. Tell me what happened.'

McLean ran through the events yet again. DCI Brooks ambled up halfway through, so he had to go over it once more. Beside him, Ritchie said nothing, which suited him fine. Had he been the officer investigating this incident, the first thing he would have done would be to separate all the witnesses and get separate statements from them before they had time to corroborate their stories. It didn't really surprise him that Dagwood missed this crucial step, but he expected more of Brooks.

'There'll have to be an internal investigation,' Duguid

said finally. 'I've already put in a call to Rab Callard over in Professional Standards.' He turned to Brooks. 'John, you can take over here.'

'I need to speak to Magda Evans, find out what Buchanan was doing here in the first place.' McLean struggled to his feet, looking for somewhere to put his mug.

'No. You don't.' Duguid's detective brain finally chuntered into life. 'You need to give a statement to DCI Brooks and then you need to go home. You too, Ritchie.'

'I can't go home. I've got to –'

'Perhaps I'm not making myself clear, McLean. Give a statement to Brooks, and then go home. That's an order. I'll see you in the morning.'

Duguid stalked off in the direction of the Range Rover. McLean watched him go, considered finishing his horribly sweet tea. Then a commotion from over by the scaffolding stopped everyone in their tracks.

'Fuck! Catch it!' A whirring sound of rope spinning through a pulley wheel. McLean watched in horrified fascination as Buchanan's body plunged downwards, picking up speed before it smashed into the roof of his bright-red Alfa.

38

A squad car dropped him off at the end of his drive, then disappeared into the late-afternoon city without a word. McLean had tried to get an idea of the damage done to his Alfa, but the area had been swarming with SOC officers and firemen. It was going to be put on a flatbed and taken back to the forensic labs for tests. He just hoped it would be repairable once he finally got it back.

Jenny Nairn looked up from the kitchen table as he walked in through the back door. 'You're home early. Something come up?'

'You could say that.' McLean went to the Aga, put the kettle on. He needed a proper cup of tea to take away the sweet sugar taste lingering from the last one. The shock had worn off now, replaced with a growing anger and frustration. And a right bastard of a headache.

'Want to talk about it?' Jenny had been reading from an old textbook, taking notes in tiny handwriting on an A4 pad. She closed the book from the back, put the pad on top of it, obscuring the cover.

'One of my colleagues died this afternoon. A detective sergeant. He fell off a walkway four storeys up. Hanged himself by accident.'

'Oh my god. Were you there?'

McLean ignored the question. He didn't want to talk about it at all. 'Emma about?'

'Last time I looked she was in the attic. Seems to like it up there. You were there, weren't you. That's why you're home early.'

McLean took the boiling kettle off the hotplate, poured water over the tea bag he'd dropped into a mug. Nodded at Jenny. 'You want one?'

'No, I'm good. And you're avoiding the question.'

'I don't really like talking about work. There's a lot of it I can't talk about, so it's easier not to start, OK?'

'OK. But if you want to talk, I'm a good listener. Just saying.'

'I'll bear it in mind.' McLean hoiked out the tea bag and threw it into the sink, fetched milk from the fridge. 'You know, you can have the evening off if you want. I'm not going anywhere. It'd be nice to spend some time with Emma for a change.'

Jenny paused to consider the offer for all of five seconds before answering. 'Sure. Thanks. I'll do that.'

The stairs creaked under his feet as he climbed up into the eaves, mug of tea held in a steady hand. Under the late-afternoon sun, it was pleasantly warm up here, and still, like being wrapped in a comfort blanket. It was quiet, too, somehow cut off from the endless thrum of the city. As he stepped into the attic, McLean noticed the door to the wardrobe was open and most of the dust sheets had been taken off the larger items of furniture. Emma was lying on the old sofa, bathed in soft sunlight shining through one of the skylights. Fast asleep, she looked like something from a fairy tale, the princess waiting for a brave prince to come and kiss her awake. A book lay open across her chest; he didn't have to see up close to know which one it was. The Conan Doyle copy of Gray's *Anatomy*, formerly belonging to the late Donald Anderson.

Movement out of the corner of his eye. McLean almost jumped, turned too rapidly, stumbling into an old carved hat stand by the door. Hot tea spilled over his hand, and he put the mug down carefully on a nearby trunk, dabbed away the damp with a handkerchief. Mrs McCutcheon's cat eyed him from the shadows, testing the air as if sight alone wasn't enough to convince it of his intentions.

'One of these days, cat, I'm going to get tired of you doing that and throw you out the nearest window.' He didn't really mean it, but felt the need to say something. Mrs McCutcheon's cat stalked past him, casually brushing its tail against his leg on its way to the sofa, where it leapt up and curled itself into a comfortable ball on the arm at Emma's feet. She didn't stir all the while, but as the sun played with the motes of dust in the air above her, McLean fancied he could see shapes forming, people almost. He shook his head and they disappeared, fog in his head from turning too quickly.

And then Emma began to speak.

She hadn't opened her eyes, and her lips barely moved. At first he couldn't even make out the words. Thinking she was waking up, he crossed the attic room to her side, but as he came close, he realized she was still fast asleep. Eyes flickered under closed lids, and her hands twitched, one laid across the book, the other trailing to the floor.

'No, no, no, no, no.' The voice didn't sound remotely like Emma's; more that of a man. McLean reached towards her, meaning to wake her up, but something stopped him. His arm froze as if a thousand tiny invisible hands held him back. Letting out a quiet hiss that was all the more menacing for its lack of volume, Mrs McCutcheon's cat stared him down. Its eyes almost challenged him to try and interfere with whatever was going on.

'Don't touch me. I don't like to be touched.' This voice was plainly that of a woman, but the accent was rich, plummy, English. Not Emma's gentle Aberdeen brogue.

'Please, I can't find her. Has anyone seen her? She was just here.' A child's voice, thick with anxiety. Emma's twitching was more pronounced now, almost a fit, and still the cat sat quietly, as if this were something that happened every day. McLean knelt down beside her, but still seemed unable to reach out and touch.

'You have to help her, Tony. Bring her back and let us go.' This voice shocked him to the core. It was a voice he knew as well as his own; a voice he'd not heard in over a decade. The voice of a young woman dead before her time.

'Kirsty?'

At the word, Emma went stiff, knocking the book to the floor. Mrs McCutcheon's cat rose up on its legs, fur prickling as if someone had passed a thousand volts through it. McLean could only watch as Emma arched her back, her head twisted further than it should surely go. He struggled to reach her, putting all his force into moving his arm.

'You cannot save her. I have her soul. She is mine.' This voice was old, deep. It wired itself straight into the fear centres in McLean's brain. The cat screeched now, wide mouth showing sharp white needle teeth. It looked for all the world like it was going to leap, attack Emma, scratch out her eyes, and as his focus shifted from her to it, so he felt his limbs lighten. The pent-up energy he hadn't realized he was exerting released and he sprung forward at the same instant as the cat, catching it in mid-air. Then gravity took over and the two of them fell on top of Emma in a tangle of arms and teeth and claws.

'Oww. What are you doing?'

Emma struggled up from under McLean, awake now and speaking in her own voice. Mrs McCutcheon's cat shot from his grasp like a bar of wet soap in the shower, disappearing into the shadows so quickly it bounced off the trunk, sending the mug of tea toppling. The crash of shattering china broke whatever spell had fallen, bringing with it the muted roar of the city back into the room. He pushed himself away, sitting down on the floor as Emma shuffled herself upright and yawned.

'What was all that about?'

McLean looked up at her, hair tousled from sleep. For the briefest of moments she was the Emma he remembered, and then the little-girl-lost expression settled back down over her face like a veil.

'You were talking in your sleep.'

'Was I? Oh. There were people all around me. So many people all trying to get my attention.' She scanned the room, craning her neck to see behind her as if looking for them. 'I can't see them.'

'It was just a dream. You're awake now. It'll be fine. You'll be OK.' McLean reached out and took Emma's hand, patted it like he would a child's. That, increasingly, was what he seemed to be dealing with.

*

Jenny Nairn was stuffing her book and writing pad into an old leather satchel when McLean entered the kitchen ten minutes later, cradling the shards of broken mug in one hand. She almost jumped when she saw him, but covered her surprise well.

'I was just getting ready to go out.' A frown crossed her face. 'You're still OK with me having the evening off, aren't you.'

'Yes, that's fine.' McLean dropped the broken pottery into the bin, then pulled out a chair, dropped into it.

'That's good. I've booked a taxi. Wouldn't want to have to cancel.'

'No, you're fine. Could do with another cup of tea though. Bloody cat knocked that one over.'

Jenny gave him a wry grin as she put the kettle on the Aga. 'I'm a carer, you know. Not a domestic.'

McLean struggled to his feet, heading for the cupboard where the mugs lived. 'You're right, sorry. I can get my own tea.'

'Sit down. I'm only joking.'

He did as he was told, grateful for the small rest. Already the incident up in the attic was fading away. True, it had been unsettling, but he'd just imagined those voices, surely. And Emma had always talked in her sleep. At least, he thought she had.

'I really should spend more time with Em. Sometimes it feels like I'm never here.'

'You finally noticed.'

'You could say that. More someone just shoved it in my face today.' He rubbed at eyes sore and tired. 'Times like this I feel like I could sleep for a week, wake up and it's all gone away.'

'Only problem is it never does. Go away that is.'

'How does someone so young get to be so wise?'

'Who says I'm young?' Jenny poured boiling water from the kettle into the waiting tea pot, set it down on the kitchen table. 'But I'll take the compliment in the spirit it was intended.'

McLean watched as she fetched mugs and milk, wondered whether he'd be chancing his arm asking her to get out the biscuits while she was at it. After Emma's strange turn in the attic he felt completely drained; the final straw in a monumentally shitty day.

'Don't forget Em's got an appointment with Eleanor tomorrow morning.' Jenny poured tea into his mug as if she'd known him all her life. McLean found it hard to care about the curious old tradition his grandmother had insisted on, that you couldn't pour tea in someone's house unless you'd known them at least seven years. He just wanted his drink, wasn't really fussed how he got it. He'd have liked a biscuit too, but right now moving was too much effort. When had he got so tired?

'I don't suppose there's any way you could take her for me?'

Jenny leaned her back against the Aga, her own mug of tea clasped in her pale, skinny hands. The smile was gone. 'You think that's a good idea?'

He shook his head. 'Probably not. I just really don't fancy sitting in on another session. The last one didn't go so well.'

'Only because you forgot to turn your phone off. Look, Tony. Emma needs you in there with her.'

'Does she really? Half the time I just fall asleep. I feel like I'm getting in the way.'

'You're not. Trust me on that.' Jenny fell silent a moment, as if in deep thought, then added: 'Why did you do it? Take her in?'

McLean slumped in his chair. He didn't have the energy for this. Jenny just stared at him, her silence demanding the question be answered.

'We had something. Before . . . Well, before. She's got no one else.'

Still the silent stare.

'And yes, dammit. I feel like it's my fault she's the way she is. I need to do everything I can to try and put it right.'

'Now we're getting somewhere. So doing everything means throwing your money at the problem. 'Cause that's what it sounds like when you pay me to take your girl-friend to her therapy sessions.'

'I . . .' McLean started to speak, realized his mouth was open, closed it with an audible click. It was never easy to admit when someone else was right and he was wrong. Jenny's words had raised questions he'd been avoiding for months now; ever since he'd found Emma unconscious, shackled to that dirty bed in Needy's underground chapel. Yes, they'd had a relationship then, Emma and him, but it had only been for a few months. More off than on, if he was being honest. And yet as soon as she'd been taken from him he'd felt like his world had collapsed. Was that because he loved her? Or because of what had happened before, with Kirsty? Christ, it was no surprise he'd lived alone for so long. Life was much easier that way.

The crunching of gravel under tyres outside broke through the whirl of thoughts, any that might have stuck around chased off by a car horn destroying the quiet.

'That'll be my taxi.' Jenny pushed herself away from the Aga, put her mug down and grabbed her bags. 'Think about it, Tony. You feel responsibility for Emma? Go talk to her. Spend some time with her. Help her yourself, don't pay others to do it for you.'

And without another word, she was gone.

39

I walk the drab city streets, scenting the air like a predator. It is not meat I hunt, but the much sweeter taste of hopelessness and despair. There is so much, each person wrapped in their own little aura of gloom. Sometimes it is hard to know where to start, but tonight my trail is clear. The sickly smell of a soul in turmoil guides me to my prey.

On the outside she is carefree, confident, happy even. But the spirit can see through to her core. The spirit knows the secrets of her heart. The failure, the fear, the darkness that has dogged her all her days. The spirit sees her true nature, and through it I know her too.

The world is so much brighter when the spirit enters me. People glow with an inner fire, and everything is pin sharp. I know no doubt when he is with me; anything is possible. I work my way through the crowd, chatting occasionally, charming people, laughing. It's so easy.

'You come here often?' Sure, it's corny. A cliché even. But that's why it works. She looks up, gives me a weary little smile. Contact.

The bar is dark, intimate. Not so noisy that you can't talk, but not so quiet that you can be easily overheard. I buy wine, and she comes with me to my favourite little alcove. I knew she would, even without the spirit guiding me. She is hungry for the happiness of others, clings to it in weary desperation.

She comes here every week, regular as clockwork. I know this because she tells me so, in her soft, bubbly voice. But I also know it because I've watched her for months now, sensing the misery in her, waiting for the spirit to come to me. Waiting for it to confirm what I'd already suspected. We talk of inconsequential things, for that is all she has. Her life has no meaning, and deep inside she knows it. She drinks the wine I have bought her, seeking courage there to admit to the failures that have dogged her. I wait patiently, the spirit coiling behind my eyes. The moment will come. Soon.

She reaches for her glass, then pauses, leans forward. Her hand slips uncertainly across the narrow table, gently brushing my own. At that touch, the spirit surges within me. I have been looking down, demure, but now I catch her gaze, hold it with my own. Her pupils dilate, a shock of electricity between us as I grasp her hand firmly in mine. Then the spirit leaps from me, fills her with its promise. She does not resist, knows that this is the fate she has been seeking. I feel a thrill of anticipation shiver through me.

'You are mine!'

40

McLean watched from the leathery comfort of the sofa as Doctor Austin conducted yet another hypnotherapy session with Emma. Once more, Dave had brought him a cup of rich, black coffee, but rather than savouring it, this time he'd downed it in one. The taste still lingered in his mouth and the caffeine was keeping him at least partly awake.

'Breathe in. Hold. And out. In. Hold. And out.' The Doctor's voice rose on each 'in', kept the same tone for the hold, then dropped with the 'out', rising and falling like waves. It was all but impossible not to get sucked in to the same breathing pattern, but he did his best.

Across the room, Emma sat ramrod straight in her high-backed armchair. She was so thin, she almost disappeared into the dark depths, her pale face framed by her black hair. It had grown since she had woken from her coma, and she'd shown no great desire to get it cut. Now it hung below her shoulders in sharp contrast to the short, spiky chaos she'd worn when first they had met.

'Now, we're going back in time. Just like we did before. Breathe in. Hold. And out.'

Something had changed in the room. McLean couldn't exactly put his finger on it. The air wasn't noticeably colder, but he had a feeling that it should be. He looked across to the door through to the reception room and

Dave. It hadn't opened, and neither had the window. Yet there was a different quality to the air, as if it had been disturbed. As if something invisible had moved through the room.

'You're at college in Aberdeen. It's your first term and you're meeting new friends. Breathe in. Hold. And out.'

New friends. McLean found himself back in Freshers' Week, Edinburgh University in the early nineties. He'd made some good friends then, ended up quite by chance sharing digs with a young Phil Jenkins. He probably ought to give Phil a another call some time. Better yet, he could take some time off, fly over and visit. It was many years since he'd last been to the States. Actually, it was many years since he'd last been anywhere overseas. That trip to Iceland where he'd finally summoned up the courage to ask Kirsty if she'd marry him. He'd met her at university, too.

'Good. You're doing very well, Emma. I think it's time we went back a bit further. To your school days. Sixth form. Breathe in. Hold. And out.'

Sixth form in that dismal English public school his grandmother had insisted on sending him to. He could still hear her voice. 'It was good enough for your grandfather and your father. It'll be the making of you.' Aye, right. And the breaking.

Sixth form at least meant the end of ten years of boarding education. Ten years of being sent away from home to sleep in draughty dormitories, endure the cruel taunting of older boys and the bewildering unpredictability of the teachers. One moment they were all praise, the next screaming at you for some wrongdoing only they could

351

see. Ten years in which he'd learnt to think on his feet, to react rather than plan. Ten years of gut-wrenching home-sickness and, yes, the occasional moments of wonder, excitement and joy. By the time he made it to his A levels, McLean had more or less got the hang of private educa-tion, but he'd also lost touch with all his Edinburgh friends. Not that there'd been many to start with.

'Back further. To your childhood.'

Is the voice different? He can't tell. It's not important. All he knows is that there is a dark place he doesn't want to go to. But the voice is insistent. He must tread that unused road, back and back and back to the frightened, angry, confused little boy. He is holding on to a hand, star-ing at the fog as it eddies and swirls in the car headlights. He is holding on to a hand as he stands at the front of a large hall, staring at a pair of pale wooden boxes, raised up on a dais. He is dimly aware they are in those boxes, his mother and father. Sleeping now. But soon the curtains will part and the flames will devour them. He doesn't want to see that. Doesn't want to hear the screams as the plane hurtles out of control towards the towering rock slab of the mountain. He doesn't want to, but the voice is impos-sible to resist.

'Well, someone's benefiting from these sessions, that's for sure.'

McLean snapped out of his dream with a start that sent his coffee cup tumbling to the thick carpet floor. Luckily for him and carpet both, it was empty.

'Sorry about that.' He stretched, covered his mouth with the back of his hand to hide a yawn. Looking up from the sofa, he saw Emma and Doctor Austin staring down at him, the one with an expression of concern writ large across her thin face, the other seeming rather amused by it all. How long had he been asleep, dreaming of the past?

'How did you get on?' he asked.

'I remembered stuff,' Emma said. 'From school and university. I knew it anyway, but this was like learning how I knew it, if that makes sense?'

'Emma's doing very well, Tony. I think with time we'll get maybe ninety per cent of her memories back.'

'Umm. Great.' He pulled himself up out of the sofa, back creaking in protest, then bent to pick up the coffee cup to more pops and snaps. Doctor Austin took it from him and handed it to Emma.

'Could you take that through to Dave, please. Thanks.' She waited until the door was closed before speaking again.

'I know about Emma's nocturnal visits, Inspector. I can't imagine that's easy to deal with.'

McLean wondered who had told her; Emma herself or Jenny Nairn? It didn't really make much difference. 'An unbroken night's sleep would be nice. Still, there's always your sofa.'

Doctor Austin smiled. 'The night terrors driving her to your bed are all part of her psychosis. She's hiding from the bad memories, and in so doing has repressed everything. But it's still all there, pretty much, and as she drifts off to sleep, it starts to come back. That can be quite overwhelming for someone who basically thinks they're about eight.'

'But you think you can cure her.' McLean tried to keep the pleading out of his voice.

'Emma's not as receptive to hypnosis as most.' Doctor

353

Austin nodded her head very gently in his direction to indicate exactly who she included in that catch-all. 'I get people like her now and then. It's just a matter of taking the time needed, and we're making progress.' She paused a moment. 'Yes, I think I can cure her. But I must warn you, it will be traumatic. A terrible thing was done to her. It's hardly surprising she's suppressed it so completely. But we need to dig it out and expose it to the light before she can start to rebuild her life.'

'It would be fair to say you and Detective Sergeant Buchanan didn't see eye to eye.'

Really not much later, the taste of Dave's coffee still lingering, McLean sat on the wrong side of the table in interview room three, trying not to feel like a criminal. Across from him, Chief Inspector Callard of Professional Standards was doing a poor job of concealing his contempt. The interview was informal, for now at least. But that didn't mean there wasn't going to be a full investigation.

'I found him obstructive, and I didn't like his methods. I've no idea why he didn't like me, but he hardly tried to hide it.'

'What were you doing at the flat?' Callard had a copy of the initial incident report in a folder in front of him, but had made no effort to look at it since McLean had given it to him.

'You know about Magda Evans being violently attacked?' McLean read Callard's expression to mean he did. 'Well, I was working on the theory it was a warning to the other prostitutes working that area. Probably someone stamping their authority on the place after Malky Jennings was killed.'

'And you went back to her flat to find out what, exactly?'

'Something didn't add up.'

'What do you mean?' Callard's scowl was a permanent feature, but its current severity suggested he had no time for excuses.

'They only did a basic forensic sweep on the crime scene. Photos, prints, that sort of stuff. It should have been sealed up after that, but somehow the message didn't get through. When I went back, the flat was wide open. Anyone could have walked in; probably every Ned in the scheme had done by then. Any forensic evidence we find in there's worth shit. At first I thought it was just a cock-up. Our fault or SEB's, doesn't really matter. It happens from time to time. But I had a set of crime scene photographs printed up anyway. Went around there to see how the flat looked in comparison to how it was originally. Someone searched the place, then trashed it to cover their tracks. I'm guessing they knew Magda had something, money probably, and beat her up when she wouldn't say where it was.'

'Interesting theory. I'm guessing you have an idea who did it, too.' Callard didn't try to hide the disapproval in his voice. McLean had been in this situation too many times now to rise to the bait.

'I'm not prepared to speculate any more, sir.'

'You think it was Buchanan though, don't you.'

'As I said. I'm not prepared to speculate, sir.'

'For Christ's sake, McLean. He's dead. He fell off a

fucking tower block. Snapped his neck. How do I know you didn't push him off?'

McLean leaned forward, rested his arms on the table. Of course it had to happen. The canteen rumours were already swirling. Nothing loved gossip quite like a policeman, and this was Grade A material.

'Isn't it fortunate that there was a witness to the events then, sir.'

Callard let out an exasperated sigh. 'I know you didn't kill him, McLean. You're many things, but a murderer doesn't fit the profile. Professional pain in the arse, yes, troublemaker, yes.'

'If you know I didn't kill DS Buchanan, then why am I under investigation?'

'Because of a little thing called procedure. You remember procedure, don't you? They taught you about it when you joined the force, yes? An officer is dead. You were present when it happened and until my investigation into exactly how it happened and why is completed you will be restricted to an administrative role. Can't risk some shite of a lawyer using your conduct as an excuse to get some scumbag off the hook. Capische?'

'What about DS Ritchie, is she on paperwork only as well?'

'For the time being, yes. So you can imagine just how happy Charles Duguid is right now.' For some reason this brought the slightest edge of a smile to Callard's face. It made him look like a snake with a mouthful of gerbil. He picked up the report and opened it for the first time. 'You'd do well to avoid him if you can.'

*

'McLean. My office. Now.'

He had to have been waiting outside. Hidden just around the corner and listening for any clues, perhaps. There was no other way that Acting Superintendent Duguid could have been in that part of the station at exactly that time. McLean considered pretending he hadn't heard, but the problem with ignoring Dagwood was that it just made him worse.

'Was there anything specific you wanted, sir?' He decided on the annoyingly helpful approach instead. Duguid eyed him suspiciously, then looked around to see who might be listening in.

'Not here. My office.'

It wasn't far, but neither was it so near Duguid might have been just passing. Neither of them said anything until they had reached their destination, Duguid paying particular attention to ensuring the door was closed.

'You're a menace, you know that, McLean?'

'I'm sorry, sir?'

'What part of "go over to the SCU and help out" do you not understand?'

McLean stared at Duguid, looking for any hint that the acting superintendent was joking. If there was one, he couldn't see it.

'Don't pretend you didn't expect me to shake things up there, sir. I'm not stupid. I know exactly why you sent me to SCU and not one of the detective sergeants like Jo asked.'

It stung to admit it, that he was so predictable even Duguid could use him. But that was what the acting superintendent had done when he'd lobbed him at Jo Dexter's

357

team. Rolled a grenade through the open door. Now the man was surprised when it had all blown up in his face. And yet here was Duguid, staring him down with those piggy little eyes as if he really didn't have a clue what McLean was talking about.

'I just don't know why McIntyre put up with you. You're supposed to be helping Jo Dexter's team, not killing them off one by one.'

OK. Count to ten. Silently. Also make sure hands are in pockets so he can't see you clenching them into fists. Ah, fuck it.

'I'm not putting up with shit like that. You so much as suggest anything as ridiculous outside this room I won't think twice about taking it up with the Chief Constable.'

'Don't be so bloody melodramatic, man. It's just a fucking joke.'

'To you, maybe. To me it's an accusation and since we're being blunt it's also fucking unfair. I tried to save Pete Buchanan's life, nearly went over that parapet myself. I'm not naive, I know the lower ranks and uniform are going to gossip and make jokes, sir. I just don't expect it from my seniors.'

'Alison Kydd. John Needham. Now Pete Buchanan.' Duguid counted the names off on his long fingers, bending them over backwards as he did so.

'What of them?' McLean knew what Duguid was doing, but he stood his ground, close to the acting superintendent's desk. For a moment he even considered sitting on the edge of it.

'They're all dead, McLean. All under your command. All in less than two years.'

'What the fuck? Under my command? Remind me again why they put you in charge here?'

Duguid's face reddened. 'Don't you dare take that tone –'

'I'll take whatever tone I bloody well please. I've had it up to here with the lot of you. Stupid gossip and nasty pranks I can take. I've done my best to ignore it because that's the only way it'll ever stop. But you start suggesting I'm some kind of pariah. Some bad luck omen or something. I –'

'I don't need to suggest it, McLean. It's out there already.' Duguid had been standing on his side of the desk, but now he slumped down into his chair. 'Look. Sit down, OK?'

McLean did as he was told, not taking his eyes off Duguid all the while. The acting superintendent looked like he was fighting a losing battle with his temper, but it was a revelation to see him even trying.

'It's the word in the canteen.' Duguid ran a hand through the remains of his hair. 'What do the Americans call it? Scuttlebutt? It's not gossip, really. More a reputation thing. There's constables asking to be taken off plain clothes just so they don't have to work with you.'

'Not much chance of that, the way you keep shifting me from team to team.'

'Well, that'll be one less thing to worry about then. You're off the SCU. Callard insisted, but I was going to do it anyway. Squared it with Jo Dexter. She's having DS Carter to pick up where Buchanan left off.'

God help her. 'What about the Magda Evans case? Is that SCU because she used to be a prostitute, or us because it was attempted murder?'

359

Duguid gave him an odd look. 'You mean the case that took you and Buchanan to the tower block where he was killed? You think Professional Standards are going to let you go anywhere near it now?'

Of course not. It was a miracle they were letting him carry on working at all.

'No, you can wrap up those three suicides. Collate the forensic and pathology reports. Write them up, close the cases. If you're very lucky I might let you investigate burglaries after that.'

'On my own? Or am I allowed a couple of detectives to help?'

Duguid glowered like a weary schoolmaster, worn down by the bright kid. 'Oh for fuck's sake. You can have anyone who'll work with you. Grumpy Bob, Ritchie, even MacBride. I don't think you'll find many others.'

'Thank you, sir.' McLean stood up, turned to leave. He was almost at the door before he thought to mention something about the malicious rumours, but Duguid spoke first.

'Why are you still here, McLean?'

'I was just leaving.'

'Not here, you idiot. Here. In this job. Why don't you just jack it in? You've got money.'

McLean turned slowly, giving himself time to think. 'I've seen that new Range Rover you've got. Hear your uncle's apartments on the Royal Mile went for a tidy sum, sir. And yet here you are. Still.'

'That's not the same. And my personal financial arrangements are hardly any of your business.'

'If you can't see the irony in that statement, sir, then nothing I say will make any difference, will it?'

McLean didn't wait for an answer. He strode out of Duguid's office, leaving the door open as it had always been in Jayne McIntyre's day, putting as much distance as he could between himself and the acting superintendent before he said anything else he might come to regret.

And yet the question kept coming back: why did he stay? He didn't have to work at all, let alone at this thankless job. He knew the answer, of course. Part of it was he couldn't think of anything else to do. Part was because of Kirsty and the things that had been done to her. He knew he could never catch all the bad guys, but that wasn't going to stop him from trying.

There was another reason why he stayed, though. One which made even less sense than the other two, and yet was so deeply ingrained with his character that he knew he'd never overcome it. That magnificent language, Scots, had a word for it: thrawn. It went beyond the pride that would cut off its nose to spite its face, it was more visceral than that. They wanted him to leave, expected him to quit, and that simple fact was all it took to ensure that he never would.

41

McLean sat in his tiny office, staring at the mountains and foothills of paperwork strewn around. A lot of it was rubbish, he knew that. There were case files in the lower strata that had been left behind by the previous unfortunate occupier of the room, and doubtless many folders that had ended up in here simply because someone hadn't known where they were supposed to be. On the plus side, if he wasn't allowed out into the field then he might at least make a start on clearing the place. Knowing his luck it would take Callard weeks to ferret out what had happened and why, so he'd have plenty of time. Then there was the small matter of preparing a list of his casework for Dagwood to reassign, and the suicide cases to wrap up. Might as well get the overtime sheets squared away as well.

The knock at the open door was DS Ritchie. She still looked pale, as if Buchanan's death haunted her dreams. McLean could hardly blame her; the image of him hanging there, arms limp by his side, one sleeve missing from his jacket was never far from his mind. Like some terrible scarecrow hung to ward off whatever mythical beast fed on the hopes of the dispossessed living in those soulless tower blocks. The noise of the rope whirring through the pulley wheel came unbidden to him too. And the horrible twang as the knot stopped it fast.

'Callard done interviewing you then, sir?'

'For now, aye. Get the impression he's going to drag this out as long as he can, though.'

'Maybe not. Word is the Chief Constable wants it played down as much as possible. Doesn't want anything rocking the boat before the switch-over.'

It made sense. The last thing Lothian and Borders needed was an investigation opening up a nasty can of worms just as the new Police Scotland came into being. Hard enough keeping track of who was supposed to be doing what anyway, without giving Strathclyde another excuse to muscle in on their territory. It wouldn't surprise McLean at all that headquarters were pushing for the whole thing to be wrapped up quickly. A tragic accident, dreadful really. Counselling for all who were involved and the whole episode tidied away. The only problem was Chief Inspector Rab Callard. Professional Standards didn't respond well to being told how to conduct their business.

'They tell you when you'll be allowed back?' he asked her.

'Depends on Callard.' Ritchie grimaced. 'Nothing but paperwork for me. I'd almost rather be down in the basement filing evidence.'

'You don't really mean that, though if you're looking for something to do it might be worth your while asking around about Buchanan. There's a reason he never made it past sergeant. I wouldn't mind knowing what it is before the top brass comes after us.'

'Isn't that a bit . . . I don't know. Callous?' Ritchie asked. 'Won't everyone think I'm just trying to cover my arse. Our arses both?'

'Probably. But a trained detective of your skill ought to be able to ferret out information without too many people realizing what you're doing.' McLean gave her a cheeky grin. He picked up the first folder that came to hand, glanced at the title without really taking it in, dropped it back onto his desk. 'Bollocks. It'll all still be here in an hour. Fancy a coffee?'

The canteen had always seemed something of a last-minute addition to the station. Stuck between the locker rooms and the stores, its windows looked out on a narrow alley and the stone wall of the neighbouring building. It was a gloomy place even on a bright day, but it was always busy. The coffee wasn't bad either, if you liked it weak and soapy.

Shift change meant the place was buzzing when McLean and Ritchie pushed through the double doors, the sound of a dozen or more conversations filling the room. An institutional cooking smell pervaded, which was at least preferable to the more usual odour of unwashed beat constable. As they walked across the room towards the serving hatch, the noise dulled down almost to silence, and McLean could feel the heat of eyes on his back. Beside him, he felt Ritchie tense.

'Ignore them,' he said, just loud enough that the silent policemen nearest could hear. At the counter he ordered two coffees and added a couple of chocolate brownies, since they looked so appetizing. When he and Ritchie turned back, looking for somewhere to sit, every officer in the room was staring at them.

'Very mature. I expect there'll be rude pictures pinned

up inside my locker next.' McLean scanned the room. In amongst a sea of uniforms, over by the window there were a couple of empty chairs at a table otherwise occupied by detectives. DI Spence and DCI Brooks, to be precise. Perhaps not who he would have chosen to sit with, but of Grumpy Bob and DC MacBride there was no sign.

'Mind if we join you?' He voiced it as a question, but was already pushing the seat with his foot, making room for Ritchie. DI Spence gave a little shrug as if he couldn't care less. DCI Brooks was less welcoming.

'You've a nerve coming in here, McLean.'

McLean stared at the fat man, took a bite of his chocolate brownie and washed it down with a swig of coffee. Disgusting, both of them, but he wasn't going to let that spoil the moment.

'I never realized it was the wild west, sir. If I had, I'd have asked DS Ritchie to bring her bow and arrows. Young MacBride does line dancing, I'm told. He could probably lay his hands on some cowboy boots and a Stetson.'

'Don't get cocky with me. A man's dead. Hardly the time to be making jokes.'

McLean studied Brooks. Like many obese men it was hard to gauge his age accurately. The excess fat in his diet kept his skin smooth, and he shaved his head, making it difficult to judge by hair colour. He was chummy with Dagwood, but happy enough to take the piss out of the acting superintendent behind his back, which suggested to McLean that he was younger. That didn't mean he hadn't been another one of Buchanan's friends in high places.

'A man's dead. Yes, sir. I did know. I was there when it happened. I tried to save him.'

Brooks let out a little snort of disbelief. 'Save him? Don't make me laugh. Everyone knows you hated Pete Buchanan, wanted him off the force.'

'Everyone, it would seem.' McLean paused, scanned the room and its gaggle of expectant faces. Like the audience at a particularly cruel comedy act. One where the so-called comedian got his laughs from tearing one of the crowd to pieces in the name of fun. 'Except me.'

Brooks narrowed his eyes, which in a thinner man might have made him look scornful, but in his case made him look constipated.

'Don't play the innocent, McLean. Everyone knows you were boning that prostitute and Pete was going to bring it up with Professional Standards.'

Fortunately for McLean, he'd finished eating his piece of chocolate brownie. Less fortunate for DI Spence, Ritchie hadn't. Had in fact just taken a mouthful along with a swig of coffee, which she duly spat out all over him.

'Oh god. I'm sorry, sir.' She patted ineffectively at the mess with a paper napkin until Spence pushed her away.

'Christ, woman. What's wrong with you?'

Ritchie couldn't answer for a while, struggling to breathe after choking on brownie. 'I'm sorry, sir. But really? To . . . DI McLean? A prostitute?'

'You deny it, then?'

'I'm not sure I'd dignify it with a response at all,' McLean said. 'But I'm intrigued as to where such a ridiculous accusation could have come from. I don't suppose you'd be prepared to tell me who told you?'

Brooks stared at McLean with a look of utter disbelief,

whether at the denial or the request, he couldn't be sure. Fair enough; he'd not readily give up his sources either.

'No. Forget it. I can guess who easily enough, and he's not around to defend himself.' McLean pushed his chair back and stood up. Nodded to Ritchie. 'Come on. There's work to do.'

Ritchie grabbed her mug and plate, scrambling to her feet. 'There is?'

'Aye, there is. And given the way everyone thinks of me at the moment, I'm going to need your help with it.'

It was late when he finally made it home. Jenny Nairn was slumped at the kitchen table, her head resting on a textbook. She stirred as he very gently put down the bag with his take-away supper in it. Looked up at him with bleary eyes.

'You should try that in bed. I'm told it's more comfortable.'

Jenny yawned, stretched and rubbed at her eyes. Considered her textbook and notes, then closed everything up. 'Sorry. I guess Cognitive Behavioural Therapy's not as interesting as I thought it was. Long day?'

'That's one way of putting it. How's Em?'

'Asleep, I think. She went up about ten. Her own bed. Can't promise she won't climb into yours again later though.'

McLean said nothing. It had been a long time since he'd managed a full night's unbroken sleep. Emma's nocturnal visits were regular as clockwork now, every morning at three. And her sleep-talking was getting worse, the voices so different from her own, the language sometimes too.

'I spoke with Eleanor today.' Jenny's words broke into his train of thoughts and it took a while for his brain to catch up. It must have shown on his face.

'You know, Emma's regression therapy?'

'Yes. Sorry. Miles away.' McLean went to the fridge, pleased to find a bottle of cold beer there. The benefits of having someone else living in the same house. 'What did she have to say?'

'She's really got the bit between her teeth. I've not seen her so fired up by a case in ages.'

'That's good. Umm, I think. It's difficult for me to tell how the damned things are going. I just keep falling asleep.'

Jenny laughed. 'Eleanor's voice can do that. She's RADA trained, you know.'

'Is that right?' McLean found it surprisingly easy to believe. There was something very theatrical about Doctor Austin.

'She said she wants to make the sessions more frequent. Said maybe next Tuesday if you can make it.'

An image swam unbidden into his mind; a tiny office filled to the ceiling with paperwork. No hope of any active cases for weeks. Just an endless succession of telling people what to do and then trying to make sense of how they'd buggered it up. 'I think I should be able to manage.'

'OK then. I'll write the details down in the diary and send a reminder to your phone.' Jenny stifled a yawn unsuccessfully. 'Now I think I'll heed your advice. Night.'

McLean wished her good night and watched as she shuffled out of the kitchen. No sooner had she gone than Mrs McCutcheon's cat appeared through the same doorway, leaping up onto the table and sniffing at the takeaway bag in that over-familiar manner of cats.

'That's mine,' he said, which earned him an imperious stare. Fair enough, there was plenty to share.

Later, with the cat happily chasing bits of pilau rice around its bowl, McLean retreated to the library and a much-needed glass of whisky. Emma had left the television on with the sound muted, flickering images of some late-night movie. He slumped down on the sofa, then realized both that the remote was too far away and he couldn't be bothered getting up again to fetch it. Instead, he just let the flashing lights soothe his brain and calm down the endless looping thoughts about Magda Evans, Pete Buchanan, Malky Jennings.

Mrs McCutcheon's cat joined him after a while, smelling slightly of korma. It leapt onto his lap, kneaded at his free hand with its head until he stroked it. The purring came as a surprise; he couldn't remember ever having heard it purr before. It was a deep vibration against his chest, as relaxing as any massage. McLean hadn't really been watching the television, but he forgot it completely, slumped back against the arm of the sofa and stared at the strange shadows cast by the cornicing on the ceiling.

Of course. The ceiling.

He sat up so suddenly the cat dug its claws into his leg in surprise. With a yelp of pain, McLean dropped his whisky tumbler, still half full. It bounced on the rug, sprayed cask strength Talisker all over the antique floor and rolled under the sofa, but he ignored it. Ignored the cat, too, now eyeing him with its more normal deep suspicion.

His phone was in his jacket pocket, on the back of one

of the kitchen chairs. When he dug it out, a message from Jenny had already appeared, noting the time and place of the meeting with the hypnotist. He swiped it out of the way, ready to call DS Ritchie, and only then noticed the time displayed at the top of the screen. She'd probably still be up, sure. But was there anything either of them could really do at this time of the night? And if he was right, then it wasn't going to change before the morning.

Pulling out the chair, he sat down and started to tap out a text message instead.

42

'We're going to get fired. I just know it.'

DS Ritchie hunched her shoulders and shoved her hands deep into the pockets of her long overcoat, shuddering against the chill wind whistling in off the Firth of Forth. Early morning and the noise of the city waking up echoed around the car park at the base of the tower block. Broken glass still glittered on the cracked tarmac where McLean's Alfa had been parked. Just as soon as forensics had finished with it, he'd send it off to the garage in Loanhead for assessment. He had a horrible feeling the insurance company would declare it uneconomical to repair, which meant that he would be digging deep. It was just as well Johnny Fairbairn had come up with a more modern alternative. Even so, he'd parked a way up the street. He didn't want to chance anything to the place now.

'There's worse things than being fired.' He looked up the street for the hundredth time, waiting for the ambling form of Grumpy Bob to appear.

'That's OK for you to say. You're loaded. Me, I've got a new mortgage to worry about.' Ritchie stamped her feet against the cold. 'Can't we wait inside anyway?'

'And you're the one worrying about getting fired? Neither of us should be here, by rights. Professional Standards and Dagwood have both said as much. At least if Bob's doing the looking we've got some small deniability.'

'That's crap, sir. And you know it.'

'You're right. It's crap. But he's got the photos. No point going in without him.'

Ritchie's reply was lost by the arrival of a shiny new pool car. DC MacBride piloted it into the space where McLean's Alfa had met its grisly fate. He and Grumpy Bob both looked up as soon as they got out, rather than greeting McLean and Ritchie. Transfixed by the spot where DS Buchanan had met his end

'You sure you want to do this, sir?' Grumpy Bob asked as he handed over a thick folder. 'Me'n the lad can go over the flat without you.'

It was tempting. He knew that disobeying Dagwood would get him in trouble, but crossing Callard was even riskier. And Ritchie was right. It was fine for him to get himself fired, but her too?

'Well, I've not done anything wrong yet.' He pulled the crime scene photos out of their envelope and leafed through them once again. There was something that had been bugging him since the first time he'd seen the place and it had finally occurred to him last night. A pity he was so bloody slow, really.

'Damn. Nothing here that's any help.'

'What're you looking for, sir?' MacBride peered over his shoulder at the photos as if he hadn't already committed every single one to memory.

'The ceiling. People never look up. Even trained detectives sometimes. Especially when they've got something else on their minds. The floors of these tower blocks are all poured concrete. Nowhere to run services, so they put in false ceilings. Like in offices. Whoever beat Magda

Evans half to death was looking for something, and they were back looking for it again afterwards. I thought it was money, the way the cushions were all cut open. Maybe it was, but what if there was something else? And where would you hide something bulky in a place like that anyway?' McLean nodded in the direction of the fourth storey and its precariously low parapet.

'Come on then, lad. Latex gloves, I think.' Grumpy Bob set off for the stairs, closely followed by MacBride. McLean shoved the photographs back in their envelope and stuck them into the report folder. He got two steps in before a hand on his arm stopped him.

'We don't need to go up there, sir.' Ritchie was the voice of reason, only more irritating.

'But what if they find something?'

'My point exactly. What if they find something and we're there? Whatever it is will be useless as evidence. I don't know about you, sir, but I don't want to be some smart-arse lawyer's reasonable doubt.'

McLean had to admit that she was right, even though he hated the thought of someone else going through Magda's flat. Of them missing some crucial detail that only he would be able to see. He shook his head at his own stupidity. How many times had he been told that being an inspector was all about delegation and management?

'OK. I'll leave it to them.' He looked around the windswept car park, feeling the morning chill. Summer was most definitely on the way out. 'I don't suppose MacBride left the car unlocked.'

'I doubt it,' Ritchie said. 'But there's a coffee shop up

the road a ways. Figure you owe me at least a latte and a muffin.'

'I do? What for?'

'How about texting me at half one in the morning? Or dragging me down to Restalrig on my day off?'

'They found Pete Buchanan's prints all over it. Blood matches Malky Jennings. Pretty much a hundred per cent it's the murder weapon.'

McLean sat in the canteen, nursing a coffee and a bacon butty. He'd managed to find a spot in the corner, more or less out of sight of the beat constables coming and going. Afternoon shift time, it was a good place to listen and find out what was going on.

'Reckon he and the whore had a thing going. Jennings hit on her one time too often, so Buchanan beat him to death.'

It wasn't anything he didn't know, of course. It had taken MacBride all of ten minutes to find the loose ceiling tile and the booty stashed behind it. One baseball bat, finest hickory, wrapped in a plastic bag from Matalan. The shape and weight of the bat matched the weapon used to beat Malky Jennings to death and the blood type was his too. DNA analysis would take a while longer to come through, but nobody in the station doubted it was the murder weapon. Several of the senior officers were less pleased about the fingerprints all over it, mostly in blood. It was probably as well Pete Buchanan had hanged himself, however inadvertently. The embarrassment of a detective sergeant of long standing beating a man to death was not something the Chief Constable needed this close to the launch of Police Scotland. It probably helped that Malky Jennings deserved everything that happened to him, but not much.

'Thought I might find you down here.'

McLean looked up into the rotund face of DCI John Brooks. He was in need of a shave, on top at least. A thin fuzz of grey-white hair furred his scalp like an advertisement for hair-restoring pills. McLean started to stand, but Brooks waved his hand for him to stay, pulled out a chair and sat down.

'Spence getting the biscuits in, is he?' McLean glanced over at the serving counter and sure enough a thin detective inspector was chatting with the girl at the till. Brooks scowled that constipated scowl of his.

'A little respect wouldn't go amiss you know.'

'I couldn't agree more.' McLean threw back the last of his coffee with a grimace; it was never as nice cold. The grease on the remains of his butty didn't look all that appetizing any more, either. 'Was there anything you wanted, sir? Only I'm a bit busy.'

'Strange how Bob Laird took it upon himself to go and check out that apartment, don't you think? And taking young MacBride with him, too.'

'I wouldn't know anything about that, sir. Not my investigation.'

'Don't be so bloody clever, McLean. You know as well as I do Grumpy Bob doesn't do anything unless he's told to. Even then chances are he'll have a nap first.'

'I think you're underestimating Detective Sergeant Laird's investigative prowess, sir. He might not move quickly, but his brain's always working away.' McLean was winding Brooks up, but there was a truth in his words too. Grumpy Bob never lifted a finger if he didn't have to, but there were two ways to look for something. You could spend a lot of time and energy turning everything over until you found it, or you could sit and think about it until the obvious hiding place presented itself. OK, so it wasn't Bob who'd done that this time, but he'd taught McLean the importance of not always rushing in head first.

Brooks shook his head, his disbelief all too apparent. 'I know it was your idea, McLean. I just hope to God you weren't stupid enough to actually go there and look for the bloody thing yourself. We might not be able to arrest Pete Buchanan, but I'm sure as hell going to put Magda Evans away. Last thing I want is someone suggesting evidence was tampered with by someone connected to the case.'

'She awake then?' McLean realized he'd not heard anything about the ex-prostitute in days.

'Not yet. She's still sedated, but the doctors reckon they'll bring her out of it soon. Her prints are on that bat too. She'll not get away with this.' Brooks eyed McLean suspiciously as he said this last bit, as if he still harboured suspicions about McLean's relationship with Magda.

'No reason she should. She'll try and play you, though. She played me pretty well.'

'Oh aye?' Brooks raised a single pale eyebrow.

'Yup. We picked her up off that ship, remember. She spun us a yarn about people trafficking, being mistaken for one of the Eastern European pros. I reckon she was doing a runner. Got herself on that boat on purpose. Bang her up for murder; that's the least she deserves. But you might want to ask yourself what was in it all for Pete Buchanan before you send her down.'

'You what?' Brooks made his constipated baby face again.

'I never knew DS Buchanan well, but he didn't strike me as the kind of officer to fall for a prostitute's charms. Sure, he sampled the wares, but this isn't a tragic love story, is it? He was round her flat looking for something. I don't think it was that baseball bat. Or at least not just that baseball bat.'

'What are you suggesting, McLean?'

'My bet's on money. Quite a lot of it, I'd guess. Probably Malky Jennings' stash as well.' McLean stood up, shuffled around the table as DI Spence arrived, carefully carrying a tray piled high with food. 'You might want to ask Magda about that when she can speak. I'd've thought it'd look good on your record if you manage to find a pile of drugs before they get back on the streets.'

43

'Right then, now I've got your attention, let's have a bit of a recap.'

The CID room, early morning. McLean had insisted everyone get in first thing, as chances were good they could have a meeting without being interrupted by anyone more senior than an inspector. Grumpy Bob had grumbled about it, but McLean knew the old sergeant was just playing the part. He might spend the day catching forty winks at every opportunity, but he was always up with the lark.

'Three suicides. All deaths by hanging. All unusual in that the subjects used a method that would break their necks, rather than asphyxiation, and they all used the same knot in the same type of rope. All three were in their mid-twenties, single, white, lived alone. Anything else?'

'All three of them left suicide notes. Textual analysis throws up some similarities, but not enough to prove they were all written by the same person.' DC MacBride was still pink and shiny from his morning shower, but he'd done all his prep work. Pictures of the three victims were taped to the large whiteboard running down one wall of the room, with details for each one neatly written alongside. There were even a few questions highlighted, and lines drawn to indicate where there might have been some connection between the three. It looked a bit like an investigation; just a shame it had taken so long to bring it all together. More so now that they were going to have to wrap it all up.

'Textual analysis?' This from Grumpy Bob, who wasn't pink and probably hadn't showered since yesterday.

'It's technical,' McLean said. 'What about other similarities?'

'Well, you know about the rope. There's the odd blood profiles for Mikhailevic and Fenton.'

'What about Sands? I thought there was something in his blood, too.'

'Initial analysis suggested it, but he'd been dead too long for a decent sample. Doctor Sharp couldn't be a hundred per cent.' MacBride didn't need to consult the report, McLean noticed.

'Same with the knots, I suppose,' he said.

'Actually the forensic expert reckons all three were tied by the same person. Or possibly machine. She's never seen three knots so closely matched, especially given that they've all been, well, used.'

McLean remembered his conversation with Miss Cairns and her fascination with all knotty things. It didn't help, though. Fascinating and unlikely though it was, the identical nature of the three knots was not in itself enough to hang an expensive investigation on. Not when Duguid was trying to control budgets and failing badly.

'So we have three deaths, all with similarities that scream one cause, but nothing that can be proven. That about right?'

'Pretty much, sir.'

'So how are we getting on finding any more solid link between these three?'

Silence filled the room.

'Nothing at all?'

'It's been kind of busy, sir. And this investigation was considered low priority.' MacBride looked embarrassed, even though it wasn't really the constable's fault. He should have been keeping on top of this himself, managing his team properly. Except of course it hadn't been a team, had it. They'd been all over the place and he'd taken his eye off the ball. McLean tried to stop himself from doing the Dagwood response of running his fingers over his face, from forehead down to chin. Failed. A horrible thought crept unbidden into his mind.

'Have we got independent confirmation of each of these victims' identities? Do we actually know these are the people we think they are?'

'Fenton's a positive ID,' MacBride said. 'I got a statement from Constable Stephen. He'd known him for years.'

'What about Sands? He had no immediate family.'

'To be fair, I don't think anyone would be able to identify Sands from his remains. If you recall, he was a bit squishy.' Grumpy Bob reminded them all of something they'd rather have forgotten.

'And Mikhailevic? We get anything back from the embassy? Anyone show his photo to the landlord of the Bond Bar? Or maybe his professor at the college? Did we check his passport with immigration?' All basic steps any detective should have known to do. Maybe Duguid was right to view him with such disdain. McLean couldn't really say he'd conducted any of his investigations well recently. Just when was it he'd started fucking everything up so badly? And why?

DC MacBride stood up, went to his desk and booted up his computer. McLean watched in silence as the detective constable tapped away at keys and scrolled with his mouse. No point asking what he was doing; it would be relevant to the question. It only took a couple of minutes anyway, then he looked up with a worried expression writ large across his round face. 'I think we might have a bit of a problem, sir.'

McLean walked around to the desk and peered at the screen. MacBride had brought up a website for Fulcholme College and somehow managed to find a page detailing the students enrolled in the current year. The thumbnail photographs weren't the most flattering, but it didn't take an ID specialist to see that the Grigori Mikhailevic on the screen was not the Grigori Mikhailevic whose face adorned the whiteboard.

Professor Bain met them in the reception hall with a worried smile. He looked a little more tired than McLean remembered, his thinning white hair unkempt, glasses slightly askew.

'Thank you for seeing us at such short notice.' McLean shook the proffered hand and introduced DC MacBride.

'Not at all. Not at all. Anything for the police.' Professor Bain's face didn't quite match his words. 'You said there had been developments, about Grigori?'

'Could we maybe talk somewhere a bit more private?' McLean nodded at a group of students loitering on the far side of the hall. Another class was obviously just finishing as yet more people streamed out of one of the doors.

'Yes, of course. Please.' Professor Bain didn't lead them to his study, instead directing the two of them down a corridor to the back of the building and an empty classroom. McLean waited until the door was closed before bringing out the photographs he had brought with him.

'I have to admit this is all rather embarrassing. Something we should have checked right at the start of the investigation. Could you just confirm that this is Grigori Mikhailevic?' He handed the first photograph to the professor, who pulled a pair of half-moon spectacles out of the top pocket of his tweed jacket and swapped them with the wonky pair already on his nose before peering closely at the picture.

'Yes. That's him.' He looked again, head bobbing like a nodding dog in the back of a car. 'This is from the college alumni web page, is it not?'

'It is indeed, sir.' McLean took back the photograph and handed over the next one. 'And can you tell me who this is?'

From his expression, Professor Bain recognized the face instantly. True enough, it was a dead man's mug shot, but the reaction was not one of horror so much as resignation.

'Oh dear me. He's dead, isn't he?'

'You don't sound surprised.'

'Poor old Duncan.' Professor Bain handed back the photograph and removed his glasses. 'When you asked me about Grigori being depressed, I thought about him.' He pointed with one spectacle arm at the picture now in McLean's hand. 'Duncan George. Used to be one of Grigori's classmates. You might almost have called them

382

friends. But Duncan . . . Duncan was difficult. I'm no great expert, you'd need to talk to Eleanor about that, but I suspect he was bipolar. Brilliant for a couple of weeks, then he'd not show up for a month. Or he'd come in late, sit at the back, not contribute anything.'

'When did you last see him?'

'When did I last see him? Now there's a question.' Professor Bain tapped the side of his cheek with a finger, an introspective expression on his face. 'Where are we now, September? Must have been back in the spring, I'd guess.'

'So he'd finished his studies, then? Do you know where he went after graduation?'

'Oh, he never graduated. Never finished. No, like I said, he'd have his moments of brilliance and then drop out. We kept his place open for as long as we could, but when he missed final exams, well, we had to strike him off the register.'

'Didn't you get in touch with his family?'

'The state is his family. Was, I should say. He came here on a scholarship, out of a care home. If I remember right, his parents died when he was four. No other family, and a series of disastrous foster-carers. Poor old Duncan. Life didn't give him much, did it? Tell me. How did he die?'

McLean shuffled the photographs together and put them back in their envelope. Losing his parents at four years old was too close to home to be comfortable.

'Thank you for your time, professor. You've been very helpful.' He held out his hand, and Professor Bain took it automatically, didn't ask the question again.

DC MacBride had stood at the door for the whole interview, and opened it as McLean approached, leaving the professor behind. It was only as he was halfway through that something the doctor had said trickled through. Stopped him in his tracks.

'Your expert on bipolar disorders. Eleanor.' McLean turned as he spoke. 'That wouldn't be Eleanor Austin, would it? The hypnotherapist?'

Professor Bain looked a little nonplussed at the question, as if he couldn't quite work out what connection it had to anything. McLean could hardly blame him.

'Yes. She runs a couple of alternative-therapy courses. Very popular with the students. Do you know her?'

44

'So, we know now that Grigori Mikhailevic didn't kill himself, but Duncan George did. And in Mikhailevic's flat. Any ideas, Constable?'

MacBride was driving, face set in concentration as he tried to get through a snarl of traffic at the bottom end of Leith Walk. The trams had been meant to come all the way down here, so the civil servants in Victoria Quay could get all the way to the airport without stopping. Incompetence that would make Dagwood look like a professional now meant that they stopped a good mile short of Leith, and got nowhere near Ingliston. Even so the roads around the old docks had been dug up and refilled and dug up again. Christ alone knew why. It made any journey fraught.

'Your man back there, Professor Bain, reckoned the two of them were friends. Maybe they were sharing the flat?'

McLean tried to remember the scene. His overall impression was of a space barely large enough for one person.

'It's not far from here, is it. I think I'd like another look.'

A U-turn was out of the question, but MacBride managed to negotiate the side streets in a zigzag route that eventually brought them to the old warehouse development where Duncan George had died. There was no sign of any police presence at the front door, but then it was many weeks on, and the scene had long since been released.

Had Mikhailevic owned the place or rented? McLean realized he knew very little about the case at all.

'I don't suppose we've got a key or anything?'

'I'll find out.' MacBride pulled out his Airwave set and started making calls. McLean got out of the car, walked around the small courtyard. The front door to the development was locked, a series of buzzers for the different flats bearing the names of their occupants. None said Mikhailevic, or even George. He picked one at random and pressed it. No response. Pressed the one below it. Still no response. He was just about to press a third when there was a buzz and the lock clicked open. So much for security.

He pushed through into the dark hallway, breathing in a smell of mould and damp quite at odds with such a new development. Up two flights of stairs, the top landing was high in the roof space, a single, small window letting in too little light from the leaden grey sky outside. He tried to remember which was the right apartment of the two available, settled for the one on his left. The front door had no nameplate or buzzer, just a fanlight above showing an unlit bulb hanging from the open ceiling, and if he took a step back, stood on tiptoes and craned his neck until it hurt, the beam over which the rope had been tied.

McLean stepped up to the door and knocked, then listened hard for any sound of movement within. There was nothing for a while, then a voice behind him said: 'Can I help?'

He almost jumped out of his skin. Turned to see a young woman standing in the doorway of the flat opposite. She had a heavy dressing gown pulled around her and eyes bleary from disrupted sleep.

'Detective Inspector McLean. Lothian and Borders Police.' He showed her his warrant card.

'This about Grigori hanging himself?' The woman nodded her head at the door McLean had just knocked on. 'Only they cleared the place out, what, two weeks ago now? Decorator's been in and all. There's been at least two couples round looking. Reckon it'll be rented out by the end of the month. S'creepy though. I wouldn't live there. Not after, you know.'

'You knew him? Mikhailevic?'

'No' well. Enough to say hi to. I work nights, so I didnae see much of him, to be honest.'

'Anyone else stay with him?'

'There was a bloke, aye. Not all the time, mind, and I'd not seen him in a while. Used to think maybe they were gay, you know. Not that I've a problem with that.'

McLean pulled the envelope with the photos out of his pocket. The picture of Duncan George was quite obviously that of a dead man. Perhaps not the thing you wanted to see just after waking up. On the other hand, it would be confirmation.

'Was it you who reported it?' He nodded his head in the direction of the other flat. The young woman blinked, nodded.

'You saw him, then.'

'Just a glimpse. Didn't notice the door was open until I got inside. I was shutting my own door and I looked across.' She gulped. 'He was just hanging there, like, not moving or anything.'

'Did you see his face?' McLean saw the look of horror passing over the young woman's own face as she relived the moment. 'Look, I'm really sorry to bring this all up again.'

'No, you're all right. It's just . . . No, I didnae see his face. He was hanging wi' his back to the door, like. Gave me such a shock. I phoned you lot and went and hid in my bedroom.'

Downstairs, McLean heard the sound of the buzzer going again. No doubt DC MacBride trying to get in. He selected the photograph of Duncan George and held it up.

'One last thing. The other bloke who came round. Is this him?'

The young woman peered at it like someone who's forgotten to put their contact lenses in. 'Aye, that's him. He deid as well? You think it was a suicide pact?'

'Something like that, aye.' McLean thanked her and let her go back to bed. He doubted she'd get much sleep now.

They were stuck in the traffic jam that was Leith Walk again, this time headed uphill, back towards the city centre and the station. DC MacBride was silent, though it was unclear whether he was deep in thought or sulking because McLean had left him chasing loose ends on the phone. It didn't really matter either way; the quiet gave McLean time to try and marshal his own thoughts.

It was, as his gran had been fond of saying, something of a bugger's muddle. Three deaths by hanging, possibly suicide but increasingly looking like some kind of elaborate pact. Quite how you could force someone to hang themselves without leaving any traces that you'd done so, McLean couldn't begin to fathom. So each of them had to have been willing participants. But only one person had tied the knots, which effectively made it murder.

Then there was the mysterious case of the missing Mikhailevic. Of course, nobody had been looking for him; they'd all thought he was dead. But neither had he turned up at work or college, so either he'd done a runner, or he too was swinging in the wind somewhere.

And looming over everything else was the simple fact that he wasn't supposed to be investigating this any more. He was meant to be sitting in his office, typing up a report that ignored all the complications and drew a line under the point where each case was a simple, tragic suicide. The problem was, his conscience wouldn't let him do that, even before it turned out they'd mis-identified one of the victims. Now the loose ends were getting tangled and out of control.

McLean glanced at the clock on the dashboard. Another day almost gone, unless you were an inspector, in which case it had hardly begun. MacBride would be needing to get back to the station for shift end though. No overtime on this one.

Almost as if he'd known it all along, McLean's unfocused gaze shifted and he realized what he'd been staring at. The shop front hadn't changed at all, still just a small door between a bookmaker's and a chip shop. The faded sign said 'Madame Rose: Tarots Read. Fortunes Told.' Below it, equally faded but somehow something he had missed before, it also said 'Esoteric and Antiquarian Books.'

'You go on back to the station, Stuart. It's near enough knocking-off time anyway.' McLean unclipped his seatbelt and climbed out of the car just as the traffic started to move again. MacBride had no time to question his actions before the car behind started tooting its horn in irritation at the added microseconds of delay. 'See you tomorrow. Briefing at eight, OK.'

The shop door creaked like something from the BBC special effects department. McLean wondered how much business was coming this way. Not much call for a fortune teller in a time of austerity. As he climbed the stairs, his feet brought up a smell of mould and stagnant air, but the reception room was at least warm. There was no one manning the reception desk though. For a clairvoyant, Madame Rose didn't seem to have much idea of who was coming to visit, and when.

'Hello?' No answer. McLean went to the door that opened onto the consulting room, knocked and then pushed it open. It was empty, but the door on the far side was slightly ajar.

'Hello? Anyone about?' This time louder. Still no reply, and then the clumping sound of large feet on loose floorboards.

'Inspector, what a pleasant surprise!' Madame Rose burst into the room like a diva, dressed for the part as well. Even at home, it would seem, the transvestite medium preferred to stay in character. Unless she really was a woman. But no. McLean found himself shaking his head. She couldn't be. He couldn't be.

'I was just passing. Thought I might pick your brains about something.'

'Of course, of course. Any time.' Madame Rose held the door wide. 'Come through to my inner sanctum.'

He'd been in the large room at the back of the building before, but it still surprised him just how crowded the space was. There were shelves on every available wall, and a couple free-standing, all filled with old books. Display cabinets heaped one upon another, their contents too dark to see or too strange to fathom. The desk, arranged under the one window so that it at least had some light on it, was covered in papers, small boxes, things McLean had no name for, and cats. It made his own office back at the station look tidy.

'Perhaps a cup of tea?' Madame Rose didn't wait for an answer. McLean was left standing in the middle of the chaos as the medium disappeared through yet another door. He hardly dared touch anything; there was a fragility about the place that put him in mind of old black-and-white slapstick comedies. Picking up a book would surely set something rolling that would knock something over that would startle a cat that would jump up at something else, and the whole place would be destroyed around him. He was still hearing the comedy sound of a metal plate rolling round and round until it clattered to a halt when Madame Rose came back in bearing a tray.

'Sit, please, Inspector. Don't mind the cats.' She, or he, put the tray down on top of the papers and proceeded to pour tea into mugs. McLean found an old armchair with only one occupant, who looked at him with feline hatred before slinking away to join some of its friends. He took his tea, and then sat down.

'So. You want to pick my brains.' Madame Rose settled into an armchair close by, not the chair on the other side of the desk where he had expected. 'About books? Or other matters.'

Faced with the question, McLean wasn't at all sure. Something had brought him here, though. He remembered a conversation he'd had with Jenny Nairn in the library back at his gran's house.

'Probably a bit of both. Book-wise, I was wondering if you'd be interested in cataloguing and valuing my grandmother's collection. I've no idea what's there, but I suspect some of it's valuable. I'd pay you for your time, of course.'

'I'd be happy to.' Madame Rose beamed a genuinely happy smile. 'As you may have guessed, there's not a lot of call for my other talents at the moment. Everybody knows the future's grim. They don't want to be told it. I'll come around tomorrow morning, if that's convenient?'

'I'll most likely be out.' McLean remembered his shout to DC MacBride about their eight o'clock briefing. 'Emma will be in, and Jenny. They'll probably try and help.'

'Ah yes, Miss Nairn. She's a strange one. And Emma. How is poor Emma? Improved at all?'

McLean shook his head. 'That was the other thing I wanted to ask about. Do you know much about regression therapy?'

Madame Rose said nothing for a while, took a very un-ladylike gulp of tea and wiped the moisture from her lips with the back of her hand. Placed the mug on the side of the desk.

'Is that what you're trying now? To help Emma get her memories back?'

McLean admitted that it was. 'I'm not sure it's working though. We've only had a few sessions. Doctor Austin seems to think it's going well. Can't say I've seen much difference myself. Emma doesn't seem to respond to hypnosis.'

'Some people don't. And I'd be very surprised if Emma did, not in her current state.' Madame Rose leaned forward in her seat, lowering her voice as if there might be spies listening in. 'Hypnotic regression can be useful at times, Inspector, but there are dangers inherent in the therapy. You can go back too far, and if you're not careful, that's where your patient stays. Correct me if I'm incorrect, but isn't that Emma's problem already? She's already regressed to the little girl she was over twenty years ago? How is regressing her further going to help?'

'What about hypnotism itself? You know, to stop smoking, stuff like that? Does it really work?'

'That depends. There's a lot of charlatans out there peddling cheap cures, but if you've got to the point you're looking for a hypnotist to help you give up smoking, you probably want to quit anyway. It's a kind of placebo effect.'

'Always? What about those shows, you know, where they make people in the audience bark like a dog or stand on one leg?'

'You mean those shows where people pay to be entertained?' Madame Rose left the question hanging for a while, then added: 'But that's not what you're trying to ask really, is it, Inspector?'

'I don't know. It sounds silly saying it. But when Emma was being hypnotized, it was almost as if I was the one – what did you call it? Going under?'

'I never said hypnotism doesn't work, Inspector. Just that it doesn't work on everybody. And in the hands of someone who isn't well tuned to the spiritual plane, it can easily go wrong.'

'What do you mean?'

393

'When you're under hypnosis, you're suggestible. That's how it can seem like a good idea to bark like a dog or stand on one leg. You're open to outside influences, but not just those of the hypnotist. Any perturbation in the ether might influence you. It could be benign and give you a sense of euphoria unlike any you've experienced. Or it could be malign. Could take over your soul and drive you mad.'

Madame Rose's gravelly voice had descended almost to a whisper, and McLean found he had leaned in closer to hear what she was saying. 'But you don't have much belief in souls, do you, Inspector? Just like you don't believe in demons and magic. They don't fit in with your science, do they.'

McLean stared at the large medium for a moment, a strange idea forcing its way through the mess of thoughts clogging up his mind. 'What about suicide?'

'I'm sorry?'

'Could you hypnotize someone to commit suicide?'

'Hypnotize? No.'

'But you're saying there are ways you could persuade someone to, say, hang themselves?'

'Like I said, Inspector. There are forces out there beyond what we perceive as normal. You've encountered them before, even if you won't admit it. I've no doubt such demons could drive a person insane, and what is suicide if not the ultimate insanity?'

As her words sank in, more mumbo-jumbo and not quite the useful insight he'd been hoping for, Madame Rose slapped her overlarge hands on her thighs and pushed herself back into the chair. Startled, McLean looked at his watch. Where had the time gone?

'I'm sorry, I need to get cracking. It's Jenny's night off tonight.'

'Then you'd better not keep her waiting.' Madame Rose stood, and McLean reflexively followed her cue. 'But think about what I've said, Inspector. And what I told you before. There are forces beyond your understanding. You've seen them in action, dealt with them in your own haphazard way.'

'There's a rational explanation for everything, however bizarre.' Even as he said it, McLean knew he didn't really believe it.

'Sometimes the rational is irrational Inspector.' Madame Rose led him out of the room, back the way he had come in. 'You of all people should know that.'

45

She's happy for the first time she can remember. The drink's got something to do with that; more wine than she's been able to afford in far too long. But there's something else, too. A fuzziness that has nothing to do with alcohol. As if something had been weighing on her mind for months, possibly years, never quite resolved. Then this evening she made a decision, and everything is fine.

What the decision was, she can't exactly recall. It's hard to think about anything but what she's doing now. Not the job with its endless weirdness. Not her studies that seem to be going nowhere. Not even the crazy infatuation she's developed with her new boss. She's not falling in love with him, of course. That would be silly. He's far older than her, for starters. And taken, as all the best ones are. But he's fascinating, complex and completely unaware of the maelstrom whirling around him.

Of course, Ellie wasn't happy when she told her, but then Ellie's always been the possessive type. Ellie really doesn't like to share. They might even have had a little argument about that, but nothing serious. And now she's heading home across the city. Walking, the way she likes to.

It's dark, as much as the city ever gets dark. This late there's not so many cars about, and hardly any people. Some fear the city at night, but not her. This is her place.

And anyway, she's made her decision; she's not afraid of anything now.

Not even the beast that roars at her from the top of the hill. Its eyes glow with malevolent fire and she can see within it the writhing forms of the people it has already consumed. They scream in agony, lost souls damnation-bound. Unless she can slay the beast, cut open its guts and set them free.

There is no moment's hesitation. She is in the now and this situation demands action. Fearless, decided, she steps into the path of the onrushing monster.

46

The tinny electronic beep of his phone on its charging stand told him that it was time to get up, but McLean had been awake for a while. Beside him, Emma slept the sleep of a small child, curled up almost foetally, and wearing her heavy fleece pyjamas with the cow print on them. She had a knack for taking up the whole bed, and stealing all the bedclothes. He could ask her not to climb in with him in the wee small hours, but there were times he'd lain awake and listened to her frightened whimpers. Sleep was not a place of solace for her, no escape from whatever monsters plagued her there.

Wearily, he hauled himself out of bed, padded through to the bathroom and began the morning ritual. He'd been mulling over his odd meeting with Madame Rose since about five, the patterns on the ceiling having lost their interest. She, he, whatever, was right about one thing at least. There were times he really did find it difficult to come up with a rational explanation for the evil things that people did. But evil was an adjective, not a noun. And when it came down to it, people did evil things for their own selfish or mad reasons, not because demons were making them do it, or had stolen their souls or whatever else was a simple way of fooling yourself that anything made any sense at all.

Happy thoughts for a grey morning. He wiped conden-

398

sation off the mirror, then rubbed at his face. Noticed for the first time the dark, saggy folds under his eyes. The stubble on his chin showed flecks of grey, otherwise he might have considered growing a beard. Except that he hated beards.

Shaking his head once more in an attempt to rid himself of his black mood, McLean doused his face in lukewarm water and set about the process of shaving.

Emma was still fast asleep in his bed when he stepped out onto the landing. The mornings were getting darker, and he almost tripped over Mrs McCutcheon's cat, which had settled itself down right in front of the door.

'Guard duty, is it?' he asked and received a withering stare in return. The house was silent, which was unusual. Normally Jenny was up even before he was. Percolator on the stove top and the cereal boxes laid out in the middle of the kitchen table. It reminded him bizarrely of school, although they'd never had percolator coffee there, and cereal had been in huge catering boxes.

But this morning the table was clear, no coffee filling the kitchen with heavenly smells.

He wasn't particularly worried. It had been her night off, after all. She'd probably met up with some friends in a pub somewhere and drunk more than she'd intended. He knew how it worked, had been there plenty of times himself. A quick glance up at the kitchen clock showed he had more than enough time to get his own breakfast, especially with his shiny new car sitting out there on the driveway. Well, new to him anyway, and barely run in. He worried that it might be a little too conspicuous, but it was an Alfa Romeo and it was a GT. That was the closest he was going to get to his dad's old car until it had been fixed. If it could be fixed.

Kettle boiled, McLean made himself instant coffee, then searched through the cupboards for the cereal. There was still no sign of Jenny by the time he'd finished and was putting the bowl in the dishwasher. He was about to go and knock on her door when he heard a noise from the hall.

'Rough night, was it?' he asked before she came in. Except that it wasn't Jenny; it was Emma, still wearing her cow print pyjamas.

'Oh. I thought you were Jenny.'

'She's gone. Not coming back,' Emma said.

'What do you mean, gone?'

'Gone. Left for ever.' Emma's shoulders slumped.

'But she didn't say anything last night. Did she speak to you before?' A flash of anger flared up inside him at the thought Jenny had walked out on the job and left him stranded.

'No. She didn't want to leave. She liked it here. With all the others. She liked you too. A lot. Said you were interesting. But she had to go.' Emma dropped into one of the kitchen chairs, pulled McLean's coffee mug towards her and peered inside. It was still half full, so she drank it. She looked like a little girl trying hard to be brave and not let the tears come.

'When did you speak to her? When did she tell you this?'

'Last night. When all the people came. She was with them.'

McLean stared at the woman sitting in his kitchen. A couple of months of loafing around and eating well had rounded out the skeletal angles from her face, but she was still thin. Her hair was beginning to regain some of its lustre, but there were streaks of grey in it now and it fell down below her shoulders. Lines crinkled around the edges of her eyes as she stared back at him, a curious, questioning frown on her face. She'd been through so much that she had quite literally lost her mind. And it was all his fault.

It occurred to him that he'd not really talked to her for weeks, possibly months. He came home of an evening and maybe had a chat, but it was inconsequential stuff, like talking to a child. More often than not she'd gone to her own room before he got in anyway, their only encounters the wordless ones when she climbed into his bed in the small hours, shivering with fear. He'd fallen into a pattern of treating her like the little girl she appeared to be, leaving the care and companionship to Jenny. It had been a wonderful house of cards, for a while. But now the simplest thing had brought it tumbling down.

'What people were these? When did they come.'

'They always come when it's quiet. Sometimes in the day, up in the attic, the nice ones come and talk to me. But late at night when it's dark, that's when the monsters come. Last night Jenny was with them. She said goodbye. Said she was sorry. Said her mum made her do it.'

He put a call in to the station as he climbed the stairs up to the attic. The phone rang longer than he would have liked before being picked up. No doubt Sergeant Dundas had been busy with his morning doughnut and didn't want to be disturbed.

'You lost another one?' was the sergeant's incredulous reply when McLean explained the situation.

'It's not a joke, Pete. Just a query. Have we got any reports of accidents involving young females in the last twenty-four hours? Hospital admissions. Something serious enough to keep her in overnight.'

A moment's furious one-finger tapping at a keyboard, and then: 'nothing on the screen, sir, but it's been acting up for days now. You want me to put a call out?'

McLean had reached the door to Jenny's room, tapped on it lightly with his free hand. It wasn't serious. Not like when Emma had gone missing. 'No, you're all right, Pete. I'll do it myself when I get in. Might be a bit late till I can find some cover to look after Em. Can you let Bob know?'

'What am I, your private messaging service?' Dundas laughed, said he'd pass it on, then hung up. There had been no response from Jenny's room, so McLean opened the door and stepped inside.

He wasn't sure what he'd been expecting. Jenny Nairn could most simply be described as alternative, so he wouldn't have been surprised if the place looked a little like a protest camp, only with better plumbing. What he found was a room almost identical to the one he remembered as a child. The narrow bed was neatly made, had obviously not been slept in recently. Over by the window, an antique dressing table had been pressed into service as a desk, and Jenny's laptop sat open on it, pad and pen lying beside. A stack of books beside the chair was the only thing in the room that was remotely haphazard. Everything else was neat, dust-free, organized.

But Jenny was nowhere to be seen.

Movement at the door was Emma, peering in but not daring to cross the threshold. 'She's not here.'

'She left her stuff. She'll be back.' McLean pointed at the laptop, noticing as he did so a small leather suitcase under the bed.

'No, she won't. She's gone. Like the others.'

'What others?' McLean hunkered down, his knees popping in protest, and pulled out the case. It was really none of his business, but on the other hand if she was in trouble . . .

'The people, Tony. You saw them. In the photographs.'

McLean had placed the case on the bed, ready to pop open the two old brass catches, but Emma's words distracted him. He turned around, still squatting down, still holding the case, and looked up at her as he opened the lid.

'What photographs?' he asked, but he knew all too well. She looked past him, eyes widening in surprise and let out a little 'Oh.'

McLean looked back around to what was in the case. A woman's wig was scrunched into one corner, grey-brown hair in elegant waves. But it wasn't that which had caught Emma's attention. He reached in with trembling fingers, aware even as he did so that he shouldn't have been touching it, and pulled out a long loop of good, stout, hemp rope.

'I'm OK, really. I can look after myself. Not a little girl, you know.'

McLean glanced at his watch as they walked back down the stairs, leaving Jenny's room and the troubling suitcase behind. It was almost eight o'clock and he should really have been at work by now. He didn't dare leave Emma here on her own, though. Her petulant words only confirmed that. But for the life of him he couldn't think who to call in to babysit.

Babysit. The word stopped him in his tracks, halfway down the stairs and looking out over the hall. When had he started thinking about her like that? She wasn't a baby, she was a thirty-two-year-old-woman. He was under no obligation to look after her if she didn't want him to. No doctor had sectioned her. But what if she wandered off again, stepped out in front of a bus or something? He'd lost Kirsty and that had been too much. Damned if he was going to lose Emma too.

The sound of the doorbell ringing brought him back to himself. Emma was already at the bottom of the stairs and hurried across to answer it. By the time he reached the ground floor, she had let their visitor in. Madame Rose stood in the lobby, rain dripping from her ankle-length coat and the brim of a wide felt hat.

'Ah, Inspector. You're still here, I see. And the delightful Miss Baird.'

'The books are all in here, obviously. You know where the kitchen is. Please, help yourself to anything you want.' McLean stood in the middle of the library as Madame Rose walked slowly around the bookcases. The medium seemed far more absorbed in scanning the books than listening to anything he had to say. Occasionally she would stop, reach up, make a little clicking noise, or a tut. Possibly touch a leather spine with one large, yet gentle finger, and then move on.

'I'll leave you the direct number for the station, as well as my mobile. Should be home by five. You sure you're OK with this?'

Something of his words must have finally got through. Madame Rose stopped her perambulation and looked around. 'What? Oh, Emma. No, of course not. Delighted I can be of help.'

'I'm sure Jenny'll be back before then anyway. She's probably passed out in some friend's front room.'

'Oh, I very much doubt that. Not unless someone spiked her drink, and it'd take a lot to get one past Jenny Nairn.'

'I didn't realize you knew her well.' McLean finished scribbling down the last of the contact numbers he could think of and ripped the page from the jotter on the desk.

'Know of her, Inspector. Miss Nairn has a reputation among the cognoscenti. But I'd hardly say I know her well.' Madame Rose took the proffered notepaper, then turned as if she'd sensed something in the air. 'And here's young Emma, and her familiar too.'

Emma stood in the doorway, Mrs McCutcheon's cat twining around her legs. She'd changed out of her thick pyjamas with the cow print and was wearing what McLean would consider going-out clothes. Faded jeans, long black boots and what he'd always thought of as a sweat-top, but which was now universally known as a hoodie. It was one of his, he noted. Not that he minded. He couldn't remember the last time he'd seen Emma wearing anything other than slouching clothes.

'You sure you're OK with this?' he asked, aware that he'd done so already.

'Shouldn't you be at work, Inspector?' Madame Rose fixed him with a gaze not unlike the one his old school matron had used to such good effect. 'Go. We'll be fine. There's enough here to keep me busy for days. Emma can be my secretary and note-taker.'

47

'Exactly what part of "no active investigation" do you not understand, McLean. You're meant to be on administrative duties only. Not swanning off all over the fucking city.'

Later than he'd have liked, and not the person he really needed to be dealing with right now. McLean stood in the all-too-familiar position on the wrong side of the desk in Acting Superintendent Duguid's office. Downstairs in the CID room, Grumpy Bob and DS Ritchie were hopefully putting some sense of order into the chaos that was the suicides investigation, aided by DC MacBride and most likely hindered by PC Gregg. Ideally he would have liked to have been down there with them, directing proceedings and trying to get his head round all the conflicting facts. Instead he'd not been in the station more than thirty seconds before a terrified young constable had passed on the message that Duguid wanted to see him. McLean had long since given up being surprised at how news of his every movement seemed to spread around the station.

'I was putting together the final report for the three hangings, sir. It turns out that we'd misidentified one of the victims. I thought it important to verify the facts myself. Didn't want to end up compounding an already embarrassing error.'

'Christ almighty. Can you not do anything right?' Duguid

slumped back into his seat, ran a hand through his straggly, greying hair. 'Misidentified how, exactly?'

There wasn't an easy way to tell the tale. Not without making all of them look like a bunch of schoolboys playing at being detectives. He'd barely opened his mouth to speak when there was a knock at the door, which then clicked open before Duguid could make any reply. McLean looked around, expecting to see the sergeant who had been manning the secretaries' desk just outside. Instead he saw the worried face of Grumpy Bob.

'What the bloody hell? Detective Sergeant Laird I'm in a meeting. How dare you just barge in.' Duguid's bluster might have worked on the younger officers, but Grumpy Bob had thicker skin. And less to lose.

'Sorry to disturb you, sir. But I thought this was important.'

'What could possibly be so important it couldn't wait ten minutes, man?'

'Seems there's been another hanging, sir. Same scenario as the three we were already investigating.'

'You . . . What?'

'Mikhailevic?' McLean and Duguid spoke at the same time.

'Not unless he's had a sex change. This one's a woman.'

'Where?' McLean asked.

'Gilmerton, sir.'

A woman. Gilmerton. A chill sensation settled in the pit of McLean's gut. Jenny Nairn's flat was in Gilmerton, wasn't it? He shook his head to dispel the thought. Many thousands of people lived in that area.

'We got a name? Who called it in?'

'No name yet. Big Andy was First Attending.' Grumpy Bob looked at Duguid as he spoke. 'Knew we were looking into the other hangings and called it in straight away.'

McLean turned to Duguid, who had gone very quiet.

'It might be nothing, sir. Just a coincidence. I'd like to have a look though, just to be sure.'

Duguid's scowl deepened, then disappeared, replaced by an evil grin.

'Doesn't really matter what I say, does it, McLean? You'll go anyway. Just don't come crying to me when Rab Callard hears about it, eh?'

Once a quiet little mining village to the south of the city, Gilmerton had long since been swallowed up in the expansion of Edinburgh. McLean took his new car; it was quicker than any of the alternatives. Grumpy Bob hunched himself uncomfortably in the passenger seat, complaining that it was too low to the ground for a man of his advanced years to get into.

'Leather's a bit posh too, isn't it?' He squirmed around like a child who's wet his pants. Well, at least it would dispel the lingering aroma of Magic Tree air freshener.

'I don't know what the problem is, Bob. You're the one's been telling me to get a proper car for years. This one's only a couple of years old. One careful lady owner.'

'Aye and three hooligans who did their best to wrap it round a lamp post, I've no doubt. Goes some, I bet.'

McLean blipped the accelerator and the car shot forward quicker than he had expected, accompanied by a very unsubtle V6 roar. He dabbed the brakes before anyone noticed he was exceeding the speed limit, felt the grin he was suppressing as a tightening around his eyes. Then he remembered why they were driving across the city.

'It's just a car, Bob. Four wheels and an engine. Only got it at all because someone thought it'd be funny to phone the local Bentley salesman pretending to be me.'

'Heard about that. Bloody idiots the lot of them. Down here, isn't it?' Grumpy Bob pointed to a side street off the Old Dalkeith Road, lined on either side with 1970s semi-detached houses. A couple more turns brought them to a cul-de-sac currently choked up with squad cars. McLean parked a decent distance away, all too aware of how clumsy even trained police drivers could be in a tight space.

A uniformed constable was rolling out blue and white tape as he and Grumpy Bob approached.

'Over there. fourteen a,' he said as McLean showed his warrant card. He didn't really need direction; there was only one house with its door open and police hanging around like lazy flies. In amongst the cars, McLean noticed Doctor Buckley's green-and-road-grime Volkswagen Golf, so whoever was in charge had at least thought to call the duty doctor. With any luck they'd have summoned the pathologist, too.

Fourteen a was an upper flat, made by splitting the already narrow hallway of number fourteen lengthways. There was barely enough room for one person to walk along the short corridor to the stairs. It never ceased to amaze McLean the ingenuity people found in creating smaller and smaller spaces to live in. Whoever had lived here must have been tiny, though the looming figure coming down the stairs made everything around him seem Lilliputian anyway.

'You're here, sir. Good.' Big Andy Houseman was a dependable sergeant, and no doubt the reason the duty doctor was already here.

'I wondered who was in charge when I saw signs of competence outside. Didn't realize you'd relocated to the sticks.' McLean backed out of the doorway. There was no way he was going to be able to squeeze past Big Andy in the hall. Not without giving him the wrong idea, anyway.

'I like it out here, sir. It's quieter than the city. Well, usually.' The sergeant looked up at the single upstairs window. The curtains had been drawn.

'Have we got a name yet?' McLean asked. Jenny Nairn had been living in as she looked after Emma, but her address was somewhere around here, he was sure.

'Neighbour says she's a Caroline Sellars. Don't know much more about her than that. I've got some constables doing door-to-door round the close, but it seems to be one of those places where people don't talk much. Don't think she'd been here long, either.'

McLean let out a silent breath of relief at the name. 'I guess I'd better go and have a look then. Doctor Buckley still in there?'

'Oh yes, he's still there. Like a bloody kid in a sweetie shop.'

The narrow stairs led up to a narrow landing with just three doors off it. Bedroom, bathroom and living room, McLean guessed. Minimal living. One door was open, leading to the room at the front of the house, and low voices in conversation filtered out. He took the one step

411

that was all he needed to get from the top of the stairs to the doorway and peered in.

She was hanging from the centre of the room, facing away from him towards the window. Like the three young men, she was naked and had gone to considerable lengths to hang herself. A small hatch in the ceiling opened up into the attic space, the stout hemp rope presumably tied to a cross-brace in the rafters above. The room was small; a much larger space that had been partitioned to form the bedroom at the back of the house. Its ceiling was high. More like the old Georgian tenements in the city centre than anything built in the seventies. Caroline Sellars had pulled a dining table across the room so that she would have had enough of a drop to snap her neck, put the noose over her head with the knot running past her left ear, and then stepped off. Her feet were just inches off the floor.

'Inspector McLean. What a pleasant surprise.'

Doctor Buckley greeted him from the other side of the deceased. It wasn't possible for him to hide behind the body, since he was enormously wide himself. McLean had been so distracted by the hanged woman that he'd missed the duty doctor anyway. Now he stepped further into the room, treading carefully so as not to disturb anything.

'It's all right, Doctor. I'm not going to ask you to give me a time of death.'

Doctor Buckley grinned. 'You're learning, then. I can tell you that she is dead, and I can hazard a cause, too. Wouldn't want to trespass on Angus's territory though.'

'Snapped vertebrae?'

'Something like that.'

McLean stepped fully into the room, looking around at a tidy, tiny living space. One wall was given over to kitchen units, with a narrow breakfast bar breaking it off from the rest of the room. The table had been pulled over from a small dining area over in the far corner, if the two chairs facing each other across an empty space were anything to go by. To the other side of the body, a bay window held a small sofa, an old armchair beside it facing towards a gas fire and telly. There were pictures on the wall, some framed photographs of smiling people, a couple of cheap prints of old masters. White IKEA bookcases held a selection of romance paperbacks and dust collectors. All so very normal. Nothing much to suggest a suicidal temperament.

'Was there a note?' McLean directed his question at the uniform constable who had obviously drawn the short straw and been told to watch the body in case it went anywhere. The young lad started, as if he hadn't noticed McLean come in and talk to the duty doctor.

'I . . . I don't know, sir. Haven't touched anything.'

McLean swept his gaze over the room a second time. A note would most likely have been left in a prominent place. On the table, perhaps, or the breakfast bar. There didn't appear to be anything obvious. SEB would probably turn something up.

'Well, I'll get out of your way. I'm sure Angus will be here soon.' Doctor Buckley negotiated his way around the body with surprising nimbleness for someone as large as he was. McLean had images of him getting stuck going down the stairs, having to call out the fire brigade. Dismissed them with a shake of his head. He moved into the

413

space the doctor had vacated and finally got a look at the face of the deceased.

She was young, Caroline Sellars. That much he'd been able to tell from behind. Her shoulder-length hair was glossy black and straight. It partially obscured her face, and the swelling and discolouration caused by the rope further altered her appearance, but there was no mistaking the fact that he had met her before.

48

McLean parked his car in front of Fulcholme College, aware that he had been seeing rather more of the place lately than he'd anticipated. Professor Bain stood in the entranceway waiting for him, half walked, half jogged up as he clambered out of his car.

'I got your message, inspector.' The professor wrung his hands together like nervous, restless snakes. He looked pale in the daylight, as if it weren't his natural habitat. His thin hair glistened at his temples, the strands that protruded from his ears quivering slightly. Since the first time they had met, just a few weeks ago, he seemed to have aged years. Having your students all committing suicide might do that.

'Can we speak inside?' McLean pointed towards the hall and the professor's office beyond. Behind him, Grumpy Bob was looking up at the building, hands in pockets.

'Yes, of course. Please.' Professor Bain led him through a crowd of students streaming out of a lecture and into the relative calm of Room 1. McLean closed the door so that it was just the two of them.

'Caroline Sellars. Tell me about her.'

Professor Bain's shoulders slumped and he collapsed down onto a nearby armchair like a deflating balloon. 'She really hanged herself?'

McLean nodded. Said nothing more. The silence hung heavy for a while before Professor Bain spoke again.

'I can't believe she'd kill herself. She was always so full of life. So bubbly, you know?'

'When did you last see her?'

The professor scratched at his bald pate. 'Yesterday afternoon, I think. She was definitely here on Tuesday. We had a tutorial group. Discussing Keynesian Economic Theory and its application in the current climate.'

'She any good at that stuff?'

Professor Bain shrugged. 'She was good enough. Not bright like Grigori, but she put in the effort, you know. Economics was always her second subject though. She was much more interested in parapsychology.'

'Parapsychology?' McLean emphasized the first two syllables. 'You teach that here?'

'Well, not teach, exactly. It's more of an informal research group. Eleanor runs it in her spare time. Very popular with the students. They come up with all manner of odd experiments.'

'Eleanor.' McLean recalled an earlier conversation with the professor, lost in the rush of everything else that was going on. 'Doctor Austin?'

'That's her. She teaches here part-time.'

'And she runs informal groups?'

The professor nodded, a worried look creeping over his face as his mind made the same connections McLean's had made.

'Was Mikhailevic involved in any of these groups? Duncan George too?'

'I really don't know, Inspector. Shouldn't be too hard to find out.' Professor Bain pulled himself wearily to his feet, headed towards his desk. 'You don't think they . . . ? Some sort of suicide pact?'

'Pact, yes. It's the suicide part I'm not so sure about.'

Grumpy Bob was chatting with a couple of students young enough to have been his daughters when McLean came out of Professor Bain's office. He couldn't tell what the sergeant was saying, but he obviously had their rapt attention.

'Come on, Bob, there's work to do,' he said as he walked past. By the time he'd got to his car, Grumpy Bob had extricated himself and caught up.

'Hot date?' McLean asked.

'Too high maintenance for my tastes.' Grumpy Bob grinned, heading for the passenger door.

'You drive. I've got to make some calls.' McLean pulled out the keys and threw them over. Grumpy Bob caught them with both hands, then looked down at the shiny, sleek shape of the car.

'You sure, sir? I mean, you've only just got it. Wouldn't want to be the first to put a dent in it.'

'It's just a car, Bob. You've driven them before.'

'Aye, but . . .' Grumpy Bob continued to mutter, but did as he was told. McLean climbed into the passenger seat and waited patiently as the sergeant familiarized himself with the layout.

'You get anything useful from the students?'

'A bit. Maybe. Seems the college isn't the picture of love and happiness yon professor chappy would like you to believe. Financial troubles, poor results. There's even talk of some scam selling qualifications so students can get visas. They don't do any studies. Find work, mostly. After a year or two they get a meaningless qualification and permanent residence.'

'What about our suicides?'

'The lot I talked to didn't seem to know much about them. A couple knew Mikhailevic. Thought he might have been in a study group with Duncan George and your Caroline Sellars back there.'

'Let me guess. Parapsychology experiments with Doctor Eleanor Austin.'

Grumpy Bob leaned forwards and started the engine, peered down at the gear stick until he could find reverse. 'See, that's what I'm on about all the time, sir. You send me off on an errand and then get the answer for yourself. Sometimes wonder why you need me about at all. Jesus, you can't see much out of the back of this thing.'

'You'll be fine. It beeps at you if you get too close to anything. Like that.' McLean tried not to tense as an electronic squawking erupted from the dashboard. He pulled out his phone and started tapping at the screen, looking for the name he wanted. Unbidden, it appeared, and it took him a while to realize that it was an incoming call from Doctor Austin herself. The call didn't take long; Grumpy Bob had barely manoeuvred the car to the exit by the time he'd hung up.

'Back to the station, sir?'

'No. Western General. Fast as you like.' He knew now why Jenny Nairn hadn't come home.

49

'They're saying she stepped out in front of a bus.'

It wasn't quite how he'd anticipated his next meeting with Doctor Austin. She'd been waiting at the front reception desk when McLean came in, obviously distraught.

'When did it happen? How is she?'

'Last night. Late, I think. After midnight. She's in the ICU.'

McLean allowed himself to be led in silence through the hospital. That Doctor Austin hadn't answered his second question directly didn't bode well for Jenny's condition.

The all-too-familiar route brought them swiftly to the intensive care unit. A uniform sergeant sat on an uncomfortable plastic chair outside the room where Magda Evans was recovering. He put down his book and stood up as McLean came towards him along the corridor. It was obvious both that he'd been warned not to let the detective inspector anywhere near her, and that he wasn't quite sure how he was going to reprimand a senior officer. McLean put him at ease with a wave.

'It's OK. I'm here for something else.'

'Right you are, sir.' The sergeant nodded and sat back down to his book. Doctor Austin raised an eyebrow.

'One of yours?' she asked.

'Long story. Not important. Tell me about Jenny.'

Doctor Austin started walking down the corridor again.

'She came to see me yesterday evening. We did what we usually do, had a bite to eat, shared a bottle of wine and talked until far too late. She wasn't drunk or anything. Perhaps a bit distracted by her studies. And looking after Emma is hard, as I'm sure you know. She left about half twelve, said she was going to walk to the city centre and then get a cab. I'd have called one for her, but she loved to walk. Espccially at night.'

They had reached the main ward of the intensive care unit. Doctor Austin stopped short of the bed where Jenny lay, surrounded by expensive machinery. McLean had seen far too many people in a similar situation for it to be truly shocking any more, but it never ceased to amaze him how small and fragile people were. It was almost impossible to see Jenny in the bed.

Doctor Wheeler was studying the readout on a screen as they approached, and turned when she heard them. It was nice to see a familiar face, but McLean knew all too well what her presence meant. Cranial trauma was her speciality. Brain damage. She looked him straight in the eye and gave the tiniest shakes of the head.

'What's the prognosis?' McLean asked.

'Not good, I'm afraid. There's too much damage to her brain. She'll never wake up. It's a miracle she survived at all, or whatever the evil equivalent of a miracle is. I guess it gives us time to inform her family. Otherwise it's just the machines keeping her body going.'

An involuntary shudder ran through McLean's back as he remembered Emma's words that morning. How convinced she was that Jenny had gone.

'She has no family. Just me.' Doctor Austin's stance was

of someone getting ready for a fight, but Doctor Wheeler just shook her head and turned her attention back to the machines surrounding the bed.

'Jenny's related to you?' McLean asked.

'Not by birth, no. But she was my protégée. She always came to me when she needed something. We were friends.'

'And she has no immediate family?'

'None.' Doctor Austin shook her head. 'Her mum died when she was sixteen. She never knew her father, but she was old enough to be an adult, as far as the law was concerned. Too young to really know what she was doing. She . . .' Doctor Austin paused as if searching for the right words. 'Came to my attention then and I took her under my wing.'

McLean let out a deep sigh. It was never easy. Sooner or later the grief would hit him, too. He was still processing that. He'd not known Jenny long, but she'd lived under his roof for a few months, cooked breakfast for him, looked after Emma. Dammit, he'd liked her, despite her strangeness.

'You said she was your protégée.' Dr Austin's earlier words finally registered. 'You taught her? At Fulcholme?'

Doctor Austin gave a little involuntary start. 'Heavens, no. Not there. I occasionally lecture at the university. Jenny was studying for a PhD. When she could afford to. Grants in her field of study are few and far between. Hence the need to take on work.'

Months and he hadn't known. Had never really bothered to find out. She'd come as a godsend, but how quickly he'd taken her for granted. How easy it was to pay to make the problems go away. Only they never really did, just hid in the shadows and multiplied.

421

'But you do lecture at Fulcholme still? And run research projects there?'

Again that little start, as if the question were a surprise. 'Yes, I still lecture there. You take the work where you can find it. Might I ask why you're interested?' Doctor Austin's gaze darted away from McLean to Doctor Wheeler, who had her back to them and was most likely not listening anyway.

'It's an ongoing investigation. A couple of your students have . . . Well, it's not really the time or the place now.' McLean shoved a hand in his pocket, dug out one of his cards and handed it over. 'Perhaps you could come to the station tomorrow?'

McLean left Doctor Austin and Doctor Wheeler to their silent vigil over the near-departed, went off in search of a nurse instead. You could ask doctors all the questions in the world, but if you wanted to know what was really going on, a nurse was a much better bet.

He found the one he was looking for quickly enough. Jeanie Robertson had looked after his gran in the months before her death, and she was still a part of the ICU team.

'Jenny Nairn? Yes, it's terrible. So young.' Her soft Western Isles accent only added to the feeling that Jenny was dead already.

'Do you know who brought her in? Who saw her first?'

'Well, she was taken to A and E, obviously. But the doctors there moved her up to us as soon as they'd stabilized her. To be honest, it would've been kinder if she'd not made it.'

The second person to make that observation. McLean

could hardly blame them. If there was no chance of recovery, then Jenny Nairn's body was blocking up a bed in intensive care. If there was a slight chance she might start breathing unaided, she was still going to be in a persistent vegetative state for the rest of her life. All that was left was a husk. She'd gone. Just like Emma had said.

'Do you know what happened to her clothes when she came in? Anything else she had with her?'

'They'll be in a locker somewhere. Did you want to see them?'

McLean's head told him no. If there was an investigation into the circumstances of the accident, then he wouldn't be allowed to conduct it. Not given his relationship with Jenny. But there was the small matter of the suitcase in her room. He'd hardly had time to think about that, but the wig, grey like the lady seen with Grigori Mikhailevic; the rope, identical to that used to hang four people. Or by four people to hang themselves, with a little help. He had a hard time squaring that with the young woman who had shared his house these past months, but if she was somehow linked, he needed as much information as he could get before the shit hit the fan.

'I wouldn't mind a wee look at them, if that was OK.'

He followed the nurse down a series of corridors, ending up in a locked backroom filled with all manner of things that had nowhere else to go. Jenny's few personal possessions were in a cardboard box. It didn't amount to much. The clothes she'd been wearing were torn and blood-stained; her phone had been crushed. Only her leather satchel with its collection of textbooks had survived largely unscathed, along with a bunch of keys that

423

would let her into his house and, presumably, her own place in Gilmerton. McLean didn't know the exact address.

'You wanting to take these away?' He was holding the key-ring when the nurse spoke, the impatience barely hidden in her voice. Fair enough, she was busy and he was taking monstrous liberties.

'No. I'll have a constable fetch them once we've opened the investigation. Probably safer here for now.' He closed the lid on the box and slid it back onto the shelf. They'd be questioning the driver and any other witnesses, of course. But there would only be a full investigation if Jenny died. The look on the nurse's face confirmed what he feared, that it would be when rather than if.

McLean thanked the nurse, left her locking up the room. He thought about going back to the ICU for an update on Jenny's condition, but he knew it would be a wasted trip. Emma had told him Jenny was gone. He couldn't begin to understand how she had known, but she was right. Gone and left him with a whole heap of trouble to sort out.

It wasn't until he was halfway to the hospital car park that he realized he still had the key-ring clasped in his fist.

First officer on the scene of the accident had been a Constable Orton. He operated out of a different station, and his shift wasn't due to start for another couple of hours, but he had logged the incident, so McLean was able to piece together something of what had happened.

Jenny had been walking back to the city centre, that much chimed with everything Doctor Austin had told him. The accident had happened on Broughton Street, near the top of the hill. The night-bus driver had been in shock when Constable Orton had spoken to him, and claimed that Jenny had simply stepped off the pavement without warning. She hadn't been wearing headphones like so many others of her generation. Nor was it a particularly dangerous stretch of road. The bus had only been doing twenty, maybe twenty-five miles an hour. But it was a bus.

Paramedics had arrived at the scene within five minutes of it being called in. Constable Orton, aided by a couple more officers who had also arrived by that time, took details from everyone on the bus. Only four people as it turned out, none of whom had seen anything. There didn't seem to have been any witnesses on the street at the time. The bus company had sent out a replacement vehicle and taken the one that had hit Jenny back to the depot, where it would sit in a garage until the police were done with their enquiries. All very simple, all by the book. A tragic accident indeed. But still there was that niggling doubt he found hard to ignore. A grey-brown wig and a length of hemp rope, too.

Closing down his computer, McLean went off in search of the one person he'd really rather avoid.

'Let me get this straight. You want me to ask DI Spence to conduct an investigation into an incident where there's no evidence of foul play? Why can't you look into it yourself? In your own time.'

Acting Superintendent Duguid sat back in his leather office chair, swivelling gently from side to side as he spoke. The desk between him and McLean was spotlessly clean, devoid of all paperwork save a copy of that morning's *Scotsman*.

'Miss Nairn was working for me, sir. As I think I told you already. I can't investigate her . . .' He was about to say death, but managed to stop himself.

'You can't investigate anything, McLean. Not until Rab Callard gives you the OK. Far as I can tell, there's nothing to investigate anyway. Your employee walked in front of a bus. Funny how these things happen to people around you.'

Christ, but the man was irritating. McLean swung his hands behind his back and clasped them together as tightly as he could. It didn't really help, other than to stop him from hitting something.

'I hardly think that's an appropriate comment, sir. She was my employee and my friend, and she had her whole life ahead of her. I owe it to her to find out what happened.'

'You owe it to her.' Duguid sat forward, planted his elbows on the desk, pointed a long, thin finger. 'You, McLean. Not Lothian and Borders Police. Not beyond what we've already done.'

The bare minimum. Probably not even that. It was like dealing with a child, and they'd put him in charge.

'Jenny Nairn's in a coma and she's not going to wake up. She's going to die, sir. Maybe tomorrow, maybe in a month. And when that happens the Procurator Fiscal will want a report. Unnatural death. That's how it works. Don't you think it would be a good idea if we've actually looked into the circumstances? Maybe while the incident's still fresh in everyone's minds?'

Duguid stared at him with piggy eyes, his brow furrowing as he considered McLean's words. It made sense, that was the problem. Duguid knew it, and hated that McLean was right.

'Dammit, man, we don't have the budget to go investigating every incident in the city.'

So it was the money, as always.

'At least have someone speak to the driver, sir. He was in shock when Constable Orton saw him. He'll be able to give us a fuller picture of what happened. It shouldn't take more than an hour. I'd ask DC MacBride, but I can't head this up. Not on paper at least.' He left it there, hanging, in the hope that Duguid would take the bait.

'You're a menace, you know that, McLean?' The acting superintendent pushed his chair back from the desk and stood up, obviously finding it hard to make a decision whilst sat on his arse. 'Very well. Have MacBride interview the driver, draw up a report and submit it to me directly. You are not, repeat not, to sit in on that interview. Understood?'

'Thank you, sir. Yes.' McLean nodded his appreciation at the same time as it occurred to him it might be worthwhile seeing if there was any CCTV coverage. For a moment, he even considered asking before he realized what a stupid idea that was.

'Thank you,' he said once more, and fled from the room.

It was far later than five when McLean finally drove through the gates and parked his new car outside the house. Lights shone from the kitchen window and lit up the lawn around the back, which suggested that someone was home. There had been no calls on his mobile either, so he had to hope everything was all right.

Except that he was going to have to explain to Emma that Jenny was near death and wouldn't be coming back.

Staring out through the windscreen, hands still resting on the leather steering wheel, he realized that Emma already knew. Emma had been the first to know. That was why she had crawled into his bed so early in the morning. That was what she had said when he'd found Jenny missing. He didn't want to know how Emma had known. He didn't want to think about the things Madame Rose had said either, and yet he'd gone to the transvestite medium for help. More than ever, he just wanted to close his eyes and sleep until it all went away. When had it all started getting so hard? So confusing? So overwhelming?

Taking a deep breath, he climbed out of the car and headed into the house.

Emma was sitting at the table as he entered the kitchen. As she saw him, a huge grin spread across her face and she leapt up, embraced him in a warm hug. It was a child's welcome, and somehow that just made him feel even more tired.

'We've been sorting out the books all day. I like Rose. She's funny.' Emma leaned close to his ear and whispered. 'And she's really a man.'

She let out a bark of laughter as if this was the funniest thing she'd ever come across. The noise brought the object of her mirth through to the kitchen. Madame Rose had a pair of horn-rimmed spectacles perched on the end of her nose. His nose. Whatever. The medium peered over them at McLean.

'You're back.'

McLean looked up at the clock on the kitchen wall. 'Sorry, it's a lot later than I realized. I found out what happened to Jenny.'

Madame Rose sank into one of the kitchen chairs as McLean told them the story. Emma fidgeted, as if she already knew it all. In the silence that fell after he'd finished, Mrs McCutcheon's cat came wandering in, leapt onto the table and walked across the middle until it could nuzzle at his hand with its nose.

'I'm so sorry,' Madame Rose said after a while. 'Is there any hope she might recover?'

McLean shook his head. 'I don't think so.'

'I told you she'd gone and wasn't coming back. She said she was sorry.' Emma reached out and stroked the cat's back, making it arch.

'I'll have to sort out all the stuff in her room. Not really sure who should have it, mind you.' McLean stifled a yawn, turning to Madame Rose. 'Can I give you a lift home?'

'I think a cab might be a better idea.'

'You sure?' McLean pulled out his phone and thumbed the screen, looking for the number of the nearest taxi firm. Emma announced out of nowhere that she was bored and was going to watch some telly, flounced out of the kitchen as if the news of Jenny's terrible fate meant nothing to her. Cab booked, McLean pulled out a chair and sat down, the weight of the day finally catching up with him.

'She's a strange one, your Miss Baird. I thought I knew what was wrong with her, but now I think I might have got it all wrong.'

'Oh yes?' McLean wasn't really listening. He could still

see Jenny Nairn's face wrapped in bandages and sunken into a pillow.

'I need to do a bit of research, but I'd like to try something that I think will help. I assume you'll be wanting me to come round again tomorrow?'

That got a bit more of his attention. 'Can you? I'm going to have to find another carer, but that'll take time. Em seems to like you.'

'I like her too. She's interesting. Anyway, we've barely made a dent on the library yet.'

'So what do you reckon you can do to help?' McLean rubbed at his eyes, hoping it might make them easier to keep open. 'Don't say hypnotism, because we've tried that. Electric shocks too.'

Madame Rose laughed. 'Nothing so spooky. I'd just like to take her to a particular place. See what happens.'

'What does Emma think about it.'

'What do I think about what?'

McLean looked up as Emma came back in and walked across the kitchen to the Aga. She put the kettle on before explaining. 'There's nothing on the telly. Thought I'd have a cup of tea.'

'I was telling the inspector about my theory. About the people you see. The ones who come and visit you in the night.'

'Jenny was with them last night.' Emma frowned, the first expression of sadness McLean had seen in her in a while. It didn't last long. 'Rose thinks he knows where the people come from.'

McLean looked at the medium, raised an eyebrow but said nothing.

430

'It's a theory, but if I'm right it might help.'

'And if you're wrong?'

'Then we'll have gone for a little walk outside. Nothing more.'

That surprised him. 'Outside?' he asked Emma. 'I thought you didn't like going out.'

Lights outside and the scrunching of tyres on gravel stopped Emma's reply. Madame Rose stood up. 'That'll be my cab. They always come quickly when they know it's me.'

50

'If you could just go over it one more time. In your own words.'

McLean stood in the observation booth looking through the one-way glass into interview room three. Detective Constable MacBride was conducting an interview with the driver of the bus that had hit Jenny Nairn. Robert Gurney didn't look anything special. Mid-forties, bald on top, chubbing up as so often happened to people who sat down for a living. He looked pale, like a man who'd not slept well. McLean could sympathize with that; he couldn't remember the last time he'd had an uninterrupted sleep. Even last night when Emma had been so positive, bubbly even after a day spent with Madame Rose, she had still crawled into his bed at half four, shivering and sobbing.

Shaking his head, he focused his attention back on the driver. MacBride was being very patient, giving the man space and time to gather his thoughts. Even PC Gregg, hovering by the door, was keeping her mouth shut. Well, there was a first time for everything.

'Been driving the late bus a couple months now.' Robert Gurney's voice was high-pitched for such a thick-set man. Not helped by the wavering tone. 'Usually that route. Sometimes south to Roslin and Penicuik. There's no' usually that many on the bus by Broughton Street. Tend to pick them up further down.'

'What about pedestrians? Many about at that time? It wasn't all that late, really.' MacBride spotted the digression and gently herded the driver back on course. Like a well-trained sheepdog.

'There's usually one or two spilling out the pubs then. Don't really remember, to be honest.' Gurney had been studying his hands, but now looked straight up at Mac-Bride. 'I saw her, though. She was walking up the hill at quite a pace, that bag slung over her shoulder. She had her eyes set straight ahead, not looking over to see when she could cross. You drive the buses long as I have, you get to read people, you know?' He shook his head. 'Least, I thought so. Till last night.'

Gurney fell silent, and MacBride let the quiet grow as he carefully took down some notes. The interview was being taped and filmed, but there was no reason not to be thorough. Only when he had finished did he speak again.

'I know this must be very difficult, reliving what happened. But if you could just take me through it, step by step. You say Miss Nairn was walking up the hill?'

First mistake. Behind the glass, McLean winced as he saw the driver stiffen. For all they knew he hadn't heard the name before. Speaking it only made it more personal.

'Is she . . . ? Did she . . . You know?'

'She's in intensive care. The doctors are doing every-thing they can for her. Don't worry about that, Mr Gurney.' MacBride's voice was soft, reassuring. 'You said you saw her walking up the hill. What happened next?'

Gurney's shoulders shook as he sobbed. 'It all hap-pened so quickly. One moment she was coming towards me, not looking at the bus, not even close to the edge of

433

the pavement, really. Then there was just this terrible bang. I never even saw her step off. By the time I'd slammed on the brakes it was too late.'

'Poor bastard. It'll be a while before he drives a bus again.'

Grumpy Bob leaned against the one-way glass in the observation booth as PC Gregg led Robert Gurney away. MacBride disappeared from the interview room too, reappearing moments later through the door.

'Sorry about that, sir' were his first words.

'No need to apologize, Constable. That was fine.' McLean still stared through the glass, even though the interview room was empty. He wasn't really all that sure why he'd insisted on the interview now. It was obviously not Gurney's fault he'd hit Jenny; probably not Jenny's either. Sometimes shit just happened. A loose flagstone, discarded Coke can, mistimed step, anything. A lurch to the side, just the wrong moment and splat, you were under a bus. But he needed to know. To be sure. That was his problem, really. He couldn't leave it alone. Wasn't that what everyone always said?

'You know if there's any CCTV coverage of that area?' McLean turned to face MacBride.

'Sure you want to be digging around like that, sir?' Grumpy Bob asked.

'I'm fairly sure I'm not involved in this investigation at all. Certainly not here in this room. That not right, Constable?'

MacBride's eyes flicked between his two superior officers, a look of confusion on his face slowly fading as his brain caught up.

'It occurs to me that following on from that interview, I really should check whether there's any CCTV footage of the area. What do you think, Sergeant?'

Grumpy Bob let out a snort of laughter and slapped MacBride on the shoulder. 'You'll go far, lad. More's the pity.'

The interview room looked very different from the other side of the glass. It was half an hour later and McLean was sitting in the chair previously warmed by the backside of DC MacBride. Taking PC Gregg's part, though less likely to talk out of turn, DS Ritchie sat beside him. Across the small table, Doctor Eleanor Austin seemed calm and relaxed. She stared at him with those wide, grey eyes of hers, very occasionally taking a little break to look at Ritchie or gaze over the room. There was nobody in the observation booth, as far as McLean was aware. Somehow he got the feeling that Doctor Austin would have known if there were.

'You run a course on parapsychology at Fulcholme College. How long have you been doing that?'

'It's not really a course as such. More a module. You can't get a degree in parapsychology, despite what you might have seen on the television.'

'OK. So how long have you been running this module?'

'Four years this August. No, I tell a lie, five years. Time flies, doesn't it, Inspector?'

McLean ignored the question. 'Professor Bain tells me it's very popular.'

'David can be such a salesman. We get a lot of students sign up, that's true. But not many of them stay after the

435

first couple of sessions. They all think it's going to be ghost hunting and mind reading, but the field of parapsychology is more about debunking the myths than anything else. Understanding the state of mind that makes people believe they've seen ghosts. Figuring out the many ways the human brain can be fooled.'

'What about hypnosis?'

'Hypnosis?' The question seemed to throw Doctor Austin for a while. 'Oh, I see. You're thinking about stage shows and the like. No, there's nothing paranormal about hypnosis. It's a well-researched tool and a useful therapy. As I think you're aware, Inspector.'

'But you teach it to your students.'

'Heavens no. I teach them about it, of course. As part of the general psychology course. I don't teach them how to do it. Wherever did you get that idea from?'

'Never mind, it's not important.' McLean shook his head, unsure how he'd strayed from the subject of the interview. 'You taught Caroline Sellars and Grigori Mikhailevic, I understand.'

Doctor Austin settled back, stared straight into his eyes. 'Not in the same class, but yes. I taught Carol and Grigori.'

'What about Duncan George?'

'Duncan was in Grigori's group. They were friends. I was very sad when he left. He had such potential, but he also had very deep problems. He needed therapy, which I would have been happy to give him.'

'Do the names John Fenton and Patrick Sands mean anything to you?'

Doctor Austin stiffened in her seat, and for a moment

McLean saw something like fear flit across her eyes. Then they seemed to widen, pupils dilating as if the lights had dimmed.

'Both of those names mean something to me. But I have to consider patient–doctor confidentiality.'

'You weren't aware that both of them were dead, then?' DS Ritchie asked the question, sparking a momentary flash of irritation in McLean. In Doctor Austin, too, if the look she gave the sergeant was anything to go by.

'Am I under suspicion here?' she asked. 'Should I have a lawyer present?'

'Not at all. We're simply trying to ascertain whether or not there is a connection between a number of recent suicides, Doctor Austin.' Ritchie appeared to be immune to the doctor's stare, much to McLean's amusement. And relief. Now that she was focusing on someone else, the tension he had not realized he was under began to ebb away.

'Well, if that's the case, then why didn't you just ask?'

'I rather thought I just had.' Ritchie tapped her notepad with her pen. She hadn't written anything down yet.

'John Fenton and Patrick Sands were both patients of yours,' McLean said.

'I didn't say that.' Doctor Austin paused, considering her words. 'But yes. They were.'

'How did they come to you?'

'Not "what were they seeing you for"?'

'I didn't think you'd answer that one. Not sure it's really all that important.'

'If you must know, they both came to me through our mutual friend.'

McLean raised a quizzical eyebrow. 'Who?'

'Who do you think? Jenny. She worked with Sands in that god-awful call centre. Nearly drove her mad. John she met in a bar, apparently. He's dead, you say?'

'Did they know each other? Fenton and Sands?'

Again a pause. Doctor Austin tried to fix her gaze on him again, but McLean avoided it. After a brief battle, she gave up.

'They met, certainly. Probably Carol, Grigori and Duncan, too.'

'All of them? Together? Where?' McLean leaned forward. Ritchie, he noticed, had started to write. Doctor Austin gave them a triumphant little smile.

'At Jenny's, of course.'

'She's lying.'

'Yes, but about what?'

McLean and Ritchie had retired to the canteen, Doctor Austin having the dubious honour of being given a lift home by PC Gregg. The coffee was especially bad that morning, but at least it was wet.

'I think she knew all of them. I think she brought them all together. Probably Jenny too. What I'd like to know is what they were doing.'

'What's the story there? I heard about the accident.'

McLean peered into the depths of his mug, saw the bottom clearly through inches of something that claimed to be coffee. 'She won't recover. If there's any fairness in the world, she'll die soon, quietly and painlessly. Mind you, if there was any justice in the world she'd never have stepped in front of that bus in the first place.'

The two of them sat in silence for a while after that,

438

which suited McLean fine. Only when she had forced down the last of her drink did Ritchie say anything.

'I'm sorry I jumped in a bit, back in the interview.'

'Did you?' McLean frowned as he tried to remember. There was a vague sense of irritation, but he couldn't quite put his finger on why he felt it. Nor could he really recall much in the way of detail from what Doctor Austin had told them.

'You were doing the silent thing. You know? Where you just sit there and stare until the other person feels they have to say something?' Ritchie made a half-hearted stab at it herself, pausing for all of two seconds before adding: 'Only you were leaving it way too long. Almost like you were falling asleep.'

McLean tried not to yawn at that, failed. He really was very tired. 'I didn't realize. Sorry.'

Ritchie suppressed a smirk. 'I was going to say every-thing all right at home. Bit bloody stupid, really. How's Emma?'

'Remarkably composed.' McLean glanced at his watch, almost two. He could grab some paperwork and take it home with him. Give Madame Rose a break and maybe make a start on finding another home help. 'Think I might go home though. Not as if we're getting anywhere here.'

Ritchie gave him an odd look, as if he'd just said some-thing really stupid. 'You want me to follow up on Doctor Austin?'

McLean almost said: 'Who?' Shook his head to try and dislodge the weariness dragging at him. Maybe he was coming down with something.

'Might be an idea.'

'I'll work up a background on her. See if there's any history.'

A rare lucid thought popped into McLean's head. 'Have a chat with Doctor Wheeler at the hospital. They know each other of old, and aren't exactly the best of friends. Actually, I'll do it. I need to speak to her anyway about Em.'

'OK. You want me to arrange a briefing for tomorrow morning?'

'Good idea. Eight o'clock in the CID room.' McLean abandoned the last of his coffee, stood up to leave. The world dimmed, and he put out a surreptitious hand to steady himself until the blood came back to his head. Maybe he really was coming down with something. That was always a problem if you spent too much time in hospitals.

'On second thoughts, let's make it nine, eh?'

The further he drove from the station, the clearer McLean's head became. Perhaps it was an allergy thing and the pollen filter in the car was clearing the air for him. He'd never really suffered from anything like that before, though. And he was still dog tired; those cats still howling.

Afternoon traffic was relatively light, which made a nice change from commuter-time snarl-ups. Avoiding the city centre and the tram works helped, too. Soon he was parked up outside the house, engine off and just staring out at nothing. It was warm, quiet and peaceful. Comfortable, too, in the deep leather seat. He could just close his eyes and drift off for a moment.

McLean shook his head to clear the cobwebs. A thick wodge of folders sat on the passenger seat, demanding his attention. He could snooze later, perhaps with a dram. First there was work to do.

The first strange thing he noticed was that the back door was locked. He'd grown so used to there always being someone in, it took him a while to remember that he had a set of keys in his pocket. Inside, the kitchen was warm, but silent. Just the tick-tocking of the clock on the wall. He went through to the hall, looked in the library, then checked the front door. It, too, was locked.

'Emma? Madame Rose?' He felt a bit stupid saying the medium's name, but he had no idea what else to call her, him. The transvestism didn't bother him at all; it was not knowing how to treat him, her, whatever, that left him uneasy. Maybe that was the point.

Either way, there was no answer, which meant they must have gone out. Reflexively, McLean checked his phone. There were no messages and no missed calls. Just a couple of texts from Ritchie reminding him to talk to Doctor Wheeler ahead of the briefing. Her subtle way of reminding him about the briefing, no doubt. Had he really been that switched off this morning?

Back in the kitchen, McLean noticed a sheet of A4 paper lying in the middle of the table with an empty mug holding it down. Written in a neat hand that had to be Madame Rose's were the words: *Gone for a little walk outside. Back soon.* The note had been written at half past two, according to the time scribbled below it. A quick glance at the clock showed that he must have just missed them. He raised an eyebrow at the word 'outside'. Emma had shown little inclination for the great outdoors after her excursion to Loanhead, and whilst Jenny had managed to coax her into

441

the garden occasionally, going any further quite obviously filled her with terror. And yet somehow Madame Rose had managed to persuade Emma not only to leave the house, but also the garden. Otherwise why bother locking up? He wondered where they'd gone.

A clattering noise from the hallway distracted him. For a moment he thought it was the front door being unlocked, but then Mrs McCutcheon's cat sauntered in, jumped up onto the table and rubbed its head against his hand. When he absent-mindedly stroked its back, it turned around jumped down and stalked back out again, pausing in the doorway to stare back at him over its shoulder. It looked absurdly like it wanted him to follow it, so he did.

Out in the hall, it strode across to the stairs before checking that he was doing as he was told. It climbed the steps in a series of bounds, stopping at each turn and looking back. When it reached the landing, it stalked purposefully off towards the narrow staircase to the attic and then disappeared into the darkness. Curious, McLean followed all the way to the closed door to Jenny's room.

Pushing open the door revealed the room much as he had left it. The suitcase still lay on the bed, the little dressing table in the window still held Jenny's laptop, the pile of textbooks still built their little Tower of Babel on the floor beside it. He took a step inside, almost tripping over the cat as it twined itself around his legs.

'Dammit, cat. Are you trying to kill me?' He struggled away from the beast, found himself standing right in front of the dressing table. Without really thinking, he pulled out the chair, sat down and tapped at a key on the laptop. The screen came to life, showed the document Jenny had been working on before she had left. Not very good security then. McLean stared at the words, trying to make sense of them. He'd been expecting some essay on Neuro-Linguistic Programming, or whatever it was Jenny had been studying. Instead he found a letter, the address on the top somewhere in Gilmerton, so presumably her home. It began:

Dear Eleanor,
I don't know how to say this without hurting your feelings, and quite frankly I'm not sure I care any more. Time was I thought you were my friend, but I can see now you were only using me to get what you wanted. Just like you used all those others before me.
I

and then the cursor blinked, waiting for something more. It would have to wait a very long time. McLean stared at the words, feeling almost dirty for peering into this private aspect of Jenny's life. It was odd, really. It wasn't as if he hadn't seen many, many secrets revealed in his career as a detective, and yet somehow this was more personal.

He looked briefly at the other items on the dressing table: spiral-bound notebook with scruffy handwriting and doodles; assortment of biros and pencils, all chewed at the ends; a half-finished roll of Polo mints. Sticking his hand in his pocket, McLean pulled out the set of keys he'd taken from Jenny's belongings at the hospital. There was a set for the house, and another set he didn't recognize, though obviously house keys. And there on the screen was an address. Almost as if Jenny had left it there for him to see. As if she were inviting him to go and look.

443

Behind him, Mrs McCutcheon's cat began to purr, a noise so loud he could almost feel it through the soles of his feet. When he turned to look, it started licking one of its paws. No longer finding him of any interest whatsoever. McLean hefted the keys in his hand, glanced quickly at the partially written letter once more. Downstairs an afternoon's paperwork awaited him, or he could make a trip out to Gilmerton and see what that might turn up. It wasn't really that hard a decision to make.

51

Gilmerton hadn't changed much in years. It was still a drab collection of housing estates, the varied architectural tastes of the different decades marked out in pebbledash and roof tile. There was an older part, though, and Jenny's address turned out to be one of the houses built when it was still a mining village separated from the big city by several miles of farmland.

McLean had assumed Jenny lived in a tiny flat; she had no money, after all. But the house formed the end of a neat terrace and had a large garden at the back, mostly given over to the cultivation of weeds. Not quite sure why he was here, he approached the building as if it were a potential crime scene, peering through the windows and clocking the escape routes. It was a waste of time; the windows were so grimy he could barely make out anything inside, and there were just the two doors. Anyone attempting to escape out the back would have to fight their way through a jungle before clambering over a stone wall into the lane behind.

The front door had two keyholes; a deadlock and a latch. It took McLean a while to find the right keys from the bundle, longer still to realize that the deadlock had not been engaged. Opening the door pushed a stack of envelopes up against the wall, where they joined forces with a growing pile. McLean stooped, picked up one at random.

An invitation to take out a credit card, much like the hundreds that had arrived for his grandmother in the months that she'd been in a coma. He shuddered at the similarities. Would Jenny hang in there for eighteen months or more? Kept alive in the loosest sense of the word by machines that cared nothing for quality of life? Modern medicine had achieved many miracles, but he couldn't help thinking it was stuck in the dark ages where death was concerned.

He noticed the smell when he stood up, and realized that it had been there from the moment he'd stepped inside. Not exactly rot, nor mould, it was something he couldn't quite place. Other than in a box marked 'unpleasant'. The air in the house was stagnant, unmoving. He doubted both that there were any windows open, and that anyone had moved from room to room for a while. Like its owner, the place was stuck in a limbo between dead and alive.

The entrance hall opened onto two small front rooms, then past the stairs to a kitchen and scullery at the back. None of them showed much trace of habitation in recent times. The house was furnished, and generally tidy, but it was as if someone had gone out the front door fifty years earlier and never come back.

Upstairs showed much the same lack of habitation. There were three bedrooms, all small, all kitted out with antique beds and old wardrobes. In the bathroom, the water in the toilet bowl had evaporated away, concentric rings of lime scale marking its slow disappearance. McLean looked out through a dust- and cobweb-covered window, down to the overgrown garden below. He'd missed it before, but there was an old garage at the end,

and a gently curving path knocked through the brush leading from the back door. Someone had been down there
often enough, even if they'd never bothered with the rest
of the property.

The back door had a deadlock and latch like the front.
There was also a heavy iron bolt, but it had long since been
painted open. As he stepped out of the dead house into the
garden it was as if someone had turned the lights and volume back up. Birds sang from the trees, cars whooshed past
on the road out the front, and the familiar, reassuring roar
of the city bypass covered everything. McLean followed the
path through brambles up to his waist, whippy elder bushes
and weed ashes that must have been growing for ten years
or more, until he finally found himself at the garage.

It was a stone-built structure, tall and narrow, with a
steep-pitched slate roof. Probably a coach house in olden
days, though it didn't seem large enough to have housed
stables. The paint on the wooden door was coming off in
thick, curly flakes, but the keyhole glistened in the sunlight
where it had been used, regularly and recently. He tried
the handle first, found it wasn't locked.

If the smell in the house had been unpleasant, it was
nothing compared to the stench that hit him now. This one
was all too easily identifiable. He'd smelled it too often
before, most recently in a tiny flat in the Colonies. But he
didn't need that cue. The body hanging from the beams by
its broken neck was clue enough. Sunlight speared through
a skylight, dappled by the trees outside. It played upon the
naked skin like a weird, moving camouflage.

McLean stepped carefully into the garage, noting the
layout. At the far end, double doors would open up onto

447

the lane. There was plenty of space for a car, but like most garages this one was used mainly for storage. The walls were lined with old wooden shelves, piled up with tin boxes, glass jars, rubbish mainly. A workbench stretched under a window whose panes of glass had been painted white. An attempt to stop sunlight fading the paintwork on a brand-new car sometime in the 1950s, no doubt. The obligatory pair of sit-up-and-beg bicycles leaned against a stack of tea chests, tyres flat, wicker baskets almost completely rotted away. An old set of wooden stepladders lay against the wall to his left, resting where they had landed after the deceased took his last, long step. And there was no doubting it was he, McLean saw, as he walked slowly around the body. Decay might have set in, but enough of his features were still identifiable.

Grigori Mikhailevic.

'He loved her so much, but she felt nothing for him. That was his undoing, in the end.'

McLean started at the sound behind him, whirled around. All he could see was an outline, silhouetted by the bright sunshine outside, but he recognized the voice.

'She killed them, didn't she. Lured them in, tied the nooses, made them do it.'

A little girl laugh. 'Jenny wouldn't hurt a fly, Inspector. She was just my huntress. My tool. The spirit's tool.'

He took a step forwards as the figure moved in the doorway. Still the sun cast it in shadow, made him squint to see a face. Then he caught the eyes, glowing like lava in the night. They held him tight, helpless as an infant, pulling him in, dragging him down, down, down.

52

He can't think straight. It's like that time Phil spiked his drink with something he'd cooked up in the lab. Only then they'd both just stared at the wall, trying to work out why the paper was patterned the way it was. For six hours, he thinks it was. Only he can't remember. He's not entirely sure who Phil is, either. Something about a place called America, wherever that is.

He's driving . . . where? Is it a good idea to drive in this condition? He doesn't know, and anyway he can't stop. It's taking all his concentration just to keep his hands on the wheel, keep the car straight.

There's someone sitting beside him, but he dare not look. There's the concentration needed to keep the car on the road, of course. But there's also memories of fire and brimstone, of burning eyes and deep despair, of a man hanging from a rope, his neck broken, his flesh beginning to rot.

Time passes, and he is no longer in the car. Did they crash? He thinks he'd remember that. His parents crashed, so long ago. Smashed to tiny pieces as their aeroplane collided with the side of a mountain. They'd left him all alone, even though they'd promised him they never would. The fires had taken them, burned them into nothing but ashes and memories.

He is in a room. A kitchen. The terrible presence is

beside him, murmuring quietly. He knows this place. His grandmother lived here. And then she left one day in an ambulance, never came back. He remembers the days dragging into weeks, the weeks into months, hope dying bit by bit until finally there was nothing left but despair.

Now he is in an attic room, small, the servants' quarters when people still had servants. A leather suitcase lies on the narrow iron-frame bed and he opens it without realizing he has been told to. Inside lies a coil of stout hemp rope. He reaches in and takes it out.

And finally, where he always knew he would end up. He stands in the middle of an attic, warm like a lover's embrace. The rope is cold in his hands. Cold like the winter's day when they lowered her coffin into the ground. The monster stands beside him, talking to him in words he cannot understand. His fingers know what to do though, carefully folding and twisting the rope, looping it round and round to a count of thirteen. Unlucky thirteen, like his life.

He has to pull an old trunk into the middle of the room, place a precarious chair on top of it so that he can reach up into the rafters, tie off the rope on a stout crossbeam, just the right length. He wouldn't want to hit the floor.

Gazing down, he is aware of movement in the dark shadows under the eaves. Something watches him with patient eyes. Watches the monster as it pulls out his pain, his suffering and loss. Lays it out for all to see. Why would he want anyone to see that? Why would he want to see it himself. He dealt with it, didn't he? Put it all behind him. Moved on.

As he steps back down to the floor, something rushes past him. Commotion, hissing, a flash of teeth and claws and fur. The monster roars: 'He is mine!' A scream like nothing he has ever heard and a tiny body falls at his feet. It gasps for breath, mewling and twitching as he looks down at it. He should go to its aid, but all he can do is stand and wait.

The monster steps up to him, kicks the cat so hard it skitters away across the dusty floorboards into the darkness. Another innocent creature hurt because of him. How much better the world would be without him in it. How much less his suffering.

He feels the hands of the monster on him then, stroking his shoulders, running a finger down the middle of his back, another up the side of his neck and into his hair. He does not fear the monster, yet neither can he disobey it. At its unspoken command he begins to undress.

53

His first rational thought was for Mrs McCutcheon's cat. Somehow it had broken whatever hypnotic trance he had been under, but now it was injured, possibly even dead. The thought of it dying filled him with even greater gloom than the depression that had already settled over him.

McLean struggled to regain control of himself, even as his body continued to respond to someone else's commands. It was almost as if he were watching from outside, only he could see everything through his own eyes, including the noose now dangling beside his head, the bottom of its loop about level with his eyes.

'It will all be over soon. The pain, the suffering, the despair.' The voice behind him was impossible to ignore. It reached into the core of him, pulled out the sadness that had dogged him ever since he had waved his parents goodbye that fateful night, never to see them again.

'No.' He forced the word out through teeth clenched tight. He was done mourning for his parents. He would never forget them, but life went on. The dead held no sway over him.

'Shush now. Calm.' A finger touch on his bare shoulder. When had he begun to undress? Why had he begun to undress? He couldn't remember. There was just the touch, and with it an overwhelming sense of grief. Yes, life went on, but with all the joy sucked out of it by the bad things that lived on with it.

'Climb up, up. You need to get as high as you can.' There was something familiar about the voice, about the person behind it. McLean wanted to shake the fog out of his head, reach up and ram his fists into his eyes until he saw stars. Anything other than what his body was doing. And yes, he wanted to get away from the sorrow, the gut-punching waves of sadness that welled up in him, one after another. But there were better ways than this, surely? Anger had helped in the past. And throwing himself into his work.

'Your anger is all spent, and everyone at work wants you to leave. What will you do without those props? How will you fend off the horrors that have been with you all these years? Better to embrace them, accept them. Take that one step and you will find peace.'

This time the voice was different, all around him, inside him even. McLean struggled against it, but it was too powerful to resist. He had climbed up onto the trunk. And then onto the chair balanced on top of it. The noose was in his hands, the rope looping down towards the floor. All he needed to do was slip it over his head, tighten it just so, and shift it round so the knot pressed against his left ear. That way when his fall was stopped, the weight of his body would snap the vertebrae, killing him instantly. Blessed relief.

'But. I. Don't. Want. To. Die.' Each word was a struggle, each a spasm in his arms as he fought the urge to lift the noose over his head. He was tense now, teetering on the edge of the chair. The floor was somehow miles away, the air between him and the wooden boards filled with darting clouds that shone and shimmered. Not clouds, but ghosts. Souls once trapped, released in a magical fire. Lost now. Searching for a way through to wherever it was they were meant to go. They sensed his ending, flocked to him as if in his despair he might lead them to their goal. Perhaps there would be some benefit in his passing, then. Some final good to come out of the suffering.

His grip on reality slipped away, inch by inch, step by step. Like poor old Pete Buchanan, staring wild-eyed and terrified as his jacket ripped stitch by stitch. McLean almost laughed at the thought that the two of them would end in such a similar manner.

'He said he didn't want to die, you bitch.'

A different voice shattered the bubble that surrounded him. It brought feelings of happiness, excitement, caring. And it had a name.

Emma.

McLean turned around, suddenly back in full command of his body. A single scene painted itself on his eyeballs. Doctor Austin, halfway through turning to see who had interrupted her. Emma with a book in her hands, heavy, leather bound, old, expensive. Sir Arthur Conan Doyle's student copy of Gray's *Anatomy*. She swung it round in an arc, putting the full weight of her body behind it, and as it connected with the hypnotist's face the spell clouding his thoughts evaporated.

Doctor Austin went down like an expertly demolished building, crumpling into a tidy heap at Emma's feet. She looked up at him, triumphant, and he saw something in her eyes that had been missing since the day she woke up.

And then the chair beneath him gave a lurch to one side. McLean had no time to remember whether he'd put the noose around his neck or not. Arms flailing, he fell.

54

A quiet beeping sound roused him from the depths of blackness. McLean was aware of no dreams; there was just nothing and then the slow realization of noise. He tried to move, but something held him back. He was warm though, and the fear had gone. He couldn't remember what the fear had been about. Something to do with his neck; his throat felt tight as if someone had tried to choke him. It was enough to know that it was over. He could relax now and let sleep wash away his exhaustion.

Later, he woke to a dull pain that seemed to run through his entire body. He didn't open his eyes at first, just lay still and listened to the noises. It didn't take long to work out that he was in hospital; the smell was as much a giveaway as anything. It was either that or he'd died and Hell was just like the Western General. With more effort than should have been necessary, he opened his eyes.

He could see that the room was darkened, the overhead lights dimmed and the blinds drawn. It still felt like he was staring into the sun. He blinked until tears ran down his cheeks, blurring everything including the plaster on his leg that anchored him to the bed. When he opened his eyes again, a familiar white-coated figure was leaning over him.

'Back in the land of the living, Inspector? We were beginning to wonder.'

'I . . .' McLean coughed at the attempt to speak. His throat was as dry as a thirsty camel. 'How long?'

'We kept you sedated for a while. Had to get those bones set properly. There's some metal pins in your leg now, will probably be a bit of a pain every time you go through airport security.' Doctor Wheeler gave him a friendly smile, looked at her watch. 'You've been under for about forty-eight hours.'

Two days. McLean let his head sink back into the pillows, tied to take stock of his injuries. His arms were stiff and sore, but unbroken. His left leg was fine, but the right was encased in plaster. Everything hurt, even blinking, and swallowing was such exquisite agony he almost passed out when he tried to clear his throat to speak again. Movement wasn't impossible, just inadvisable for the time being, even if he had the energy. He tried not to think about needing to go to the toilet.

'What happened?' He vaguely remembered driving across the city. Had he been in an accident? Bloody typical to finally give in and buy himself a car, only to wrap it around a lamp post before he'd had it more than a couple of days.

'You fell off a chair balanced on top of a trunk. That's all anyone's told me. You'll have to ask Emma for the rest of it.'

'She's here?'

'Hasn't been away since you were brought in. I think she's asleep in the waiting room. I'll go and fetch her.' Doctor Wheeler paused a moment. 'She's improved enormously, you know. I have to say I had my doubts about regression therapy, but it seems this time Eleanor has actually succeeded at something.'

'This time?' It was painful even forcing out a couple of words.

'I shouldn't really be gossiping.' Doctor Wheeler pulled a chair closer to the bed, dropped wearily into it. 'Who am I kidding? She bad-mouthed me for years.'

McLean kept silent. He might have said he was leaving a space for Doctor Wheeler to fill in her own time, but the truth was he didn't think he could speak even if he wanted to.

'She was my supervisor, when I was studying neurobiology. Gods, that was a fair few years back now.' Doctor Wheeler shook her head in disbelief. 'I thought she was brilliant. To be fair, she was brilliant. But completely self-obsessed. As long as you were useful to her, she'd tolerate you. But if you dared question her. Oof.'

Another pause. McLean looked sideways at the doctor. She was leaning right backwards, head tilted up to the ceiling, eyes closed. For a moment he thought she might have fallen asleep; couldn't find it in him to be annoyed. If anyone looked like they needed a good kip it was Doctor Wheeler.

'She got interested in the whole hypnosis thing about ten years ago. Maybe twelve. I read a couple of her early papers and it looked like she was onto something. But then there was a problem with one of her study groups. A couple of her students committed suicide. There was an investigation. The ethics committee got involved. I was about to head off overseas for a few years. Won a scholarship to study best practice in neurobiology around the world, would you believe. But dear old Eleanor put the kybosh on that. Wrote to the head of the charity that was funding the trip, told him a whole load of lies about me.'

'Why?' McLean forced the word out in a hoarse whisper.

'Because I was the one called in the Ethics Committee. Like I said, she can be a bit self-obsessed. She put her test subjects through the wringer without having any of the obvious safeguards in place. A couple of them just couldn't cope.'

McLean didn't know whether to be grateful that she was telling him this, or annoyed that she'd known it and let Doctor Austin treat Emma anyway.

'Hanged themselves?'

'What . . . ? Oh, no. One of them slit his wrists. John Phimister, that was his name. Poor old John. The other one jumped off the ferry from Rosyth to Rotterdam, somewhere in the middle of the North Sea. Half a dozen people saw him do it. That was Alastair Burns. Quiet chap. From what I recall, neither of them should have made it through the initial screening to be in the test group anyway. Eleanor just fudged the scores to make up the numbers.' Doctor Wheeler straightened up in the chair, looked over at McLean. 'Dear me, I'd not thought about any of this in a while. We patched things up about five years back, when she went into therapy rather than research. She's a brilliant therapist, really. Just not an easy person to like. Sorry, Inspector. You must think me a terrible tell-tale.'

'Not at . . .' McLean got no further before his throat gave up in a spasm of painful coughing.

'Rest, Tony. That's what you need. Take it easy and I'll go tell Emma you're awake.'

McLean closed his eyes for a moment, his memory coming back in disjointed chunks, mixed in with the latest information on Doctor Austin. Brilliant or not, the hypnotist hadn't done anything for Emma, so it must have been Madame Rose. The two of them had gone off for a walk. Was that all it took? And regression therapy. He recalled the first session with unusual clarity now. That was when it had all started to go downhill. He'd been tired, sure. Ever since Duguid had effectively doubled his workload. Or was it when Emma came home and started waking him in the middle of the night? But the rot had really set in after the first session with the monster. Doctor Austin.

He tried to sit up and immediately regretted it, winced through the pain lancing through his arm and leg as he looked across at the bedside table for his phone. Of course, it wasn't there, and he wouldn't have been able to use it anyway. He needed to talk to Grumpy Bob, or Ritchie. Even MacBride might understand. Collapsing back into the pillows, he stared up in frustration at the ceiling tiles. He knew now how they had all died: Duncan George, Patrick Sands, John Fenton, Grigori Mikhailevic, Caroline Sellars. Hell, probably even Jenny Nairn.

The problem was that it would be impossible to prove, and worse he'd probably be called insane for even suggesting it.

'Oh my God. Tony. You're awake.'

He barely had time to register the voice before she was

at his side. McLean stared up, his vision blurred by the overhead lights and for a moment thought he was looking at someone else entirely.

'Kirsty?' The word died in his throat. It couldn't be Kirsty; she'd been dead more than a decade now.

'Shhh.' Emma knelt beside the bed, put one hand on his forehead, the other on his chest. 'Caroline told me about your throat. The rope must have crushed your larynx or something.'

Doctor Wheeler hadn't been lying when she had said Emma was much improved. The little-girl-lost eyes had gone and now her face glowed. Unless that was just a strange effect of the lighting. He'd seen it before, but only just realized how much her hair had changed, the spikes become gentle waves of darkest black, shot with here and there a few streaks of grey. That was why he'd thought it was Kirsty come for him. She looked just like her, even down to the mannerisms.

'It's nice.' He lifted a weak hand, took a few strands between his fingers and felt how soft they were. 'Suits you.'

Grumpy Bob was the first to show up from work, once word got out that he was fit for visitors. The old sergeant had brought a bag of grapes with him, which he proceeded to eat without offering any to McLean. Probably be too painful to swallow, what with his neck and everything, was all he gave by way of explanation.

'You any idea how long you're going to be in here for?'

'Day more. Maybe two.' McLean poked at the cast on his leg. 'Don't think I'm going to be back at the station for a while though.'

'Probably for the best. Gives the rumour mill time to burn itself out.'

'Oh Christ. What are they saying?'

'Well, the best one I've heard yet is that you were indulging in some weird auto-asphyxiation erotic thing. Apparently you've always been into that sado-masochistic stuff and the only surprise is you've not hurt yourself this badly before.'

McLean tried not to laugh. Laughing hurt too much. 'What's the worst? I bet it can't top that.'

Grumpy Bob's grin disappeared. 'Aye, well. Mebbe. A couple of folk think the job was getting too much for you and you tried to hang yourself.' He pointed at McLean's neck. 'You might want to wear a cravat or something til that rope burn's gone down a bit.'

Reflexively McLean's hand went up to his chin, fingers lightly brushing the bruised skin just below. He didn't have to guess who those folk were, or what the fallout from their supposition would be. 'I guess I'm going to have to come up with a better story then. I really don't fancy being pensioned off.'

'They'll not do that, Tony. We're short enough good detectives as it is.'

There was an uncomfortable silence then, while Grumpy Bob continued to munch his way through the grapes. In all their years working together, it was the first time McLean had seen the sergeant eating fruit.

'You found Mikhailevic's body? Out in Gilmerton?' Had he told anyone about that? It was all such a blur, he could hardly remember.

'Aye, once we'd worked out what you were blethering on about. Almost as bad as the other lad, Sands. The Doc reckons he'd been hanging the longest, which just makes things even more complicated.'

'Not really. He bought the rope, after all.' McLean had already joined up all the dots in his head, but then he'd had a long time to think about it. 'What happened to Doctor Austin?'

'Who?' Grumpy Bob spoke through a mouthful of half-chewed grape.

'Doctor Austin. The hypnotherapist. Emma clocked her a good one with that book.' It was one of the few clear memories McLean had of the whole afternoon of what he was coming to refer to as 'the incident'.

'Oh, her.' Grumpy Bob wiped at his face with the back of his hand. 'She's not going to press charges.'

It took a while for McLean's brain to catch up with this. 'She's . . . what?'

'Way she told it, she could understand why Emma walloped her like that. Thought she was attacking you, whatever.'

McLean dropped his head back into the pillow, spoke to the ceiling. 'She was the one who killed them all, Bob. All of the hangings, probably Jenny Nairn too. They all came through her study groups at that college. She picked them out, marked the ones who were depressed, did something. I don't know how. Made them hang themselves. She nearly killed me too. That's why she was round the house in the first place.'

Grumpy Bob was halfway through scrunching up the

463

empty paper bag that had contained his grapes, prior to throwing it at the bin and missing. He stopped, mouth hanging slightly open. 'You what?'

'Hypnosis, Bob. That's what she did to them all.'

'Don't be daft, sir. You can't hypnotize someone into doing something that'll harm them. Something they don't want to do.'

Uncomfortable thoughts hovered around McLean's consciousness. He concentrated on the central strand of his theory. Worry about the ramifications later. 'That's the whole point. They were all of them severely depressed. They all wanted to kill themselves. She latched onto that, fed on it somehow.' Like she was being controlled by something larger, more deadly. Something he didn't want to think about.

Grumpy Bob stared at him for a while before saying quietly: 'So how did she get her claws into you?'

'Come on, Bob. Time was you and old Guthrie wouldn't leave me alone for five minutes. Back when Kirsty died. It was subtle, I'll give you that, but you roped all my friends into suicide watch too.'

'Aye but you pulled through, didn't you? You're no more suicidal than my finger.' Grumpy Bob waggled it, just in case, then threw the bag at the bin. Missed.

McLean didn't argue the point. Instead he just stared at the ceiling. 'That's the problem though, Bob. It never goes away. You can bury the past, or lock it away in a little room in your mind. But it's always there. And she brought it all back out. I couldn't work out why I was so tired, so pissed off at everything. I thought it was Dagwood being in charge, and working at the SCU. Pete Buchanan's death didn't help either, but all the while it was Doctor Eleanor bloody Austin messing with my head.'

Another long silence as Grumpy Bob digested the information, weighed it and found it wanting.

'You might want to keep that theory to yourself.'

'I know. Might as well write my resignation letter otherwise, eh? Think I'd rather act my way through a dozen therapy sessions with Matt Hilton.'

'That few? You'll be lucky.'

'Aye, well. It still leaves the problem of Doctor Austin. Who's she going to go after next?'

'I'll get the lad onto firming up that connection between all the victims, then. If they can all be tracked back to her, we'll get her in for questioning.' Grumpy Bob blew out his cheeks, then let the air out in a long low whistle. 'Not sure what we can do about her, though. I mean, how the hell do you prove she did something like that?'

The chair still sat outside the ICU room where Magda Evans was recovering, but it was unoccupied as McLean clumped his way down the corridor, trying to get to grips with crutches. He remembered a time at boarding school, back in the eighties, when one of the boys had come back with his leg in plaster. He'd been the cool kid for a while, deciding who did or didn't get to sign his cast and speeding along on his crutches. Teachers couldn't tell him off and even the bullies hesitated to pick on him, at least for the first couple of weeks. Every boy in the school wanted a broken leg and a plaster cast then. Now, thirty years on, he really couldn't understand why. It was a pain, quite literally.

He paused at the door. The chair looked very inviting, but lowering himself into it for a rest was almost as difficult as standing, and then he'd have to get back up again. Emma was coming to pick him up in an hour or so, after which there would be the fun of stairs to learn about.

Who was he kidding? McLean knew damned well why he'd come this way in the first place, and the fact that there was no police officer on guard was hardly his fault. He knocked lightly on the door, then pushed it open.

Magda was healing, that was about as much as you could say. Her face was still a mess of bruising and cuts, only now the swelling was almost gone, just the colours remaining. Yellow and purple and grey, slashes of dark red hatched with black stitches. She was watching the television hung on the opposite wall, but her eyes flicked across to him as he clumped awkwardly in, up, down, widened in surprise. She barely moved her head, he noticed.

'Wha' ap'n you?' Magda struggled with the words, the stitches tugging cruelly at the slashes to her mouth and cheeks.

'Someone tried to hang me.' McLean reached up for his neck where the rope burn still stood proud. His throat was less painful now, at least for talking. Eating anything solid would have to wait a week or two.

'Why?'

McLean manoeuvred himself to the end of the bed, wedged the crutches up against the frame so he could rest his weight on them for a moment.

'It's not important. I wanted to talk about you, not me.'

Magda said nothing, just stared up at him from her ruined face.

'They told you about Pete Buchanan, aye?'

She blinked her eyes in the most minimal of nods.

'Nasty way to go. Let me tell you.' He rubbed at his neck again. 'Did they tell you about the bat we found in your apartment?'

Another nod, and this time McLean saw the wince of pain that went with the movement. Nerve damage from the attack, likely to leave her in permanent pain. At least that was what Doctor Wheeler had said.

'It was DS Buchanan who did this to you, wasn't it.'

McLean waited for the nod. For a long while Magda just stared at him, then finally she blinked. 'Eff.'

'He killed Malky Jennings too. No, you don't need to answer that one, we know that. I've just been trying to work out what your angle on the whole thing was. Took me a while, but I've had nothing much else to do these last couple of days. So here's my idea of what was really happening.' McLean shuffled slightly to ease the pressure on his wrists. How the hell did people use crutches for more than ten minutes at a time?

'We know you'd had enough of Malky. You tried to get away a couple of times, but that didn't work. The police were no help either. Can't say I've got much time for the Devil You Know approach myself. It wasn't just you, either. All those other girls, the Eastern Europeans who'd been brought over here with promises of good jobs, learning English, sending money back home? Yeah, I know how it goes. So you decided to do something about it. It was bloody clever, too. Get Buchanan on your side. Not sure how, not sure I want to know how. He kills Malky because he thinks he's your protector now. But you keep the bat, hidden away somewhere safe. I'm guessing you've been creaming money off Malky's operation too. Maybe some drugs as well. Am I warm?'

Magda said nothing, just stared at him. Her eyes were all he needed to see though. He could read the relief when he got it wrong, and so far there'd been none.

'You organized the boat, too. Anyone who wants to go home. Something like that anyway. The only problem is we got wind of the whole thing and rounded you all up. I'm guessing Buchanan wasn't best pleased when he found out you'd tried to do a runner. What was the plan, anonymous tip-off as to where the bat was hidden once you'd made it to safety? Drop him in the shit?'

Magda blinked again. 'Aw ee zerrved.'

'You won't find me disagreeing with you there.'

'Appens ow?' Magda grimaced as she tried to form the question.

'To be honest, I don't know. Not my case any more. We've got Buchanan for Malky Jennings' murder, so my boss is happy. But you were an accessory to that, at the very least. I can't see a judge letting you off. I might put in a good word, plead mitigating circumstances. Not quite sure how I feel about being played right now. Still, it's going to be a while before you're fit to stand trial, and there's the small matter of it being a police officer who tried to kill you.' McLean let that last thought hang in the air. He really wasn't sure he could stay angry with Magda Evans. Not after what had been done to her.

'Ugger girls?' This last word gurgled up from deep in Magda's throat like a death rattle.

'Clarice Saunders has taken them under her ample

wing. I know everyone laughs at her, but her charity does good work. They'll be given shelter, re-housed, sent home, pretty much whatever they want. No one's going to charge them for being on that boat.'

'Goog.' Magda blinked once more. A single tear formed in the corner of each eye before trickling into the scabs on her ruined cheeks.

PC Jones was back in his seat when McLean let himself out of the room a few minutes later. He looked up, startled.

'Inspector, sir. I didn't . . . You shouldn't have been in there.'

'Relax, Reg. I wasn't in there.'

'I . . . But . . .' He pointed at the door as it clicked shut.

'And you weren't nipping off to the toilet without any-one to cover for you.' McLean smiled, then clunked off down the corridor back to his room.

55

It was a small cemetery, tucked away on a piece of land the property developers would have paid a king's ransom for, were it not for the bodies interred beneath the grass. McLean knew it well from his childhood. Summer days spent exploring the green spaces beyond the garden of his grandmother's house. Out through the little gate in the wall at the back, and you could almost imagine you'd left Edinburgh behind. At least it had been like that back then. Nowadays there was always the roar of traffic, and more and more people. The lock on the gate was rusted solid too, so you had to go around the long way.

Emma led them through the gravestones, once more forgetting that on crutches he couldn't move all that quickly. Not over this uneven ground, for sure. The grass could really have done with a mowing, and the bramble vines seemed determined to trip him at every turn. He wasn't labouring as much as Madame Rose though. The transvestite medium was not built for speed, more of a taxi ride kind of person. McLean got the feeling he was going to have to pay him, her, whatever, a fairly large sum, but it was worth it just to see Emma so much improved.

And now, if the two of them could be believed, he was going to find out how it had been done.

'Here we are. This was the first one.' Emma had stopped

in front of a gravestone, fairly new in comparison to those around it. McLean shuffled an awkward route through the undergrowth until he was standing next to her and could read the words carved into the stone.

In Loving Memory
Rosie Buckley
12-7-1972 25-12-1998
Taken Before Her Time

A cold weight settled in the pit of McLean's stomach. 'Is this some kind of joke?'

'Far from it, Inspector.' Madame Rose lumbered up alongside the two of them. 'This is the final resting place of Donald Anderson's penultimate victim. It took me a long time to track her down, and quite by chance Diane Kinnear is buried just over there.' The medium pointed towards the edge of the cemetery, where it gave way to mature woodland.

'What . . . ? I don't understand. What's this got to do with anything?'

'This is everything, Inspector. This is what has been causing Emma all her problems.' Madame Rose laid a large hand on the headstone, her ornate rings clinking lightly against the granite. 'I have to admit I was wrong, and that's not something that happens often. I thought Donald's book had taken a piece of Emma's soul. Turns out that wasn't the case.'

'They're all here. With me.' Emma tapped the side of her head and twirled her finger like a schoolgirl indicating looniness in one of her chums. 'Well, apart from Rosie and Diane. They're gone now. And the others are much quieter. Makes it easier to think.'

McLean looked sideways at Emma, standing beside him. She reached out and took his hand, a simple gesture but not one he could remember her having done before. They'd not really known each other that long, and were both too old for the teenage infatuation that could not bear to be physically separated for more than a few seconds. It was more like the touch of an old friend, a re-acquaintance with someone he'd loved a long time ago and not seen for years. And as he thought it, so the wild story that Madame Rose was spinning began to take on another layer.

'When you destroyed the book in that fire, you set free all the souls it had trapped down the centuries. Every victim, everyone who tried to read it and was found wanting. They were all in there and they all had to go somewhere. I thought they'd just passed on, gone beyond the veil. Maybe some did, but many of them followed that small piece of Emma back to her. I can't blame them, Inspector. They were scared, traumatized beyond anything you can imagine. Some of them have been trapped inside that book for centuries. They took refuge in Emma, and in the process very nearly killed her.'

He didn't believe it. There was always a rational explanation; that was what he had been trained to look for, after all. But there was no denying the difference in Emma; the slow transformation of the past couple of months. She'd changed as she'd recovered from her time in a coma. His own preoccupations had stopped him from seeing it, perhaps. Now there was no denying how much she looked like her.

'Kirsty.' The word was barely a whisper. For some reason he found it hard to speak. Had he not been propped up on the uncomfortable metal crutches, he would probably have sunk to his knees there in the damp graveyard.

'She loved you so much. She still does.'

'She's in there somewhere, isn't she.'

Emma nodded, and it was a punch to his gut. Never mind what Doctor Austin had done to dredge up his past, with that one simple movement he was transported back to the darkest days, the dawn of the new millennium when only his innate stubbornness had kept him from taking his own life.

'Which is why I have to leave.'

If he thought nothing could shock him more, Emma's words proved him wrong. 'Leave? Why?'

'I have to free them all. I'll never be right until they're gone, and they need this.' Emma pointed at the headstone and its simple, terrible inscription. 'Their deaths were so violent, they need to be reunited with their mortal remains before they can accept what happened and move on.'

'But . . . How many? How long?'

Emma bowed her head, as if the weight of all those souls was almost too much to bear. 'I don't know.'

She came to him in his room that night, as he lay awake staring at the ceiling. The dull ache of his mending leg made sleep difficult, as did the long hours of sitting around doing nothing each day. Enforced rest didn't suit him well.

He didn't look at her, knew the drill. Just shuffled across to one side of the bed to make room. He'd hoped that the night terrors were lessening now; Emma had certainly seemed much more composed, more adult. If not really anything like her previous self. The selfish part of him wondered if this meant she would stay.

Her hand was cold, but not unpleasantly so as it reached through the cover for his chest. She snuggled up against him, stealing his warmth, and that was when he realized she wasn't wearing her thick fleece pyjamas. Wasn't wearing anything at all.

'Em–' A single finger stifled the word before it could escape from his lips. She leaned over, kissed him, her long black hair flowing over his head like a drowning tide.

56

It wouldn't have been a proper day back at work without a summons to Dagwood's office. Still on crutches, McLean had to shuffle his way through the door, but at least standing on the wrong side of the desk wasn't a problem. The acting superintendent hadn't exactly gone out of his way to redecorate Jayne McIntyre's office, but he couldn't help noticing the cardboard boxes piled along one wall, those few personal items that had made their way up to this floor now being packed away again.

'I hear they've finally appointed someone.' He didn't need to point out who hadn't got the job.

'Not for another week yet, so don't push your luck.'

'Actually, sir, it'll be good to have you back in CID. We're always short-staffed and this' – McLean tapped at the cast on his leg – 'well, it doesn't really help. Looks like I'm going to be off active duty at least another six weeks.'

'Way I hear it, you probably ought to be off for good.' Duguid leaned back in his seat. It was always good to hit him with a compliment, put him off guard. 'You wouldn't be the first detective self-destructed under the pressure.'

McLean didn't point out that most of the pressure was due to one particular senior officer. So far the interview wasn't going too badly, no need to jeopardize that.

'I didn't try to hang myself, sir.'

of putting it all together. Not without either making himself look like a lunatic or, worse, someone who had harboured a mass murderer for several months.

'And?' Duguid wouldn't let it go. Damn him.

'They all knew each other. All five of them. They'd all had therapy at one time or another from Doctor Austin, so it's safe to say they all had mental health issues.'

'So it's looking like a suicide pact after all.'

'Yes, sir. It does.'

'This Doctor Austin. She was the one round your place the day . . .' He nodded at McLean's leg again.

'Yes. She was working with Emma. Trying to help her get her memory back.'

For a moment McLean thought Duguid was going to ask him who Emma was. The no-longer acting superintendent certainly looked puzzled.

'So that's why she was at your house?'

Tell the truth? Or lie and keep his job? It wasn't hard, really. 'Yes, sir.'

Duguid made a noise that suggested he didn't really believe it but was willing to let it slide. 'Have you interviewed her about the suicides?'

'Like I said, sir. I've been off for two weeks. I'm sure Grumpy Bob will have talked to her though.'

Duguid snorted. 'Not if he wasn't told to, I don't doubt. Get on it, McLean. I want this investigation wound up by the end of the week.'

McLean opened his mouth to protest, then thought the better of it.

'Yes, sir,' he said, and clumped wearily out of the room.

*

'Good to see you back, sir. How's the leg?'

DS Ritchie sat at her desk in the CID room tapping away at a smart new laptop computer. She was all alone save for the five images still taped to the whiteboard. Lines spidered between them, questions now answered, more or less. One name was conspicuous by its absence. He hoped he could keep it that way.

'Sore.' McLean tapped the plaster cast, leaned into his crutches. 'Awkward. Where is everyone?'

'Brooks has got them upstairs chasing actions on his latest investigation. I'm only down here because I've been away at Tulliallan all day.'

'So no one's been working on this.' McLean pointed at the whiteboards.

'Nothing really to work on. We found Mikhailevic where you said he was. PM was pretty clear. He hanged himself like all the others. No sign of foul play. Only difference was he had hemp fibres under his nails.'

Almost as if he could have been the last in the line, were it not for the fact he'd died first.

'It's all written up then?'

'Stuart left it on your desk. The other four as well. Brooks wants it signed off soon as.'

'Him and Dagwood both. They're probably right, too. The last thing the PF wants is a complicated case with no end to it.' McLean shuffled uncomfortably with his crutches, turning himself around so he could leave the room. 'Anyone speak to Doctor Austin? Her name's not up there.'

'Wanted to, but there's a bit of a problem there.'

'There is?'